THE CHRONICLES OF MAVI[N]

In her first trilogy of novels: *King's* [...] and *Wizard's Eleven*, Sheri Tepper cr[...] lands of the True Game – where society is structured by the rules of a game much like chess. On the basis of these inventive and highly original fantasies (published by Corgi as *The True Game*), Tepper was nominated for the Campbell Award honouring the best new talents in the SF/Fantasy field. She followed up this success with a very different work, an epic high fantasy titled *The Revenants.* Now she has returned to the world of the True Game with a new trilogy, exploring its history and telling the tale of Mavin Manyshaped – the most notorious shifter of them all.

'*Mavin* demonstrates considerable originality and literary skill. Recommended'
Fantasy Review

'This . . . gem of a book features fine characterization, a beautifully drawn, original society . . . Another fine effort by Tepper'
Booklist

'A plot of many switches, eccentric and developed characters, and a setting in a wonder-filled fantasy world'
Voya

Also by Sheri S Tepper

THE TRUE GAME
THE REVENANTS

and published by Corgi Books

The Chronicles of Mavin Manyshaped

Sheri S Tepper

comprising
THE SONG OF MAVIN MANYSHAPED
THE FLIGHT OF MAVIN MANYSHAPED
THE SEARCH OF MAVIN MANYSHAPED

CORGI BOOKS

THE CHRONICLES OF MAVIN MANYSHAPED

A CORGI BOOK 0 552 12834 1

Originally published in the United States of America as THE SONG OF MAVIN MANYSHAPED, THE FLIGHT OF MAVIN MANYSHAPED and THE SEARCH OF MAVIN MANYSHAPED

First publication in Great Britain

PRINTING HISTORY

Corgi edition published 1986

This book is set in 10/11pt Plantin.

Corgi Books are published by Transworld Publishers Ltd., 61-63 Uxbridge Road, Ealing, London W5 5SA, in Australia by Transworld Publishers (Australia) Pty. Ltd., 15-23 Helles Avenue, Moorebank, NSW 2170, and in New Zealand by Transworld Publishers (N.Z.) Ltd., Cnr. Moselle and Waipareira Avenues, Henderson, Auckland.

Made and printed in Great Britain by The Guernsey Press Co. Ltd., Guernsey, Channel Islands.

The Song of
Mavin Manyshaped

CHAPTER ONE

Around the inner maze of Danderbat keep – with its hidden places for the elders, its sleeping chambers, kitchens and nurseries – lay the vaster labyrinth of the outer p'natti: slything walls interrupted by square-form doors, an endless array of narrowing pillars, climbing ups and slithering downs, launch platforms so low as to require only leaping legs and others so high that wings would be the only guarantee of no injury.

Through the p'natti the shifters of all the Xhindi clans came each year at Assembly time, processions of them, stiff selves marching into the outer avenues only to melt into liquid serpentines which poured through the holes in the slything walls; into tall wands of flesh sliding through the narrowing doors; into pneumatic billows bounding over the platforms and up onto the heights; all in a flurry of wings, feathers, hides, scales, conceits and frenzies which dazzled the eyes and the senses so that the children became hysterical with it and hopped about on the citadel roof as though an act of will could force them all at once and beforetime into that Talent they wanted more than any other. Every year the family Danderbat changed the p'natti; new shaped obstacles were invented; new requirements placed upon the shifting flesh which would pass through it to the inner maze, and every year at Assembly the shifters came, foaming at the outer reaches like surf, then plunging through the reefs and cliffs of the p'natti to the shore of the keep, the central place where there were none who were not shifters – save those younglings who were not sure yet what it was they were.

Among these was Mavin, a daughter of the shapewise Xhindi, form-family of Danderbat the Old Shuffle, a girl of some twelve or fourteen years. She was a forty-season child, and expected to show something pretty soon, for shifters came to it young and she was already older than some. There were those who had begun to doubt she would ever come through the p'natti along the she-road reserved for females not yet at or through their child-bearing time. Progeny of the shifters who turned out not to have the Talent were sent away to be fostered elsewhere as soon as that lack was known, and the possibility of such a journey was beginning to be rumored for Mavin.

She had grown up as shifter children do when raised in a shifter place, full of wild images and fluttering dreams of the things she would become when her Talent flowered. As it happened, Mavin was the only girl child behind the p'natti during that decade, for Handbright Ogbone, her sister, was a full decade older and in possession of her Talent before Mavin was seven. There were boys aplenty and overmuch, some saying with voices of dire prophecy that it was a plague of males they had, but the Ogbone daughters were the only females born to be reared behind the Danderbat p'natti since Throsset of Dowes, and Throsset had fled the keep as long as four years before. Since there were no other girls, the dreams which Mavin shared were boyish dreams. Handbright no longer dreamed, or if she did, she did not speak of it.

Mavin's own mother, Abrara Ogbone, had died bearing the boy child, Mertyn – caught by the shift-devil, some said, because she had experimented with forbidden shapes while she was pregnant. No one was so heartless as to say this to Mavin directly, but she had overheard it without in the least understanding it several times during her early years. Now at an age where her own physical maturity was imminent, she understood better what they had been speaking of, but she had not yet made the jump of intuition which applied this knowledge to herself. She had a kind of stubborn naiveté about her which resisted learning some of the things which other girls got with their mother's milk. It was an Ogbone trait, though she did not know it. She had not before now understood flirting, for example, or the reasons why the men were always the winners of the processional competitions, or why Handbright so often cried in corners or was so weary and sharp-tongued. It wasn't that she could not have understood these things, but more that she was so busy apprehending everything in the world that she had not had time before to make the connections among them.

She might have been enlightened by overhearing a conversation between two hangers-on of the Old Shuffle – two of the guards cum hunters known as "the Danderbats" after Theobald

Danderbat, forefather and tribal god, direct line descendent, so it was said, from Thandbar, the forefather of all shifters – who kept themselves around the keep to watch it, they said, and look after its provisioning. So much time was actually spent in the provisioning of their drinking and lechery that little enough energy was left for else.

"Everytime I flex a little, I feel eyes," Gormier Graywing was saying. "She's everwhere. Anytime I've a mind to shift my fingers to get a better grip on something, there she is with her eyes on my hands and, like as not, her hand on mine to feel how the change goes. If there's such a thing as a' everwhere shifter child, it's this she-child, Mavin." Gormier was a virile, salacious old man thing, father of a half-dozen non-shifter whelps and three true-bred members of the clan. He ran a boneless ripple now, down from shoulders through fingers, a single tentacle wriggle before coming back to bone shape in order to explain how he felt. Some of the Danderbats would carry on whole conversations in muscle talk without ever opening their mouths. "Still, there's never a sign she knows she's female and I'm male, her not noticing she gives me a bit of tickle."

" 'Tisn't child flirtiness." The other speaker was Haribald Halfmad, so named in his years in Schlaizy Noithn and never, to his own satisfaction, renamed. "There's no sexy mockery there. Just that wide-eyed kind of oh-my look what you'd get from a baby with its first noisy toy. She hasn't changed that look since she was a nursling, and that's what's discomfiting about her. When she was a toddler, there was some wonder if she was all there in the brain net, and she was taken out to a Healer when she was six or so, just to see."

"I didn't know that! Well then, it must have been taken serious; we Old Shuffle Xhindi don't seek Healers for naught."

"We Danderbats don't seek Healers at all, Graywing, as you well know, old ox. It was her sister Handbright took her, for they're both Ogbones, daughter of Abrara Ogbone – she that has a brother up Battlefox way. But that was soon after the childer's mother died, so it was forgiven as a kind of upset, though normally the Elders would have had Handbright in a basket for it. Handbright brought her back saying the Healer found nothing wrong with the child save sadness, which would go away of itself with time. Since then the thought's been that she's a mite slow but otherwise tribal as the rest of us. I wish she'd get on with it, for I've a mind to try her soon as her Talent's set." And he licked his lips, nudging his fellow with a lubricious elbow. "If she doesn't get on with it, I may hurry things a bit."

The object of this conversation was sitting at the foot of a slything column in the p'natti, in full sight of the two old man things but as unconscious of them as though she had been on another world. Mavin had just discovered that she could change the length of her toes.

The feeling was rather but not entirely like pain. There was a kind of itchy delight in it as well, not unlike the delight which could be evoked by stroking and manipulating certain body parts, but without that restless urgency. There was something in it, as well, of the fear of falling, a kind of breathless gap at the center of things as though a misstep might bring sudden misfortune. Despite all this, Mavin went on with what she was doing, which was to grow her toes a hand's-width longer and then make them shorter again, all hidden in the shadow of her skirts. She had a horrible suspicion that this bending and extending of them might make them fall off, and in her head she could see them wriggling away like so many worms, blind and headless, burrowing themselves down into the ground at the bottom of the column, to be found there a century hence, still squirming, unmistakably Mavin's toes. After a long time of this, she brought her toes back to a length which would fit her shoes and put them on, standing up to smooth her apron and noticing for the first time the distant surveillance offered by the two granders on the citadel high porch. She made a little face, as she had seen Handbright do, remotely aware of what the two old things usually chatted about but still not making any connection between that and herself. She was off to tell Handbright about her toes, and there was room for nothing else in her head at the moment, though she knew at the edges of her consciousness the oldsters had been talking man-woman stuff.

But then everyone was into man-woman stuff that year. Some years it was fur, and some years it was feathers. Some years it was vegetable-seeming which was the fad, and other years no one cared for anything except jewels. This year was sex form changing, and it was somewhat titillating for the children, seeing their elder relatives twisting themselves into odd contorted shapes with nerve ends pushed out or tucked in in all sorts of original ways. Despite the fact that shifters had no feeling of shame over certain parts – those parts being changed day to day in suchwise that little of the original topography could still be attached to them – the younglings who had not become shifters yet were tied to old, non-shifter forebear emotions which had to do with the intimate connections between things excretory and things erotic. It could not be helped. It was in the body shape they were born with and in the language and in the old stories children were told, and in the things all children did and thought and said, ancient as apes and true as time. So the children, looking upon all this changing about, found a kind of giggly prurience in it despite the fact that they were shifter children every one, or hoped they were soon to be.

All this lewd, itchy stuff to do with man and woman made Mavin uncomfortable in a deep troublesome way. It was by no means maidenly modesty, which at one time it would have been called. It was a deeper thing than that – a feeling that something indecent was being done. The same feeling she had when she saw boys pulling the wings off zip-birds and taunting them as they flopped in the dust, trying, trying, trying to fly. It was that same sick feeling, and since it seemed to be part and parcel of being shifter, Mavin decided she wouldn't tell anyone except Handbright she was shifter, not just yet.

Instead, she smoothed her apron, pointedly ignored the speculative stares of old Graywing and Haribald, and walked around the line of slything pillars to a she-door. At noon would be a catechism class, and though Mavin made it a practice to avoid many things which went on in Danderbat keep, it was not wise to avoid those. Particularly inasmuch as Handbright was teaching it and Mavin's absence could not pass unnoticed. Since she was the only girl, it would not pass unnoticed no matter who was teaching, but she did not need to remind herself of that.

Almost everyone was there when she arrived, so she slipped into a seat at the side of the room, attracting little attention. Some of the boys were beginning to practice shifter sign, vying with one another who could grow the most hair on the backs of their hands and arms, who could give the best boneless wriggle in the manner of the Danderbats. Handbright told them once to pay attention, then struck hard at the offending arms with her rod, at which all recoiled but Tolerable Titdance, who had grown shell over his arms in the split second it had taken Handbright to hit at him. He laughed in delight, and Handbright smiled a tired little smile at him. It was always good to see a boy so quick, and she ruffled his hair and whispered in his ear to make him blush red and settle down.

"I'm nye finished with you bunch," said Handbright, making her hair stand out from her head in a tangly bush which wriggled like a million little vines. "You're all coming along in one talent or another. I have to tell you today that it looks like Leggy Bartiban will be going off to Schooltown to be fostered. Seems he's showing signs of being Tragamor. Not unexpected, eh Leggy?"

The boy ducked his head, tried to smile through what were suspiciously like tears. True, it wasn't unexpected. His father had been a Tragamor, able to move great boulders or pull down mountains by just looking at them, but it was still hard for him to accept that he must forget the shifters, forget the Danderbat citadel, go off to a strange place and become something else again when all he knew was shifter. He could take comfort from the fact that he wouldn't grieve. He wouldn't even remember a week hence when the Forgetters had done with him. Still, looking at it from this end, it must seem dreadful. Mavin ducked her head to hide her own tears, feeling for him. It could have been her. She might not have been shifter, either. No one knew she was, not yet.

"All right, childer. I'm not keeping you long today. Elder Garbat Grimsby is coming in for a minute, just to ask a few simple questions, see how you're coming. Since two of you are off to Schlaizy Noithn in the morning, he'll just review two or three little shifter things and let you all go. Sit up straight and don't go boneless at the Elder, it isn't considered polite. Remember, to show politeness to elders and honored guests, you hold your own shape hard. Keep that in mind. . . ." She broke off, turning to the door, as she heard the whirring hum of something coming.

It came into the room like a huge top, spinning, full of colors and sounds, screaming its way across the room, bumping chairs away, full of its own force, circling to stop before them all and slowly, slowly, change into old Garbat, hugely satisfied with himself, fixing them all with his shifter eyes to see if they were impressed. All of them were. It was a new trick to Mavin, and when reared in a shifter stronghold those were few and seldom, with every shifter challenging every other to think of new things day on day. The Elders came infrequently out of their secret place deep within the keep, or at least so it was said. Mavin thought that if she were an Elder, she would be around the keep all day every day, as a bit of rock wall, a chair, a table in some dusty corner, watching what went on, hearing what was said. It was this thought which kept her behavior moderately circumspect, and she looked hard at the Elder now. He might have been the very pillar she had sat under to shift her toes. She shivered, crouching a little so as not to make him look at her.

Handbright managed some words of welcome. Old Garbat folded his hands on his fat stomach and fixed his eyes on Janjiver. "What about you, Janjiver. You tell me what shapes shifters can take, and when."

The boy Janjiver was a lazy lout, most thought, with a long, strong body and a good Talent which went largely unused. There were those who said he would never come out of Schlaizy Noithn, and indeed there were some young shifters who never did. If one wanted to take the shape of a pombi or a great owl or some other thing which could live well off the land, one might live in Schlaizy Noithn for all one's life without turning a hand. "A shifter worth his net," said Janjiver in his lazy voice, "can take any shape at all. He can bulk himself up to twenty times bigger, given a little time, or more if the shape is fairly simple. He can conserve bulk and take shape a quarter size, though it takes practice. The shape he cannot take is the shape of another real person."

"And why can't he do that, Janjiver?"

"Because it's not in our nature, Elder. The wicked Mirrormen may mock mankind but we shifters do not. All the Danderbats back to the time of Xhindi forbid it."

"And you, Thrillfoot. What is the shifter's honor?"

"It is a shifter's honor to brook no stay, be stopped by no barrier, halted by no wall, enclosed by no fence. A shifter goes where a shifter will." Thrillfoot threw his hair back with a toss of his head, grinning broadly. He was looking forward to Schlaizy Noithn. In the citadel he was befamilied to death, and the desire for freedom was hot in him. He rejoiced to answer, knowing it was the last answering he would do for many a year.

"And what is a shifter to the rest of the world, Janjiver?"

"A shifter to the rest of the world, Elder, is what a shifter says he is, and a shifter always says less than he is."

"Always," agreed Thrillfoot, smiling.

This was just good sense and was taught to every shifter child from the time he was weaned. The shapes a shifter could take and the shapes he would let the outside world think he could take were two different things. Shifters were too sly to let all they could do become general knowledge, for in that shiftiness lay the shifters' safety. One wouldn't look for a tree-shaped shifter if one thought shifters couldn't shift into trees. So it was that most of the world had been led to believe shifters could become pombis or fustigars or owls, and nothing much more than that. Indeed for some shifters it was true. It was possible to fall in love with a special shape and ever after be able to take only that shape besides one's true one – or for a few, only that shape forever. It had been known to happen. Shifter childer were warned about it, and those who indulged themselves by staying pombis or fustigars for a whole season or more were pointed out as horrible examples. So now in the classroom everyone nodded in agreement.

Garbat manifested himself as pleased, gave each of the boys who were off to Schlaizy Noithn a handmade Danderbat token – at which they showed considerable pleasure, intricate handmade things being the only things shifters ever bothered to carry – and then took himself away, soon followed by most of the others.

Leggy Bartiban did not go out with them. He had tears running down his cheeks openly now. "That's a shifter secret, teacher, not letting the world know what shapes we can do. How do you know for sure I won't tell all the shifter secrets when I'm gone away from you?"

"Ah, lad," Handbright came to hug him, drawing him tight into the circle of her arms. "You'll not remember. Truly. I have never lied to you, Leggy, and I'll not lie now. It is sad for you to go, and sad for us to lose you, but you will not suffer it. We have contract with the good Forgetter, Methlees of Glen, who has been our Forgetter for more seasons than anyone remembers. You'll go to her house, and the people from the school will be there, and she'll take your hand, like this, and you'll know the people, and remember them, and will forget us like a dream. And that's the way of it, Leggy, the whole way of it. You'll be a Tragamor child born, always friendly to the shifters, but not grieving over them a bit."

"Do they need to forget me my mother?" The boy was crying openly now.

"Shush. What silliness. Of course they'll not forget you your mother. You'll remember her name and face and the sound of her voice, and you'll welcome her happily to visit you at Festival. You'll see her as often as you do now, and most of the other boys at school will be the same, except for those who came to the Schoolhouses as infants and do not know their mothers at all. Now go along. Go ask anyone if that isn't so, and if anyone tells you otherwise, send them to me. Go on, now, and stop crying. I've got things to do."

Then all had gone but Mavin, who sat in her seat and was still, watching the back of Handbright's head until Handbright turned to see those keen eyes looking into her as though she had been a well of water. "Well, little sister, and you still here?"

"It was a lie, wasn't it, Handbright, about his mother?" Her voice was not accusing.

Handbright started to deny it, then stopped, fixed by that birdlike gaze. "It was and it wasn't, she-child. He will remember her name, and her face, and the sound of her voice. He'll welcome her at Festival, if she chooses to visit him. But all the detail, the little memories, the places and times surrounding the two of them will be gone, so there'll be little loving feeling left. Now that may build again, and I've seen it happen time after time."

"And you've seen the other, too. Where no one cares, after."

After a long weary silence, Handbright said, "Yes, I can't deny it, Mavin. I've seen that, too. But he doesn't see his mother now but once or twice a year, at Assembly time. So it's not such a great loss."

"So why can't he stay here, with us. I like Leggy."

"We all like him, child. But he's not shifter. He has to learn how to use his own Talent or he'll be a zip-bird with wings off, all life long, flopping in the dust and trying to fly. That'd be hateful, surely, and not something you'd wish for him?"

Mavin twirled hair around one finger, shook her head from side to side, thinking, then laid her hand upon Handbright's own and made her fingers curl bonelessly around Handbright's wrist. Handbright stiffened in acknowledgement, her face showing gladness mixed with something so like shame that Mavin did not understand it and drew her hand away.

"Lords, child! How long?"

Mavin shrugged. "A little while."

"How marvelous. Wonderful." Handbright's voice did not

rejoice; it was oddly flat and without enthusiasm. "I have to tell the Elders so we can plan your Talent party. . . ."

"No!" It came out firmly, a command, in a voice almost adult. "No, Handbright. I'm not ready for you to do that. It hasn't been long enough yet . . . to get used to the idea. Give me . . . some time yet, please, sister. Don't do me like Leggy, throwing me into something all unprepared for it." She laughed, unsteadily, keeping her eyes pleading and saying not half of the things she was feeling.

"Well . . ." Handbright was acquiescent, doubtful, seeming of two minds. "You know the Elders like to know as soon as one of us shows Talent, Mavin. They've been worried about you. I've been worried about you. It isn't a thing one can hide for very long. As your Talent gets stronger, any shifter will be able to tell."

"Not hide. Not exactly. Just have time to get used to the ideas. A few days to think about it is all. It won't make any difference to anyone." And she saw the dull flush mounting on Handbright's cheeks, taking this to mean that yes, it did make a difference, but not understanding just what that difference might be.

"All right. I won't tell anyone yet. But everyone will have to know soon. You tell me when you're ready, but it can't be long, Mavin. Really. Not long." She leaned forward to hug the younger girl, then turned away to the corridor as though more deeply troubled than Mavin could account for. Mavin remained a long time in the room thinking of what had happened there that day.

The tears of Leggy, sent away to forget.

The words of Janjiver, in answer to the question of the Elder, what is a shifter, to the world?

"A shifter to the rest of the world, Elder, is what a shifter says he is, and a shifter always says less than he is."

"I, too," she said to herself, "could be wise to follow the words of the catechism. I could say less than I am."

She went out into the day, back to the alleys of the p'natti, fairly sure that though Handbright would be upset and worried for a time, she would say nothing about Mavin's Talent until Mavin told her yes. And Mavin had begun to feel that perhaps she did not want to tell her yes. Not today. Not tomorrow. Perhaps, though she did not know why, not ever.

CHAPTER TWO

Had it not been for the fact that Assembly time was only days away, Handbright would have worried more over Mavin, would have been more insistent that the Elders be told that Mavin had shown Talent, was indeed shifter, might now be admitted to full membership in the clan Danderbat and begin to relieve some of the endless demands made upon Handbright for the past half-dozen years. Though she was fond of Mavin – and of eight-year-old Mertyn, too, if it came to that – it did not occur to her that Mavin knew no more than Mertyn did about what would be expected of a new shifter girl by Gormier and Haribald, and by the others. Though Handbright had never told Mavin any of the facts of life of shifter girl existence, she assumed that Mavin had picked it up somewhere, perhaps as she herself had done, from another young she-person. In making the assumption, she forgot that there were no other shifter girls to have giggled with Mavin in the corners, that Handbright could have been the only source of this information unless one of the old crones had seen fit to enlighten the child, an unlikely possibility.

Indeed, if she had had time to think about it, she would have known that Mavin was as innocent as her little brother of any knowledge of what would happen when it became known she was shifter. Who could she have observed in that role except Handbright herself? Who else was there behind the p'natti to share responsibility or provide company? Had there been a dozen or so girls growing up together, as there should be in a clan the size of Danderbat, Handbright herself would have been far less weary and put upon for she would have been sought out by the old man things no more often than she could have found bearable. Part of the problem, of course, was that she had not conceived. If she had been pregnant, now, or had a child at the breast. . . . Or better yet, if she had borne three or four, then she could have gone away, have left the keep and fled to Schlaizy Noithn or out into the world. Any such realization made her uncomfortable. It was easier simply not to think of it, so she did not consider Mavin's ignorance, did not consider the matter at all except to think without thinking that with Mavin coming to a proper age, the demands on herself might be less.

When Handbright had been a forty-season child there had been others near in age. Throsset of Dowes. The twin daughters of old Gormier, Zabatine and Sambeline. At least three or four others. But the twins had soon had twin children, two sets of sons, had left them in the nursery and fled. And Throsset had simply gone, with a word to no one and no one knowing where. And all the others had had their children and gone into the world, one by one, so that for four years Handbright had been alone behind the p'natti – alone except for a few crones and homebound types who were too lazy to do else than linger in the keep, and the Danderbat granders who were there to keep watch. That was all except for peripatetic clan members who visited from time to time. Well, at least the last of the babies was now out of loincloths and into trowsies. And Mertyn was eight. And Mavin now would be available to help . . . help.

So she thought, in the back of her head, not taking time to worry it because Assembly was so near and there was so much to do. Of course more hands were assembled to do it, too, for the Danderbat were beginning to gather. The kitchens were getting hot from fires kept burning under the ovens. Foods were being brought by wagon from as far away as Zebit and Betand. All during the year shifters might eat grass in the fields or meat off the bone, but at Assembly time they wanted cookery and were even willing to hire to get it done. That was the true sign that Assembly was near, when the cooks arrived by wagon from Hawsport, all wide-eyed at being surrounded by shifters. Of course the kitchens were underground and there were guards on them from morn to night so they didn't see what non-shifters shouldn't see, but the gold they were paid was good gold and more of it than a pawnish chef might make in a season otherwise.

Mavin, aware that Handbright was distracted by all this flutter, decided it would be best to lose herself in the confusion. She knew a half-hundred places in the keep in which one might crouch or lie totally unobserved and watch what went on. Now with the

Danderbat gathering from all the world, and sensible that it was a time of great change for herself whether she wished to change or no, she took to hiding herself, watching, staring, learning from a distance rather than being ever present and handy as old Gormier had noticed her being. But he was now so mightily enthralled by gossip from a hundred places in a hundred voices, so distracted by the clan members gathering in their beast-headed cloaks of fur, full of tall tales and babble, that he forgot about Mavin or any intentions he may have had toward her. Mavin, however, had merely exchanged ubiquity for invisibility, hiding herself in any available cubby to see what it was that went on as the Danderbat clansmen came home. As Gormier was a man of restless, lecherous energy, full of talk, a good one to watch if one wanted to learn things, she followed him about as she had done for years, peering down on him from odd corners above rafters or from rain spouts. It was thuswise she finally lost her stubborn naiveté.

Gormier and Haribald were helping unload a wagon of vegetables which had been hauled all the way from Zebit up the River Haws and the windy trail to the top of the table mountain on which the keep sat, just east of the range of firehills which separated it from Schlaizy Noithn. As they were about this business, they heard a drumming noise and looked out through the p'natti to see a vast brown ball, leathery hard, with arms at either edge, cudgeling itself to make a thunder roar. They set up a hail which Mavin heard, hid as she was under the edge of the keep roof in a gutter, and the drum ceased pounding upon itself to make a trial run at the p'natti. It assaulted the launching ramps, rolling upward at increasing speed, propelling itself by hand pushes along its circumference, to take projectile form as it left the ramp, then a winged form which snagged the top of a slything pillar with a hooked talon only to change again into a fluid serpent which slythed down the pillar before launching upward once more in a flurry of bright veils which floated upon the sky, the veils forming a brilliant parachute against the blue. Even Mavin gasped, and the granders made drum chests for themselves, beating with their arms, an answering thunder of applause. So the falling parachute, making itself into a neat bundle as it dropped, became a shifter man on the ground before them, the parachute veils gathering in and disappearing into the general hard shape. Mavin recognized him then as Wurstery Wimpole, for he had won the tournament in a previous year and been much glorified then by the Danderbat.

"Damfine, Wurstery. Damfine. Like that parachute thingy, soft as down." Gormier, pounding him on his hard shape back, shaking his hand in sudden pain as Wurstery made a shell back there to take the blows. "Haribald was just saying he hadn't seen veils used so – or such a color! – in a dozen years. Amblevail Dassnt used to do some parachute thing, but his was pale stuff beside yours. You going to use that coming in during procession?"

"Oh, might, might. Have another trick or two I've been practicing. Might use them instead. Anyhow, that's days away and there's days between! I've been bringing myself eager cross country thinking of the drink and the cookery and the Danderbat girls."

Gormier shook his head, sadly, Mavin peering down on him from the height and hearing him breathe. "No girls, Wustery. Not a one save Handbright, and she's tired of it. Hardly worth the effort. She doesn't make it enjoyable. I've been at her bed this past two, three years, and Haribald, too, seeing she's of breeding age, but there's no good of it at all."

"You don't mean it! Only one girl shifter behind the p'natti? Lords, lords, what are the Danderbat coming to. Last time I was here, there were a dozen – two dozen."

"Naa. Last time you was here was four years – twelve seasons ago, and there weren't all that many. Throsset was here then. And my daughters, but they were just weaning the twins, one set each. And there was a flock of visitors, of course, but right after Assembly they left. After that there wasn't another girlchild behind the p'natti save Mavin, and she's only now maybe coming of age or maybe not. Lately the Danderbats've borne nothing but boys. Who would have thought there could be too many boys! There's talk among the Elders that the Danderbats may be done, Wurstery. Talk of that, or of bringing back the women who've gone out, whether they're willing or no . . ."

"So howcome Handbright's stayed so long? What is she, twenty-four or so?"

"She doesn't bear. Never been pregnant once, so far as we know. One of these days, she'll give up hope and take off for Schlaizy Noithn, I doubt not. She's thought of it before, but we've discouraged her, Haribald and me." Gormier gave his head a ponderous shake at the pity of it all. "So if you're looking for female flesh, best ask a friend to shift for you, old Wurstery, or visit some other keep of some other clan, for there's naught here for you save one old girl not worth the trouble and one new one not come to it yet."

And it was in this wise that Mavin realized what Handbright's flushed face had meant and why it was that Mavin's being a shifter would make a difference. The truth of it came to her all at once, a complete picture, in vivid detail and coloring. She went inside to the privy and lost her lunch.

There was no time to steam over it then, for Wurstery had been only one of the latest batch of Danderbats who were flowing in from all directions, laughing and shouting in the Assembly rooms downstairs, drifting up and down to the cellars to see what the cooks were preparing and whether the wine was in proper supply, taking their chances on the lottery which told them off into food service crews day by day during Assembly. Mavin, no longer invisible, was hugged, kissed, hauled about by the shoulders, congratulated on her growth, questioned as to her Talent, and sent on a thousand errands. It was impossible to escape. There were eyes everywhere, Danderbats everywhere, both grown ones and childer ones, for some Danderbat shes chose to take their childer with them rather than leave them in the nurseries of the keep. And a good thing, too, thought Mavin exhaustedly as she counted their numbers and went for the twentieth time escorting a small one to the privy. It was only that night, long after darkness had come and the keep had fallen into an almost quiet that she went to find Handbright, waking her from an exhausted drowse.

"Mavin? What's wrong? What do you want?"

"Sister. I need to ask things."

"Oh, Mavin, not now! I've been standing on my own feet since before dawn, and weariness has me by the throat. You've asked questions since you were born, and I can't imagine what's left to ask!" Handbright pulled a shawl around her shoulders and sat up in her narrow bed. This room at the top of the keep was her own, seldom visited, mostly undisturbed, and it was rare for anyone, Mavin included, to come there. Handbright herself usually slept near the nurseries, and she had sought this cubby now only because there were visitors aplenty to care for the children.

Mavin, slightly ashamed but undeterred, drifted to the window of the room and looked out across the p'natti to the line of fire hills upon the western horizon. Beyond them was Schlaizy Noithn, the ground of freedom where her schoolmates had gone to try their Talent and learn their way. Of course, she ones could go there too, if they liked, after they had had a lot of childer, or when they knew they could not. This had never been important before. She had known that fact as well as she knew her own name, or the sight of Handbright's face, or the feel of a fellow shifter through a changed hide, knowing this was shifter kin even though he looked or smelled nothing like himself. But it had never really meant anything to her until now.

"Handbright, I want to go to Schlaizy Noithn." And she waited to hear the proof of all her assumptions.

"You can't do that, child. You're a she-child. Danderbat womb keepers don't go. You know that."

"Of course I know it. But I said, I want to go to Schlaizy Noithn. I want to go regardless of what the Danderbats say. Suppose I go to a Healer in the Outside and ask her to take my womb away."

"She wouldn't do it. If she did, the Elders would kill her."

"Suppose I changed me, so that I don't have a womb at all."

Handbright made the ward of evil sign, her face turning hard and wooden at the thought. Her voice was no longer kindly when she replied. "That's a disgusting thought. How could you think such a thing?"

"Ah. Well, as to that, sister, answer me this. If I have my Talent party in a day or so, or say right after Assembly, when the visitors are gone, how long before I have to do man-woman stuff with old Gormier? Or Haribald? Or maybe old Garbat himself?"

The older girl turned away, face pale. "Ah, Mavin. I don't want to talk about it. You'll learn to manage. It's part of being a shifter girl, that's all. You'll live through it. Besides, you've known all about that . . . you've known. . . ." Seeing Mavin's face, she stopped, reddening. "You *didn't* know?"

"No. I didn't know. Not until this morning. I should have known, maybe, but I didn't. I need to understand all this, Handbright. I have to know what this change is going to mean to me. Suddenly it's me the old Danderbats are leching for. Now if I'd been Tragamor, you'd have turned me over to the Forgetter to take all my memories and send me out in a minute. Wouldn't you?"

"Yes. It's necessary. We always do that."

"Even if I was a she-child Tragamor, you'd do the same. Womb or no womb, you'd turn a Tragamor she-child away to Schooltown in a minute."

Handbright nodded, stiffly, seeing where the argument was going.

"But because I'm shifter, a she-child shifter, the Elders have said I have to womb-carry for them. I can shift my legs and arms, grow fur or feathers, make me wings for my shoulders, but I can't fly or leap or turn into any other thing, for it might change womb and make it unfavorable for carrying baby shifters. If I'm biddable, though, after I've had three or four or so, or once I can't have any more, they'll let me go to Schlaizy Noithn. Or out into the world. Isn't that right?"

"You know it is. You've known those who went."

"Oh, yes. I've seen them when they went, Handbright, and I've seen them when they come back. They say Throsset fled, and there's a penalty on her if she comes back. She's gone away far, and none have seen her."

"Throsset was in love with a Demon, and he took her with him into the Western Sea. That's what's said."

"She went. That's what I mean. She didn't stay here in the keep and carry babies for the Elders."

"The word is she couldn't. She had no proper parts to do it."

"Then maybe I'm not the first to think of disposing of the proper parts," Mavin said angrily. "Handbright, remember how you used to tell me you'd shift into a great sea bird when you had your Talent? You'd be a great white bird, you said, and explore all the reaches of the western sea. You used to say that. But here you are, teaching, baby watching, cooking and carrying for the Elders, and I know for a fact that there's been much breeding done on you and no end of it planned, for I heard old Gormier talking of it and of how he'd discouraged your leaving. . . ."

The older girl turned away, face flaming, half angry, half shamed. Undaunted, Mavin went on.

"You stayed here, and let yourself be used by old Gormier, and Haribald, and I don't know how many others – and because you didn't have childer, they kept at you. And the years go by, and it gets later and later. You don't shift, you don't do processionals, you don't go to Schlaizy Noithn to learn your Talent, you don't practice, and it still gets later. And maybe it's too late to dream of becoming a great bird and going exploring, too."

"Don't you understand!" Handbright shouting at her, face red, tears flowing freely down the sides of her tired face. "I stayed because of Mertyn . . . and you. I stayed because our mother died. I stayed because there wasn't anyone *else*!" She turned, hand out, warning Mavin not to say another word, and then she was out the door and away, so much anger in her face that Mavin knew it was the keep angered her, the world, the Elders, the place, the time, not Mavin alone. And yet Mavin felt small and wicked to have put this extra hardship upon Handbright just now during Assembly, when she must be bearing so much else. Even so, she did not regret it, for now she knew the truth of it. It was a hard bit of wisdom for the day, but it came to Mavin as a better thing than the fog she had been wandering about in until the overheard conversation of the morning.

"Still," she whispered to herself, "I have doubts, Handbright. For you may have stayed out of grief for our mother, and out of care for baby Mertyn . . . and me. But there have been eight long years since then. And four long years since Throsset left. And I have been strong and able for at least four or five of those years. So why not have gone, Handbright? Why not have taken us with you? There must be some other reason."

"Perhaps," said the clear voice which had spoken to her from within her own mind that morning, "She is afraid or too tired or believes that it is her duty to stay in the Danderbat keep, oldest of the Xhindi keeps. Or because she believes she is needed here." Mavin left the room thoughtfully, and went down the long stairs past the childer's playground. Mertyn was there, sitting on the wall as he so often did, arms wrapped around his legs, cheek lying on his knees while he thought deep thoughts or invented things, a dark blot of shadow against the stars. Mavin considered, not for the first time, that he did not look like a shifter child. But then, Mavin had not thought of herself resembling a shifter child either and had grieved over that. Perhaps Mertyn was not and she could rejoice. She sat beside him to watch the stars prick out, darkness lying above the fireglow in the west.

"You're sad looking, Mertyn child."

"I was thinking about Leggy Bartiban. He was teaching me to play wands and rings, and now he's gone. They took him to the Forgetter, and he's gone. If I see him again ever, he won't know me." The child wiped tears, snuffling against his sleeve, face already stained. She hugged him to her, smelling the fresh bread smell of him, salt sweat and clean breath.

"Ah. He may know us both, Mertyn. Handbright says they don't forget everyone. He'll know us. He'll just forget the shifter things it's better he forgets, anyhow, if he's not shifter. Why clutter up your mind with all stuff no good to it? Hmm? Besides, I can teach you to play wand-catch."

He looked at her in surprise. "Well if you can, why didn't you? I should've learned last year. I'm getting old fast, Mavin. Everyone says so."

"Ah. Do you think you're getting older than I am? If you could manage that, it would be fine, Mertyn. Then you could take me with you and we'd go travel the world."

"I'm not catching up to you, Mavin," he said seriously. The boy had little humor in him, and she despaired sometimes that he would ever understand any of her little jokes. It upset him if she told him she had been teasing so she pretended serious regard.

"No, of course you're not. I was just wishing, thinking it would be nice to go traveling and shifting."

"Oh, it would. If you go, you mustn't leave me all alone here, Mavin. I had Leggy, and he's gone, and there's only Handbright except you. I want to go traveling and shifting more than anything. I dream about it sometimes, when I'm asleep and when I'm awake. I want to go. But you can't go until you've had childer, Mavin. Girls aren't supposed to. Janjiver says it messes up their insides."

Mavin bit her lip, wanting to laugh at his tone of voice, unable to do so for the tears running inside her throat. "Tell me, Mertyn, why it is it doesn't mess up a boy shifter's insides? Boys have baby-making parts, too, don't they? But I've seen them shift their parts all over themselves and then put them back and make a baby the same day. So why is it only she-shifters have to be so careful?"

The boy looked doubtful, then thoughtful in that way he sometimes had. "I don't know. That would be very interesting to know, wouldn't it. What the difference is. I'll ask Gormier Graywing. . . ."

"Don't," she said harshly. "Let me find out, brother child, I'd rather." She left him sitting there under the stars, went out only to return and whisper to his shadow crouching dark against the wall, "Mertyn, if I were to figure out a way to go traveling, would you go with me?"

His voice when he replied was all child. "Oh, Mavin, could you? That would be fun!"

Could she? Could she? Could she do what Throsset of Dowes was said to have done? Leave in the dark of night, slipping away in silence, losing herself in the fire hills or the roads away north to Pfarb Durim. Oh, the mystery and wonder of Pfarb Durim, city of the ancients!

This was only dream stuff, only thoughts and ruminations, not intentions. She was not yet at the point of intention. Meantime it was Old Shuffle time, Assembly time, and she no less than any in the keep would watch the processions on the morrow.

For it was tomorrow that the visitors would come, tomorrow that the first procession would come through the p'natti, through Gormier's new pillars and doors. Even now those of the younger clans were probably roaming about in the fire hills in pombi shape or fustigar shape or flying high overhead, endlessly circling like great waroo owls, ready to assemble with first light, making themselves a great drum orchestra to beat the sun up out of bed. She went to sleep in a cubby which faced the sunrise, so that the coming of the shifters should not take her by surprise.

They began before dawn, drumming, hooting, whistling, a cacophonous hooraw which woke every person in the keep and brought them all to the roof where today's kitchen crew gave them hot spiced tea and biscuits made of ox-root, all nibbling quietly in the pre-morn darkness while out in the firehills that un-gamish hooraw went on and on, rising and falling. Mavin huddled in her blanket, perched within the rainspout once more, out of sight and therefore out of anyone's mind at all, she told herself. She did not want to see Handbright's face.

It came toward dawn, and the Elders put their score pads on their laps, ready to note what it was they liked about the procession, already seeing shifting shapes out beyond the p'natti, high tossed plumes, lifted wings, whirlings and leapings just at the edge of the light. Mavin waited, holding her breath. She had told herself that she was not so childish as to be excited, but the breath stuck in her throat nonetheless.

Full light. Out at the edge of the p'natti a hedge of prismed spears arose, shattering light in a thousand directions, then broke into shapes which came forward to the music of their own drumming. They came low, then upward to fly, to catch, to slide down, to rear upward again, to sparkle in jeweled greens and blues, fiery reds and ambers, scales like emerald and sapphire – the mythical jewels of heaven – and eyes which glowed a hundred shades of gold. Beyond the narrowing pillars they thrust upward into trees of gems, glittering from a million leaves, slid forward between the pillars and confronted the square-form portals in contracting shapes of bulked steel, gleaming gray and shiny. Around the slither-downs they came, erupting now into different shapes, some winged, some coiled like leaping springs, some vaporous as mist, all to break like water upon the barrier of the slything walls and take the shapes of fustigars and pombis and owls, tumbling and leaping over the walls and the ways until they were at the walls of the keep itself where they became whirling pools of light and shadow, towering higher and higher, drawing up, up, up to meet at the zenith above the keep in a dome, a shining lattice of drawn flesh, all the time the drumming going on and on, louder and louder, until a crash came to make their ears fall deaf.

And in that moment the high lattice fell, drew in upon itself like shadow to become the visitors from Bothercat the Rude Rock and Fretowl the Dark Wood and a dozen other Xhindi keeps, laughing outside the walls and demanding entrance. So was the first processional ended. Mavin sat in the high hidey hole, mouth open, so full of wonder at it that she could not wake herself from the dream.

Still there were some hundreds to be fed, and it would have taken advance planning and great determination to hide from so many. She was winkled out and set to carrying plates within the hour, and thereafter was not let alone for so much as a moment during the days or nights.

It was on the last day of Assembly that one of the Xhindi from Battlefox the Bright Day sought her, making a special thing of asking after her and begging her company for a walk in the p'natti. He told her his name was Plandybast Ogbone. "Your thalan, child. Do you know what that is?"

She looked at him mouth open. "Full brother of my mother? But she was Danderbat! Not Battlefox!"

"Oh, and yes, yes, child. True. But your grandma, her mother, was Battlefox right enough. Bore six for Battlefox, she did, before taking herself away into the deep world for time on her own. And it was here she met a scarfulous fellow called young Theobald, so it seems she told Battlefox Elders. And he got twins on her, which was your mama and me, and then she died. And young Theobald, he took the girl child and brought her back to the Danderbats knowing their deep scarcity of females, but me he kept with the Battlefoxes, reminding me frequent that I was thalan to any of her childer. He died some time back. And so I am thalan to Handbright, and to you, and to young Mertyn.

"Time ago I invited Handbright to come visit Battlefox the Bright Day, but she pled she could not leave young Mertyn. Today I asked her to bring him, and you, if she would, but these here have convinced her the walls of Danderbat keep are Xhindi gold. It seems a slavey in Danderbat is equal to an Elder in Battlefox – or so she believes. No, no, I lie if I say that's true, for I've talked with her and talked with her, and it's something other than that. Something is awry with her, and she seems unable to decide anything. She simply does and does and tries not to think about it. Well, you know the old saying, 'Vary thought, vary shape.' Since we do not take the same shapes, it is silly to expect us to think alike." He shook his head. "Though, weary as she looks, I would expect her to have accepted my invitation. Though I have a kinsman or so there who may be a bit difficult – most particularly one kinswoman, of whom the least said the best – she would have companions and help at Battlefox."

"She's the only girl behind the p'natti," whispered Mavin, so moved by this intelligence that she forgot to be wary of telling anyone, and him a stranger man for that. "Until she tells them about me."

So Plandybast Ogbone looked at her, and she at him, sharing a wordless kind of sympathy which she had not felt from any of the Danderbats. "So that's the way of it. And when they are told about you, all the oldsters will be at your bedroom door night on night, won't they? Ah, surely Danderbat keep may be the oldest and the original, but it has fallen into a nasty sort of decay. We do not so treat our she-children at Battlefox and would have you welcome there. Or are you too convinced that the keep walls are Xhindi gold?''

''No,'' she whispered. ''I want out.''

''Ah. Well. There's young Mertyn. He'd miss you no doubt.''

''Bring him with me,'' she said. ''I would. Couldn't leave him here. To hear unkind things. About me, as I have heard about mother.''

''What is it they say about my sister Abrara?''

''That she shifted forbiddens while she carried Mertyn, and died from it.''

''Oh, Gamelords, what nonsense. I've known many who shifted before and during and didn't die of it, though the Healers do say the child does best which isn't shifted in the womb. This all reminds me of my other sister, Itter, going on and on about Abrara whom she never knew and knows little enough about. There are some who must find fault somewhere, among the dead if they cannot find enough among the living. Abrara died because she was never strong, shifter or no. That's the truth. They should have had a Healer for her when she was young, as they did for me, but they didn't, for the Danderbat Xhindi set themselves above Healing. Lucky I was the Battlefoxes are no such reactionary old persons, or like I'd have died, too. She should have been let alone, not made to have childer, but the Danderbats are so short of females these two generations, and she had had daughters. She should have been let alone.''

''At the Old Shuffle, we are not let alone.''

He looked at her seriously, walked around in a circle, as though he circled in his thoughts. ''You know, child, if I took you away from Danderbat with me, there'd be fits and consternation by the Elders. Particularly since Danderbat is so short of females just now. There'd be hearings and meetings and no doubt unpleasant things for me and you both. That's if I took you. Stole you, so they'd say, like a sack of grain or a basket of ripe thrilps. If you came to me, however, at Battlefox the Bright Day, you might have a few nasty words from Itter, but I'd not send you away empty-handed or hungry. You've seen maps of the place? You know where it is?''

She stared at him, but he did not meet her eyes, merely seeking the sky with a thoughtful face as though he had said nothing at all of importance.

''Yes,'' she said finally in a voice as casual as his own. ''I know where it is. It lies high upon the Shadowmarches, northwest of Pfarb Durim. If I came to visit you some day, you'd be glad to see me?" she offered. "More or less."

"Oh. Surely. More or less. I would be very glad to see you. And Mertyn."

"Ah," she said. "I'll remember that, my thalan, and I thank you." She turned to leave him, full of dignity, then turned to hug him briefly, smearing his face with unregarded tears. "Thank you for telling me about my mother." Her gait as she left was perfectly controlled, and he looked after her, aware of a kind of envy at her composure. It was better done than he had seen from many twice her age.

CHAPTER THREE

The Assembly was concluded. The visitors left. The cooks departed in their wagon looking weary and half drunk, for they had had their own celebration when the last banquet was over. Up in the small room at the top of the tower, Handbright slept in total exhaustion, and for once the old ones were so surfeited with food and frolic that they left her alone. Mavin, watching, made sure of this. She had set herself to be Handbright's watchdog for the time Mavin remained at the keep. That would not be long. She had resolved upon it. But she was still too untried a shifter to take child Mertyn into the wide world trusting only on her own abilities to keep him safe. As the shifter children were often told, there were child markets operating in the Gameworld, and whether a child might be shifter or no, the bodies of the young were saleable.

She knew that when they went safety would depend on covert, quiet travel over many leagues, for the way to Battlefox the Bright Day lay a distance well beyond Pfarb Durim through the Shadowmarches. And covert travel would be totally dependent upon Mavin's Talent, child Mertyn having none of his own save a sensible and thoughtful disposition. Her Talent had to be tried, and exercised, and practiced. Each night when the place was still, Mavin went beyond the p'natti into the woods – a forbidden excursion – or deep into the cellars – empty now – to try what it was she could do with herself.

It took her several nights to learn to damp the pain of shifting, to subdue it so that it did not distract her from what she was attempting. She spent those nights copying herd beasts from the surrounding fields, laying her hands upon them and feeling her way into their shapes, hide first as it were, the innards coming along as a consequence of the outer form. She learned to let discomfort guide her. If there was a feeling of itchy wrongness, then she could let the miraculous net within her sort it out, reach for a kind of rightness which felt both comfortable and holdable. There were parts which were difficult. Hooves were troublesome. And horns. They had no living texture to them, and making the hard surfaces took practice. She learned the shape of her own stomach by the forms it took in shifting, the fineness and texture of her own skin, the shape and function of her own female parts, for she had determined to ignore the proscription against shifting placed upon females by the Danderbat. Reason said that if men could do it and still produce progeny, then women could do it also. And if not, then not. She would do without childer. Whatever she might do or not do, she would not end like Handbright.

Each morning she woke Handbright with a cup of tea – aware that this sudden solicitude evoked a certain suspicion – and repeated that she did not want the Elders told, not just yet. Each day Handbright would reluctantly agree, and Mavin would go to sleep for a few hours before finding some deserted place to practice in. Day succeeded day. Gormer and Haribald were gone from the keep on a long hunting expedition, for the food storage rooms were virtually depleted. In their absence Handbright stopped insisting that the Elders must be told, and Mavin relaxed a trifle, sleeping a few more hours than she would have done otherwise.

She developed her own systems for rapid acquisition of Talent, reminding herself how quickly the babies in the nursery learned to talk once they had begun. If one spent hours every day at it, it came fast. Even the boys who began to show Talent were not usually allowed as many free hours for practice as Mavin took for herself, for they had to attend classes and spend time with the Elders listening to history tales. With the Assembly so recently over, however, everyone was tired. The Elders themselves were off in the woods in easy shapes which required no thought. The children were left to their own devices and seemed to spend endless days playing Wizards and Shifters. In a few days the keep would pull itself together to resume its usual schedule, but just now it was open and relaxed, ideal for Mavin's purposes. She thanked the Gamelords, prayed to Thandbar it would last as long as she needed, and practiced.

She knew she did not have time to learn many different things. She could not trifle with herself, learning the shape of a whirlwind or a cloud. She must take what time she had to learn a few things well, learning even those few shapes in wonder and occasional chagrin. She worked endlessly at her horse shape, believing that a boy the size of Mertyn could best be carried farthest on some ordinary, acceptable animal. Besides, horses could fight. Horses with hooves honed to razor sharpness could fight particularly well, and she spent prodigious hours rearing and wheeling herself, striking with forefeet and back ones, all in absolute silence so that no one would hear and come to investigate. She practiced gaining bulk, all the bulk one needed to become a horse, practiced doing it quickly and leaving it just as quickly. Taking bulk was not an easy thing. One had to absorb the extra bulk, water or grain or grass – organic things were best. Then one had to pull the net out of the extra bulk to return to one's own shape, quickly, neatly, with no agonizing tugs or caught bits of oneself lingering. It was not an easy thing, but she learned to do it well. Not knowing what she could not do, she did everything differently than other shifters would have done it, comforted herself by naming herself "Mavin Manyshaped," and did little dances of victory all alone.

She began to pay attention to other shifters, to the way she knew them, could identify them, even inside other shapes, and discovered at last a kind of organ within herself which trembled in recognition when another shifter with a similar organ was near. It was small, no bigger than a finger, but it was growing. A few days before, she would not have known it was there. Desperately, she set about shifting that organ itself, veiling it, muffling it, so that it could not betray her. She wanted to be horse, only horse, with no shifter unmasking her as anything else. The difficulty lay in the strange identifier organ, for when she muffled it directly, it was as though she had become deaf and blind, unable to walk without losing her balance. Not knowing that it was impossible – as any Elder of the Xhindi would have told her – she invented a bony plate to grow around it which allowed it to function inside her body without betraying itself outside. The plate was bulky. She could not contain it in a small shape or a narrow one, but she could do it as a horse, and the night she achieved it she slept for hours, so drowned in sleep that it was like waking from an eternity.

Waking to find that Gormier and Haribald had returned, and with them Wurstery and half a dozen others. The hunt had been successful; the kitchen courtyard was full of butchery, with smoky fires under the racks of meat, drying it for storage.

And Handbright was there with great black rings around her eyes, looking cowed and beaten, as though she had not slept for days. "I told them," she said to Mavin, not meeting her eyes. "I had to. I can't go on."

Mavin looked up to find Gormier's eyes upon her, full of a gloating expectation. Ah, well. She had had more time than she had expected. "When?" She did not reproach Handbright. The strange identifier organ would have betrayed her sooner or later, and what she intended to do would be reproach enough.

"They want to have your Talent party today. They're drawing lots who stays with you first tonight. Well, it's time for you, Mavin. You'll live through it, though. We all have."

"I'm sure I will. Of course I will. Don't fret. Come with me to the kitchen and have a cup of something hot. You look exhausted."

"They woke me in the middle of the night, the three of them. They . . . they put . . . I . . . I had to tell them."

"Of course." Soothing, kindly, hypocritical, Mavin led her to the kitchen. "Handbright, listen to me. I want you to go to Battlefox keep in the Bright Day demesne. Our thalan, Plandybast Ogbone, wants you to come. Promise me?"

Handbright shook her head, a frantic denial. "Mertyn. Mertyn needs me."

Mavin thought it was only habit and a weary inertia which made Handbright speak so. "He doesn't need you, Handbright. He's fine. The youngest child in the nursery is five years old, and you've spent long enough taking care of them. You should know by now you're not going to conceive, and you'd have been long gone if you had conceived. So you must go. There are lots of Danderbats can come in to take care of the childer. Besides, I'll be here."

"But . . . alone. It's so hard alone . . . and Mertyn . . ."

"You did it alone. After you have some rest, you can come back and help me if you like. But I want you to go, Handbright. Either to Plandybast, or to the sea, as you once said you would do. Today." She bent all her concentration upon her sister, willed her to respond. "*Now*, Handbright."

"Now?" Hope bloomed on her face as though this had been the secret word of release; but there was a wild look in her eyes. "Now?"

Mavin wondered what had happened to make the woman respond in this way. It could not be her own pleading, for she had pled before and nothing had happened. No. Something else had happened. She did not take time to worry about what it might have been.

"Now. Become a white bird, Handbright! Fly from the tallest tower. From your bedroom, up there in the heights. Nothing carried, nothing needed – to Battlefox. Or to the sea."

Handbright rose, a look almost of madness in her face, eyes darting, hands patting at herself. "Now. Mavin. Now. I'll go. Someday, I'll . . . you'll come. Mertyn's all right. He's a big boy. He'll be fine. Now." And she fled away up the stairs, Mavin close behind but unseen, as though she had been a ghost.

Clothes fell on the stone floor. Handbright stood in the window, naked. From the doorway Mavin gasped, seeing bruises and bloody stripes on the naked form which changed, shifted, wavered in outline to stand where it had stood but feathered, long neck curled on white back, beak turned toward Mavin, eyes still wild and seeking.

"Fly, sister," she commanded, fixing the maddened eyes with her own. "Fly, Handbright. Go."

The wings unfurled slowly, the neck stretched out tentatively, cautiously, then all at once darted forward as the wings thrust down, once, twice, and the great bird launched itself into the air, falling, falling, catching itself upon those wide wings at the last possible moment to soar up, out, out, away toward the west.

Mavin found herself crying. She flung herself down on Handbright's narrow bed, aware for the first time of the basket in the corner, the ropes, the little whip carelessly thrown down upon the stones. It was a punishment basket, the only true punishment for a shifter, to be confined, close confined, unable to move, to speak, to change into any other shape. The baskets were woven in Kyquo, tightly woven, tightly lidded. And this one had been used on Handbright, or she had been threatened with it.

So. Threatened or used; what did it matter. Handbright was gone. Mavin wiped her face in a cold, unreasoning fury and without knowing how she did it, or even that she had done it, took on the very face and features of Handbright; the well known expression, the tumbled hair, the tall, slender form bent with work and abuse, the eyes dark-ringed with pain to look upon herself reflected there – Handbright's own form and face.

"Everyone knows," she whispered, "that it is impossible for a shifter to take the form of another living person. Everyone knows that it lies outside our nature, that it is forbidden. Everyone knows that. But – but, someone has done it." She smiled at herself in the mirror, a cold smile, and went slowly, with fearful anticipation, down into the smoke of the kitchen court to confront Gormier's truculent stare.

"Well?" he demanded. "She's been told there's been enough of this holding back, has she? Celebration for her this day and for me this night. I've won the draw." And he grinned widely at her as he displayed the red-tipped stick he had drawn. "Time I had a little luck after too long of your dead body, old girl. Time we had some fresh blood behind the p'natti."

"She doesn't want a celebration." This in the very tone and substance of Handbright's own voice, dull and without emotion. "She's sick to her stomach. She's up in my room, and you can go up there, come dark, but she'll have no celebration."

"Well, and go up I will. And after me Wurstery, and after him Haribald, for that's the way it falls."

Still in Handbright's voice Mavin let her curiosity free to find the limits of the old ones' abuse. "Couldn't you have pity on her this night? Make it only one of you?"

Wurstery had overheard this from his drying rack duties and intervened to make his own demands. "We've been days in the woods, old girl. Make a nice homecoming for us. Besides, best begin as we mean to go on."

"Well then," Mavin said in Handbright's voice, "she'll have to bear it, I suppose."

"Let's hope she bears better'n you've borne, old girl." And they went back to their smoky work in a mood of general self-righteousness and satisfaction. Mavin went back into the keep, into a shadowy place, and leaned against the wall, weeping. When she had done, the Handbright shape had dropped away, and though she tried, she could not bring it back. She went to find Mertyn to tell the boy they would leave Danderbat keep that night.

She went over it with him several times, though the boy understood well enough even at first. "The horse will come to the corner of the p'natti wall farthest toward the fire hills. You'll have all your clothes and things in this sack, everything you treasure, lad, for you'll not be back. And I will meet you on the road. . . ."

"And I must not say anything about it to anyone," he concluded for her, puzzled but willing. "Especially not to any of the Danderbats."

"That's right. Especially not to the Danderbats. And you're to wait. Even if it gets very late and scary, and you hear owls or fustigars howling. Promise."

"Promise." He put his small hand in hers, cold but steady. "I'll wait, Mavin. No matter how late."

She left him, trusting him. Then to the cellars for two more of the punishment baskets, thick with dust, hardly ever used. Except by shifters like Gormier, for Mavin had no doubt it had been his idea – to spice things a bit. Then to the kitchens for a sack of grain. Then to Handbright's room. She would have to be ready by dark, and it would take that much time to gain the bulk she would need to become a horse – to become a horse, but first to become something else indeed, only a part of which would resemble Mavin.

She did not know that what she was doing was impossible. She knew only that she would not rest and could not go until Gormier and Haribald and Wurstery knew what Handbright had known, the sureness of pain, the tightness of confinement. And another thing. One other thing. When they knew that, it would not matter that there were no Danderbat girls behind the p'natti in future.

In the deep middle of the night her horse shape came to Mertyn, exactly where she had told him to be. She whinnied at him, pushing at him with a soft nose, letting him feel her ears and neck to reassure him that all was well. He scrambled clumsily onto the low wall, and from that to Mavin's back, the sack of possessions balanced in a lump before him.

"Nice horse," he said doubtfully. "Are you going to take me to Mavin?"

The horse's head nodded, and the beast stepped away from the wall, into the forest which Mavin knew as few others of the keep had ever known. By dawn they would need to be leagues away, down the cliff road which led to Haws Valley and well buried in the woods which lay along the upper stretches of the River Haws. She could not let the boy know she was shifter. His mind would be open to any Demon riding along who might choose to Read him, and it was better if he simply did not know. So, there would be play acting aplenty in the hours and days to come.

They would be safe from pursuit for at least this day. The three in the tower room would not be found for hours, perhaps not for days. Each one of them had struggled, frightened half out of his wits and mad with the pain of missing vital parts of himself. Struggle had been useless. Mavin had prepared for the encounter by taking more bulk than the three of them put together, part of that bulk a Mavin-shaped piece, and the rest a huge, tentacled thing which swumbled them up and thrust them into the baskets no matter how they howled, pushing and squashing until they were forced to take the shape of the basket, without lungs or lips or eyes. Gormier had been first, arriving full of explicit, lewd instructions for the cowering girl, ready to force them upon her, only to be thrust into agonized silence by the hugeness that was Mavin. Then Wurstery, then Haribald, each coming into the dark room expecting nothing more than a bit of the usual. Well, usual they now had. Handbright's usual. They would probably live, if they were found before they starved, but they would not father any more Danderbats. A shifter might shift as he would: once that part of his self was gone, it was gone forever. He might shift him a part which looked similar, but he would take no pleasure from it. Beneath Mertyn's drowsing form the horse shuddered, half in horror, half in satisfaction.

Now that the boy was soundly asleep, Mavin grew tentacles again, small ones to hold him securely on her back, and began to run. The horse shape was well and fully practiced, constructed for fleetness with eyes that could spy through the dark to see every hollow or bit of broken ground. Night fled past. Behind them in the keep a hysterical Wurstery managed a hair-thin tentacle to lift the latch of his basket. Behind them in the keep was consternation, fury. The Elders were summoned out of their inner privacies by bells. "Handbright," they said. "It was Handbright!" No one was thinking to look for Mavin or for Mertyn. A shifter girl only just come to Talent could not have done this thing. It could only possibly have been done by someone older, someone who had practiced secretly. Ah, yes, that is why she never conceived. Surely it was Handbright. The Danderbats had only thought the creature looked like Mavin. The room had been dark. It had been Handbright, shifting shape, desirous of protecting (protecting?) her little sister.

Jealous, Gormier offered. Jealous that the younger girl would get all their attention. At which there was much clucking of agreement, save among the crones who looked knowingly at one another but said nothing.

The Xhindi did not believe in Healers, but one was sent for nonetheless. The three Danderbats were in too much pain to let nature heal them. Pain and fury.

Far off to the north, the horse ran on, the boy cushioned soft on its wide back, as dawn leaked milky into the edges of the sky. She stopped, laid him down, went off into the woods to give up bulk and clothe herself. When she came out into the clearing, he was rubbing his eyes, looking up at her in gladness. "Mavin. You said you'd be here, but I thought maybe you'd forget."

She took him in her arms, glad that he could not fully see her face. "Oh, no, Mertyn," she said. "Never fear that about Mavin. Mavin does not forget."

He slept curled in her arms, as secure as though he had been in the childer's rooms at the keep, waking full of deep thoughts about the day. Mavin had brought with her a handful of the seeds of the fruit of the rainhat bush, used by the crones in the keep whenever shallow, quiet sleep was needed by someone ill or wounded. She fed half a dozen of these to Mertyn with his stewed grain, and then made him up to look like quite another boy. She had brought dye for his hair and bits of false hair to tuft his eyebrows out and a brush to make freckle spots on his clear skin. When she had done, he smiled at her in his sleep, quite content, looking utterly unlike himself. She wanted him passive, unable to take fright or betray them by recognizing someone, for they would need to travel part of the day on the Hawsport Road which led along the River Haws all the way from the far northern lands over Calihiggy Creek and down to the sea. Later, when there was time, she would explain it all and trust to his own good sense, but there was no time now for any explanation, and she dared not trust his guile.

The horse form she took was sway-backed and old, with splayed hooves which turned up at the edges. A horse ridden by an unaccompanied child might be coveted by someone stronger, but this horse could be coveted by no one. So she took bulk and changed, scooping the sack and the child onto her back with a long, temporary tentacle and holding them in place with nearly invisible ones thereafter. Then they wandered down through the woods to the road, empty in either direction. She began to plod along it, heading north, the river on her right and on both right and left, leagues away, the crumbly cliffs of Haws Valley. On that western height, well behind her, lay Danderbat keep. It was from that height that search would come, if search came, but it did not cross Mavin's mind that the search might be for Handbright.

The sway-backed horse shape was unbearable. It was inefficient and it ached. Without in the least meaning to do so, Mavin changed herself to remove the aches and make it easier to move along the road, only to come to herself with a sense of impending danger at the sounds of something coming along the road after her. A quick self check – she thought of it as a kind of patting the pockets of herself to see what she had in them – showed her a form so unnatural and strange as to have evoked immediate interest in anyone except a blind man. Hastily, and barely in time, she shifted back into the old horse form, plodded off the road and into a clump of bushes to let the travelers pass her by. She knew them for shifter the moment they came into view as dark, moving splotches against the moon-grayed loom of the forest. She even knew which shifters they were, Barfod Bartiban, thalan to Leggy Bartiban, and Torben Naffleloose. She knew them by the fustigar shapes they had taken, ones often seen in processionals at the Danderbat keep, as familiar in their way as the actual shapes of the two shifter men. The two shapes were hard run, panting, lagging feet in the dust to stir up a nose-tickling cloud. Mavin repressed a sneeze and tightened her grip on Mertyn, praying they would not see her, know her, somehow spy her out in the horse shape with the bony plate around her shifter organ.

They did not. Instead, they slowed to a dragging walk, and then into a breath-gulping halt, sagging into the dust of the road with heaving moans of exhaustion.

"No way Handbright could have come so far north lugging two younglings," panted Barford. "So we've got to figure we're in front of her if she came north. Not that I think she did."

"Think she went west? On no more than that crone's say so?"

"Only place she ever talked of going. Beyond Schlaizy Noithn to the sea. Wanted to do a bird thingy over the ocean. Fool idea, but that's what the crone said."

"What'd she expect to do with the childer? Put them in a nest on a cliff and feed them fish?" Torben Naffleloose chuckled, hawking through the dust phlegm of his shifted throat. "Take a big bird to carry a girl the size of Mavin."

"Well now, you're forgetting Mavin had turned shifter herself. Wasn't that what all the ruckus was about?"

"Oh, well, still. A just turned shifter is useless, Barfod, useless as tits on a owl. All they do for the first half year or so is fiddle with fingers and toes. You know that."

"I remember that. Fingers, toes, and some other interesting parts, eh, Torben. Remember when you was a forty-season child? Out behind the p'natti? Hah. All the shifter boys seeing who could . . ." He paused, listening. Mavin had shifted her weight, rustling some branches. "What was that?"

"Owl, prob'ly. No shifters around. I could feel 'em if there were. No. Just night noises. Owls. Maybe a shadowman, sneaking around behind the bushes like they do. This is the kind of mild night they like, I hear. They come out and sing on nights like this. Did you ever hear 'em?"

"Oh, sure, when I was in Schlaizy Noithn. Playing flutes, playing little bells, singing like birds. There's lots of them around the Schlaizy Noithn hills. There was one or two shifters when I was there claimed they could talk the shadowman talk. All full of babble-pabble it is, goes on and on. They'll sing for a half night, words and words, and then you ask what it was all about and get told it was shadowman talk for 'Look at the pretty moon.' Ah, well. Now that we're as far north as Handbright could have come, what's the next thing, old Barfod?"

There was a moment's silence while the two sat quiet, thinking, then Bartiban replied, "Now I think we start off through the woods heading south again, you on one side of the road and me on the other, casting back and forth to see can we smell hide nor fang of whatever Handbright is up to. There's others gone away west, and I'm betting my coin that they find her there. She's an unpracticed female, Torben, and unpracticed females aren't up to much, as you well know. Which is why we keep 'em unpracticed, right?" And he chuckled in a liquid gurgle before rising once more to take another, more forest ready shape. The two went off into the underbrush, and Mavin stayed silent, hardly breathing, to let them get clear of her.

So. They were seeking Handbright, a shifter burdened with two children. They were not seeking Mavin. Then so much for the horse shape, not-Mavin shape of the journey. She laid Mertyn upon the shadowed grasses and went away a little to give up the bulk she had taken, most of it, keeping some, for she wanted not to appear a child. There were child hunters, child takers in the world, and it would be better not to appear a child. Better not to appear a woman, either, for that. So. Well, first she would need to explain to Mertyn, and after that they would decide. She lay down beside him and let the night move over her like a blanket, quiet and peaceful, with no harm in it except the little harms of night-hunting birds doing away with legions of small beasties between their burrows; the slaughter of beetle by night-stalking lizard; the trickle of melody running through the forest signifying of shadowmen, shadowmen unheard for Mavin was asleep.

In the morning she woke to the child stirring in her arms, woke to a crystal, glorious morning, so full of freedom that her heart sang with it and she thought of Handbright wonderingly. How could she have waited so long? How could she have given up all this to stay prisoned within the p'natti, within the keep, prey to those old granders and their salacious whims? It was a puzzle to her. She, Mavin, would not, ever, could not, ever. She tickled Mertyn awake and fed him from their small stock of foodstuffs, knowing she would have to hunt meat for them soon, or gather road fruits, or come to some place where such things could be worked for.

"Where are we going, Mavin? You never said."

"Because I didn't have time, Mertyn. You see, you and I are running away from Danderbat keep."

"Running away! Why are we doing that? I didn't know that! You mean we can't ever go back?" The child sounded crushed, or perhaps only surprised into a sense of loss.

"You said you wanted to go traveling more than anything, Mertyn child."

"I know. I just – just thought I'd come back to Danderbat keep and tell everyone where I'd been and what I'd been doing. Like the shifters do at Assembly. Like that."

"Unlikely for us, Mertyn. We are going to Battlefox the Bright Day, high on the Shadowmarches, for there is your thalan and mine. Plandybast Ogbone." She patted the boy while he thought on this, chewing away at the tough dried meat they had brought with them.

"He was at Assembly. He gave me a thingy." The boy rummaged in a pocket, coming up at last with a tiny carving of two frogs grinning at one another on a leaf. It was the kind of intricate handwork which the shifters loved, tiny and marvelous, done with fanatical care and endless time in the long, dark hours of the keep nights of the cold season. "He told me he had brought it for Handbright, but that I looked as though I needed it. What did he mean by that, Mavin?"

"He meant that he thought you were still young enough to be tickled by it, child, and to keep it in your pocket forever. He could see that Handbright was beyond such things, beyond hope, beyond saving, perhaps. Perhaps not."

He looked questions at her, started to ask, bit his lip and did not. Mavin, sighing, took up the story. He would need to know, after all, child or not. "You see, Mertyn child," she said, "this was the way of it with Handbright. . . ." So she told him, everything, he flushing at the harsh telling of it but knowing well enough what it was she meant. Once in a while she said, "You know what that is? You understand?" to which he nodded shamefaced knowledge.

When she had done, he whispered, "You know, the boys . . . they say . . . the ones like Leggy and Janjiver . . . they say the girls like it. That's what they say. They say that the girls may say no, but they really like it."

Mavin thought a time. "Mertyn child, you like sweet cakes, don't you?"

He nodded, cocking his head at this change of subject.

"Let us suppose I put a basket of sweet cakes here, a big one, and I held your mouth open and I crumbled a cake into your mouth and pushed it down your throat with a piece of wood, the way the crones push corn down the goose's neck to fatten it, so that your throat bled and you choked and gasped, but I went on pushing the crumbled cakes down your throat until they were gone. You could not chew them, or taste them. When I was done and your throat was full of blood and you half dead from it all, I would take the stick away and laugh at you and tell you I would be back on the morrow to do it all again. Then, suppose you came crying to someone and that someone said, 'But Mertyn, you *like* sweet cakes, you really like sweet cakes. . . .' "

The boy thought of this, red-faced, eyes filling with quick tears. "Oh, Mavin. Mavin. Oh, poor Handbright. I hope she has gone far away, far away. . . ."

Mavin nodded. "Yes. She was bruised and the blood had spotted her skin, Mertyn. She had had no joy of the granders, nor they of her except the ugly joy of power and violence and the despising of women that they do. So. We have run from Danderbat keep, but they do not know that we are gone one way and Handbright another. So, we will stop going as boy and horse and go as boy and something else. For I am a shifter, Mertyn, and shift I will to keep us safe and fed and warm of nights."

"But Mavin, you are only a beginning shifter. Everyone says they are not up to much."

"Well. Perhaps they are right. So, I will not shift much. I will only be your big brother instead of your big sister, and that only so that no one disturbs us as we walk along."

"What will we do with the poor horse?" he asked gravely.

She began to laugh, then stopped herself. No. Let him go on believing there had been a horse. "I turned it loose back in the woods. It will graze there happily all the rest of its life, so we will leave it. Come, now. Let's pack all this stuff and be on our way. We have spent long enough in one spot, and it is many such spots before we come to the Shadowmarches."

She pulled him to his feet and busied him about the camp, burying the scraps and packing all the rest. Then, when she had changed herself under his wondering eyes into something not unlike herself but indisputably male, they went out onto the road to take the way north.

CHAPTER FOUR

The road was thick with dust of a soft, pinky color, powdered rose as it fluffed upward in small clouds around their feet, coating them to the knees with a blushing glow and velvety texture. At the sides of the road grew luxuriant stands of rainhat bush, the conical leaves as stiff as funnels, furry tan fruit nestling in each. The fruit was blue-fleshed and sweet beneath the furry, itchy skin, and they amused themselves as they went, spiking the fruit out without touching it and slitting the skin away to reveal the turquoise juiciness beneath. Small boys considered it great fun to hide rainhat fruit skins in one another's beds or clothing, laughing uproariously at the frenzied scratching which would ensue. Mavin warned Mertyn with a glance when she saw him furtively hiding a fingerlength of skin, and he flushed as he threw it away.

Beyond the stands of bushes to the west the forest began, first a fringing growth of yellow webwillow, then the dark conifers building gloom against the bronze red cliffs which reached upward at their left. The cliffs were crumbly piers eaten away by ages of rain and sun into angled blocks stacked far upward to the ivory rimrock where the brows of the forest peered down into the valley. To their right the river ran silver, silent, slithery as a great snake, making no murmur save at the edges where it chuckled quietly under the grassy banks, telling its own story. Small froggy things polluped into the pools as they passed. Reeds swayed as though lurkers traveled there, though nothing emerged from the green fastnesses but stalking birds, high on their stilts, peering and poking into the mire with lancelike beaks. Sun glittered, spun, wove, twisted into a fabric of light and air and shining water, and they walked as though at the center of a jewel to the muffled plopping of their own steps.

Beside the river were hayfields, few and narrow between the

water and the road. Across the river were more fields, with twisty trails leading onto the high ridge where villages perched upon the rocks like roosting owls, windows staring at them as they passed. That was the Ridge of Wicking, between the River Haws and the Westfork, which lay in a great trough north of Betand. Not far ahead, to the east, the high plateau at the north end of the Ridge bulked vastly against the sky, its black stone and hard outline menacing, the bare rocky top fisting the sky like a blow. There was supposed to be a Wizard's Demesne on Blacktop, but Mavin thought it unlikely anyone would nest there save Armigers, perhaps, or other Gamesmen who flew. Dragons or Cold-drakes, perhaps. Gamesmen of that kind. There appeared to be no comfort in the place, no kindness of wood or water. She preferred it where they were and said as much to Mertyn, who sighed, hummed, trudged along the road not talking and seeming unthinking in the warm and the light.

"Elators, maybe," she mused. "Perhaps they are initiated by being taken up there on some long, climby trail, and then once they have seen the place and can remember it, they flick up onto the high rock from the far places, flick, and there they are, the place full of Elators as a thrilp is full of seeds. . . ."

"I think Seers," Mertyn offered. "It would be nice for Seers, up there, where they could really see for a thousand leagues in every direction." He hummed again, smiled up at her as though drugged, and trudged on once more. She thought that she herself must seem as drugged as he on the sunlight and the quiet, for she was in a mood of strange and marvelous contentment, so quietly peaceful that she almost missed the sound of hooves behind them on the road.

Mavin moved into the bushes at the side of the road, pulling Mertyn along with her. "Remember," she cautioned him. "I am your older brother. You may still call me Mavin, for that could be man or woman, but do not for the love of all the powers and freedom call me 'sister'." It was easy enough for her to seem male, the changes were superficial and easy; and if Mertyn did not forget, she would pass well enough. The horse sounds came on, more than one animal, and she turned at last to see what moved toward them in the morning.

They were two Tragamors, one male and one female peering through their fanged half helms, and a rough-looking man dressed in a strange garb which Mavin did not recognize. She had been told that the school in Danderbat keep was not good for much except teaching some shifterish skills and policies, and she knew that they had paid little enough attention to the Index. She wished at the moment that they had spent more time upon it, enough time at least to recognize what he might be. Not Tragamor – their fanged helms were unmistakable – therefore probably not having the Tragamor skill of moving things from a distance or tossing mountains about at will. It would probably be some complementary talent. The man was clad in skins and furs, and he had a long glass slung at his shoulder. She had barely time to look him over before the horses pulled up and the male Tragamor leaned from his saddle to hail them in a voice both unpleasant and challenging.

"Hey there, fellow. We are told there is a way into the highlands along this River. Would you know how far?"

Just as Mavin was readying herself to reply, Mertyn spoke, his childish treble firm and positive. "Just before you come to Calihiggy Creek, Gamesman, there is a trail leading back to the southeast onto the heights. Or, if you need a better road than that, there is one which goes south from Pfarb Durim to Betand, but that is many leagues to the north."

"Ah, a scholarly scut, isn't it," drawled the skin-clad man. "And where did you learn so much about the world, small one." He seemed to be struggling with his face, attempting to keep it in its frowning mold.

"I studied maps . . . sir. I'm sorry, but I don't know what your title should be, Sir Gamesman. I mean no offense. . . ." Mavin looked at the boy, fascinated, for he was smiling up at the men, a kind of light in his face, and they all smiled back, kindly, with no hint of trouble.

Mavin shook herself, drew herself into the persona she had adopted and said, "Indeed, we mean no offense, Gamesmen. We are country people and see few travelers."

The skin-clad one turned his eyes from the child to Mavin, face still kindly and happy. "No offense, young man. No offense. I am an Explorer, and there are few enough of my kind among all the Gamesmen in these lands. We go into the high country in search of fabled mines, and we must find a way the wagons can come after, for why should Tragamors delve when pawns can dig? Eh?"

"Why, indeed," caroled Mertyn. "Well, it is more than one day's journey to the trail, Gamesmen. We wish you speedy journey and comfortable rest." And he smiled, and the Gamesmen smiled and rode away, and Mavin was once more trudging in the dust which had been so full of sparkling light and peace.

She shook herself. "What did you do to them?"

"Do?" He was all innocence. "Do?"

"Do, Mertyn. When that Tragamor spoke to us first, his fanged helm practically dripped menace at us, ready to bite us up in one gulp if we did not tell him what he wanted to know. Then, in moments, in a breath, he was all kindly thalan to us both, full of good will as a new keg is of air."

The boy frowned, seemed to concentrate. "I don't know, Mavin. It's just something that happens sometimes when I don't want people to be cross. It's nicer to be happy and contented, so I do the thing and everyone feels better." He stared at his feet, flushed. "I guess I make them love me."

For a moment she did not understand what he had said. She confused it in her mind with something natural and childish he might have said, "I guess I make them love me. . . ." What could he have meant? Some childish game? Some pretend magic? Then came a sickening combination of horror and understanding as she understood what he meant, a kind of nausea, yet with fascination in it. "Did you . . . did you do that to Handbright, Mertyn?"

He nodded guiltily. "Otherwise she would have gone away. I would have been lonely. That's the real reason she stayed, Mavin. I made her stay."

She could not keep the words inside. They spilled out. "I wonder if you have any idea how horrible that was for her. . . ." Her anger went away as quickly as it had come at the response she saw. The boy wept, his face flushed and red, tears flowing in a stream, his thin chest heaving with the pain of it, all at once bereft and cast down by tragedy, lost to it.

"I'm so sorry, Mavin. I'm so sorry. I didn't know, really until you told me. They said . . . they said it wasn't so bad, not really. They said women just complained to be complaining. When I saw her so sad, I should have known better, Mavin. Truly. Shall we find her and tell her? Will she forgive me?"

She was distressed at his grief, as distressed as she had been at what he had said. A child. Eight years, perhaps twenty-five seasons in all? Certainly no more than that. And yet, to have bewitched Handbright, kept her behind the p'natti to be abused, used, beaten. . . . She pulled herself together. "There, child. There. No one really expects that you should have known better. I don't myself. Handbright is gone. I told her she must go away . . . as soon as we were gone. She isn't there any more, so we needn't go back. I'm all adrift, Mertyn. I don't know what to say to you. I'm just amazed that you can do this thing. But I've never felt you do it to me, Mertyn."

"I wouldn't do it to you, Mavin. You're childer, like me. It wouldn't be fair."

"Ah. Do you know what it means, Mertyn child? It means you're probably not shifter. It means you must be Ruler, King or Prince or one of those high-up Beguilers. But you only eight years old? A twenty-four or -five season child, and showing Talent already? I've never heard of that."

"I didn't think it was Talent. I thought it was just something I could do."

"Well, that's what Talent is, boychild. That's all Talent is, something we can do. Well." She looked at him in amazement, seeing that the world around them had become less shining, less marvelous, less peaceful. "You were doing it this morning."

"Not to you. Just to me, to the world. To make it prettier for us. You know."

"What I know, Mertyn, is that you'd better keep that thing you can do very quiet to yourself. Don't use it unless there's need. I'm worried now that those men may begin to think, there on the road, of how sweet a child you were, and thinking may lead them to more thinking, which might lead them to deciding you have a Talent. And there's a market for any child, much more a child with Talent. I worry they may start thinking and come back for us. Me they'd hit over the head and leave for dead, but you they'd sell, I think."

He considered this, thinking it over gravely before saying, "I don't think so, Mavin. Truly. No one has ever thought it was Talent. Not in all this time. . . ."

"All this time? How long have you been doing this thing?"

"Oh, since I was a fifteen-season child, at least. I used to do it at Assembly, to the cooks, to get sweets. They didn't mind. And

I did it to the shifters, too, and to the granders when I wanted something. And to Handbright."

A fifteen-season child. Five years old. And already with a Talent seeming so natural that no one knew he had it. Mavin tried this thought in a dozen different ways, but it made no sense to her. Children did not have talent. That was one of the things that made them children. And yet here was Mertyn. Slowly, hesitantly, she moved them on their way. "It will still be best to use it only when we must. Elsewise you may do some unconsidered damage with it. So. Agreed?"

He nodded at her, rather wanly, and they went on their way, Mavin cautioning herself the while. "He is only a child. Because he seems to have this Talent, you will begin to think that he is more than a child, that he understands more than a child can understand. You will make demands upon him, you will expect things from him. He will make childish mistakes, and you will blame him. Don't do it, Mavin. He is child, only child, and that is quite enough for the time being. Let him live with his thalan, Plandybast, at least for a little time. Let him not have to *make* people love him. . . ." Shaking her head the while, impressing it upon herself, demanding that she remember. The light had gone out of the day, and she longed for it, longed to have Mertyn bring it back, but would not allow him to do it even if he would. "Child," she said to herself yet again. "A child." She had the feeling that she herself had never been a child, having to remind herself what she had been until the past few days. Before the Assembly she had been a child. Before she overheard the granders she had been a child. Before she had seen Handbright's body striped with the whip, before she had known what it would be not to be a child. . . .

"Don't worry, Mavin," he whispered to her. "It's really a good thing to have. You'll see. I'll only use it to help us."

They went on toward the north for that day and most of the day following. The latter part of that day they accepted a ride on a farm wagon hauling hay from the fields along the river to the campground at Calihiggy Creek. Mavin had grown used to her boyish shape, had managed to hold it constant even while sleeping. Mertyn nagged at her from time to time. "I thought shifters couldn't take other people shapes, Mavin. They taught us that. Handbright taught us that."

To which she replied variously, as the mood struck her. "I think most shifters can't,'' or ''It was a lie,'' or ''I think it's only other real people we can't shift into,'' knowing that this last was as much a lie, at least, as any other thing he had been told.

''You need a fur cloak,'' he said seriously to her. ''With a beast head. Barfod had one with a great wide head on it, he said it was a monstrous creature from the north. I like pombi heads best. Let's get you one of those.''

''Mertyn, child, I don't want anyone to know I am shifter. I don't want anyone to know that either one of us are anything except – just people.''

''Pawns?'' he asked in a disgusted voice.

''Well, maybe not pawns. But whatever is next to pawns that would make the least problems. I don't want anyone carrying tales about us back to Danderbat keep. I don't want any child stealers coming after you. I don't want any woman stealers to be taking me. So, we're just two – whats?''

He began to think about this, laying himself back in the haywagon and staring at the sky. It was growing toward evening, and the lights of the campground were showing far ahead of them on the road. ''I know,'' he whispered to her at last. ''You shall be a servant to a Wizard. No one wants to upset a Wizard or trifle with a Wizard's man. I shall be the Wizard's thalan, son to his sister. That way no one will trifle with me either.''

She considered it. It had a certain audacious simplicity which was attractive. ''Which Wizard? We'd have to say which Wizard?''

''It couldn't be a real one with a Demesne around here, or we might get caught. I heard of one. There's one called Hagglefree who has a Demesne along the River Dourt.''

''You know some very strange things,'' she said.

''There are lots of old books and maps at the keep that no one paid any attention to,'' he replied. ''We should have learned all about them at school. Someone must have learned about them long ago, or they wouldn't have been there.''

''We had become decadent,'' she said. ''That's what Plandybast said to someone at the last dinner. That Danderbat keep was decadent. That we hadn't any juice anymore.''

He nodded solemnly. ''So. If he's still alive, Hagglefree, I mean, then we should be all right.''

''If he had a sister. If she had a boy. If he keeps servants, for some do not. We might be better to make up a name, Mertyn. Make one up.''

He thought for a moment, said, ''The Wizard Himaggery. That's who we are connected with.''

''And where is his Demesne?''

''Ah . . . let's see. His Demesne is down the middle river somewhere, toward the southern seas. There's lots of blank space on the maps down there. No one knows what's there, really.'' He put his hand in hers, ''Shall we swear it, Mavin? Shall it be our Game?''

''Let it be our game, brother. The campground is ahead, and we will see how it sits with the people there when I buy us supper and a bed.''

''Do you have money, Mavin? I brought a little. I didn't have much.''

''I didn't have much either, brother boy, but I took some from the cooks' cache before they left. It will get us to Battlefox the Bright Day – if we are careful.''

The wagon driver leaned back toward them, gesturing toward the firelights down the road. ''That the place you were going, young sirs? There it is. Calihiggy Campground. I'll take the wagon no further, for I've no mind to have my hay stolen during the dark hours. I'll sell it to the campmaster come morning.''

They thanked him and left him, then wandered out of the gloaming into the firelight before a half hundred pairs of eyes, both curious and incurious.

It was the first time Mavin had been anywhere outside the keep of the Danderbats where she had needed to speak, bargain, purchase, seem a traveler more widely experienced than in fact she was. She did it rather creditably, she thought, then noticed that the man to whom she spoke smiled frequently at Mertyn with a glazed expression. Shaking her head ruefully, she accepted the bedding she was offered and allowed them to be guided to a tent pitched near the western edge of the ground, near Calihiggy Creek and a distance from the privies.

''I thought I told you not to do that,'' she hissed.

''I had to,'' he said sulkily. ''The man was beginning to think you were a runaway pawn from some Demesne or other. You stuttered.''

''Well. I haven't practiced this.''

''You've got to seem very sure of yourself,'' he said. ''If you seem very sure of yourself, everyone believes you. If you stutter or worry, then everyone else begins to stutter and worry inside their heads."

"I thought you had Ruler Talent, not Demon Talent to go reading what's in people's heads."

"It isn't like that. I can just feel it is all. Anyhow, it didn't hurt anything. Now you've got to practice walking as though you knew just where you were going, and when you talk, do it slowly. As though you didn't care whether you talked or not. And don't smile, until they do. I'm tired. What did you get us to eat?"

"I got hot meat pies, three of them, and some fruit. You can have thrilps or rainhat berries."

He had both, and two of the pies. Mavin contented herself with one. They weren't bad. Evidently some family from a little village along the road brought a wagonload of them to the camp every day or so, and the campmaster heated them in his own oven. When they had done, they wandered a bit through the camp, trying to identify all the Gamesmen they saw, and then went back to their tent. "No one is looking for us," Mavin said. "No one at all. They've all gone back to Danderbat keep. And likely we will not see Handbright again until we come to Battlefox. Well, it's less adventurous than I'd thought."

"It's adventurous enough," the child responded, voice half dazed with sleep. "Enough. Lie down, Mavin."

She sat down, then lay down, then pulled the blankets up to her chin. They were only three days away from the place she had lived all her life, and already the memory of it was beginning to dim and fade. She was no longer very angry, she realized in a kind of panic. The anger had fueled her all this way, and now it was dwindled, lost somewhere in the leagues they had traveled. Something else would have to take its place.

She thought about this, but not long before the dark crawled into her head and made everything quiet there.

When morning came, she went out into it, telling herself what Mertyn had told her the night before. She watched how the men of the camp walked, and walked as they did, watched their faces as they talked and made her face take the same expression. She went first to the campmaster to ask whether he knew of a wagon going to Pfarb Durim, following his laconic directions to a large encampment among the trees in the river bottom. There she confronted a dozen faces neither hostile nor welcoming and had to take tight control in order that her voice not tremble.

"I greet you, Gamesmen," she began, safely enough, for there were a good many Gamesdresses in the group. "My young charge and I travel toward Pfarb Durim. Our mounts were lost in a storm in the mountains through which we have come, and we seek transport and company for the remaining way."

There was among the group a gray-headed one, still strong and virile-looking, but with something sad and questioning about his face. He looked up from his plate – for they were all occupied with breakfast – and said, "As do we all, young man. You have not told us who you are?" He set his plate down beside him, the motion leading Mavin's eyes to the spot, and she saw a Seer's gauze mask lying there, the moth wings painted upon it bright in the morning light.

"Sir Seer." She bowed. "I am servant of one Wizard, Himaggery of the Wetlands and I have in my care thalan to the Wizard, the child Mertyn."

"So. Would you have us escort you against future favors from your Wizardly master? Can you bargain on his behalf?" This was shrewdly said, as though he tested her, but Mavin was equal to this.

"Indeed no, sir. He would have me in . . . have my head off me if I pretended such a thing. I ask only such assistance as my master's purse will bear, such part of it as he entrusts to me." She felt a small hand creep into her own, and realized that Mertyn had come up beside her. A quick glance showed that he was simply standing there, very quietly, with a trusting expression on his face.

"Ah." The Seer seemed to think this over. He had a knotty face, a strong face, but with a kind of strangeness in it as though it were hard for him to decide what expression that face would wear. His hair was a little long, thrust back over his ears in white wings, and he had laid the cloak of the Seer aside to sit in his shirt and vest. The others around the fire watched him, made no effort to offer any suggestion. These were mostly young men, no more than nineteen or twenty, with a few among them obviously servants. The horses at the picket line were blanketed in crimson and black, obviously the colors of some high Demesne around which Gamesmen gathered. At last one of the young men walked over to them to stand an arm's-length from Mavin and look her over from toe to head, his own head cocked and his expression curious and friendly.

"Windlow, our teacher, does not make up his mind in any sudden way. You still have not told him who you are – your name."

"His name is Mavin," said Mertyn in his most childlike voice. "He is very nice, and you would like him very much."

"My name is Mavin," she agreed, bowing, and pinching Mertyn's arm a good tweak as she did so. "A harmless person, offering no Game." She glared at Mertyn covertly.

The man who had been named Windlow spoke again from the fire. "There is always Game, youngster. The very bunwits play, and the flitchhawks in the air. There is no owl without his game, nor any fustigar. You cannot live and offer no game."

"He means . . ." began Mertyn.

"I meant," she said firmly, "that I seek only transport, sirs. Nothing more."

"Surely we can accommodate them, Windlow?" the young man said. "After all, we're going there. And we have extra horses. And neither of them weighs enough for a horse to notice, even if we had to carry them double."

"Oh, ah," said Windlow. "It isn't the horses, Twizzledale. It's the vision. Concerning these – this. I had it the moment they walked into view. Curious. It seems to have nothing at all to do with anything happening soon, or even for quite a while. And it wasn't this one at all" – he pointed to Mavin – "but what seemed to be his sister. Looked very much like his sister. And this child grown up and teaching school somewhere. Most unlikely. But you were in it, too, Twizzledale, and you didn't seem unhappy about it, so one can only hope it is for the best."

The young man laughed and turned back to offer his hand, which Mavin took in her own, grasping it with as manish a pressure as she could, so that he winced and shook his own in pretended pain. "So. Then it is settled. You will come with us the day or two to Pfarb Durim. I am Fon Twizzledale, like to be, so they tell me, Wizardly in persuasion. Yon is Prince Valdon Duymit, thalan of High King Prionde of the High Demesne. Our teacher, Seer Windlow, you have met. These are our people, all as kindly in intent as you yourself claim to be. Welcome, and will you join us for breakfast?"

Mertyn let his childish treble soar in enthusiasm. "Oh, yes sirs. I am very tired of smoky meat." And more quietly to Fon

Twizzledale, "Did he truly have a vision about us?"

"He truly did," the young man asserted, "if he said he did. I have never known Windlow to say anything which is not strictly and literally true."

"I thank you for your kindness," Mavin interjected, "but you have not yet told me what price you place upon your company."

Windlow shook his gray head impatiently, as though the idea were one which did not matter and distracted him from some other idea which did matter. "Oh, come along, come along. There is no payment necessary. The Fon is quite right. We have extra mounts, and neither of you appears to be a glutton. Have you eaten? Did they say they had eaten?" he appealed to Prince Valdon, saturnine in his dress of red and black.

That one's mouth twisted in a prideful sneer of distaste. "The child seems ready to eat, Gamesmaster. Children usually are, if I remember rightly."

"Yes, please," said Mertyn, casting his grave smile at Valdon's face, on his best behavior, edging away from Mavin's clutching fingers toward the Seer. "I would like some of whatever you are having. It smells very good."

The Seer's face lightened, an expression of surprising sweetness which drove away the slightly peevish expression of concentration he had worn since they had walked into the camp. Mavin thought, "He was having a vision, but he couldn't quite get it, and it was like a dream he was fishing for. Now it is gone." In which she was quite correct, for Windlow had had a vivid flash of Seeing somehow wrapped around the two of them, but it had eluded him like a slippery fish in the stream of his thoughts. Now it was gone, and he turned from it almost in relief. Too often the Seeings were of future terror and pain.

"Well, come fill a bowl, then," he said to Mertyn. "And tell your sister – no. No. How stupid of me. Tell your . . . cicerone to join us, too." He turned to Mavin. "Forgive me, young sir. Sometimes vision and reality confuse themselves and I am not certain what I have seen and am seeing. I seemed to see the boy's sister. . . ."

Mavin bowed slightly, face carefully calm. Across the fire she could see Twizzledale's face fixed on her own, an expression of bemusement there, of thoughtful calculation. "No forgiveness necessary," she said. "The boy's sister is far from here." And that, she thought, is very true. She accepted a bowl of the food. It was indeed very savory smelling.

"My good servant, Jonathan Went, that scowling old fellow over there by the wagon, saves all the bones from the bunwits whenever we have a feast. I'm talking about you, Jonathan! Well, he saves the bones and cooks them up into a marvelous broth with onions and lovely little bulblets from the tuleeky plant and bits of this and that. Then he uses the broth to cook our morning grain, and sometimes he puts eggs and bits of zeller bacon into it as well. Remarkable. Then we are all very complimentary and cheerful, and he goes over by the wagon and pretends he does not hear us. Modest fellow. The best cook between here and the High Demesne. King Prionde himself made the fellow an offer, but he would not leave me and the King was kind enough not to press the matter. Ah. Good, isn't it?"

"Very," gasped Mertyn, his mouth full.

"It is delicious," agreed Mavin. The grain was tender, rich with broth and bunwit fat, and she could taste wood mushrooms in it as well. She sighed, for the moment heavily content. Across the fire Fon Twizzledale stared at her, his head cocked to one side. Farther away the proud Prince sat looking toward her but across her shoulder as though she did not exist, his small crown glittering in the early sun. She found herself liking the one, wary of the other. "Careful," she warned herself. "There was a time you liked old Graywing, too."

The meal was soon done. In her role of servant, Mavin moved to help those who were packing the wagons and loading the pack animals. There were indeed many extra mounts, and she found herself atop one of them with no very clear idea what to do next. Being a horse and riding a horse were two different things, but she kept her face impassive and paid careful attention to those around her. With Mertyn on the pad before her she clucked to the horse as others around her were doing, and it moved off after them, head nodding in time to its steps in an appearance of bored colloquy. Mertyn leaned comfortably against her and whispered, "You won't need to do anything, Mavin. This horse will follow that one's tail. I heard some of the visitors talking at Assembly time, too. About riding horses, I mean. They say you're supposed to hold on with your legs. Can you hold on with your legs?"

"Brother mine," she whispered in return, "remember that I am the well schooled servant – upper servant – of a Wizard. Of course I can ride a horse. Didn't you tell me I can do anything I think I can?"

He giggled, then lapsed into silence, rolling his head from side to side on her chest to see the country they were traveling through.

Calihiggy Creek was a sizeable flow, emptying into the River Haws at the conjunction of two valleys, the narrow north-south one of the Haws, the wide, desolate east-west one of the Creek. Here the waters had cut deep ravines into the flat valley bottom so that the water flowed deep below the surface of the soil. What plants grew there were dry and dusty looking, more suited to a desert than a river valley, though at the edges of the cliffs there were scattered groves of dark trees. They clattered briefly over a long wooden bridge, high above the Haws.

"Why is it so high up?" Mertyn wanted to know.

The Fon had ridden alongside and answered him promptly. "Are they not built so high in your country? Here it is built high to escape the spring rains which come in flood down those barren gullies. The water is so low now that we might have waded over, as it always is at the turn of the seasons, but when the spring rains come it will be a muddy flood once more. I have seen it almost at the floor of such bridges after the rains." He adjusted the flowing sleeve of his Wizardly robe, burnishing the embroidered stars at the cuff with a quick rub and breath from his lips.

Mertyn, remembering that he was supposed to be thalan of a Wizard of the Wetlands, very sensibly shut his mouth and merely smiled his understanding.

"Why do you go to Pfarb Durim?" the Fon went on. "Does the Wizard travel there?"

Mavin had been prepared for this question. "We are to await further instructions in Pfarb Durim. Young Mertyn has been visiting his mother."

"Ah," said the Fon. Mavin had the distinct impression that he did not believe her. "A very small entourage for a Wizard's thalan. If the boy were my thalan, I would not send him so little accompanied."

"Mavin is quite enough," said Mertyn in a firm voice. "It isn't nice for you to say he isn't. Besides, what is a Fon, anyhow?"

"Sorry," laughed Twizzledale. "I withdraw my comment, young sir. As for *Fon*, it is only a word used in my southernish Demesne for eldest-important-offspring. It means I will inherit certain treasures and lands held by my family and learn if I can hold them in my turn. Good travel to us all." And with that he was off at top speed, raising the rosy dust in a great cloud as he sped past the other riders and dwindled away on the northern road between the two lines of cliffs, Prince Valdon in pursuit.

Now the Seer Windlow was riding beside them, his gauze mask draped on the saddle before him, casually picking his teeth with a bit of wood. "A bit along the road here," he remarked, "where the woods begin to thicken once again, we will need to climb the cliffs. If we stay on this road along the valley it will take us to the place called Poffle, below Pfarb Durim, and it is my understanding that one would do well to avoid the place."

"Why is that, sir?" Mavin asked politely.

"Ah, well, the place has a bad name. Said to be a den of Ghouls. Old Blourbast rules there, and he is not a Gamesman others speak of with friendship."

"Is that the place called Hell's Maw?" piped Mertyn. "I saw it on a map."

"Shhhh, my boy. Not a name which is generally spoken aloud. However, yes. You're right. People speak of Poffle, but they mean Hell's Maw. At any rate, it will not matter. We will not come near the place except to look down on it from the walls of Pfarb Durim, for it lies in the chasm below those walls, shut away from light and sun as it properly should be if all that is said of it is even half true.

"I heard you say to Twizzledale you will be met in the city. I think that is well. Travel is safer in larger numbers. Not that you are not fully competent, I'm sure. Merely that . . . well, you are young." He smiled to take the sting from what he said. "Forgive my mentioning it. If you are like most young men, you hate having it mentioned."

Mavin could not help laughing. "I hate having it mentioned. Yes. Perhaps . . ." She paused a moment before going on, "it is because young people are not that sure they are competent."

"There is always that," agreed the Seer. "But that feeling does not necessarily diminish with age. It is merely challenged less frequently. When one has over sixty years, as I do, then the world assumes we would not have survived without competence. With someone your age, it could always be sheer luck." He patted Mavin's arm and nodded at her. Mavin soberly thought it over. Next time she shifted, it would be into something more bulky and older-looking. Why tempt fate?

"May I ask why your group travels to Pfarb Durim, Sir Seer? Do I understand you are Gamesmaster to the young men in your party?"

"Ah, well yes, in a manner of speaking. At the moment I am sworn to the High King, Prionde, he of the High Demesne away south in the mountains near the high lakes of Tarnoch. Prince Valdon Duymit is son of Valearn Duymit, full sister to the King, therefore thalan to the King. The boy riding off there to the left is his full brother, Boldery Duymit. We call him Boldery the Brash, for his thirty seasons have been full of troubles as a cage of thrilpats. You have met the Fon, offspring of some great Demesne away south where I have never traveled though I would much like to go. He says he is a Wizard, and one does not ask too many questions of Wizards, as you know. I am inclined to believe much of what he says although he is given to flowery passages and glittering nothings. A good boy, though. I like him.

"There are two other young men awaiting our group in Pfarb Durim, thalani of Demesnes to the north and west high in the Shadowmarches, and a youngster named Huld whose schooling has been arranged through negotiators with the King. I know nothing about him save that he shows early signs of becoming a Demon. Well, when we have all the students there, we will swing down through Betand – Betand? Yes. That is where the Strange Monuments are. You know of the Monuments? Ah. One of the wonders, so it is said, of the world. No one knows who built them or what their purpose is. Some hint that they were not built by men at all. Well, then we go on to the south picking up another student in Vestertown and then up into the mountains to the High Demesne to my newly built school. A small school. Only a dozen young men and a few boys. The young men have mostly shown Talent already, so much of the confusion and exasperation of teaching is eliminated thereby. I remember . . . seem to remember my own schooldays. What a time, wondering whether there would be any Talent at all, wondering whether it might be some horrible kind one would rather not have, some Ghoulishness or other. . . .

Though, come to think of it, I have never known one who would be repelled by Ghoulishness to receive that Talent. It is almost as if our Talents prepare us for their coming. Well, all that is of no import. It will be a small school, as I said, mostly for the benefit of the King's thalani with a few others to keep them company. This trip to Pfarb Durim is likely one of the last few I will make."

All of this was explained in a slow, ruminative fashion which Mavin could hear with half her attention while her busy mind attended to the road and the river and the canyon at either side. Valdon and Twizzledale were still far ahead, Boldery the Brash riding back from time to time to inspect the face of the sleeping Mertyn and inquire whether they might ride and play together, at which Windlow shook his gray head and warned him away. "Let the boy sleep, Boldery. Time enough for your games when he wakes. Likely he slept little enough last night. Campground beds are hard as stone." Then, to Mavin, "It would probably do your charge good to have some boyish company, even of such mischievous kind as this. I have no doubt they will be deep into trouble before supper." And he nodded to himself as if in considerable satisfaction at this prediction.

The canyon walls, which had been close upon their right, began to retreat into the east; they had come to a widening of the river bottom, and fields began to appear once more between the river and the cliffs to the east of the river even as the cliffs drew closer to the river on the west. Boldery came riding back toward them in a cloud of pink, his face and short cloak liberally dusted, only his eyes shining at them in the rosy fog. "The trail to the top is only a little way on. Valdon says we need not take it. There is a road between Poffle and Pfarb Durim we can pick up beneath the walls of the city. . . ."

"No," Windlow said firmly. "We do not wish to approach . . . Poffle . . . so closely. We have allowed time for the extra leagues, and we are not short of either energy or provisions."

"But Valdon says . . ."

"I am Gamesmaster here, Boldery. We know that Valdon seeks adventure, always, believing that the name of the High King is enough to protect him. It may not always be so. The Ghoul Blourbast holds . . . Poffle. He may care little for the High King."

"Everyone fears the name of the High King," the boy asserted, flushed skin showing through the pink dust.

"Not everyone, lad." Windlow patted him gently. "I mean no disrespect to your thalan to say so. You have not been so far from the High Demesne before or you would know. If you think I am telling you fibs, then go ask Twizzledale. He will tell you aright, for he has traveled far enough to know that what I say is the truth."

"Valdon says he's a pawnish churl, no Wizard at all."

"If Valdon said that, then Valdon was either silly or drunk." Windlow's voice held anger, and the boy flushed again as he turned away.

"He was drunk, Gamesmaster. He would be angry I told you. Please don't tell him."

"I won't mention it. You might remember it, however. It is never wise to drink so much that you say things others remember to your discredit. Now – ride on back to the young Gamesmen and tell them we take the cliff trail."

Mavin had been somewhat embarrassed by this interchange, not knowing where to look, whether to seem interested or not to notice, though it would have been impossible not to hear. Windlow shook his head as the boy rode away. "Do not attach too much importance to that, Mavin. The boy worships his older brother, as is often the case. The brother is not worthy of such worship, as is often the case. Valdon is prideful. Over prideful. It would have been better had he not known since childhood that he would be a Prince."

"Known since childhood?" She was startled. "How could anyone know in childhood what Talent they would manifest later? Why even in . . . the places I have been, they have not . . ." Her voice trailed away into betraying silence. She had almost spoken of Danderbat keep.

"I will tell you," he said, seeming not to notice her confusion. "Prionde, when he was no older than Valdon is now, took his own full sister to wife, she being Queen in her own right and talent. My studies of history lead me to believe that such breeding is often unwise. It is true that traits – perhaps Talents – are intensified by such breeding. It is also true that dangerous and deadly tendencies are also intensified. There is a certain rashness in Prionde and in his sister-wife, Valearn, as well. It is amplified, greatly, in both Valdon and Boldery. I fear for them sometimes."

"And so, the King was sure his children – his thalani would have the Talent of Ruling, Beguilement?" Within her arms she felt Mertyn stir and knew that he had heard the conversation. "He knew it when they were children and let them know it?"

"He was so sure that if they had not, I think he would have sent them away and not have seen them ever again."

Mavin gulped, possessed by a frantic curiosity which she did not attempt to find reason for. "What did she think about it. Her. His sister?"

"She has not spoken of it in the High Demesne. She seemed to like her life well enough. However, she had complained of illness since bearing Boldery, and the Healers have been unable to cure her. Which makes me believe it is not her body which ails her." He fell silent, biting his lip, then adopted a more casual tone. "Well, what a conversation to be holding with a casual acquaintance. I would appreciate it if you did not repeat what I have said. I am a loquacious old man, and on occasion I forget myself."

Mavin nodded her agreement, feeling Mertyn tense against her, then relax. A shout from close ahead drew their eyes forward, and there at the beginning of the cliff trail Twizzledale waited for them. One of the wagons had already turned behind him and was lurching upward on the narrow way.

"We cannot get by the wagon," he called. "The way is too narrow. Shall we have tea to give them time to get to the top?" His laughing eyes met Mavin's. She flushed and looked away, though she did not know why.

From between her arms Mertyn spoke calmly, his shrill voice carrying over the sound of hooves and wheels. "Thank you, Wizard, sir. I am very thirsty. Besides, I have to get off this horse."

And as Mavin followed him to the ground she thought that she, too, had to get off the horse. The world seemed to move beneath her feet, and she was hard put to it to seem balanced and secure upon her legs. Still, she managed a manly smile of thanks for Twizzledale's hand and a cheerful offer to collect some wood along the slope to make them a fire. Once away from them all, she sighed deeply and let her face sag into its own girlish shape, just for a moment, just to know who and what she was. This role-playing demanded more of her than she had guessed it might, and the strain of it tugged at her muscles, tugged at the shifter net within her, making concentration difficult. She breathed deeply, heard Mertyn call, "Mavin? Where are you?" and managed to find both an armload of wood and a feeling of calm before she walked back toward the group, waving to the child with one hand.

CHAPTER FIVE

They came to the city of Pfarb Durim at noon of the day following, for they had lingered on the road to investigate the Strange Monuments which the Seer Windlow had longed to see. The wagons had taken some time to get up the narrow path, and Valdon had been throwing unpleasant glances at the Seer long before the way was clear, sprinkling his displeasure with remarks made just loudly enough to be heard concerning the width and smoothness of the road along the valley floor. Perhaps Windlow did not hear them, but at the least he gave no evidence of hearing the sneering remarks, and when the trail to the highlands was clear, they made their way upward in some appearance of amity. The first of the Monuments stood over the road within spitting distance as they came over the lip of the cliffs, and from that time on the journey was one of continual expostulation and wonder.

"I had no idea they were this close to Pfarb Durim," marveled Windlow. "I had always thought they were further south, nearer Betand. Though, as I think of it, some of the authorities – if any are to be considered authorities on such subjects as this – have said that these Monuments have a strange tendency to wander, seeming first nearer and then farther away."

"Oh, come, Gamesmaster." Twizzledale laughed. "You do not expect us to believe that. The things are ten man-heights above the road, anchored on pedestals which appear to be part of the mountain we ride upon. Surely you don't take such stories seriously."

The older man shrugged, eyebrows high to indicate his own wonder at the idea. "I repeat only what I have read, Gamesman. At certain seasons, these arches glow. All authors agree to that. At certain seasons, those who live hereabouts are in agreement that it is wise to avoid this road. Since that season coincides with the time of storms, during which wise persons avoid travel in any case, perhaps no one has seriously tested the notion that the arches are dangerous then. Or, if not dangerous, something else. Something stranger, perhaps."

Mavin was following along behind, marveling as much as the two riding ahead, but less vocal about it. "Did you know these things were here?" she whispered to Mertyn.

"I read about them," he answered. "But the book didn't say much. Just that no one knows who built them or why. I can't even figure out how anyone could have put them here."

Mavin agreed. The arches might have been made of green stone, or metal, though they seemed more crystalline than metallic, giving an impression of translucence without actually letting any light through. Two man-heights broad at the base, they narrowed as they rose, dwindling to a knife's edge straight above the road. Where the shadow of the arches lay upon the way, the horses hopped and skipped like zeller kids, sidling across the shadow as though it formed some mazy barrier which only they could see and only such frolicking progress could penetrate. Each transit of the shadow made Mavin think she heard twanging chords of music, rapidly blending, echoing briefly on her skin when they had come through, and – most interesting she thought – each passage of shadow seemed to take time totally out of keeping with the actual width of the shadow on the road.

"Remarkable," breathed Windlow, trying to stay on his jigging horse. "I hear music. Quite remarkable."

"Shadowpeople," breathed Mertyn to Mavin. "Shadowpeople are supposed to have all kinds of musical magic, Mavin. Could the shadowpeople have built these?"

"Shadowpeople aren't builders, are they? I thought they just sang in the wilderness and made music and ate a few travelers now and then."

"I don't think so. I don't think they eat travelers, I mean. They trick people. Lead them over cliffs, or into bogs, but only if the people are doing something bad to them."

"Children's tales, brother boy."

"Maybe. There's some truth in children's tales, though, or they wouldn't go on being told. You're right, though. No children's tale I ever heard mentioned the shadowpeople building anything. Just the same, whenever the horse dances through one of those shadows,

I think of shadowpeople."

"Wise beyond your years, young one," said Windlow, coming up from behind where he had stopped yet again to inspect one of the Monuments. "I, too, think of shadowpeople. As a Seer, I have learned thinking of some oddity is often prelude to other oddity following. It is tempting to wonder what actually does happen here in the season of storms."

"I'd like to know where the road goes," said Mavin.

"Why, it goes to Pfarb Durim."

"No, I mean the other end."

"To Betand?"

"Betand is just a human city. If the Monuments were built on a road, then it must have been important where the road went. It couldn't have gone to a human city, because the human city wasn't there. So it must have gone somewhere else." She fell silent, noting that Windlow had fixed her with a somehow calculating eye, as though she had surprised him. Before he could reply, however, a cry came from before them.

"Pfarb Durim!" A cloud of dust bustled toward them, full of hoof clatter. It was Boldery. "Pfarb Durim is just down the hill."

They jigged through the last of the arches to see the city spread before them, its high walls bulking hugely in the center of a saucerlike depression resulting from some long ago subsidence of the cliff's edge. Around the rim of this saucer the road ran, making a wide circle to the east before turning north once more. To their left they could see a narrow road winding up from the valley, from Poffle, and from the circling road several broad avenues ran downward to the city which gulped them in through strangely shaped gates. These gates and the many doors made tall keyholes of black against the lighter stone. Vast iron braziers stood on the wall at each corner, twisted iron baskets hung before the gates, all stuffed full of grease-soaked wood which would be lit at nightfall to send a smoky pillar hovering over the place. The smell of burned fat reached them first, then the smell of the markets outside the gates, spices and fish, raw hides and incense, the stench of commerce carrying a wild babble of voices which rose and fell as the sound of moving water.

"Pfarb Durim," said Windlow. "City of legends. Here, so it is said, when our forefathers came to this place a thousand years ago, they found the city already built by other than we, by not-men, perhaps by those who built the arches."

"It smells very human to me," said Mertyn, wrinkling his nose.

"It has been occupied by humans for some time," he replied.

They led their animals through the market, fascinated to see so many things being bought and sold, hearing the cries of the merchants as they would have heard strange birds in a forest, with as little understanding. The gate was guarded by several red-nosed men who looked them over casually, inquired whence they had come, and seemed inclined to accept Mavin and Mertyn as part of Windlow's group without any special inquisition as to their origins. Once inside the walls, Mavin handed the reins of her horse to Twizzledale, who was riding a bit behind the others, and bowed to him from the street.

"We appreciate your kindness, Gamesman. Now we must leave you with our thanks."

"Where are you meeting your . . . whoever?" he asked, looking more closely at her than she found comfortable. "You're welcome to stay with us until you are met." Giving the lie to this, Prince Valdon shouted from the street corner.

"Leave the pawnstuff, Wizard! There's wine waiting!"

Twizzledale flushed, but did not move. Mavin said, "Thank you again, Gamesman. But we will not inflict ourselves upon you further. I must obey the instructions I was given." She smiled, more warmly than she had intended, backed away from him, and set out around the corner, Mertyn's hand clutched firmly in her own. There she took refuge in a deep doorway while she tried to decide where to go next.

"Brother child, we need some cheap lodging to roost in while we find the best road to the Shadowmarches and Battlefox."

"If you don't want to run into the Seer and his students, we'd better see where they go," said Mertyn, leaning around the corner, his voice betraying the sadness he felt. He had been looking forward to a few more hours with Boldery in pursuit of some form of exciting mischief. "It would have been nice to . . ."

"Yes, it would have been nice to. But I didn't dare. That Twizzledale kept looking at me as though he could see through to my smalls. I don't think I made a convincing man. There's something more to it than shape, and he was suspicious of something the whole time. I could smell it.''

"But he liked you."

"That might have been the trouble," she answered. "If he'd despised me, as Prince Valdon does, he would not have looked at me so closely."

The boy was peering around the corner still, then turned to her, sighing. "They've gone into a big inn right at the wall. I guess we should go on into the city. Should we ask someone?"

"We should," she agreed, and set about doing so. Within a few moments she had the names of three cheap lodging houses, all within a short distance of one another, as well as three sets of instructions how to reach them. They set off in a hopeful frame of mind which changed to a kind of dismay as they left the open ways near the gate and began to wend down damp alleys, shadowed by protruding stories in the buildings to either side and threatened by a constant shower of debris from the windows and roofs. "Gamelords, what a warren," she said. "I had no idea."

As they made a last turn, Mertyn ran full into a staggering man who gurgled ominously, supporting himself against the wall. Mertyn reached out to catch him, then drew back, fastidiously wiping his face where the man had drooled on him. "Play . . . play . . ." the man gasped, his eyes protruding with the effort. "Play . . . ch'owt . . ." And then he crumpled onto the stones, fingers scrabbling weakly at the slimy cobbles.

"Come on!" ordered Mavin. "We can't help him, but we can send help." And they ran on, coming into a wider area in which the lodging houses they had sought all stood, one bearing a sign THE BALD BADGER near at hand.

The door jangled as they opened it, and a voice screamed at them from some other room. "Wait! Don't move, now, just wait and I'll get to ya. A minute. That's all. I swear, only a minute, and I'll get to ya. Are you there?"

"We're here," Mavin replied in a doubtful voice.

"A minute. I'll get to ya. Everybody's so impatient. Run, run. I'll get to ya." There was no sign of the person getting to them immediately. They looked at one another, then turned as a soft footfall whispered on the stairs behind them.

"Sirs," said a gray voice. "You desire lodging?"

"Just a minute," screamed the other voice. "Run, run."

"A thrilpat," exclaimed the colorless woman who owned the gray voice. "Over trained. A vocabulary of over twenty phrases, none of which are in the least useful. I'd sell it, except it has the mange."

"Are you there?" screamed the voice hysterically. "Everyone is so impatient."

"We need a room," said Mertyn. "And there's a man down the alley who fell down. I think he's sick."

The gray woman smoothed her tightly knotted hair, slick upon her skull as paint. "A room I can provide. Assistance for men who fall ill in alleys is outside my competence, young sir. When I have shown you what we have – little enough, but cheap. Lords, yes, cheap is the name of the house – when I have shown you, I'll get the kitchen girl to run tell the watch about the sick man. Will that satisfy your sense of the appropriate? The honorable? The kindly? This way. Watch the step, second from the top. It wants nailing down."

They followed through half darkness until a door opened, flooding the corridor with light. "Step in. You'll need to share the bed, there's only one, but it's fresh straw and linens washed only last week." The slant-roofed room peaked over the open window which let in the turmoil of the street. The bed was low, wide, and the place smelled clean. "How much?" asked Mavin, in her bargaining voice.

"Coin or trade? Three minimunt in coin. If you were a Healer, I'd give it to you for a bit of work. You're not, though, nor anything else useful to me at the moment. Well, then, three minimunt. With a bit of supper thrown in. Nothing fancy, a cup of this and that and some beer. By the by, my name is Pantiquod Palmfast. They call me Panty. Nothing to do with intimate trousering, young sir, so do not giggle in that unfortunate way. No, it has to do with breath, with breathing, with climbing these ghastly flights of stairs. Well, enough. Three minimunt, is it?" She smiled, a smile as gray as her voice, and went away, closing the door behind her. Mertyn was already on the bed.

"Will you remind her about the sick man, Mavin. I think she'll probably forget it."

"I think you'd better not worry about it, brother child. I've a feeling there are more unfortunates in Pfarb Durim than you could possibly give worrying time to. Still, I'll remind her, for what good it may do. Next thing is to see where we might get some maps, don't you think?"

"Shadowpeople, too," he said drowsily, burrowing into the bed. "I'll pull the latchstring in behind you and take a nap."

"It isn't like you to sleep in the bright day, child."

"Well, Boldery was telling stories last night, about ghost pieces. Boldery tells good stories, but I didn't get much sleep."

"All right then," she agreed. "But I'll hammer on the door when I come back, so be ready. And you're not to go out by yourself, even if I'm late." She did not leave the door until she saw the end of the latchstring slide through the hole, then she went down the way they had come, stopping for a moment to speak to the gray woman who emerged, like a phantom out of smoke, at the bottom of the stairs.

"Yes, I've sent the girl to tell the watch, young sir. Not that it will do much good. They'll send a wagon after him, sooner or later, and it will take him to the infirmary of the Healers – though with all the Healers gone, who knows what good that will do."

"Healers gone? Why?"

She put on a mysterious face. "There is talk in the marketplace of a dispute between the Healers and a certain inhabitant of . . . Poffle. You know of Poffle?"

"I've heard of it," she admitted.

"Ah. Well, Healers were summoned there from Pfarb Durim. Evidently they did not go or would not heal, it is uncertain which. Then others were sought and brought – some say involuntarily, which is a mistake in dealing with Healers – and something unfortunate happened, so it is alleged, which caused all the Healers to leave Pfarb Durim and set a ban on the city."

"But if the dispute is with Poffle, why set a ban on this city?"

"The connection is always assumed, young sir. The place below is somewise dependent upon Pfarb Durim. Or, other end up, possibly. Whatever. May I offer you any help or direction?" she added, looking curiously at Mavin's cloak. And, upon Mavin's telling her that she needed a mapmaker or guide or geographer or any combination of them, the lodging keeper gave her directions to Chart Street.

It was almost dusk when she returned, the lights of the city were being lit and the great firebaskets upon the walls had been set ablaze. In the red, smoky glare, ordinary citizens began to assume the guise of devils. Every face seemed either frightened or menacing or closed around some ominous secret. Laughing at herself for these fantasies, Mavin nonetheless hurried to return to the lodging house, thinking of Mertyn and dinner with about equal intensity. She had purchased half a dozen cheap maps of the Shadowmarches, from different chartmakers, on the theory that the features common to all might be assumed – only might be assumed – to indicate a close approximation to reality. On the other hand, she told herself, it might not be wise to discount the odd, dangerous feature shown on only one. That one might have been the result of an exploration while the others were only popular fiction or speculation.

She knocked at the door of their room for a long time before Mertyn dragged it open. He stood peering at her blearily, eyes and face swollen and red. She touched his forehead and cheeks and felt a feverish heat. He seemed unable to focus on her.

"Brother child, what's the matter with you?"

"I feel – all sort of sick," he said. "Everything keeps fading."

"Have you been asleep since I left?"

"I slept a long time," he said, staggering back toward the bed. "Then I woke up feeling funny, and it comes and goes."

"Stay here," she instructed him, though he showed no inclination to go anywhere. "I'll get you some broth from the kitchen and see where the nearest Healers are to be found."

"Danderbats don't seek Healing. . . ." he murmured.

"Battlefoxes do," she said grimly, remembering her conversation with her thalan. As she went down the stairs, however, she remembered a more recent conversation, the one with Pantiquod. The woman came out of her hidey hole as though summoned.

"You'll be wanting supper, young sirs," she began.

"I'll be wanting some broth for Mertyn," Mavin cut her off. "He's sick. Did you tell me true, earlier, when you said there were no Healers in Pfarb Durim?"

"According to the tittle-tattle of the marketplace, there is not one Healer left in Pfarb Durim. Healers are clanny, young sir, and if one of them was injured in Poffle, why – I suppose none would come near us after that. 'Who injures a Healer goes without Healing.' Isn't that the old saw? Well, perhaps not. Maybe it's only something I thought I had heard somewhere."

"But the end of all this is what you said earlier. No Healers in Pfarb Durim. Where would the closest ones be, then?"

The gray-faced woman nodded in mixed sympathy and satisfaction. "He's truly ill, then. I thought that might be coming. We seem to have ghoul-plague in the city. So rumor hath."

"Ghoul-plague? I have never heard of it."

"I thought of it when the boy spoke of the sick man in the alley. I was almost certain of it when the wagon came suspiciously soon. Plague has been muttered of for days. They say it began in Poffle. The Healers were summoned and would not – some say could not – heal. An attempt was made to force them. Now the plague has come to Pfarb Durim, and the Healers are gone." Then, seeing the horror on Mavin's face, she relented. "Let us not be so quick. Come, I'll get you some broth. Perhaps he is only weary from his journey."

But when they returned to the room, Mavin could not get Mertyn's attention at all. He was in some deep well of delirium from which she could not arouse him.

"It's too quick," complained Mavin. "We only arrived today."

"The disease is sudden in those it takes," said Pantiquod from where she hovered in the doorway, not coming any closer than she needed to see the boy's face. "And he said he touched the man in the alley."

"Do they recover?" Mavin whispered. "Does it kill many?"

"Some recover," Pantiquod said. "Most die. It is said that the shadowpeople can cure it, which is like saying a flask of sun will gild thrilps. First one has to fill one's flask." The woman left her, turning in the doorway to say, "Do not try to move him. Sometimes, so I have heard, persons ill with ghoul-plague are transported, perhaps in search of a Healer, or some more salubrious air. If they are moved, they invariably die. So I am told. Do not move him. In any case, you could not. The gates will soon be locked against any leaving." And the door swung shut behind her, leaving an impression upon its surface as though she stood there still, dim and smokelike, inhabiting the lodging house like mist, a smile almost of satisfaction upon her face.

It did no good to feed Mertyn the broth. It ran out of his mouth. She could not get him to swallow. She sat with him cradled against her, terrified and helpless, not knowing what to do next. When she began to pull herself together, it was fully dark outside.

She did not know whether to believe the woman or not, but for the time being she would not attempt to move Mertyn. He was hot, unconscious, but he breathed steadily and when she put her ear to his chest, his heart thudded away evenly. So. She covered him warmly, set herself frantically to make some sensible plan.

First she must determine whether what the woman said was true. She left the room, wedging the door shut behind her. At the foot of the stairs, she looked inside Pantiquod's hidey hole. It was empty, more than merely empty. It had an air of vacancy about it. Suddenly suspicious, she found her way to the rear of the place. The kitchen was empty also, and the little area way opening from it. She went back up the stairs, opening each room she came to. Empty. So. If there had been plague rumored for the past days, then those who heard the rumor would have left the city. The woman herself? Had she stayed? Or did she have some secret way out?

No matter where she might be, Mertyn and Mavin were alone in the place now, and the street outside was quieter than it had been since she had entered the city. She opened the heavy door onto the street. It creaked, and the wall torch showed her the crudely painted words, "Plague here," on its rough outer surface. The warning had been painted after she had returned, within moments, perhaps of that time. Mavin found some curse phrases she had not remembered knowing and used them freely, harshly, whispering into the silent street. She would have to leave Mertyn alone in the place while she sought some kind of help. Perhaps the sign on the door would protect him as well as anything could. She closed the door softly behind her and went back down the dark alley, the way they had originally come, unaware until she was halfway to the city wall that she was going to find the Seer Windlow. Then she realized that it was the only sensible thing to do.

She found the inn at the city wall without trouble, could not have avoided finding it, for there was a great mob gathered around it full of threats and brandished weapons, like a gathering of devils in the light of the great braziers and the torches. Above them the city walls were crowded with people looking outward, shouting down to those below. "It's King Frogmott from the north. He has Armigers and Elators with him." And these cries were contradicted by others, "No, they come from the Graywater Demesne of the

Sorcerer Lanuzh!" Mavin forced her way through the crowd, tucking in a rib here and bending a shoulder there. Everyone was so full of panic that they paid her no attention. From the wall she looked out to see the City gates guarded from some distance by an array of warriors and Gamesmen, torches flickering along their lines, lighting the pennants flickering over their heads.

"Why are they here?" she asked the nearest watcher. "Who are they?"

"I've heard six people say six different things about who they are," her informant muttered. "As to why, well, young man, that should be obvious to anyone. We've plague in the city, and those out there are determined we shall not bring it out of these walls."

"Surely there are Elators within the walls who could transport themselves away in an instant? Armigers who could fly over their lines? Others, perhaps, who escape such sieges as this every day of their lives? The place cannot be closed tight!" Mavin was beginning to feel the crowd's panic as her own. Her heart pounded and her muscles twitched with the need to do something.

"Well, and if it gets bad enough, they'll probably try. The Healers have set a proscription on all who leave the city, however, and not many will risk that until they must. Even an Elator must come out somewhere, and it is said they have the countryside for leagues around under watch."

"It's true, then? What someone told me. A Healer was injured – forced, down in Poffle."

"So the story goes. There is plague there, in Poffle. And now there is plague here."

"Has anyone approached the Healers? Surely they know there are people here innocent of any involvement with Poffle. Travelers."

"Young man, ask someone who knows. I am a merchant, here doing trade, and as innocent of involvement as yourself. Wait! See there. A Herald comes. Now you will have some answer, and so will I."

A knot of glaring light had separated from the flaming line along the hill and was coming toward them, lighting the upper half of a Herald's body so that he seemed a half person, floating upon the dark. The light came from a large, shallow brazier floating between two Tragamors, and its evident purpose was to light the Herald's face so that he could be recognized. He stopped outside the walls, far enough away that all could see, yet close enough to be heard. Mavin had been told of Heralds' Talent, but she had never heard the trumpet voice with which Gamesmen of this persuasion made their pronouncements. When the voice came, it startled her as well as others along the wall so that they moved as one with a reflexive grunt.

"People of Pfarb Durim give ear," the Herald cried. "I am the Herald Dumarch-don, servant of the great King, Frogmott of the Marshes, and of his allies in this endeavor, the Sorcerer Lanuzh, the mighty Armiger, Galesbreath of Rockwind Demesne, and other Gamelords and men of unquestioned honor and unlimited might. I cry siege upon the city of Pfarb Durim and upon that pit of Hell which lies at its feet. Siege shall be maintained until all within have died or until a cure has come. Let none within seek to escape, for our vengeance will be dreadful upon him and upon his house, his Demesne, and his kindred." The Herald wore a tabard of jewels. His face was proud and high-nosed, and his voice like an orchestra of brass, mellow and challenging at once. Mavin could not get her fill of looking at him, so marvelous he was, but he turned his back on all within the city and rode away, back to that flickering line of light along the mountain.

When she turned back to ask yet another question, the man had gone, and she stood for long moments upon the wall staring out at the gathered host. Even as she watched, a hilltop was crowned with moving figures, newly arrived besiegers tightening the grip upon the city. She fought her way down the stairs and through the crowd gathered around the inn. Huge, burly men guarded the door, pretending not to hear her as she asked for the Seer Windlow. Giving up in frustration, she slipped away, around the side of the place and into a narrow, blank alleyway where the trash from the place was dumped. There was a small window, high above. She looked around to see that she was not observed, then lengthened an arm and used it to pull herself up and through the narrow opening. She came down into the place, casually, stopping a scurrying servant in the hall.

"I am seeking the Seer Windlow. I carry an important message for him. Can you tell me where he is?"

"There's no Seer here, young sir. Was you wanting that one with the young men and the boy? He was here eating a meal, but then he went with the others. To the Mudgery Mont, so they said at dinner. And sensible it was of them, too, for the Mont is above all this clamor." And she was off down the hallway, answering a screamed summons from below.

Mavin used the same window to leave the place and set about finding the Mudgery Mont, growing more frantic by the moment as she thought of Mertyn left alone.

Now it was necessary to fight her way through the streets, packed from wall to wall with the inhabitants of the inner city as they tried to get to the walls, to the gates, to learn for themselves that the city had been closed like a trap with themselves inside. She gave it up before she had gone two streets, melting into a dark sideway and from that swarming up the side of a building and onto the roofs. When she had come to a less crowded place, she descended, picking out a small group who seemed disinclined to join the general pack.

"The Mudgery Mont? Surely. At the top of the hill which caps the cliffs, young man. They'll never let you in there, though. It's guarded like a treasury."

Mavin nodded her thanks and was off again, swarming onto the roofs once more to lope across them in some long legged form more usual in forests than in such a place as this. She could see the hill against the western sky, crowned with squat towers and another set of walls. It was closer, actually, to the place she had left Mertyn than the gateway inn had been, and she wasted some small breath giving thanks for this as she ran and climbed and swung across gaping chasms of street.

Behind her came the hooting of a great horn, an outcry of bells, a welling shout as from a thousand throats. Something had happened where the mob was gathered, but she did not look back. Soon she was at the foot of the hill where streets widened to sweep upward around mansions and palaces and one brightly lit and elegant hotel. Before it stood a dozen Gamesmen in livery, Heralds and Tragamors, leaping to do the bidding of those who went in and out. Mavin came to ground and walked into the light, approaching the door as though she had business there. They did not let her go by unchallenged.

"Just hold a minute there, young man," said one of the Tragamors, moving toward her purposefully. "What business have you here?"

"I have come to Mudgery Mont to find the Seer Windlow. I have . . . a message for him."

"Does he expect you?"

"I think – yes, he may well. Can you tell me if he is here?"

"Give me your name. Wait here. It may be he will receive you, and it may be he will not."

"Tell him, please, that Mavin waits without. With news which he should have."

She waited. The Tragamor showed no indication of passing on her message or of going himself. Time passed. She fidgeted from foot to foot, strode back and forth. Then she saw another petitioner approach the Tragamor, give him money, and the man went within on the moment.

"Gamelords," she said to herself. "I have no coin to pay the man. What I have must be kept for Mertyn's sake." She melted back into the darkness, into the shadows of the streets and up to the roofs once more. Trees grew in the gardens of the Mont, and she was able to go across to the roof of the hotel itself, leaping like some great thrilpat among the branches. From there it was only a few moments to find a stairway leading down, and from there only a matter of time until she encountered a servant.

"I seem to have lost my way," she said, trying to give an appearance of puzzled calm. "I am looking for the Seer Windlow, or any of his party."

"Certainly, young sir," she replied. "Will you follow me." She trotted away, down a flight of stairs, to knock on a door and beckon Mavin forward. The door opened and she said, "This young man wandering about the hotel, sir, looking for a guest." Before she could react, Mavin found herself held fast by yet another Tragamor in the livery of the place confronting an irritable-looking Armiger who held a glass of wine in one hand and a sword in the other.

"A spy," he grated. "The hotel is full of them. They gather in closets and leap out at one from under the stairs. And who are you working for, young spy?"

She had no time to invent anything new. Taken by surprise, she fell back upon the story she knew. "I am the servant of the Wizard Himaggery, sir. I traveled here in company with the Seer Windlow and his group of students. I seek him now, with a message." She tried to keep the face which she wore calm, slightly aloof, not dismayed, even though her nerves screamed at the thought of Mertyn, alone in the empty lodging house, burning with fever.

"Humph," the Armiger snorted. "A silly tale, but silly enough to be true. How did you get in?"

"The guards were busy talking with someone, sir. I just came in." She tried to sound surprised at this. Evidently the propensity of the guards for unguardly behavior was sufficiently well understood that they believed her. "Raif, go up and get someone from the Seer's party to come down here and vouch for this youngster.

"You'd better be telling the absolute truth, young man, for if you are not we'll have a Demon delving into your skull within the hour, and he'll not rest till he knows who spies upon the guests of Mudgery Mont." He went grumpily to his chair, taking the wine with him, but sheathing the sword. Mavin breathed a bit more freely, and the two men who held her relaxed somewhat. It was not long before the door opened, and the Tragamor called Raif returned with a youth, scarcely more than a boy, whom Mavin had not seen before.

"Gamesman Huld offered to take a look at him," said Raif, standing aside. Behind him the youth paused, posed in the doorway, and fingered the jeweled dagger hung at his golden belt. He was elegantly, almost foppishly dressed, wearing a Demon's half helm so over ornamented that it appeared top heavy. Beneath it a narrow, white face looked out through swollen-lidded eyes, a lizard's look, calculating, without warmth.

"Who does he say he is?" The voice was as chill as the eyes, as uncaring. "Who does the pawnish churl say he is?"

Mavin took tight rein on her temper, recoiled within herself as if she had seen a serpent rearing before her, and spoke quietly, without emphasis. "I am the servant of the Wizard Himaggery, Gamesman. I seek the Seer Windlow to give him a message."

"You can give it to me," he said carelessly. "The Seer is occupied."

She breathed deeply, aware of danger. "My deepest apologies, Gamesman. I may give the message only to the Seer."

Anger flared in the pale youth's face, turning it into a livid mask. He turned to the Armiger, sneered, "It does not know its place, does it, Armiger? I suggest you teach it its place, and bring it to me when it is ready to give me its so-called *message*. This is no

Wizard's servant, for Wizards have better taste. . . ." His hand began to play with his dagger, half drawing it from its sheath, and Mavin knew he was about to Read her to find the truth.

"Do they, now?" The drawling voice came from the doorway, which still stood open. Seeing the tall figure which lounged there brought sudden tears of relief to Mavin's eyes. It was Twizzledale. "Do Wizards indeed have better taste? The youth told you, I suppose, that he is the servant of the Wizard Himaggery. Did he not, Huld?"

"Nonsense," spat the Demon. "Lies and trickery. Likely there is no Wizard Himaggery. . . ."

"Oh, indeed there is, Huld, and I am he." Twizzledale strolled into the room, one hand playing with the knife at his own belt, almost in mockery of the Demon.

The pale youth barked laughter. "You? You are the Fon, whatever a Fon may be, of some place no one has ever heard of."

"Am I a Wizard, Huld?" Twizzledale's voice purred, all the mockery gone from it, menace dripping from every sound.

"So you say!"

"Would you care to test the notion, Huld?"

The bulky Tragamor crossed the room in one heaving motion. "My lord, Huld. The revered Ghoul Blourbast, your thalan, would not forgive us if some misunderstanding were to result in any injury to you, or even any discomfort. Surely the matter is not worth a major confrontation. The Seer is here under the protection of the High King Prionde. The High King's sons travel with him. This Wizard is with them, also, and it is said that you will join the group. . . ."

"I will not," the Demon sneered. "I have looked it over. I have smelled it. It was my thalan's wish that I be *educated* at some advanced school, but this Seer is no Gamesmaster. He is a charlatan, a fake. I will have nothing to do with it." He turned and stalked from the room, leaving the Armiger still mumbling.

"Raif, go with him. No doubt he'll leave the city by way of the tunnel. Let him go. But double the guard behind him." Baring his teeth, he frowned at the man's back, then turned back to Twizzledale and Mavin. "You say you're this man's master? Well, then get him out of here, and I don't want to find him wandering about the hotel again. You've just put me between the jaws of a cracker, and I like not the feel of it. Do you know who he is?" And he pointed the way Huld had gone.

"I learned," said the Fon. "Tonight. When the Seer learned. We had not been told that the young Demon, Huld, was ward or thalan or what have you of the Archghoul, Blourbast, holder of Hell's Maw."

The Armiger lifted off the ground, hung in the air, burning with annoyance. "Don't say that. Don't say that word."

"Hell's Maw," repeated Twizzledale. "From which no good thing comes. Is that not the saying here in Pfarb Durim? I have heard it seven times since entering the city, Guardmaster. Come now. Settle. You are using power to no purpose. We will leave you in peace."

He took Mavin by the shoulder and led her out of the room. "Mavin, what possessed you to try that here? The place is guarded like an old pombi's one kit."

"I know," she whispered, reaching for his hand. "Listen, Fon. There's plague in Pfarb Durim. . . ." And as they walked she murmured rapidly of all that had brought her to Mudgery Mont.

When they came to the door of the suite of chambers which were occupied by the Seer and his students, Twizzledale opened the door softly, peering around it before entering. He drew her into a side room, shut the door behind them, and then went to still another door, half hidden behind a hanging. "I didn't want Valdon to see you," he explained. "It was he who sent Huld down to identify you. There was much sympathetic feeling between the two." He passed through the door, leaving it ajar, and she heard a rapid murmur of voices, Windlow saying "No! Here!" and more rustling of clothing as the voices went on. The Seer came into the room, belting a robe around him.

"Where is the place young Mertyn lies ill?" he demanded.

She went to the window, oriented herself by the slope of the hill and the line of distant towers, pointed. "There. Near the round-roofed building. Perhaps six or seven streets over. The woman who runs the place – who ran the place. She left – said not to move him."

"I doubt it would hurt him to be wrapped well and carried here, if it were done quickly. Twizzledale will go, and I'll send men from the Mont."

"Valdon won't like it," said the Fon. "He grows more annoyed with every passing hour."

"Valdon is frustrated that the world has not yet fallen at his feet," said Windlow. "His expectations of this journey were unrealistic. He awaited some great event, some recognition of himself. He must blame someone. Well, we will not speak of it to him."

"What will they think?" Mavin murmured. "About your going out to get a boy, just a boy."

"Why, Mavin." Windlow was surprised. "What would they think if the Wizard Himaggery did not go out to rescue his thalan? Since the Fon has said he is the Wizard Himaggery – and who am I to say he is not, particularly if both you and he say he is – and since everyone, including Boldery, knows that Mertyn is the Wizard Himaggery's thalan, why then of course he must be rescued." He turned to Twizzledale, frowning. "Though how you will explain it all to Valdon, I do not know. I leave it to your necessarily fertile imagination."

And from that moment it was only a short time before they came to the empty lodging house with a troop of the Mont's guards and carried Mertyn back to that place, up the back way, quietly, into a room separated from the body of the hotel, where the Seer awaited them. Only Twizzledale had touched him, though the Seer now laid a hand upon his forehead and sighed.

"The woman said ghoul-plague, did she? And that is what the host outside the gate is besieging us for? Then I am deeply worried, lad."

"What is this disease?" Mavin asked. "I had never heard of it."

"It begins, some say, with the eating of human flesh. For this reason it is called ghoul-plague. In my reading of history, however, I have found that it may not be human flesh but the flesh of shadowpeople which causes the disease. Once begun, it is like other plagues, crossing from those who have eaten the forbidden flesh to those who have not. It is carried from place to place, and none know how."

"Mertyn touched the sick man, in the alley. The man drooled on him. On his face."

"That may have been enough. A very ancient book spoke of disease being spread by the bites of small creatures, little blood suckers or flitter bats. I have seen plagues of similar kind. Some do recover." He did not sound hopeful.

"The woman said the shadowpeople are said to cure this plague," said Mavin. For the past hour she had been making plans, moving pieces of information about in her head. "I'm going to go find them, Gamesmaster."

"Find the shadowpeople?" The Fon was amazed. "They can't be found by anyone wishing to do so."

"Perhaps not. But I must try. Will you care for Mertyn while I am gone? I would not ask this thing of you, except that you are kindly and good, and you cannot leave the city anyhow."

"And you," murmured Windlow. "How will you leave the city?"

"The way that Demon did," she said. "The Armiger said he went through tunnels."

"By all the Gamegods, child. Those tunnels lead to Hell's Maw. And I do not know, nor do any in this city know for all I can tell, whether there is any way out of Hell's Maw at all."

CHAPTER SIX

Though both of them tried to dissuade her, speaking quietly so as not to disturb Mertyn, she would not be moved.

"I must go. Never mind about Poffle. I'll get through Poffle. Never mind about shadowpeople, I'll . . ." And still they argued.

Until suddenly old Windlow stiffened where he stood, his face turning rigid and pale, his hands stretching out as though to touch something the others could not see.

"He's having a vision," whispered the Fon. "Quiet. It affects him in this way sometimes when he is very upset." They watched, not touching him, as he swayed upon his feet, his eyes darting from side to side as though watching some wild movement or affray they could not see. Then his eyes shut, he swayed, caught at the bed to keep himself from falling, and gasped deeply, like a man coming from under water and desperate for air.

"We must let her go, Twizzledale," he said at last.

"Let . . . *her* go? Mavin? Oh, come now, Windlow. Or have I been unwizardly?" He turned to give Mavin a keen look, swiftly up and down.

Mavin, staring at the Seer, knew that the Fon had penetrated at least part of her identity, but let the feminine identification go by without protest. "You saw something. What was it?"

"I'm not sure," he sighed. "It was dark and there was a great deal of confusion. But Mertyn was there, and his sister, Mavin. And Mavin had a trick or two in her left ear, or so Mertyn said. There was something evil. Valdon was involved. Something terrible, huge. Lords, Twizzledale, but at times I hate being a Seer." He grabbed at his head with both hands as though he would tear it off. "Sometimes I think I am not a Seer at all, but something else."

The Fon accused her, quoting Windlow. "His *sister* Mavin, eh?

What are you, young person? Charlatan, as Huld accused us of being? Or something else?"

"Hush," said Windlow distractedly. "Don't snarl at her, Wizard. Whatever she has done, she's done for the boy. Go with her. Help her if you can. But don't snarl. Don't worry about Mertyn more than you can help, Mavin. Whatever can be done for the boy, I'll do."

"You won't move him, Seer?"

"No farther than he's been moved, child. Go with Twizzledale. Take what you need from our goods, food, whatever. There's a puzzle about you that my Seeing didn't do a thing to solve, you know. Until we meet in happier times, then." He embraced her. She felt a dew of clammy perspiration on his cheeks, a trembling in his hands, but his mouth was firm as he turned her out the door, Twizzledale following, still in his mood of irritation.

"I don't like it when people don't tell me things," he grumbled. "Particularly important things."

She sighed, moved by his exasperation, not to an answering anger but to some soothing words, some kindliness. He looked so spiky, hands rooting at his hair, eyes sparking with annoyance.

"Wizard. I know you are angry with me, but how could I trust you? Someone just met on the road? I barely felt I could trust the Seer, and I wouldn't have come to him if I had had any choice. Please." She stopped, holding him by his arm. "Where are we going?"

"Back to our rooms. To pack you some – whatever you need. Food, I suppose. A change of clothing."

"I won't need any of that. Wizard, if you want to help me, come with me to the entrance, the tunnels, the way to go through that place . . . Poffle. Don't go on being angry. It has nothing to do with you, truly."

They stood in confrontation, he clenching and unclenching his fists, shifting his weight as though he wanted to hit her; she, head cocked, poised, prepared for flight if he decided to grab her. So they stared, glared, until he began to smile, then to laugh. "I'd like to strangle you." He coughed. "You're impossible."

She smiled warily. "I'm really doing the only thing I can."

"You're shifter, aren't you? I should have guessed. The minute Windlow said 'sister,' I should have guessed. I did guess. Except that . . ."

"Except that you don't like shifters," she said in a flat, emotionless tone. "Other Gamesmen, yes. But not shifters."

"Hold! I've never known a shifter. Surely, shifters are supposed to be – well, what are they supposed to be. Stranger than the rest of us? Less understandable?"

"Less trustworthy?" Her smile was sweet, poisonous. "Less reliable? Less honorable?"

"More tricky," he said, amused again. "More devious, more challenging, more entertaining."

"Less destructible," she said in a firm voice, putting an end to the catalogue. "Which is why I think I can get through Poffle to the outside world. Which is why I think maybe I can find shadow-people, though others possibly have been unable to do so."

"How old are you?" he asked, apropos of nothing.

"Fifteen," she said, before she thought.

"Young. Have you had talent long? I mean . . ."

"You mean, have I had it long enough to learn to use it. Yes, Wizard, I have. Probably better than you have learned to use your own. I had to." And she turned away from him to march out into the dark through a side door, he following mutely, feeling it a better idea to hide his curiosity than to annoy her with any more questions. Once outside he led her in a circuitous route through the grounds of the Mont and onto a narrow walkway curving along the rim of the escarpment. The way was unfrequented, littered with small trash, ending in a parapet surrounded by a low wall.

"Down there." He pointed.

She looked over to see the narrow crevasse which fell below the wall, a walkway there lined with needled, misshapen trees. At the end of the walkway a lonely lantern burned beside a grilled arch, and outside the grill a platoon of guardsmen moved restlessly back and forth. The archway led into darkness.

"This is the Ghoul Blourbast's private highway into Pfarb Durim," said the Fon. "It was pointed out to us by Huld. The Seer was not happy to learn of that young man's true identity."

"How was it that you did not know?"

"The arrangements were made through third parties, Negotiators and Ambassadors. That alone should have warned Windlow that something was amiss. What use has an honest Gamesman for Ambassadors!"

"It seems Huld didn't care much for the arrangement either."

"Valdon is an example of humility compared to Huld. After some time in Valdon's company I thought him the epitome of arrogance, but I was wrong. I believe Huld has never asked for anything, no matter how outrageous, which he has not been given. Who is he, really? No one seems to know, except that Blourbast holds him dear. And he went back down that hell hole, Mavin, so watch out for him."

"He will not see me," she said soberly, then, taking him by the arm, "Fon, can you help me? With the shadowpeople? What language do they speak? What would they ask of me in return for healing Mertyn?"

He shook his head. "I wish I knew, Mavin. I would help you in any way I could, if only because you tricked me and teased me and made my mind work in odd ways. You must find them first and then try to do them a service, as you would for anyone, Gamesman or pawn. If they are peoplelike – and I have heard that they are in some ways – then they will seek to do you a service in repayment. How you will speak with them, I do not know. I have never seen one of them. At times I have doubted they exist." He pulled her to him and squeezed her, quickly releasing her, so that she felt only breathless and wondering at the suddenness of it. "Let us make a pact, however. If you have need of me, you will send word – let me think! The word shall be the name of that place you stayed, BALD BADGER. Or, if there is no way to send word, then the first letter of your name in fire or smoke or stone or whatever. Given that word, that signal, I'll get to you somehow."

"You can't get out," she said. "The city is closed."

"You can't get out either," he replied. "And yet you are going. So. Strange are the Talents of Wizards. Leave the way of it to me." And he released her, standing away from her, and looking at her in a way no one had looked at her before. Mavin shook her head, trying to clear it, then gave it up and turned from him to slide over the low parapet at the edge of the declivity. She cast one look over her shoulder to see him walking steadily away. She had not wanted him to watch her as she changed. Seemingly he had understood that.

She shifted into something which could climb walls, rather spiderlike if she had thought about it, which she had no time to do. At the bottom of the ditch, she skulked along behind the twisted trees until the light of the torches splashed amber on the stones before her. She had already decided what to do next. Using an arm much stronger than her own, she heaved a paving stone high onto the opposite bank, some distance behind her. It crashed through the branches with a satisfactory sound of someone thrashing about. The guards ran toward it, not looking behind them, and she slipped through the bars of the gate into darkness, resuming her own shape once hidden in shadow. Only a shifter could have come through the gate – a shifter or a serpent. The bars had been set close together.

There was no light in the tunnel. Far ahead she thought she could see a faint grayness in the black. She fumbled her way forward, stopping close to the walkway, feeling a slimy dampness on her hands where they touched thc walls or floor. Furred feet made no sound. Soon she was walking four-footed, making a nose which would smell out trails and paths. A sharp sound broke the silence, echoed briefly like a shout into a well, and was gone. Still, it had given her direction in the darkness. The grayness grew more light. She turned toward it, out of the widened corridor and into a side way. It was torchlight, reflected off wet walls around several sinuous turns. The torch burned outside another barred gate which was no more trouble than the first had been. Now the corridor was lighted, badly, with smoky torches at infrequent intervals.

She became aware of sound, a far, indefinite clanging, an echoing clamor, a whumping sound as though something heavy fell repeatedly into something soft. Through it all came a thin cry of song, high, birdlike, quickly silenced. She shivered, not knowing why. The sounds were not ugly or threatening, and yet heard together they made her want to weep. She sneaked along the way, now finding windows cut into the stone which looked out into black pits. As she went, she tossed bits of gravel through the openings, listening for the sound. Her ears told her some were merely small rooms or closets while others were bottomless. The sounds came closer, and suddenly—

"Wait a minute, will ya. I'll be with you. Run, run, so impatient. Wait a minute!" The voice screeched, whined, almost at her shoulder, and Mavin fell against the wall, crouched, ready to be attacked.

"I'll be right with ya," the voice screamed.

She reached out, patting the air around her. Another of the openings was just above her head, and hung inside it, far enough inside that no light struck it at all, was a cage. Mavin found the ring on which it was hung, drew it down and into the light. Inside it crouched a ragged-looking beasty, eyes dilated into great, brown orbs, teeth bared, patches of its hide missing as though they had been burned away. "Run," it screamed at her. "Run, run."

Without thinking, Mavin opened the cage and shook the creature out onto the stones where it lay for a moment, too shocked to move. Then in one enormous leap, it crossed the corridor and disappeared down a side way, shrieking as it went. Thoughtfully, Mavin hung the open cage back where she had found it and followed. "Run, run," it screamed, fleeing at top speed into darkness. "I'll get to ya."

"I hope you do," she muttered. "To one Pantiquod, one strange, gray woman. To one someone who talks, who can be overheard, who knows the way out of here."

She had need of her nose again, for the little animal lost itself in darkness. The stench of it – part illness, part dirty cage, part the beasty itself – lingered on the stones, however, and Mavin tracked the little animal through dark ways into lighter ones to a heavy door upon which the little creature hung, still trying to shriek, though its voice had wearied to a whisper. "Run," it whimpered. "Run. I'll get to ya."

Mavin stood to one side, pressed down upon the latch and let the door swing open. The thrilpat was through it in an instant. Hearing no alarms, Mavin followed. She was now in a well lit corridor ending in a broad flight of stairs. A small balcony protruded to her left, half hidden behind embroidered draperies. She oozed into the cover of these, hearing voices from below.

"I thought I told you to get rid of that animal!" The voice was heavy gasping, full of malice and ill humor. Peering between the railings, Mavin could see where the voice came from – a vast, billowy form lying in a canopied bed. Only the bottom half of the form was visible to her. She could see all of the other persons in the room, however, and was unsurprised to recognize the gray woman from the lodging house, now dressed in an odd, winged cap with a feathered cape at her shoulders. It was Pantiquod, the mangy animal now clinging to her ankle as it sobbed and pled.

"I gave it to one of your servants, brother, and told him to dispose of it."

"Which servant was that?"

"I don't really know. One of those who stand outside this room from time to time."

"Well, find out which one. Have him chained to the long wall in the tunnel. If you can't find out which one, have the whole lot of them chained. Let them hang there till they rot."

"Which they assuredly will. Have you not had enough of rottenness, brother Ghoul? Has it not brought you to this pass? Perhaps it would be well to dwell less on rottenness for a time?"

"Shall a trifle of sickness make me forsake my life's work?" The bulk upon the bed heaved with laughter, and Mavin, watching it, found a kind of fascinated nausea in the sight. The figure heaved itself upright, and the sight of its face made her stomach heave, for it was covered with hideous growths from which a vile ichor oozed. The hands which stroked an amulet at the creature's throat were as badly afflicted. "My bone pits are not yet full, Panty, my sister, my dove. Panty, my dear one, mother of my delicious twins, Huld and Huldra, my dear boy and his delightful sister. And though she has obviously learned aplenty about the world – and will soon enough bear us yet another generation – my dear boy is not yet fully educated. Though it seems he does not want to go into the world to mix with his inferiors."

"It was a foolish idea," she said calmly, seemingly unafraid of this monster on the bed. "You have not reared him to care what others do, or think, or say. How then should he care for education, for is that not the study of what others care about? Hmmm?"

"He says we have taught him enough, you and I. Har, ahrah, enough, he says. Enough that he can use what we have taught him to conquer the world. Harar, aha." The vast figure shivered with obscene laughter, and Mavin trembled upon the balcony.

"I have taught him to dissemble, my lord. To pretend. To play the Gamesman of honor. To mock the manners of others, if it seems wise – or amusing – to do so. What have you taught him?"

"To care for nothing, my love. To be sickened by nothing, repelled by nothing, to be capable of anything at all. Between us, he has been well educated."

"Well then, why this mockery? Why all this effort expended to put him in the company of Prionde's sons? He cared not for them. Should he have?"

"Softly, my dove, my cherub. He did all that was needed. He

found in Valdon's mind the way to the King, to Prionde. That was all he needed to do for now. It will be useful for some future Game. They will not suspect him of plotting, not at his age. But he and I – we have planned, sister. We have planned."

"But does it not seem now all those plans are for naught?"

"Araugh," the man screamed in rage. "Beware, sister. Do not be quick to condemn me to death. Blourbast does not die of ghoul-plague. My thalan made me immune to ghoul-plague when I was younger than Huld. I have eaten forbidden meat all my life, and the plague has not touched me!" The bulk heaved, quivered, drew itself upright, then collapsed once more.

"It has not touched you until now," she said, her face as cold and empty of emotion as a mask. "Until now. It amused you to hold the shadowpeople to ransom for their relic. So they came at your command. I told you they were sick, but you sent them to your kitchens nonetheless. You gave the meat to those destined to be sent above, to Pfarb Durim. Well enough. But it was foolish to dine from the same dish, brother. You have not had ghoul-plague before, but you had not used the disease to empty a city before, either. In fact," she turned an ironic glance upon him, "there had been no ghoul-plague for some tens of years. For most of our lifetimes, yours and mine, Blourbast. Now the disease comes again. Perhaps it is a new strain to which you are not immune."

"Ghoul-plague is ghoul-plague," he growled. "I am immune, I say. I ate only what was necessary so that they should not suspect what meat I fed them. I have eaten this meat many times before."

"No," she contradicted him. "You have not. I tell you again, brother, this is not any disease which has come upon us before. You are not immune, and now the Healers have spread the ban against you. You should not have tried to force healing out of them."

"In Hell's Maw, Gamesmen play as I will."

"But in Hell's Maw they did not. I told you that shadowpeople are reputed to cure this disease. What have you done to learn the truth of this?"

"I have a few dozens in my cellars, madame. Since they speak no tongue I can understand, what good to question them? I had a little man once who spoke their tongue, but he is dead now. My Demons have attempted to Read their little minds, to no end. So let them hang there and starve."

"You have given up eating them, then? You do not fatten them in their cages?"

"Let them starve, I say. I hold their relic here," and he stroked his breast once again, the motion of those horrid hands holding Mavin's eyes fixed. "Here. So let them starve. Let them all die. It is nothing to me."

"Nothing? What if you are ill to death, Blourbast?"

"I will recover, woman. I will recover, shadowpeople or no. This is only a temporary inconvenience."

"But there is Huld, brother. If he sickens, will he recover?"

"You are late with your motherly concern, sister. He is gone to the far reaches of Poffle where the ways open upon the woodlands. I sent him thence, with his lovely sister-wife. He will be served only by his own people. Then, when Pfarb Durim is emptied and the winds have washed it clean, I will give it to him for a gift, as I promised him. He may fill it with his followers, and the revenues will be his and his fortune great, for no city garners more from trade than Pfarb Durim." Exhausted by this speech the bulky form seemed to collapse in upon itself. "Leave me, woman. You were ever contentious."

The woman bowed, moved out of the chamber through a door at the far side, taking one of the torches with her as she went. A kind of gloom fell in the chamber, a heaving dusk, the thick breathing of Blourbast filling it as might the petulant waves of a foul and polluted sea.

Mavin waited for that breathing to soften before creeping down the stairs and into the chamber. She was invisible against the shadows, silent as a shadow herself, as she crept around the chamber and to the door Pantiquod had left through. She eased it open, but it shrieked at her, and she found herself confronting the mad eyes of the little thrilpat, shut in with the Ghoul and dying on the floor.

"Harrah?" from the bed. "Who's there? Come into the light, you vermin."

She did not wait, but oozed through the crack and pulled it shut behind her, hearing the whisper, "Run, run, run," as she ran indeed, down the long way which arched into emptiness before her. What she had heard had been enough to give her an idea. Now she had only to find the place the shadowpeople were kept. After all, had not the Fon told her to do some service for them? What better service than to save them from this place?

Which was easier thought of than accomplished. Pantiquod walked for a great distance, through balconies which stretched over vast audience halls, down twisting corridors, up curved flights of stairs and down similar ones, but at the end of it she came only to a wing of the place devoted to suites of ordinary rooms, small kitchens, servants' quarters, more luxuriously furnished bedrooms and sitting rooms among them. Here there was a certain amount of coming and going, and Mavin's journey was interrupted by the constant need to hide. After the fifth or sixth such occasion, she decided that too much time was being wasted. It took only a little creeping and spying to see what livery the servants of the place wore, and then only a brief time more of experimentation to shift into that livery and guise. Thereafter she walked as a servant, obsequious and quiet, so ordinary about the face as to be anonymous. Pantiquod entered a set of rooms which were evidently set aside for her use, and did not emerge from them. She was obviously alone, and there was nothing Mavin could overhear or oversee to her advantage.

Well then, one must risk something. She returned the way she had come, stopping at the first large hall in which there was any appreciable traffic. "I have taken a wrong turning," she said to an approaching servant. "I was told by the woman, Pantiquod, to carry a message to the guard of the chambers . . . below. Where the shadowpeople are."

The servant stopped, stared, at last opened his mouth to show a tongueless cavity there. Mavin's first reaction was to run, or to vomit. She restrained herself, however, and grasped the man firmly by one shoulder. "Do you understand what I say?"

He nodded, terrified.

"Do you know the place, the door?"

He nodded again.

"Then lead me there. You may return here and none know the difference."

Still fearful, shivering, the man set out at a run, Mavin striding alongside. They twisted, turned, then the man stopped just before coming to a corner and pointed around it, keeping well back, face white and contorted. Though she had no Demon's talent for reading minds, his was easy to read. "You were down there? That's where they cut out your tongue? I understand. Go." And he scurried back the way they had come, in such frantic haste that he stumbled, almost falling.

Mavin lay down upon the floor, peeked around the corner from floor level. At the end of the hallway was another of the guarded grills like those at the tunnel entrance to Hell's Maw. Before this gate, however, was no casual assembly of guardsmen but an armed line of Armigers, shoulder to shoulder, naked swords gleaming in their hands, a line of lounging Sorcerers behind them, blazing with power in that silent place.

"Oh, pombi piss," she muttered. "Filth and rot and foul disaster." Then she simply lay against the wall, exhausted, unable to think what to do next. How long had it been since she had had anything to eat? How long since she had slept? Probably a full day. They had had breakfast the day they entered Pfarb Durim. She had not eaten after that. Nor slept. She sighed. Well enough to know the way into the dungeons, but no help if one were too weak to go there. "Food," she murmured. "Food first. Then whatever comes next."

CHAPTER SEVEN

She cursed herself tiredly for not having brought the food which Windlow had offered. What food she might find here in the depths of Hell's Maw had little likelihood of being healthful, "You are too rash, my girl," she lectured herself in silence. "You have done well so far, but what have you had to oppose you? A few old lechers in Danderbat keep, that's all. Now, here you are, run off in a sudden frenzy without any thought at all." Sighing, she rose and went skulking off in search of something to fill her empty belly.

The woman Pantiquod had looked more or less normal, that is, unghoulish, and she had seemed to live in a part of the caves and tunnels which was cleanly, not smelling of rot and mold. Mavin returned there, staying out of sight, poking about until she found a larder with fruit in it and loaves of bread smelling of the sun. Evidently not all those who lived in Hell's Maw were of Blourbast's persuasion. Perhaps only a few were, or none except the Ghoul himself. She wondered what diet the arrogant Huld had eaten, whether he had been cossetted with dainties from Pfarb Durim or fed from childhood on the horrors of the pit. None of this wondering did anything to destroy her appetite, which was ravenous. The tunnels were chill, and her shifting had drawn what power she carried with her, leaving her weary and weak. After a short rest, she began to feel stronger. "Able to shift for yourself again, girl," she said. "Able to shift." She created a capacious pocket to carry some of the food with her, knowing it might well be a long time before she would find more. She thought longingly of sleep, then rejected the idea. There was no time, not with Mertyn lying sick in Pfarb Durim and the image of Blourbast's ravaged face before her as a threat. Mertyn might come to this if she did not find help for him.

When she returned to the guarded hall it was to find the entrance to the lower realms unchanged. The line of Armigers still stood shoulder to shoulder; the Sorcerers behind them still lounged against the wall. They seemed not to have moved while she had been gone, as though some power she could not sense kept them in that utter stillness and concentration, entranced to their duty. It did no good to speculate. She had to get past them, preferably without alerting the warren to her presence.

Nothing came to her. She peered down the sides of the corridor, searching for any gap in the line. There was none. None. Except above the guardsmen's heads where the corridor arched into gloom above the glare of the shaded lanterns. Stretching from side to side below the vaulted ceiling was a line of wooden beams which tied the walls together, knobby and convoluted in the shadow, for they had been carved into likenesses of thick vines and bulbous fruits with pendant sprays of leaves fanning across the stone walls at either end. She examined them, then began to thin herself, to flow upward, to draw in upon herself while stretching out, becoming limbless, earless, hairless, softly scaled and quiet as a dream, relentlessly pouring up and onto the beam where she twisted about it in a bulky knot no different in outline from the carved vines.

The beam on which she rested was in the cross corridor. Now her serpent's head reached out into the guarded corridor, hidden in the gloom above the light, weaving out a little, silent, silent, until it rested on the next beam and anchored there. A long loop of body followed, knotting and unknotting slowly, moving forward as the sinuous body bridged the shadowy space, beam by beam. At last she lay above the guardsmen, twined onto the last of the beams, her endless neck reaching into the shadow behind them, over the Sorcerers' heads. There was nothing to hold her there except the lintel of the arch itself, and she descended by tiny tentacles sent deep into the mortar between the stones, holding herself to the wall as a vine holds, pulled tight to the rock until her serpent's head could pass through the iron grill, fingerlength by fingerlength. She lay at last beyond the grill and behind the guards, they not having moved during all that time. When the last scale of her tail slipped through the grill, her head was halfway down the flight of stairs behind, body stretched between the two points like a single reaching arm.

Now she heard again the sounds she had heard on first entering

Hell's Maw, the clangor, the heavy pounding, the fragment of birdlike song, cut off abruptly. The stairs wound around a pit, down onto the floor of a well from which more of the arched corridors spread in all directions. The place was lit by the omnipresent torches. There were torches and lanterns everywhere in Hell's Maw, an insufficiency of light in all those depths, a gelid half shade thick with fumes and smoke. After a time she had stopped noticing the light, had only moved through its dusky inadequacy like a fish moving through water, not noticing the medium. Now, however, as she came to the bottom of the well, she saw that one of the tunnels to her left was lit in a stranger way, by a flickering which receded and advanced, receded and advanced, accompanied by a sound as of clattering wooden twigs upon stone. She stared toward this way, then stopped as a stench poured out of the tunnel toward her, an effluvium so dense as to seem impenetrable. The wisp of birdlike sound came from behind her, and she turned, seeking the sound, finding any excuse not to go toward that flickering light.

Song led her into a darker way, one smelling of soil, but a cleaner stench than the corruption behind her. Roots dangled through the ceiling stones, brushes of dense hairy fiber dragging across the lean furred form she had taken. Snakes were all very well, she told herself, but stone was cold upon belly scales and the placement of the eyes left something to be desired. A twitter sounded ahead, and she melted into the darkness behind a pillar, searching. Nothing. No, perhaps a tiny movement. A scampering. Song again, a single, disconsolate trill. Then again. Silence. She snaked out a lengthened arm and grabbed into the gloom, then bit back a howl as needle teeth sank into her hand. Fighting down her instinct to drop whatever it was and run, Mavin toughened the flesh around the small thing she had caught and dragged it into the half light.

To stare in wonder, for it was like nothing she had ever seen before. Huge, fragile ears; wide lipless mouth; large dark eyes wild with fury and fear; teeth bared, slender form fluffed with soft fur, crying, crying words . . . words. She knew in an instant that it was no mere animal she held. The eyes, while frantic, were full of alert intelligence, and the sounds were too consecutive, too varied to be mere animal cries of panic. She sat down on the chill stone and crooned to it, without thinking, using the same tone she had used to Mertyn when he had hurt himself. "Ahh, ahh, it's all right. I won't hurt you. Shh. Shh. See, I'll hardly hold you at all. Now, who are you?''

She asked the question with an interrogative lilt and a cock of her head, waiting for an answer. The little creature stopped shaking and regarded her quietly, chest heaving with enormous sobs, quieting until only an occasional tremor ran through the muscular limbs she held so gently. ''Mavin,'' she used one hand to point at herself. ''Mavin.'' Then she pointed to her captive and cocked her head once more. ''Who?''

''Puh-leedle-addle-proom-room-room,'' it warbled. ''Puh-leedle-addle-proom-room-room.''

Mavin shook her head, laughing. ''Proom!'' she pointed to him, relaxing her grip. ''Mavin. Proom.'' This matter settled, she sat with the manikin on her lap, wondering what to do next. A final, sobbing breath passed through the creature, then it collapsed into her lap, sighing, such a sigh of despair and sadness as she had never heard. ''What's the matter, little one?'' she asked. ''Are you as lost in this terrible place as I am?''

Proom tilted his head – Mavin was sure it was a ''he,'' though she could not have said why – and thought about this for a moment. Then he reached up to lay one slender, three-fingered hand across her lips. The other he held behind his ear, the delicate pink nails curved above it. More clearly than with words he said, be still and listen. Then he sang, birdlike, a clear warble of sound in the ponderous dusk of the cavern. Mavin held her breath. She thought she heard a reply, or was it only an echo? No, it was a reply, for Proom's hand whipped away from her ear to point into the dark. A reply. There were others here, others in this place, and she knew already that they were not here by chance. Something tickled at her mind, fled away.

Proom started to leap away, but she held him, placing him on her shoulder as she stood and moved in the direction he indicated. ''I'll help you,'' she said, forgetting everything for the moment except the longing and despair in the little one's voice. ''This way?'' And she strode into the darkness. Torches were fewer along this way, but she compensated for the lack of light by making her eyes larger, her ears wider, not noticing Proom's astonishment at this, nor his obvious interest as she brought her reaching arms back to a more normal length.

"Andibar, bar, bar," he murmured.

She paid no attention. She was busy listening. They came to a fork in the way and she paused, looking to Proom for guidance. He warbled again, and again she heard a ghostly reply, thin, almost directionless, but Proom seemed to have no trouble knowing where it had come from, for he pointed down one of the branching ways without hesitation. They went on in this way, turn after turn, branch after branch, until Mavin had lost all sense of direction or place. Still, the answering voice grew more distinct each time they turned, and Proom's excitement was manifest as they went into the almost total dark. So it was Mavin almost impaled herself upon the spiked gate before she saw it. It was another of the ubiquitous grilled gates, this one with a mesh so small even a creature the size of Proom could not get through. He had pressed himself against it with a piteous cry, fingers thrust through the mesh as though he would pull himself through by an act of will. She knew he had been this far before. His despair could mean nothing else.

"Shh, shh," she said, tugging him away. Pressing herself against the mesh, making her eyes wide to gain all the available light, she could see the latch, high inside the gate. "Nothing to it," she murmured to the little one. "Nothing at all." A finger extended into a tentacle which wove its boneless way through the mesh, pushed upward and outward until the latch opened with a satisfying *tlock*. At first the gate would not move, but then as she threw her full weight against it, it screamed at her and sagged open on rusty hinges. Mavin stopped pushing to listen. Proom pushed past her and ran on down the corridor, the quick birdsong running before him in greeting. This time she heard the answer clearly, no mistake about it and no confusing echoes. Whoever sang in reply sang close before them.

She followed the sound, the two sounds, call and reply, as they grew louder, rounding a dim corner to find herself in a room hung with cages like that one which had held the unfortunate thrilpat, cages hung high on slender chains. They were out of reach of little Proom, no matter how he jumped and warbled to reach his imprisoned kin, and all the cavernous room thrilled with their birdsong twittering until Mavin was dizzy with it.

The song was interrupted by a monstrous clanging, as though from a gong unimaginably huge. All the little people writhed in pain on the bottom of their cages, tiny hands clamped across their ears. The clanging stopped, but the little creatures still cowered, sobbing, Proom also from his place on the stones. From some distance came a burst of evil laughter and the word "Silence . . ." shouted in a great voice. Then there was quiet, broken only by despairing whimpers from dozens of throats.

Mavin, at first confused by the noise, was now angry. Without stopping to think about it she began to stork upward, taller and thinner, so that she teetered to the height of the cages, then above them where they were fastened to rings in the high ceiling. She began to lower them, one, two, a dozen, twenty. Some of the cages held only one of Proom's people while others held two or three. She let them all down into the troubled quiet, and Proom gathered himself up to move among the cages, whispering, gesturing. He tugged at her ankle, pointing high where the ring of keys hung, and she passed them down to him, almost falling, for she had forgotten what a stiltwalker she had become. She folded into herself, suddenly weak and wan, aware that she had used up her strength and power again, depleted as it was in this chill place. She fished a piece of fruit from her pocket, bit into it, then saw some dozens pairs of eyes focused hungrily upon her. She gave them the other food she carried, watched with amazement as each creature took a single bite before passing it on. The food circled quickly, came back to her to be urged upon her again. She took her single bite and gave it back once more. Proom climbed into her lap and patted her on the head. "Mavin," he said. "Mavin, vin, vin."

"Introductions are all very nice," she said, "but I assume what you really want is to get out of here." She staggered to her feet and went back into the corridor, turning the way they had come. At once a dozen hands patted at her, pushing her in the opposite direction. Proom chattered, sniffed at the air, then agreed, following the others in their scamper toward a break in the corridor wall, thence into root-hung tunnels, and finally between two great knobbly tree roots into a rocky cavern of a different kind. Sunlight came upon them from above, the warm amber light of a distant afternoon. Around them hung icicles of stone, bulging buttresses of rock, walls of ochre and red and a long, straight path leading upward into leafy forests. She found strength she did not know she had to follow them up and out into a clearing among great trees.

On a distant hill she could see the bulk of Pfarb Durim rising beyond its walls.

"Ahh?" called the little ones. "Ahh? Ahh?" They looked around, jigged uncertainly, called again and again, in some distress. It was obvious they did not know where they were. They had smelled their way out, but could not identify this location. Mavin hoisted Proom high on her shoulder where he could see the city through the trees. "Durim, rim, rim," he called, leaning down to give a hand up to others of his kindred. Mavin staggered under the load as twenty of them climbed her like a tree. There was pointing, argument, finally agreement, and most of the burden dropped away and vanished in the brush. Proom waited with her, regarding her with thoughtful eyes. After a time he beckoned, vanishing like the others in the shadow of the trees. The answer came then, simply, as if she had known it for some time. "Shadowpeople," disbelieving, yet knowing it was so. "These are the shadowpeople, and I have already done as the Fon suggested. I have done them a service. Now, shall I follow to see if they will do one for me?"

They traveled for a time in an arc, a long, curving line which kept Pfarb Durim always visible, high on its cliffs to their left. Once Mavin heard water, the sound of a considerable flow, making her believe that the River Haws ran no great distance from them in the forest. Others came back to them from time to time, bringing nuts and fruit and loaves of bread. Others came with messages, after some of which they changed direction. Mavin followed, uncomplaining, telling herself that now was a time for patience, for waiting to see what might happen next of its own accord, without her intervention. This patience was about to be exhausted when they arrived. The place of assembly was a hollow in the woods with a straight, tall tree at one side. The shadowpeople were gathered near it, staring upward. Mavin could see nothing from where she stood except a lumpish blob hanging high among the branches, swaying a little in the wind.

"Agirul," the shadowmen sang, dancing below the tree with its pendant form, swaying their bodies in time to the swaying of whatever it was above them. "Agirul, rul, rul."

Slowly, so slowly that she was not sure she saw it move at all, the lump turned its head over so that it faced downward, showing a tiny, three-cornered mouth, a shiny, licked-looking nose, two dark lines behind which eyes might be hiding. The mouth opened. "Ahhh, shuuush," it said with great finality. "Shuuuush."

"Ahh shuuuush," sang the shadowmen, laughing, falling down in their laughter. Several of them ran off into the forest to return bearing slender bundles of long grass, the top of each stem tassled like a feather. They began to splice these together, making long, fragile lengths with which they tried to tickle the pendant creature, fluttering the tassled ends around its invisible ears, over its hidden eyes. One shadowman, more venturesome or inventive than the rest, concentrated his attention on the creature's rear, evidently touching some sensitive spot for the creature opened its tiny mouth once more and roared.

At this sound every one of the shadowpeople, down to the smallest cub, sat down at once with expressions of severity and solemnity sitting awkwardly upon their cheerful faces. Above them the creature went on roaring as it swung to the trunk of the tree and began to descend, ponderously, long leg after long arm, like a pendulum swinging on its way downward, tic by toc, to slump at last on the ground at the roots of the tree, long legs and arms sprawled wide and helpless. It began to draw itself into some more coordinated posture, and two of the shadowpeople ran to help, murmuring, patting, easing the creature onto its haunches with its monstrously long arms folded neatly into its lap.

"Naiii shuuush," it complained, scratching its head with two curved nails, "Mumph, mumph, who is this person?"

A warbled answer came from the assembly. The beast considered, then turned its head to Mavin.

"I suppose you'll insist that this wasn't your idea," it bellowed at her in a petulant voice. "The little beasts won't let me alone."

"No – it was not my idea. Not letting you alone, I mean. Since I didn't know that you exist, I could hardly . . ."

"No. No, of course not. No one has any idea, not ever. Don't they teach languages in the benighted schools you people attend? Why shouldn't you learn to speak shadow-talk? Why shouldn't they speak whatever ugly tongue we are speaking now? But no. No, it's always come to Agirul for translation, because that's easier. Shush. Get away, you," and it pushed ineffectually at the crowd of shadowpeople who were still busy propping it up and cushioning its back with leafy twigs. It did not look comfortable. Its arms and legs were not designed for living on the ground, sprawling uncontrolled as though the muscles would not work out of the trees. One look at its hands told Mavin that it was a tree liver which never came to the ground of its own will, for it had curved hooks of bone growing from each palm.

"They didn't hurt you, did they?" she asked.

"Of course they didn't hurt me. They woke me! They know I dislike being wakened. It has been sleeping weather recently, good sleeping weather, and I hate having it interrupted. I'm not unwilling to acceed to emergency, however, and these little people always seem to have one. I suppose it's you they want to talk with?"

Mavin cast a wondering glance around. "I suppose so. I helped them get out of Hell's Maw. I want to talk to them, very much. I need their help."

The Agirul sighed. "Hell's Maw. Blourbast the Ghoul. I heard he had ghoul-plague. Why isn't he dead?"

"I don't know. He looks half dead. His hands and face are covered with sores, but he claims he will recover. Does it always kill? The plague, I mean?"

"Obviously not always. Ah, you brighten at that? It means something to you that some recover? Well, we will explore the notion soon. Just now it seems that Proom is ready to explain why I was awakened."

There was a brief colloquy, then the Agirul murmured to Mavin that it would attempt to make a simultaneous translation of the explanation which was about to follow. "Woman, it may be you will understand nothing at all, in which case I will explain when they have finished. It is the desire of Proom that you be honored by a song – and since his people are quite decent in the matter of gifts, fruits, you know, and nuts, and even a bit of roast meat from time to time – I will accommodate them. Sit comfortably now, this may take some time."

The hooked hand drew her gently close, and she squirmed about until her head lay near the Agirul's mouth. For a moment, she feared she would go to sleep, thus disgracing herself, but once the singing started, she did not think of sleep again.

"*Hear the song of Proom!*" It was a solo voice which sang this phrase, each syllable dropped into the clearing as a stone may be dropped into still water. The echoes of it ran in ripples across the gathered faces, gathering force, returning from the edges to the center amplified. Agirul murmured the words, but she did not hear the words, only the song. When the echoes had died, the voice sang again.

"*Summoned, Proom, by those who live forever.*
Summoned, Proom, on a great journey.
Far to go. Many seasons spent. Doubt shall he return.
Ah, Proom, Proom, keeper of Ganver's Bone."

Now those gathered in the clearing took up the song, a full chorus. Some of these little ones had deeper voices than she had heard before, and these deeper voices set up a drone beneath the song, dragging, ominous.

"*Shall the Bone go? Far from the people?*
Shall the Bone travel far from its own place?
Shall the Bone depart from Ganver who gave it?"

Three voices sang alone, joined by flutes and bells.

"*Leave the Bone, Proom, before answering the summons.*
Leave the holy thing among its people.
If Proom does not return, the Bone remains."

Now there were drums, little and big, cymbals ringing, and a solo voice, awe filled, chanting.

"*Now see, listen all, Proom left it in the high place.*
In the sacred place. Forbidden place. Guarded place.
Farewell, Proom. Go with song around you."

Now a solo drum, high-pitched, frenetic, full of panic, one voice, very agitated.

"*See who comes. Blourbast the Ghoul.*
Riding.
Riding.
Blourbast does not see the things which guard.
Blourbast does not feel forbidden place.
Blourbast cannot tell sacred from his excrement hole."

Full chorus once again, full of wrath.

"*The Ghoul sees it.*
The Ghoul takes it.
Ganver's Bone, Bone, Bone,
Gone, gone, gone, alas."

Now the voices lamented, high, keening.

"*Terror, terror, monstrous this evil.*
The holy thing lost in dreadful's hands.

One must go recover what is lost."

Now drums, fifes, cymbals clashing, something that sounded suspiciously like a trumpet, though Mavin thought it was a voice.

"*Come to the place, the evil place.*
Call out for the return of Ganver's Bone!"

Now an old, old female rose, her voice a whispery chant in the clearing, barely heard over the humming of the multitude.

"*Comes one from Hell's Maw,*
An old, gray man,
Servant of Blourbast,
Lo, he sings the words of Blourbast.
Lo, he sings them in the people's song.
'Let twelve of the people come or Ganver's Bone will be destroyed!' "

Now a quartet of strong voices, in harmony.

"*Ah, ah, Proom, thou art far away. Ah. Ah.*
Aloom is old, is sick, Aloom sings.
"I will go, I will go, that Ganver's Bone shall never be destroyed."
Aloom goes, and behind her others go.
Twelve gone. Old ones, sick ones, twelve gone.
This is one time.
Time passes."

There was a moment's silence, then the voices went on.

"*The old, gray man sang once more, 'Let twelve come.*
Ah, ah, Proom, thou art far away. Ah. Ah.
Duvoon is quiet, is loving, Duvoon sings.
'I will go, I will go, that Ganver's Bone shall never be destroyed.'
Duvoon goes, and behind him others go.
Twelve gone. Male ones, female ones, twelve gone.
This is two times.
Time passes."

Again silence, again the voices.

"*The old, gray man sang once more, 'Let twelve come.'*
Ah, ah, Proom, thou art far away. Ah. Ah.
Shoomdu is Proom's child. Shoomdu sings.
"I will go, I will go, that Ganver's Bone shall never be destroyed."

Shoomdu goes, and behind her others go.
Twelve gone. Children ones, little ones.
This is three times.
Time passes."

Now the chorus again, ugly in wrath, full of fury, quickly, almost shouting.

"*Oh, behold, plague comes on Blourbast.*
Oh, behold, Ghoul has eaten our flesh.
Oh, behold, he is maddened, he kills the old gray man.
Oh, behold, Proom, Proom, Proom returns."

Hearing his name sung, Proom stood up and began to chant, waving his arms high, leading the chorus and the drums.

"*Hear the song of Proom, Voice of the Songmakers.*
'No more shall go to Hell's Maw.
All who went shall come again to us if yet they live.
Holy Ganver will forgive us this.'
Hear the song of Proom, 'I will go in.' "

"Daroo, roo, roo," sang the multitude. "Daroo, roo, roo, pandillio lallo lie, daroo."

"*So he went, wandered, wandered, wandered,*
in the dark, the smell, the pain,
Lost, he wandered into the very hands of her
Mavin who takes many forms.
Now of her we sing.
Now we sing the song of Mavin."

"I suggest you make yourself comfortable," said the Agirul. "They are about to begin singing."

"Gamelords," whispered Mavin. "What do you call what they have been doing?"

"Oh, that was just getting warmed up," it replied. "They have sung their song. Now they will sing the song of Mavin who . . ."

"Mavin Manyshaped," she said to the beast. "Mavin Manyshaped." He did not hear her. The chorus was already in full cry.

Afterwards, Mavin supposed it had been a kind of enchantment. Certainly while it was going on there was nothing she could do about it or herself. She was the center of a whirlpool of song, drawn down into it, drowned in it, surfacing at last with a feeling that some heavy, nonessential part of her had been washed away leaving her as light and agile as the shadowpeople themselves. When they had finished their song, they went away into the forest, leaving only a few behind.

"I could translate for you the words of the song they have just sung, Mavin Manyshaped, but the words do not matter." The Agirul nodded to itself. "They have made a song of you, and that is what matters, for they do not make songs of every little happening or every chance encounter. Quite frankly, I do not know why they have honored you in this way. You were at little risk of your life in that place, so far as I can tell. Whatever their reason, you are now brought into their history, and your song will be sung at the great convocations on the high places until you are known to all the tribes wherever they may be. You may call upon the people for help, and they will be with you in your times of need.

"I trust that now I may be allowed to go back to sleep." And with that, the Agirul turned to begin climbing back up the tree.

Mavin cried out, "No. Don't go. I came for a reason, Agirul. I have need now. I must talk to them."

Proom had heard the tone of her voice, and he came to her with brow furrowed. Mavin reached out to him even as she began speaking, hastily, words tumbling over one another. "Mertyn," she said. "Brother . . . sick . . . woman said shadowpeople . . . cure . . . graywoman . . . Pantiquod . . ."

"Hush," said Agirul. "Start again. Slowly. What is the trouble?"

So she began again, telling it more slowly, giving Agirul time between thoughts to translate her meaning. Proom's face changed, gave way to horror, then despair. When Mavin said that Mertyn lay ill with ghoul-plague, he cried out, tearing at his fur with both hands. Others ran toward him, questions trilling on their tongues, only to begin keening when he explained.

"What is it?" cried Mavin. "What's the matter?"

Agirul shook its narrow head. "Mavin Manyshaped, you have come on a fruitless quest. The disease you speak of is one which long ago took great toll of their lives. Then came Ganver, Ganver the Great, Ganver of the Eesties, to tell the people he would give them a gift in return for a song. So they made a song for Ganver, and he gave them his Bone. It is only by using the Bone they may cure the illness, and the Bone is gone – gone down there, in Blourbast's hands, where you may have seen it yourself."

"Is that the thing Blourbast took? The thing he wears around his neck? The thing he was holding for ransom?"

"It is. And Proom believes that when Blourbast found the shadowpeople had escaped, he probably destroyed the Bone as he threatened to do. Proom says he could not leave his people, his own child, to be eaten, not even for Ganver's Bone, but now he is unable to repay his debt to Mavin Manyshaped. He says he will kill himself at once."

"No!" she shrieked. "Tell him no. Mavin forbids it. Ganver forbids it. Tell him whoever forbids it so that he won't do it. That's terrible. Oh, Gamelords, what a mess."

She set herself to think. It did not come easily. There was too much in her head, too many squirming thoughts, Blourbast and Pantiquod, the caverns below, the flickering lights and horrible smells, Pfarb Durim high on the cliff surrounded by the host, the song of the little people, the face of Agirul. Too much. "I want the Fon," she said, not even knowing she had said it.

"The Fon?" asked Agirul.

"A Wizard. But he's shut up in Pfarb Durim, so even if I sent the message we agreed upon, it would do no good."

"A Wizard? I would not be too sure about that. If I were you, I would send the message and leave it to the Wizard to decide whether it will do any good or not. Is there not a saying among your people? 'Strange are the Talents of Wizards?' What was the message?"

"The letter M, in any form, set so he could see it."

"Well then. Dark comes soon. We will send him a message he cannot fail to see."

Though she fumed at the delay, she could think of nothing else to do. She had not slept since leaving Pfarb Durim, and when the Agirul suggested she do so, and when Proom's people made her a leafy nest cradled in the roots of a great tree, she told herself that she would need to sleep sooner or later, so it might as well be done now. Though she was sure worry would keep her awake, the shadowpeople were singing a slow, calm song which reminded her of wind, or water running over stones, and she sank into sleep to the sound of it as though she had been drugged. She went down and down into dreamless black, and did not come up until the stars shone on her through windwoven trees.

"Be still," said the Agirul from a branch above her. "Look through the trees to your right."

She sat up, stretching, seeing through the branches a long slope of meadow on which dozens of tiny fires burned in long lines.

"You cannot see it from where you are," the lazy voice from above her mused, "but the fires make your name letter on a slope which faces the city. They have been burning since dusk, half a night's length. The shadowpeople have been bustling about dragging branches out of the forest for hours. They will keep the fires alight until dawn."

"No need," said a firm voice from the trees. "They may let the fires die."

"Twizzledale!" cried Mavin. "How did you get out? How did you find me? How . . ."

"Ah," as he came silently across the grass, a moving blackness across the burning stars, "it took much longer than it should have done. However, when I went to one of the watchtowers, I found that the watchmen had gone – for tea, perhaps, or to quell some disturbance in the city. They had left a rope ladder there, useful for climbing down walls."

"But the armies? The besiegers?"

"Evidently there had been some attempt to leave the city by some half-score merchants, and a group of the besiegers had gone to drive them back, leaving the road unguarded. Quite coincidental, of course, but fortuitous . . ."

"Fortuitous," murmured the Agirul. "Coincidental."

"Whom have I the honor of addressing?" asked the Fon in measured tones, as though he were a Herald preparing to announce Game.

"The Agirul hangs in the trees above you," said Mavin. "It is a translator of languages. The shadowpeople wakened it so that they might talk with me."

"And kept me awake," said Agirul in an aggrieved tone. "I will not catch up on my sleep for a season or more."

"I have great honor in speaking with you," said the Fon, "though I would not have wished your discomfort for any purpose of my own convenience. . . ."

The Agirul tittered. "Wizards. They all talk like that. Unless they are involved in some Game or other." The titter turned into a gurgle, then into a half snore.

"Well, Mavin," said the Fon, seating himself close beside her in the nest. "What have you been up to?"

As she spoke, the fires died. Proom returned to sit beside them, ashy and disconsolate. The Agirul was roused from time to time to ask a question or translate a response. Night wore on and the stars wheeled above them, in and out of the leaves like lantern bugs. At last the Fon had asked every question which could be asked and had set to brewing tea over a handful of coals, humming to himself as he did so. Proom crouched by the fire, humming a descant, and soon a full dozen of the shadowpeople were gathered at the fire in full contrapuntal hum, which seemed to disturb the Fon not at all. When he had the tea brewed to his satisfaction, he shared a cup round with them then brought a full one to share with Mavin.

"Blourbast has not destroyed the Bone," he said.

Over his head, Agirul murmured, and a sigh went round the fire.

"He would not. He would think that a thing held in such reverence by the shadowpeople must be a thing of power or value. Blourbast would not destroy anything which might be a source of power. He is vicious, wantonly cruel, irredeemably depraved, but he is not stupid. He would not discard a thing of value merely to avenge himself upon those he despises. He would keep it, study it, perhaps even seek out those who might know of such things. Now I have heard of Eesties, as have we all. Myths, I thought. Legends. Stories out of olden time. This thing, whatever it may be, whether Eesty bone or artifact or some natural thing, must be obtained if we are to work a cure upon your brother and the others who lie ill and dying in Pfarb Durim. There are some hundred of them in the city. Mertyn is no worse than he was, but he is no better either. So a cure is needed, and if not for him then for the others. The Healers will not relent. Heralds have been sent to them – even Ambassadors, with promises of magnificent gifts – but they stand adamant. Until Blourbast is dead they will bring no healing to Pfarb Durim."

"Why?" cried Mavin. "Pfarb Durim is not Hell's Maw. Why hold the city ransom for what Blourbast has done?"

"Because the city profits from what Blourbast does," replied Twizzledale. "It stands aloof, pretends it does not share in Blourbast's depravity, murmurs repudiation of his horrors, but sells to Hell's Maw what Hell's Maw buys and takes in return the coin Blourbast has stolen or extorted or melted out of the bones of those he eats. The Healers lay guilt where guilt is due. No. Pfarb Durim is not innocent, nor are those who trade there innocent."

"And we," mumbled Mavin, white-lipped, "we who came there unknowing, but still spent our coin on lodging, on food? Are we guilty?"

The Fon shook his head, smiling, reached out to touch her face – then thought better of it, for she was close to tears. "Mavin, did you know of all this before entering the city? Well, neither did I, nor Windlow either. I do not hold us guilty of anything but ignorance, though we will be guilty indeed if we come this way again or buy anything which comes from Pfarb Durim. Enough of this conscience searching. We must find this thing, this Bone."

"Blourbast had a thing around his neck, something long and white, which he stroked. He spoke of it to that woman, his sister, stroking it with his awful-looking hand, covered with sores. She wore a kind of cap with birds wings at the side, and there were feathers on her shoulders. I don't know what Talent she has. . . ."

"Harpy," he replied. "His sister, a Harpy, mother of that Huld whom we so much enjoyed meeting. Not only Blourbast's sister, seemingly, but his emissary as well. She who arranged for the plague to be spread in the city. Did she assume herself immune?"

"Probably she was simply careful not to touch anything, not to become infected. But Blourbast thought himself immune. Even now he thinks he will recover."

"Perhaps," mused the Fon while the Agirul translated what they said to the shadowpeople amid much twittering and warbling. "And perhaps he only blusters. If what you say is true, however, if he wears it upon him, touches it, then we may not think of your going to fetch it. You would become ill and we would be no better off. No, we must get him to bring it out – find a way to use it without touching it. . . ."

The Wizard got up to stride to and fro, rooting his hair up into spiky locks with both hands, as though he dug in his brain for answers he could not find. "He sought to compel healing from the shadowpeople, what would happen if it were offered to him? Can Proom tell us in what way the Bone is used in preparing the cure?" He waited for the usual twittering exchange before the beast replied in a sleepy voice.

"It is a matter of music, Wizard. One note of which is summoned from Ganver's Bone."

"Need the Bone be in Proom's hands? Could any person holding it summon the note as needed?"

This time there was a lengthy colloquy, argument, expostulation, before the beast said, "Proom acknowledges that the note could be struck by any. He denies that any has that right except himself, but it is not a matter of impossibility."

"Ah," said the Fon with satisfaction, "Then, then . . ." And his hands waved as he sketched a plan, improvising, leaping from one point to the next as the Agirul muttered along and Mavin watched in fascination.

When he had finished, Mavin said, "But . . . but, your plans call for several shifters. Three, four, more perhaps."

"That is true," he murmured. "No help for it. We must have them. Well, shifter girl? Have you no kin to call upon?"

"Danderbat keep, from which I came, is not within a day's travel," she replied. "I was traveling to Battlefox keep, somewhere in the Shadowmarches to the north. My thalan is there, and my kindred and Mertyn's. Is it within hours of travel? I do not know. Shall I run there seeking help which may arrive too late?"

The Agirul began its murmuring and twittering while the little people chattered and trilled. "Battlefox is within a few hours, Mavin," it said at last. "One or more of the people will go with you as your guide."

The Fon was staring at the ground where his busy hands made drawings in the dust. At the edge of the world dawn crept into the sky. "When must it be done?" he asked of Proom. "What time of day or night?"

"In the deep of night," replied the beast. "When the blue star burns in the horns of Zanbee. Do I say that right?"

"You do." The Fon smiled. "Were you translating, or did you think of that yourself? It is an odd bit of esoterica for you to know. Well then, Mavin, you must return to that road south of Pfarb Durim which we have traveled once before. Beneath the Strange Monuments there, at midnight, we will find a cure. Come with whatever help you can muster. You do understand the plan?"

"As well as I may," she said distractedly, "having heard it only once. You will probably change it, too, as the day wears on. Nonetheless, I will do what I can. Do you, also, Fon, for my hope rests in you." She was very sober about this, and the tears in the corners of her eyes threatened to spill.

He took her hand in his to draw her up but then did not release her. Instead he pulled her tight to him. At first she struggled, fighting against the strength of his arms as she would have fought the constraints of a basket in Danderbat keep, full of panic and sudden fear. Then something within her weakened, perhaps broke, and she found herself pressed against his chest, hearing the throb of his heart beneath her ear, aware for the first time that he was seeing her, holding her, in her own shape, in her essential Mavinness. He did so only for a moment, then let her go with a whisper.

"Go, then. Trust in me so far as you may, Mavin. It is your Wizard, Himaggery, who promises it after all. Bring what help you can and we will put an end to this."

She did not trust herself to say anything more, but turned to run from him in that instant. From him, or in order to return to him, but she did not really think of that.

CHAPTER EIGHT

"I run," she said between her teeth, putting one foot before another on her long-legged form, feeling the clutch of shadowperson knees behind her shoulders where the little creature rode astride, whooping its pleasure at the speed of their movement. "I run," concentrating on that, trying not to think of the plan the Fon – Himaggery – had sketched before them, vaporous now, too many details missing, too many things that could go wrong. "I run," chanting it like an incantation, moving in the direction the little heels kicked her, up long slopes under the leaves spangled with sun, out into green glades where flowers bloomed higher than her head, then into shade again and down, down into gullies where gnarled black branches brooded against the sky, making a cold shade over the wet moss. The way tended always upward, coming at last to a leg-stunning climb beside a tumbling fall of water, all white spray and wet, slick rock where ferns nodded in time to the splashes. "I run," she panted, trying to convince herself, making the back legs longer to kick herself up with and the front ones clawed to scratch at the slippery rock. It was not a run, more like a scrambling climb. At the top, however, the land leveled into long shadowy rides among the groves of sky-topped trees, and the little heels kicked her into a lope once more.

"Away northwest," the voice on her back trilled, and she needed no Agirul to translate the song. It sang of sky, tree, and direction, and she understood it in her bones. The shadows dwindled but it was still short of noon when she topped a long ridge to look downward upon Battlefox keep sprawled wide in the center of its p'natti. And here she was, come to Plandybast's place – not with a modest appeal for lodging and food, perhaps for friendship if kinship should not be enough. No, here she was to beg followers, warriors, fighters, shifters to shift for something they had probably not heard of and would not care for.

Well then. How did a shifter enter a keep? Or, how best might Mavin enter a keep to make such demands upon short acquaintance?

She urged the little one down from her back so that she might sit herself down, back against tree, to eat a bit and think. The shadowperson sat comfortably beside her, snuggled close for warmth, but making no protestations at the sight of the place before her. After all, she told herself, the creature had guided her here. It probably knew as much about the place as Mavin did. Once it trilled, but her hand stilled it, and it merely hummed quietly like a kettle boiling.

Suppose that Battlefox Demesne was not so hidebound as Danderbat keep. Still, they were shifters, full of shifterish Talent and seeming. Would they respect her need? Could they offer help where they did not respect? Could she ask from weakness what she could not demand from strength? How did Plandybast stand within the walls? Was he high up in the way of things, or a mere follower after? All in all, well – all in all, would it be better to do something shifterish and fail at it or to do nothing shifterish at all and leave them wondering? She chewed and ruminated, unable to make up her mind, wishing the Wizard were there to give her some firm instructions to take the doubt away.

Finally she swallowed, sighed, pointed firmly at the base of the tree where they sat and said to the shadowperson, "You stay here."

The little head cocked. A narrow hand was placed on the trunk of the tree, and a voice warbled, "Quirril?"

"I suppose," she said. "Quirril. Until I come back."

She stood long upon the hill, remembering the way Wurstery Wimpole had come into Danderbat Keep, the drumming, the rolling, launching, flying, slything down, then up once more into veils which fell as soft as down. She sighed. She had never flown, had no idea how. Serpent forms were easy, but those immediate transitions were something she had never practiced. Better not to try anything of the sort.

And there was always the she-road, cutting through the p'natti straight as a shadow line. But if Plandybast had been correct, then only pregnant women used that road coming into Battlefox. What to do, to do, to do?

"Well, girl," she said to herself. "What would you have done if you and Mertyn had come here as you planned? You'd have walked up to the gate in your own shape, holding Mertyn by the hand. For aren't you the thalani of Plandybast, and hasn't he invited you to come? There's no time for anything else, no time for making a show of yourself, so go, go, go." And before she could talk herself out of it or think of anything else to worry about, she stepped out into the light of the sun and began walking toward the keep.

The drum sounded when she was only halfway there. It boomed once, then once again, not in any panic sound, more as a warning to let those in the keep know that someone was on the road. She did not hurry, merely kept walking, her eyes upon the walls. Forms materialized there as she watched, dozens of them, still as stone and as full of eyes as an oxroot. No sound. No welcome, only those eyes. What were they looking at? Nothing to see upon the road but one girl, dressed in whatever old thing she had shaped around herself. Mavin stopped suspiciously. They were entirely too silent. She turned her head slowly. There, behind her, was her guide – her guide and two or three dozen of his kindred.

"Gamelords," she said. "What have I done now?"

The shadowperson who had ridden her shoulders so happily came forward to take her dangling hand. "Quirril?" it asked. "Quirril?"

For a moment she could not think what to do. Then she shrugged and hoisted the little one onto her shoulders, beckoning the others to come on. "Come," she cried aloud, "Let us visit my thalan, Plandybast."

She stopped within a few man-heights of the gate, peering upward at the watchers along the wall. "Plandybast," she cried, making her voice a trumpet, full of sonority, dignified and pleading at once. "Plandybast, I come at your invitation, I, your sister's child, Mavin." Then she waited, ready, so she told herself, for someone to call down in a cold voice that Plandybast was not at home, or had never lived here, or was long dead.

Instead the gate began to creak, and she saw the almost familiar face peering at her from around the corner. "Mavin? May I come out? Will I frighten them? Some are saying they are . . . shadowpeople? Could that be true?"

She wanted to giggle. All her worry and concern, and here was her thalan as full of wonder as some child seeing Assembly for the first time. "Come out, Plandybast. I don't think they'll frighten, not so long as I am here."

He came to her, put his hand out to her, watching the little rider on her shoulder the while. "Where's Mertyn?" he asked. "What's happened?"

"Thalan, there is no time to tell you everything that has happened. I can only tell you two important things. Mertyn lies ill of ghoul-plague in Pfarb Durim. That is the first thing. The second is that a cure may be wrought by these little ones, if I bring some of my kindred to help. I need you, you and some others."

Plandybast looked up, called to the watchers, "It is as we heard. Ghoul-plague. In Pfarb Durim."

There was an immediate outcry, a kind of stifled protest or moan, and he turned back to her, shaking his head in a kind of fussy sympathy which hid his curiosity only a little.

"You must be frantic with worry," he said. "I can see that. You say there's little time? Surely you have time to come in? To eat a little something? Have a warming drink?"

She shook her head, looking sideways at the shadows, seeing how they stretched now a little east, a little past high noon. "We must be there by midnight. The Agirul said when the blue star burns in the horns of Zanbee. A Wizardly saying, evidently. Midnight. No later than that, and it is a way from here. As far as I have run since dawn, and farther. We must be there. Will some of you come, Plandybast? Do we have other kin here who will help us?"

"I will come with you if you need me, of course. But to ask others – we must at least tell them where. And what the plan may be. And why they are needed. They will be so curious, so delighted to see you. Can you come in?"

She moved toward the gate, a bit uneasily, at which all the assembled shadowpeople began to cry out, moving away from her, and her shoulder rider began to scramble down, bleating.

"They won't come in," she sighed. "They have no good experience of walls. If I come in, they may all go – and I need them to guide me back. No. Better I stay out here. Could you bring us something to eat? I had some food with me, but not enough. . . ."

"Don't distress yourself, child. Or them. This is so great a wonder, why should we spoil it with ordinary behavior. If they will not come in, we will come out." He called up to the watchers again, and there was a bustling among them as some went off at his request. It was not long before two or three of the shifters came out of the gate carrying baskets laden with fresh loaves split open and filled with roasted meat. There was no need for the shadow-people to pass the food about or share it for each of them had both hands full. By that time a dozen of the Battlefox shifters had gathered at Plandybast's side, and Mavin found herself trying to explain once more.

There were long looks from the Battlefoxes. Long looks and pursed lips, shaken heads and skeptical eyes. Among the most doubtful-looking was one Itter, a narrow-faced woman introduced as Plandybast's sister – at which Plandybast merely looked uncomfortable, saying nothing to confirm or deny this claim. "Who is he?" the woman asked when Mavin spoke of the Fon.

"A Wizard," she replied for the third time. "From the southlands."

"A Wizard," the questioner repeated after her, making the words sound slick and unreliable. "From the south."

"Yes," Mavin said, beginning to be angry. Everything the woman said was an accusation, an allegation of dishonesty or stupidity, unspoken but most explicitly conveyed in her words. "A Wizard. A young Wizard. Perhaps too young to be much regarded by the dwellers of Battlefox. As I am young. As Mertyn, who will die if a cure is not found, is young." She clenched her fist, turning from them to her thalan who stood shifting from one foot to the other at the edge of the group. "It comes to that in the end, doesn't it, Plandybast? The Fon and I are young enough to need help, therefore too young to be trusted when we ask for it."

"Now, child," he objected, "don't be so quick with blame. Itter didn't mean to sound . . ."

"Oh, but I did," said Itter sweetly. "Your other sister, Plandybast, was known for her eccentricity, her individuality. Are we to assume that her child – her children – are any less . . . individual?" In the woman's mouth the word became a curse, an indictment.

"Now, now, no need to rake up old troubles. Let's take a little time to talk this out."

"There's no time!" Mavin cried. "Tonight it will be done. The little people will be there, and the Fon, and old Blourbast with his armies and his foul sister. And I am supposed to be there, too, with help from the shifter kindred. They will expect me, and I will not fail them no matter what the people of Battlefox do or don't do."

"Why not let the Ghoul alone?" the woman asked in her sharp, accusing voice. Her eyes were calculating and cold. Her mouth curved but her eyes were chilly, and the shadowperson cringed away from her when she stepped closer. "The Ghoul does no more than any Gamesman. He plays in accordance with his Talent. From what you say, the Wizard's plan will work well enough without shifters. The cure will be wrought. The people will be healed. What matter that the Ghoul returns to his tunnels? What business is it of ours? Our business is the education of our young, not interfering with Ghouls. When he is cured, you bring Mertyn here to be educated, and forget the Ghoul. All will be as it was before."

"But it will not be as it was before," said Mavin, gritting her teeth. She had already said this twice. "The disease is one which afflicts the shadowpeople from time to time. They have always been able to cure it before, with the Bone. If Blourbast is left alive, if he returns to his tunnels with the Bone, then the disease will strike again, and again. As it returned again and again in the ancient time." The little creature on her shoulder trilled, and Mavin understood the meaning. "My friend says it may strike next time at you, Madam Itter, and at the children you are so eager to see educated, perhaps your own. It would not be wise to return to that ancient time, before Ganver."

Hearing this name the shadowpeople began to sing, a lamenting song, full of runs and aching sadness, so engaging a song that they put down the food they held to put their arms about one another and sway as they sang.

"What are they doing?" asked the woman in sudden apprehension.

"They sing of Ganver. A god to them. Perhaps Ganver would have been a god to us as well. It is Ganver's Bone the Ghoul has. Listen to them, woman! Listen to them, Plandybast! To you they were legends? Myths? Now they are here before you, singing, and you owl me with those doubtful eyes and will not promise to help me." She flung her arms wide in a despairing gesture and moved away from them toward the shadowpeople.

Plandybast came after her. "Some of them will probably come, Mavin. Just give them a little time. Itter is a kind of sister to me.

At least, her mother said she was my father's child. But you've heard her. She always assumes that others are stupid, or evil, or both. It isn't only you, she behaves so to all of us. And she does have a point, you know. There seem to be a lot of details you're not sure of. And none of us relish the idea of having anything to do with the plague, or with the Ghoul, come to that. We don't really interfere in the business of the world that much, we Battlefoxes. Oh, we hire ourselves out for Game from time to time, but there seems to be no fee and no honor in this. . . .''

''Fee! Honor! I have seen these little ones so frightened that their faces run with tears and shuddering so hard with sobs they can scarcely stand, and they go on while they are crying! I call that honor, Plandybast. You would respond better to a call to Game? If I had come with a Herald, announcing challenge, would that have made it easier? I could have done that! Watch, now, thalan. See the Herald come?'' She was angry and tired. She shifted without thinking as she had done once before in Danderbat keep, without planning it, letting her shape become that of the Herald she had seen outside the walls of Pfarb Durim. She made her voice a bugle, let it ring across the walls of Battlefox keep. ''Give ear, oh people of Battlefox Demesne, for I come at the behest of the Wizard Himaggery, most wise, most puissant, to bring challenge to the sluggards of this keep that they stay within their walls while Game moves about them!'' Then she trembled, and the shape fell away. There was only silence from them, and astonishment, and – fear.

''Impossible,'' Plandybast quavered. ''Shifters cannot take the form of other Gamesmen. But your face was the face of the Herald Dumarch-don. I know him. Your voice was his voice. Impossible. You're only a child.''

''I'm a forty-six-season child,'' she agreed. ''It is said to be impossible, but I can do it. Sometimes. You have not asked how we escaped from Danderbat keep, thalan. You have not asked how I came out of Pfarb Durim, a city under siege. It is better, perhaps, that you do not know, but I made use of this Talent to do it. I have been long on the road to you, coming to you at your invitation. Now look to your kin. They are all fainting with shock.'' And she turned away bitterly, knowing that fear had done what politeness might have prevented – made them refuse to help her.

Itter was already cawing at the group. ''You see! What did I tell you! She is no true shifter! Can a true shifter take the shape of other Gamesmen? Can they? I said her mother was guilty of individuality, and so she was. Now will you believe me?''

''Go with them,'' Mavin said wearily to Plandybast. ''I will wait out here for an hour, perhaps two. I will sleep here on this sun-warmed hill and make strength for the journey back, among my small friends who account themselves my kindred while my kindred sort out whether they are my friends or not. Any who will come with me will be welcome. If none will come – well, so be it.'' And she turned away from him to move into the welcoming arms of the shadowpeople who snuggled about her on the slope, a small hillock of eyes watching the walls of Battlefox Demesne.

A voice spoke calmly from above her head. ''They are not eager in your aid, your kinsmen.''

She looked up. The Agirul hung above her head. ''How did you get here?'' she cried. Around her the little people twittered and laughed.

''I have been here,'' said the Agirul. ''All along.''

''Then you're not . . . the one who . . . you don't know . . .''

''What the Agirul knows, the Agirul knows,'' said the creature in a voice of great complacency. ''Which means all of it, wherever its parts may be.'' It released one long, clawed arm to scratch itself reflectively, coughing a little, then twittering a remark to the shadowpeople which made them all sigh. ''I said that you are saddened by your reception in this place.''

''Old Gormier would have been biting on the bit by now,'' she said. ''Him and Wurstery and the others. They may be evil old lechers, but they would have been full of fire and ready to move.'' Then she added, more honestly, ''Of course, I don't really know that to be true. They might have been willing to be involved, but might not have responded to a plea from me, or Handbright, or any girl from behind the p'natti.''

''Wisdom,'' growled the Agirul. ''Painful, isn't it? We assume so much and resist learning to the contrary. Well, neither Danderbat nor Battlefox meets our needs at the moment. Shall we consider other alternatives?''

''Our needs, Agirul? I didn't know you were involved.''

The beast swung, side by side, a furry pendulum, head weaving on its heavy neck. ''Well, girl person, if we were to speak strictly of the matter, I am not involved. If we speak of curiosity, however, and of philosophy, and of being wakened and not allowed to go back to sleep – there are consequences of such things, wouldn't you agree? And consequence breeds consequence, dragging outsiders in and thrusting insiders out, will we or nil we, making new concatenations out of old dissimilitudes. Doesn't that express it?''

She shook her head in confusion, not sure what had been expressed. ''Are you saying I shouldn't bother to wait for Plandybast?''

''Leave him a note. Tell him to meet you on the road south of Pfarb Durim tonight with any of his people who will assist or to go to Himaggery and offer himself if you are not there. In that way, you need not linger, wasting time, and it is indeed a waste. If one may not sleep and one may not act, then what use is there sitting about?''

After a moment's thought, she did as the Agirul suggested, finding a bit of flat stone on which a charcoaled message could be left. He could not fail to see it. The letters were as tall as her hand, and the Agirul assured her there would be no rain, no storm to wipe them away in the next few hours. ''Where, then?'' she asked him. ''Back to Pfarb Durim?''

''I thought we might seek assistance from some other source,'' the Agirul replied, lapsing into shadowperson talk while the little ones gathered around in a mood of growing excitement. ''I have suggested they take you to Ganver's Grave. It is not far from here, and the trip may prove helpful.''

''Ganver's Grave? We have no dead raisers among us, Agirul. And truth to tell, after Hell's Maw, I have no desire to see or smell any such.''

''Tush. The place may be called Ganver's Grave, girl, but I did not say he is dead. Go along. It is not far, but there is no time to spend in idle chat.''

''Are you coming?'' she inquired, offering to help it down from the branch it hung upon.

''I'll be there,'' it said, humming, still swinging. ''More or less.''

Shaking her head she allowed herself to be led away, following the multitude which scampered ahead of her into the trees. A tug at her hand reminded her that a small person waited to be carried, and she lifted him onto her shoulder once more. He kicked her, and she shifted, making it easier for him and herself to catch up to the fleeing shadows before them.

They led east, back toward the River, she thought, and the long valley in which it ran. The land was flat, easy to move across, with little brush or fallen wood to make the way difficult. After they had run for some little time, Mavin began to wonder at the ease of the travel and to look at the land about her with more questioning eyes. It looked like – like park land. Like the land at the edge of the p'natti, where all the dead wood had been cut for cook fires and all noxious weeds killed. It looked used, tended. "Who lives here?" she panted, receiving a warble which conveyed no meaning in answer. "Someone," she said to herself. "Something. Not shadowpeople. They would not cut brush or clear out thorns." Someone else. Something else. "Maybe some Demesne or other. Some great Gamesman's private preserve." But, if so, where were the thousand gardeners and woodsmen it would take? She had run many leagues, and the way was still carefully tended and groomed and empty. "If there are workers, where are they?"

She heard a warbling song from far ahead, one which grew louder as she ran. The shadowpeople had stopped, had perhaps arrived at their goal. She ran on, feeling the warmth of her hindquarters as the sun rolled west. There through the trees loomed a wall of color, a towering structure which became more and more visible, wider and wider, until she emerged from the trees and saw all of it, an impossibility, glowing in the light. "Ooof," she whispered, not believing it.

"Ooof," carolled the shadowpeople in sympathy, coming back to pat her with their narrow hands and bring her forward.

It was stone, she thought. Like the stone of which the strange arches were made. Although they were green and this was red as blood, both had the same crystalline feel, the misleading look of translucence. The wall bulged toward her out of the earth, then its glittering pate arched upward at the sky. "A ball," she marveled. "A huge ball, sunk a bit in the ground. What is it? Some kind of monument? A memorial? Agirul called it Ganver's Grave. Is Ganver buried here?"

"Unlikely," said the Agirul from a tree behind her. "I don't think the Eesties bury their dead. I don't think Eesties die, come to think of it. At least I never heard one of them saying anything to indicate that they might. Not that I've been privileged to hear them say that much. No, I've probably not heard a word from an Eesty more than a dozen times in the last two or three thousand years."

"You're that old! Two or three thousand years!"

The beast shifted, as though uncomfortable at her vehemence. "Only in a sense, Mavin. What the Agirul knows, the Agirul knows. It may not have been precisely 'I' who spoke with the Eesties, but then it was in a sense. The concept is somewhat confusing, I realize. It has to do with extracorporeal memory and rather depends upon what filing system one uses. None of which has any bearing on the current situation at all. We came, I believe, to seek some help, and should be getting at it." The Agirul came painfully out of its tree and began dragging itself toward the red ball, moving with so much effort and obvious discomfort that Mavin leaned over and picked it up, gasping at the effort. The Agirul was far heavier than its size indicated, though she was able to bear the weight once it had positioned itself upon her back. She would need more bulk if she were to bear this one far, but the creature gave her no time to seek it. "Around to the side, to your left. There's a gateway there. It will probably take all of us to get it open."

The gateway would have taken all of them and a hundred or so more to open, had it not stood open already, a curved section a man-height thick, peeled back like the skin of a thrilp to show a dark, pointed doorway leading inside.

"You want us to go in there?" she asked. "In the dark?"

"Not we," said the Agirul. "You. Mavin. Don't worry about translation. If you meet an Eesty, you'll be able to understand him. Or her. Or thir. Or fle. Or san. Whichever. The polite form of address is 'aged one.' And the polite stance is attentive. Don't miss anything, or you may find you've missed it all. Go on now. Not much time left." It dropped from her back and gave her an enormous shove, one which propelled her to the edge of the black gateway, over which she tripped, to fall sprawling within, within, within. . . .

There was no within.

She stood on a shifting plain beside a row of columns. Upon each column rested a red ball, tiny in comparison to the great one she had entered, and translucent, for she could see shapes within, moving gently as though swayed by a quiet sea. A gravel path ran beside the column, gemmy blue and green and violet stones, smoothly raked. Mavin turned to see a small creature pick up a round stone from the side of the path, nibble at it experimentally, then nip it quickly with his teeth, faceting the stone, polishing it with a raspy black tongue before raking it to the path with its claws. It moved on to another stone, taking no notice of her. When she knelt to look at it more closely, it did not react in any way. It had no eyes that she could see, no ears, only two pale, clawed hands, a mouth like a pair of steel wedges, and two pudgy legs on which to move about. It faceted another stone, then extended its neck and its hands to roll rapidly away on its feet, its hands, and the top of its head, like a wheel, disappearing into the distance.

This drew her eyes to the horizon, a very close one, as though the ground beneath her curved more than what she was used to. On that horizon marched a line of towers, each tower topped by a red ball, in each ball a hint of movement as of something moving slightly in its sleep or a watchman shifting restlessly upon a parapet. Between these towers giant wheels were rolling, creature wheels, stopping now and then to polish one of the towers with great, soft hands or trim the grassy verge with wide, scissory teeth before rolling on like huge children turning endless handsprings. Mavin moved toward them, noticing the sound her feet made on the jeweled gravel, an abrupt, questioning sound, as of someone saying "what' over and over again. She moved to the grass, only to leap back again, for the grass screamed when she stepped upon it, a thin wailing of pain and outraged dignity. So she went on, the gravel saying "what" beneath her feet, the grass weeping at her side, each section taking up the complaint as she passed.

Flowers began to appear along the verge, gray blossoms the size of her hands, five-petaled, turning upon their stems like windmills with a shrill, determined humming. Creeping, grublike things lay upon the stems of the flowers. Mavin watched as the creepers extended long, sharp tusks into the whirling petals, cutting them into fragments which floated upon the air only an instant before opening like tiny books and flying away.

Bushes along the road began to lash their branches, each branch splitting into a bundle of narrow whips which exploded outward into a net. The nets cast almost to the road, missing her, though not by much. Some of the flower creepers were caught and dragged back toward the bushes while they plied their tusks frantically, trying to cut free. The gravel went on saying "what".

She came near to the first of the towers, stepping aside to avoid the nets, paying no more attention to the crying grass. The gravel fell silent beneath her feet, and she stood gazing upward at the ruby globe, twice her own height in diameter, with something moving in it. Was this an Eesty? Was it alive? How did one attract its attention? There was nothing in this place to tell her the time, to tell her how many hours there might be between now and midnight. How many of these globes dared she knock upon, if knocking was the thing to do?

Then she remembered what Agirul had said. Remembered, stood back from the globe, and cried in a voice which would have broken rock had any been present to be broken, "Aged one. Oh, oho, aged one! I cry for assistance!"

At first there was only an agitation within the globe, as though a bubble of air had burst or some small thing whipped around in its shadowed interior, but then lines began to glow down the sides of it, golden lines, from the apex down the sides, running beneath the globe where it sat on its pillar, glowing brightly and more brightly until she could see that they were actually lines graven into the globe, pressing down into its mirror-smooth surface. The lines darkened, deepened, turned black with a sudden cracking sound as of breaking glass. Then the sections began to fold outward, five of them, opening like a flower's petals to the sky, crisp and hard at first, turning soft, beginning to droop over the pillar to disclose what sat within.

Which was a star-shaped mound, one leg drooping over each opened petal, the center pulsating slowly as though breathing, the whole studded with small, ivory projections. As she watched, the thing began to draw itself upright, one limb rising, two more pushing upright, until what faced her was a five-pointed semblance of her own shape, two lower limbs, two upper ones with a protrusion between them containing what might be interpreted as a face. At least it had a slit in it which could be a mouth. Or could equally well be something – anything else.

She waited. Nothing further happened. Taking a stance which she defined in her own mind as attentive, she tried once more. "Aged one. Most honorable and revered aged one. I cry for help."

The voice formed in her brain, not outside it, a whispery voice, like wind, or the slow gurgle of a stream over stones, without emphasis, constantly changing yet unchanging. "Who calls Ganver for help? Ganver who gives no help? Ganver who does not interfere?"

"I was sent," she said. "Agirul sent me." There was no response to this. She tried again. "My name is Mavin. I am a shifter girl, from the world" – she waved vaguely behind her – "out there. The Ghoul Blourbast has stolen Ganver's Bone."

There was nothing, nothing. Beyond the pillar she could see another of the little jewel cutters, or perhaps the same one, burrowing into a pile of stones at the side of a branching path. It nibbled and scurried, paying no attention to her or to the star-shaped creature which confronted her. Finally the voice shaped in her mind once more.

"What is a Ghoul?"

"A Ghoul – well, a Ghoul is a person with the Talent of dead raising. Not only that. Most Ghouls eat dead flesh. And they kidnap people and kill them. And Blourbast is particularly horrible, because it is said he fastens live people to the walls of his burrows and leaves them there forever, animating the bones. And . . ."

"Such a creature, how did it come by Ganver's Bone?"

"Proom had the Bone. Do you know Proom? No, probably not. Well, Proom is a shadowperson. It is he who had the – what would you say – the *custody* of Ganver's Bone. But someone, someone very powerful, I think perhaps some one of you, that is of the Eesties, sent Proom on a journey, and he didn't want to take the Bone. So he put it in a safe place – an old, sacred, guarded place. But Blourbast came riding, and he didn't care whether it was sacred or not, so he took it. And the little people went to sacrifice themselves to get it back, but it didn't do any good. He won't give it back. And if he doesn't they'll all die of disease. Of ghoul-plague." She ran out of words, unable to go on without a response. She did not know whether the thing before her had even heard her. Again she waited. Again it was long, long before the voice formed in her head.

"It is not ghoul-plague. It is a disease of the shadowpeople.

"Long before there was any such thing as Ghoul, there were shadowpeople.

"Long before Ghoul ate shadowperson flesh, shadowpeople ate shadowperson flesh. Small creatures, beasts, with such aspirations, such longing for holiness.

"Ah. Sad. So sad, such longing for holiness. So it was Ganver came to them and made them a bargain. If they would stop eating flesh, Ganver would give them a Bone, a part of Ganver, a thing to call a note from the universal song that they might sing. And holiness would follow. In time. In forever. But you say the sickness is returned."

"We call it ghoul-plague, because Ghouls get it. Some of the shadowpeople were sick, but not with the plague."

"So. Then they have kept their bargain. How long? Do you know how long ago I bargained with Proom's people?"

She tried to think. What had Agirul said, that there had been no plague among the little people for what? A thousand years? More, perhaps? "A thousand years," she said. "Since Proom's many times great-grand-father. But they still do eat meat."

"True," whispered the voice. "Their bodies require it. But they do not eat each other. That is good. Good. Thank you for coming. I will relish this news of the shadowpeople, for it has been a thousand years or more since I have seen them."

The petals on the pillar began to harden, to draw upward. Mavin cried out in a voice of outrage: "No. You can't go. Don't you understand, the Bone is in Blourbast's hands. The little people believe they cannot cure the illness without it."

"They cannot," said the voice unemotionally. "What matter is that? If they do not eat one another, they will not become sick with it."

"The Ghoul ate shadowpeople, the Ghoul became sick with it," she cried. "And he has given the sickness to my brother, a boy, only a child. And others. Others who have done nothing wrong. Innocent people . . ."

"We do not interfere," whispered the voice.

"You did interfere," she shouted, stamping her foot on the gravel so that it shrieked, kicking at the grass until it wailed beneath her feet. "You gave them the Bone in the first place. That's interference. If you hadn't given it to them, they'd all have died. Then they wouldn't have been around for Blourbast to eat, and he wouldn't have gotten sick, and Mertyn wouldn't be lying in Pfarb Durim, dying, my own brother. You did interfere!"

This time there was a long silence. One of the wheel things rolled up to the pillar, lowered itself onto four limbs and polished at the pillar with the fifth before standing up once more and rolling away. As it rolled, it made a whipping sound, like the wings of a crow, receding into the distance.

"It is hard to do good," the voice whispered.

"Nonsense," she muttered. "You have only to do it."

"Shhhh," the voice hissed, sounding rather like Agirul. "Think. Ganver heard the music of the shadowpeople and saw them dying. Ganver longed to help them. Ganver gave them his Bone. Was that good? At first, perhaps. Then the Bone was stolen, the shadowpeople were sacrificed, now they are in danger of their lives once more – and so is another people who were not even there when the Bone was given. If the Bone had not been given, you have said what would have happened."

"They would have died," she said, mourning. "They would all have died then."

"And their song with them. All their songs. The song of Ganver, the Song of Morning, the Song of Zanbee, the Song of Mavin Manyshaped."

"But if they die, the songs will die," she argued. "We must save them. We must save Mertyn."

"A good thing. Of course. And what evil thing will come of that? Oh, persons of the world, why do you pursue the Eesties? Have we not yet learned to do nothing, not to interfere?"

"It seems to me," she said, "if you ever interfere at all, you just have to go on. You can't just say, 'Well, it isn't my fault,' and let it go at that. It is your fault. You admitted it. And aged one or not, you've just got to do something about it."

There was a feeling of sighing, a feeling beside which any other sigh which might ever be felt was only a minor thing, a momentary discomfort. This sigh was the quintessential sigh, the ultimate sigh, and Mavin knew it as she heard it. She had asked more than she had any right to do, and she knew that as well. Gritting her teeth, she confronted the drooping Eesty and said it again.

"It's up to you to fix it."

"Tell me," whispered the voice, "what is to be done."

So she told, for the manyeth time, what was to be done. The armies of King Frogmott assembled to confront the armies of Blourbast. Blourbast himself led beneath the monuments on the road, settled there with his immediate retinue. The ritual –

whatever that might be – conducted by the shadowpeople. The cure wrought – Mavin had no idea how; presumably the Eesty did, since it was the Eesty's bone which was involved. Then, when the cure was wrought and Blourbast tried to leave, then the shifters would rise up about him from their disguise as stone and tree and earth, rise up and consume him, all but Ganver's Bone. Which would be returned to the shadowpeople. . . .

"Which will be returned to me . . ." whispered the voice. "I did not intend it to be used in these games of back and forth. I am not a bakklewheep to be used in this way, cast between players in a Game I do not choose. Oh, I have been long asleep, Mavin Manyshaped, but I know of your Game world. Tell me, if I gave you my Bone, would your people cease their Game of eating one another as Proom's people stopped their own?"

She bowed her head in shame. "I do not know, aged one. Truly I do not know."

"No," it said sadly. "You do not know. Perhaps in time. There are some of you who talk with some of us. Perhaps in time. Now I have interfered once, and my holiness is dwindled thereby. I may not take myself away from it all but must continue in the way my foolishness led me. So. We will come to your place of monuments, which is also my place of monuments – for they are my people as well – when the blue star burns in the horns of Zanbee. And later, Mavin Manyshaped, I will regret what I have done, and you must pray peace for me."

The thing came down from its pillar, all at once, so quickly that she did not see it move. It rolled, as the smaller creatures had rolled, and it made a music in its rolling, a humming series of harmonic chords which caught her up into them so that she could not tell where she was. She felt herself move, or the world move beneath her. It was impossible to tell which. There were stars overhead, and a sound of singing, and she heard Himaggery's voice crying like a mighty horn.

CHAPTER NINE

It was dark. She could hear Himaggery shouting at someone, his voice carrying fitfully on the shifting wind which whipped her hair into her eyes. There were stars blooming above her, and Zanbee, the crescent moon, sailed upon the western edge of the sky. She searched for the blue star, finding it just below the moon. Soon it would hang upon the moon's horns, or appear to do so, and she had no idea where the hours had gone since afternoon.

She stared into the dark, making her eyes huge to take in the light, blinding herself at first on the arcing rim of fire which burned at one side until she identified it as the torches of King Frogmott's army gathered on the high rim about Pfarb Durim, between her and the city. Soon her eyes and mind began to interpret what she saw, and she located the place she stood upon, a small hill just west of the road where the Strange Monuments loomed among lights which moved and darted, hither and thither, and from which the Wizard's voice seemed to emanate.

"The Agirul says they've left the place below. It will take them almost till midnight to get here. Help the shadowpeople with that cauldron. . . ."

She couldn't see enough through the flickering lights to know what was going on. But the closer she came the more confused things became, and when she stood at Himaggery's side while he fumed over some drawing in the dust, she knew less than she had to begin with. She laid a hand upon his shoulder and was surprised to feel him leap as though he had been burned.

"Mavin," he shouted at her. "You . . . where have you . . . they said you might not . . ." Then as she was about to make soothing sounds, he said more quietly "Sorry. Things have been a bit hectic. I had word that you probably wouldn't make it back, and that you wouldn't bring any of your kin to help. Except the fellow who brought the message, of course. Your thalan, is it? Plandybast? Nice enough fellow. A bit too apologetic, but then it doesn't seem that the Battlefox branch of your family has much to recommend it outside himself, so perhaps he has aplenty to apologize for."

"Plandybast came then," she said in wonder. "I really didn't think he would." She leaned over the dirt where he had been drawing diagrams. "What are we doing? Have you changed the plan?"

"Of course. Not once or twice, but at least six times. At first we couldn't find a Herald, but then I managed to locate one I knew slightly. Subborned him, I suppose one might say, right out of Frogmott's array."

"And you sent him to Blourbast."

"To the front door. What there is of it. Most of Poffle is underground, as you well know, and what shows above ground isn't exactly prepossessing. Well, the fellow went off to Blourbast full of Heraldish dignity and made his move, cried challenge on the Ghoul to bring the amulet – that's what we decided to call it, an amulet. Why let the Ghoul know what he's holding? – to the Monuments at midnight tonight to assist in preparing a cure for the plague. We didn't let on that we know he has the disease himself. The Herald just went on about honor and Gamesmanship and all the rest."

"Was there a reply?"

"Not at first. We thought there's wasn't going to be, and I'd started to re-plan the whole thing. Then this woman came out. It must be his sister, the Harpy. . . ."

"Pantiquod."

"Right. She came out and gave us a lot of double talk which meant that Blourbast would show up but that he didn't trust us. So he would come with a retinue. That's what she called it. A retinue. By that time it was getting on evening, and Proom showed up with the Agirul. Or rather Proom showed up and we found the Agirul hanging in a tree by the side of the road. Fortuitous."

"Fortuitous," repeated Mavin, not believing it.

"Among the three of us, we decided that 'retinue' probably means the entire army of Hell's Maw as well as a few close kin and men sworn to the Ghoul. And about that time your thalan arrived to tell us you probably wouldn't be coming if you weren't here already. You'd left him a note or something?"

"Or something, yes."

"Which meant I had to plan it again. And then Proom's been busy with his kindred. Evidently this ritual hasn't been performed for a thousand years, and there's only a song to guide them in the proper procedures, so it's been sing and run, run and sing every moment since dark. Now we've just received word that Blourbast and his retinue – we were right, it is the army – are on the road coming up from Hell's Maw. So. Now here you are."

"I'm sorry I'm late," she said, starting to tell him about the Eesty, wondering why the Agirul and Proom had not already done so, only to find that she could say nothing about it at all. The words stuck. She thought them clearly, but her throat and tongue simply didn't move. She did not choke or gasp or feel that she was being throttled. There was not any sense of pain, but the words would not come.

Then for the first time she wondered about the Eesty and looked around for it. Nothing. Dark and stars and the flicker of torches: shouting, fragments of song from the area around the arches, nothing more. And yet the darkness was not empty. She could feel it boiling around her, something living, running its quick tentacles through her hair, its sharp teeth along her spine. She shivered with a sharp, anticipatory hunger, a hunger for action, for resolution, a desire to make something episodic out of the tumbled events of her recent past.

"You're forgiven," he said distractedly. "Some day you must tell me all about it. But right now we've got to figure out how to accomplish everything that needs doing in this one final do."

She crouched beside his diagram. "Show me."

"King Frogmott's army is here," he said, retracing a wide circle just inside the line that was the arc of road outside Pfarb Durim. "From the cliff's edge south of the city, all along the inner edge of the road, curving around and then over to the cliff at the north side of the city. On high ground, all the way, able to see everything."

"Except a Wizard who may want to get out," she remarked in a quiet voice, not expecting the hand he raised to stroke her face.

"Except that," he agreed in a satisfied voice. "There's another line back a few leagues, one which encloses Pfarb Durim and Poffle, but those besiegers cannot see what is going on. Now, the road which comes up from Poffle to the top of the cliff is *outside* Frogmott's lines, so Blourbast can bring his ghoulish multitude up and along toward the Monuments. The Agirul and I believe he will marshall his own army in a long array between him and King Frogmott's men. He will want to be protected against the besiegers, for they have threatened anyone who comes out carrying the plague. Then, having protected himself against King Frogmott, he will bring a considerable group with him to the Monuments – to protect himself against whoever is here. The Herald challenged him in my name. Huld may have mentioned me to him. I don't know who else he expects to find here, but he certainly won't come alone."

"I was supposed to shift . . . where he'd be."

"You were supposed to shift. Right. You and a dozen more just like you. Well, two of you just aren't enough, that's all. I had hoped we could make a very natural-looking setting, one he wouldn't hesitate to sit himself down in comfortably, but with only two of you, what could we manage? A couple of rocks, trees?"

"I've never tried a tree," she said in a small voice. "Or a rock either. I haven't had much time for practice."

"Rocks aren't easy," said a voice from behind them. "I hate to do them myself. Trees are easier, but they do take practice. I could probably show Mavin how in an hour or so. . . ."

"Plandybast." She turned to him gladly. "I didn't think you'd come. I really didn't. I thought Itter would talk you out of it."

"Itter is always perfectly logical," said Plandybast, rather sadly. "But she's frequently wrong, and after a while I just get very tired of listening to her. The others haven't been disillusioned, not yet, but the time will come. Until then I'll just have to do what I think is right and let her fuss if she wishes. And she will."

"What are the shadowpeople doing?" she asked. "Is it anything we could help with?"

"I think not," said Himaggery. "They located an ancient cairn near the road and moved it to disclose a huge old cauldron underneath. They rolled that over to the middle of the road under the arches, dragged in a huge pile of wood for a fire, and now they're out on the hills gathering herbs and blossoms and who knows what. Meantime they've assembled an orchestra all over the hills – I have never seen so many drums in my life – and what seems to be the greater part of several other tribes. For a creature that I have always considered to be mythical, it seems to be extremely numerous."

"I doubt we'd ever have seen them in the ordinary way of life,"

Mavin said. "If it hadn't been for Blourbast and the plague."

"And Mertyn," he said, touching her face again. "And Mavin."

She flushed and turned away toward the dark to hide it. She wanted, didn't want him to touch her again; wanted, didn't want him to look at her in that particularly half-hungry fashion; wanted, didn't want the time to wear on and things to happen which would take him from her side and throw them both into violent, unthinking action. "Why should I feel safer fighting Ghouls," she asked herself, rhetorically, not seeking an answer, not wanting an answer.

"You'll have to give me something to do," she said. "I can't have run all this way just to sit and do nothing."

He sighed, looked for a moment older than his years as the firelight flickered across his face. She could imagine him as he would be at age forty, tall, strong, but with the lines deep between his eyes and at the sides of his mouth, lines of both laughter and concentration. And some of anger, she told herself. Some of anger, too. He said, "Whenever Blourbast and his crew get themselves settled, try to get close to him, as close as you can. Then when the cure is done or made or created, if you can do it without getting hurt – remember, there are no Healers closer than Betand – if you can do it without getting hurt, try to get the Bone. Then get away from him."

"You don't want us to try to dispatch him?" asked Plandybast.

"If there were a dozen of you, yes. With two of you, no. Just get the Bone and get out. The dispatching of Blourbast will have to wait for another time."

They sat, the three of them, staring down at the lines in the dirt, the curving arc of the road, the waving line of the cliff's edge, the *x*'s marking the army of the King. The Strange Monuments loomed beside them, and on the road the shadowpeople scampered and sang to one another, short bursts of music which sounded harsh and dissonant.

"One of Proom's people says the Ghoul is almost at the cliff's top," said the Agirul from behind them. Mavin had not known it was there, and she tried to see it, but saw only the massed bulk of foliage against the lighter sky.

"Who does he have with him?" asked the Fon.

"In addition to the army, there is his sister and her twins, Huld and Huldra. Then there are a few guards, a Sorcerer, two Armigers, two Tragamors."

"And here, with us?"

"Me," said Himaggery. "And you two shifters. Proom and his people. The Agirul. And my friend the Herald. He is waiting in the trees to make whatever announcements may seem most useful."

"Windlow?" she asked. "Mertyn?"

"I haven't been back in the city," he said softly. "I don't know, Mavin. Believe me, Windlow will have done everything possible for him."

"I know," she admitted. "Except that it is hard to let someone else do it while I am out here, not knowing."

"We'd better get out of the light," he said. "I'll go down near the road. We found some logs to use as seats for Blourbast, arranged where we want him, in the middle of the road. We'll try to get him there. Once he is there, do what you can. . . ."

He left the two shifters, taking the torch with him. They sat for a moment silent, then Mavin said, "A log should be easier than a tree."

"It is," Plandybast admitted. "Much."

"We couldn't be much closer than to have him sitting on us."

"If the small ones do not make the cure . . ." Plandybast said, "and he is sitting on us . . ."

"They'll make it. Plandybast, I've seen them do wonderful things. Don't doubt it for a moment." And she drew him up to follow her down into the darkness of the road where the shadow-people had lighted the fire beneath their cauldron and a pungent smoke poured into the night sky, making her dizzy yet at the same time less troubled. It was not difficult to become a log. She shifted once or twice, then simply lay there and let the smoke wreath her around, driven as it was by a downdraft of the fitful wind.

She heard Huld's voice first, a petulant whine, a sneering tone, "They have made a place for you, dear thalan. The seats are not what you are accustomed to, I fear. There is no velvet cushion."

"Hush, dear boy. I have no need for velvet cushions. Does one need a velvet cushion to witness a wonder? Hmmm? And are we not to witness a wonder tonight? The making of a plague cure? Who has heard of such a thing? The Healers will be frantic with embarrassment and envy. Not a bad thing, either. I am not fond of Healers."

Another voice, so like Huld's that it might have been mistaken for his, yet higher, lighter. "Dear brother, dear thalan, indeed we would all dispense with cushions to see this thing. And to take – what may I say? – advantage of it."

"Be silent, girl," said Pantiquod, following them down onto the road where they clustered around the logs with their guardsmen, all staring suspiciously into the darkness. "Say nothing you would not like to have overheard. The dark is all around us, and it trembles with ears."

"Of course, mother," said the voice sweetly. "One would not wish to be overheard saying that a cure of the plague is of great interest to us."

"Your mother said hush," grated the Ghoul. 'Now I say to you hush, Huldra. You may think that child in you protects you from my displeasure, but I have no care for that. If you trouble me, girl, both you and the child may go into hell for all me."

"Not so quick, thalan," purred Huld. "I am thalan to the child in her womb, you know. Mine own. And mine own child, too – as is the teaching of the High King, away there in the south – a child linked to me doubly if not to you at all. So, Blourbast, go quietly with my gentle sister or I will make your sickness seem a day's walk in the sun."

"Let us all be still," said Pantiquod. "We are here for a reason. Let the reason be manifest. I see nothing except fitful torches and scampering shadows. Is this a mockery?"

"No mockery, madam," came Himaggery's voice from the dark. "The blue star moves towards the horns of Zanbee. The little people of the forests have lit their fires beneath the great cauldron. They will begin to sing soon. There will be drums, voices, manifestations. At some point in the ritual, I will call to you to strike the . . . amulet you carry. Strike it then, and the cure will be made.

"I will return in time. Until then, seat yourselves and do not disrupt what must occur." They heard him moving away into the shadows.

"Where will this cure be made?" asked Huldra, seating herself on Mavin's back with a moue of discontent. "What form will it take?"

"They have spoken of a cauldron," said the Harpy Pantiquod. "Undoubtedly the cure will be therein. When it is made, we must move quickly to take it. If the cauldron is too heavy to be carried, then we will take what we can in our flasks and dump the rest upon the ground."

"How dreadful for Pfarb Durim," said Huld. "They will not receive their portion."

"I have promised you Pfarb Durim," said the Ghoul. "When it is empty."

"I am glad you remember that promise," said Huld, fingering the dagger at his side. "It is a promise I hope much upon. There are some in that city who may not die of plague, and I wish to be first among them like a fustigar among the bunwits. They have not pleased me."

"Did the old Seer speak nastily to my dear brother?" the woman beside him drawled. "Did the little Wizard make him unhappy?"

"Be still, girl. There are things I could do to you which would not affect the child, so do not count too much upon my forbearance. Hush. What is that?"

The sound was of many drums throughout the hills near the road, drum heads roaring to the tumbling thump of a thousand little hands, like soft thunder far among mountains. Flutes came then, softly, a dawn birdsong of flutes, then gentle bells, music to wake one who had slept a long sleep.

The fire beneath the cauldron blazed up, and they could see the tiny shadows which crossed before it, black against the amber light, some dragging more wood to the fire, others tossing their burdens into the cauldron. Steam rose from the cauldron to join the smoke of the fire, and this moist, woodsy mist waved back and forth across the road, wreathing the bases of the Monuments, seeming to soak into the crystalline material of which they were made, making them appear soft and porous. One could almost see the mists sucked up into them, the softness moving upward on each arch, out of the firelight into the high darkness.

The smell of the mist reached them at the same time the voices began to sing, taking up the bell song and repeating it, close, far, close again, first the highest voices and then the deeper, again and again. A lone trumpet began to ride high upon the song, higher yet, impossibly treble above the singing, while some bass horn or some great stone windpipe blew notes almost below their hearing so that the ground trembled with it.

The earth trembled, trembled, then moaned.

Beside them the base of the Strange Monument shivered in the earth. The pedestal beneath it shifted, groaned, and then was still.

Mavin created eyes in the top of her log shape and looked up. The arch was glowing green: diagonally across the width of it a dark line appeared, deeper with each moment. Then the sound of breaking glass cracked through the music and the top of the arch split in two lengthwise, each part coiling upward like a serpent to stand high above its base, each arch becoming two tapered pillars which waved in the music like reeds in wind.

The watchers shivered. The Monuments danced, reaching toward one another across the road, beside the road, bowing and touching their tips, two great rows of tapered towers, dancing green in the night as the drums went on and on and the mists from the cauldron rose more thickly upon the shifting wind.

"Keep your eyes on that cauldron," hissed the Ghoul. "Move to capture it as soon as I strike the amulet." The men behind him murmured assent even as they shifted uneasily, feeling the earth teeter beneath them.

Now the contents of the cauldron began to glow, a pillar of ruby light rising out of the vessel toward the zenith. The singers had moved closer to the road, their voices rising now in an almost unbearable crescendo. Mavin held herself rigid, though she wanted to weep, faint, curl up where she lay into as tiny a space as she could. She heard the voice of Himaggery calling from the sidelines. "Be ready, Blourbast."

Then all that had gone before faded in a hurricane of sound, a storm of music, a shattering climax in which there were sounds of organs and trumpets and bells so huge that the world shivered. "Now, Blourbast!" came Himaggery's voice, barely audible over the tumult, and the Ghoul held up the amulet and struck it with his dagger.

One sound.

One sound, piercing sweet in silence.

Tumult over, singing over, all the terrible riot of drum and trumpet over, and only that one sound singing on and on and on into the quiet of night. The cauldron blazed up in response, the red light pouring out to spread like an ointment across the sky, into every face, onto every surface, high and low, hidden or visible, like water which could run everywhere, over the drawn battle lines of the armies, over the walls of Pfarb Durim, onto every roof, down every chimney, into every window and door, closed or open, through every wall. Only Mavin heard the *whip, whip, whip* as of great wings and only Mavin saw the huge, cloudy wheel flick through their midst in an instant, taking Ganver's Bone with it and leaving the Ghoul standing, his mouth open, his hands empty except for the dagger he had used to strike that note.

And Mavin knew why the Eesty had taken its Bone back again. It would not have done to leave that note in the hands of Gamesmen. Among the shadowpeople, perhaps, for they were attempting to be holy, though they failed from time to time, but not among the Gamesmen.

In the silent flicker of the distant fire, they saw the shadowpeople tip the cauldron over and let it empty itself on the roadway.

The Ghoul roared, spitting curses. From the roadside, Himaggery said, "You need not threaten and bluster, Ghoul. The bargain was kept. You are cured."

And Huld's voice, hissing with a scarce concealed fury, "And are those in Pfarb Durim cured as well?"

"All," said Himaggery. "All within reach of the light, and it spread as far as my eyes could see."

Huld turned on the Ghoul, dagger flicking in his hand, "Then you have not kept your promise, thalan. You have undone what you promised me."

"But, but . . ." blustered the Ghoul, the only words he had time to say, for the dagger stood full in his throat and the blood rushed behind it in a flood, soaking his chest and belly, spurting upon those who sat near him so that they recoiled, Mavin recoiled, becoming herself near the place that Himaggery stood, both to stand with shocked eyes while Huld drew his dagger out again and turned toward Himaggery with madness in his eyes.

"Your fault, Wizard. You tempted him with this cure. Pfarb Durim would have been mine except for you." And he came rushing toward Himaggery, dagger high, and Himaggery with no protection at all—

Save Mavin, before him, furious, suddenly taking the shape of another Gamesman, without thinking, without planning, so it was Blourbast stood before Huld's onrush and roared into his face like some mighty beast with such ferocious aspect and horrible, bleeding gash of throat that Huld stopped, eyes glazed, screamed, and turned to stumble away into the night. The others, also, Pantiquod and

Huldra and the guardsmen, frantic, overwrought, driven half mad by the music and then fully mad to see Blourbast's body stand before them again.

The shape dropped away. Mavin found herself standing bare in the roadway, covered with Blourbast's blood, too weary to shift a covering for herself. She felt Himaggery's cloak swing around her, his arms draw her close. A quivering voice asked, "Is it all right to change now?" and Himaggery replied,

"Yes, Plandybast. It's all over. You can unlog yourself."

"I'm glad there wasn't any real violence," said Plandybast. "I've never been able to handle violence."

"I'm glad, too," said Himaggery, lifting her up and carrying her away to the comfortable shelter of the trees.

"Is she all right?" asked the Agirul.

"She's covered with blood," said Himaggery. "See if you can get someone to bring water." Then he sat beneath the tree, cuddling her close in his arms. She could not remember being so held, not ever, not even by Handbright in the long ago. She sighed, a sigh very like the Eesty's sigh, and let all of it fade away into dark.

CHAPTER TEN

When morning came, they went into Pfarb Durim. The armies of King Frogmott were no barrier. The sickness had been spreading among the besiegers, and the cure was as evident to them as it was to those in the city. Indeed, when Mavin and Himaggery passed, they were already taking down the tents and putting out the fires, preparatory to the long march back to the marshes of the upper Graywater, to the northeast.

They found Mertyn still in the room in which they had left him, Windlow still by his side, though both were sound asleep on the same bed, and Himaggery forbore to wake them. Instead, he ordered a room for Mavin, and a bathtub, and various wares from clothiers and makers of unguents. By the time Mertyn wakened, she was more mistress of herself than she had ever been in Danderbat keep or since.

All of this had gone to make her a little shy, not least by the fact that she knew things the others did not, and could not tell them. She had been unable to speak of them even to the Agirul when she had wakened beneath his tree that morning. She had tried, and the Agirul had opened one slitlike eye to peer at her as though it had never seen her before and would not see her again.

"Many of us," it said at last, "remember things that cannot be shared. Sometimes we remember things that did not really happen. Does that make them less true? An interesting philosophical point which you may enjoy thinking about at odd times." Then it had gone back to sleep, and she had given up. She did not for one moment believe that she remembered a thing which had not happened, but she was realist enough to know that it would be her own story, her own memory, and only that.

Now she sat at Mertyn's side in her luxurious room – he had been moved as soon as he woke – looking out across the cliff edge to the far west. "Schlaizy Noithn is there," she said to him. "Southwest, there beyond the firehills. Perhaps Handbright is there."

"There was more to her leaving Danderbat keep than you told me, wasn't there?" He was still pale and weak from not having eaten for some days, but his eyes were alert and sparkling. "Are you going to tell me?"

"Perhaps someday," she said. "Not now."

"That Wizard is in love with you," he said. "I can tell. Besides, he was talking to Windlow about it."

She didn't answer, merely sat looking at the horizon. The sea was there, beyond the firehills. She wondered if she could find her way back to Ganver's Grave. She wondered if Ganver's Grave had not been moved elsewhere.

"He'll probably ask you to go with them."

"Where are they going?"

"Windlow has a school at the High Demesne, near the Lakes of Tarnoch. That's far to the south, west of Lake Yost."

"That's right," she mused. "Valdon is the King's son. And Boldery. Windlow is to educate them both."

"Not Valdon," Mertyn went on, a little cocky, as though he had had something to do with it. "Valdon and that Huld got along so well that Windlow had words with Valdon about it, and that made Valdon mad, so he took the servants and went riding out at dawn. He says Windlow may school Boldery all he likes, but Valdon will have none of it."

"That's too bad," she said. "If he follows Huld, it will be the death of him." She turned to find the boy's eyes fixed on her in wonder.

"That's what Windlow says. He had a vision about it," he said.

"It doesn't take a vision. Anyone would know. Huld is walking death to anyone who comes near him. Well, he's gone, for a time at least."

"And the plague is cured. And Windlow says so long as no one eats shadowpeople – yech, I wouldn't – no one will ever get the plague again. You don't think anyone ever will, do you?"

She shrugged. "Many strange things happen, Mertyn, brother boy."

There was a light knock on the door. She opened it to let Windlow and the Fon come in, Boldery close behind them bearing a wrapped gift.

"I brought it for Mertyn," he said. "Really, it's for us both." Then, "It's a game," he announced proudly to Mertyn. "I came to play it with you."

"The Seer and I thought – that is, we felt the boys might like to play together for a time while we have a meal downstairs." The Fon held out his hand to her, but she only smiled at him, using her own hands to gather her skirts. They had not been much for skirts at Danderbat keep. She rather liked the feel, the luxurious sway of the heavy material at her ankles and the warmth around her legs, but they still took a bit of managing.

"I'd like that." She smiled at them both, going out the door and preceding them down the stairs. There was a table set for them on a paved terrace beside a fountain, and the servants of the Mont were busy in attendance. There was fruit and wine already on the table. She sat and stared at it, smiling faintly, not seeing it.

"Mavin." She did not reply. "Mavin, what are you thinking about? Are you troubled by the Ghoul's death?" She looked up to find Windlow's eyes fixed on her, his face full of concern.

Briskly she shook her head, clearing it, giving up the dreamy fog she had moved in since waking. "I'm sorry, Seer," she said. "Today has been . . . today has been like a dream. It is hard to wake up."

"It's the first time in days you have not had to do something outrageous," he replied, spooning thrilp slices into his mouth. "Quite frankly, it's the first such day for me, too, in a very long while. Prince Valdon was not an easy traveling companion. Huld was worse, of course, but not by much. I understand he made off into the woods?"

"No doubt he is back in Poffle by now," she said. "His sister is pregnant. By him, he says. Their mother the Harpy is with them. I would say Huld is master in Hell's Maw now."

"I had hoped the place was empty."

"Not now, not soon," she said. "Though it is bound to come, one day."

"Aha," he laughed. "So now you are a Seer."

"No." She frowned. "Now I am beginning to learn to use my brain." She laughed in return. "It is like Seeing in one way. It, also, can be wrong from time to time."

The Fon sat while they talked, watching her hungrily, eating little.

When the waiters had brought fresh bread and bits of grilled sausage, he said, "Mavin, will you be going to Battlefox keep, now that you have been there once and seen the people?"

"No. No, our thalan, Plandybast, is a good fellow, as you yourself said, Fon. But that is not what I want for Mertyn. Mertyn has Talent, you know. Beguilement. He has had it since he was a fifteen-season child. It is a large Talent, and he must learn to manage it. They could do nothing for him in Battlefox save savage him and make him vicious with it. No. He must have a good teacher." She was looking at Windlow as she said it, half smiling. "I spoke with him about it, and he told me what teacher he would prefer. Of course, I cannot pay much in the way of fees."

"I will pay the fees," choked the Fon. "In return for saving my life, Mavin. Huld would have killed me."

"He would have tried. I think you might have stopped him quite successfully."

"And you, Mavin?" asked Windlow, quietly, softly, like a child trying to capture a wild bunwit without scaring it. "You?"

"Will you come with Mertyn?" The Fon, less wary, too eager.

"No," she said.

"No? Never?"

She shook her head, biting her lip over an expression which might have been part smile. "I did not say never. I only said no, I will not come with Mertyn." She folded her napkin as she had seen other diners do, reached out to take their hands, one on each side.

"I am Mavin of Danderbat keep? What is a Mavin of Danderbat keep? What shape is it? What color is it? What does it feel and know in its bones? Does it fly? Crawl? Does it grow feathers or fur?

"What places has it seen? What Assemblies has it attended? You who are not shifters do not know what an assembly is, and neither really does a shifter girl who has not left her keep to go into the wide world.

"What is in Schlaizy Noithn? For me?

"No, Fon. I will not come with Mertyn now. Though I may, some day. Some day."

And she would not let them try to dissuade her, nor would she let the Fon be near her with the two of them alone, for she knew what her blood would do and how little her head could manage it. Instead, a day or two later, she stood beside the parapet with him, with Boldery and Mertyn playing at wands and rings nearby, and told him farewell.

"My sister is out there somewhere. I would like to find her, see if I can help her. She may need my help. As for you, Fon, you do not need my help, not now."

"Do not call me Fon. You named me before. I am the Wizard Himaggery, and I will be that Wizard until you name me else."

"The Fon is dead." She laughed shakily. "Long live the Himaggery."

"So be it." He was not laughing at all. "Will you make a bargain with me, Mavin?"

"What sort of bargain?"

"If you go out into the world, and if the world is exciting, and you forget me, and time spins as time does, and the world passes as the world does, will you return to this place twenty years from now and meet me here if you have not seen me before then?"

"Twenty years? So long? Do you think I will not seek my friends out long before that?"

"Well, and if you do, better yet. But will you promise me, Mavin?"

"I'll be old, wrinkled."

"It will not matter. Will you promise me?"

"Oh, that I'll promise!" She laughed up into his unlaughing face.

"On your honor?"

"On my honor. On my Talent. On my word."

"Twenty years?"

"Twenty years." She turned away, biting her lip, afraid that her calm might break and the tears spill over. "Now. I am going west, my friend. I have made my farewells to Mertyn." She reached out to stroke his face as he had done so many times to hers, then turned down the stairs and away down the street of the city, without looking back.

Windlow came to him where he stood, looking after her. "Did she make the promise?"

"Yes."

"Did she know it was a Seeing of mine?"

"I didn't tell her."

"Does she know she will not see you again until then?"

"I didn't tell her," he said. "I could not bear to say it. I can not bear to think of it now."

The road south of Pfarb Durim is arched by great, strange monuments. Mavin Manyshaped walked that way, seeing the arches with new eyes. She felt eyes from the branches of the trees watching her pass. On the hills, voices added to a song, spinning it into a lazy chant which made small echoes off the Strange Monuments, almost like an answer.

As for her, her eyes were fixed on the horizon where Schlaizy Noithn lay, and the western sea. There was something in her mind of wings. And something of places no other eyes than hers had ever seen. "I am the servant of the Wizard Himaggery," she sang, quoting the Mavin of a younger time. "Perhaps," she sang, making a joyful shout at the sky. "But not yet!"

The Flight of Mavin Manyshaped

CHAPTER ONE

From her perch on the side of the mainroot,Beedie could lean back at minor peril to her life and look up the Wall, the mainroot dwindling away in perspective until the solid, armspan width of it had shrunk down to a mere hair's breadth line at the rim of the chasm. So much height above was dizzying, and she slapped at the right piton to hear the comforting thwunging sound which indicated it was solidly set. Setting her spurs more deeply into the bark, she thrust back against the strap to look up once more at the light falling through the leaves of the flattrees, huge even at this distance, a ten-day climb from the rim. She didn't want to miss the noonglow, that vivid, emerald moment when the light came directly down through the leaves, making the whole chasm shine with the same verdant light it now shed on the western, morning-light, wall. Sometimes birds could be seen in the noonglow, enormous white ones, messengers – so the Birders said – of the Boundless.

It was in the noonglow that the birdwoman had come, slanting down in the green rays, white plumes streaming from the edges of her wings, to alight on the bridge rail of Topbridge, almost within the arms of Mercald the Birder. And Mercald had had her ever since, ever since he caged her that day only to find a girl in the cage the following morning. It had been either bird or girl every day since, with no one able to say for sure what it meant or why she had come in the first place. Still, the Birder caste had gained more status from that event than they had in all the history of the bridges – so much so that there was serious consideration of elevating them to the same high status as the Bridgers, Beedie's own caste. Not that she cared.

"Not that I care," she advised herself. "It makes no difference to me," knowing that it made considerable difference to some. There were three Bridger families in the chasm, and while the Beeds and the Chafers were not jealous of caste status, the Banders certainly were. She would bet that old Slysaw Bander would do everything in his power to prevent any Birder being considered *his* equal. "Thank the Boundless he isn't the eldest," she reflected. "If old Slysaw were the eldest, the whole chasm would regret it."

Judging noonglow to be some time off yet, she dug in her spurs and began climbing upward; chuff, heave, chuff, heave, chuff. The roll of measuring cord at her belt had unreeled almost to its end. Chuff, heave, chuff. Left, right, heave the strap, left, right, heave the strap. The measuring cord began to tug. She leaned out on her strap once more, judging how close she had come to her starting mark. Immodest self-congratulations. Within an arm's reach; not bad. She began to set pitons on the mark, right and left. Might as well set them deep. She would be back to this place with others of the Bridgers soon, getting ready to set the lines, tackle and winches. Topbridge had become crowded, too crowded, many thought, and the elders wanted the bridgetown widened. Even from this distance she could hear the sounds of the crowd from Topbridge, cries from the market, the rasp of a saw from the middle of the bridge where the Crafters House stood, hammers banging on anvils. She took up her own hammer, concentrating on the job. When the pitons were set deeply she leaned on her strap once more, waiting for the noonglow.

High above the bridgetowns the rim of the chasm was edged with flattrees, wider than they were high, one set of roots anchoring the trees to the rock of the plain, another set dropping down the chasm wall into the dark pit of the bottom with its unseen mysterious waters. Here and there the mainroots bulged into swollen, spherical water-bellies, sole source of water for the bridge people. At intervals the mainroots sent out side roots, smaller though still huge, which grew horizontally along the wall before plummeting downward. The side roots put out ropey, smaller roots of their own, and the ropey roots were heavily furred in hair roots, the whole gigantic mass curtaining the sides of the chasm like a monstrous combed pelt, a matted shag of roots so dense that none of the chasm wall could be seen. In shadow, the roots appeared dark and impenetrable, but now in the emerald light of glorious noonglow the shaggy mass blazed out of shadow in jeweled greens as bright as the high glowing leaves, each strand an individual shining line. A chorus of floppers began to honk somewhere in the mass; flocks of birds from the distant rim to circle in the light like devotees circling the altar of the Boundless. All the noises of Topbridge ceased – the other cities were too far down to be heard except as a murmur – the sound of the bell and the call to prayer coming from the Birder's tower in a thin, cutting cry, sharp as broken glass.

Below her right foot she could see the Bridger house of Topbridge and the bridge itself, wide and solid, diminishing into a long wedge stretching across the chasm to the far wall, 2000 paces away. On either side of it were nets looking like lace, dotted with the fallen flattree leaves they were put there to catch.

Below her left foot she could see the narrower wedge of Nextdown, too tiny to seem real, and beyond it to the left, up-chasm, the thin line of Midwall. Down there somewhere lay Bottommost, barely visible, shining sometimes at noonglow as the merest thread. Potter's bridge and Miner's bridge were up-chasm, hidden by the bulk of Topbridge, but she could see Harvester's far off to her right, just at the place the chasm began to turn away west. Seven cities of the chasm. And the broken one above. And the lost one below. The lost one which had disappeared, so it was said, all in one night into the depths of the chasm together with all its people and all its fabled treasure – punished, the Birders said, because of some insult to the Boundless. Lately, though, there had been talk of other reasons, perhaps other bridgetowns in jeopardy – talk of something down in the depths which threatened them all. She made a religious gesture, a ritual shiver at the thought of the lost bridge, then put it out of mind.

The Birder had finished calling prayers. Already the glow had moved from morning wall to evening wall. Time to get on with the task.

She had begun the job the day before by climbing the great mainroot which supported Topbridge in order to measure it from midpoint to the place it left the wall in its long catenary. She had started early in the morning, shivering a little in the mists at the edge of Topbridge commons as she fastened on her belt and spurs. None of the Bridgers had been out and about yet. She had touched the bell outside the Maintainer's door as she came by, and a 'Tainer had come running – or giving that appearance. Hairroot Chafer gave as his opinion that 'Tainers were bred for slowness, like the slow-girules the Harvesters used to gather root nodules, and only gave the impression of running by leaning forward, wherever they went – to give her a cup of nodule broth and a crisp cake of wall moss.

"A fine morning, Bridger." It was the Maintainer called Roges, a tall, strong man, who seemed often to be the one available when Beedie needed something.

"Fine enough," she had answered shortly. It did not do, she had been told, to become too friendly with the Maintainers. Pity. This one seemed to have good sense and he was not slow, no matter what Hairroot Chafer said. "I seem to be about the business early."

"It was the Birder feast last night," the Maintainer murmured, looking politely away while she finished the broth. "To discuss the elevation of the Birder caste. Everyone drank a great deal. You had not yet returned from the mainroot, Bridger." Though he did not breach courtesy, she could tell he was curious about that. She toyed with the idea of making up some story to keep the 'Tainers occupied in myth-building for a day or two – everyone knew they were frightfully superstitious – but her sense of fairness prevented.

"I broke a spur, 'Tainer. Unfortunately, I also broke the strap. I had a spare spur, as what Bridger would not, but not a spare strap, and it took a little time to braid one out of root hair." She was a little embarrassed at his look of concern. A broken strap was nothing. "True, I was late returning. Was it you put the meat and moss cake by my bed?"

He nodded. "I saw you had not returned. It is difficult to sleep if one is hungry."

"And difficult to sleep if a hungry Bridger comes hammering on your door," she said, grinning. Roges must have been thinking of his own sleep as much as of hers. She handed him the cup, checked the fastening on her belt, then began to climb the side root. The great mainroot of the city was only a little above her head at this point.

"May the roots support you as they do the city," the 'Tainer called from below, looking up after her for longer than necessary before moving away toward his house. Beedie did not reply. Getting from the side root to the mainroot took a bit of tricky maneuver, and she wanted her attention on her work. Once on the top of the mainroot, she fastened the end of her measuring cord to the root just over the bulge that marked the center point and then began to walk along the root toward the evening-light wall, slightly uphill.

When the curve grew steeper she threw her strap around the root, dug in her spurs and started to climb, the measuring cord unreeling from its container at her waist. It was a good climb, steeper the closer to the wall she came, higher and higher above the bridgetown, until at last she could reach out and touch the wall through the tangle of rope roots and hairs. She marked the place.

Now she had to locate a new mainroot, one straight and supple, with no soft spots or water-bellies, and measure it downward from a place on the wall even with her mark, her own white-painted signs which showed bright even against the shadow. She had spent the rest of the day prospecting among the likely mainroots for the best possible one as close to the existing bridge as possible. That had been yesterday's work.

Today she had started early again, climbing to the mainroot she had selected and marking it carefully. She fastened her measuring cord at that point, then climbed down as she checked each arm-length of the root for imperfections. Sometimes a mainroot would look solid, with unblemished bark, but there would be soft spots hidden away. One tapped with the hammer while listening for the telltale dullness, the soggy sound which would hint at rot. One tapped and listened, tapped and listened, and then one prayed anyhow, for there were rots set so deep no Bridger could find them except by luck and the help of the Boundless. The root she had chosen seemed good throughout its length. She had fastened her cord at the bottom and climbed back up the root, measuring once more to come to her present perch. "Measure twice, cut once," she told herself wearily. Bridger youngsters were reared on the story of Amblebee Bridger who measured once, cut once, and found he had cut too short the only mainroot near enough to use. "Measure twice, cut once." Well, she had measured twice, and tomorrow she would start preparing for the cut. She thwapped the pitons with her hand one final time, then started the climb down. On the far side of the chasm, Byle Bander should have completed his own measurement today. Likely he would be preparing to cut soon as well.

After they were cut, the two great roots would be hauled up, the cut ends rising, coming closer and closer in the middle of the chasm until they almost touched. Then one end would be shaped into a socket, the other into a join, the join would be doused with plant glue, the two would be hauled together and secured with lines while they grew together. In a couple of seasons the join would be callused over, bulging a little, stronger than the mainroot itself.

She hoped Byle Bander would cut his mainroot long enough to make a good socket. Last time he hadn't left enough to allow chopping away all the wood they had set hooks into, and roots made a better join if all the hook-damaged wood was cut away before socketing. Last time had only been a side root, one meant to carry a footbridge and stairs between Topbridge and Nextdown. It hadn't had to carry much weight. Still – it would have been better to cut a little longer. And a mainroot, one meant to carry a city, well – she just hoped he cut it long enough. It wouldn't do to suggest it to him. Though Byle Bander had received his tools and titles in the same season Beedie had, to hear him talk he'd been rootwalking two lifetimes at least. Any thought of Byle Bander made her uncomfortable and brought back a memory of the summer that the root broke, one she would rather not have recalled.

The summer the root broke, Beedie had been about ten, living in the Bridger House on Nextdown with her father, Hookset, her mother, Rootwalker, and assorted aunts, uncles, cousins and remoter kin. Uncle Highspurs was the eldest Bridger on Nextdown, which made the Beed family head of caste and main occupiers of Bridgers House. The other Bridger family on Nextdown was the Bander family who said they preferred to live by themselves in a wallhouse at the far, evening-light, side of the chasm. They had moved up from Midwall, some said, though others thought it was from Bottommost itself, and they did not talk as the Nextdowners did. There were only half a dozen Banders in the family: Slysaw and his wife, two grown sons, one old aunt and a boy Beedie's age, Byle. There were known to be many more members of the Bander family at Topbridge, and still more at Miner's bridge, but the family at Nextdown was neither numerous nor considered very important. Beedie thought about that sometimes, how common and unimportant the Banders had seemed.

The elders had decided to expand Nextdown on the up-chasm side. The discussions about it had gone on for a long time, at least a season, with a good deal of exploration among the mainroots to locate proper candidates to carry the new part of the bridgetown. Beed had even been allowed to try her own little spurs up and down the roots, being shown the water-bellies and how to find soft spots, learning how to judge the direction of side roots. Both the first and second pair of support roots had been located, and the first pair was due to be cut, morning-light side first, then the evening-light side. The Beed family had made the decisions, but they'd invited old Bander, him they called Slysaw, to be part of the cutting crew. He'd told them no thank you very much, but his family had planned to visit kin downstairs at Potters' bridge that day and some days to follow.

"Besides, you Beeders have plenty hands," the man had said, sneering a little, the way he always did. "Mighty prolific family, the Beeders. You've got hands aplenty. Just take Highspurs and Hookset and a few uncles and you've got the job done in a jiffy." Then he and his family had gone off to the stairs, seeming eager to make the two-day climb it would take with the old woman, though the younger ones might have made it in a day, going down.

"Well," said Beedie's dad. "We offered, 'Walker. You heard me make the offer. The old fart won't cooperate worth a flopper's honk. We try and make work for him to earn his space and he goes to visit kin. We don't make work for him and he complains to the elders we're shutting him out. Don't worry what would satisfy the Bander family, tell true, and I'm about tired of trying to find out."

Beedie remembered it, all of it, the conversation around the hearth where the deadroot fire gleamed and the 'Tainers were stirring the soup pot. Next morning six of the Beeds, including Uncle Highspurs and Beedie's parents, went down-root to make the cut, and that was the last anyone saw of them, ever. Hookset and Rootwalker. Uncle Cleancut, Uncle Highspurs, Cousin Rootcutter, Cousin Highclimb, the one who had gone all the way to the rim and brought back most of a fresh leaf from a flattree to astonish them all with the color of it when she unfolded it and it covered the bridgetown from side to side.

All the elders of the family were gone, including the eldest Bridger. They had started the cut right enough, but seemingly the root had broken, broken away while they were working, and carried them all to the bottom, into the dark and mystery of the Bounded, among the rejected dead but without the ceremony of the flopper-skin kites, the memorial clothes. Six of them, gone, gone with all the tools and the hooks and the lines. All but one rootsaw that Aunt Six found wedged in the cut and brought back to Beedie, for it had been her mother's.

"Something wrong there, Beedie," she had mourned. "That root is all black up inside, as though it had been burned. Looky here at what I found. . . ." She had shown the black lumps. "Charcoal. I took that right out of the root at the back, next to the wall, down a little lower than they started the cut. Oh, from the cut side it looks solid, but from the back, it's only a shell. . . ."

"Daddy wouldn't have cut burning wood," Beedie had objected. "Mother wouldn't. It isn't safe."

"Oh, no, child, they wouldn't have done it. Not if they'd known. If it was burning up inside when they got there there'd be no smoke to smell. Not until the saw cut through to the center, where the fire was, and then the smoke. . . ." She didn't need to say anything more. Greenroot smoke was lethal. Everyone knew that.

A day later, Beedie had put on her spurs and climbed down against all custom and allowances, for she was too young to be allowed on a mainroot by herself. Still she went, chuff and heave until she thought her arms would drop off, to come at last to the end of the mainroot and see for herself. Someone had been there in the meantime. Someone had chopped away all the char with an adze, leaving only clean root, but Beedie went on down a side root and found pieces of the char caught in the root hairs, back near the wall. She looked down, sick and dizzy from a climb considerably above her strength, seeing not far below her the stair to Potter's bridge. It would have been easy to climb onto the stair from the mainroot. Easy to get to the mainroot from the stair, come to that. Easy. She cut the thought off. Why would anyone burn a mainroot? Greenroot made poisonous smoke. Deadroot was always dried for a long time before burning. Besides, Nextdown needed that root. Meddling with it was unthinkable, so she resolutely did not think it.

The Potter's bridge stairs were so close, so easy in comparison to the long climb upward on spurs that she almost decided to get back to Nextdown that way, but something dissuaded her. Afterward, it was hard to remember what the reason had been, but she connected it to the return of the Bander family that night.

Nothing was the same after that. Slysaw was now the eldest Bridger on Nextdown, which meant he held Bridgers House. He wasn't the most even-handed of holders, either, though elders weren't supposed to play favorites, and it wasn't long before the remaining Beed cousins were moving up to Topbridge or down to Potter's or Midwall. Finally, there had been only Beedie and Aunt Six left, and when old Slysaw told Aunt Six she had to move out of her old rooms because he meant to give them to a Bander cousin from Midwall, Aunt Six decided to leave. The two of them moved up to Topbridge next day, carrying what they could on their backs and leaving the rest for the Banders. "Ill-wished on them," said Aunt Six. "Every table and chair ill-wished on them, and may those who sit there have the eternal trots."

On Topbridge the Bridgers were more mixed; there were some Banders, true, but there were more Beeds and more Chafers and plenty of housing for them all. The Bridgers House was held by Greenfire Chafer – who was killed soon after, some said by a rogue flopper – and Beedie and Aunt Six were given rooms in the Bridgers House at the morning-light end of the bridge right away. Then Beedie got on with her schooling. Still, every now and then she would wake in the chasm night to the sound of floppers honking in the root mat, half dreaming about hiding on the rootwall, lumps of charcoal in her hands, looking up at the adze-cut end of the mainroot while hearing from below that phlegmy chuckle as Slysaw Bander came climbing up the stairs.

And now it was a Bander again, Slysaw's son Byle, come to work on Topbridge, cutting the roots too short, putting his hands on Beedie every chance he got, and bragging as though he were a Firstbridger himself. Beedie wondered, not for the first time, if she and Aunt Six moved to Bottommost whether they might escape from Banders once and for all.

The bridgetown grew larger and louder as she climbed down toward it, chunk, chunk, chunk, the spurs biting into the bark. She felt lucky to have found a mainroot right where it was wanted, with good, clean length and no water-bellies. Sometimes, so she had heard, there were no suitable mainroots within a great distance of the existing bridge. Then it was necessary to build elsewhere, or haul a distant root closer with hooks and ropes, a procedure which took half a lifetime and was as deadly as it was dull. Well, it wouldn't be necessary. As one of the youngest Bridgers, prospecting had been assigned to her, and she had found a good root. That one and the one Byle Bander had found would make up the first pair. After the haulers were started, she'd have to start looking for her half of the second pair. From what the elders had said, this could be a four or five pair job. They wanted the expansion built wide, they said. Enough to absorb all the growth Topbridge might make for the next several lifetimes. Of course, to hear Aunt Six tell it, elders were always like that, always planning more than other people could build. Since the elders didn't actually have to do the job, it was always easy to plan large.

She amused herself going over the steps it would take to make the cut on the morrow, how the Bridgers would ring the root with hatchets, then fit the loop saw into the groove, two of them braced against the root as they pulled alternately, cutting through the mainroot until the whole massive weight of it fell away into the chasm with roaring echoes which seemed to go on forever. It would be the first town root Beedie had helped cut, but she well remembered the sound from the time the root fell at Nextdown. What happened to the roots that fell, she wondered? Did they end up propped against the chasm wall? Or fallen over into the bottom river? Did they rot? Or dry? Did floppers build nests in them? No matter, really. They ended up far below Bottommost, and whatever might happen below Bottommost could not be reckoned with at all. Except, she reminded herself, for whatever this new worry was. Though whether that was coming up from below Bottommost was anyone's guess.

After cutting the root, the Bridgers would bore hook holes in the end of it, set the great hardwood hooks in place, then run rope from the hooks back and forth through the tackle and across the chasm to the hooks set deep in the other root end there. After which everyone on Topbridge would spend a part of their days hauling at the windlass. Everyone, that is, but the Bridgers.

The Bridgers would be making a detailed chart of every side root on the mainroots, every bud, every ropey growth. Once the mainroot was hauled into its long supporting curve, the Bridgers would use many of the verticals hanging from it to support the base of the new bridge. There would have to be other verticals reaching all the way to the distant Bottom and its nourishing waters if the mainroot was to be kept alive and healthy. Still other side roots would be needed for the stairs which were planned to link Topbridge directly to Potter's bridge, replacing the current link by way of Nextdown. Any side roots that didn't fit the plan would have to be trimmed away as they budded; otherwise the mainroot would turn into an unmanageable tangle which could never be maintained properly.

"Hey, skinny girl," came a call from below. She looked down to see Byle Bander leaning from the bridge rail, staring up at her with the half sneer he always wore. "Hey, Beedie, slow-girule. What are you doing, girl? Harvesting nodules?"

There were several slow-girules in the roots nearby, their hooked hands tight around the side roots, moving now and then to clip root nodules from the root with the sharp edges of their claws, like scissors. One just below her had a pouch almost full, and she whispered to it, "Nice giruley. Give us? Give us, hmmm?"

"Hnnn," it growled at her, half in complaint. "Hnnno. Minnnne."

"Ah, come on, giruley. Give us one little root mouse to tide us until supper time. One little juicy one. Hmmm?" She reached out to scratch the creature in the one place its own claws could not reach, the middle of its back. The whine turned into a purr, and the creature handed her a green, furry nodule. She leaned against her belt once more to peel it with her Bridger's knife. Anything for delay's sake. She didn't want to descend with Byle there.

"The Harvesters' caste will be fining you, Beedie," Byle Bander called. "You know you're not supposed to fool with the 'rulies."

"I'm not fooling, I'm hungry," she replied, her mouth half full of the juicy, crunchy root nodule. "I could have picked it myself." If she had behaved in accordance with the rules, she would have picked it for herself. It was uncastely for a Bridger to receive food except from a Maintainer's hands, though the rules did permit harvesting from the roots if one was kept past meal time. The rules did not allow Bridgers to invade Harvesters' caste by taking food from the slow-girules, however, and Beedie flushed. Though it was something all the Bridgers did from time to time, it was precisely the kind of thing Byle Bander would make an issue of, or harass her about until she would be heartily sorry for having done it. He liked to couple his attempts at fondling with threats, and neither were welcome. His presence on the walkway below her made her uncomfortable. Still, delaying any longer wouldn't help. She finished the nodule and wiped her hands on her trousers, moving on down the root to the edge of the bridge. Bander reached out a hand to her, which she ignored. He had the habit of pulling one off balance and then laughing, or, worse, grabbing parts of her she didn't want grabbed.

As she stepped onto the bridge, she saw a group of Bridgers striding toward her at the same time she saw the expression of amused superiority on Byle Bander's face. All of the Bridgers in the group were Banders, interesting in itself. What were they up to?

She waited little time for an answer. One of the Bridgers, a ruddy, fussy little man called Wetwedge, bustled up, peered at her as though he had never seen her before, then said, "You getting ready for the cut, girly?"

"That's what I've been doing," she replied, wondering what this was all about. Certainly it was no chance encounter. It had the feeling of a delegation.

"Not today, girly. No. Big business, this. Got to have it checked at least twice, you know. Can't cut until we check it twice."

"I did," she said, amazed at his open-faced stupidity. What did the man think? That she was witless?

"No, no. I mean you got to have it checked by someone else. Gotcher measuring cord?"

Something deep inside Beedie sat up and looked around with sharp eyes and a sharper nose. Something smelled. "My measuring cord is put away safe, yes."

"Well, trot it out, girly, and we'll check it. Old lady Slicksaw here will climb it down for you, down to your mark, just to check."

"That's not the way it's done," she said, somehow keeping her voice from shaking with anger. "If you want Slicksaw Bander to check my measure, go ahead with my blessing. But she'll use her own cord and compare it to mine before witnesses from Bridgers House, and any difference will be checked by an impartial eye. That's the way it's done, Wetwedge Bander-Bridger, and I'm surprised you should suggest anything different."

The man looked quickly from side to side, seeking support from one or another of them, but they shifted feet uncomfortably, not looking at him. He laughed, trying to put a good face on it. "Well then, takes more time that way, but it's according to rule. So, take a day off, then, Beedie."

She saw deceit on his face, an evil intention which she couldn't read but one made clear in those shifty eyes, darting up and down like a flooper's wings. Besides, he wasn't enough elder to her to tell her to take a day off, and him not even from her own family.

"My mark is sealed with my knot," she announced loudly. "Slicksaw can't mistake it." Or alter it, she said to herself. One might mistake an accidental scarring for a hatchet mark, but one would not mistake any accidental tangle in the hair roots for an individual Bridger's own knot, complicated as an alphabet, tied and then doused with paint to make it stand out. "It's tied once at each side, top and bottom," she said. Then, as they began to turn away, "Of course, I'm going to Bridgers House to see that they check Byle Bander's measure as well. Otherwise it would be unfair, wouldn't it, and not something the elders would tolerate. Since you're all Banders checking a Beed, I'll ask the Bridgers House to send Chafers or Beed to check Bander. Fair's fair, after all."

She had the satisfaction of seeing Byle Bander's face full of anger as she stalked away. Nor did she miss the hesitation among the other Banders, the glances, the stuttering lips as one or another of them tried to think of something to say. She did not look back, contenting herself with a call. "Good day to you, Bridgers."

As she walked away to Bridgers House, she could hear their whispers behind her. Well, what had they thought? That she would let a clutter of Bander hangers-on presume to double-check her competence without having some Beed fellows check on Byle's ability as well? Did they think if they called her girly, as they would some curvy Maintainer wench, wriggling her hips between the tables at dinner, that she would not hear what it was they were really saying? Not likely.

She went directly to Bridgers House. She wanted to talk to Rootweaver Beed, second eldest, a white-haired woman with young eyes whom Beedie admired for her good sense and friendly demeanor toward the younger Bridgers. The woman was curled up on a windowseat, weaving carded hairroot fibers to make a new climbing belt.

"Checking you, are they?" Though Rootweaver was not young, she was straight and supple as a side root, and Beedie had seen her using spurs not four days before. Rootweaver considered the matter now, frowning a little. At last her face cleared and she said, "With all the troubles from below we have to worry us just now, leave it to the Banders to come up with something fretting. Well, it's never a bad idea to check a measure, 'specially when it's a mainroot in question. We'll take it as though it were friendly meant and send a crew along to check the Bander whelp as well. Have a day off, Beedie. You might help your Aunt Six with the moving. She's found a place she likes better than Bridgers House again." The woman laughed, not least at Beedie's expression of dismay.

Aunt Six had moved house at least two or three times a year since they had come to Topbridge, never able to settle into the same comfort she had known in the Bridgers House on Nextdown. She had moved into and out of Bridgers House on Topbridge seven times – this would make eight. Having Aunt Six behaving as usual made the day somehow merely annoying, an almost customary irritation taking the place of that extraordinary discomfort she had been feeling since she had been hailed by Byle Bander. If Aunt Six was moving house, it must be assumed the world was much as usual.

So she spent the afternoon with a cart, hauling Aunt Six's bedding and pots and bits and pieces from the pleasant rooms in Bridgers House to some equally pleasant ones on the far edge of Topbridge, about mid-chasm, from which the latticed windows looked out toward Harvester's bridge, a lumpy line against the bend of the chasm wall behind it. Beedie wondered what the view was like from Harvester's. Since it was at the turn of the chasm, could the chasm end be seen from there? Was there a chasm end? Odd. She'd never wondered about that until this very minute.

"Beedie! What are you dreaming about, Bridger-girl? You'll only have this one day to help me, so help me! I've got all the rugs yet to bring."

"Aunt Six, do you think this place will suit you? Will you stay here for a while? Now that I've got my tools and titles, I'd like to get some things of my own for this room, but not if you're just going to move us again."

"Girl, you get your own things and make it your place, you can stay whether I go or not. For Boundless' sake, Beedie. You're a grown-up girl." She compressed her lips into a thin and disapproving line and began to bustle, accomplishing little but giving a fine appearance of activity.

Beedie smiled to herself. The only time Aunt Six referred to Beedie as a grown-up girl was when there was moving to be done, or something else equally boring or heavy. Still, the new place did have that marvelous view of the chasm, being right at the edge this way. Shaking her head, she went to fetch the rugs.

Slicksaw Bander said she found no fault with Beedie's measure. Rootweaver Beed was not so favorable about Byle's. The Beeds found him marked short, as Beedie had feared, and told him so in front of half the Bridgers and a full dozen Maintainers with their ears flapping. Byle was so angry he turned white. Beedie tried not to look superior, failing miserably. Perhaps now he would keep himself to himself and pay attention to his own Bridger business rather than hers. It had a consequence she had not foreseen, however, when she was called to Bridgers House for conference.

"Byle's root was marked short, Beedie," said Rootweaver, the half-dozen assembled Bridger elders behind her nodding and frowning. They had summoned her without warning, always a slightly ominous occurrence, but this time there had been nothing discomforting in it for her. "Not merely a little short," Rootweaver went on, "but far short. As though he had not measured at all, and certainly not twice – or got his cord tangled up on the climb, and that's a child's trick. So we're going to go down there with him tomorrow, check his measuring technique and check his axe work, too. Short in one thing, short in all, isn't that the saying? So. You can go ahead and start cutting a groove on the root you've measured, but we've no one to help you cut root. After we get young Byle straightened out, you'll get your crew. Do what you can alone, and we'll send the crew next day."

"Byle's in the classroom right now," said one of the other elders, indignantly. "Fulminating and fussing. We're keeping him here tonight, doing a little review of technique, and he's mad as a hooked flopper. Madder than he should be. You'd think he'd been planning a lovers' meeting or something the way he's carrying on. Demands to be let go home."

"Bridgers House is home for all Bridgers," said Rootweaver calmly. "Let him go get a change of clothing if he pleases, but I want him to stay here tonight. We'll see if we can't talk some sense into him."

All of this made Beedie quite uncomfortable, and she was glad Byle hadn't seen her with the elders. If he thought she had been privy to his embarrassment, he'd never have permitted her a peaceful day. Since she thought he didn't know, she had a peaceful night. Come morning, though, she thought he had probably found out, for she was visited by a Harvester elder with an annoying sniff and his pen ready to record her words.

"It's been reported you've been interfering with the slow–girules, girl," he pinch-mouthed at her, pulling his nose back as though she smelled.

"You may call me Bridger," she said, holding her fury carefully in check. "And I have never interfered with a slow-girule in my life. I did take a nodule from one, yesterday, when I was delayed on the root and missed a meal."

"Report is you interfered with it. Rassled it about. Maybe bothered it in its work."

"I scratched its furry back, and it purred at me. So much for your 'interference.' "

"You could have injured it." The man was white around the mouth, wanting to storm and yell at her, but afraid to do so seeing her own anger and knowing what Bridger wrath meant.

"Nonsense," snapped Aunt Six from behind her. "You can't injure a slow-girule with an axe. Be done, Harvester. Beedie took a nodule from one of your beasties and she must pay a fine for it, for it's against the rules. So impose your fine and be done. It's no large thing, and you'd best remember it. The good will of Bridgers is given freely, but it's taken freely, too, when there's cause."

The Harvester did not reply, merely threw the piece of paper at them and stalked away. "Parasites," hissed Aunt Six, just loud enough that he could not fail to hear. "No skills of their own, so they must live by preventing others from using common sense. Sorry the day the Harvesters ever became a caste, Beedie. And sorry the day any Bridger takes one like that seriously."

The man heard. He turned and made a threatening gesture, mouthing something they could not hear.

"Still," Beedie said, "I did break the rule, Aunt Six. It was seeing that Byle Bander waiting for me on the bridge, like some old crawly-claw, hiding in a root hole. I didn't want to come down where he was, so I played with the 'rulie instead. They like it."

"Of course they like it, child. The Harvesters may think they own the slow-girules, but no one has ever convinced a slow- girule of that yet. It's that which makes the Harvesters so angry. They'd like nothing better than to have the 'rulies turn clipper-claws on all except the Harvesters. That would suit them right to the bridge floor. And what kind of a Bridger is Byle Bander to report one of his own caste.

"A miserable one," Beedie replied in a grim voice. "A miserable bit of flopper flub, for all he's a Bridger."

All this caused Beedie some delay, and it was late in the morning before she started down, chuff, heave, chuff, humming to herself, throwing a glance upward now and then to see if there were birds. It would be wonderful, she thought, to fly like that, up to the flattrees and the plain – not even dangerous for a bird. A bird wouldn't have to fear the gnarlibars, the giant pombis, the ubiquitous d'bor hiding in every pool and stream, the poison bats, the were owls. A bird wouldn't be bothered by the monsters of the plain, the monsters who had almost wiped out the people, would have wiped them out if they hadn't moved down into the chasm to build the bridgetowns where the monsters couldn't get at them. Not the Firstbridge, of course. That hadn't been built far enough down the chasm, and the monstrous forest pombis had climbed down the mainroots to it as they would have climbed a tree. The site of that disaster was the broken city, still hanging high against the light, a network of black in the up-chasm sky. Then there had been the lost bridge, the one that had disappeared one night, never to be seen again – disappeared between dark and dawn without a sound. Built too low, some said, though legend said it had been built only slightly lower than Bottommost. Trouble in the depths, they said. Then and now, they said. Well, all this conjecture wouldn't help get the job done. She spotted her marks, moved beyond them, readied her hatchet to make the groove, then clung to the root with a sudden, giddy disquietude, overcome by a wave of familiar horror. She had felt like this before. There was something. Something wrong? Something not as usual? Uneasily she shifted on the root, moving around it as a flopper moves when hiding from the hunters, listening to silence, tasting the air, smelling . . . smelling.

What was it? An odor so faint she could hardly detect it? But what? She wished for the crew, the other Bridgers, suddenly aware of her solitude.

She began to move lower on the root, sniffing, tapping at the root with her hammer. The sound was wrong, wrong. She moved lower still, still tapping, then abruptly astonished, feeling the heat beneath her palms as a hallucination, an unreality, outrageous and impossible. Roots were cold, her mind said, and therefore . . . therefore . . .

Even as her mind toyed with a dozen irrelevant notions, her body reacted, leaping upward in three quick movements of arms and legs, chuff, heave, chuff, heave, chuff, hands frantically feeling for cool, not sure they had found it, upward once more in that same panic-ridden gallop, until there was no possibility of mistake. She smelled it then for the first time, that harsh scent of poison smoke, barely detectable. She longed in an instant to be one of the slow-girules, able to turn head down on the root, able somehow to see below her feet. And yet she didn't need to look. She could smell it. The mainroot was burning.

Back in the old times, she had heard, this was the way roots were severed. A Bridger would climb in between the root and the wall, hack away a hole in the root, then put burning charcoal in there to burn away and burn away until the thing dropped. Sometimes the fire didn't go out, however. Sometimes it got into the heartwood and kept on going, poisoning the air, no matter how one cut at it and chopped at it. So the Bridgers had stopped burning roots and began cutting them. But someone had burned a mainroot at Next-down, and someone had set fire to this one Beedie sat upon, the one Beedie should have arrived at with a full crew of Bridgers, earlier than this. If she went back and told about it the fire would have burned the root away by the time they returned, burned it too high, and it was the only useful one in the right place on this side.

So – so what? So cut it off before it went any further. Cut it off right below the mark, working against time, trying to get it cut through before the fire reached the saw cut and the smoke killed her. Her body began it, even while her mind was thinking through the right procedures. She was high on the root in a moment, setting her pitons and hooks for safety lines, one after the other, running the lines through and down to her belt, checking the buckle, checking the lines, setting them high above the mark, so high that no matter if the root fell, she would be left hanging – if a side root didn't lash her head off, or a tangle tear her away from where she hung.

The axe in her hand flew at the bark, making the first cuts, up and down, overhand, underhand, chips flying out into the chasms to flutter away like crippled birds, down and out of sight forever. The pungent smell of the milky root juice made her nose burn, a corrosive stench. She shifted rapidly to the right, cutting around, keeping her lines straight. When the root was ringed, she went back, doing it again, cutting deep so the saw loop wouldn't slip. Then the hatchet went into the belt, the saw loop came out. She had to throw it from behind the root, with free space all around. She held one handle in her right hand, whipped the length of the saw out and left, praying it would wrap around the root, smacking the handle into her left hand.

No. The saw tangled in a mass of root hairs, dangling. She moved down a little, lashed the saw outward again. The loop spun out, around the root, came back into her waiting left hand with a solid thwack. She eased the blade into the groove, dug her spurs deep and began to pull, right, left, tugging against the saw line with its myriad diamond teeth, seeing the puffs of sawdust fly into the air.

The sawline resisted her for a moment, then bit deep, cutting its own groove deeper, dust puffing at either side. At first she thought the amount of sawdust ridiculously large, then saw that it was mixed with smoke, smoke rising in little clouds from the cut, making her eyes stream, her throat burn. It was deadly. Deadly. Everything in her urged her to get away, to climb outward, away from that hideous smoke, but instead she moved around the root to find an updraft of clean air and went on heaving at the saw. It was well used, supple, only recently reglued with jeweled teeth for which she had paid a pretty price, the supply of gems being so short. Aunt Six had always said that good tools repaid their keeper, and she chanted this to herself as she went on heaving, feeling the root beneath her spurs begin to grow warm. The fire was eating its way up, toward the mark.

"Bite teeth, cut deep, saw line chew, job to do, pull, Bridger, pull. . . ." then six deep breaths and chant again, over and over. This was not a job for one Bridger! She should have had a full crew, spelling one another as they tired, encouraging one another. "Bite teeth . . ." It was getting a little easier as the groove bit deeper, there was less surface to pull against. "Bite teeth, cut deep, saw line chew. . . ." In older days, there had been plenty of gems, plenty of saw gravel. Maybe she should have paid for another dipping. Pull. Pull. The root quivered.

Quickly she shifted her feet upward, bracing out above the groove, lying almost horizontally from the root as she heaved the line, heaved, heaved, feeling her shoulders start to burn and bind, beginning to choke in the smoke once more, unable to move from this stance, unable to shift her position, trying to hold her breath against that one too many which would bring the poison full strength deep into her lungs.

A quiver again, this time a mighty one, a shaking, a groaning sound, a rending as the world began to drop from beneath her. The root below her fell away – but only a finger's width, whipping the entire root to one side as it did so, throwing her to the end of her lines, breaking two of them with lashing side roots. She hung, nose dripping blood, suspended between her remaining two lines, turning like a hooked flopper, gagging at the smoke. One incredibly strong cable of fiber held the root, kept it from falling away, one bundle no thicker than her leg, groaning as though it had human voice, toward which the fire crept, upward, upward – taking what seemed an eternity to burn it through.

She fainted, came to herself, began to go in and out of blackness as though it were a garment put on and took off. Through a veil of swimming gray she saw the mass of the mainroot dropped away down the endless depth of the chasm, lashing side roots as it went so that they twitched and recoiled, knocking Beedie against their rough sides. She swung still at the end of her lines, thrashed into semiconsciousness, eyes staring upward at the rim.

Far above the noonglow came, through emerald light, a kind of singing. Was it the Birder on Topbridge or the singing of her own blood? High in the light she saw wings, white wings, circling down and down, huge and mysterious, wonderful as a myth, beautiful as a song.

"It will stop at Topbridge," she told herself in her dream, "like the other one." But it did not. It came down and down until it perched on a side root spur just beside her and turned into something else. Something with a woman's face, but with hands and arms like a slow-girule, arms to hold fast, and legs to reach out and pick Beedie from her lines as though she had been no heavier than a baby. Then the bird person wiped the blood from her face and cradled her, cradled her there on the root and whispered to her.

"My name is Mavin, little root climber. It seems to me you need some help here, whatever strange wonderful thing it is you are so determined to do."

CHAPTER TWO

After a time Beedie came to herself lying on a horizontal shelf of side root, carefully fastened to it with her own belt and pitons, having the blood washed from her face and neck with something that looked suspiciously like a furry, wet paw. The paw owner went away. There was a sound of water near by, splashing and trickling, then Beedie's head was lifted and a cup thrust at her lip. She drank, trying not to look at the cup, for it had appeared magically where the paw had been. When the paw/cup/person retreated from her side again, she turned her head to follow the creature/woman/bird as it went to the water-belly and burrowed into it through a sizeable hole in the tough shell which had not been there when Beedie had passed it earlier in the day.

"How did you cut it?" she asked, her voice a mere croak in the sound-deadening mat of the rootwall. "It takes a drill, and a blade saw. . . ."

"Or a sharp beak and determination," said the bird/person/creature. "You reached toward this place when I carried you past, mumbling something or other about being thirsty, so I figured there was water inside this what you call it. . . ."

"It's a water – belly," Beedie murmured. "It stores the water the root brings up from the bottom, down there. . . ."

"Down there, eh? A very long way, root climber. Do you go down there often?"

"Never." She shook her head and was frozen into immobility by the resultant pain. "Never. No. Too far. Too dark. The Boundless punished the Lostbridgers by sending them down there, so they say. Maybe for greed, because of the gemstones. We're running out, you know. All the ones left from that time have been used up. Dangerous. Dangerous creatures on the Bottom, they say. As dangerous as the plain, up top, where you came from."

"Plenty of creatures up there, all right. Gnarlibars. Pombis bigger than any I've seen elsewhere. There's a kind of giant bunwit with horns on its rear feet, did you know that? Strangest-looking thing I've ever seen. And I've seen wonders, oh, root dangler, but I've seen wonders. Oceans and lands, lakes and forests, all and everything in a wide world full of wonders. Among which, may I say, is this place of yours, what you call it?"

"The chasm? We just call it the chasm, that's all." If Beedie lay perfectly still, she could speak without really feeling discomfort. So she assured herself, at least.

"Do you know what it looks like from up there?" the bird/woman/person asked. "Let me tell you, it's a remarkable sight. To start with, the roots from those trees extend out onto the plain like great cables, bare as pipes. I saw them from up there, my soaring place, and had to come down just to see my eyes didn't lie to me. Leagues and leagues of these great roots laid out side by side, like the warp threads of some giant loom all ready for the weaving. Then, after leagues of nothing but bare root, a few little stalks pop up; short, stubby things, with one leaf, maybe, or two, gossamer leaves, spread to the sun like the wings of something bigger than you can imagine. Then the stalks grow higher, higher yet, bigger and bigger, until all you can see is the leaves, overlapping each other like scales on a fish, thin as tissue, and green – Gamelords, girl, but it's a lovely green."

"I know," murmured Beedie, entranced by the rough music of that voice. "We see it every day, at noonglow."

"And then a shadow in the green, slightly darker, with a mist rising up through it. At first I thought it was only a river under there, but then I saw how wide the shadow was, a long, dark stripe on the forest, going away north to tall, white-iced mountains; bending away to the south west into a desert hot and hard as brass, and that mist coming up full of food smells and people smells.

"Well, I came down, girl, working my way down through those gossamer leaves, eyes all sharpened to see what I could see far down, and what should I see but this great root thrashing about and a small girl person hung on it being smoked like a sausage, the smoke roiling nasty to my nose."

"I saw you coming down," said Beedie. "At first I thought I was dreaming it, that you were the other one."

There was a long silence, then the bird/creature/person said, in a voice even Beedie recognized as carefully noncommital, "What other one is that?"

"The white bird. The great white bird who came down, oh, a long time ago. A year, almost. It came down in the noonglow, and it perched on the railing of Topbridge commons. Mercald was there, Mercald the Birder?" She started to make an inquiring gesture, to move her head questioningly, but desisted at the swimming nausea she felt. The expression on the bird/person's face had already told her it did not know what Birders were. "White birds are the messengers of the Boundless, you know?" Beedie tried again. The bird/person nodded helpfully, indicating this was not impossible. "And the Birders are the servants of the Boundless. They do our judging, and our rituals, and dedicate the festivals, things like that. So, birds being sacred, and Mercald being a Birder, naturally, he took the white bird to the Birders House. Only later on it changed into a person, a woman. Like you did."

"Ah," said the bird/person in a flat, incurious voice. "Tell me your name, will you girl? And call me by mine. It will make it easier on us both. I'm Mavin."

"Mavin," said Beedie. "I'm Beedie. Beed's daughter, really, but they call me Beedie. I'll get some other kind of name after I've worked at Bridging a while – something like, oh . . ."

"Smoked sausage? Root dangler?"

"Probably." She raised one trembling hand to feel along her ribs. They were bruised, terribly tender, and it hurt when she took a deep breath or moved her head. She put the hand down, carefully, and was still once more. "More likely something like "Rulie-chaser' or 'Strap-weaver.' We like to be named after big things we've done, but some of us never do anything that big."

"Well, Beedie, what did this other bird have to say for itself? When it changed into a woman, I mean?"

"It never said anything, not that I heard of." The question made her a little uncomfortable, as though there were a right answer to it, one she didn't know. "It sings. Mercald used to bring it out in the noonglow and it flew. It circled around and around in the light, singing. Lately, though, it hasn't changed into a bird at all. It's stayed a woman."

"What does the woman do?"

"Sits. She sits in the window of the Birders House and brushes her hair. They feed her fruit and moss cakes, and bits of toasted flopper. They give her nodule beer to drink, and water. They dress her in soft dresses with ribbons woven by the Weavers' caste, especially for her. At festival times she watches the processions, and the jugglers, and the root walkers. And she sings."

"And never speaks? Never at all?"

"Never at all," said Beedie, in a definite voice. "Now, best you tell me what she is to you, for the people up there" – she moved her eyes to indicate the woven bottom of the great bridge above which threw an enormous shadow across them – "those people think she's sacred. You go asking too many questions, like you have with me, and they won't be contented just wondering where you came from, like I do. They'll wonder if maybe you're a devil from the Bottom. Or another messenger from the Boundless, in which case they'll lock you up, just to keep you safe, until they decide you've delivered the message, whatever it's supposed to be." She fell into a gray fog, exhausted by this speech.

"Dangerous, then, to be a messenger! Well, who else could I be? Who could visit you without stirring any curiosity at all?"

Beedie's head was swimming, but she tried to consider the question carefully. "You could be someone from Harvester's bridge. We hardly ever see anyone from Harvester's, because it's such a long way down-chasm. There's a Harvesters House on Topbridge, so you'd have someplace to stay." She sighed, the pain pulsing insistently.

"Ah. Well now. Tell me, Beedie, do you owe me for saving your life?"

She had not thought about it until that moment, and it was an odd question, all things taken into account, but still it was a question she could answer. "Yes," she said. "I owe you."

"Good. I want you to tell me all about this place, the chasm, the – what did you call them? – the bridgetowns. About Harvesters and Bridgers and whatever else there are about. Then, when you've done that, you won't owe me anymore and we can talk about some other arrangement."

"You're . . . strange," Beedie commented. "If you hadn't pulled me off that root and got me out of the smoke, I'd be dead by now, though, so I guess strange doesn't matter."

"A remarkable conclusion for one so young. So, sausage girl, tell me about this place. I am a stranger. I know nothing. You must tell me everything, even the things you know so well you never think of them.''

It was an odd session, one Beedie was always to remember. Later in her life, the memory was evoked by smoke smell, always, or by sudden jolts of pain. Even after, she was to recall this time whenever she was ill or injured. Now she lay as quietly as she could on a furry root, soft as her own bed, cushioned somehow in the arms or person of whoever it was called herself Mavin, and talked through her pain about the chasm, sometimes as though she were present, sometimes as though she were dreaming, in both cases as she had never talked or heard anyone talk before.

''Our people came here generations ago,'' she said. ''Down from the plain above. I didn't know about the trees and the roots up there, because all the records of that time were lost when Firstbridge was destroyed. All we know is that the people were getting eaten up by the beasts, so the Firstbridgers came down into the chasm and built a bridge. Firstbridge. It wasn't far enough down, and the beasts got at it, so the survivors came down further to Nextdown while they built Topbridge. You can see Firstbridge if you look, way up against the light. We call it Brokenbridge sometimes. There isn't much left of it but the mainroots and a few dangling verticals. When my cousin Highclimb went to the rim, she saw it. She says the mainroots are still alive.''

''Ah. Humm. Are there any – ah – Gamesmen, among you?''

''Gamesmen? You mean people who play games? Children do, of course. There are gambling games, too. Is that what you mean?''

''Are there any among you who can change shape? Who can fly? Who can lift things without using their hands?''

''Demons, you mean. No. There's a story that before we came down into the chasm, there were Demons or something like that over the sea. We used to trade with them in the story, but it's only a story. According to the story, we came to this world before they did. When we came, the animals weren't so bad, so we lived on top. Then, later, the animals got bad. That's when we moved down.''

''All of you? All the persons this side of the sea?''

Beedie shook her head and winced. ''I don't know. I don't think anyone knows. We keep hearing stories about lost bridges or lost castes. People who survived some other way. Aunt Six says it's all myths, but I don't really know. Do you still want to hear more about the chasm?''

''I didn't mean to interrupt. It was just a thought. Yes, go on.''

''Well, let's see. After Topbridge was built, they finished Nextdown. Then the Potters built their bridge down-chasm, because there were clay deposits in the wall along there, and coal. They use that for the firing. Then came Miner's bridge, further down-chasm, because that's where the mines were. Metal, you know. And gems for the saws, though they don't seem to find many of those. . . .

''Then Midwall, up-chasm, the other side of Nextdown, then Harvester's bridge, away down-chasm where it bends, and last of all came Bottommost. Aunt Six says Bottommost is rebels and anarchists, but then she talks like that about a lot of things. I think it's Fishers, mostly, and Hunters, and some Crafters, and Banders and casteless types.'' She stopped to take a deep breath before continuing, gasping. Her ribs cut into her like knives. The arms around her tightened, then pillowed her more deeply.

''Tell me about castes. What are they?''

''Top caste is Bridgers. They're the ones who build the bridgetowns and maintain them and build the stairs and locate the water-bellies and all that. Then there are Crafters, who make things out of wood, mostly, though they use some metal, too. And Potters, and Porters, and Miners, and Teachers. And Harvesters. They train the slow-girules to harvest the nodules from the roots, and they harvest the wall moss, and fruits from the vines and all like that. And the Messengers. They have two jobs to do. We don't talk about one of them. The other – well, they fly. Not how you meant it when you asked. They put on wings, and then they jump out into the air when it rises, and they fly between the bridgetowns with messages or little things they can carry. Medicine, maybe. Or plans, to show the Bridger in the other city what's going on. Maintainers. They're the ones who take care of the Bridgers, feed them, clean their houses and all. Birders I already told you about. Then there are the Fishers, two kinds of those, one that fishes for floppers from the Fishers' roosts and those who drop their lines from Bottommost into the river down there, so far they can't even see it, and bring up fishes. And the Hunters who track game through the root mat. . . .'' She stopped, exhausted.

''And you said something about casteless ones?''

Beedie sighed, weary beyond belief. "There are always some who don't fit in. Weavers – did I mention Weavers before? – who can't weave. Or Potters who can't do a pot. Or even Bridger children who get the down-dizzies when they look down. They may get adopted into some other caste, or they may ask to become Maintainers – some say Maintainers will take anybody, though I don't know if that's true – or they may just stay casteless. It's all right. No one hates them for it or anything. It's just that they don't have any caste house to live in or any special group to help them or take them in if they're sick or old or have a baby."

"Do people marry?"

"Oh, yes. In caste, usually, though not always. They say if you marry in caste, your kids will have the right aptitudes. That isn't true, by the way. Aunt Six says it never was true. She says having a child is like betting on a flopper's flight. They always go off in some direction you don't count on."

"What are caste houses?"

"Oh, like Bridgers House on Topbridge. Whenever there are enough of any one caste on one bridge, they build a caste house. Usually the elders of the caste live there, and any other caste members there's room for. One elder from each castehouse makes up the bridge council, though we usually just say 'the elders,' and they decide when to expand the bridgetown or build new stairs or pipe a new water-belly. I don't know what else to tell you. Except I hurt. Please let me stop talking."

"Just a moment more, sausage girl. What about clothing? Do the castes dress differently?"

Beedie could not understand the question. She tried to focus on the question and could not. Dress? How did they dress? "Like me," she whispered. "More or less. Trousers. Shirt. Only Bridgers wear belts like this. Harvesters wear leather aprons. Potters have very clean hands. Miners have dirty ones. . . . I can't . . . can't . . ." There was only a heavy darkness around her, a sense of vast movement, easy as flying, as though she were cushioned in some enormous, flying lap. Then there were voices.

"Are you her Aunt Six? The root she was working on . . . burning . . . the smoke . . . don't think she's seriously hurt . . . from Harvester's Bridge myself . . . just happened to see her as I was coming up the stairs . . . thank you, very kind of you. Yes, I would be glad to do that. Boneman, you say? In the yellow house next to Bridgers'? Never mind, ma'am, I'll find it. . . ."

Inside the darkness, Beedie felt herself amused. The bird/woman/person was leading Aunt Six about by the nose, pretending to be a Harvester from Harvester's Bridge. Beedie was enjoying it, even through the black curtain. It was very humorous. They had sent for the Boneman, to find out if anything was broken. So, she was home, home on Topbridge, in Aunt Six's new place. Now that she knew where she was, she could let the darkness have its own way. Though the voices went on, she stopped listening to them.

There seemed to be no next day, though there was a day after that. She swam lazily out of quiet into the light, feeling hands holding her head and the rim of a cup at her lips once more. This made her laugh, and she choked on the broth Aunt Six was trying to feed her, then couldn't explain what the laughter was about.

"Lucky you were, girl, that a doer-good came along just then. I was in little mood to trust any Harvester, as you can imagine, seeing what an arrogant bunch they are, as you well remember from just a few days ago. But this one, well, she told me someone had fired the root. . . .

"I sent the elders. They saw no sign of it, except the smell of smoke clinging. Greenwood smoke does cling, so they don't doubt the story at all, or the word of the doer-good, Mavin, her name is. I suppose you wouldn't remember that, being gone to all intents and meanings from that time to this." Aunt Six used her handkerchief, blowing a resounding blast. "A bad thing to take almost a whole family that way, your daddy and mother, all the uncles, then to try it with you, girl." The pillow was patted relentlessly into a hard, uncomfortable shape. "We can't imagine who. Who would it be?"

For some reason, all Beedie could think of was that phlegmy chuckle of old Slysaw Bander, the sneering eyes of Byle Bander, the two of them like as root hairs. Making mischief. But why? Why? Why would even a Bander do hurt to his own caste? What could he gain from it? How did he know I'd be going down there alone?

"Well, fool girl," a voice inside her head said, "He knew no such thing. He thought there'd be six or seven Bridgers, including a few elders." Then her head swam and accusations fled through it like birds through air. He must have thought he'd take six away with the root . . . the way he did before . . . the way he did before . . . the way he did before.

Gradually her mind slowed and quieted. Well, if it hadn't been for the doer-good, one Bridger would have fallen to the Bottom, but there could be no proof it had been planned or who by. Byle had probably been companied by five or six Bridgers all day, including at least one or two Chafers or Beeds. No proof. No proof, and all a waste, for the trap hadn't killed six, hadn't even killed one. Was that why Byle was so eager to get away from Bridgers House last night? To get someone else to set the fire he had planned to set himself?

Could she accuse him? Them? Byle hadn't had a chance to set that fire, so someone else had. Who? Slicksaw and her friends, while they were down there checking her measure? No. Too early to set it then, though they may well have made ready for it. And if so, was it a general thing, then? A conspiracy among all the Banders? To accomplish what? To kill Bridgers, evidently, but why?

Dizzy from the unanswerable questions in her mind, Beedie drifted off into gray nothing again, unable even to be curious about Mavin, the person/bird/woman who might be doing anything at all while Beedie slept.

She awoke to find a leather-aproned Harvester sitting in the window, the Harvester sipping at a cup while reading one of Aunt Six's books about religion; the steam from the tea curled over the lamp beside the bed. At first Beedie did not recognize the woman, but then something in the tilt of head said bird/person/creature, and Beedie smiled. "Good morning."

Mavin put down the tea cup and turned to pour another, offering it to the swaddled figure on the bed. "Say 'good evening,' sausage girl. You've spent a good time muffled up there, recovering from your wounds, I thought, but then, hearing your Aunty Six talk for a time, I figured it was only to escape the constant conversation."

Beedie tried to laugh, turning it into a gasp as her ribs creaked and knifed at her. "I don't think I'm better."

"Oh, yes. You've got a few cracked ribs where you hit the mainroot with the side of your ownself. The Boneman strapped them. He says they'll heal. You've got a nasty blue spot on your forehead spoiling your maidenly beauty. The Skin-woman put a foul-smelling poultice on that. Aside from that, there's not much wrong with you a few days lying about won't cure. Meantime, I've met the people at your Bridgers House and been thanked by them for saving you. There's been a good deal of climbing up and down as well, trying to figure out what set the roof afire – or maybe *who* set it afire. Far as I can learn, no one knows for sure, though there seem to be whispered suspicions floating here and there. Your Bridger elder, Rootweaver, says I have a strange accent and must come from the farthest end of Harvesters where no one talks in a civilised manner, but she was kind enough for all that."

"Rootweaver is a good person."

"True. She is such a good person I told her some of the things I had seen 'on my way up from Harvesters.' To which she replied by trading confidences, telling me that something seems to be eating the verticals of the bridgetowns. Killing them dead, so she says. Giving me a keen look while she told me, too, as though she thought I might have been eating them myself. Had you heard about that?"

"Something of the kind," murmured Beedie. "The Bridgers are very upset about it."

"Indeed? Well, I heard her out. Since then, I have waited for you to recover so that you can take me to see the greatest wonder of Topbridge."

"And what's that, Mavin doer-good?"

"Doer-good, am I? Well, perhaps I am. The wonder I speak of is the birdwoman, sausage girl. I'd rather visit her with someone discreet by my side. Someone who knows more than she says. That is, unless your praiseworthy silence results from inability to talk rather than discretion."

"Oh, I can talk," Beedie said, proving it. "But when there are strangenesses all about, better maybe to keep shut and wait until talk is needed. My father used to say that."

"Pity he didn't tell your Aunt Six. Why was she named Six, anyhow?"

"She was named Six because when she was a girl, she always insisted on carrying six spare straps for her spurs. Not four, nor five, but six. And if my father had tried to tell her anything, she wouldn't have listened. She would have been too busy talking. And" – she shifted uncomfortably – "I have to go."

"If you mean you have to *go*, the Boneman who looked at you said you could. Get up, I mean. Just take it easy, don't lift anything, don't bump yourself. Is there a privy in here?"

"Of course. Do you think we live like floppers?" Beedie struggled out of the bed and across the room, feeling the cold boards on her feet with a sense of relief. Until that moment she had not been sure she could stand up. She left the privy door ajar, letting the heat from the bedroom warm all of her but her bottom, poised bare over the privy hole, nothing but air all the way to the Bottom and all the night winds of the chasm blowing on her. "All the houses on all the bridges have privies. That's why we don't build bridges one under the other, and that's why we put roofs on the stairs."

When she returned to the bed, Mavin handed her a piece of paper and a pen. "Draw me a plan, girl. Looking end on, how are these bridges of yours arranged? How do we get from one to another supposing – as it would be wise for us to suppose – neither of us can fly?"

Beedie sipped at her tea, propped the paper against her knees and thought. Finally, she drew a little plan on the paper and handed it to Mavin. "There. These are the ends of the bridges. There's a stair from Topbridge to Nextdown. There are two stairs from Nextdown; one on down to Midwall, another winding one across under Topbridge to Potter's. From Potter's there's a stair down to Miner's; and from Miner's there's a stair up to Harvester's. Then, from Midwall, there's a stair down under Nextdown to Bottommost. There are rest places on that stair, and from Bottommost there's a long stair which leads along the Wall to mine entrances way below Miner's and then goes on and meets the Harvester's trail way below Harvester's. Some of these stairs are at the morning-light end, and some at the evening-light end of the bridgetowns, so it can be a long walk between Potter's and Topbridge. That's why we have messengers, if word needs to be carried quickly on wings. There's one hot spot right below us, off the edge of Topbridge."

"Hot spot?"

"Where the air rises, where the Messengers fly. Remember, I told you. There are other hot spots here and there, every bridge has at least one close by. There's a big one near Harvester's, around the corner of the chasm. No one knows what causes hot spots, though some of the old books say it's probably hot springs, water that comes out of the ground hot."

"And you've never been to any of these places?"

"I was born on Nextdown. And I came here. And that's all."

"Ah. Well, if I go journeying while I'm here, perhaps you'd like to go along? But first, you'll sleep some more and recover entirely. I hear your aunt coming. Time for me to get along to Harvesters House. . . ."

"They took you in then, at Harvesters House?" Beedie whispered.

"Why shouldn't they? I'm a Harvester, aren't I? I work well with the slow-girules, don't I? Besides, you can tell by my apron." And Mavin winked at her, making a droll face, strolling out of the room and away.

"A very pleasant doer-good," said Aunt Six. "Well spoken and kindly. You're a lucky girl, Beedie, to have had such a one climbing the stairs from Nextdown just at the time you needed help. And one not afraid Of root climbing, either. What if it had been a Potter? Or a Miner? Not able to climb at all for the down-dizziness in their heads?"

"I'm very lucky," Beedie agreed, saying nothing at all more than that.

By afternoon of the third day from then, her ribs rebandaged by the Boneman, she was able to visit the Skin-woman who lived just off center lane, midchasm, by the market, in order to have another poultice put on her forehead. A train of Porters had brought in a great load of pots from Potter's bridge, and the Topbridgers were out in numbers, bargaining in a great gabble for cook pots and storage pots and soup bowls. Mavin and Beedie walked among the stalls, half hearing it all, while they spoke of the birdwoman at Birders House.

"Of course they'll let you see her!" said Beedie. "As a messenger of the Boundless, she can be seen by anyone, for any person might be sent a message from the Boundless, and the Birders wouldn't know who."

"I've been in places they would tell you they did know," said Mavin in a dry voice. "And tell you what the message was, as extra."

"Why, how could anyone know? Would the Boundless give someone else my message to tell me? Silly. Of course not. If the Boundless had a message for me – which I am too unimportant to expect, mind you – it would give it directly to me, no fiddling about through other people."

Mavin laughed. "There are things about your society here that I like, girl. Your good sense about your religion is one of them."

Beedie shook her head in confusion. "If a religion doesn't make sense, what good is it? It has to make sense out of things to be helpful, and if it isn't helpful, who'd have it?''

"You'd be surprised, sausage girl. Very surprised. But here we are. Isn't this Birders?'' They had stopped outside a tall, narrow house which reached up along the Wall, its corners and roof erupting in bird houses and cotes, its stairs littered with feathers and droppings, and with an open, latticed window just before them behind which a pale figure sat, smiling heedlessly and combing its long dark hair.

"Aree, aree,'' it sang. "The boundless sea, the white wave, the light wave, the soundless sea.''

"Can we get closer?'' asked Mavin in a strange, tense tone. "Where she can see us?''

"We can go in,'' Beedie answered. "We'll have to make an offering, but it won't be much. I'll tell them you have confusions and need to be blessed by the messenger.''

"You do that, sausage girl. For it's true enough, come to think of it.''

They went up the shallow stairs to the stoop and struck the bell with their hands, making it throb into the quiet of the street. A Birder came to the door, his blue gown and green stole making tall stripes of color against the dark interior. When Beedie explained, he beckoned them in.

I'm Birder Brightfeather,'' he said, nodding to Beedie. "I know you, Bridger, and your parents before you. Though that was on Next-down, and I am only recently come to Topbridge to help in the House here, for young Mercald was no longer able to handle the press of visitors. Will you offer to the Boundless before seeing the messenger?''

"If we may,'' answered Mavin easily, moving her hand from pcoket to Birder's hand in one practiced gesture. The Birder seemed pleased at whatever it was he had been given.

"Of course. Go in. Stay behind the railing, please. She becomes frightened if people come too close. If you have a question, ask in a clear voice, and don't go on and on about it. The Boundless knows. We don't have to explain things to It. Then if there's an answer, the birdgirl will sing it. Or perhaps not. The Boundless does not always choose to answer, but then you know that.'' The Birder waved them into the room, through heavy drapes that shut away the rest of the House. They found themselves behind a waist-high barrier, the birdgirl seated before them, half turned away as she peered out through the lattice at the street, still singing as she combed her hair.

"No sorrow, tomorrow, tomorrow go free, to high flight, to sky flight, the boundless sea."

"Handbright," said Mavin, in a husky whisper. "Handbright. It's Mavin."

"Aree, aree," sang the birdgirl, slowly turning her head so that she could see them where they stood. She was dressed in a soft green robe, the color of the noonglow, with ribbons of blue and silver in her hair. Her face was bony, narrow, like the face of a bird. She looked like something out of the old tales, thought Beedie, something remote and marvelously beautiful, too wonderful to be human. And yet, this Mavin spoke to her. . . .

"Handbright. Sister. See, it's Mavin. Come all the way from the lands of the True Game, all the great way from Danderbat Keep, from Schlaizy Noithn, from cliffbound Landizot and the marshy meadows of Mip, over the boundless sea to find you. It's been more than fifteen years, Handbright, and I was only fifteen when you saw me last."

"No sorrow, no sorrow, the soundless sea," sang the birdgirl, her eyes passing across them as though they did not exist. "Aree, aree." She stood up and moved about the room behind the railing, around her chair, half dancing, her feet making little patterns on the floor. Then she sat back down, but not before Mavin had seen the way the soft gown fell around her figure, no longer as painfully thin as it had been when Mavin had seen her last, no longer slender at all. Her belly bulged hugely above the thin legs.

"Ah," said Mavin, in a hurt tone. "So that's the way of it. Too late for you, Handbright. So late." She stood in a reverie, seeing in her head the great white bird, plumes floating from its wings and tail, as it dived from the tower of Danderbat Keep, as its wings caught the wind and it beat itself upward into the blue, the high blue; a colour which these people of the chasm never saw, preserved only in these ribbons, in the ritual garments of their Birders. She saw herself, pursuing, asking here, there, high on the bounding cliffs of Schlaizy Noithn; among the seashore cities of fishermen who wore fishskin trousers and oiled ringlets; in Landizot, the childless town; high in the marshy mountain lands near Breem; among the boats of the hunter fleet which never came to land but plied from Summer Sea to Winter Sea, its children born to the creak of wood and the rattle of sheets; along the desert shore of this other land beyond the Western Sea, where there were no Games nor Gamesmen, coming at last to this people living pale and deep, beyond the light of the fructifying sun; fifteen years spent in searching, asking, following. "Well, I have found you at last, sister," she said to herself. "And your face is as peaceful as a candle flame in still air, burning with its own heat, consuming itself quietly, caring not. You sing and your voice is happy. You dance, and your feet are shod in silk. Oh, Handbright, why do I need to weep for you?"

She turned to take Beedie by the arm, her strong hands making pits in the girl's flesh so that she gasped. "Sorry, sausage girl. It is a sad thing to come too late. Ah well, let's go back to your place, my dear, and drink something warming. I feel all cold, like all the chasm night winds were blowing through me."

"What is it, Mavin? Why are you so upset? Do you know her? Is she truly your sister?"

"She is truly my sister, girl. Truly as ever was. I was fifteen when she left, when I told her to leave, but she is my sister, my Shifter sister, mad as any madman I have ever seen, and pregnant as any mother has ever been. And if I understand your religion, my dear, and the respect that would be due to a messenger of the Boundless, the fact that my sister will bear now – though she did not bear in years past, to her sorrow – bodes ill for the Birders. And, sausage girl, from what I have seen traveling the width of the world for fifteen years, when a thing bodes ill for the religion of a place, trouble follows, and anarchy and rebellion and terror." Her voice rang like a warning bell, insistent and troubling.

Beedie trembled at her tone. "Oh . . . surely, surely it is not such a great thing. . . ."

"Perhaps not. We will hope so. But I think best to consider it, nonetheless. There is time to be tricksy, child, and best to have plans made before needs must." She smiled and laid a hand gently on the girl's shoulder. Strange, to have come so far and made such an odd alliance at the end of it all. "Tush. Don't frown. We will think on it together." And she squeezed Beedie's shoulder in a gesture which, had she known it, was one Beedie's father had once used and thus won the girl to her as no words could have done.

CHAPTER THREE

Trouble came more quickly than Mavin had foreseen, more quickly than Beedie would have thought possible. It was the following morning that they left Beedie's house on their way to take a breakfast cup of tea at one of the ubiquitous stalls, when they saw a Birder – not a person they would have recognized except for her robes – fleeing with loud cries of alarm from a group of youngsters intent upon doing her some immediate harm. The expressions on their snarling faces left no doubt, and when Mavin and Beedie came among them like vengeful furies, pushing and tossing them about like so many woodchips, they responded with self-righteous howls. "They're blasphemers, the Birders. . . . They've blasphemed the Boundless . . . else she's no messenger . . . need to be taught a lesson. . . . My dad says they should be whipped." Indeed, one of the leaders of the child pack had a whip with him.

"And who are you to be judge of the Birders? And what have they done that is blasphemous?" Mavin demanded in a voice of thunder, drawing a good deal of attention from passers-by, including the parents of some of those cowering before her who shifted uneasily from foot to foot wondering how far they might go in interfering with this angry stranger. Beedie, throwing quick looks around, was horrified to note that a good part of the child pack was made up of Bridgers – Bander whelps – as good a guarantee as any that they might go about their evil business without being called to account for it.

"My dad says . . . no fit judges for us anymore . . . did a bad thing. . . . Either that or she's no messenger. . . ."

Mavin seized the speaker and shook him. "Before you decide to run a mob behind you, boy, better wonder what vengeance the Birders might take if you are wrong! Have you thought what may come from the Boundless as messenger . . . to you . . . in the dark night . . . with no mob about to protect you?'' Her voice shivered like a maddened thing; wild-eyed, her hands shook as though in terror. The boy began to tremble in her grasp, eyes widening, until he broke from her to fall on his knees, bellowing his fear. Beedie was amazed. Anyone within reach of Mavin's voice could feel the terror, the awfulness of that messenger who might come. The boy took his fear from her pretended feeling, cowering away as though she had threatened him with immediate destruction. The adults gathered about were no less affected, and several of the young ones were hauled away by parents abruptly concerned for their own welfare though they had been egging the children on until that moment.

The other whelps ran off down an alley, yelping as they went. Mavin spun the boy with the whip around, kicking him off after them, and wiped her hands in disgust. The Birder, who had paused at the turn of the street, returned to thank them.

''This riot and attack is all up and down the chasm,'' she said, still breathless. ''I came to warn the Birders House here on Topbridge, for our house on Nextdown is virtually under seige, and no sooner set foot upon the street than that gang attacked me. They were set on me! I saw their fathers or older brothers urging them on from a teahouse door.''

''You'd best let us take you to the Birders House,'' ventured Beedie.

''You'd best stay there when you arrive,'' Mavin instructed her. ''There is a kind of animal frenzy can be whipped up sometimes among fools and children, often using religion as an excuse for it. When it happens, it is wise to be elsewhere.''

They escorted the Birder to the House, much aware of gossiping groups falling silent as they passed, much aware of eyes at windows, of chunks of root thrown at them and easily fended off by either Mavin or Beedie, who walked virtually back to back in protection of the robed woman. Once at the Birders House, Mavin asked for Mercald and learned that he had been sent to the far end of Topbridge to gather the shed plumes of gongbirds, used by the Birders in their rituals. ''He will return momentarily,'' dithered Brightfeather. ''I told him to set his robes aside and go. With all this confusion and the violence outside, I wanted some time alone, to think. I don't understand what is happening.''

''Violence outside?'' The newly arrived Birder was peering from the window. They could see no sign of trouble, but the Birder assured them there were small groups of ill doers lurking just out of sight.

This was confirmed as they came from the house after the visit. They encountered a group of Topbridgers skulking just inside an alleyway, keeping watch upon the Birders House.

"There's some. Ask'm" muttered one of the loiterers, thrusting another out of the alley at them. "Ask'm whether it's true. She's puff-belly, right? Ask'm."

" 'Ja see the birdgirl?" panted the thrustee. "There's some saying she's swole. Been havin' at her, those Birders, some say. Mercald's had atter. 'Ja see her?"

Beedie started to say something indignant, but the pressure from Mavin's hand stayed her. "Oh, I have indeed," said Mavin. "There are three schools of thought, good people, among those from Harvesters. One school teaches that the birdwoman was pregnant when she came to us, but a long pregnancy of a strange, messengerial kind, and that it is the desire of the Boundless that we foster her child. Then another opinion teaches that she became pregnant sometime after she came, and that it will be her child who carries the message from the Boundless. And a third opinion teaches that it was the intention of the Boundless she become pregnant, but only to illustrate that the holy and the human are of like kind. Be wary, people, for we do not yet know the truth of this, and it would not be wise to anger the Boundless." And Mavin fixed them with eyes which seemed to glow with a mysterious fire even as she, herself, seemed to grow taller and more marvelous. It was less overt than the technique she had used upon the youths, but it worked no less well. The men stopped muttering and merely gazed at her, their mouths gaped wide like that of the puffed fish lantern above them, working over the phrases they had rehearsed, now impotent to arouse themselves with their litany of hate. When they had thus gazed for a little time, Mavin brought them back to the present. "You might ask," she said in a voice of portentous meaning, "among your acquaintancnes, which of these theories they subscribe to. Which, for example, do you yourselves believe? You may be held accountable for your belief."

There was a muttering, a scuttling, and the two of them were quite suddenly alone.

"I'd love to know where you learned to do that with your voice," Beedie said. "Where you learned to do that trick you did earlier, with the boys, and this one, with these fellows. It's in your eyes and your face. Suddenly they forget what they were about to do. They get real worried about themselves. You'd been planning that, hadn't you? You were ready for those brats, for these folk. You knew they'd been put up to that talk." Then, in a voice of sudden revulsion, "Someone's been stirring a vat of chasm air about the Birders."

"Oh, assuredly they'd been put up to it. But I've given them other matter to chatter on. The interesting part of it is, who did it? Who blamed the Birders right off? Who blamed Mercald? And why?"

"To prevent the Birder caste being raised," she answered, sure of it. "Though why it should matter to them, I cannot tell."

"Ah. Tell me, Beedie, what is this lantern we stand under, and why have I not seen them before?"

"Because there aren't many of them, Mavin," she replied, confused at this change of subject. "Most of them are very old and rare. They come from the Bottomlands. Fishers catch them sometimes. They glow, you see. The Fishers take out the insides and blow up the skin, then when it's dark, the skin glows. The fishers say there are many glowing things deep in the chasm. These are about the only one they can catch, however."

"Interesting. It glows. You know, root dangler, the bottom of your chasm is a wonderful and mysterious place, wonderfully attractive to such an adventurer as I."

"I told you before, it's dangerous down there, Mavin."

"I think it's going to get dangerous up here, girl. Now use your head to help me think. Why would anyone not want another caste raised up? You told me that the Bridgers were top caste. What does that mean in simple language?"

"Simple language is all I have," she said with some dignity. "It means the eldest Bridger is the head of the chasm council."

"That's all?"

"That's enough. Head of the chasm council can do almost anything. The head can decide to build a new bridgetown. Or send off an expedition. Or assess new taxes. Or get up an army, not that we've ever needed one since we came down from Firstbridge. Or assign duties to a caste, or take duties away."

"All by himself, he can do this?"

"Or herself, yes. Not that they do go off all on their own like that. Mostly they're quiet kinds who do a lot of talk before they decide anything. You've met Rootweaver. Likely, she'll be next head of council. Her cousin, old Quickaxe, is head now, but he's getting very feeble. Either he'll resign or he'll die or become so ill the council will declare him honorably dis-casted."

"And how old is Rootweaver?"

"How old? I haven't any idea."

"How old is – oh, the Bander from Nextdown, Byle's daddy, Slysaw?"

"Almost as old as Rootweaver, I suppose."

"So, if Rootweaver died, and maybe a few others younger than she but older than Slysaw, who would be the eldest Bridger in the whole chasm? Hmmm, girl?" Mavin paused, smiling dangerously while Beedie considered this. "And you think the bottom would be dangerous, do you? I'll tell you, nothing is so dangerous as ambition in a man who cares not who stands in his way."

"Slysaw Bander? Oh, the day he became eldest Bridger is the day we would all change caste. It's disgusting! No one would have him."

"Oh, girl, girl. So speaks the naivete of youth. Why, I have seen such tyrants as you would not believe cheered and carried on the shoulders of their countrymen in that same frenzy the boys were whipped up to this morning. I'll wager you, girl, you'll find some in the teashops today who are talking of Slysaw, telling of his generosity, and what good ideas he has, and how much things would be improved if he were eldest Bridger. I'll wager there are casteless ones and bitty members of this caste and that one, including more than a few Bridgers, probably, all with sudden coin in their pockets and free time to talk endlessly, all talking of Slysaw Bridger and what a fine fellow he is."

Beedie, who had learned something about Mavin in the last day or so, said, "You'll wager what they're saying in the teashops because you've heard them."

"Right first time, sausage girl. There seem to be many visitors from Nextdown in your bridgetown, more than I can figure why they've come. They seem to have no business but talk. But they are talking, endlessly."

"But why – I still can't figure why, Mavin. If old Slysaw lit the fire that killed my daddy and mother, well, I'll believe anything of him including he's a devil. But I can't figure why."

"Because there's power to be had, girl. I'll tell you a tale, now.

Suppose these talkers go to the teashop and go on with their talking, fuming and blowing, saying how terrible it is what the Birders have done, maybe how terrible it is what the birdgirl has done. . . ."

"Maybe saying she's no messenger from the Boundless at all?"

"Words like that. The sense of it doesn't matter much, so long as the sound is full of indignation and fire. So, they talk and talk, getting fierier and fierier, until at last some of them go to set matters right. How will they do that?"

"Bring Mercald and the Birders up before the judges."

"Ah. But it's Birders *are* your judges, girl, and Birders they claim are doing evil. So, what is it they'll cry then?"

"They'll cry the judges are corrupt; they'll say they'll have to do justice on their own. . . ."

"Right again. And their justice will mean killing someone, maybe Mercald, maybe half a dozen other Birders or all of them, maybe the birdwoman. . . ."

"Which you won't . . . you can't let happen," whispered Beedie, beginning to understand for the first time what a tricksy person sat beside her.

"Which I won't let happen. Meantime, there's confusion and threats and maybe a few little riots. You've got no kind of strong arms in this chasm except the Bridgers themselves, perhaps, and you'll have to forgive my saying it, girl, but they seem half asleep to what's going on."

"They've never – had to . . ."

"That's obvious. Well then, with all the confusion, this one and that one could get killed. And wouldn't it be strange if among those killed were a number of elderly Bridgers? And at the end of it strange that Slysaw Bridger would happen to be eldest Bridger in the chasm and thus head of council. And in the meantime, of course, everyone too upset and confused to wonder who fired the mainroot you almost died on."

"How could any Bridger do such a thing?" she demanded, white around her eyes, mouth drawn up into an expression of horror and distaste. "Even a Bander shouldn't be able to think of such things. I wouldn't have thought that, ever."

"Which is what he counts upon, sausage girl. He counts on no one believing ill of a fellow caste member. He counts on being able to sow distrust without being suspected of it or blamed for it. He cares nothing for the religion, so does not fear to meddle with it. He's no believer, that one. Else he wouldn't have trifled with a messenger of the Boundless."

"I thought she wasn't – that she was just your sister, Mavin. I'm all confused. . . ."

"She's my sister right enough. But who's to say what messengers the Boundless sends? Why not my sister?"

"Why not you?" asked Beedie, whispering.

"Ah. Why not me, indeed. Well, then, this messenger needs a word with your lady Rootweaver, and it's up to you to arrange it, Beedie. Arrange it quietly, and in a way no one will wonder at, for I've things to tell her and her fellows, things to ask of her as well, and I want no prying ears while I'm doing it."

"You're not going to tell them that you . . ."

"I'm not going to tell them anything except what any Harvester might have overheard, in a teashop, say. Or at a procession. And if you're asked, girl, you know nothing about anything at all except that I saved your skin on the mainroot one day as I came climbing up from Nextdown. That way, whatever I say, you know nothing about it."

"I could help you," Beedie pleaded.

"Not yet. Come necessary time, then yes, but not now. Just go along to Rootweaver, child, and give me the space of a few minutes to think what I'm going to say to her." She turned to lean on the railing of the bridge, leaning out a little to let the updraft bathe her face in its damp, cool movement, full of the scent of strange growths and pungent herbs. Behind her, Beedie dithered from foot to foot for a moment before moving off purposefully toward the Bridgers House. Mavin put her face in her hands, letting herself feel doubt and dismay she would not show before the girl. She felt disaster stirring in every breath of air and was not completely sure she could save Handbright, either her life or the life she carried.

Far out on a Fishing bridge, which jutted from the mainbridge like a broken branch, she saw a Fisher blowing into his flopper call, making a low honking that echoed back from some distant protrusion of the wall. He put the call away to stand quiet, flicking his line above his head in long, curled figures as a chorus of honks came from inside the root wall. Too quickly for the eyes to follow, a flopper dropped from the root wall, planing across the chasm on the skin stretched from forelegs to backlegs, folding up from time to time to drop like a plummet in the intermittent flops which gave the creatures their name, then opening the stretched skin to glide over the chasm depths once more. The fisher's line snapped out, the weighted hooks at the end of it gleaming in the evening light, missing the flopper by only an arm's breadth. Another flopper fell from the root wall, and this time the hook caught it firmly through the skin of its glider planes. The flopper honked, a long, dismal hoot into the dusk, and the Fisher began hauling in against the struggling weight.

"Caught," breathed Mavin. "Handbright, you dropped out of Danderbat Keep on wings, on wings, girl, and you've been hooked here in this chasm, the hook set so deep I may never get you loose." She fell silent, thinking about the technique she had used in diverting the mob of boys, the one she had used on the men. When had she learned to do that? And how? It seemed a long time past, a great distance gone.

There had been a town, she remembered, along the coast north of Schlaizy Noithn, separated from the world of the True Game by high cliffs and from the sea by a curving wall of stone around a placid harbor, such a wall as might have resulted from the inundation of some ancient fire mountain. The people of that town had called it Landizot. She came there seeking Handbright and the company of humankind but found a people hesitant and wary, uneasy with strangers and as uneasy among themselves. Yes, they said, there had been a white bird high upon the cliffs – those they called the dawn wall – earlier in the year. The young people had pursued it there, setting nets for it, mimicking its call in an effort to entice it down, but the bird had avoided them easily, circling high above the cliffs in the light of early morning or at dusk, when it gleamed like silver against the mute purple of the sky.

When had it last been seen, Mavin asked, only to be confronted with shrugs and disclaimers. The children had not been allowed to play outside lately, she was told. Not for some time. So they had not seen it. No one went outside much, certainly not alone at dusk, and the bird had always avoided groups. Perhaps it was still there. Perhaps not.

Mavin decided to stay a while and look around for herself. When she asked why people no longer ventured from their locked houses with the barred windows and doors, she did so in that flat, incurious voice she had learned to use in her travels, one which evinced a polite interest but without sufficient avidity to stir concern among casual talkers.

"Because," she was told, "they have released the Wolf." The person who told her this glanced about with frightened eyes and would say nothing else. Stepping away from this encounter, Mavin looked into the faces of others to find both fear and anger there.

When she enquired, they said they were not Gamesmen, that they repudiated Gaming as a wicked thing, if indeed even a tenth of what was said about it was true. They did not want to be thought of as pawns, however. They were an ancient people, they said, with their own ways of doing things. Mavin smiled her traveler's smile, said nothing about herself at all, but made a habit of sitting about in the commons room of her inn at night, listening.

At first there was little conversation. The people who came there at the supper hour were the lone men and women of the town, those without family. They ate silently, drank silently, and many of them left once they had eaten so that the room was almost empty by dusk. As the evenings wore on, however, a few truculent men and a leathery woman or two found their way to the inn to drink wine or beer and huddle in the warmth of the fire. Mavin, with a laconic utterance, offered to buy drink for those present. Later in each evening that courtesy was returned. On the third or fourth night she sat near one old couple who, when the wine had bubbled its way through to their tongues, began to talk, not much, but some.

"Stranger woman, you'll stay here in the place after dark at night, won't you?"

"I'd planned on it," said Mavin.

"Don't go out at night. You're not young as most of the girls or children who've been et, but you're female, and the good Guardians witness the Wolf has eaten older."

Mavin thought about this for a while, not wanting to seem too interested. "Is that the same Wolf I'm told was let out?"

"There is no other," said the old woman. "And thanks be to all the Guardians for that."

"What had he done, to be locked up?" She kept her voice calm, almost uninterested, so the woman would not feel it would be troublesome to tell her.

"Killed a woman. Drank her blood. And after crying remorse

and swearing he would not do such a thing again."

"Oh," said Mavin. "Then the Wolf had been locked up before."

"Aye," responded the oldster. "Twice, now. First time he was young, the Wolf. There were those said young ones find society troublesome and strange, so it wouldn't do to set him down too hard for it. So, that time they locked him up for a season, no time at all."

"And the second time?" Mavin prompted.

"Well second time they locked him for a full year. A full year. That's a weary long time, they said. A full year. Tssh. Seems years go past like autumn birds to me, all in a flock, so fast you can't see them clear. But then, I'm old."

"So they've let him out?" Mavin prompted again.

"Well, the time they set for him was done. Since it's done, they let him out."

"The time seems very short. For one who ate a young woman and drank her blood."

The oldsters shifted uncomfortably on their chairs, and Mavin changed the subject. Still, she thought a year seemed a very short time indeed.

When all had gone save the innkeeper himself, she yawned her way past him on the stairs, remarking as she did so that the two oldsters had seemed upset at the short confinement of the Wolf.

"Those two," snorted the innkeeper, wiping his hands on his protruding, apron-covered belly. "They're among those howling loudest at the cost of it. Wolf isn't eating them, they say, so why should they want to pay for it?"

"Pay for what?" asked Mavin, unable to keep the curiosity out of her voice.

"Pay to keep him locked up, woman! You think it comes free?" And he snorted his way to his rest, shaking his head up all three flights of stairs, calling back down to her, "Tell truth, though. They've got nothing. It's all they can do to keep their own hovel warm without buying firewood for the Wolf."

Next day Mavin had strolled about the town, seeking among the children for any who might have seen the white bird. In her walk she passed the prison lately vacated by the wolf. Though it looked like a dreary place, it had every comfort in it of warmth and food and drink and soft mattresses and a shelf of amusements and a place to run in for exercise. Seeing it, Mavin well knew it had cost treasure to keep it, for the wood to burn to warm for it for a winter alone would have cost many days' labor, and the food many days' labor more, to say nothing of the guards who would have been needed night and day.

A number of children claimed to have seen the bird. One lovely girl of about ten years believed it had flown away south. Her name was Janine, called Janny, and she tagged after Mavin for the better part of five days, talking of the bird, the dawn cliffs, of life and the ways of the world while begging for stories of that world in return. The child was artless and delightful, full of ready laughter. Though Mavin had learned all there was to learn about the white bird, she put off her travels for a time out of simple joy in the girl's company.

One night there was a new face at the inn, a local preacher of Landizot, one Pastor Kyndle, whose house had been burned down by someone or something and would live at the inn while it was being rebuilt. Seeing Mavin was a stranger to the place, he set about making himself pleasant with the intent of converting her to the faith of Landizot and the Guardians. Talk turned, as it often did, to the Wolf.

"Why didn't they kill the Wolf when they caught him?" she asked. "Or, if they won't do that, why don't they lock the Wolf in a cage of iron here in the village square and let him shiver when the nights are cold. Surely he would be no colder than the corpses of the young women and children who lie in your burying ground?"

The pastor was much disturbed at this. "It would be cruel." he said. "Cruel to treat a person so. We are *good* people. Not cruel people."

Mavin shook her head, but withheld any judgment. If there was anything she had learned in long travels here and there, it was that to most people in the world, every unfamiliar thing was considered unacceptably strange. She told herself she was undoubtedly as odd to them as they were to her, and let the matter go. She determined to continue her search for Handbright as soon as the weather warmed only a little. She stopped asking questions and settled into the place, merely waiting for the snows to melt.

But before the thaw came a wicked murder of a young girl child of the town. Her body was found at the edge of the woods, dragged there by something. There was blood on the snow, and tracks of someone who had struck her down and drunk her blood. The tracks disappeared in the hard-packed ice of the road, however, and could lead them nowhere. The little girl was Janny, and Mavin learned of it with a cold horror which turned to fury.

That night in the inn were only murmurings and sideways glances, and more than once Mavin heard this one or that one speaking the Wolf's name. She expected before the night was over to hear he had been taken into confinement once more, but such was not to be.

He had not left the tavern, they said. He had been in his room drinking with his friends. All night. Never alone, not for a minute. His friends swore to it – Hog Boarfast, and Huggle, the brick-maker's son, and Hot Haialy, the son of Widow Haialy who had beggared herself trying to help him out of one scrape after the other.

"With them all night, was he?" murmured Mavin, controlling her voice with some difficulty.

"So they say."

"Trustworthy men, these? Those who say the Wolf was with them?"

"Well . . . there's no proof not. I mean, who's to say not?"

"Where did they get to know one another? The Wolf and these friends of his?"

"By the hundred devils, traveler, how would I know? All of 'em were born and raised here. Wolf, now, he came more lately, but I don't keep track of him. Most likely they got to know one another while they were locked up – all of 'em have been at one time or another. Or over the wine jugs at the Spotted Fustigar."

Mavin smiled a narrow smile and bought the man a drink. As days wore on, her fury did not abate. In a few days was another killing, and once more the three friends of the Wolf swore he had been with them in the tavern. Mavin had known this child, too – one like Janine, trusting, joyous, kind. The next day Mavin left town with some noise about it, saying she would return in a few day's time. Instead, she returned that evening in the guise of a wastrel youth who took a room at the Spotted Fustigar and bought drinks for all and sundry in the tavern. It took no time at all to be introduced to Hog, Huggle, and Hot, and when one met them, one met the Wolf.

He had yellow eyes, and a slanted smile. His eyebrows met over his nose, and he had a feral, soft-voiced charm which had the new young barmaid, who was scarcely more than a child herself, bemused and troubled before the evening was half done. Hog, Huggle, and Hot were youths of a type; one fat, one meaty, one lean, but all as ignorant of the world as day-old bunwits and covering that ignorance with noise. Mavin set herself to be agreeable – which no others in that place did – and before much had been drunk or more than a dozen disgusting stories told, Mavin too, was among the Wolf's close friends. During the fits of lewd laughter, Mavin had looked deep into the faces of the other friends of the Wolf to see the mindless excitements stirring there, gleaming in their eyes like rotten fish on tide flats.

Each day that passed there were fewer people on the streets, each night was closer locked and tighter fastened. The childlike barmaid seemed to stop breathing when the Wolf came near, yet she could not stay far from him. She was always within reach of his hands, always seeking his eyes with an open-lipped fascination. Mavin, watching, made angry, silent comments to herself.

Came an evening the Wolf said, "I'll be here all night tomorrow, won't I, Huddle?" He giggled, a high-pitched whine of excitement. "It's time for a good boozer, eh, Hog, all us good friends together, up in my rooms. Time for hooraw till the cock tries to get up and can't!"

There was a shifting, eager laughter among the three, in which Mavin joined beneath Wolf's speculative eyes. "I'll be back for it," she gasped from her wastrel's face, pretending drunken amusement. "Got to go to Fanthooly in the morning, but I'll be back before dark."

"What's of such interest in Fanthooly?" drawled the Wolf, his suspicious eyes burning in his face so that they seemed to whirl like little wheels of fire. The others hung on his words, ready to laugh or strike, as he bid.

"Old aunty with money, Wolf. Every year, money left me by dead daddy. She has it ready for me, same time, every year in Fanthooly." Mavin appeared too drunk to have invented this, and the four had been drinking at Mavin's expense for some days, so they laughed and believed, saying they would save a drink for him. Mavin, in her wastrel guise, set off in the direction of Fanthooly the following morning.

Only to return, under cover of the forest, entering Landizot once more at the first fall of dark.

She went to the alleyway behind the Spotted Fustigar. There was a door into an areaway in which the trash could be dumped, and if Mavin had read the signs aright, it was there the young barmaid would come, charmed as a bird is said to be charmed by a serpent. And she came, sneaking out without a lantern, wrapped tight in a thick shawl, face both eager and apprehensive. Mavin took hold of her from behind in a hard, unpleasant way which would leave her with a headache but do no other damage, then dragged her unconscious form into the stables. Shortly, the same shawl was in the areaway once more, wrapped around someone else.

The Wolf came there, as she had known he would.

He did not waste his time with words or kisses. The knife was in his hand when he took hold of her, and it stayed in his hand when she took hold of him.

Mavin had been curious about his eyes. She wanted to know if they would glow in that way if he were afraid, if he were terrified, if he knew he was about to die. She found he could not believe his own death – later she thought that might be why the deaths of so many others had meant nothing to him – so, she tried her voice to see whether she could convince him. After a time she caught the knack of it; by the end of it, the Wolf was truly convinced.

It was Hog who found him later that night, lying in his blood, yellow eyes filmed over and tongue protruding from between his slanted lips, the knife still in his hand.

In the morning, Mavin returned to Landizot as herself, full of tsks and oh-my's at the Wolf's sad end. She was questioned about the Wolf's death, as were others, but there was no proof. A stranger young man had been among the Wolf's friends, and it was thought he might have committed the deed except that he had been seen leaving for Fanthooly earlier that day.

As far as Mavin was concerned, the matter was done with. She could not restore Janine to life, but no other Janine would die. She was no longer angry, and she felt she had repaid whatever hospitality had been shown her.

One of the officials of the town came to Mavin afterward, however, with many suspicious questions and lectures on morality. Mavin was sure Pastor Kyndle had cast suspicion on her because of her views. She was sure of it when the official talked on and on about the Wolf's demise.

"Why?" he asked, attacking her, apropos of nothing.

"Why was he killed? Why, I suppose because he made a habit of killing others. Surely no one except himself expected him to do it forever?" Mavin asked it as a question, but it seemed only to agitate the man.

"We had no proof he was still killing. Perhaps it was someone else who was killing the women."

"Perhaps," Mavin shrugged.

"Whoever killed the Wolf had no right . . . " the official began.

"Explain to me again," asked Mavin, "because I am a stranger. Why was it you could not subject the Wolf to the cruelty of a cage? Why did you not simply kill him the first time? You had proof then."

"Because he is – was human."

"Indeed? how did you know that?"

"Why, because his mother was human, and his father."

"Ah. And is that all humanity is? To be born from others who appear human? What does it mean, humanity?"

"It means," said the official with some asperity, "that he was born in the ordinary way and therefore had a soul. We cannot subject someone with a soul to cruel or horrible punishment."

"Ah," said Mavin, cocking her head in a way she knew to be particularly infuriating. "And the young women and children he killed? Did they also have souls?"

"Of course."

"And by Landizot's failure to restrain the Wolf, were they not cruelly treated and horribly punished? Was your town not guilty, therefore, of a grievous and very cruel punishment of the innocent? Ah – I see from your face I have missed some subtlety and fail to understand. Forgive me. I am a stranger and quite stupid." By this time she was also very angry, for the man had begun to bluster and threaten.

Though she had intended to leave the town at the first thaw, the thaw came while she lingered near Landizot in a cave high upon the dawn wall. The town had acquired a new Wolf. She spent the next season and a half stealing all the children of that town up to the age of ten or so and carrying them away, far away, to be fostered in desmenes beyond the mountains, over the chasms in the world of the True Game. The people of Landizot were much upset, but they had no proof, so could do nothing. When she had taken all the children to the least, newest baby, she entinced the inhabitants

inhabitants of the town out onto the beach, then burned the town behind them, leaving them weeping upon the shore.

She appeared to them then, only that once, in the guise of a terrible, wonderful beast, using the voice she had learned to use in the alley with the Wolf. "I will teach you my teaching, people," she roared at them. "No man gets a man's soul by birth alone. That which behaves like a Wolf is a Wolf, no matter who bore him. I have judged you all and found you guilty of foolishness, and this is the punishment, that you shall walk shelterless and childless until you learn better sense."

After which she left them.

She remembered this now as she stood beside the rail on Topbridge, roiling with the same kind of fury she had felt in Landizot, seething with a hundred ideas for intervention, wondering how much of it she could justify to herself. She had been young then, only eighteen. Even so, she had not been able to excuse having been judge and executioner as a youthful prank. It had not been without consequence. There were still nights when she wakened from a dream of the Landizot children mourning that they would not see their people again. And yet, even so, she still believed they were better in the lands of the True Game, whatever might befall them, than in the town of Landizot beside the ancient sea. At least in the lands of the True Game, people who gambled with women's lives did not claim to do it out of morality.

In the last several days she had stood in the Birders House more than once, hands resting upon the railing, listening to the voice of Handbright singing. There was no sorrow in that voice, and it was that as much as anything that had stayed Mavin from precipitous action. She had not yet seen Mercald. With Beedie off talking to the Bridger elders, perhaps now would be time to do it, though Mavin dreaded it. When she thought of Handbright and her pregnancy, she could think of it only in terms of the abuses of Danderbat Keep, and her anger envisioned what the man would look like and how she would hate him.

In which she was wrong.

He was slight and pale as a boy, soft-spoken, mild as mother's milk, timidly diffident, stuttering, his fingers perpetually catching to twist on one another as a baby's do in the crib. He was dressed in the blue and green of the Birders, but on him it looked like festival dress, a child got up in costume, at once proud and shy, and his smile was a child's smile abruptly radiant. In that instant, Mavin knew she had been wrong and in what degree, for Mercald was like Mertyn, Handbright's younger brother and her own, Mertyn who had held Handbright in Danderbat Keep out of love long after she should have left it out of pain.

"You're Beedie's doer-good," he said breathlessly, holding out his hand, trembling in his desire to thank her. "We have all blessed the Boundless that you were there when needed to help her and save her."

"Yes," she said, changing her mind suddenly, as she sometimes did. "I am Beedie's doer-good. I am also the sister of the person you call the birdwoman. Her name is Handbright."

His skin turned white, then flushed, the hot blush mounting from his neck across his face to the tips of his ears, onto his scalp to glow through his light hair like the ruddy glow of a lamp. His hands went to his mouth, trembling there, and his eyes filled with tears. Mavin found herself wondering who had beat him as a child, why he felt this fear, finally deciding that it was merely an excess of conscience, an over-sufficiency of religious sensibility.

"Come" she said harshly. "If I can forgive you, surely the Boundless will do no less."

"Forgive . . ." he muttered in a pathetic attempt at dissimulation. "What . . . is there to forgive?"

"She's pregnant, Birder. Having seen you, I can tell you how and why and even when, mostlike. You didn't plan it, did you? Didn't even think of it. It was just that she had been here for some time, sometime weeping, and you held her, and then – well, whist, it happens. She didn't mind at all, no doubt."

"No," he wept. "I prayed forgiveness of the Boundless, so to have treated his messenger with such disrespect, but then as time went by, I thought perhaps it had been intended. Oh, but I am soiled beyond all cleansing. . . ."

"Nonsense," said Mavin impatiently. "You are silly beyond all belief, but that is your sole sin I am aware of, young man. I have no doubt that even now you do not know what trouble this will cause."

"I will be disgraced," he said in a sorrowful voice. "And it is right I should be."

"If that were all, we could possibly bear it with equanimity," she said, but there is more to it than that. There is a deal of riot and murder involved. Well. I have seen you, Mercald. Having seen you, I may not become angry with you, for I do not become angry with children."

He flushed again, this time offended.

"Ah," she thought. "so he is capable of anger. Well and good, Mercald." To him, aloud, she said, "Think, now, if you are disgraced, will you be disgraced alone?"

"It was my fault alone. No other Birder would . . ."

"Tush, boy. I wasn't talking of Brightfeather out there. I was speaking of *her*, Handbright. If you are disgraced, so will she be disgraced. If you are punished, so will she be punished. If you are put to death – as I have no doubt someone will try to do – then do you think they will not try it with her as well?"

His expression took on all the understanding she could have wished, horror and terror mixed. "But she is a messenger of the Boundless. They would not dare so offend the Boundless. . . ." Then he thought of this and his expression changed. She knew then that there was a functioning mind behind all the milky youth of him, for his eyes became suddenly aware and cold. "By the Boundless, but they would. Those piles of flopper excrement would try it, to discredit our judging of them. . . ."

Mavin smiled. "Who? Who are they, boy?"

He drew himself up, blazing. "I am not 'boy'. I am a Birder of the third degree, judge of the people of the chasm. I will examine mine own conscience, doer-good, if that is warranted, but I will not submit to disgrace which uses matters of conscience as a starting point for revolt. As to who they are, if you know so much, you know as well as I. The ones from Nextdown. Bridgers, mostly, though with casteless ones mixed in, and Porters and people from Bottommost."

"Led by whom?"

"I don't know. Nor why. But led by someone, I have no doubt."

"As to that, I can enlighten you. Which I will do, young judge, if you will come with me towards Bridgers House. Beedie has gone there to arrange a meeting with the Bridger elders – only those of Topbridge, mind you."

"It is customary for Bridgers to wait upon the Birder caste," he replied in a stiff voice, now growing accustomed to his anger and making use of it.

"Come off it, Birder. If the rebels have used Handbright's condition to discredit your caste, it was you who gave them the opportunity. Take off your robes. Put on something dark and inconspicuous, and we will walk outside the light of the lanterns. We are sneaking away to a secret meeting, not leading a procession of dignitaries." And she smiled at him, nodding toward the door to give him leave to go, listening throughout all this to the voice of Handbright behind her, threading endless chains of unstrung words with her song.

They left Handbright singing, making no attempt to guard her, Mavin doing so in the hope the skulkers had not been directed to start overt trouble so soon, and Mercald with the conviction that she was safe, would always be safe in a Birders House. Leaving dignity behind, they skulked down the twisty ways among the dwellings and shops, up and down half flights of stairs, out onto Fisher platforms and back again, staying out of the light of the lanterns away from the alley corner gapers and chatterers. They encountered Beedie only a little way from the Bridgers House.

"Rootweaver says she can meet with us in about an hour, Mavin. Mercald. You look very different without your robes. Was it you got Mavin's sister pregnant?"

He began the stuttering, fluttering, pale then red once more, only to be stopped in midflutter by Mavin's saying, "Of course he did, sausage girl. He's the only one innocent enough to have done it without realizing what a mess it would make. Don't tease him about it. He's troubled enough as is, and will be more when we finally figure out what needs to be done."

CHAPTER FOUR

The buildings of Topbridge burgeoned at the edges of the bridge like growing things, room atop room, lump on lump, anchored by fine nets of twig roots to the buildings below, connected across alleys by twisting, tendril-like flights of Fishers' roosts jutted like rude tongues from this general mass; every roomlet sprouted corbeled parapets; machicolations perforated the edges, allowing a constant shower of debris to float downward. The city was fringed with vertical roots which fell from the great supporting catenaries into the everlasting murk of the far-below, pumping life up into the mainroots and thus into the city. Along some of these verticals, new towers spun themselves in airy insubstantiality, a mere hinted framework of hair roots and a plank or two awaiting the day they would be strong enough to support a floor, a wall, a roof.

Water fell occasionally from the green leafy sky, a kind of sweet rain or sticky dew, and children ran about in it with their mouths open and tongues stuck out, whooping thier pleasure at the taste as their elders made faces of annoyance and wiped the dew from their hands with gestures of fastidious displeasure. Everyone wore fishskin hats on days like this, to keep the sticky rain from coating their hair, and all the awnings were put up, adding to the general appearance of haphazard efflorescence.

This clutter of room upon room, tiny balconies jutting over other such balconies, flat roofs forming the front porch of still other dwellings, all the higgledy piggledy disarrangement of the place gave way here and there to more open spaces, commons where market stalls surged at the foot of the surrounding structures, flapping with woven awnings and banners like a net full of fishes. Wide avenues ran the length of the bridgetown; narrower alleys twisted across it. Carts rumbled up and down, hawkers cried the flavour of tea, the strength of liquor, the fieriness of exotic spices from Midwall – culled from the parasitical vines which grew there and there alone. Harvesters stalked about vending quantities of root nodules from gaping sacks, or wall moss in bulk, as well as vine fruits, thickic herb, dried strips of net-caught flattree leaves and fifty other viands as strange and odd-smelling.

The favourite place for meetings, whether planned or spontaneous, was Midbridge Market, and the most favored of the stalls there was that of Tentibog the Teaman. There were those who said Tentibog traded with the pombis aloft, that nothing else would explain how he obtained herbs unobtainable by other men, at which Tentibog only laughed and talked of the quality of his water, procured at great expense from some distant, secrct water-belly. Whatever his secrets, his place was so crowded that it virtually assured anonymity. Anyone might be there, might meet anyone else, might engage in a moment's conversation or a morning's philosophical discussion without anyone else wondering at it or commenting upon it. So it was that Beedie and Mavin encountered Rootweaver there, and the three of them happened upon Mercald the Birder – dressed in simple trousers and shirt and unrecognizable therefore – and the four of them drank Noon Moment tea while deciding the fate of the chasm.

Rootweaver had ordered the third pot by the time Mavin had finished talking, Beedie marveling the while at the things she had said and had not said. "Because we are what we are, my sister and I," Mavin had emphasized, "does not mean we are not what you supposed my sister to be – a messenger of the Boundless. Indeed, by this time, I believe we are both such messengers, sent to help you out of a difficulty."

"Out of mere kindness, I suppose," Rootweaver had said, somewhat cool in manner.

"Oh, I think not. If the Boundless uses us as its messengers, surely it takes into account what will make us act. I am moved out of sympathy for my sister, whom I owe a debt. And out of regard for your people, who until now have treated her kindly."

Rootweaver toyed with her teacup, one of the Potters' best, circled with lines of rippling colour and pleasant to the touch. When she spoke at last, it was with some hesitation. She did not wish to offend Mavin, nor the Boundless, if it came to that, but she was acting eldest, and that carried certain imperatives. "Mavin – see, I call you by your name, thus offering a measure of friendship and trust – you ask that we take your . . . sister into Bridgers House. You make a persuasive case that her life is in danger where she is. No! You need not cite further incident. I am inclined to believe you. We are not so blind in Bridgers House we cannot see unrest or hear the result of manufactured demonstrations of discontent.

"So, well and good. But what would occur if this woman were taken into Bridgers House? Those responsible for rumor and riot would soon learn she is gone from Birders. They would seek her out. Our house is full of Maintainers and workmen who come and go. There is no locked room so remote that its existence might not become known if a search were going on. So on the one hand a woman will have disappeared, on the other hand there will be a locked room at Bridgers House. What will the rumormongers make of that?"

There was a lengthy silence. Beedie sighed, tapping the table with her own teacup. "She's right, Mavin. That wouldn't keep the birdwoman safe."

"Besides which," Rootweaver went on in her calm voice, "you give us no real reason to assist you in this way. We would be more sensible to disinvolve ourselves, to stand remote from this Bander-Birder conflict so that our own position would not be threatened."

"The Banders killed my family," Beedie burst out, in a barely suppressed whisper. "Tried to kill me . . ."

"Where is your proof? What proof do you have, child? A cough heard on the stair from Potter's bridge? A sneering look? Suspicious absences? A bit of harassment by officious Banders? Well, here is a judge. Tell me, Mercald, would you convict the Banders on this evidence?"

Mercald flushed, then turned pale. "I could not," he whispered. "As you know, Bridger."

"You see," said Rootweaver. "If we have no proof, we cannot take action against the Banders. We cannot even be sure to prevent what evil they may attempt in the future. Because we have not proof, we Beeds and Chafers must protect ourselves. We cannot openly ally ourselves with Birders who may fall into disrepute. We cannot have ourselves accused of blasphemy because we offer protection to a person alleged to be a false messenger, perhaps a servant of Demons. . . ."

"I have said Handbright means much to me. I cannot take her away with me until she is delivered of the child she carries. If she remains here, it is at peril to her life. And you say you will not help me?" Mavin spoke in that flat, incurious voice Beedie had heard before, an ominous voice in that it gave nothing away.

"I didn't say that," replied Rootweaver, pouring Mavin more tea. "I merely said that you asked a great deal and offered nothing much in return except information we were already aware of. Now – if you were willing to take on a job of work for us. . . ."

"Ah," said Mavin. "So now we come to it."

"We come to it indeed, if you wish. I have something in mind." Rootweaver leaned forward to speak softly, intently, making closed, imperative gestures with her fingers, hidden from others in the room by their huddled bodies. Mercald and Beedie listened with their mouths open.

Mavin feigned uninterest. When Rootweaver had done, however, she leaned back, stared at the ceiling for a time, then dried her hands on her trousers and held them out. "Done," she said. "Agreed. If you will keep Handbright safe."

"We can only try," the Bridger replied. "We may not succeed once it is known she lodges with us."

Mavin gave her one, brilliant smile. "I think we can improve her chances in that regard. It may not be necessary for anyone to know that the birdwoman is with you at all. And while we are at it, may we test to see if proof of our belief may be found?"

"You may test. You may not foment insurrection merely to see who falls into your mouth." Mercald said this firmly, without doubt, and Beedie gave him a surprised look. For all his milky youth, still he had some iron in him.

"Very well then," agreed Mavin. "Here is what we will do. . . ."

The following day, an hour or so before noonglow, a procession of Bridgers and Birders was seen to enter the marketplace, dressed in the full regalia of office, obviously on some portentous mission. The assembly of so many top caste persons was enough in itself to attract attention, and by the time the call for prayer cried silence upon Topbridge, there were people in every alley and every market stall, on every roof and balcony, waiting to see what would happen.

It was Rootweaver who mounted to the announcement block on the market floor at the very center of the commons, she who cried into the attentive quiet of the place. "People of Topbridge, I speak for the eldest Bridger, Quickaxe, head of chasm council, who is too feeble with age to attend upon you. I am next eldest, next in line to be head of chasm council. I am here to speak about disorder, for disorder has come to the chasm. There has been talk and dissention. A Birder has been assaulted – no, do not draw horrified breath. There is not one of you who did not know of it.

"As you all know, Mercald the Birder received a visitation from a messenger of the Boundless. This is a mystery. We do not understand why the messenger has come. Some, in their foolishness, have accused the Birders of ill doing. Others have gone so far as to question the validity of Birders' judgments, their place to judge at all.

"I come to you all with a message. Tomorrow, during noonglow, the messenger will depart Topbridge. It has come to lead a small group on a quest, toward a greater mystery than any we have spoken of. Mercald, the Birder, will attend upon that quest. Beed's daughter, Bridger, will attend upon it. The Maintainer Roges will attend upon the quest. They go to find the lost bridge. I invite you to witness the going forth.

"There will be no disorder! I serve notice here upon you all. If there is language unfitting the occasion, if there is unruly behaviour, if there is childish rebelliousness displayed, those responsible will be brought before swift judgment under chasm rule." Then there was indrawn breath from everyone present. Mavin had been prepared for that, and she heard it with satisfaction. Chasm rule allowed immediate execution of rebels against the order of the bridgetowns by tossing them into the chasm. Privately, she thought it a bit too good for the Banders – at least, those involved in the conspiracy, as she felt most of them probably were. From the corner where she stood, she watched faces, eyes, searching for the quick sideways glance, the covert whisper, the betraying signs of those who had plans that were upset by this announcement. There were many. Too many. Most of them casteless ones, but there were Bridgers among them, and Fishers, and a knot of belligerent–looking Harvesters. She shook her head. Proof! She had all the proof she needed.

"Ah, well. Much to do before the morrow. Much explanation, much preparation. Rumor must be spread in the market place concerning the treasures of the Lostbridgers. Beedie must be outfitted for travel, and Mercald, and the 'Tainer Roges. Beedie had not wanted him along, had become rather flushed about it, as a matter of fact, but Rootweaver had insisted. "Where a Bridger goes, a Maintainer goes, Beedie, and that's the rule. In times of danger, a Maintainer is a Bridger's spare eyes, a Bridger's spare nose."

"I can take care of myself," she had replied rebelliously. "I don't need Roges."

"If you will not accept him as a quest mate, then we must send some other Bridger," Rootweaver had replied. "We will not begin a holy quest by breaking the rules. You may be sure someone would notice, and it would throw doubt upon the whole endeavor."

"Rootweaver is right," Mavin had said. "Let be, Beedie. I've met Roges. He's strong, sensible, and seemingly devoted to you, though why he should be, I cannot tell you." At which Beedie had flushed bright red and shut up.

In the night, at the darkest time, a small group of people left Birders House unobserved, carrying something fairly heavy. They placed it in a cart with muffled wheels and took it along the main avenue. The avenue was much darker than usual, for all the lanterns had gone out simultaneously. This happened rarely, but it did happen. If anyone lay wakeful at that time to hear the muffled squeak of a wheel, no one remarked upon it at the time or later. At Bridgers House the cart was unloaded and those who had accompanied it dispersed into the dark. When morning came, there was no evidence of the trip. The cart was back behind Harvesters House from which it had been borrowed. The visiting Harvester, Mavin, who had enquired about the cart, had departed the evening before. There were those in the house sorry to see her go. She had been interested in everything, a good listener to all their tales, all their woes and dissatisfactions, and she had been remarkably good with the slow-girules, almost as though she understood their strange language. Two of the Harvesters, meeting over breakfast tea, remarked that it was sad she would miss the beginning of the quest which was to start at midday.

"Though she's probably on the stairs to Nextdown by now, and from there she'll probably see as much as we will. Likely more. With the crowd there'll be, likely we'll see nothing or less." Mavin preparing herself in the back room at Birders House, would have been amused.

Time moved toward noonglow. Mercald came out of the Birders House, together with Brightfeather and half a dozen others of the Birders, all in their robes and stoles, tall hats on their heads with feather plumes nodding at the tips. In their midst walked a birdwoman in her green dress, silver and blue ribbons flowing as she walked, calm and easy, humming her song in a quiet voice.

The woman who had once worn that dress now sat in a high, comfortable room at Bridgers House, guarded both day and night. She wore clothes of quite a different kind. Her hair had been cut and dyed. She did not resemble the birdwoman at all.

Anyone who went to the Birders House would find it empty; anyone who looked at the birdwoman in the procession saw that she was lean as a sideroot. There was murmuring, consternation in some quarters. How could one accuse the Birders of having interfered with a messenger of the Boundless when the messenger did not seem to have been interfered with? Byle Bander, watching from a convenient doorway, slipped inside the house to report to his dad.

"No sign at all, Dah. None. She was swole like a water-belly three days ago. I swear. Saw it myself. Not now, though."

"There's some can use herbs," said the old man in a dire voice. "We can give it out that they used herbs on her, made her lose it.'

"Ah, but Dah, those herbs come nigh to killing anyone who takes 'em. Everybody knows that. This one is healthy as anything. No sign she was ever sick, and there are those know she was swole three days ago.They're saying it's a miracle already on the street."

The man heaved himself up, face dark with fury.

"What are they up to, those Beeds, those Chafers? I ask you. What do they know?"

"Nothing, Dah. How could they?"

"Well it's strange, I tell you. All suddenly now, after doing nothing for days and days, the whole Bridger bunch is talking quest. Talking miracle. Talking to the Birders as though they was cousins. And you noticed how they go around? There's never a time they don't have a Maintainer within reach, knife in his belt, looking, looking. What are they suspecting?"

"Well . . . a lot of 'em have died, Dah. You can't expect they shouldn't notice."

"Accidents," said the old man, sneering. "All accidents. It's that Beeds daughter girl. She's come up from rootburn all full of fury, spreading stories."

"I haven't heard any, Dah. Swear I haven't."

"Well, hear it or not, it's her, I'll tell you. Come up on the roof, boy. We'll see what they're about."

Outside, the procession moved into the commons. The birdwoman moved toward the railing to stand framed by two verticals, posed, all soft as feathers in dress and demeanor, gazing around her with mild eyes. Some of those who had been busy assaulting the Birder only days before had the sense to look ashamed of themselves, and more than one wife whispered angry words to her husband. "You see! You can tell she's holy. You men, putting your filthy mouths on everything wonderful. . . ." "Pregnant, is she? Well, she's about as pregnant as my broom handle, husband. If you'd spend more time making nets and less time in chatter, we'd be better off and the Boundless would be gratified, I'm sure." Mavin, looking at them out of Handbright's face, read their lips, their expressions, and smiled inwardly.

The Birders moved toward her, setting up poles, banners, making a screen around her on all sides except outward toward the chasm. They roofed it with scarves, and Mavin was hidden from their view. The call for prayer sounded, a narrow cry, a climbing sound which rose, rose, upward into the green sky. Floppers honked in the root wall. Birds sang. High above them a breeze shook the leaves of the flattrees and the sweet dew fell. Noonglow came. The Birders drew the screen away.

All the assembled people gasped at the white bird which perched at the edge of the chasm, unbelievably huge and pure, more a symbol than a living thing, hierarchic and marvelous.

Mercald moved forward, a traveler's pack on his back, Beedie coming to stand beside him, then Roges.

"Show us the way," Mercald called to the bird in his high, priest's voice. "Show us the way, messenger."

Mavin spread her wings, dived from the edge of the bridge, caught the air beneath her and whirled out into the hot, uprising draft. She circled upward, twice, three times, gaining height with which to circle above the bridge, crying in a trumpet voice as she did so, then outward once more and down, down into the depths and out of sight. Mercald struck the bridge floor with his staff, cried, "We follow, messenger. We follow." The three of them moved resolutely toward the stair to Nextdown as the crowds pushed back in religious awe. A group of ordinary people Messengers assembled at the chasm side, strapping on their flopperskin wings, leaping one by one out into the same warm updraft to circle away up-chasm and down-chasm, carrying word of what had happened.

Behind the questers on the roof of his house, Sly-saw Bander pounded the parapet with his fists. "They know something, Byle, I tell you they know something. They've got something in their teeth. Something big. Something wonderful. The lost bridge went down in the long ago, so they say, with treasure on it. Treasure we can't even think of, boy, because we've lost the secrets of it. Can you imagine? Well, I've need of treasure right now. I need to put it in many pockets, boy, and the Banders are running shy of enough of it. So I'm not going to let them get it all by theirselfs. Pack us some gear, boy, and go tell your cousins. There'll be two expeditions going down, one to lead and one to follow – one to find, and one to take it away from them."

"But, Dah! It makes me fearful to hear you talk so. Fearful to think what they may be up to. There's only a few of the old Beeds and Chafers to have done with and you'll be eldest. Why go away now? We're close, Dah. Real close."

"Because they're onto something, boy. And whatever it is, we've got to know. The other'll wait. None of 'em'll get younger while we're away. Come on now, hop." And Byle Bander hopped, unaware that when the group left the house and headed for the stairs down which Mercald had gone, they were observed with considerable satisfaction by Rootweaver herself.

"You see, cousin," she said to the eldest, who sat well wrapped in an invalid chair at the teashop table. "While it won't do as proof, still it goes far to establish that Mavin was right.

"But who is she?" the old man said wonderingly. 'What is she?"

"A wonder, a Demon, a messenger of the Boundless," replied Rootweaver. "Mavin Manyshaped. One who can see farther than we have had to learn to do, cousin."

"Well then," he said, "what is to happen now?"

"According to Mavin, the announcement of a quest, particularly one rumored to have treasure as a part of it, will draw the villains out where they may be seen and proof assembled against them. Mercald goes with the questers to witness such proof and to remove him as a subject of rumor. Beedie goes because Mavin asked for her, and because the girl has an adventurous spirit. Roges goes where Beedie goes.'' Rootweaver refilled their cups, meditatively, gazing at the stair head, now almost vacant. She remembered her own youth, her own adventurous spirit. For her, too, there had been a certain Maintainer. . . .

''Actually, Eldest, they go to find out what is killing the roots of the bridges. We do not say that, for to say it would mean panic, but that is why they go – that is the bargain we have made with Mavin. 'Find out', we said, 'and put a stop to it.'

''Privately, I believe Mavin would have gone into the chasm to explore it whether we asked her to do so or not,'' she said. ''She is an adventurer first, and whatever else she may be second. This is in her eyes, in the very smell of her skin. Well, as for us, we will wait and see. Guard the pregnant birdgirl, guard ourselves against assassination, warn our fellows on the other bridges, and wait and see.''

The old man shook his head. Despite his fragility, his concern for the people he had so long cared for, he found himself in a curious mood. After thinking about it for a very long time, he decided the feeling was one of envy. Wait and see was not what he really wanted to do, and he thought of Beedie and Roges as he had seen them marching off to the stairs with a longing so sharp that he gasped, and Rootweaver had to put his head between his knees until he recovered.

CHAPTER FIVE

There was no one else on the stairs when the small group began the descent. They looked back to see the whole rim of the bridge edged with white disks of faces, mouths open in the middle so that it looked like hundreds of small, pale O's along the railing and at every window. "We are already a legend," said Beedie, not without some satisfaction.

"I pray there will be more to the legend than a last sight of us disappearing into the depths," commented Roges. He was staying politely behind her, and Beedie was surprised to find that the thought of him so close rather pleased her. Well, it was a new thing she was doing, unused to travel as she was. It was always good to have familiar things about, rugs, bits of furniture, ones own 'Tainer. With uncustomary tact, she did not mention this to him, knowing that he would not like being compared to cooking pots and sleeping mats. Then, too, perhaps the comparison was not quite fair. Roges was a good deal more useful than a sleeping mat. She flushed, and began to think of something else.

"Do I understand that the white bird was not actually the . . . the messenger which we had received before?" Roges asked. "Actually, Bridger, Rootweaver told me very little."

"Maintainer, the white bird we are following into the depths is named Mavin. She, whatever she is, is sister to that white bird Mercald had in Birders House – the one all the fuss was about. However, everyone thinks it is the same white bird, so if they are intent on doing it harm, they'll have to follow us into the depth to do it."

"And we are not actually upon a quest to find the lost bridge? I gathered that much."

"Roges," Beedie sighed, calling him by name for the first time in her life without noticing she was doing it, "We're going to find what's eating the roots. Because Rootweaver and all the elders are frightened half out of their wits. And they're afraid to talk about it or go down into the depths themselves for fear it will cause an uproar. So they've maneuvered Mavin into doing it for them. Now that's the whole truth of it."

"Ah," said Roges, turning pale, though Beedie did not see it, for which he was grateful. "There's been talk about something eating the roots. Whispers, mostly. No one seems to know anything about it, except that some of them are dying. Well. How . . . interesting to be going on such a mission."

Then he fell silent and said nothing more for quite some time while he tried to decide how he was going to act now that he knew what the mission was about. Eventually he reached the conclusion that he would still have volunteered to come even if he had known the whole truth; that being part of the group selected for such a mission was gratifying; and that while the journey had suddenly gained certain frightening aspects, he did not regret that aspect of it. Besides, nothing could have kept him from going wherever Beedie went, though he carefully did not explain this to himself. After a little time he felt better about it, and actually smiled as he followed Beedie on down the seemingly endless stair.

"What was it you said about not stopping at Nextdown?" Mercald asked her. "I didn't understand that part."

"Mavin said she would meet us on the stairs before we get to Nextdown, and she doesn't want us to go to Nextdown at all if we can help it. She thinks old Slysaw has been building strength there, and likely we'd be set upon. It's important that they not lay hands upon you."

"How would they know we are coming? Are the Banders set to assault any Birder who shows up?" Mercald was edgy with uncertainty, fearful and made touchy by his fear.

"Mavin thought old Slysaw had probably hired a Messenger or two. We know Slysaw is up on Topbridge. One of the Chafers from Bridgers House saw him. So he might have sent word ahead of us to Nextdown. She says she'll be very surprised if he didn't."

"I didn't know there was a way around Nextdown," commented Roges, hearing this for the first time.

"Neither does she. But Mavin says if there is a way, she will have found it by the time we get there. She thinks there may be some construction stairs used by the Bridgers in times past that will duck down this side and join the stairs to Midwall farther on."

"If so," said Mercald, "I'll wager they've rotted away by now. Nextdown is the second oldest of all the bridges, and it hasn't been renewed at all. Any construction stairs would be lair for crawly-claws by now."

"I thought Topbridge was the second bridgetown built,"said Roges. "Before the fall of Firstbridge."

Mercald shook his head. "Nextdown had been started before Firstbridge was destroyed. There were already stairs down to it, which is how a few Firstbridgers escaped. Then, it was from Nextdown they moved up to build Topbridge. It's all in the records we have left at the Birders House. Not that they're complete in any sense. Mostly they're things that were rewritten from memory after Firstbridge was broken."

"Do they say where we came from, Mercald?" Beedie had been curious about this ever since Mavin had spoken of the wide world above the chasm.

"Only that we came from somewhere else, long ago. We lived on the surface under the trees until the beasts drove us out. And why that happened is a mystery. Some say it's because we sinned, disobeyed the Boundless. Others say the Demon Daudir brought it upon us out of wickedness."

"I haven't ever heard of the Demon Daudir!" Beedie was indignant. "If it's an old story, why haven't I heard it?"

"Because it's accounted heresy," replied Mercald. He had stopped for a moment at a place the stair root they were on switched to another one, heading back along the root wall. Stairs were made by pulling a sideroot diagonally along the root wall as far as it would go, then cutting steps into it and building rails where necessary. Except for the short stretch between Potter's bridge and Miner's bridge, one root was not sufficient for the whole distance and crossovers were needed. At these crossover points, small platforms gave space to rest. Travelers caught between bridges by nightfall sometimes slept there, too. Mercald stopped to take off his high feathered hat, folding it up with some care and stowing it away in his pack wrapped in a handkerchief. His robes were next, and when he had finished all the regalia was hidden away and he appeared to be merely another traveler. "Daudir was supposed to be a Demon who arrived out of the Boundless in the time of our many-times-great forefathers. She brought disaster upon our world, so it is said, and our own troubles were the result. However, this is not in accordance with the Birders' teaching, so we don't talk of it."

Beedie wondered if Mavin knew the legend, and if so what she thought of it. "Why isn't it in accordance, Mercald? Is it a story?"

"Everything is a story," muttered Roges, unheard.

"It isn't a story," Mercald said. "But it is doctrine. Do you want to hear it?"

"If it isn't too much trouble."

"As a Birder, I have no choice. Trouble or no, I must tell what is to be told. That's what Birders are for. So. Let me follow you and Roges, and that way you can hear me as I talk. . . .

"*The Story of the Creation of All.* Ahem. Time was the Boundless lived alone, without edge or limit, lost in contemplation of itself. Time was the Boundless said, 'I will divide me into parts and compare one part against the next to see if I am the same in all parts of me, for if there is difference in anything, in this way may I discover it.'

"So the Boundless divided itself, one part against another part, and examined all the parts to see if difference dwelt among them, and lo, there was difference among the parts for what one part contained was not always what another part contained.

"So the Boundless was lost in contemplation, until the Boundless said, 'Lo, I will divide me smaller, in order to see where the difference lies.' And the Boundless divided itself smaller yet, finding more difference the smaller it was divided ...."

"I don't understand that at all," murmured Beedie to Roges.

"It would be hard to tell the difference between Beedie and Beedie," Roges whispered. "But if you divided yourself in pieces, I suppose it would be easy enough to tell your left foot from your elbow." He smiled behind his hand.

"Until at last," Mercald went on in full flight of quotation, "the Boundless was many, myriad, and the differences were everywhere. Then did the Boundless hear the crying of its parts which were lost in the all and everything. 'Woe,' they cried, 'we are lost'."

"I should think so," muttered Beedie. "What a thing to do to oneself."

"So it was the Boundless created Bounds for its parts and its differences, and places wherein they might exist, that the differences might have familiarities in which to grow toward Boundlessness once more. . . ."

"And a good thing, too," said Beedie. "Now, what has that to do with not believing in Daudir the Demon?"

Mercald shook his head at her, provoked. "Obviously, this chasm is a familiarity, a Bounded place which was created for us by the Boundless. We are the differences who live here. If it was created for us by the Boundless, then it can have nothing to do with Demons or devils or anything of the kind. All of that is mere superstition and beneath our dignity as people of the chasm. Doctrine teaches that all differences are merely that – differences. Not necessarily good or evil." He then fell silent, climbing a little slower so that the other two drew away from him

"Try not to tread on him," said Roges. "All the really religious Birders are sensitive as mim plants. You touch them crooked, and they curl up and ooze. As judges go, Mercald isn't bad. He's true to the calling."

"You speak as though some might not be," she said, surprised.

"Some are not. I come from Potter's bridge, and we had Birders there as judges I would not have had judge my serving of tea for fear they'd condemn me under chasm rule. It was pay them in advance or suffer the consequences, and those among us too poor to pay suffered indeed."

"Wasn't it reported to the chasm council?"

"Oh, eventually. Before that, however, there was much damage done. In the end, it was only three of them were judged by their fellows and tossed over, two brothers and a sister, all corrupt as old iron." He moved swiftly to one side of the stair, reaching out toward a ropey root that hung an arm's length away. It was dotted with tender nodules, the green-furred ones called root mice, and he cut them cleanly fom the root to place them in the pouch at his belt. "Enough for the three of us," he said. "And some left over for breakfast ." He knelt, peering through the railings. "Ah. Look there, Bridger. In that little hole in the biggest root along there, see – behind the three little ones in a row."

She knelt beside him, searching until her eyes found the waving claws, moving out, then in, then out once more. "A crawly-claw," she whispered. "Do you suppose we could get him?"

"Do you suppose we should? With a judge following after? We're not Hunter caste." He was laughing at her, she knew, but at the moment she didn't mind.

"I caught one once," she confessed, blushing at the memory of her illicit behaviour. "A little one. I had to hunt all up and down the root wall for enough deadroot to cook it, but it was worth it. Isn't it all right if we're out on the root wall?"

"We're not on the root wall. We're on the stairs. And there's likely to be a party coming up or coming down past us any time. No. Likely hunting a crawly-claw would take longer than would be prudent."

"It's true. They pull back in and disappear, and you have to burrow for them. Well, all right," she agreed.

"But we'll keep an eye out for any wireworms. And if we see any, we get them, whether there's a Hunter around or not." Beedie had never had enough fried wireworms, and there were never enough in the market to satisfy her appetite, even if she had had enough money to buy them all.

Mercald had caught up with them, evidently restored to good humor by his time alone. He moved ahead of them now, after admiring the crawly-claw and quoting in great details several recipes for preparation of the beasts, and they continued their downward way. Beedie, her legs accustomed to hard climbs by hours each day spent in spurs, did not feel the climb, but she noticed that both the others stopped from time to time, wriggling their legs and feet to restore feeling numbed by the constant down, down, down.

They had not come far enough yet for the quality of light to change much. It was still that watery green light the Topbridgers knew as daylight, full of swimming shadows cast by the leaves as they moved in winds from outside the chasm. Beedie remembered the light on Nextdown as being less watery and more murky, darker. She had heard that on Midwall and Miner's bridge, lanterns were used except at midday, and of course on Bottommost they were needed at all times. She had heard, also, that the eyes of the people on Bottommost were larger, but this might well not be true. Surely travelers from Bottommost would have come to Topbridge from time to time, but she had never noticed any strangers with very large eyes.

They went on. A group of chattering Porters passed them going up, followed not much later by a second group, their legs hard and bulging with climbing muscle. A Messenger swooped by on flopperskin wings, calling to them as they went, "Luck to the quest, Bridger. . . ." before falling away out of sight in the direction of Potter's bridge. The light began to fail; the stairs became hard to see. Far below them lights began to flicker in a long line, stretching from the root wall out across the chasm in a delicate chain, growing brighter as they descended. They stopped at the railing to look down, hearing the voice behind them without surprise, almost as though they had expected it.

"What took you so long?" asked Mavin. She stood in the shadow, half-hidden behind a fall of small roots, almost invisible.

"We had no wings, ma'am," said Roges, grinning at Mavin with what Beedie considered astonishing familiarity.

"Fair blow Maintainer. Well, I had hoped to tell you of a sideway by this time, some kind of trail or climb around Nextdown. I've looked. Up the wall and down it, behind the roots and before them. Nothing. What was there has rotted away and been eaten by the wireworms long since."

"So we must go to Nextdown after all,"said Beedie.

"Where needs must, sausage girl. However, we'll not do it without a little preparation. There's a house full of Banders near the stair – the very house your Aunt Six told me you used to occupy, Beedie. Evidently all the Bander kin from upstairs and down have come to fill it full, and every window of it has eyes on this stairway. They've been warned we're coming. There's talk of assault and the taking of a Birder hostage. So, lest harm fall . . ."

"Lest harm fall?" questioned Mercald, fearfully.

"We shall commit a surprise. As soon as we figure one out. However, why don't we have something to eat first. Have you supplies, Maintainer?"

"Fresh root mice, ma'am. And things less fresh brought from Topbridge. We can have a cold supper."

"No need for that. There's a cave in the wall, just here, behind these roots, and a pile of deadroot in it enough to warm twenty dinners. There is also a convenient air shaft which guarantees we will not suffocate in our own smoke. Even if all this were not so near and so convenient, I would want it to be a good bit darker before we attempt to go past that Bridgers House. So we might as well rest a while and enjoy our food."

"We saw a crawly-claw, Mavin. I wanted to hunt it, but Roges said the Hunter caste might catch us at it."

"Are they especially delicious, girl?"

"They are the best thing next to wireworms. Even better, sometimes."

"Then we'll have to try and hunt one down, somewhere along the way, Hunter caste or no." She wormed her way behind the bundle of roots, showing them the way into the cave. The sight of it surprised them all, for it was lit with one of the puffed fish lanterns glowing softly to itself in the black. Snaffled from Nextdown by a strange bird, said Mavin with some amusement. There was also a vast pile of deadroot, looking as though it had fallen there rather than been gathered in. Roges set about building a fire, laying his supplies ready to hand on a spread sheet of flopperskin.

"I didn't know there were caves in the root wall." Mercald was indignant, as though the existence of anything he did not know of was an affront to his priestly dignity.

"I think your people have become so caste-ridden, priest, that they do not use their humanish curiosity any longer. You have no explorer caste, do you? No. Nor any geographers? Your adventurous young are not encouraged to burrow about in the root wall?"

"Well, in a manner of speaking," Beedie interrupted. "Bridger youngsters climb about from the time they can walk. I did."

"Always under supervision, I'll warrant. Always learning methods or perfecting skills. Well, it doesn't matter; it's only a matter of interest to me. In looking for a way around Nextdown, you see, I have found a number of curiosities, and I merely wonder that the people of the chasm seem unaware of them. For example, there is another cave somewhat below us which happens to be occupied by a strangeness."

"Occupied?" Roges looked up from his folding grill, interested. "Someone living in the wall? A Miner, perhaps?"

"A person. He tells me his name is Haile Sefalik; by profession, a theoretician; in actuality a stranger, an outlander, not belonging in this chasm at all. He tells me he has come here for difference, for where he was before was same. I invited him to join us for supper."

Roges made a face and turned to his pack for another handful of the root mice. He was slicing them into a pan with bits of dried flopper meat and a bulb of thickic. He did not comment. Mavin watched their faces, interested in the ways they received this news: Mercald fearfully; Roges with housekeeperish resignation; Beedie with delight.

"How wonderful! What is he, Mavin? I don't know what a theo – a theor whatever is."

"I'm not at all certain, sausage girl. That's why I invited him. He looks hungry, for a start, so I presume a theoretician is not anything practical like a Harvester or a Bridger. He is living in an unimproved cave, so I presume it isn't something useful like a Miner or Crafter. There is a sort of dedication in his expression which reminds me of you, Mercald, but he has no regalia at all."

"What is he doing, then? In his cave?"

"So far as I can tell, he sits and thinks."

"Only that?" asked Mercald, scandalized.

"Only that. He's being fed by the slow-girules. I saw two of them come in and leave him a few nodules while I was there. They talked at him, and he talked back at them, and they purred." She smiled again, then held up one finger. "Shhh. I think I hear him on the stairs."

There was a slow tread on the stairs, interrupted by frequent stops. Beedie ran to the cave entrance and peered between the roots, seeing a dark shape silhouetted against the lights of Nextdown, below them. "I know why it does that," said a voice in a tone of pleased amazement. "It's obvious."

"You know why what does what?" asked Beedie, coming out onto the stairs. "Why what does what?"

"I know why it feels colder here than it does up above, among the trees. They always say it is because we are closer to the river, here, with more moisture in the air. Nonsense. We've come down a long way. There's more atmosphere, more heat capacity, and the thicker air cools us faster. That's all. I hadn't thought about that until now. Interesting, isn't it." The person turned toward her, not seeing her. "Different. Not the same at all." He moved blindly toward the place in the roots from which she had emerged, feeling his way between them to the firelit space beyond.

"Who's they?" asked Beedie. "I never heard 'they' say that, about the river and the moisture."

"They," said the man, moving steadily toward the fire and food. "You know. Them."

Beedie had no idea about them. She shook her head and followed him, seeing Mavin grasp him by one arm and lead him to a convenient sitting stone. He was dressed all in ragged bits and pieces, and his face was one of mild interest, unfocused, as though he did not really see any of them even while he took food from Roges' hands. He had shaggy, light hair and a wild-looking moustache and beard which drooped below his chin, wagging gently when he spoke. The colour of his eyes was indeterminable, somewhere between vacant and shadow. After a long pause during which no one said anything, he murmured, "Perhaps it was some other place they said it about. That it was cooler lower down. Because it was wetter. Perhaps that was it."

"What other place was that?" Mercald asked, suspiciously. "Nextdown? Midwall?"

The man chewed, swallowed, spooned another mouthful up before considering this question. "Oh, not any place very local, I'm afraid. Elsewhere, I think. Before I came here at all."

"You came from elsewhere," commented Mavin. "Perhaps from the place the ancesters of these chasm dwellers came from? Or from the southern continent?"

"Elsewhere," he replied, gesturing vaguely at the rock around them, as though he had permeated it recently. "It started with liquids. They didn't understand liquids. Local geometry is non-space-filling. Icosohedra. Triginal bipyramids. Oh, this shape and that shape, lots of them. More than the thirty-two that fill ordinary space, let me tell you. That's why things are liquid, trying to pack themselves in flat space, and that's what I told *them*.

"*They* couldn't deal with it. *They* wanted order, predictability, regularity. Silly. Local geometry can be packed, I said, just not in flat space. So, I said, give them a space of constant curvature and they'll pack. All *they* did was laugh. I took some liquids to a space of constant negative curvature to show *them* it would crystallize, and it sucked me up. One minute, there. Poof. Next minute, somewhere else. Somewhere different, thank the Boundless. Boundless. That's a local word for it. Picked it up from someone on the stairs out there. *Boundless.* Good name for it."

"I'm sure the Boundless would be gratified at your approval," said Mercald, much offended.

"Shhh," calmed Mavin. "The man's a guest in our midst."

"*They* said every place was like the place I was. Infinite replications of sameness. They called it translational symmetry. Well, I determined to find difference no matter what it took. So I left there and came here.It's different here. It's local. Poof and feh on translational symmetry."

"I thought you said you got here by accident," said Beedie, trying to make sense out of the person. "By some curvature or other."

"Yes. Both. Hardly anything is mutually exclusive when you really think about it. You can't look at things too closely. The more precisely you look at one thing, the more uncertain the others get. If we locate me precisely here, how I got here becomes increasingly unsure. Tell you the truth, I don't remember."

"Reality has many natures," said Mercald in his most sententious voice.

"That's the truth," said the theoretician, focusing on the priest for a moment before drifting away again.

"That's the truth, so far as it goes, at least." He chewed quietly to himself, smiling at his own thoughts. "Surfaces," he murmured. "Edges. Reality has edges."

"That's the truth," Beedie muttered to herself. "So far as it goes." She glared at Mavin. "What did we need him for?"

"Need? Well, sausage girl, what do we need you for? To make life more interesting. He's different, isn't he?"

Mercald circled the theoretician in slow, ruminative steps, eating, staring, eating. At last he said, "What do you mean, reality has edges?" Receiving no response, he repeated the question, finally driving it through with a kick at the stone the man was sitting on. "Edges?"

The theoretician put his plate down, picked up a length of root from the floor of the cave. "You see this? This is a system. It has surfaces. It has extent. It has size and corners and edges and impurities and irregularities." He put it down, searched for a stone, found one. "This one, too. Here's another. Not the same, not the same at all. And another one yet. All local. Everything's local. Local."

The other three looked at one another, Mercald kept on with his circling; at last it was Roges who said, "So?"

"Not to *them*! Oh, no, not to *them*. To them, everything is the same. In all directions. Forever. No edges. No corners. *They* used to scream at me. 'What do you do about surface states?' As though that meant something. I thank the Boundless for the surface states. Show me something, anything without surface states! Anything at all! There's nothing like that in reality. But they didn't understand. Just went on inventing 'ons. Palarons. Plasmons. Phonons. Exitons. Vomitons and shitons soon to come. Feh."

Beedie murmured, "I don't know, Mavin. It seems to me we ought to let him go back to his cave and start worrying about the Banders."

"Banders," screamed the theoretician in a sudden expression of fury. "Infinite lattices. Homogeneous deformation. Idiots."

"I really think it's something religious," said Mercald to Mavin in a thoughtful voice. "There's a fine kind of frenzy about it. Of course, it might be heretical, but it sounds quite like doctrine." He regarded the theoretician almost with fondness.

"We'll take him with us," said Mavin. "If he wants to go. Thinker, do you want to come with us?"

The man shook his head, then nodded it, reaching into the general pan for the last of the fried root mice. "If it will be different where you are going. I've modeled this place. There's nothing left to do here."

"He means he has realized it," said Mercald with satisfaction. "I'm beginning to understand him. It is definitely religious, after all." He stroked the theoretician's shoulder, wrinkling his nose at the feel of the rags. "I've got an extra shirt I can lend him."

"Ah," said Mavin. "I'm glad you find him sympathetic, Mercald. I wonder if he has any practical use at all." She stretched herself on the cave floor, seeming, to Beedie's eyes, to flow a little, as though she shaped herself to the declivities of the place. "Thinker, will you solve a problem for me? Give me an answer?"

"Answers? Of course. I always know the answer. After I see the problem, of course. Not before. They're always terribly simple, answers. Which one do you need?"

"We need to get to the stairs below Nextdown – that's the bridge just below us – without being seen by anyone on Nextdown. There is no other stair and no root climbable by any of us but perhaps Beedie here."

"Ah," said the theoretician. "Might one ask why?"

"There are a dozen large men at the end of this stair who are determined to do us harm," said Mavin, without changing expression. "Is that reason enough?" She had been watching

Beedie's bright, excited face and was determined not to change into some huge climbing shape which would solve all problems and take all the fun out of the expedition. Besides, shifting was too easy. Sometimes it was more fun to plot one's way out of trouble. This praiseworthy thought was interrupted.

"Shhh," said Roges, moving to throw his jacket over the fish lantern. "I hear voices. Someone coming down." They fell silent, listening, hidden as they were in the dark of the cave, the last glowing coals of the fire hidden from the entrance by their bodies. There was the sound of a dozen pairs of feet, a malignant mutter, a phlegmy cough.

"I smell smoke," said someone from outside. Byle Bander's voice. "Smoke, Dah."

"Well of course you smell smoke, idiot boy. There's Nextdown no more than a few hundred steps down. This time of evening when don't you smell smoke? Everybody's cooking their dinner, and good time to do it, too. I'm hungry enough to eat for six."

"You think the Birder's gone on down? You think our fambly took 'em at Nextdown, Dah?"

"I think that's probable, boy. In which case, we'll have a high old time finding out from that Birder what they're going after."

"And Beedie. I get to ask Beedie, Dah. That and a few games, huh? She's one I've been wanting to play a few games with for a long time. . . ." The voices faded away into silence, footsteps echoing up the stair for a time, then nothing.

"Ah," whispered Mavin. "So we are not only expected below, but followed after as well."

"They won't find us down there," said Beedie. "But they'll know we have to be somewhere."

"It's all right, sausage girl. They won't come searching back up the stairs until morning. Well, Birder. Was their conversation proof enough for you?"

Mercald gestured impotently. "What did they say? They would ask me questions. They would play games with Beedie. Can I prove dishonorable intent?"

"Rootsap," said the theoretician. "I've been thinking about rootsap. The way down, you know. Rootsap."

"Poisonous," said Beedie. "Eats through your skin."

"Not at the temperature of the chasm at this altitude at this time before midnight,'' said the theoretician. ''Which is the coolest time of the daily cycle in the chasm. A phenomenon which awaits explanation but is undoubtedly the result of a warming and cooling cycle on the surface.'' He stood up and patted himself, as though taking inventory, though he carried nothing at all. ''Knife,'' he said. ''Or hatchet. We need several good sized blobs.''

''Knife is quieter,'' commented Mavin.

Beedie nodded. Mavin took a knife from her hip and went out of the cave, Mercald following her silently. The theoretician merely sat by the coals, his eyes unfocused, staring at the stone around them, muttering from time to time. ''Suitable viscosity. Alpha helix. Temperature dependent polymerization. Glop. All local.''

Beedie dumped her pouch on the ground and re-packed it, taking a moment to put her hair in order, coiling the dark wealth of it neatly into a bun when she had finished. She caught Roges looking at her, and he flushed. ''You have lovely hair,'' he whispered. ''I've wanted to say that, you know.''

''That . . . that kind of talk isn't customary, Maintainer,'' she said stiffly. Then, seeing the pain in his face, ''Roges. You embarrass me. I'm sorry. Nobody ever said I had nice hair. Aunt Six always says I'm a scatter-nonny.''

''You're not a scatter-nonny,'' he said. ''Don't be embarrassed. It's just . . . just, I've never had anyone trying to do me harm before. If anything happens, I wanted . . . I wanted to have said . . .''

''I don't think they're going to do you harm, Roges. I think it's me they're after. And Mercald, maybe. They don't even know Mavin is here.''

His face darkened in a kind of remote anger. ''Harm to you, Beedie, is harm to me. Maintainers are not mere servants. We are a good deal more than that.''

''Polymer,'' said the theoretician, loudly. ''About now.''

Mavin reentered the cave, carrying a huge milky blob of rootsap on a piece of bark, Mercald just behind her similarly burdened. They put the blobs down where the theoretician could see them. ''Well, Thinker?''

''Cooler,'' he directed. ''Wherever it's cooler.''

Beedie rose, moved around the cave. ''It's coolest just at the entrance, Mavin. There's a draft there.''

They put the rootsap down and waited as the theoretician

wandered about, examining roots that came through the cave top, smiling at rocks. At last he came to the cave entrance and peered at the blobs. "There," he said with considerable satisfaction. "You can see the polymerization beginning." They looked at the whitish blobs which were turning transparent. "Cut it," he suggested in his mild voice. "Into four pieces. No. Five. I'll go with you."

Mavin shrugged, took her knife and cut the blobs into five parts. They resisted cutting, piling up around the blade. She pushed the blobs apart, for they seemed to want to rejoin.

"That's funny," said Beedie. "I've never seen it behave that way before."

"Nighttime," said the Thinker. "You'd have to have seen it at nighttime, when it's cool."

"You've seen it at nighttime before?"

"Well, no. But I thought about it."

"Now what?" asked Mavin. "We've got five blobs, rapidly turning transparent. What now?"

"When they are totally clear, you'll need to pull it through a hole of some kind. Lacking any method of precise measurement, I would say something roughly finger size. Small finger size." He watched with interest as Mavin carried the blobs and the fish lanterns out into the dark. There she found a chunk of tough rootbark and drilled a hole in it with her knife.

"So?" she asked. "Why don't you do one."

"Madam, I am not an experimentalist!" The theoretician turned his back on her, as offended as Mercald had been earlier.

Mavin snorted. "Well, if you won't soil your hands, you won't. Have you any suggestion what I should do next?"

He turned, very dignified in his rags. "You'll need to push the blob through the hole. You'll need to fasten that chunk to something that will hold your weight."

She found a convenient fork in a root and wedged the chunk behind it after pushing some of the blob through the hole with a stick of deadroot.

"That should do," said the theoretician, taking a firm hold on the part of the blob which protruded from the hole and leaning outward into space. "Be sure to make all the holes in the bark just that size. The yield at that diameter will be approximately one hundred man heights. . . ." The blob stretched. He grasped it firmly. It stretched further. He stepped into air, and the blob stretched, becaming a thick rope, a line, a line that went on stretching, bobbing him gently at the end of it like a child's balloon as he sank down below the light of the lantern into darkness. "I thought it would do that," his voice came plaintively up. "I could theorize, but does anyone know what's down below?"

"For all our sakes, I hope it's the stair to Potter's bridge," muttered Mavin, leaning out into the chasm. "Well, let's make another chunk with a hole in it, sausage girl. However, let me try it first. What works for our strange guest might not work for us. He's fond of saying everything is local."

After another session with knife and bark chunk, Mavin stepped into the chasm and dwindled away at the end of the stretching line, bobbing as she went. The sapling made a thin humming noise as it stretched, a kind of whirring. After a time, when the blob had shrunk almost to nothing, the whirring stopped, and Beedie heard a muffled call from below.

"I guess we try it," she said to Roges, wiping her hands up and down her trousers.

Mercald was dithering at the edge of the drop, peering down once more. "I . . . I . . . can't . . . let . . . I can't"

"Oh, foof," she spat. "He's got the down-dizzies. I might have known. Mercald. Don't look. I'm pushing some of it through, now take firm hold of it. *Wipe* your hands, ninny. They're all slippery and wet. Here. I'll use my belt to fasten you to it so you can't drop. Now. Roges and I are going to hold you by the hands. Shut your eyes. Now! I mean it. Do what I say, or I'll call the Banders and let them have you. We're holding you. Now. I'm going to let go. You're going down. Just keep your eyes shut. Shut!"

She checked the straps of her pack, wiped her hands once more. "Are you ready, Roges? Roges?"

"Hnnn," he whined through his teeth. "As ready as I'm likely to be, Bridger. I, too, suffer from the down-dizzies, but I suppose it's time to get over it."

She surprised herself, and him, by touching his face, stroking it. "Honestly, Roges. You can get over it. It just takes getting used to. Do what I told Mercald. Just don't look down." She watched as he eased himself over the edge, teeth gritted tight, sweat standing out on his face. He began to drop, and she took firm hold of her own blob, jumping outward with a strong thrust of her legs, stretching it abruptly, so that it twanged, bobbing her up and down in midair. She clung for dear life, cursing her own stupidity.

When she stopped bobbing, she was beside him, falling down the side of the wall in a dream drop, the hairs of the roots tickling her face, occasional small creatures fleeing with squeaks of alarm. She could see only the light of the fish lantern above them, fading into distance, and the lights of Nextdown which came nearer and nearer on her left, until she and Roges were bathed in their glow. He still gritted his teeth, but his eyes were open, darting this way and that, and she knew that he searched for danger to her even as he fought fear for himself.

Then the lights of Nextdown were above them, becoming only a glow against the root wall as the bulk of the bridgetown eclipsed the lanterns. From below she could hear the voice of the Thinker raised in complaint.

"*They* would never have thought of that. *Their* systems have no surfaces, and it's totally dependent upon surface. . . ."

"I think I'm going to get very tired of that voice," she said to Roges plaintively.

"I'm tired of it already," he agreed. "Still, we're past Nextdown. We didn't get captured or tortured or held for ransom. We're all alive. And I'm confident we'll find out what's eating the roots, and then we can go home."

Beedie was silent, watching the glow of Nextdown fade above her. "I'm not sure I want to think about . . . home, Roges. Not just yet. I know you get the down-dizzies, but . . . isn't it exciting? Aren't you enjoying it at all?"

There was no time for him to answer. Mavin's voice came out of the blackness nearby. "The stairs are to your right, sausage girl. I'll toss you a line." Then they were drawn down onto the stairs, and she forgot she had asked the question.

CHAPTER SIX

"Where are we?" asked Mercald, his voice still trembling.

"On the stairs to Potter's bridge. Which is not where we particularly want to be," said Mavin. "Nextdown is slightly above us on one hand, Potter's bridge a long way below us on the other hand. Midwall, which is where I need to go in order to reach Bottommost, eventually, is beyond Nextdown, quite the other direction."

"We can work our way along the root wall under Nextdown," said Beedie, not looking at all sanguine about it. "That will bring us to the Midwall stairs."

"I think not," said Mavin. "At least two of us, possibly three, would find such a traverse difficult. I'd rather find another way, if possible."

"Is the idea to escape from those who followed? Who may follow?" The theoretician seemed only mildly interested in the answer to this question.

"No," said Mercald firmly, surprising them all. "The idea is to stay out of reach, but not out of touch. We need proof they are murderers, and for that we must remain within distance to see and hear what they do, but I'd just as soon not fall into their hands."

"Hurrah," said Mavin, laughing a little. "Mercald, you put it cogently. We don't want to lose them, Thinker. Only avoid them. Which means I must go up yonder and leave a few clues or whisper a few rumors indicating we've passed them by, don't you think? I suggest the rest of you curl up on the steps – they're rather wide along here – and sleep if you can. I'll return before light."

"Couldn't we go all the way to the Bottom on the rootsap?" Beedie had enjoyed the drop, once she had quit bouncing. Even that had been interesting. Now she saw with disappointment that the Thinker was shaking his head.

"Limits," he sighed. "Surface to volume, temperature changes, weight a factor, of course. We came about as far as one blob will allow. And now it's too warm."

Beedie hadn't noticed, but the midnight cool had passed. The winds which swept down the chasm each day from midafternoon to midnight had stopped, and now the warm mists were rising once more. "What would happen if you tried that in the day time?" she asked.

"Plop," said the Thinker, making a vividly explanatory gesture. "Plop. Nothing much left of you, I should think."

Mavin had already gone. They settled themselves upon the step, backs against the stair risers. Knowing Mercald's fear of heights, Beedie planted pitons and belted him to them. Knowing Roges' pride, she did not do the same for him. Instead, she placed herself between him and the edge, as though unintentionally, a little dismayed at his quiet, "Thank you, Bridger." They settled, not believing they would sleep, but falling asleep almost at once out of sheer weariness.

In remembering it afterward, Beedie was never sure quite what had wakened her. Was it a scratching sound from the stair root itself? Something moving in the root wall? A slight shaking of the stair they rested upon? As though tugged by something pulling at it from below? At first she thought it a dream and merely dozed in it, without concern, waiting to see what odd thing would happen next. Then her eyes snapped wide against the glow of Nextdown, and she felt Roges stiffen behind her, his foot kicking at her involuntarily as he awoke.

"What is it?" he hissed.

"Mnn, um," said Mercald. "Wassn. Morning?"

"Unlikely to be volcanic or tectonic," said the Thinker calmly. "Biologic in origin, I shouldn't wonder. Probably zoologic, though there's too little evidence to be sure."

The mists were rising around them, bringing the odors of Bottom, a rich, filthy smell, of rotted things, a soupy odor of growth. Suddenly a miasma struck them, a stench, foul as decaying flesh, sweetly horrible, and they all gagged and gasped in the moment before a rising draft of air wafted it away. The root trembled again, purposefully.

"Something climbing on it, I should say," said the theoretician. "I can compute the probable bulk, knowing the modulus of the root stair we are on, and the degree of movement . . . say something on the order of a thousand two hundred man weights, give or take a hundred."

"How big would that be?" gasped Beedie as another wave of stink flowed over them.

"Oh, something roughly six or seven men long and a man height and a half through."

Seeing her look of incomprehension, Roges said, "Put another way, something about as long as a four-story building is tall, and as thick through as the Bridgers House living room." The root shook beneath them, a steady, gnawing quiver accompanied by aching vibrations of sound.

The noise covered the sound of Mavin's return, but they heard her voice as she said, "Gamelords! How long has this been going on?"

"Just started," said Roges through his teeth. The smell had grown worse in the last few moments.

"Stay here," she hissed at them in a voice of command. "Don't move. I'll be back in a moment." They had not seen her leave, or return, or leave again, but Beedie's mind flashed quick images of the white bird, and she thought she could hear the whip of air through feathers. They clung to the stair, waiting. It was not long before Mavin returned, calling urgently, "Up. We've got to get off the stair. Either back into the root wall or up onto Nextdown, one or the other. There's a something eating the stairs, something too big to fight." They heard a frantic fluttering among the roots along the wall, exclamations, expressions of fury, a quick hammering, water falling. "Beedie, light a bit of deadroot and get over here."

Roges had it ready, even as Beedie wondered why they had forgotten the fish lantern. Sparks flew, went out, flew again, as Roges cursed at them. Then they caught and the deadroot flared up, centering them in a weird, shadowy dance of light. They saw Mavin along the root wall, perched on a water- belly, a round hole carved into it and another at its bottom draining the water away.

"Tie something to Mercald and I'll haul him over. Roges, help the Thinker. Beedie, put your spurs on."

"I already have them on," she said. "I put them on when the shaking started." She tied Mercald to her with a safety belt and thrust him along a side root, hissing at him. "Close your eyes and crawl, Birder. Crawl, and don't look at anything. Pretend you are crawling under Birders House to check for wall rot. It is very quiet and unexciting, and you'll get to Mavin in just one moment. There." She turned to find Roges at her heels, teeth clenched, eyes fixed ahead. Behind him the Thinker walked along the root, examining the bark as though he had been a Bridger since birth.

"Do you know, the formation of water-bellies occurs at precises intervals dependent upon the diameter of the root involved. I've been thinking . . ."

"Later," snarled Mavin. "Get in here with the rest of us and think about it silently." They slithered together into the water-belly just as the last of its contents drained away, piled untidily in the spherical space, still wet, feeling the tickly brush of little capillary hairs as they huddled, each trying to see out. Mavin had gone out as they came in, and she was perched well above them now, holding the burning deadroot to cast a light upon the quivering stair. The light blinded them; they could not see what shape she had, and only Beedie knew enough about Mavin to wonder. The thought distracted her, and she did not see what the others did until their indrawn breath drew her attention.

It was vast and gray, covered with scabby plaques of hardened ichor or flaking skin, oozing between the plaques thin dribbles of greenish goo which stank. It had an upper end, but no head that they could see. Still, from beneath the upper end came the sound of chewing, gnawing, the rasp, rasp, rasp of hardness biting into the stair root. The thing moved up, up, not seeing them, not looking for them, merely chewing blindly as it came. Then the chewing stopped. The thing quivered obscenely. Its top end began to rise up, sway, a horrible tower of jiggling jelly ending in a circular mouth which sucked, chewed, sucked – and somehow sensed them. The terrible head moved in their direction, cantilevered out from the root stair toward the water-belly, toward the place they crouched, staring, unable to breathe.

Then something flew at the creature's head, something bearing flame, beating at it, burning it. The monster screamed a hissing agonized sigh like a kettle boiling dry. It lashed itself upward, striking blindly, without a target. The torch darted upward, back, down once more, striking at the mouth, again and again. With a last, horrible scream, the mass began to withdraw down the stair, faster than it had come, folding in upon itself, sliding on its own slimy juices, a trail it had laid as it climbed up, going now away and down and out of sight.

Beedie shuddered and then embarrassed herself by beginning to cry. Roges held her tightly, and she could not tell if the wetness on his face was from her or from them both. Mercald was beneath them, his face hidden at the bottom of the water-belly, half suffocated, and she could not imagine how he had come there. The Thinker had withdrawn a pad from among his rags and was making notes, murmuring to himself as he did so.

"Lignivorous. Purulent dermatitis. Unlikely to be a survival trait, therefore pathological. Recently invaded areas would indicate a newly arrived natural enemy perhaps? Or, possibly, use of a toxic substance ..."

"What do I understand you to say, Thinker?" demanded Mavin, arriving at the opening in the water-belly, panting, holding the torch high so that she could see them. She wore her own shape, or one Beedie thought of as hers.

"The thing is sick," said Thinker, putting his pad away. "If not dying, at least not at all well. That skin condition is not normal to the species. So much is evident."

"It wasn't evident to me," muttered Beedie with some hostility. "Does he know everything?"

"Within certain limits, yes," replied the Thinker. "Your attitude of irrelevant hostility is one I have encountered before." He sniffed.

"It's not sick enough that it wouldn't have eaten us, is it?"

The theoretician cocked his head, ruminated over this for a little time, then pronounced: "No. It was eating voraciously. I imagine it will eat almost anything it can get at, though my guess would be it prefers flesh, moist roots and whatever small creatures live upon them."

"There are places not far from where I grew up where they domesticate things like that," said Mavin thoughtfully. "Not exactly like that, of course. Not so big. Rock eaters. There are said to be smaller ones that eat plants further north. I've never seen them. . . ."

"Quite possibly the same genus," said the Thinker.

"What did you think made the thing sick?"

"A natural enemy, or some accidental ingestion of a naturally toxic substance, or some purposeful contamination by a toxic substance.

In other words, something is eating it, it ate something which disagreed with it, or someone is trying very hard to kill it."

"Whoever it is, I'm for them," said Beedie. "I don't blame them a bit."

"Whoever?" asked Mercald, slightly dazed. He had burrowed his way up from the bottom of the water-belly and was now one of them once more, though slightly slimy in aspect. "We would have heard! Where? Even on Bottommost, we would have heard! If anyone had seen one of these things, we would have been notified!"

"Something was destroying the roots, the verticals, Mercald. Rootweaver told us. It's just – no one supposed anything like this." Beedie fell silent, suddenly aware of the implications. "You mean . . . someone is trying to kill those things . . . besides the people on the bridgetowns? Thinker? You mean someone else?"

"My dear person, I have no idea. The who is unimportant. I merely recited the possibilities. If you want me to extrapolate probabilities, it will take me a few moments."

"I don't think we need to belabor our ignorance," Mavin said, heaving Beedie out of the water-belly. "One reason that we came upon this journey was to find this thing – these things. So. We've found it. One. Perhaps there are more. But to find the cause of peril was not the main reason for coming; the main reason is to put an end to that peril, and we are a very long way from knowing how to do that. That we are not alone in the attempt changes nothing, really.

"A thing I do know, however, is that the creature didn't climb all the way up here in one night. That means it didn't go all the way back down, either. I think I saw it ooze itself into a hole some distance below. It's probably been working its way up, night after night, for a long time. It's likely no other of them, if there are more of them, has worked up this high until now, which would explain why they have not been seen or smelled before."

"But now that we have seen, we must send word," said Roges. "The Bridgers must be told."

"Yes, we must send word," agreed Mavin. "We can leave a note nailed to the stair. The first group up from Potter's bridge this morning will find it – and word will be sent. The chewed stairs alone would probably be enough, but we'll describe the creature for them."

"Tell them it fears fire," said Roges. "They'll need to know that." He fell silent, thinking in horror of a bridgetown invaded by such a monster, or monsters, the crushing of little houses, the shrieking of children, the steady rasp, rasp, rasp of its teeth, the stink.

"Light," said the theoretician. "The thing avoids light. It shrank not only from the heat of the torch, but also from the light of it. At least, so I think."

"We will say fire, certainly, and light, possibly," agreed Mavin. "Now. It is written. Do you have a spare piton, Beedie? So. Nailed fast. No one could possibly miss it. I see light above, green light through the leaves. It's time for us to move on before the Banders arrive. Like it or not, we're going to cross the root wall."

"Madam," said the Thinker, "Is it your desire to reach Bottommost?" At her nod he continued, "Bottommost is almost exactly beneath us now."

"Down," said Beedie indignantly. "Three days climb down. Past that thing. Maybe dozens of them. And I'm the only one of us with spurs."

"Down," agreed the Thinker. "With warm updrafts and otherwise calm air, and Bottommost precisely below. I suggest we float."

The others in the group turned to Mavin, exasperated, annoyed, yet despite their annoyance sure that the weird creature had thought of something. "Mavin . . ." Beedie pleaded. "I don't know how to talk to theo–theor-whats-its. Will you talk to him? He makes me tired."

Mavin sighed. "Well, Thinker. Explain yourself. In short and sensible words."

"Well, in layman's terms, there are flattree leaves lying in the Nextdown nets, which are slightly above us. Climbable, I should think. By the young woman with spurs. Or even reachable from the stairs, for that matter. There are half a dozen of them there, at least, very large, tissuey things, soft, pliable, almost like fabric. It has occurred to me that they might be used to manufacturer a kind of hyperbolic air compression device . . . let me see, 'wind catchers.' Then, we leap off, one by one, and after an interesting float, we arrive at Bottommost."

"Splashed into a puddle on the commons, no doubt," said Beedie. "Going about a million man heights every heart beat."

"Dropping at about one man height per heart beat," said

the Thinker, annoyed. "Please do not dispute scientific fact with me. It is annoying enough when qualified people do it."

"Would it work?" Beedie pleaded to Mavin. "We could always work along the root wall to the stairs to Midwall. If we take it carefully . . ."

"If we take it carefully, it would take us five days," sighed Mavin, muttering almost inaudibly. She knew that she could solve the problem in a number of ways, all of which required that she gain bulk and shift into something large, crawly or winged, which would involve her in endless explanations. She preferred to remain only a messenger from the Boundless, bird or woman, nothing more than that. It would be safer for Handbright if her sister was not thought to be a devil of some kind even by this friendly group. "Look, I'll test the Thinker's idea. I can always become a bird, so there's no danger. If it works for me, then the rest of you can try it."

"Become a bird?" asked the theoretician. "Is that metaphorical?"

"Never mind," said Beedie, irritated. "Just explain to Mavin what this 'wind catcher' thing is!"

By the time she had climbed to the net, folded and extricated five of the flattree leaves and returned them to the stair, light was shining clearly through the flattrees high above. Rigging the wind catchers seemed to take forever, and Beedie kept reminding herself how long a traverse of the root wall would have taken. Mavin had more or less figured out what the Thinker had in mind and had drawn a little diagram of the way the cords should be strung, from the edges of the leaves to a central girdle. When the first one was done, Mavin fastened the cord girdle around herself then spread the folded leaf along the railing as she climbed over.

"This should be very interesting. It would probably help to jump out as far as possible." The Thinker had observed all this rigging with great interest but without offering to help. "It should unfold nicely, if it doesn't catch on the railing."

"If it doesn't tear, if the ropes hold, if the leaf doesn't rip in the air, if Bottommost is really straight down," muttered Beedie. "Mavin, are you sure you want to do this?"

"It's all right, sausage girl. Besides, I think you can rely on the white bird to help out if anything goes wrong. Now, if it works well for me, rig the others in the same way. You come last. That way you can help the rest of them." And with that she leaped out into the chasm, the faded green of the flattree leaf trailing away behind her. The leaf was small as flattree leaves went, only large enough to carpet a large room, and it caught the air, cupped it, turned into a gently rounded dome that seemed to hang almost motionless in the air as it dwindled slowly, slowly downward.

"Lovely," came Mavin's voice. "Toss Mercald over."

They had already decided that Mercald would have to be tossed. He had turned up his eyes and gone limp at the thought of being dropped into the chasm and was now completely immobile. It was Roges who heaved him over, out into the chasm like a lumpy spear, and they all held their breaths until the leaf opened above him.

"I thought that would work," said the Thinker, tying himself to the girdle. He waited with no evidence of impatience while Mavin spread the leaf behind him, then stepped far into the chasm.

"All right, Roges," she said, knowing without looking that he was sweating again. "Don't look down."

"Beedie."He reached out to touch her shoulder. "You're very pretty, did you know that? Ever since you were little, when you first came to Bridgers House on Topbridge. Even then, you were pretty."

She stared at him, disconcerted again. "I always had skinned knees," she said. "And Aunt Six said my face was never clean from the time I was born."

"Maybe," he replied, trying to smile. "But pretty in spite of it."

"Is this like the hair business?" she asked, growing angry. "You think you're going to get badly hurt or die, so you want to tell me now? Well let me tell you, Roges, I don't go throwing my friends over railings if I think they're going to die. Mavin says she'll catch any of us who have trouble, so if there is trouble just yell and keep yelling. Get up there over that railing and let me spread this thing out." She pushed at him, getting behind him so that he couldn't see the tears on her face. All she seemed to do lately was cry! When he was poised to go, however, shaking so uncontrollably that she could not fail to see it, she could not let him go without a word.

"Roges. When we're down. When we're finished with all this. When we've got the proof that the Banders are murderers and Mavin figures out how to kill those things, tell me then that I'm pretty, will you?" And she pushed him. He fell silently, without a sound, and she found her nails cutting small, bloody holes in her palms until the leaf billowed behind him, cupping air, and he floated after the others.

She spread her own leaf carefully, being sure it would not snag on the railing, then leaped outward – into terror. Her heart thrust upward into her mouth, clogging her breathing. She gasped, sickened, eyes wide with fear, horrified at the weightless, plunging feel of falling, she who had never been afraid of heights before. "You never fell before," she screamed at herself. "Oh, I'm going to die. . . ."

Then the leaf opened above her. Warm air rose around her,and the root wall drifted past.

Silence. It was the first thing she noticed. Stairs drummed and clamored beneath feet. Bridgetowns were full of chatter and whine. On the root there was always the noise of the spurs digging in, the chafe of the straps, the blows of hammers or hatchets. But here, here was silence, only the drum of one's blood in one's ears, only the far, falling cry of a bird. Below her, slightly to one side, she could see a movement in the root wall as small creatures burrowed there, then a bare spot where a strange rock . . . a scabrous, oozing rock – the *creature*. There it was, piled into a cave in the wall, only part of its horrid hide exposed. It heaved, breathed, lived, and she dropped below it. The peace of the drop had been destroyed and her stomach heaved in sick revulsion.

She heard Roges calling, twisted herself around to find him. The mound of his leaf was below her, and she called down to him. "Just above you, Roges. Can you see Mercald?"

"Under . . . me . . ." came the call. "Hear . . . town . . ."

She listened, hearing it at last, the far, rattling clamor of a town. What was the word Mavin used? "*Gamelords*!" More and more lately it seemed like a game, some strange, silly game in which no one knew the rules. Would old Slysaw come down after them? Likely he would, if the stairs were passable. She considered for the first time that the creature, whatever it was, might have cut the stair root, eaten the stairs themselves. In which case, Slysaw couldn't follow, and where would their proof be then? And Mercald might be permanently out of his head, in which case they didn't have a judge. So, so, "Gamelords," she swore fervently.

The sounds from below grew louder, even as the light around her grew dimmer, more watery. Now it was dusky, shadowy, an evening light. She searched the darkness below her for lights, lanterns, torches, seeing nothing. She looked up at the wall once more, watching it float past, thinking.

She had to think about Roges. Roges, by the Boundless. A Maintainer. Though she knew some Bridgers who were married to Maintainers. Several of them. Quite happily. Rootweaver herself had been married to a Maintainer, so it was said. He had been killed during a storm, a great storm of rain which had almost drowned Topbridge and all who lived there, but he had saved Rootweaver's life, so it was said. She recalled what Roges had said. "We are more than servants, much more." That was true. It wasn't always remembered, but it was true.

"Beeeedieeee," came a call from below. Roges' voice again. She looked down, seeing the lights now, glowing fish lanterns making green balls of light, yellow and blue balls of light all along the bridgetown mainroots, two glowing necklaces of lights in the depths. She was not quite above the town, and for a moment she felt panic, believing she would fall on past, but then there was a brush of wings and a voice, "Well, sausage girl. You and Mercald are the only ones I've had to fish in. Roges and the whatsit fell straight as a line. Hold on, now, I'll tow you a little. . . ." Her straight line of fall turned into a long, diagonal drop that brought her over the open avenue of Bottommost.

"I'll not appear like this," Mavin called in a whisper from above. "Join you later. . . ."

The bridge grew larger, larger, more light, more sound, wondering faces looking up, a great tangled pile of flattree leaves below with Roges reaching up from the middle of it, reaching up, to grab her – then they stood together as the leaf fell over them, closing them in a green fragrant tent, away from the world. He was holding her tightly. She was not trying to get away. Neither of them were saying anything, though there was much chatter from outside.

Mercald was saying, "Get them out from under there before they suffocate," and Beedie was thinking quietly that she would like to suffocate Mercald and to have done it yesterday. Then the leaf was pulled away amid much shouting, and Roges untied the lines from her waist.

"I'll save the cord," he said in a strangely breathless voice. "We'll need it later, I don't doubt."

She needed to say something personal to him, something real. "The fall – I was scared. When I jumped, all of a sudden, I was really frightened."

He looked at her with a kind of joyousness in his eyes that she didn't understand at all. "Were you really, Bridger? So was I." Then Mavin in her persona of birdwoman came calmly through the crowds and the moment's understanding was behind them.

"Come on," she whispered. "Though I must pretend to be the birdwoman once more, I have serious need of breakfast, and tea, and a wash. And poor Mercald needs a change of clothing. Unfortunately for him, his unconscious state did not last until he landed. And then we all need to revise some plans, or make some. It seems things are worse then we knew."

They had landed just outside the Bridgers House of Bottommost. It was a small house, not as well kept as the one at Topbridge, but with a guest wing, nonetheless, though one barely large enough for all five of them.

After a quick wash, they went along to the House dining hall, Mercald resplendent in his robes and hat – the only garb he had to wear while his others were being washed. As for the rest of them, they were only cleaner, not otherwise changed except that Mavin was once more playing her silent role of birdwoman. The food was quickly provided and almost as quickly eaten before Roges and Beedie were taken aside into a smaller room where the eldest Bridger of Bottommost awaited them, wringing his hands and compressing his lips in an expression of concern.

"The Messenger came yesterday, Bridger. We did not expect you for many days still, and yet here you are! I thank the Boundless you have come, for it was only two days ago we first saw the *thing*. I have sent word to the head of chasm council, but we cannot expect a response from old Quickaxe – or from his junior, Rootweaver – for some days."

"By *thing*," said Beedie, "I suppose you mean the gray monster with the oozing hide." At his expressions of awed dismay, she went on, "We encountered it on the downward stair. Eating the stair, I should say. Just the other side of Nextdown."

"Is it true what my Bridgers say?" the old man asked, hoping, Beedie knew, that she would say it was all an exaggeration.

"It is a thing some six or seven man heights long, as big around as this room, Elder. A . . . man who is with us says he believes it is sick. He believes it has been poisoned, perhaps purposely, by . . . Roges, what can I say? By what?"

"By people, Beedie. The . . . ah, the messenger of the Boundless who is with us says that there may be . . . people in the depths. That is, if it was not done by people from this town, Elder."

Beedie sighed. "Elder, have you made any attempt to kill this thing? Or have you had any word of any intelligent creatures living below you in the depths?"

"Never." He wriggled the thought around in his mouth for a time, trying it between various pairs of teeth, finally spat it back at them. "No, never. As for killing the thing, I would not know where to begin. As for the other, my Bridgers go down the roots as Bridgers do, and up, and out across the root wall. We see the usual things. Crawly-claws. Slow-girules. Wireworm nests, sometimes. Leaves fall from above, and sometimes the nets of Topbridge or Nextdown miss them so we catch them. It is true that the Fishers bring up strange things from time to time, oddities which we cannot explain. But intelligence below . . . well, I've never heard any allegation of it."

"The lost bridge?" prompted Beedie. "That would be below you, wouldn't it?"

"Oh, but my dear Bridger. What is the lost bridge? Sometimes I wonder if it ever existed! And if it did, is it not surely gone? No one has seen or heard of the lost bridge for what? – hundreds of years."

She shook her head. "When there was a lost bridge, before it was lost, Elder, how did people get to it? Was there a stair?"

He made a face at her, age grimacing at the silly ideas of youth. "There is said to have been a stair. Yes. At the morning-light side. We even have some books with adventure tales for children concerning the stairs and the lost bridge and all the rest of it. Would you like to see them?"

Beedie started to say no, indignantly, then caught sight of Roges' face, intent upon the old man's words. "I would, yes, Elder. If you would be so kind."

"I will have them sent to the guest rooms. Have you any other word for me, Bridger? We are very much afraid of these creatures. . . ."

"They are afraid of fire," said Beedie firmly. "It is thought they might be afraid of light.''

''Not of our lanterns, I'm afraid. The one we saw two days ago was on the stair trail which leads to the mines below Miner's bridge. It is a little used way built for the convenience of the Miners, to bring loads of some materials across to us for processing. It was lit by fish lanterns, and the thing had eaten great pieces of the stair, lanterns and all, when first we saw it. Fire – that's a different thing. Torches. We do not use torches. It is damp this far down in the chasm. Except during the wind, smoke lies heavy upon Bottommost. Still, if fire will drive the monsters away, we must somehow learn to use fire once more. . . .'' And the old man turned away, weary and fearful, yet somehow resolute.

They walked back toward the guest rooms, Beedie's hand finding Roges' as they went, silent, dismayed not a little. They slipped into the room Mavin shared with Beedie and told her what had transpired.

''So the Thinker was right,'' said Mavin. ''The things have only recently been seen so far up in the chasm. Well, they must somehow be made to go back where they have been. We will stay here in Bottommost today, perhaps tonight. Read the books when they are brought, sausage girl.'' Then, seeing her annoyed expression, ''Read them to her, Roges, if you will. I will return after dark. If anyone asks, the messenger of the Boundless is asleep,'' and she slipped out of the room, disappearing down the corridor.

''Do you want to sleep, too?'' asked Roges. ''Our rest last night was interrupted.''

''Later perhaps. Not now. Now I want to see Bottommost, the mysterious bridgetown I have heard of since I was a child! Aunt Six says it is all rebels and anarchists here, that there is no custom worthy of the name, that bad children gravitate to Bottommost as slow-girules to root mice. We are here and I must see if she lied to me.''

They left Mercald curled up on a clean bed, quietly asleep. They left the Thinker sitting in a window, staring at nothing, a small muscle in his left cheek twitching from time to time. Beedie had had the generous intent of asking him if he wanted to go with them. One sight of him changed her mind. The two of them went out together, out of Bridgers House onto the main avenue of Bottommost.

''It's narrow!'' she exclaimed. ''It's little.'' Compared to Topbridge, it was narrow and confined, the lines of lanterns which marked the mainroots only two hundred paces apart, beads of light softly glowing in two arcs that met at the far wall. "And it's like night-time!" Far above them the light of the chasm could be seen as a wide line of green, slightly shifting, as though they looked upward into a flowing stream, but the light upon the bridge came more from the ubiquitous fish lanterns than from the sky. Every corner carried at least one of the scaled globes; every market stall was lined with them, blue orbs and green, with an occasional amber one here and there. Those which were amber, Beedie noticed, bore horns and warts and protuberances of various shapes and kinds as well as a discouraging set of fangs. "I would not like to be the Fisher who caught one of those," she remarked to Roges.

Bottommost was quieter then Topbridge. It buzzed with a muted sound, as though it did not wish to attract attention to itself. The cries of the hawkers were melodious and soft, a kind of repetitive song. "They don't look like rebels and anarchists," said Roges. "They look rather sad"

"It's because there's so little light. It's an evening sadness, a perpetual dusk. If I lived here, I would cry all the time." The colours of the place were strange to her high chasm eyes. Soft greens and grays and blues. No white or red, no yellow. "Look how narrow their nets are." The nets on either side of the railing were mere handkerchiefs, of no extent.

"Look up and you'll see why," murmured Roges. High against the light were the twin bars of Topbridge and Nextdown, bracketing Bottommost on each side. "If the nets were any wider, they'd be catching all the fall-down from up there. Not very pleasant for the net cleaners."

"Well, there's got to be something good about the place. Let's try a teashop." And in the teashop they began to appreciate the true flavor of Bottommost as the calls of the hawkers, the bells in the Birder House, and the soft light blended into music. If there were rebels in Bottommost, they were rebels of an odd sort, rebels of silence, of shadow, of gentle movement. "I haven't seen any Banders," she said. "None in the House."

"There are some here," he replied. "I asked the Maintainer who brought us blankets whether there had been any unrest on Bottommost concerning the messenger of the Boundless. She said yes, rumor and story telling, a small attempt to whip up frenzy, resulting in nothing much. Still, there are some of them here, enough to do us harm if we are not careful.''

''Enough to carry the word back to old Slysaw?''

''I should judge so.'' He did not sound as though he cared greatly about it, about anything. He had been sitting, sipping, smiling at her for hours. She blushed. She, too, had been sipping, smiling. Resolutely, she got to her feet. ''Roges. We promised Mavin we would read the books about the lost bridge.'' She took his hand, dragged him upright.

They went out onto the avenue, still hand in hand, lost in the gentle music of Bottommost, to remember it always as magical and wonderful, more wonderful than any of the truly wonderful things which were to follow.

CHAPTER SEVEN

Lantern-eyed, fluff-winged she flew along the root wall, soft as down, observant as any owl in the dusk, peering at this, that, the other thing. There were many small creepies, many larger ones as well-claws gently waving, and things that came to the claws thinking they were something else; shelves of fungus in colours of amber and rose, washed into grays by the green light; other fungoid growths hanging upon the roots themselves in pendant fronds, projecting horns and antlers and mushroomy domes, pale as flesh, moist as frogs.

There was a chorus of smells, rich and fecund stenches, rot and mildew and earthy green slime. There were greens innumerable, bronzy green and amber green and the blue-green of far seas not remembered by the people in the chasm. The air was wet, wetter the lower she went, full of mist wraiths which seemed in any instant almost to have coherent shape. Her wings were wet and heavy, and she changed the structure of her feathers to shed the damp, bringing a clear set of membranes across her eyes at the same time.

Those who might have known her in the white bird shape would not have known her in her present form, and she took pleasure in this, in this renewed feeling of anonymity, of remoteness. Beedie was a good girl; Roges a treasure; the theoretician an interesting find; Mercald a necessary burden – and not good enough to be a partner for Handbright as she had been, though perhaps better than one could have expected for Handbright as she was now – but there was much to be said for solitude. There was time for contemplation, time for feeling the fabric of the place, time for memory.

There had been another place, not unlike the chasm in its watery light, a pool-laced forest, green under leaves, full shadowed in summer warmth and breathless with flowers. Mavin had come there in the guise of a sweet, swift beast, four-legged and lean, graceful as the bending grass. It had been a shape designed for the place, needful for the place, and her body had responded to that need without thinking. So she had unaware she was observed, wandered, unaware until she came one dawn to the shivering silver pool and saw her own image standing there, head regally high, crowned with a single spiraled horn like her own, male as she was female, unquestionably correct for that place, that time, without any requirement for explanation.

And there had been a summer then, without speech or thought or plan for the morrow; a summer which spun itself beneath the leaves and over the welcoming grass, sparkling with sun shards and bathed in dew. Morning had gone into evening, day into day, as feet raced upon the pleasant pastures and across the mysterious hills. And then a day, a day with him gone.

She had never named him in her mind, except to believe that whoever he was, he was Shifter like herself, for there was no such supernally graceful beast in the reality of this world, had never been, probably now would never be again. And when a certain number of days had gone without his return, she had shifted herself and left the place behind her, sorrowing that she would not know him again if she met him in a street of any town or upon the road to anywhere at all. Outside of that place, that stream-netted garden of gold-green light, what they had been together would have no reality.

It was the sight of Roges' face that had made her think of this, Roges' face as he brooded over Beedie who, though she was beside him, did not see the way he looked at her. In that silken passionate look which reverberated like soft thunder was what she had felt in the summer garden. And it made her think of something more, of that same expression seen fifteen years before on the face of the Wizard Himaggery. *Twenty years*, he had said. Return to him in twenty years. Over three-quarters of that time was gone. Well, she could not think of that now, not with Handbright's child soon to be delivered, and Mavin soon to take it away to be safely reared as a Shifter's child should be reared – not with the chasm to be explored – and all these lands beyond the sea.

She moved out into the chasm, away from the root wall, attracted by a hard-edged shape which spiraled down toward her. It was one of the rigid frameworks webbed with flopperskin which the Messengers used to fly between bridgetowns, gliding on the warm, uprising air to carry messages from Topbridge to Harvester's. She flew close, wondering what brought a Messenger to these depths.

It was no Messenger. The kite held a young man's body, shrouded in white upon the gliding frame, staring with unseeing eyes into the misty air. There were embroidered shoes upon his feet, a feathered cap upon his head, and his hands were tied together before him with a silken scarf. Someone had decked the beloved dead for this last flight. Someone had set dreams aside, love aside, to grieve over this youth, and in that grieving, had realized there would be no more time in which to dream.

She flew aside, eyes fixed upon those dead eyes, as though she might read something there, accompanying the body down as it fell, turn on wide turn into the narrowing depths. At last she let it go, watching as it twirled into the chasm, softly as a leaf falls, the bright feather upon the cap catching at her vision until it vanished in mist.

No more time in which to dream. Twenty years. The bird body could not hold the pain which struck at her then, a shiver of grief so great that she cried out, the sound echoing from root wall to root wall, over and over again, in a falling agony of sound. She did not often think of herself as mortal.

"I will return," she promised herself. "I will return."

And was Himaggery still alive in that world across the sea? Must be, her mind told her sternly. Must be. I would have known if anything had happened to him. I could not have failed to know.

There, in the chasm mists, the Mavin-bird sang its determination and decision, even while it sought for mystery in the chasm with wide eyes.

Back in the guest rooms of Bridgers House, Roges lay with his head in Beedie's lap and read to her.

" 'In the time of the great builders, the outcaste Mirtylon (he whose name came from the ancient times above the chasm) took captive the maiden daughter of the designer of Firstbridge, the Great Engineer, she whom he called Lovewings after the love he bore her mother who had died. For the Great Engineer had forbidden his daughter to marry Mirtylon, though he had sought her in honor and in love, for the Great Engineer feared to lose her from his house.

" 'And Mirtylon fled from the wrath of the Great Engineer, into the bottomless depths of the chasm, root to root, with his followers, losing themselves in the shadowy lands beneath the reach of the sun. Then it was the Great Engineer wept and foamed in his fury, for taken from him was what he held most dear in all his life, for Lovewings had gone with them. And he fell into despair. And in his despair he failed to set the watch upon the bridge, and in the night the great pombis came, lair upon lair of them out of the darkness, driving the people of Firstbridge down into the chasm to the half – built city of Secondbridge, called by some Nextdown. And though many came there for refuge, the Great Engineer was slain together with the Maintainers of his house.

" 'But unknowing of this was the outcaste Mirtylon and unknowing of this was Lovewings – who would have been greatly grieved, for she loved her father – so she married Mirtylon of her own will and lived with him in a cave at great depth upon the root wall while those who followed him drew great mainroots together for the establishment of the town of Waterlight. In those depths the light was that found deep in river pools of their former lands, mysterious and shadowy. And in time the bridgetown of Waterlight was built, and Bridgers were sent from it to build a stair along the morning-light wall which should reach from Waterlight upward to the rim of the chasm. And in time the Bridgers so sent met the Bridgers of Nextdown upon the root wall, and the news of the death of the Great Engineer, her father, came to Lovewings.

" 'Then did she feel great guilt and great despair, accounting herself responsible for what had occurred, for she well knew with what value her father had held her. And she went to Mirtylon and told him she would go away for a time, to expiate her guilt in loneliness after the manner of her religion, but he would not let her go.

"And by this time the stair which Mirtylon had ordered to be built stretched upward from the depths into the very midst of the chasm, to the new-built bridge of Bottommost. Forbidden to expiate her guilt Lovewings took herself to the highest point which had yet been built and threw herself into the depths so that none saw her more. This is the story told of her, for none knew the truth of it save that she had climbed the stair and came no more to Waterlight.

" 'And Mirtylon despaired, ordering that the stair be shattered, that none might walk that way again. So it was broken, and all connection between Waterlight and the other cities of the chasm was cut off.

" 'Still the Messengers flew between the bridges, and there was trade of a kind between them, with much gathering of gems and diamonds from the Bottom lands by those of Waterlight, and much trading of this treasure for the foodstuffs which grew high above. And though people of the bridgetowns were curious as to the source of the treasure, the secret was well kept by the people of Waterlight who would say only that the treasure was gathered at great danger to themselves from that which dwelt in the Bottomlands below.

" 'Until came a day the Messengers flew to Waterlight to find it gone, its place empty, the roots severed, the people gone, all in one night, vanished as though taken by a Demon or devil of the depths.

" 'And of Mirtylon many songs are sung, and of Lovewings, and of the vanished bridge which is called Lostbridge, and of the shattered stair. . . .' "

"And that," Roges said, "is that. There's another story here about Lovewings. You want to hear it?"

"No," said Beedie definitely. "It's depressing. All that guilt and' foolishness and throwing themselves about. I would like to know where the bridge went, though."

"So would Mavin," said Roges. "And I doubt not she'll find out, one way or another. Whatever she may be, she is very positive about things. I wonder who she is – what she is. . . ."

"I don't know. She's like the birdwoman. I mean, there are two of them, sisters. That's all I know. What I think about how she came when I was caught on the root, dying in the smoke, I know I should be frightened of her. But I'm not. She's just not scary."

"I think she's scary." Roges was serious, worried. "Though I try not to show it. She knows things. That's scary."

"Oh, the theo . . . theor . . . the whatsit knows things, too. And I know things. And some are the same things, and some are different things. That's all. It doesn't matter to *her*! It shouldn't matter to you."

Roges laughed, burrowed the back of his head into her lap, reached up to touch her face. "Beedie, you don't have any doubts at all, do you?"

"Hardly any," she agreed, in surprise that he should ask. "It seems an awful waste of time. You just do things, and if it doesn't work, then you do something else next time. Sitting around having doubts is very wasteful. At least, it seems so to me."

"Don't you ever worry about whether things are right or wrong?"

"Daddy and mum taught me what wrongs are. I don't do wrongs. I take care of my tools, and I don't risk my neck on the roots, and I'm castely in my behavior – mostly – and polite to my elders. I don't tell lies. What else would you like to know about me?"

"Are you religious?"

"Oh, foof, Roges. You know I'm not. Just enough to make sort of the right responses to noon prayers, and that's about it. Are you?"

"Some," he admitted. "I wonder about the Boundless a lot."

"Maybe you should have been a Birder."

"Maybe I was born a Birder. No one knows. I was found on the root wall, a foundling."

"Oh, Roges. That's very sad. Why, do you suppose?"

"I don't know. Never knew. Tried not to wonder."

"I'm sure I know," she said, grinning at him, not letting him see she was beginning to tear up again. "You were so beautiful a baby that everyone looked at you all the time. Your aunt had an ugly baby no one ever looked at, and it made her so jealous that she stole you away from your mum and daddy and hid you on the root wall, giving out the slow-girules had carried you away. And ever since then they've been longing for you, unable to find you at all."

"Not very likely," he said. "They'd have found me by now."

"That could be true. Well then, we'll say they got very sick from their loss, and they both almost died from despair. And their elders told them they had to give the mourning up."

"Now who's making stories about guilt and despair?" he asked her in mock fury. "Beedie. You're a crazy child."

"I'm not a child," she said, suddenly deciding it was time to prove it to him. "Not a child at all."

They were interrupted by Mavin's voice from the doorway, warm and amused. "I see I interrupt. Well, such is my fate. I have found the broken stairway, young ones." They turned to her, a little dizzy and unaware, not believing her at first, faces questioning. "True! Surprisingly, it is still there. Nothing has eaten it. It hasn't rotted. It is hatcheted away at the top end, but the rest of it goes down and down – overgrown a little, true – into the depths."

Then they were both on their feet, the books – and other things – forgotten for the moment. "Did you go to the bottom? Have you seen it? Shall we go now?" asked Beedie, ready as ever for action.

"I saw only a little. The light is scant enough at this depth, and what is there is waning. I think we will go at first light tomorrow. While I saw no signs of the gray oozers on the morning-light wall, it should be easier to avoid them in light. So. Let us go in light, such as it is." And she stretched herself upon the bed in the room. "Go on with whatever you were doing. . . ."

"Oh, Mavin," Beedie growled. "You are not always very funny."

"Not always," agreed Roges in a wry voice. "I think it would be a good idea for all of us to get some rest and a good meal here at Bridgers House tonight." He took up the books, placing them in a neat stack on the table beside Mavin's bed.

Mavin leafed idly through one of the books, scanning a few pages while Beedie talked about the story of Lovewings and Mirtylon and how sad it was, then let her eyes close.

"Mavin . . . Mavin. Are you asleep?"

"Trying very hard to be, sausage girl."

"Do you think old Slysaw is still following us?"

"I can guarantee he is, child. At this moment, he is two-thirds of the way down the stair to Midwall. He will rest in Midwall tonight. Two nights hence he will rest here in Bottommost. And the day after that, someone will show him where the broken stair is."

"Do you think we will get proof he killed my family? That he set fire to the mainroot?"

"I don't think it matters, root dangler. Whether we get proof Mercald would accept or not, I have enough to suit me. You may depend upon it. Old Slysaw Bander will not return from the depths." And then there was only the gentlest of snores, like a dragon purring, as Mavin slept.

There was a traverse of considerable extent across the root wall between the morning-light end of Bottommost and the place the old stair began, its splintered end well hidden behind a cluster of side roots and a fountain of fungus. The Bridgers of Bottommost were so excited at the thought of finding the old stair, however, that they had worked most of the night while the expedition slept to build a temporary footbridge across the root wall. Except for Mercald, the expedition crossed it without difficulty, and Roges solved the Mercald problem by carrying him over on one shoulder. Once the stair was reached and they had burrowed into it with hatchet and knife and much flinging aside of great blobs of fungus, Mercald was able to stand once more, though it took him a little time to be steady on his feet.

"It's hidden," Beedie said, looking down the stair in the direction they would go. "The roots have grown all over the outside of it." Indeed, it was like walking through some dusky cloister, the roots on the outside of the stair making repeated windows into the chasm so that they walked first in shadow, then in half light, then in shadow once more. "How far down does it go, Mavin?"

"I didn't find out. Just found that the stair was here, then flew up above to check out old Slysaw. Shh. Here's the Thinker coming along behind. I'd as soon not talk with him about my private habits. Hush now."

They set a slow pace at first, warming up to it as the day warmed, easing up again when they had eaten their midday meal, then slowing still further when the afternoon wind began to blow down the canyon, whipping the root hairs over the stairs, making their eyes water.

"I postulate a desert at the lower end of this chasm," said the Thinker, wiping his eyes so that he could see his note book. "Quite large, very dry, very hot. At the upper end of the chasm a range of mountains, perhaps a tall, snow-capped range. . . ."

"Actually," said Mavin, "it's a glacier. A monstrous big one."

He did not ask her how she knew, but simply plunged on with his explanation. "The sun heats the air over the desert. It rises. The air in the chasm, being cooler, flows out onto the desert. The air over the glacier, being cooler still, flows down into the chasm. We have wind each day from afternoon through about midnight, by which time the desert has given up all its heat. Then the hot springs in the chasm begin to warm the chasm air once more. The lower we go in the chasm, the stronger the winds will become. That is, unless there are many barriers down there, narrowings, turns, fallen rock. In that case, it might be strongest above the bottom. . . ."

"Is that true?" Beedie whispered to Mavin. "Is that really why the wind blows every day? The Birders say the Boundless does it to move the smoke away, so we won't suffocate."

"Is there any reason it couldn't be both?" laughed Mavin. "I suppose the Boundless can use deserts and glaciers to sweep smoke away if it wants to."

"The way I would use a broom," said Roges. "Why not. Still, it makes traveling difficult." He wiped away a clot of wet root hairs the wind had driven into his face. "It wasn't this strong on Bottommost."

"It was stronger than you felt. The buildings on Bottommost are all built facing down-chasm, away from the wind. Besides that, they're all built with curved backs, I noticed, and there are wind shields along the streets." Mavin leaned out into the chasm to look down. She was now the only one of the party not constantly wiping streaming eyes, though the others had not noticed the clear lids she had closed to protect her own eyes from the wind. "We may have to find a sheltered place and wait until the wind drops before we go on. I've brought fish lanterns, so we needn't camp in the dark. Hss. What's that?" She pointed away along the root wall, toward a distant shadow. Roges and Beedie thrust their heads out, drawing them in immediately.

"I can't see anything," Roges complained. "What did you think it was?"

"A shape," she replied, still peering into the chasm. "Only a shape. Vaguely manlike. Perhaps it was nothing, only a shadow."

"Probably just a shadow. Our eyes are tired. I think stopping for a time would be a very good idea," said Mercald apologetically. "We've been climbing down since early this morning, and my legs have cramps in them. Both."

"Well then, why not. Start looking for some kind of declivity or protected spot. We'll stop as soon as we find one." Mavin drew her head in and clumped along behind them, her face both thoughtful and apprehensive.

Beedie moved ahead, Roges close beside her, searching the root wall. There were many small holes, but none large enough to offer shelter to the group. Then they came to a fairly flat stretch of stair solidly overgrown on the chasm side with only a shrill shiver of wind entering from the bottom end. "We could close that off," said Beedie, measuring it with analytical eyes. "I can cut some short lengths of ropey root, and weave a kind of gate across it, then we can put a blanket or two across it to shut out almost all the wind." Without waiting for the others, she began to hack at the wall, pulling down lengths of shaggy root. Roges tugged them to the opening, thrust ends into the root wall and began weaving them together, hauling and tugging until the woven gate was in place.

By this time the others had arrived, and Mavin fastened her blanket to the gate, tying it along the sides. It felt as though the temperature on the stair went up at once, just from excluding the cold wind.

"I suppose it would be too much to hope for that there'd be some deadroot along here," Mercald commented. "I'm thirsty for tea."

There was usually deadroot up under the thatch along the wall, and a few moments' scratchy burrowing brought a pile of it to light. It was brittle enough to break and dead enough not to threaten them with lethal smoke, but it was soggier than they were accustomed to burning. Roges had trouble lighting it upon the portable hearth. However, once started, it burned readily enough, the smoke roiling upwards along the stair. They sat in the firelit space, hearing the wind howl outside, all of them aware of some primitive, fearful feelings concerning darkness and the creatures which dwelt in it. Mavin found herself listening to the wind, listening through the wind, trying to hear what other sounds there might be in the chasm. There had been a manshape upon the root wall, and yet not exactly a manshape. It should not have been there. There were no men in the bottoms. She knelt, thrust her ear against the root stair, but there were no hostile sounds, no rasp of great slug teeth, only the thrumming of the wind upon the root fibers, the monotonous hum of steadily moving air.

They sat, dozed, woke with a start only to doze again. The light faded and Mavin took the fish lanterns out of her basket to hang one upon the staff she carried, one upon Mercald's staff. The light was not the warming amber-red of firelight but the chill blue-green of water, and they found themselves shivering.

"The wind will let up about midnight," said Mavin. "I suggest we wrap up tightly, get as close together as possible to share warmth, and wait until then to go on." She heard no dissent, not even from the Thinker, though he did not lie down among them but sat under the chill green lanterns muttering to himself, making notes in his little book.

The wind began to howl loudly, rocking the stair, moving it in a curiously restful motion, so that they all slept as in a cradle, or, thought Mavin, as on the deck of a sea-going ship.

It was the cessation of motion that wakened Mavin, that and the stillness. The Thinker still sat, still muttered, eyes fixed on something the rest of them could not see. In the darkness, she could see firelight glittering on Beedie's open eyes.

"So. You're awake, sausage girl."

"I'm sore," she complained. "Next time I'm going to bring something softer to sleep on."

"How often do you plan to go on such expeditions?"

"Whenever I can. Don't you think it's exciting?"

"Umm," said Mavin. "What does Roges think?"

"I'm sure he thinks he'll be very glad when he can get me back to Topbridge and maybe marry me and probably talk me into having babies."

"What do you think about that?" Mavin sat back, pulling her own blanket around them so that they half reclined between Roges and Mercald, warmed by their sleeping bodies. "Is that something you would enjoy?"

"When Roges and I are – when we're . . . ah . . . involved, I don't mind the idea. Then, other times, like now, I *do* mind the idea. I want to go to Harvester's bridge and around the chasm corner and see what's there. I want to see that thing you told the Thinker about, that glacier. I can't do that if I'm all glued down on Topbridge with babies and Aunt Six being grandma. Whoof. I'd sooner eat dried flopperskin."

"By that, I presume you mean the idea lacks flavor."

"Flavor, and chewability, and a good smell. Oh, Mavin, I don't know. Were you ever in love?"

Mavin considered this. In the lovely summer forest, once, she had loved. In the long ago of Pfarb Durim, when she had been the age Beedie was now, she had looked into love's face, had heard its very voice. Since she had seen the dead youth fluttering like a dry leaf into the chasm, she had been aware of mortality in a way she had never been before. If she were honest, she would admit that the five years which stretched between now and that time she would meet Himmaggery seemed a very long time, a time she would shorten if she could. And yet it would be hard to say why, for little had passed between them in that long ago time. Little? Or perhaps much?

Finally she answered. "I believe . . . believe that I love, yes. Someone. And yet, I have not sought him out in many years. I do not go to him or call him to me."

"How do you know he's still alive? People die, you know. Things happen to them." Beedie had thought of this in the night hours, had wondered how she would feel if she put off Roges until some future time and then found there was no future time for them. "If I had to choose, I suppose I'd rather have a child now than never do it at all."

Mavin shivered at this expression of her own thoughts. "You would rather love Roges now than never a do it at all? Even though it might keep you from that far turn of the chasm?"

"Hmm. I think so. How do I know? Would there be someone else who would make me feel the same way? Would I have cheated him if I did not?"

Mavin chuckled, humor directed at herself rather than at Beedie. "I know. Since I met . . . the one I speak of, all other men have seemed to have . . . too much meat on their faces. I find myself longing for a certain cast of feature, a strong boniness, a wide, twisty mouth, eyes which seem to understand more than that mouth says. . . ."

"Eyebrows which meet in the middle over puzzled, sometimes angry eyes," whispered Beedie. "A certain smell to skin. A certain curl of hair around an ear. . . ."

"Ah, yes, sausage girl. Well, I will say only this one thing to you. If you would regret forever not having done a thing, then do it. But you need not give up your dreams in order to have done it. Go, if you will, and take your man and babies with you."

"Roges has the down-dizzies." She said it sadly, as though she had announced a dire and deadly disease.

"Well then, leave him at home with the babies and tell him you'll see him when you return." She stood up, stretching her arms to hear the bones crack. "Midnight?" she announced loudly into the silence. "Are we ready to go on?"

They rose, groaning from the hard surface. "Stairs should be carpeted," said Beedie. "Either that, or they should put way stations with beds every half day along them."

"Shhhh." Mavin's hiss quieted them all. She had pulled the makeshift windshield aside and was leaning out over the stair rail, peering into the depths. "Look."

Below them in the suddenly calm air, the chasm was full of lights, globes of pearly luminescence which swam through the moist air, collected in clusters like ripening fruits, then separated once more to move in long, glowing spirals and curving lines. As they watched, several of the globes swam up to their level, peered at them from the abyss with wide, fishes' eyes from bodies spherical and puffed as little balloons of chilly light. One of them emitted a tiny, burping sound, then dropped with a sudden, surprised swoop to a much lower level and fled. The other, a smaller, bluer one, with quick, busy fins, followed them as they continued the downward way. There were smaller things in the chasm, also, vibrations of translucent wings, shivering dots of poised flight, darting among the glowing fish to be gulped down whenever they approached too near.

Other blue fish joined the one which followed them, and then still others, until they were trailed by a long tail of blue light, shifting and glowing. "There," said Mavin suddenly, pointing ahead of them. After a moment they saw what she had seen, huge stumps of mainroot, projecting into the chasm like broken corbels. "This is where the city was."

"*Waterlight*," said Beedie and Roges together.

"What was that?"

"Waterlight," said Roges. "The name of Lostbridge was really Waterlight. At least, according to the books up in Bottommost."

"I can see why," murmured Mercald. "I haven't seen a bird of any kind since way before Bottommost. Do you think these fishes keep them away?"

"I think the air is too wet for them," said Mavin, not bothering to tell him that she knew so from experience. "Feathers would get soggy, heavy in this air. It would be almost impossible to fly."

"No Birders, then," he said. "I wonder what religion the people had to come uncomplaining into this depth."

"Follow the leader, I should think," said Roges. "The man who built Waterlight was named Mirtylon. From the tone of the stories we read, the people followed him and him alone."

"Always a mistake," said Mercald. "To follow men instead of the Boundless."

"On the other hand," remarked Beedie, "if you're following a man, he can at least tell you what he really expects you to do. Sometimes it seems to me the Boundless is a little vague."

Mavin was examining the end of the severed mainroots, noticing that they did not appear to have been chopped through or sawn.

The ends were blunted, as though melted. She shivered. "Down," she said. "We're spending too much time in chitchat. This was the level of the city; now we'll find out where it went."

Though Beedie had expected the stair to end at the site of the ancient bridgetown, it went on down, doubling back on itself onto a new root system. They clambered around the turn, carrying the lantern fish which seemed to attract other, living ones, so that they continued to walk with a growing tail of lighted globes.

"Electron transport," said the Thinker suddenly, almost yelling. "Hydrogen segregation through cytochromes."

"What are you saying now?" asked Mercald in a kindly tone. "What is it, Thinker?"

"That's how they float. Hydrogen. They crack it out of water, using heme or hemelike proteins . . . remarkable." He did a little jig on the stairs, scratching himself as he sought his little notebook among his rags. "We could test it, of course. Try lighting one of them. It should go up in a puff of flame."

"Difficulty to light a flame down here, Thinker. Have you noticed how damp you are? How damp everything is?"

He had tried to separate the pages of his notebook which sogged into a kind of pulp in his hands, and he merely looked at her with an annoyed expression. Beedie felt the increasing weight of her hair, the knot on her neck as waterlogged as it was possible to be. Also, the air had grown warmer during the past hours so that they seemed to move through a thin soup, almost as much liquid as gas. "I've been in fogs as thick as this before," said Mavin, as though talking to herself. "But not many. I hope we're nearly down, for if it gets any thicker, we'll be swimming."

She stopped, amazed, for the light of the fishes showed a net reaching out from the stair in every direction, as far as she could see on every side. Fish swam up and down through the meshes, some large, some small, and below the net they gathered by the thousands. The stair burrowed through the net, and they followed it down, silent, wondering, one man height, two, three, four. Then Mavin stepped off the root onto stone, the others crowding after. "Shhh," she said. "Listen. Water running."

The sound seemed to come from all around them, a light splashing, babbling sound, an occasional whoosh of air, a chuckle as of streams over stone. "The fish are all above us now," said

Beedie. "None below us. We must be at the Bottom." At that moment her feet struck solid stone.

"Look up," said Roges. "Noonglow." There, so far above them that it did not seem they could have come from that height, was the narrow ribbon of green light which meant noonglow, a mere finger's width shining through the fish-spangled gloom. "Bottommost is only a day and a half from the Bottom. I thought it was much farther than that."

"No one has tried to find out for a very long time," said Beedie. "Because everyone believes it is dangerous. I told you that, Mavin."

"Indeed you did, root dangler. I haven't forgotton. But I remember also that you did not tell me why it is dangerous, or for whom. So – let us go carefully, watchfully."

"And well prepared," said Roges, taking his knife from his belt. "I thank the Boundless we have sure footing beneath us if danger comes."

"I, too," murmured Mercald. "I thank the Boundless for having seen such wonders. What must we do next?"

"The promise I made to Rootweaver, priest, was that we would put an end to whatever it is that eats the roots of the towns. So much; no less, no more. In return for which she keeps Handbright safe, awaiting our return. Well, we know it is the gray oozers which eat the roots. I have seen none of them on the root wall below Bottommost. So – I presume we must search." She had been speaking moderately loudly, loudly enough to attract a circle of curious fish, loudly enough that they were not really surprised to hear a voice answering her from outside their circle. . . .

It was a breathy voice, the kind of voice a forge bellows might have, full of puffing and excess wind. "You need . . . not search . . . far . . . travelers." The word was stretched and breathed, "*traaahvehlehhhrs*."

They turned as one, peering into the shadowy light, seeing nothing at first, locating the speaker only when it spoke again.

"What are . . . you looking . . . for . . . travelers? Is it . . . only . . . the bad beasts . . . of the ... Bottomlands?" *Bhaaahtahmlahhhnds*

Even Mavin, more experienced than the others in the variety of which the world was capable, shivered a little at this voice. There was something ominous in it, though the robed figure which stood in the shadows of the root wall did not menace them in any way.

It merely stood, occasionally illuminated by a passing fish, its hood hiding its face. Mavin shivered again. "We do indeed, stranger. We seek certain beasts, if they are gray, and huge, and eat the roots on which the bridgetowns depend. And we are greatly surprised to find any . . . any person here in the Bottomlands, for we believed them occupied only by creatures. . . ."

"Ahhhh. But . . . you knew . . . of Waterlight." *Whaaaahtehr laihhht.* "Is it believed . . ." – puff, puff – "that . . . those on . . . Waterlight ... perished?"

Beedie started to say something, but Mavin clutched her tightly by the shoulder, bidding her be silent. "Nothing is known of Waterlight, stranger. Nothing save old stories."

"Do the . . . stories . . . speak of . . . Mirtylon?"

"They do, yes," said Roges.

"I am . . . Mirtylon," *Aihh ahhm Muhhhrtihlohhn.* . . . said the figure, moving a little out of the shadow toward them, stopping as they took an involuntary step back, away from it. It was robed from head to toe in loose folds of flattree leaf; a veil of the same material covered its face; its hands were hidden in the full sleeves. It regarded them now through mere slits in the face covering, a vaguely manhigh thing, but with only a line of shoulder and head gleaming in the fish light to say that it had anything resembling manshape.

"Ah," said Mavin. "Waterlight has not been heard of for some hundreds of years. If you are indeed Mirtylon, then you have lived a long time, stranger."

"The . . . Bottomlands are . . . healthful. Things . . . live very . . . long here."

"Enzymes," murmured the theoretician, patting his pockets in search of the notebook which had turned to moist pulp. "Cell regeneration. . . ."

"We desire . . . to welcome . . . you . . . properly," the form went on. "Our . . . village is . . . only a . . . little distance, . . . toward the wind. . . ."

"One moment," said Mavin. "Let us confer for a time." She drew them into a huddle, watching the robed thing over Roges' shoulder. "There is something here I do not like," she muttered. "And I do not want all of us in one heap, like jacks to be picked up on the bounce – Aha, you play that game, do you? Well, I am not about to have it played upon us.

"Beedie, I want you and Roges to go back up the stairs, quick and hard. Keep going until you're *above* where Waterlight used to be. Keep going until the air is dry enough to get a fire going, then build a deadroot fire on the hearth and keep it burning until you hear from me. Don't let it go out. If anyone comes from above, it will be Slysaw. Hide yourself and the fire as best you can and let him come down. If anything comes at you from below, use torches. Do not seem surprised at anything I say, and do . . . not . . . argue with me!" This last was at the rebellious expression on Beedie's face. "I would send Mercald if I thought he could make the climb fast enough. He can't. The Thinker would forget what he was told to do in theorizing about something else. I have no choice. Our lives may depend upon having someone up there who can go for help if we need it, so get going."

Still resentful, Beedie turned toward the stairs, Roges close behind.

"Surely . . . you will not . . . go so soon," puffed the stranger. "We would . . . show . . . our . . . hospital . . .ity."

"We have others waiting for us a little way up the stairs," called Mavin, urging Beedie and Roges upward. "I'm sending the young ones to bring them down. Can you have someone meet the party here when they return?"

There was a doubtful pause, almost as though the figure engaged itself in conversation, for the figure poised, bent, poised again in a way that had a questioning, answering feeling about it. Then at last the breathy voice answered, "We will . . . meet them. Now . . . we will . . . go to our . . . village."

Without looking back, the figure moved along the chasm floor, winding its way between fallen rocks and huge, buttress roots which emerged from the root wall like partitions, ponderous in their height, thickly furred with hair. Mavin looked up at the net spread above them, seemingly stretching from wall to wall of the chasm, from which more root hairs dropped into the rocky soil to make fringed walls along the path on either side.

"Protection," the Thinker muttered. "To protect them from stuff falling off the rim and from the bridgetowns. I would imagine the nets cover the entire area they occupy. And the net is living, of course, because of all these root hairs hanging down, which must mean that they cut these paths through it. No. No. Ah. Look," and he pulled one of the fringing root hairs up before Mavin's face.

"Not cut. Rounded. As though it just stopped growing. Hmm. Now, what would make it do that. . . ."

Mavin did not answer. She was too busy considering that Mirtylon, seemingly so eager to offer hospitality, had not turned to see whether they followed. She looked behind her, seeking Mercald's face, pale as a fish belly. "Are you all right?"

"No," he whispered. "My heart is pounding. I smell something strange. It makes me sweat and shiver."

"Pheromones," said the Thinker. "Something exuded by a living thing to attract mates or warn predators away. Perhaps exuded voluntarily by some kind of water dweller. . . ."

"Perhaps involuntarily," murmured Mavin. "By something that calls itself Mirtylon."

CHAPTER EIGHT

As they walked through the fibrous hallways of the Bottom following the robed stranger, Mavin felt all her senses begin to quiver and extend. Unseen by Mercald or the Thinker, she sharpened her eyes, enlarging them and moving them outward so that she could have a wider range of vision to the sides. What light there was was not much diminished by the netted roof they walked beneath for lantern fish swarmed through the whiskery jungle, casting pale circles of cold light.

Just above and slightly to her left, Mavin saw a hardedged diamond shape upon the net, a thing of some weight, making the net sag beneath it. One of the rare amber fish nosed at the shape from above, and in that sunny glow she caught a glimpse of bright colour, knowing it at once for what it was – the bright feather upon the cap of the young man whose body she had seen two days before, slowly circling upon its kite into the depths. The hallway led beneath it, and when she was almost below, she looked upward, quickly, to see the cap, the kite, the wrappings of white. There was no sign of the body which had been wrapped and decked in the clothes. She made no comment, merely trudged on, keeping close watch on the figure before her.

The sound of water grew louder, a bubbling and boiling with plopping heavings in it as of seething mud. They set foot upon a wooden bridge which led across this noise, through rising clouds of hot mist and the hiss of escaping steam. The bridge was made of short lengths of root, tied with bits of root hair to long, horizontal beams. The robes of the person before her moved in the rising steam without flapping loose, evidently being fastened at the ankle so that no surface of the body could be exposed. Mavin thinned her lips and marched on. Behind her the Thinker muttered once more about tectonics, rift valleys, plate separation. She had no idea what he was talking about, but naive intuition told her that the chasm Bottom burrowed near the great, hot heart of the world and was heated thereby. She needed no theorist's language to tell her that. Her own nose told her, full as it was of sulphurous, ashy stenches and the acrid smell of hot metal.

"We must . . . come to . . . shelter before the . . . winds begin," puffed their guide. "Else we . . . will be crushed."

"Crushed?" wondered Mavin. Certainly the winds were strong, but they had not been of crushing strength. What kind of creature might be crushed by such winds? She checked the two who followed, seeing them trudging along behind her, the one with his eyes fixed firmly upon his boots, the other staring placidly at everything he could see, muttering the while as though he stored away a million facts for later consideration. They had been walking for some time in a winding path that would have confused anyone other than Mavin. She had opened an additional eye in the top of her head and kept it fixed upon the green sky at the chasm top. Though they had walked a considerable distance, they had not come far from the stair. She estimated the distance Beedie and Roges might have climbed. They should be halfway back to the broken roots of Waterlight by now. Keeping her eye fixed on their direction, she went on.

At a conjunction of the hairy hallways they found two other robed strangers waiting. One was silent. The other spoke in a manner no less breathy than the first, but with an unmistakably feminine voice, "We greet you . . . travelers. My name . . . is Lovewings."

Something tugged at Mavin's memory, an insistent, nagging thought which she could not take hold of. "It seems our arrival is not a surprise."

"You were . . . seen on the . . . Shattered Stair. No one has . . . climbed that . . . stair for . . . a long time. The one who . . . saw you was . . . surprised. When we thought . . . about it . . . we knew it . . . must happen sometime. Sometime . . . bridge people must . . . come down." This short speech took an interminable, windy time. It appeared to have exhausted the speaker, and Mavin wondered if they ever spoke to one another in this watery depth or whether they communicated in some other fashion. Certainly their voices seemed unaccustomed to regular use.

"How long has it been since you had commerce with the bridgetowns?" asked Mercald.

"Since . . . since Waterlight . . . fell. Since then. Except . . . there have . . . sometimes been . . . people fall. Into the . . . nets." For all its breathiness, the voice was wistful. Why did Mavin distrust that wistfulness? Could it not reflect an honorable desire for company?

"Why did Waterlight fall?" demanded the Thinker. "Was it conflict? Rebellion? Something eating the roots?"

"Aaahhh," breathed the first guide.

"Aaahhh," echoed the second. There was silence, then the third figure spoke.

"It was . . . was the desire of . . . those on . . . Waterlight. To . . . to go into . . . the Bottomlands . . . and live there. . . ."

"In expiation for those who died on Firstbridge?" demanded Mercald eagerly. "Because of all the deaths that were caused then?"

"Oh, yes . . . yes," all three of the figures sighed, in breathless unanimity. Suspicious unanimity, Mavin thought. They sounded like children caught in some naughtiness who seized upon an offered excuse with relief that they did not need to make up a story of their own. What was going on here? Was it so easy to put words into their mouths?

She spoke quickly. "You have lived here, then, since your scouts first explored here, before Waterlight was taken down. You took Waterlight down yourselves, of course, after you had moved here."

"Of course," sighed the breathy, male voice of the one who called himself Mirtylon. *Ahhhv cohhhhrz.*

"Of course," said the female voice, almost simultaneously.

So she calls herself Lovewings, thought Mavin. Lovewings. What was it she could not remember about Lovewings?

The beard-walled hallway opened into a larger space, a clearing near the morning-light wall through which a quick, cool stream ran down into the steamy lands behind them. Mavin's eye told her that she was only a few wing beats from the stair, though their pathway had wound back and forth across the chasm a dozen times in the last hours. A few score openings gaped in the chasm wall before them, carefully rounded, some of them decorated by a carved fretwork at the sides and top. Around each opening a cloud of fish lanterns hovered, nibbling at the fungus which grew there.

"Saprophytic," murmured the Thinker. "Living upon waste and decay, to be eaten in turn by the fishes, which may be eaten in turn by the occupants. Though I wonder if they would digest at all well? Phosphorous poisoning? I would need to look that up."

"Will you . . . enter?" The robed figures inclined themselves in a mere hint of bow. "Soon the . . . wind will . . . blow."

"My friends will stay here," said Mavin in a firm voice, "until I have seen whether these accommodations are suitable. Mercald? Thinker? Thinker! Can you concentrate on simply standing here for a few moments?" She had succeeded in jolting his attention away from the lantern fish, at least for the moment. She walked up the little slope to the cave, giving no appearance of hurry or distress. The cave was shallow and sandy-floored with a hinged screen standing ajar. Not large, she thought. Large enough for the three of them to lie down in, not large enough for anyone else to come in. And not furnished with anything. Not a pot of water, not a rag to wash one's face, not the semblance of a chair or bed to soften the sandy floor.

She knelt, taking a handful of that sand in her fingers. It was dotted with bright, smooth stones which gleamed at her in blues and violets and greens. Gems. Some of them huge. They were not faceted, but smooth, as though worn by water. Looking back through the gate, she saw sparks of light thrown from many places in the clearing. Well now, she thought. That is interesting. No furnishings of any kind. But protected places, out of the wind. And gems. Everywhere.

"Very nice." She went out. "Very comfortable. Do come up, Mercald. Thinker. We offer our thanks, *Mirtylon.* And to you, *Lovewings*." The robed figures confronted her still, offering no food or drink, no comfort or company.

"Aaahhh," murmured the one.

"Aaahhh," echoed the others.

"We will find water when we need it in the stream, of course, and root mice growing upon the wall, and edible mushrooms. You mean us to take food and water as we need . . . of course."

"Of course," sighed the one.

"Ahhhv cohhhrz," echoed the others.

Mercald and the Thinker came in as Mavin pulled the gate across the opening and peered through it at the figures outside. For a time, they did not move. At last, the three turned away as though joined by invisible strings and moved across the clearing where they halted against the dangling root hairs and did not move again.

"You notice," Mavin asked, "no offer of food, or drink. No beds. No chairs."

"Persons living a life of religious expiation would hardly be expected to think of such things," said Mercald in a sententious voice. "It is likely that they fast for days at a time. Probably they engage in self-mortification as well, flagellation or something such, and robe themselves both to avoid licentiousness and to hide their wounds from one another's eyes."

"I don't know what they engage in, priest, but I do know that hospitality to strangers is a duty of every religion I have ever encountered with no exceptions. None. I am inclined to believe, therefore, that all your blather about expiation and fasting and what not is just that – blather. I don't know what's going on here, but it isn't religious."

"Besides which," said the Thinker, "it's unlikely that Lovewings, who committed suicide several hundred years ago, could be still alive. To say nothing of Mirtylon, who would have to have lived for about nine hundred years. Unlikely they would still have any licentiousness to cover."

"Of course!" Mavin struck her forehead with one hand, waving the other at the Thinker. "That story Beedie was telling me about the lost bridge. Lovewings was the one who threw herself off the stairs."

"The Boundless might extend the life of any worthy . . ." Mercald began, only to be cut off.

"The Boundless might, but I'll bet my socks the Boundless didn't. No, Mercald. Something other than the Boundless is at work here. Best rest while you can. They say they are concerned about the wind, and yet they stand out there in the clearing, not taking shelter. Something is awry here, so let us be cautious." She lay on the sandy floor, accommodating herself to it, placing her head where she could see through the woven gate, hearing Mercald burrowing in his pack, smelling the food he unwrapped but refusing a share of it when he offered.

The sides of the sandy clearing were hung with thick mats of root hairs, like the pelt of some giant beast, and against this shaggy background the robed figures stood out plainly, as silent and unmoving as when they had first arrived there. There were some dozen of the forms around the clearing, all standing with hooded heads slightly down, hands and arms hidden in the sleeves of the flattree-leaf robes. Mavin nagged at herself, wondering what was odd about the grouping, realizing at last that the creatures stood at strange, out-facing angles one to the other, not toward one another as people tended to do in groups. "Thinker," she whispered. "Look here."

When he lay beside her, she said, "Look at them. Are they talking with one another?"

He stopped breathing for a time, mouth half open around a chunk of cold fried root mice. Then he sighed. "No. Not talking. But something is happening. Look at the shifting, at the far end of the group, then the next one, then the next, as though they are moving slightly, one by one along that line. You don't think they are people at all, do you? Well. I have my doubts. We should see what's under those robes. Do you want me to postulate?"

"No. Better just find out what's under the robes. I'm going to sneak out, get around through the root wall. I think you'd better stay close to this cave, not wander about, and you'll probably be safer if you keep the gate shut until I return."

"The root hairs out there are impenetrable. The mean density of root hairs per square. . . ."

"Never mind," she said. "I'll manage." She pulled the gate open, slipped through and sidled along the root wall until her relocated eyes told her she was out of direct line of vision from any of the fretted arches. The group across the clearing still stood, heads down. She Shifted.

Spidery feet with sharp claws levered long legs up the rootwall. Spidery eyes, multifaceted, searched for any sign of movement. Once she had climbed above the level of the netted roof, she stopped to peer away toward the stairs, seeking upward for a fugitive gleam of light. There was still too much light in the chasm to tell whether it burned or not. She thought she saw a little, golden gleaming upon the wall but could not be sure. Well, that matter would wait. Both Roges and Beedie were sensible; they would not take chances.

The net bounced beneath her as she moved to the place the kite had rested. Once there she turned it over with angled legs, searching with mandible and claw. Only the wrappings, the clothing. Nothing else. Except – except a smell. A scent. Not unpleasant, but odd. Odd. Making her shiver and sweat. What was the word the Thinker had used. Pheromones? Well, and what was that? Stinks. Emitted by things. So, there were stink bugs and stink lizards and perfume moths. Back in the long ago, she had met an Agirule. It had had a strange, fungus smell, earthy and warm. Himaggery had smelled like autumn woods. Pheromones. So, these wrappings smelled like the creature that called itself Mirtylon. Which meant, so far as Mavin was concerned, that Mirtylon or one of his fellows had been here. And now the body of the youth was gone. Only his bravely feathered cap, his funeral wrappings remained. She shifted uneasily on her many legs, jigging upon the net until it quivered beneath her.

Then she made her way across the net until she was above the quiet forms where they stood, silent and unmoving.

The wind had begun to blow by the time she reached the place, moving very slowly. The only light lay high upon the evening- light wall, only the eastern end of Topbridge breaking the line of shadow, a hard, chisel shape against the glow. The other bridgetowns hung in darkness. Beneath the net the lantern fishes swarmed in their thousands, moving now toward the walls where they dwindled, diminished, becoming dark egg shapes fastened tightly to the walls. Beneath the net the robed forms stood as they had first arranged themselves, the robes flapping a little in the wind. Mavin lay upon the net, let her legs dangle through it, appearing to be only another set of skinny roothairs dangling into the clearing, invisible among countless others.

She took hold of a sleeve, pulled it gently, gently, tugging in time with the wind. It was fastened tight. She sent an exploratory tentacle along it, not believing what she found. The sleeve had no opening. The two sleeves were joined at the ends. If there had been arms and hands in these sleeves, they had never been expected to reach the outside world.

Her tentacle dropped to the sandy floor, probed up upward at the top of the clumsy shoe shapes. No opening. Shoes and robe were one. The thing was a balloon, all in one piece. On the net, Mavin snarled to herself, a small, spider snarl. Well and well, what was the sense of this?

The end of the tentacle grew itself a sharp, ivory claw and cut a slit in the robe, moving like a scalpel along one rib of the flattree leaf of which the garment was made. When the slit was large enough, the tentacle probed through.

After which Mavin lay upon the net in furious thought. Whatever she might have suspected, she would not have suspected this. She slid down a convenient root hair, spent some time exploring the area very carefully, with great attention to the boiling springs, then went back up onto the net, finding her way quickly from there back to the cave.

She paused before entering, searching the high wall for the gleam of amber light, sighing with relief when she found it unmistakably. So. Beedie and Roges were there, above harm's reach if Mavin had reasoned correctly. Above one harm's reach, she corrected herself. Slysaw would have reached Bottommost by now. On the morrow, he would come down the Shattered Stair. Well and well once more. After midnight, when the wind stopped, would be time enough to worry about that. There were other things to think of first.

She slipped inside the cave, pulling the gate tight behind her and taking time to lash it with a bit of thong. Evidently Mercald had ventured out, for there was a pot of steaming tea upon the sandy floor. She looked around for the fire, before realizing there was no smoke.

"I ventured just as far as that boiling spring," said Mercald in an apologetic tone. "The Thinker kept watch. It's only at one side of this clearing. We both wanted something hot. I thought you would, too."

Mavin listened to the wind rising outside and nodded. It had been sensible of him, she had to admit. If one set aside the man's fear of heights, he was brave enough for all ordinary matters. Wishing she could like him more, for Handbright's sake if for no other reason, she crouched beside the steaming pot and took the cup he offered. If one could not have fire, this would do. There was a long silence. At last she looked up to see both pairs of eyes fastened upon her and realized that they were waiting for her.

"Can you still see the figures out there?" she asked Mercald who was sitting near the gate.

He peered into the dusk, nodded. "The wind is fluttering them a little, but they still haven't moved."

"They aren't likely to," she said. "They're anchored to the roots. Besides, they're empty." She waited for expostulation, surprise. There was none.

"When Mercald went out for the water," said the Thinker, softly, "he said they looked like the cloak room at the Birders House. Hanging there. The minute he said it, I thought that's why they were left out in the wind – because there was nothing in them."

Mavin peered through the gate, head cocked to one side. They did have that look, a kind of limpness even though she knew they were supported from within by a framework of wiry greenroot.

"They are made like balloons," she began, going on to describe the framework of flexible strands inside, with the flattree leaves stretched over. "There are two slits in the veil, probably to appear as though the beings have eyes, but I doubt it. Then there are no soles to the shoe parts. There is a smell there, at the bottom of the things, as though something flowed out of them and along the soil, away into the root tangle. There are places along there where the roots don't reach the ground, places about ankle high and an armspan wide, where the roots look burned off or chewed off. No, the ends are smooth. They look – rounded, somehow.

"Digested off," suggested the Thinker.

"Perhaps," she agreed, silent for a time after that trying to visualize a being shaped like a flatcake, with an odd smell, which could eat greenroot without dying from it. "Of course, once I saw the greenroot framework inside those things, I knew they couldn't have been people."

"It would poison people," agreed Mercald. Fresh greenwood sap on the skin, even small quantities of it, caused ulcers which did not heal. He had been listening to all of Mavin's discoveries, sadly shaking his head from time to time, not in disagreement but in profound disappointment that what he had thought was a religious community was likely to be something quite different.

"And then," she went on, "I found a burial kite – what do you call them?"

"Wings of the Boundless," said Mercald. "Which carry the dead into the Boundless sky. Or, sometimes, into the Bounded depths. Depending upon what kind of life they've lived, of course."

"Of course. Part of the duty of the Messenger caste, as I understand it? Manufacture of wings and dispatch of the dead thereon? Yes. Beedie told me. Well, two days ago I saw one of the . . . wings . . . descending into the chasm. There was a bright feather on the . . . well, on the fellow's cap. That wing now lies on the net a short way from here. The cap is there, and the white wrappings, and the other clothing, but the body is gone."

"Of course it's gone," said Mercald with asperity. "It went into the care of the Boundless."

"I thought the ones that went up went into the care of the Boundless. This one came down."

"Well, naturally, both end up in the care of the Boundless, it's just that . . . our . . . theology is a little indefinite about . . ."

"It's just that you don't know, Mercald. Do you really think that the Boundless cares about bodies? Well, no matter. In my experience across the lands of this world, bodies invariably vanish because something buries them or burns them or eats them. Beetles, usually. Or things that look like beetles. Except that I could find no beetles around the kite. Excuse me, Mercald. Around the Wing of the Boundless.

"I did find the smell of whatever. Whatever wore those robes. Whatever greeted us in human language. Whatever guided us here. Whatever has now gone elsewhere, probably because the wind has started to blow and whatever is afraid of being crushed."

"The inescapable hypothesis is, then, *whatever ate the people of Lostbridge*," said the Thinker.

"Whatever," agreed Mavin. She leaned forward to fasten the rattling gate more tightly. The wind kept up its steady pressure on the thong, stretching it.

"How horrible," said Mercald, making a sick face. "How dreadful."

"Dreadful, certainly," she agreed. "But helpful. I think we can draw some conclusions from what we know, can't we, Thinker?"

"Ahhm. Well. Yes. A form of life which absorbs some – how much, I wonder? – of the mental ability *or* memory of whatever it eats. Hmmm. Yes. Language for example? Yes. Hmm. Doesn't manage it any too well, but does have the general idea. Tends to use it reflectively. . . ."

"They don't think very quickly," said Mavin. She had come to this conclusion some time ago. The poor creatures, whatever they were, did not think well. They struggled with thought, struggled to put ideas together, like a partly brain-killed Gamesman trying to do things he had once done easily, not able to understand why these simplicities were now impossible. She had seen that. More than once. She clenched her teeth at the memory, set it aside.

"What would explain this masquerade? Why the robes? Why the names of the long gone?"

Mercald cleared his throat. "Because, Mavin, they told the truth when they spoke of expiation. No. Listen. Let us suppose these creatures, these whatever, came upon Waterlight in the darkness those hundreds of years ago, came upon it and ate the people, only to take into themselves all the memories of those people, and the thoughts, language, feelings. All the sorrows. All the pain.

"Before that, they had been animals. They hadn't had any 'thinking' at all. Now, suddenly, they would have language and thought and guilt. For the first time, guilt. Oh, what a terrible thing. A simple animal of some kind, with only animal cleverness or skill, and then suddenly to have all that thinking. No way to get rid of it. No way to go back as they were before. Only the idea of expiation which they had swallowed at the same time they swallowed guilt, but no way to do that, either. And the thinking perhaps gets less and less useful as time goes on. . . ." He fell silent, sorrowing, hearing the wind sorrowing outside as though it agreed with his mood.

"Probably asexual reproduction," said the Thinker. "Which means clones. Which means no change, no natural selection. Every generation the same as the preceding generation, and every individual – though there really wouldn't be individuals in that sense – the same as every other. So, whatever ate Mirtylon is still Mirtylon. And whatever ate Lovewings is still Lovewings. . . ."

"Because she didn't die when she jumped," said Mavin. "She landed in the net and the whatevers got to her while she was still alive."

"Possibly more than one of them," the Thinker went on. "And possibly learned from her that there was good eating on Waterlight bridge. If that was the case, then we have to assume that the total effect of thought didn't come about immediately. Maybe it took some time for it to be incorporated into the beings, the whatevers. . . ."

"Poor things," said Mercald, sadly. "Poor things."

"Well, if they are such poor things, tell me how to help them, Priest. Would you have them expiate, finally, what it was they did? Perhaps we could arrange it. That is, provided they don't eat us first."

"Surely not. Having once felt guilt . . ."

"Having once felt guilt, Priest, there are those who court it, believing that more of the same can be no worse. No, there may be sneaky slyness at work here. I will believe only what these creatures do, not what they say. I do not think they understand words very well, though they use them. I have known people like that in the world above. They say human words, but from an unhuman heart. Even a thrilpat may speak human language, often with seeming sense, but that does not mean I would trust one with my dinner."

"But you speak of expiation. . . ."

"Yes. Something is trying to kill the oozers that threaten the bridgetowns, or so Thinker says. We know of nothing which could be making that attempt save these whatevers. So. If these creatures, whatever they are, succeed in killing gray oozers, then they will have expiated their guilt at wiping out Lostbridge – Waterlight. We will give them . . . what is it you give penitents, Priest? Forgiveness? We will give them that. Perhaps it will satisfy them."

"Perhaps," agreed Mercald, giving her a narrow and suspicious look. "And do you intend to give them Slysaw Bander and his followers, as well?"

Mavin smiled a slow smile at him, a wicked smile which burrowed into him until he shifted uncomfortably, unable to bear the stare. "Well, Priest. I thought of it, yes. And I decided against it. Can you tell me why?"

He sighed in relief, wiped his forehead which had become beaded with perspiration. "Because you are a messenger of the Boundless, Mavin, and would not judge without proof?"

"No, Priest," she said in the same wicked tone. "Because I am a pragmatist. I do not want one of these whatevers sliding about in the Bottomlands with Slysaw's evil brain alive inside it, moving it. It may be we are fortunate that none of those who were eaten on Lostbridge desired power. If they had wanted power or empire, the creatures that ate them might not have stopped with Waterlight. If Slysaw Bander had eternal life, clone or no clone, I would not sleep soundly in my hammock anywhere in this chasm or, it may be, in this world. Even though the things seem to have trouble keeping their train of thought, I would not risk it. It may be they merely find language difficult."

Mercald flushed. "You mock me, Messenger."

"I instruct you, Priest. Pay heed. When you believe that messengers arrive from God, it is wise to listen to everything they say, not merely when they recite accepted doctrine." She was ashamed of herself almost immediately. He turned so pale, so wan. Well. It was only as she had suspected from the beginning. Many men had a strong tendency to tell God how to behave, and religious men were more addicted to this habit than most.

"All of which," she said, changing the subject, "is not relevant to our current need. We need a way to destroy the oozers. The whatevers evidently have not found a way, not yet. It would help if we knew whether the whatevers think at all. Do they think, Thinker?"

He shrugged. "What is thought? No current theories explain it. I suggest you attempt what it is you wish to do and see whether it works. Though I am not an experimentalists, at times one must simply sit back and observe what experimentalist manage to accomplish. In the interest of acquiring data. No other way. Sorry. Sometimes, one simply must."

"Well, then, Thinker, we are stymied until the wind stops. Whatever they are, they will not come out until midnight. I suggest we sleep until then, keeping watch turn about. Priest, you seem wide awake."

"I am troubled," he said with dignity. "I will watch first. It is unlikely I would sleep in any case."

"I have abused you," said Mavin, "if only for your own good. So watch then. Wake me when you grow sleepy."

She curled into a ball on the sandy floor, covering herself with her blanket. Though the gate of the cave was loosely woven, it seemed to be out of the wind, protected on the up-chasm side by a protrusion of the root wall. The wind was cool but it did not feel as cold as it had the night before upon the stair. She drowsed, half dreaming, half remembering.

Near the source of the River Dourt was a town called Mip. It lay in the valley of the Dourt, below the scarps of the Mountains of Breem, far east of the Black Basilisk Demesne of which the people of Mip spoke often, softly, and with some fear. As far to the east as the Black Basilisk lay west was the Demesne of Pouws, and between the desmesnes a state of wary conflict had become a way of life and death. Mip, lying as it did between, strove quietly to be invisible. The people around were small holders, farmers, those to the south raising livestock while those in the river valley grew vegetables and fruits for towns as far away as Vestertown and Xammer in the south or Leamer in the north. Thus the town itself was largely devoted to commerce of an agricultural kind, full of wagons and draft animals, makers of harness and plows, seed sellers, animal Healers and minor Gamesmen who would dirty their hands and Talents with ordinary toil.

Mavin had come there, pursuing the white bird, coming south from Landizot, down the rocky shores of the Eastern Sea, past Hawsport, with its harbor full of fishing boats behind the breakwater, down along the mountains to the Black Basilisk Demesne which was mad with celebration over the birth of a boy child named Burmor to the family of the Basilisks. Mavin went quiet there, anonymous, answering fewer questions than she was asked, learning at last that the white bird had been seen. "Ah, yes, stranger. Seen by the Armigers on duty at the dawn watch. Two of them flew off in pursuit of it, losing it in the haze above Breem Mountains. It would have gone to water along the Dourt, no doubt. But that was some time ago. Ask in Mip."

So she had gone to Mip.

A quiet little town, on both sides of the Dourt, which so early in its flow was little more than a brook, full of inconsequential babble and froggy pools. A town full of trees, planted there, most of them, generations before by the first settlers in the area. "We feed the Basilisks," she heard whispered. "We feed Pouws. They have no wish to go hungry, so leave us alone."

And, indeed, there was little sign of Great Game in Mip. No tumbled rocks to show that Tragamors had heaved the landscape about. No piles of bones to show where Gamesmen had pulled the heat from the very bodies of the townsmen to fuel their Talents. An occasional Armiger from the Black Basilisk Demesne high in the western sky, light shattering from his armor; an occasional highly caparisoned Herald from Pouws stopping for beer at the Flag and Branch on his way to or from some other place. Mavin had settled into the town, found a quiet room on the upper floor of the Flag and Branch and moved about to ask questions.

There was a hunter in Mip. "I saw the bird, Gameswoman, in

the marshes. The source of the Dourt lies there in the ready marshes, and the wild fowl throng there between seasons, moving north or south. I did not attempt to take the bird. I do not take the rare ones. Only the common ones, those we may eat without feeling we have eaten the future and so kept it from the lips of our children. It seemed contented there, though without a mate or nest or nestlings to rear. If you go there, likely you will find it, though if you go to harm it, I would beg you to reconsider.''

''I am a Shifter,'' Mavin had said. ''As is the white bird. My sister.''

At which the hunter had moved away, with some expressions of politeness, his face suddenly hard and unpleasant. It was not the first time Mavin had seen that expression when Shifters were mentioned. Seemingly no other Gamesmen – no, not even Ghouls and Bonedancers, who moved among hosts of the dead to the horror of multitudes – were held in such disrepute. It was fear. Seemingly some pawns did not believe the carefully constructed mythology which Shifters were at considerable effort to put about. Seemingly some pawns believed they had special reason to distrust, to fear the Shifter Talent. It was a reaction Mavin found curious. She promised herself she would learn the cause of it some day.

Come that day when it would come; she took herself off to the swamps at the source of the Dourt. This was high country, much wooded, with little meadows surrounding the streams and the low, marshy places grown up with reeds. It reminded her a little of another forested place, and she was almost contented there, in one shape or another, searching for the white bird.

The streams came down out of many shallow valleys into a myriad meadowlands. Searching was no matter of high flight and sharpened eyes. She had to seek along each separate creek and gully, among each separate set of marshes. It was not until ten days had passed that she caught sight of the bird, the white bird, helplessly beating her wings against the net which held even as the hunter closed in to take her. If it was not the same hard-faced hunter she had left in Mip, it was his twin, and the anger that was always close to the surface in Mavin boiled up in a fury. Still, she held back, seeing the way he peered about, face sly and full of hating intensity. She knew then what he meant to try. This white bird, a Shifter, was to be bait for another Shifter, herself. The fact that he brought nothing but a net showed his ignorance. He believed, then, only the common knowledge about Shifters, much of it spread by the Shifters themselves. He thought a Shifter could be either human or one other thing – a wolf, a pombi, a fustigar, a bird.

"I am Mavin Manyshaped," she sang to herself in the treetop from which she watched him. "You have done a foolish thing, Hunter." Then she followed him as he put the white bird in a cage, a cage too small, painfully too small, and carried it away in a wagon.

Mavin, seeing him through flitchhawk eyes, circling high above him, saw each plodding step of the team.

He did not go far. Only to an open meadow where the white bird would be very visible for a long way, and where he tethered her tightly to a stake driven deep into the ground and set his nets to drop if that stake should be touched.

Mavin, watching him from mountain zeller eyes, merely smiled.

Dusk came, and after that darkness, and the hunter curled beside his dying fire to rest. What did he think? she wondered. Did he believe Shifters could not stay awake at night? Did he think that because one Shifter flew as a bird in the daylight that her sister would also fly only in the day? Foolish man. Her serpent's eyes saw him clearly by his warmth, even in the dark.

She slid beside the stake, found the thong that bound the white bird's leg, whispered, "Handbright? Handbright? It is Mavin, your sister."

There was no whispered answer, only the glare of mindless bird eyes, gleaming a little in the light of the embers. Well and well. It was a thing known to Shifters. Sometimes one took a form too long, too well, and could not leave it again. Well and well, sister, she thought. So you are sister no longer. Still, because of what you were and your protection of me. . . .

The serpent's form bound about the white bird, grew little teeth to chew the thong away, slithered away into the night to lead the white bird stumbling in the dark to the forest's edge as though it had forgotten how to Shift eyes for night vision, only the maddened gleam showing. "Stay," Mavin murmured, as she would have to some half wild fustigar. "Stay. I will return."

Then she returned to the stake, began to take on bulk, eating the grass, the leaves of the trees, whatever offered. At last, when she was ready, she trembled the stake and let the nets fall over her howling.

The hunter tumbled out of sleep, half dream-caught yet, snatched up a torch and thrust it into the embers, then held it high, uncertain whether he still dreamed or was awake, to confront the devil eyes within his gauzy net, to see the claws which shredded that net, the fangs which opened in his direction. . . .

Mavin thought, later, that perhaps he stopped running when he reached Mip, though he might have gone all the way to Hawsport. It had been a good joke.

Too good. The white bird had been no less terrified and had flown. All the search had to begin again, be done again. Still, when next she heard word of the white bird, that word had been clear. The white bird had flown west, over the sea.

Over the sea. To strange lands and far. To this chasm. Outside the wind had dropped. Through the woven gate she could see the glowing lanterns emerging from the root wall. It would not be long before the whatevers sought to fill their strange, manshaped garments once more. She sat up, seeing Mercald's eyes in the fishlight.

"You didn't wake me, Priest?"

"I was wakeful enough for both, Mavin. I knew you would be about as soon as the wind dropped. I will sleep in a while, perhaps, while the Thinker keeps watch. If you need me – though I do not suppose you will – call me."

"Ah," she thought. "So you are still unhappy with me, Mercald."

She sidled out through the gate, surrounded at once by a great cloud of blue fish. Across the clearing, one of the flattree garments moved purposefully toward her.

CHAPTER NINE

"You are not Mirtylon," she cried.

The balloon dress, twitchy upon its framework, stopped where it was, trembling in indecision.

"You are not Mirtylon," Mavin cried again, "but that doesn't matter. You do not have to be Mirtylon to talk to us."

"Am Mirtylon," it puffed *Ahhm Muhhrtuhhlohhn.*

"No." She moved across the clearing, thrusting her way through a cloud of importunate fishes to stand beside it, almost within touch. "No. You ate Mirtylon. Now that you have eaten Mirtylon, you think Mirtylon. You have his name and can use it if you like. But you are not Mirtylon. What did you name yourself *before* Mirtylon?"

There was only an edgy silence during which the balloon quaked, shifted, and did not answer. At last an answer came, from another of the forms.

"No name . . . had no name . . ."

"Ah. Well. If you did not call yourself by human names, what other name would you have?" The Thinker had suggested this line of questioning in an effort to determine whether the things thought at all, whether they could deal with conditional concepts. Everything the creatures had said until now might have been mere stringing together of phrases the humans might have said – or so the Thinker thought. She waited. Silence stretched thin. She could feel the Thinker's eyes, behind her in the cave, watching every tremor.

"We . . . bug . . . sticky."

Mavin's mouth fell open. What in the name of the Boundless or any other deity was she to make from that? She heard the Thinker hissing from the cave. "See if you can get it to come out of cover! Let us get a look at it."

"Come out of that shape," she commanded.

"No." The word was strong, unequivocal, from several of them at once. "No. Ugly."

She scratched her head. "Ugly" was a human word and therefore represented a human opinion. Which meant it was possibly what the dwellers of Waterlight had thought of these creatures. Which had a great many implications. "Ugly is all right," she said at last. "Thinker is ugly." She waved at the cave behind her. "Many things are ugly."

"Ugly . . . things . . . are . . . bad." *Ahhhr bahhhd.*

"Not . . . always." She shook her head, understanding what horror these words conveyed. She could visualize what had happened on Waterlight bridge. It would have been night, people would have been asleep, then would have come the invasion of these whatevers, the terror of being eaten alive, consumed, only to find after one had been eaten that thought and personality did not end but went on, and on, and on. Still, there must have been some self-awareness in the creatures before. Otherwise they could not have named themselves at all.

"All things which eat us are ugly-bad. Being eaten is ugly-bad. If you do not eat me, I do not think you are ugly-bad." There, let them chew on that, she thought, turning to rejoin the Thinker. "What do you think?"

He shrugged. "I postulate mentation prior to their having eaten people. However, seemingly they had no visual or symbolic communication. They obviously had some form of language, however, and it may have been in smell. They had a concept of number – the thing said 'we'. They had a concept of otherness – it said bug. They had a concept of relationship – sticky. It's possible we'll find they're a kind of mobile flypaper.

"However, if the people of Waterlight used the phrase 'sticky-bug' then these creatures may just be using it because they swallowed it. In that case, all we're left with is the fact one of them used a plural."

"All of which means?" sighed Mavin, understanding about one word in five.

"That I can't say at this point how intelligent they are, leaving aside for the moment that we don't know what intelligence is. I have always eschewed the biological sciences for exactly that reason;

they're unacceptably imprecise." He peered over her shoulder, eyes suddenly widening.

Mavin turned. Something was flowing out at the bottom of the balloon dress, something thick and oleaginous, shiny on the top, puckered here and there as though the substance of it flowed around rigid inclusions. When it stopped flowing, it was an armspan across, ankle high, and it quivered. Out of the centre of it, slowly edging upward as though by terrible effort, came the shape of an ear, a bellows. The ear quivered. The bellows chuffed. "Not . . . eating . . . you . . ." it puffed. "Not . . . ugly . . ."

While Mavin considered that, trying to think of something constructive to say next, a cloud of small flutterers swept through the clearing. As though by reflex action, the thing that had spoken lifted a flap of itself into their path. Wings drummed and struggled. There was a momentary agitation of small bodies upon the surface of the thing, then the smooth shininess of it closed over the disturbance.

"What did I say?" asked the Thinker, triumphantly. "Mobile flypaper!"

"Not ugly," said Mavin, firmly, trying not to laugh. "Very neat, very good-looking. Very shiny. You are . . . Number One Sticky."

Across the clearing another puddle of glue thrust up its own ear and bellows. "I . . . Number . . . Two . . . Sticky."

"Well, that answers a lot of questions," said the Thinker. "They certainly have self-awareness."

"And they can count," commented Mercald. "So, it is not beyond the bounds of possibility that they . . . "

"I don't want to hear it," said Mavin. "There isn't time. Whether they are religious or not, Mercald, I don't want to consider the matter now."

"Well. So long as you don't expect them to do anything that would offend against . . ."

"I don't want to hear that, either, Mercald. My understanding of what would offend against the Boundless is at least as good as yours. As you would remember if you reflect upon recent history!" Mercald flushed and fell silent, obviously distressed. Mavin turned to see the ears quivering at full extension, and cursed herself for having yelled. Undoubtly she had confused them. "Pay no attention to the arguments we humans have from time to time. It is our way. Often, it means nothing."

"We . . . remember," blob said. "Number . . . Two . . . Sticky . . .?" It repeated with an unmistakably questioning rise in tone.

"Number Two Sticky," agreed Mavin. "But you will have to mark yourself somehow, so that we will know which one you are. We cannot smell the difference as you probably do. We must see it."

Ears and bellows disappeared into the flat surface. The blobs quivered, flowed toward one another, seemed to confer through a process of multiply extrusions and withdrawals. Finally the surfaces of both began to form a dull fibrous pattern against the overall shine. The figures were clear, a large figure "1," an even larger figure "2."

"They've moved some of their bottom membrane onto their tops," said the Thinker. "That stands to reason. They couldn't move around at all if they were sticky on the bottom."

The conference among the Stickies went on, and more numbers began to appear, 3, then 4 and 5 in quick succession. When all those in the clearing had identified themselves, there were fifteen.

"Handsome," announced Mavin in an approving tone. "Very handsome. Very useful."

"And very fortunate that the poor people of Waterlight were literate," sighed Mercald. "I wonder if any of these creatures ate the babies on Lostbridge. Poor things. They wouldn't have enough language yet to talk with us."

"There . . . are . . . more. . . ." said One, breathlessly. "In . . . the . . . place we . . . stay."

"How many?" asked the Thinker. "How many of you?"

The glue blob quivered, shivered, erupted in many small bubbles which puckered and burst, then became calm, slick, only the fibrous identifying number contrasting upon its surface. The bellows gasped, puffed hugely: "Three thousand . . . nine hundred . . . sixty-two now. One was . . . crushed in the last . . . wind."

"And that," said the triumphant Thinker, "proves they can reason with quite large numbers. Well. Most interesting."

"Do all talk human talk? All understand?" Mavin's keen sense of survival quivered to attention. How many people had there been on the lost bridge, after all? Surely not almost four thousand of them.

The ear drooped, the bellows pumped. "Only . . . four hundred . . . seven. All. We . . . want . . . ed . . . did want . . . did want . . . not now . . . understand . . . not now."

"What did you want?" asked Mavin, already sure of the answer.

"Did want . . . people . . . to eat. For . . . the . . . others."

"Noble," sighed Mercald. "Risking their lives to help their brethren. Giving it up when they learn it is a greater wrong. . . ."

"Mercald, I am not at all sure they have learned any such thing," Mavin hissed at him, cupping her hands around her lips and standing close so that the stickies should not hear her. "They have said they do not wish to be ugly. Very well. But they desire to acquire more of – well, whatever it is they acquired when they ate the people of Waterlight. They're outnumbered nine to one by those who speak only in smells. Now, no matter how ugly I might wish to avoid being, that kind of desire would speak strongly to me. We will do them a courtesy by not putting temptation in their way."

"Of course not," he said with offended dignity. "I wouldn't."

"Then don't adopt them, Mercald. Don't make them into some kind of Bottom-dwelling holiness. I've had some experience with promises of expiation and reformation. I've seen what happens when people act on such promises prematurely. We must not risk our lives on some religious notion you may have." She realized she was glaring, panting, that her face was flushed. "Oh, foosh, Mercald. I feel like we've been arguing about this for days. Can't you simply leave the religious aspects of it alone until you can get back to Topbridge and have a convocation or something to decide what it all means." She turned away, sure he had not heard a word she had said.

She turned to the stickies. "We have come here to find the big beasts that are eating the roots." Mavin had started to say "Great, gray oozers," and had then remembered what Mirtylon, nee Sticky One, had called them. "Do you know about those big beasts?"

"Beasts . . . eat . . . stickies . . . too," puffed Sticky Seven, quivering in indignation.

"We put . . . rootsap . . . on them. . . ." puffed another. Mavin could not see its number, hidden as it was behind two or three others. "Make little . . . ones sick. . . . die. . . ."

"There, you see!" demanded Mercald. "Our interests are similar. We can help them!"

"We're going to have to help one another," muttered Mavin. "Rootsap won't kill the big ones? Is that what you're saying?"

"Too big . . ." came the disconsolate reply.

"Can the net hold the beasts? Do the big beasts crawl around on top of the net?"

"Go on . . . top, yes." Puff, puff. "Sometimes, net . . . breaks . . . beasts fall . . . down . . . eat us. Crawl around . . . eat ... everything." This was the same sticky that had spoken before. By extending her neck a little, Mavin could read its number. It was Sticky Eleven.

"How many beasts?" she asked. "Many?"

There was a quivering conference among the glue blobs, with much extrusion of parts and emitting of smells. At last number Eleven struggled to the front of the group. "Nine . . . big ones . . . left . . . near here. Sap . . . killed . . . little ones. Always had . . . little . . . ones here . . . making pretty stones. First time . . . big beasts . . . come here. They come from . . . down-chasm." Puff, puff, puff, collapse. Eleven thinned to a pancake, bellows pumping impotently.

Sticky One took up the story. "Eleven is . . . right. Nine big ... ones ... left."

All right, thought Mavin. I'll need to think about this. She turned to Mercald and the Thinker, hammering a fingertip into her palm. "Now's the time to negotiate. None of the three of us is a representative of the bridge people – I speak of the governance of them, Mercald, not their religion. So, we need to get Beedie down here promptly. As a Bridger, she should serve nicely as ambassador. I can think of a few things we can try, but the agreement needs to be between the stickies and the chasm people so that it can't be repudiated later by some collection of Banders or whatnots."

"I am glad to hear you say so," murmured Mercald. "Whoever speaks for us should be open-hearted. There is too little love and trust in you for that. You are too cynical. I do not think you are a real messenger from the Boundless, Mavin. The white bird . . . your sister . . . now, she is a different matter. I can believe she is a messenger."

Mavin stepped back, stung, angry. *Ah, my sister,* she thought. *Poor, mad Handbright. Yes. She is a different matter indeed. Besides, she doesn't argue with you, you pompous, self-righteous idiot!*

Aloud, she said, "You have not heard me, Mercald. I'm sorry. I have tried to tell you there are dangers in the unknown."

"And opportunities," he said. "Opportunities to extend the hand of friendship, the hand of . . ."

"And I have asked you not to extend anything yet," she snapped. "Wait until Beedie and Roges get down here. I'll fetch them now and be back by the time it gets light. Just wait here, both of you, and don't . . . do . . . anything."

She cast one quick look in the Thinker's direction, remembering that he had not yet seen her change shape. Bidding the stickies loudly to wait until she came back, she drew upon the power of the place to Shift into the great bird-bat form she had put together which could fly even in the soggy air of the chasm. Around her the place grew chill. She saw the Thinker shudder with cold as he stared at her. As she lifted through the cold in a whoosh of wings, she heard him cry out behind her.

"Marvelous! Revolutionary! A verification of the ergotic hypothesis!"

"Oh, by Towering Tamor," Mavin muttered. "Now I've done it. He'll want to talk to me about how I do this, and I can't explain because when I try to explain or even think about it I can't do it at all!" Resolutely, she turned her mind to other things, not thinking about flying as she circled upward toward the amber gleam of Beedie's fire.

As she came closer, however, she saw that it was the gleam of a torch they carried in a headlong dash down the stairs. She Shifted into her own form and met them.

"Mavin!" cried Beedie. "Whoosh, I'm glad it's you. There's a hundred Banders clumping down behind us, and I wanted to warn you. I know you told us to stay put, but we didn't expect so many."

"A hundred?" Mavin was doubtful. "Surely not so many as that."

"One hundred seven," said Roges, putting down his pack in order to stretch his arms. "When we heard them coming, Beedie went back up to a place she could count them as they crossed a break in the stair. One hundred seven of them, each with much cursing and many weapons. They think they are to find some great treasure down below, something the Beeds and Chafers have kept secret from them for generations."

"You're right," admitted Mavin. "I expected neither so many nor so soon. Let me carry part of that for you. I think we'd best hurry to get as far ahead of them as possible. Throw the torch over; it will go out on the net below. The fish make enough light. Come. . . ." She led them on down, carrying some of their burdens so that all could move faster, ignoring all attempts at conversation.

When they had come some little way, she left them in order to fly up along the stair and see the descending Banders for herself. There were over a hundred, as Roges had said, old Slysaw in the forefront, all galumphing down at a steady pace and cursing the stairs as they came. She hovered just out of their sight, listening to their mutinous threats as to what they would do if they were not allowed to rest soon, then dropped on her bat wings down the chasm once more with a feeling of some relief.

"You've gained good distance on them," she told the others. "And they'll soon stop to rest. Evidently they've been climbing in the wind, and even though many of them have strong Bridger's legs, they are tired and hungry. Come, give me that pack again, and we'll go a bit more slowly."

Beedie refused to relinquish the pack until she was told what Mavin and the others had found in the depths. Then there were squeals of astonishment at the descriptions of the stickies and still greater astonishment when she was told they would soon meet Mirtylon and Lovewings – or what remained of them.

"The Thinker is ecstatic at all the new theories he has about them," said Mavin. "But Mercald is determined that they are something very holy, somehow sanctified through guilt or some such. I have begged him to simply wait until we know a bit more before doing anything, but he accuses me of cynicism."

"Mercald is such an uneven person," said Beedie. "He can be brave as a pombi if it is a question of faith in the Boundless, and in the next minute he is peeing in his pants because he has the down-dizzies. I hope he will listen to you, Mavin, because I think he is not very realistic."

"And I hope you've had time to discuss a few things besides theology," panted Roges. "We may have gained on the Banders, but they will arrive at the Bottom eventually. When they do, they'll expect to do away with us, I imagine."

"I have a few ideas," said Mavin modestly. "A few things that might work out." Her foot jolted upon the solid floor of the chasm, and she sighed with relief. "Follow me. I've found a shorter way than the one we were led in by."

She led them at a fast trot through the whiskery halls beneath the net, pointing out the features of the place as she did so; the boiling pools – including one very large, deep pond alive with steam

– the flopperskin kites that dotted the net, the ankle-high holes connecting between the hallways. Though her way was much more direct than the path the stickies had led them before, daylight was shining through the flattrees on the rim when she brought them into the clearing to find – no one. No Thinker. No Mercald. No stickies.

"Now what?" Mavin sighed in frustration. "Where have they gone? I told them to stay right here. I begged them not to do anything until I returned."

Roges moved through the open gate into the cave. "Here's the Thinker behind the door," he called. "He seems to be Thinking."

The others came in to see him crouched against the wall behind the gate, gesturing to himself as he babbled a string of incomprehensible words over and over. "Thinker!" Mavin demanded. "Where's Mercald? What happened to Mercald?"

"Mercald? Does one care? When one has verified the ergotic hypothesis at last, does one care about Mercalds? It seems that in order to describe the statistical state of a system, one needs an ensemble. There are those who believe the ensemble has physical reality, that the occurrence of a particular state corresponds to the frequency with which one observes the phenomenon. Others think the ensemble only a mathematical construct. It is now established that all systems must go through all states in the ensemble. Ergo, you can fly. This place is merely a rare event, sitting out in the tail of distribution of all places, non-representative. . . . I shall present a paper before the physical society at the fall meeting. . . ."

"Oh, flopper poop," Beedie. "He saw you change shape, didn't he? He doesn't believe in the Boundless, like Mercald; and he isn't open-minded, like Roges and me; so he's theo . . . theor . . . thinking his way through it and has dropped off his bridge completely. He probably thinks I'm a rare event too, and no more real than anything else." She shook him. "Thinker! Where's Mercald? Tell me about Mercald!"

"Absolution," grated the Thinker distractedly, his eyes unfocused. "He wanted to give absolution to Sticky One. He wanted to lay on his hands in forgiveness, and he did, and he couldn't take his hands off, and he . . . ah . . . wah . . . aaahhh dissolved . . . aaahhh slurp!" The last word was uttered with a hideously descriptive sound which made them all recoil in disbelief.

"By the Pain of Dealpas," moaned Mavin. "By the Great Flood and the Hundred Devils. By the p'natti of my childhood. By . . . by . . ." She stuttered her way into silence, beating her head with one hand.

"A paper for Physical Review would be out of the question," muttered the Thinker. "It would never get by the idiot referees."

"By the Boundless," Mavin sighed at last. "Did Mercald think they had voluntary control over their stickiness?"

"I don't imagine he thought at all," murmured Beedie sadly. "Often he didn't, you know."

"Don't speak of it as though it were in the past," Mavin urged. "If he has been slurped up by Sticky One, he is still with us, still Mercald, and he will have a lot of time to consider what he has done." *Oh Mercald, I told you to be careful. Because I did not speak in syrupy words, you would not listen.* She shook her head again, then laid down her pack and went out into the clearing.

"Sticky-One-Mirtylon-Mercald! Sticky Two! All the stickies! Come out, come out, wherever you are!"

Then she disgraced herself by weeping.

Beedie took her hand in sympathy. "It's awful, isn't it. I really want to throw up, but I haven't anything in my stomach at all."

Across the clearing the whiskery wall trembled. Moments passed. A sticky crawled out, slowly, so flat in aspect that Mavin wondered if it had suffered some accidental crushing. When it emerged completely, she saw that it was Sticky Two. "It's Lovewings," she sighed to Beedie.

"Sticky Two," she said, loudly, then waited for the ear to emerge, which it did only reluctantly. "I know what happened. It was not your fault. Not . . . your . . . fault."

"Sticky . . . One . . . fault . . . it was. . . ." puffed Sticky Two.

"No. It wasn't any sticky's fault," Mavin sighed. "It was the man's fault. He didn't think. Where is Sticky One, now?"

"Very . . . sick. Sticky . . . One has . . ." There was a long, long pause . "Has . . . too many . . . things inside . . . all at once." The ear trembled, retracted, the bellows sighed dismally to itself.

"I'll bet he does," said Beedie. "Can you imagine trying to digest Mercald? Oh my, I shouldn't joke about it. But then, it shouldn't seem funny, and it does."

"Sticky Two." Mavin was trying not to hear what Beedie said, for it made her want to laugh unbecomingly. "There are ugly men coming. We must do things very quickly. We cannot wait for Sticky One, or anything else. We must talk with all the speaking stickies at once. Will you fetch them?"

The glue blob dithered for a moment, then flowed away under the wall. Roges came out of the cave nibbling on a piece of bread, offering some to Mavin and Beedie with the other hand. "Thinker is all tied up in knots talking to himself about you, Mavin, and birds and some law or other he claims you broke. I haven't seen him like this before, and I don't think he'll be much use to us."

"That's all right," Mavin replied distractedly. "At least he'll be out of the way." She began explaining to Beedie and Roges what she had thought they might do, with much waving of arms and pointing here and there. Roges did not accept it without question.

"That's dangerous for Beedie, doer-good. She could be hurt!"

"She won't be, Roges. I'll take care of that part myself."

Beedie had a doubtful comment. "You know how Mercald would feel about doing it this way. We still don't have any proof he would accept that the Banders are what we know they are."

"He's not in any position to complain about it," she laughed bitterly. "We can give the Banders fair warning, if that would make you feel better. They won't heed it, but we can try. Then, if it's the wrong thing to do, Mercald can figure out later how we can expiate for it. All of us, including the stickies who help us do it."

"Are you sure they will help us?"

"Well, sausage girl, it's up to your eloquence. I think there's a good chance for building excellent relations with the stickies. If they do the chasm people a favour, then they'll be in good odor with all. If we do the stickies a favour, they'll want to treat us well in future. It's up to you, Beedie. You've been reared to work on the roots, to manage a crew. Now we need you to work on the root net, and the stickies will be your crew. Right now I think they're very eager to please. Let's see how eloquent you can be!"

At almost midday the Banders came down to the vast net which spread across the chasm, making a ceiling above the Bottom. The net was made up of many ropey roots, tugged sideways from the forest of verticals, which were knotted or grown together at armspan intervals, again and again, until the whole chasm was divided horizontally by a gridwork of thick, strong lines. each individual polygon of rope-sized roots was further connected by a finer mesh of knotted root hairs. When Beedie had first seen it, she had known at once it was sufficiently strong to catch something large and flat dropping from above or perhaps even a person who might fall on his face while running across the grid. She had known at once it would not stop large rocks plunging from the rim – or the crawling gray oozers whose weight had torn ragged holes in the fabric already.

It was not unlike the floor of a bridge before the main planks were laid, and the Banders looked across it as a natural and familiar arena for exploration, whereas the Bottom, with its steams and stinks, was both strange and intimidating. Only one small group of the Banders went to the Bottom, found themselves in the maze of hallways, and promptly rejoined the others above the net level where they stood peering at the distant root wall, wondering where to go next.

It was not long before one of them, more sharp-eyed – or more acquisitive – than the rest, spotted a bright sparkle on the net, bounced his way out to it, and brought it back to be passed around among the others

"Jewels," shouted Byle. "Dah, it's jewels. Laying there on the net like so much flopper flub. See yonder, there's another sparkle."

The gems, in glittering clusters, had been glued onto the grid with rootsap to form a twisting path. They were stones like those Mavin had discovered in the cave – gizzard stones from the small oozers, polished to a fine, high shine by the tumbling of the creatures' great guts. All the stickies who spoke human language had been at the labor of placing them until moments before the Banders arrived. Now the stickies crouched upon the net, and their shiny tops camouflaged with nonsticky bottom membrane, half-hidden with bits of root hair and leaf. The trail of gems wound out across the chasm; some of the younger Banders were already following it and collecting them.

Slysaw bellowed at them. "You all get off there! I didn't say go, and you don't go till I say. Now get back here and let me look at those. Well, well, what a wonder. So this is what the Birder and the Beedie wench were after. I'll be dropped off a bridge by my ears if this isn't something. . . ."

There were mutterings from the others in the band. One or two looked as though they were going to disregard orders, but these were cuffed into line by some of Slysaw's close kin.

"Now, boys. Now then. Think what a shortage of saw gravel there's been lately, and all the time pots of it here in the Bottom to be picked up by the pocketful! And won't we have fun taking all this back and showing it around. All this secret stuff the high and mighty Beeds and Chafers and Birders never told us about. Let's be orderly, now. Byle, you and your cousin get out there first, and the rest of us'll come after." And soon the hundred were moving across the net in a long line which undulated from side to side as jewels were found and picked and popped into pockets – though some were hidden in shoe tops or behind ears in the expectation of avoiding the eventual sharing out.

Up-chasm, others waited. Roges and Beedie were upon the net; Roges at the root wall, securely anchored to the mainroot, Beedie more or less at the center of the chasm, on the up-chasm side of the steamy place above the boiling pool. Before her, and to either side, stickies lay upon the net, almost invisible in the steam, their ears carefully extruded between bits of leafy litter as they listened for the signal.

Mavin, hovering high above, peered down through the veils of steam. The mists made seeing difficult, but she had planned for it to be difficult. She did not want the Banders able to see clearly. They must be greedy, angry, and with obscured vision. She lifted a bit higher to see farther, then dropped down to whisper. "Beedie, are you ready?"

Beedie waved her away impatiently, trying to remember her lines. At her direction, the largest, brightest stones had been placed in the steamy place. Now she could hear the result of that placement; raised voices, argument, the sound of blows. She heard Slysaw's voice as he intervened, his own greed making him half-hearted. "Doesn't matter who finds 'em," he shouted at his men. "We'll share alike when we're done. Just keep gatherin' 'em in, and soon we'll come to the source of it all. . . ."

The group tumbled on, stooping, grabbing, pushing one another in their haste.

"Stop right there, Banders!" Beedie cried in a fine, trumpety voice.

The men stumbled to a halt, their eyes widening in surprise, searching through the steamy veils for the source of the voice. Then one of them glimpsed her, pointed, shouted. Behind him, others pushed close.

"Stop!" she cried again. "You have no business here, Byle. Nor you, Slysaw. The rest of your ruffians should be back at work on the bridgetowns that pay them. I give you warning, you are at peril of your lives, so take care. Go back to the stairs and up where you belong."

"And who're you, wench?" Slysaw thrust through the pack, leaning on Byle's shoulder. "Who appointed you head of chasm council, heh?" The Banders heaved and pushed at one another, drawing into a smaller, tighter group. Behind them stickies moved across the net.

"Yeah," interrupted Byle Bander, bouncing and posturing on the net. "Who're you, Beedie? I'll tell you. You're gametime for me, that's what. And after me, as many of these kin of mine as are interested in your skinny body."

Cheers and animal howls rose at this sally. Mavin, hearing this from above, recalled old, bad memories of Danderbat Keep, and boiled with fury. Still she hovered, close above the place Beedie stood.

"I tell you to go back. You are meddling in things that are none of your business. You do not belong here. You are in danger here. Don't be stupid, standing there threatening me. Just turn yourselves around and go!" Beedie no longer needed to remember lines she had rehearsed. She was now so angry that they came of themselves. Beside the root wall, Roges heard her anger and sizzled with protective wrath.

"We'll see, Beedie girl. We'll see. . . ." Byle plunged toward her through the rising steams, the entire pack pressed at his back. Slysaw was carried along in the rush even as his native suspicion made him try to stem the stampede. They came in all together, individually sure-footed yet stumbling against one another, so intent upon their own beastly mob noises they did not hear Mavin's scream.

"Stickies. Now. Now. Now. Now."

Roges at the root wall began to echo the sound, through Mavin's amplified voice could have been heard by any creature not deafened by its own howls. Beedie, too, cried out, and the three voices rose together. "Now. Now. Now. Now"

Stickies had moved into a circle around the Banders, a circle that had already cut many of the main grid roots supporting the mesh above the boiling pool. Abruptly, with a loud, tearing sound, the fabric ripped to one side of the close-pressed mob. The flap of net they stood upon dropped to one side, throwing many of them flat, dropping others so quickly that arms and legs broke the finer meshes and dangled below, waving frantically at nothing.

Those at the rear of the pack nearest the torn edge were first to realize that there was nothing below but the sound of seething water, occasional glimpses of its bubbling surface appearing through the gusts of steam. Those who saw what lay below tried to climb over the bodies of those above them on the net, shouting and kicking. Those above them retaliated by kicking and pushing in return. Two or three men toppled through the hole and fell, screaming only for a moment before striking the water with a splash, a final agonized gargle and silence.

The entire pack was silent, only for that moment, not realizing what had happened but aware that something was wrong, that the net was no longer horizontal, that Beedie was moving away from them in the veiling mists, her face drawn into an expression of – what was it? Sorrow? Horror? At what? Even as shouts and howls arose once more, Byle, with his usual sensitivity, let voice follow wonder.

"Whatcha starin' at, bone body? Heh? Run if you like, Beedie, girl, but I'm faster then you are. . . ." Slysaw was grabbing at his shoulder, but the boy shrugged it off, blind and deaf to any needs but his immediate desire to do violence. Slysaw dropped and was trampled under the climbing hands and feet of a dozen others, kicked downward, beneath half a hundred struggling bodies, to lie at last half-dazed upon the very edge of the tear, clinging with both hands to a mesh of root hair.

The stickies had continued with their work. The tear widened, the finer lacework ripping with an audible shriek, ropey roots breaking under the increased weight with repeated, snapping sounds which made Beedie think of a drum rattling, faster and faster. "Go back," she screamed, unheard in the general din. "Go back." It was too late for any of them to go back, and she knew it only briefly before they did.

Now a second tear opened, across from the first. Those who remained upon the net were caught now upon a kind of saddle, low at the sides, high at the ends, with those ends growing more narrow with each breath they took. Beedie stood just beyond one end so that she looked straight into Byle's face when the far, narrow strip broke through and the entire flap of net hung down for an instant's time, laden with clutching forms, shedding other forms amid shouted words she could not understand and some she could, old threats and obscenities, all ending in a liquid gulping, diminishing echoes, and quiet.

Beedie stood at the edge of the torn net, unable to move. Seeing her safe, Mavin dropped from her guardian's post through the roiling steams, past fringy edges of torn net and the quivering stickies poised there awaiting her word, down to examine the simmering surface of the pool. Nothing floated in it. She had not measured its depth, but now knew it must be a vast cauldron to have swallowed so many without a sign remaining.

Above, where Beedie stood, the net bounced from some weight hanging below it which jiggled and fought against falling. She looked between her feet to see him hanging upon a remaining shread of root just as his hand took her by the ankle. Byle Bander. She screamed his name.

And Roges drew his knife, cut the root hairs which fastened him safe at the root wall and ran upon the gridwork, sure-footed as any Bridger, not looking down, not remembering to be afraid, thinking of nothing except the sound of her voice. He came to her while she still struggled against the hands that were pulling Byle Bander upward on her body while he cursed at her and called her filthy names.

Beedie's cry had summoned Mavin back in that instant. She was too late. Her great bird's beak was too late to strike those climbing hands away. Roges' knife had already done so, and he stood with Beedie wrapped in his arms on a net which shook and shivered and threatened to collapse beneath them at any moment.

"Come on, young ones," she said quietly. "There's other time for that, and better places." And she led them back to the root wall and down, not letting either of them go until she was sure they were safe.

Later, when they thought of it, they went looking for the Thinker. They could not find him. Mavin was suspicious of the stickies for a time, but they convinced her of their innocence at last. He had gone, gone as he had come, into some other place, through some wall only he could see or understand.

"Now I'll never know how I do it," Mavin thought with some disappointment. "I really thought he'd figure it out and would explain it to me." The disappointment was not sufficient to keep her from curling up upon the cave floor and sleeping for a very long time.

CHAPTER TEN

It was some days later that they sat in the small commons room of Bridgers House on Topbridge. Beedie and Roges were unpacking a small bag they had brought from the Bottomlands, laying the contents upon the table before Rootweaver's interested eyes. Old Quickaxe sat in one corner where his blanket-wrapped body could catch the last of the day's light through a grilled window. Mavin sprawled before the hearth, playing with a stick in the deadroot fire which burned there to warm their supper.

"And you think all the great oozers are dead?" asked Rootweaver, fingering the gems on the table. "Though you did not see them killed?"

"We saw the first two killed," said Mavin. "The first time wasn't very efficient. The stickies hadn't quite figured out what smells were most attractive to the beasts, so the first one tended to wander about. The second time –"

"The second time was perfect," said Beedie. "They stretched a net-road right over the Stew Pot, that's what we named the boiling pool. Then they laid stink all over it, to attract the oozer. Then more stink to where the nearest oozer was, and it wasn't close at all. It must have come a long way. Then, when it went out on the net-road, they cut the net, and down it went. Stewed beast. That didn't smell very good either, but eventually it will all wash away."

"The stickies will have killed them all by now, ma'am," said Roges, "even the one we saw on the root wall above Bottommost. The Bridgers from Bottommost were driving it down into the chasm with torches when we came that way. Evidently there was only the one who climbed that high, and both they and the stickies were very eager to have the beast gone."

"Why now?" quavered Quickaxe from his corner. "What brought the huge beasts into the chasm? We have never had anything eating the roots before.''

Mavin nodded in time with the dance of the flames. ''I knew you would want to know, so I went down the chasm to see. There had been a rock fall there, just beyond the bend of the chasm. Evidently, a few of these very large beasts were trapped on this side of the fall. There are many of them further down, where it is even wetter and warmer and where a different kind of vegetation flourishes.''

''But you say there are small ones below us?''

''Not the same kind,'' said Mavin off handedly. ''The little ones are a different beast entirely. They don't eat the roots deeply, for one thing, and they stay away from the stickies, for another. The stickies have been killing them off with rootsap as long as any one of them can remember – certainly long before they ate the people on Waterlight.''

''And it was gizzard stones they traded with the Waterlight people long ago?'' Quickaxe asked.

''Gizzard stones, from which our saw gravel is made, yes. And our supply of it had been laid up since that time. Even hoarded and used thriftily, as we did, it would soon have been completely used up. . . .'' Rootweaver sighed. ''Now there is enough of it we may deck ourselves in gems as in the old stories.''

''They traded different kinds of fungus, too,'' offered Roges. ''And fish lanterns. Things like that.''

''We made a treaty with them,'' said Beedie. ''I hope the chasm council will ratify – is that the word, Mavin? – ratify it. The stickies won't hurt us if we don't build a bridge below the level of Bottommost, because it isn't wet enough for them that high up in the chasm. And if we aren't silly, like poor Mercald, and try to touch them, they can't do us any harm.''

Mavin nodded in agreement. ''I think you can act on that assumption, ma'am. But take my warning. There are thousands of them down there that still speak in stinks, and they would really like to have living, thinking humans to eat. I don't think they're evil, but I don't think they're holy, either, and I'd continue to be careful.''

''Poor Mercald,'' sighed the old man. ''I remember his father. No practical sense at all. Still, Mavin, there is a certain temptation there.''

Mavin rose slowly, looked the old man in the eye, thought carefully before she spoke. "Old Sir, I will not presume to guide you. But before I would consider any such thing, I should have myself carried to the Bottom, and there I would speak with that which was Mercald. He is a confusion now, some Mercald, some Mirtylon, and some Sticky One. Still, he has gained . . . insight."

Beedie and Roges both looked horrified when they finally realized that the old man meant that he felt a temptation to do what Mercald had done, but Rootweaver considered the idea calmly.

"Did he say anything to you? Mercald, I mean. Before you left?"

"He said he could find very little guilt or expiation in Mirtylon. And he said Mavin had been right. And he sounded very disappointed," said Beedie. "I felt so sorry for him I forgot and almost patted him on the shoulder."

"He also said," Mavin spoke for the old man's ears alone, almost in a whisper, "that it didn't hurt. It surprised him, of course, since he wasn't expecting it. But it didn't hurt."

The old man gave Mavin a fragile, tremulous smile. "If one were to do such a thing, one would have to do it fairly soon. While there is still time."

Mavin did not answer. She had found a great poignancy in Mercald's disappointment. His voice had puffed out of the sticky shape as all sticky voices did, windy and full of huffs, but the intonation had been very much his own. She recalled he had told her she had too little kindness in her, and this made her sad. Perhaps he was right. She had power, and had used it, and had made her own judgments. She did not regret them. But still . . .

She remembered the weeping children of Landizot.

The frightened hunter of Mip.

The slim, silver-horned beast she had loved in the pool-laced forest.

"What are you thinking about, Mavin?" Beedie whispered to her.

"I am thinking, sausage girl, that I wish Handbright would hurry with what she is about so that I may take the baby and go. Being among you has made me doubt myself, and that makes me fractious."

"Oh, pooh. You mean Mercald. That was his job, Mavin. Birders are supposed to make us doubt ourselves so we don't get too proud. Do you think you are too proud?"

Mavin shook her head, seeing Rootweaver's eyes on them from across the table. "Perhaps I was."

The older woman nodded. "Sometimes each of us is. Now, I think from the smell that food is cooked. Will you share it around, Roges?" And she rose to seat them all at the table.

They were only half through the meal when a Maintainer woman entered, beckoning Rootweaver into the hall. She returned with a sad face. "Your sister is not young, Mavin. Among our people, we would not want to bear children at her age."

"She's almost forty," said Mavin "Is there trouble?"

"The birther women are concerned, worried. She has been in labour for a very long time now. She does not seem concerned. She sings, and does not concentrate. She seems to feel nothing. We have medicines, but they are dangerous. . . ."

"Well," Mavin rose. "I will come. No – alone. Beedie, you stay here. I'll see if I can help her, but I must do it with as few as people around as possible."

Handbright was lying on a white bed, her legs drawn up, the muscles in her belly writhing, but her face was as calm as a corpse as she sang a little, wordless song. Mavin motioned the women out of the room, asking only the head birther to stay. The place smelled of the sea, salt and wet.

"Tell me what she must do," she directed the birther, taking Handbright's head between her hands to make the blind eyes stare into her own. She began to speak. It was the voice she had used in Landizot and in Mip; the voice she had used on the Banders mobs, utterly confident and compelling.

"Handbright. White bird. Shifter. Sister. You have seen birthing before. This is a good child. Like Mertyn, Handbright. Mertyn. Mertyn. A good child. You must save this good child, you must birth it, Handbright. Think." The birther woman gestured, thrusting down. "Push. Birth the good child."

Something fled behind Handbright's eyes, the singing stopped. Mavin went on, demandingly. "Save this good child, Handbright. Concentrate. Push. Think. This is a good baby. Handbright always wanted a baby. Think. The birther says now, Handbright. Push. See. That makes it easier. Now again, push."

Handbright cried out, a sound completely human rather than the strange birdsongs she had made before. The birther nodded, encouraged, and felt the swollen belly. Mavin spoke on, and on, and on.

There was a thin cry, and she looked down to see a wriggling form, all blood and wetness, in the birther's hands. Sighing, exhausted, she released her sister's hands and sat back. There was a scurrying. Others came in from the hallway. Handbright cried out once more and the birthers moved even faster around the bed, lifting another child in their hands. Mavin looked on only, bewildered.

"Twins," cried one. "Twin boys."

"Ah, now, now," thought Mavin, tears in her eyes. "One would have been quite enough. More than enough." She rose unsteadily and went out into the hall, breathing deeply. She had seen dcath in Handbright's eyes. If not now, soon. Soon. Well, she could have come more quickly. She could have interfered less in the world's business and paid more attention to her own. She leaned against the wall, weeping, not knowing Beedie was there until she felt the strong young arms tight around her.

The birther came into the hall, her face strained and tight.

"Never mind," said Mavin. "I know."

"She's asking for you," the birther said. "She's come to herself. She's asked for the babies, too."

"Well then," Mavin responded. "Well then."

She sat in that quiet room for the rest of the day, and most of the day following. The birthers put Handbright's children on her breasts, though she had no milk for them yet and none of them expected that she would have. Still, she asked to have them. And Mavin. She talked of Mertyn and their mother. And died, lying quietly there with the babies in her arms.

The Birders came the next day, expecting to send Handbright's body to the Boundless. Mavin told them it had already gone.

"What are their names?" asked Beedie, poking one of the babies with her strong, Bridger fingers to make it smile.

"Swolwys and Dolwys," said Mavin. "Dolwys has hair that is a little darker, I think."

"Will you let me have them?" asked Beedie, all in a rush. "Me and Roges. We decided together we'd like to have them. We'll have some of our own, too, of course, but we'd like very much to raise Handbright's sons."

"No, sausage girl. You'll have enough of your own to keep you busy. These are my own kin, my own Shifty kin, and they will need to be reared by those who understand our ways. I'll take them with me, as soon as they are a tiny bit older and able to travel."

"How will you carry them, Mavin? How can you manage with two?"

"I'll manage," she said. "I'll figure out a way."

It was in the summer season that the people of Battlefox the Bright Day, a Shifter demesne on the high downs of the shadowmarches, looked out across the p'natti to see a great beast. The beast would not have been considered extraordinary by any Shifters' demesne. Shape and size and aspect are all infinitely variable in Shifters' lives, and they are not surprised by fur or fang or feather. Still, there was something surprising about this beast: the red-haired twin boys who rode upon its back.

The beast opened its mouth and bellowed, "Plandybast!" at which one of the inhabitants of Battlefox Demesne trembled with mixed apprehension and delight.

By the time he had threaded his way through the p'natti, Mavin stood there in her own shape, holding her toddlers by their hands. "Plandybast," she said. "Thalan. My mother's brother. You told me once Handbright would have been welcome at Battlefox Demesne. Tell me now that her sons are equally welcome!"

After which was a time of general rejoicing, story-telling, lying, and welcoming home. Plandybast's half sister, Itter, had left the Demesne long before and was believed dead. Mavin sighed with relief and offered polite consolation. Itter had been the one thing she had doubted about Battlefox Demesne. Now there was nothing to doubt, and even Mavin herself felt at home.

Still, in a few seasons, after the babies were accustomed to the place and had found dozens of kin to care for them, she took quiet leave of the demesne.

"Can you tell me why you're leaving us?" begged Plandybast, who had grown fond of Mavin.

"Oh, thalan, you will think it a silly thing."

"I would rather be told and think it a silly thing than think myself not worthy of being told."

"Well then, hear a tale. Some almost twenty years ago, I came with Mertyn to Pfarb Durim. He was a child, and so was I, scared as two bunwits in a bush when the fustigars howl. So, we made it up between us I would say I was a servant of a Wizard. Himaggery. Mertyn made up the name."

Plandybast nodded. "Not a bad stratagem. Wise men don't fool with Wizards, or the servants of Wizards."

"That's what Mertyn thought. So, I told my tale, but during the next few days I came into danger and told my tale to unbelieving ears. Then came one who said, 'This is my servant, and I am the Wizard Himaggery."

"Ah," said Plandybast.

"And the end of the tale was I sworn him an oath, thalan, that in twenty years time I would come once more to the city of Pfarb Durim, to find him there."

After a thoughtful silence, "Will you be back for Assembly?"

"Perhaps not then. But I will be back. I'll be back for the boys when they're old enough. I want to take them to Schlaizy Noithn myself, if they turn out to be Shifter. If they turn out to be something else – or nothing else – well, I want to decide what should be done in that event."

"Not the Forgetter?"

"No. Not the Forgetter. We have tried to convince the world we are . . . limited, thalan. So they would not fear us, or hate us. We have woven mystifications around us, and the world does not believe them. Shifters are not well liked in the wide world. That being so, why should we commit evil deeds to protect that which can't be protected?

"Ah, well. I don't intend to get the demesne in an uproar raising the question now. It'll be ten years or more before we know what Handbright's sons will be. It may be best to take them back oversea to their father's people."

"Who is their father?" asked Plandybast, curious about this matter for the first time.

Mavin thought briefly she would tell him, "A glue blob in the bottommost lands of a chasm, over the sea." Instead she contented herself with a larger truth. "A priest," she said. "A good and kindly if imperfect man."

She turned when she arrived at the bend in the road beyond which the demesne dissappeared behind the hill. He was waving to her, smiling, weeping a little. Beedie had wept a little, too, and Roges, when she had left them. It was pleasant to be wept over in such kindly fashion.

And the better part of twenty years was gone since she had promised she would keep tryst in Pfarb Durim, twenty years from then.

And the better part of twenty years was gone.

"I am the servant of the Wizard Himaggery," she hummed, remembering that refrain. "Perhaps. Almost. But not quite yet."!

The Search of Mavin Manyshaped

CHAPTER ONE

The season of storms had begun in earnest when Mavin Manyshaped rode down the Ancient Road, beneath the strange arches, toward the city of Pfarb Durim. It was almost twenty years since she had been there last; twenty years since she had promised to come there again. "The Blue Star hangs upon the horns of Zanbee," she sang to herself, not sure she was remembering it correctly. It was something Himaggery had said, was it? Something Wizardly, a specific time which had to do with the season and the arches? The tall horse she rode tiptoed into the shadow of each arch with shivering skin, dancing as he came out again, and she adjusted to this fidgety movement with calm distraction. Twenty years ago they had promised to meet upon the terrace of the hotel Mudgery Mont in the city. Looking down from this height upon the labyrinth of walls and roofs, she was not sure she could find her way to the hotel. Ah. Yes, there it was. Upon the highest part of the city, almost overlooking the cliff wall. She chirruped to the horse, urging him to stop fidgeting and move along.

Just beyond the last of the Monuments was a small inn, a dozen empty wagons scattered around it, as though parked there until the weather cleared, and a fork in the road with one branch leading down to the town. A distant rumble of thunder drew her attention to the clouds, boiling up into mountainous ramparts over the city, black as obsidian, lit from within by a rage of lightning and from the east by the morning sun. This was the weather during which the Monuments were said to dance. While it was never alleged that they had any malevolent intent, it was true that certain travelers caught on the Ancient Road during storms arrived at Pfarb Durim in no condition to pursue their business. If they had the voice for it, and unfortunately sometimes when they did not, they tended to lie about with unfocused eyes singing long, linear melodies which expressed a voice of disturbing wind. Mavin shivered as the horse had done, encouraging him to make better speed toward the distant gates.

A few she knew of had actually seen the Monuments dance. Blourbast the Ghoul had seen, only to die moments later with Huld's dagger in his throat. Huld the Demon and Huldra, his sister-wife had seen, as had their mother, Pantiquod the Harpy. Mavin spat to get the memory of them out of her mouth. She had heard they had gone away from Hell's Maw, left that warren beneath the walls of Pfarb Durim to inhabit another demesne: Bannerwell, beside the flowing river. It was, so her informant had said, a cleaner and more acceptable site for a Gamesman of power. Kings and Sorcerers who could not be enticed to Hell's Maw for any consideration would plot freely with Huld in Bannerwell. She spat again. The memory of him fouled her mind.

Two others had seen the Monuments dance, of course; Mavin, herself, and the Wizard Himaggery. They, too, had gone away separately after promising to meet again when twenty years had passed. Now Mavin Manyshaped rode her tall horse along that Ancient Road, so lost in memory of that other time she paid little attention to the clouds towering over the city. Two decades ago there had been wild drumming in the hills, a fury of firelight, and a flood of green luminescence from the dancing arches. The murmur of present thunder and the threatening spasms of lightning merely rounded out the memory.

A challenging shout brought her to herself. A gate guard, no less fat and lazy than those who had been here long ago. "Well, woman? I asked were you bound into Pfarb Durim or content to sleep on your horse?"

"Bound in, guardsman. To Mudgery Mont."

He gave her a curious glance, saying without saying that he thought her a strange guest for the Mont. Most of those who stayed there came with retinues of servants or with considerable panoply. She gave him a quirky smile to let him know she read his thought, and he flushed slightly as he turned away. "Go then. The gates are open to all who have business within."

As indeed they always were, she reflected. There was no city in all the lands of the True Game so open, not even Betand, which was a crossroad itself. And, as in other of the commercial cities of the land, there was little large scale Game – though much small scale stuff, Games of two, family duels and the like – and a minimum of Game dress. Helmed Tragamors could be seen around the inns and hotels. Even here guards were often needed. A gaudy band of Afrits entered the square as she crossed it, bound away south, no doubt, to the Great Game lately called in the valley land beside Lake Yost, in the midland. Everyone had heard of that; the first Great Game in a decade and half. The Gamesmen in the land headed to it or from it, as their own needs struck them.

The streets were shrill with hawkers, bright with banners, alive with a smell she remembered, rich and complex, made of fruit both rotted and fresh, smoked meats, hides, the stink of the great cressets upon the wall full of grease-soaked wood. The pawnish people of Pfarb Durim had a distinctive dress; full black trousers thrust down into openwork boots (which let the dust and grit of the road sift in and out while somewhat hiding the dirty feet which resulted) and brilliantly colored full shirts with great billowy sleeves. The women belted these garments with an assortment of sashes and chains, topping all off with an intricately folded headdress; the men used simple leather belts and tall leather hats. Both sexes fluttered like lines full of bright laundry or a whole festival of pennants, and were shrill as birds with their cries and arguments. The tall horse picked his way through this riot fastidiously, ears forward, seeming interested in all that went on around him.

As she came farther into the city, the noise quieted, the smell dwindled, until, between the rumbles of thunder, she could hear the wind chimes and smell the flowers in the Mont gardens. The courtyard wall was surmounted with huge stone urns spilling blossoms down the inner wall where a dozen boys plied wet brooms to settle the dust, though by the look of the sky this task would soon prove redundant. The Heralds at the entry looked up incuriously, and then returned to their game of dice, dismissing her in that one weighing glance. "Of no importance," their eyes said. Mavin agreed with their assessment, content to have it so.

A liveried stableman came to take the horse, and she let him go thankfully. It was no easy matter to ride upon another's four legs where she could go easier upon her own. But Shifters were not always welcome guests, not even among Gamesmen notable in treachery and double dealing, so she came discreetly to the Mont, clad in softly anonymous clothing of sufficient quality to guarantee respect without stirring avarice or curiosity.

Now, she thought, I will meet him as I promised, and we will see. What it was she would see she had not identified. What it was she would feel, she had carefully avoided thinking of. Each time her mind had approached the thought it had turned aside, and she had let it turn, riding it as she might a wilful steed, letting it have its own way for a time, until it grew accustomed to her – or she to it. She went into the place, shaking her head at the man who would have taken her cloak, wandering through the rich reception halls toward the terrace she remembered. It lay at the back, over the gardens which stretched down to the cliff edge and the protecting wall, bright under their massed trees, their ornamental lanterns. The door was as she remembered it, opened before her by a bowing flunkey –

And she stood upon the terrace, shaken like a young tree in a great storm.

"Gameswoman?" She didn't hear him. "Gameswoman. Are you well? A chair, Madam? May I bring you something to drink?"

Evidently she had nodded, for he raced away, stopping to say something to some senior servant at the doorway, for that one turned to look at her curiously. She took a deep breath, grasped at her reason with her whole mind.

"Come now, Mavin," she said to herself in a stern, internal voice seldom used, always heeded. "This is senseless, dangerous, unlike you. Sit down. Take a deep breath. Look about you, slowly, calmly. Think what you will say when he returns, how you will set his curiosity aside. Now. He is coming. Careful, quiet."

He set the glass of wineghost before her and she took it into her hand, smiling her thanks. "I was here last many years ago at the time of the great plague," she said in a voice of calm remembrance. "It was a tragic time. We lost many dear to us. The memory caught me suddenly and by surprise. You are too young to remember." She smiled again, paid him generously, and waved him away.

At the door he spoke once more to the other man, shaking his head. The other man nodded, said something with a serious face, but did not look in her direction. So. All was explained. All was calm. She sipped at the wineghost, staying alert. No one was interested in her. The few on the terrace were talking with one another or admiring the gardens or simply sitting, looking at nothing as they soaked the last of the morning sun slanting below the gathering clouds. Was Himaggery among them? Had he seen her come out without knowing her?

She examined the others carefully, one by one, discarding each as a possibility. She knew what he would look like, had visualized him many times. And yet – could it be that plumpish fellow by the wall? Perhaps it was. Her stomach knotted. Surely not. Not. No. He had turned toward her with his pursey mouth and heavy-lidded eyes. Not Himaggery.

One of the men by the stairs, perhaps? The tall, martial- looking man? "Silly," she said to herself. "He has a Sorcerer's crown. Himaggery, if he wore Gamesman's garb at all, would wear Wizard's robes." She finished the wineghost, stood up abruptly and left the terrace. She had been so sure that he would be here when she arrived, so sure. So certain.

Inside she dithered for a moment. She could wander about the place, spend half a day doing it, without knowing whether he was here or not. There was a simpler way.

"Your title?" demanded the porter, officiously blocking the door of his cubby. "Your title?"

"If there is a message for me," she said, "it will be addressed simply to Mavin. I am Mavin, and my title is my own business."

He became immediately obsequious, turning to burrow in the untidy closet among papers and packages, some of them covered with the dust of years. It was obvious that nothing was ever thrown away on the Mont. She was ready with significant coin when he emerged, the sealed missive in his hand. "Who brought it?" she asked.

His eyes were on the coin as he furrowed his face, trying to remember. "A pawn, Gameswoman. A lean, long man in a decent suit of dark clothes. Many lines in his face. A very sad face, he had. The air of a personal servant about him. He did not stay at the Mont, you understand. He just left the message with me, along with the payment for its safe keeping and delivery." He looked at the coin once more, his expression saying that the previous payment could not have been considered sufficient by any reasonable person. She flipped it to him, left him groveling for it in the dusty closet as she turned the packet in her hands. So. Not Himaggery. A message delivered by a man who could only be Johnathon Went, old Windlow's man. Windlow. Himaggery's teacher. Himaggery's friend.

The last of the morning light had gone and rain was falling outside. She found a quiet corner in one of the reception rooms, behind a heavy drapery which held away the cold. The note in the tough parchment envelope was not long.

"Mavin, my dear," it said. "I have no doubt you will be in Pfarb Durim, faithful to your promise. Himaggery will be there, too, if he can. If he is not, it is because he cannot, in which case you are to have the message enclosed. Over the years, each time he has left me to go on one of his expeditions he has left a letter with me for you. This one was left eight years ago. I am sending someone with further information. Please await my messenger upon the Ancient Road – where the Monuments danced. . . .

"I think of you often and kindly. My affectionate regard. Windlow."

It was sealed with Windlow's seal. Another letter lay within.

She stuffed them both into the pocket of her cloak, rose abruptly and went out into the courtyard, shouting for her horse, though the threatened rain had begun. When he was brought to her, she mounted without word and clattered through the city, almost riding through the guards at the gate. The rain had become a downpour and the roadway ran with water, but she urged the horse into a splashing canter up the hill toward the crossroad. She would not, could not have stayed in Pfarb Durim another moment. The city seemed to swallow her. She needed a smaller scope, with trustworthy walls around her.

The tiny inn ghosted into existence through the slanting knives of rain. She shouted to bring a stable boy out of the barn; his mouth was half full of his lunch. Inside the inn she found a room, acceptably clean though sparsely furnished, with a fire ready laid upon the hearth. Food was brought, and beer, and then the kitchen girl was gone, the door shut behind her, and Mavin sat beside the fire with the unopened letter in her hand.

"Well," she said. "Well and well. So all this hurry was for nothing, Himaggery. All this long ride from Schlaizy Noithn, this Shifting into acceptable form with an acceptable face and acceptable clothing. All for nothing. Nothing." Her thumb nail moved beneath the seal. It broke from the paper with a brittle snap, flying into the fire to sizzle upon the wood, hissing like a snale. "For nothing?" she said again, opening the page.

Mavin, my love:

Though I have called you my love often in these past seasons, you have never heard me. If you read this, the chance is great that this is the only time you will ever hear me.

I am going into the Northlands tomorrow, first to see the High Wizard Chamferton – who, I am told, knows much of the true origins and beginnings of things which have always intrigued me – and then farther north into places which are rumored often but seldom charted. There is a legend – well, you probably are not much interested in such things. If you were her now, Mavin, I would not be interested in them either.

Since it is not likely you will read this – I have been, after all, fairly successful at looking after myself for some dozen years – I will allow me to say the things I could not say to you if you were here for fear of frightening you, sending you off in one shape or another, fleeing from me as you fled from Pfarb Durim so long ago. I will say that you have been with me each morning and each night of the time between, in every branch which has broken the sky to let sunlight through, in every deep-eyed animal I have caught peering at me in the forests, in each bird cry, each tumult of thunder. I will say that the thought of you has held me safe in times of danger, held me soft in times of hardship, held me gently when I would have been more brutal than was wise or fair.

Mavin, if I am gone, treasure how deeply I loved you, how faithfully, how joyously. Live well.

Yours as long as I lived,

Himaggery.

She sat as one frozen into stone, eyes fixed on nothing, the room invisible around her. So she sat while the food chilled and the fire died; so she sat until the room grew cold. "Ah, Himaggery," she said at last. "Why have you laid this on me, and you not here."

She rode out at dawn, spending the day upon the Ancient Road, waiting for Windlow's messenger. That day she did not eat, nor that night. The next day she ate something, though without appetite, and stayed again upon the road. The third day she told herself would be the last. If Windlow's messenger did not come, then no messenger would come, and she would ride south to Tarnoch to talk with Windlow himself.

So for this last day she sat upon the tall horse as he fidgeted beneath her, sidling in and out of the shadows once more. "Be still, horse," she said, patting him without thinking. "We are waiting for a messenger.''

The horse did not care. He had waited for three days and was not interested in waiting more. He jumped, hopped, shook his head violently until the links upon the bridle rang and jingled.

She dismounted with a sigh and led him upon the new grass of the hill. ''Here then. Eat grass. Founder upon it. I'll not sit on your twitchiness longer.''

She stretched her arms toward the threatening sky, shifting her ribs experimentally around the soreness remaining from the long ride east. She had left Battlefox Demesne last year, had spent the intervening seasons in Schlaizy Noithn – trying, without success, to remedy an unpleasantness in that tricksy land – and had come out not long ago to Shift into her own shape and equip herself for the journey. So, horse legs instead of her own legs; real clothing instead of mere Shifting; her own face instead of the grotesqueries she had used lately. There was nothing Shifty about her now, nothing to betray her except the quivering Shifter organ deep within her which would announce the presence of another of her kind.

As it did now.

She crouched, ready to assume fangs and claws if needed for her own defense. There was no one on the road in either direction. She searched the dark forest from which a questioning howl rose, abruptly broken off, and her teeth lengthened slightly and her feet dug into the soil. The plump fustigar which trotted from the trees did not threaten her, however. It sat down a good distance from her, peering about itself with attention to the road and the surrounding thickets, then Shifted into a woman's shape clad much as Mavin was in tight breeches and boots.

''Mavin Manyshaped?'' the woman said, beating the dust from her trousers. ''I am Throsset of Dowes, and I come from the Seer Windlow.''

Mavin's mouth dropped open. Throsset of Dowes? From Danderbat Keep? Mavin's own childhood home? Such as it had been. Well and well.

''Throsset of Dowes?'' she asked wonderingly. ''Would you remember Handbright of Danderbat Keep?''

The woman grinned. She was a stocky person with short, graying hair, bushy dark brows and eyes which protruded a little, giving her the look of a curious frog. Her shoulders were broad and square, and she shrugged them now, making an equivocal gesture. "Your sister, Handbright! Of course. She was younger than I. I tried to convince her to come with me, when I left the keep. She would not leave Danderbat the Old Shuffle."

"They said you were in love with a Demon, that you went across the seas with your lover."

The woman frowned, her face becoming suddenly distrustful. "The Danderbats said that, did they? Well, they'll say anything, those old ones. Likely Gormier said that. Or old Halfmad. Or others like them. I left, girl. So did you. It's likely we left for the same reasons, and lovers had no part in it."

"It was Handbright told me, not the old ones." Mavin felt an old anger, for Handbright, for herself.

"Ah." Throsset's voice turned cold, but her mouth looked tired. "She had to believe something, Mavin. She couldn't allow herself to believe that I simply *went*, that I got fed up with it and left. Girls of the Xhindi aren't supposed to do that, you know. We're supposed to be biddable – at least until we've had three or four childer to strengthen the keep. Well, it would be better to say the truth. I am not only Shifter, Mavin. When I was sixteen or so, one of the old ones tried something I didn't care for, and I found a new Talent. It seems I had Shifter and Sorcerer Talent both, and the Danderbats didn't know how to handle that. One Talent more and I'd have been a Dervish, and time was I longed for it, just to teach them a lesson. Still, there's no basket discipline will hold a wary Sorcerer, though they tried it, surely enough. I burst the basket and the room, and then I left. I'm sorry Handbright didn't go with me. How is she now?"

"Dead," said Mavin flatly, not caring to soften it.

"Dead!" The woman slapped at her legs, hands going on of themselves, without thought, as though they might brush the years away with the dust. "I hadn't heard. But then, I haven't been back to Danderbat Keep."

"They wouldn't have been able to tell you had you gone there. She died far away, across the western sea. She was mad – until the very end. She had two sons, twins. They're fifteen-season childer now, five years old, at Battlefox Demesne, with Handbright's thalan and mine, Plandybast Ogbone."

"So she did leave Danderbat at last. Ah, girl, believe me, I did try to get her to go with me. She said she stayed for your sake, and for Mertyn's. She loved him more than most sisters love their boy-kin. I could not break her loose."

Seeing the distress in the woman's face, Mavin tried to set aside her own remembered anger and to dissipate the chilliness which was growing between them. Handbright's servitude and abuse had not been Mavin's fault, or Throsset's. "Mertyn made her stay," she said sadly. "He had Beguilement Talent even then, and he used it to keep her there because he was afraid she would leave him. He was only a child. He did not know what pain it cost her. Well. That is all long gone, Throsset. Long gone. Done. Mertyn is a man now. Though his Talent was early, it has continued to grow. He is a King, I hear. Lately appointed Gamesmaster in some school or other."

"Windlow said to tell you he is in Schooltown." The woman stopped brushing dust and frowned. "Look, Mavin, I have traveled a distance and this is a high cold hill. There is threat of rain. I have not eaten today, and the city lies close below. . . ."

"We need not go so far as the city. There's an inn at the fork of the road, called The Arches. I have a room there." She lifted herself into the saddle. "Come up with me. This twitchy horse can carry double the short way." The woman grasped her arm and swung up behind her, the horse shying as he felt two sets of knees Shift tight around him. Deciding that obedience would be the most sensible thing, he turned quietly toward the road, going peaceably beneath each of the arches as he came to it with only a tiny twitch of skin along his flanks. The women rode in silence, both of them distressed at the meeting, for it raised old hurts and doubts to confront them.

It was not until they were seated before a small fire in a side room at the inn, cups of hot tea laced with wineghost half empty before them, that old sorrow gave way to new curiosity. Then they began to talk more freely, and Mavin found herself warming to the woman as she had not done to many others.

"How come you to be messenger for Windlow? A Shifter? He was Gamesmaster of the school at Tarnoch, under the protection of the High King. I would have thought he would send a Herald."

"I doubt he could have found a Herald to act for him. Windlow has little authority in the Demesne of the High King Prionde. Did you know the High King's son? Valdon?"

Mavin shuddered. Memories of that time – particularly of Valdon or Huld or Blourbast – still had the power to terrify her, if only for the moment. "I met him, yes. It was long ago. He was little more than a boy. About nineteen? Full of vicious temper and arrogance. Yes. And his little brother, Boldery, who was a little older than Mertyn."

"Then if you met him it will not surprise you to know that Valdon refused to be schooled by Windlow. His pride would not allow him to be corrected, so says Windlow, and he could not bear restraint. He announced as much to the King, his father, and was allowed license to remain untaught."

Mavin had observed much of Valdon's prideful hostility when she had been in Pfarb Durim before. "But he wasn't the only student!" she objected. "Windlow had set up the school under the patronage of King Prionde, true, but there were many other boys involved. Some were thalans of most powerful Gamesmen."

"Exactly. You have hit upon the situation. Prionde could not destroy the school without hurting his own reputation. He could let it dwindle, however, and so he has done. Windlow is now alone in the school except for the servants and two or three boys, none of them of important families. Since Himaggery left, his only source of succor is through Boldery, for the child grew to love him and remains faithful, despite all Valdon's fulminations. Valdon is a Prince of easy hatreds and casual vengeance. A dangerous man."

Mavin twisted her mouth into a sceptical line. "Fellow Shifter, I sorrow to hear that the old man is not honored as he should be, and I am confirmed in my former opinion of Valdon, but Windlow has not sent you all this way from the high lakes at Tarnoch to tell me of such things."

Throsset gulped a mouthful of cooling tea and shook her head. "Of course not. I owed the old man many things. He asked me to come to you as a favor, because I am Shifter from Danderbat Keep, and you are Shifter from Danderbat Keep, and he believed you would trust my word. . . ."

"Trust you because we are both from Danderbat Keep!" Mavin could not keep the astonishment from her voice.

Throsset made a grimace. "Unless you told him, what would he know about the lack of trust and affection in Danderbat Keep? That wasn't what he was thinking of, in any case. He asked me because we were both women there. That old man understands much, Mavin. I think you may have told him more about yourself than you realized, and I certainly told him more than I have told anyone else. He senses things, too. Things that most Gamesmen simply ignore. No, Windlow didn't send me to tell you of his own misfortune. He sent me to bring to you everything he knows about Himaggery – where he went, where he might be."

"But he is dead!" Mavin cried, her voice breaking.

"Hush your shouting," commanded Throsset in a hissing whisper. "It is your business, perhaps our business, but not the business of the innkeeper and every traveler on the road. He is not dead. Windlow says no!"

"Not dead? And yet gone for eight years, and I only hear of it now!"

"Of course now. How could you have heard of it earlier? Did Windlow know where you were? Did you send regular messengers to inform him?" Throsset was good-natured but scornful. "Of course, now."

"He is a Seer," Marvin said sullenly, aware of her lack of logic.

"Poof. Seers. Sometimes they know everything about something no one cares about. Often they know nothing about something important. Windlow himself says that. He knows where Himaggery set out to go eight years ago; he Sees very little about where he may be now."

"Eight years!

"It seems a long time to me, too."

"Eight years. Eight years ago – I was . . . where was I?" She fell silent, thinking, then flushed a brilliant red which went unnoticed in the rosy firelight. Eight years ago she had wandered near the shadowmarches, had found herself in a pool-laced forest so perfect that it had summoned her to take a certain shape within it, the shape of a slender, single-horned beast with golden hooves. And then there had been another of the same kind, a male. And they two . . . they two . . . Ah. It was only a romantic, erotic memory, an experience so glorious that she had refused to have any other such for fear it would fail in comparison. Whenever she remembered it, she grieved anew at the loss, and even now she grieved to remember what had been then and was no more. She shook her head, tried to clear it, to think only of this new hope that perhaps Himaggery still lived. "Eight years. Where did he set out for, that long ago?"

"He set out to meet with the High Wizard Chamferton."

"I know that much; his letter said that much. But why? Himmagery was Wizard himself. Why would he seek another?"

Throsset rose to sidle through the narrow door into the commons room in the inn where she ordered another pot of tea. She came into the room carrying a second flask of wineghost, peeling at the wax on the cork with her teeth. "Two more cups of this and I'll be past the need for food and fit only for bed. Don't you every get hungry?"

Mavin made an irritated gesture. It was no time to think of food, but her stomach gurgled in that instant, brought to full attention by Throsset's words. The woman laughed. When the boy came in with the tea, Throsset ordered food to be prepared, then settled before the fire once more.

"You asked why he sought another Wizard. I asked the same question of Windlow. He told me a tale of old Monuments that danced, of ancient things which stir and rumble at the edges of the lands of the True Game. He told me of a time, perhaps sixty years ago or so, when great destruction was wrought upon the lands, and he said it was not the first time. He had very ancient books which spoke of another time, so long ago it is past all memory, when people were driven from one place to another, when the beasts of this world assembled against them. He spoke of roads and towers and bells, of shadows and rolling stars. Mysteries, he said, which intrigued Himaggery and sent him seeking. Old Chamferton was said to know something about these ancient mysteries."

Mavin tilted her head, considering this. "I have heard of at least one such time," she said. "Across the seas there is a land which suffered such a cataclysm a thousand years ago. The people were driven down into a great chasm by beasts which came suddenly, from nowhere."

"Stories of that kind fascinated Himaggery," Throsset mused, "as they do me. Oh, we heard them as children, Mavin! Talking animals and magical rings. Swords and jewels and enchanted maidens. Himaggery collected such tales, says Windlow. He traveled all about the countryside staying in old inns, asking old pawnish granddads what stories they remembered from the time before our ancestors came from the north."

"You say our ancestors came from the north? In Schlaizy Noithn I have heard it rumored we came from beneath the mountains! And across the seas, in the chasm of which I spoke earlier, the priests say the Boundless – that being their name for their god – set them in their chasm."

Throsset turned up her hands, broadening the gesture to embrace the space near the table as the boy came into the room with their food. "Ah. Set it here, boy, and bring another dish of that sauce. This isn't enough for two! Good. Smell that, Mavin? Cookery like this always reminds me of Assembly time at Danderbat Keep."

Mavin did not want to remember Assembly time at Danderbat Keep. "The food was the best part of it," she remarked in a dry tone of recollection.

"It was that," Throsset agreed around a mouthful. "But we have enough sad memories between us without dragging them out into the light. They do not grow in the dark, I think, so much as they do when well aired and fertilized with tears."

Mavin agreed. "Very well, Kinswoman, I will not dwell on old troubles. We are here now, not at the Keep, and it is here we will think of. Now, you tell me Himaggery had heard all these tales of ancient things. I can tell you, for you are in Windlow's confidence, that Himaggery himself saw those arches dance, those Monuments where we met today; and so did I – Yes! If you could see your face, Throsset. You obviously disbelieve me. You don't trust my account for a moment, but it's true nonetheless. Some future time, I'll tell you all about it if you like – Well, I saw the arches dance, but afterward I was willing to leave it at that, perhaps to remember it from time to time, but not to tease at it and tear at it. Not Himaggery! Himaggery had a mind full of little tentacles and claws, reaching, always reaching. He was never willing to leave anything alone until he understood it.

"Strange are the Talents of Wizards, so it's said, and strange are the ways they think. Once he had seen, he couldn't have left it alone, not for a moment. He'd have been after it like a gobble-mole with a worm, holding on, stretching it out longer and longer until it popped out of its hole. And if he heard the High Wizard Chamferton knew anything – well then, off he'd go, I suppose." She felt uneasy tears welling up.

Throsset confirmed this. "Yes, he heard it said that Chamferton knew about the mysteries of our past and the past of the world and ancient things in general. So. He went off to see Chamferton, and he did not come back."

"But Windlow knows he is not dead?"

"Windlow knows Himaggery lives."

"Not mere wishful thinking?" Mavin turned away from the firelight and rubbed her eyes, suddenly a little hopeful, yet still hesitant to accept it. "Windlow must be getting very old."

"About eighty-five, I should say. He is remarkably active still. No. He says that Gamesmen, often the finest and the best of them, do disappear from time to time into a kind of nothingness from which the Necromancers cannot raise them, into an oblivion, leaving no trace. But Himaggery's disappearance is not of that kind."

"How does he know?"

"For many years, Windlow has been collecting old books. He sends finders out to locate them and get them by beggery, barter, or theft, so he says. During the last several years he has asked these finders to search for Himaggery also. Some of them returned to say they felt Himaggery's presence, have sought and sought, felt it still, but were unable to find him. And this is not old information; a Rancelman came back with some such tale only a few days before I left there."

"So Windlow has sent you to tell me Himaggery is not dead but vanished and none of the Pursuivants or Rancelmen can find him." Mavin said this flatly as she wiped sauce from her chin, keeping both her voice and her body still and unresponsive. The tears were in abeyance for the moment, and she would not acknowledge them. It would do no good to weep over her food while Throsset chewed and swallowed and cast curious glances at her over the edge of her cup. It would do no good until she could think of something else to do besides weeping. Despite her hunger, the food lay inside her like stone.

She pushed the plate away, suddenly nauseated. The firelight made a liquid swimming at the corners of her eyes.

"Tush," mourned Throsset. "You're not enjoying your dinner at all. Cry if you like! We don't make solemn vows over twenty years unless there is something to it besides moon madness. Was he your lover?"

She shook her head, tears spilling down her face in an unheeded flood, dripping from her chin onto her clenched hands. Her throat closed as in a vice, almost as it had done when she had read his letter.

Throsset got up and closed the door, leaning a chair against it. Then she walked around the room, saying nothing, while Mavin brought herself to a gulping silence. When that time came, she brought a towel and dipped it into the pitcher on the table. "Here. Wash the tears away before they begin to itch. You have a puddle on your breeches. They'll think you've wet yourself. Come to the fire and dry it. Now, you don't need any more wineghost, that's certain. It won't cure tears. Take some of the tea for your throat. You'll have cried yourself hoarse . . . "

After a time, Mavin could speak again. "I am not much of a weeper, Throsset. I have not wept for many years, even when I have made others weep. I don't really know why I'm doing it now. No, Himaggery and I weren't lovers. We could have been. I was very much . . . desirous of him. But I kept him from it, kept me from it. I did not want that, not then. There was too much of servitude in it, too much of Danderbat Keep."

The woman nodded. "Anyone who grew up in Danderbat Keep would understand that. Still, there was something between you, whether you let anything actually happen or not." She took the towel and wrung it out before handing it to Mavin once more. "Windlow told me of some joke between you and Himaggery. That Himaggery was not his true name at all, that you had made up the name."

"Mertyn and I made it up on our trip north from Danderbat Keep. To avoid being bothered by child stealers and pawners, I was to say that I was the servant of the Wizard Himaggery – which was a name we invented – and that he, Mertyn, was thalan to the Wizard. In this way, we hoped to avoid trouble or Gaming as we traveled north. For a time it worked. Then we were accused of lying – accused by Huld." She shivered, remembering the malevolence in that Demon's voice and manner.

"And then this casual young man came into the room saying the accusation was nonsense; that he was himself the Wizard Himaggery and that I, Mavin, was indeed his servant. And so the threat passed. Afterward, he said he would keep the name. I thought at the time it suited him better than his own."

"And that was all that passed between you?"

"That. And a night together on a hillside among the shadowpeople. And a few hours in Pfarb Durim at the hotel Mudgery Mont when the plague and the battle and the crisis were all over. And a promise."

"And yet you wept . . . "

"And yet I wept. Perhaps the weeping was for many things. For Handbright, because you knew her. And for the young Throsset of Dowes as well. For old Windlow, perhaps, who has not received the honors he deserves. And for me and the eight years I have wandered the world not knowing Himaggery was gone. I had imagined him, you know, many times, as he would look when I met him again at last. I saw his face, clearly as in a mirror. It is almost as though I had known him during these years, been with him. When I rode to Pfarb Durim, I knew how familiar he would look to me, even after all this time . . . " She wiped her face one final time, then folded the towel and placed it on the table near her half-emptied plate. "Well. I am wept out now. And I know there must be more to this than you have told me. Windlow could have put this in the same letter he sent to Mudgery Mont."

"He could," agreed Throsset, piling the dishes to one side before returning to her cup. "He could. Yes. He did not, for various reasons. First, there are always those who read letters who have no business reading them. Particularly in Pfarb Durim. Huld still has great influence there, I understand, and every second person in the city is involved in gathering information for him."

"That's true. Though I was told at Mudgery Mont that Huld repented of Blourbast's reputation and will stay in Bannerwell from now on."

"No matter where he stays, spies who work for him will still sneak a look at other people's letters. In addition, however, there are those abroad in the world who have no love for Himaggery. I speak now of Valdon. Windlow did not tell me the source of the enmity. Perhaps he does not even know. But Windlow would put nothing in writing which might be used to harm him.

"In any case, that was not the main reason Windlow sent me. He says he had a vision, years ago, when you were all here before, in which he saw you and Himaggery together in Pfarb Durim. Somehow in the vision he knew that twenty years had passed. So, says Windlow, if Himaggery is to come here again and the vision to be fulfilled, then you, Mavin, must be involved in it."

"He wants me to go searching, does he?"

"He thinks you will. He never said what he wanted."

Mavin made a rather sour smile, thinking of the leagues she had traveled since her girlhood. "I spent fifteen years searching for Handbright, did you know that? No, of course you didn't. I could have done it in less time. I might have saved her life if I had been quicker. When that search was done, I was glad it was over. I am not a Pursuivant who takes pleasure in the chase, Throsset. My experience is that searching is weary work. I don't know what I will do, Kinswoman. As you say, we were not lovers."

"Still, you made a promise."

"To meet him here. Not to find him and bring him here."

"Still, a promise . . . well. It is no part of my duty to chivvy you one way or the other. Only you know what passed between the two of you long ago and whether it was enough to send you on this journey. Only you know why you have been crying as though your heart would break. I have done as I promised the old Seer I would do – brought you word. No. I have not done entirely. He sent a map of the lands where the High Wizard Chamferton dwells, if indeed he dwells there still. It is a copy of the one Himaggery took with him. It is here on the table."

"Are you leaving? So soon?"

"No. I am taking a room in this place for the night, unless you will let me share yours. Whichever, I will go there now to sleep. Which you should do, unless you are determined to linger by the fire and think deep thoughts. If I thought I could help you, I would offer to do so, for long ago I cared about Handbright. Cared for her, failed her. There should have been something more I could have done, but at the time I thought I had done everything." She stared into the fare herself, obviously thinking deep thoughts of her own.

Marvin, curious, asked, "Is there a name for this combination of Talents you have, Throsset? I have gone over and over what little I know of the Index, and I cannot remember what Gamesname you should be called."

Throsset flushed. "There is a name, Mavin. I would prefer to be called simply Shifter, if you must call me. Or Sorcerer, if Shifter is not enough. I sometimes think those anonymous ancestors who made up the Index suffered from an excess of humor. Their name for one of my Talents is not one I choose to bear. Well. No matter what I might have called myself, Handbright would not hear me when I spoke to her. You have not said how it was she left at last."

Mavin murmured a few words about the lateness of the hour, indicating she did not want to talk about it then. The thought of Handbright saddened her always, and she was sad enough at the moment over other things. Throsset nodded in return, signifying that another time would do. The time did not come, however. When Mavin woke in the morning, the bed beside her was empty and Throsset was gone. The map lay on a chest beside the door. The innkeeper said the account had been paid.

Outside in the stableyard Mavin's tall horse whickered, and after a time of thought Mavin sold him to the innkeeper. Somehow in the deep night the matter had become decided, and she needed no flesh but her own to carry her to whatever place Himaggery had gone.

CHAPTER 2

There was a note attached to the map with a silver pin. "Mavin, my dear child, this is a copy of the map Himaggery and I made up before he left. Most of the information is from some old books I had, but we got one or two things from some recent charts made by Yggery, the Mapmaker in Xammer. Himaggery was to go first to Chamferton, who is reputed to have access to an old library. If you decide to go looking for Himaggery, there is no point in coming here. Everything I know is on the map or Throsset will have told you. I hope you will want to go after him. I would do so if these aging legs would carry me, for he is very dear to me." It was signed with Windlow's seal, and she stood staring at it for a very long time.

She bought a few provisions from the Arches, more for appearance's sake than anything else. It was better to let those who saw her upon the road, those who might speak of her to others, think she had had to sell the horse to buy food than that they know her for a Shifter who could live off the countryside as well as any pombi or fustigar. Shifters were not highly regarded in the world of the True Game, not by Gamesmen or pawns, and there was recurrent unpleasantness to remind her of it. Better to be merely another anonymous person and wait until she was out of sight of the inn before Shifting into a long-legged form in which she could run all day without weariness – in which she had run day after day in Schlaizy Noithn.

According to the map, the High Wizard Chamferton dwelt in the Dorbor Range, east of the shadowmarches, in a long canyon which led from the cliffs above the Lake of Faces northward among the mountains. Mavin knew her way to the shadowmarches well enough. She had traveled there before; to Battlefox the Bright Day, where her own kin lived in a Shifters' demesne; to the lands of the shadowpeople where Proom lived with his tribe, wide-eared and bright-fanged, singing their way through the wide world and laughing at everything; to Ganver's Grave, the place of the Eesties, or Eestnies as some called them; to that enchanted, pool-laced valley she remembered in her dreams where the two fabulous beasts had lain together in beds of fragrant moss. North. The location did not surprise her. If she had been told to seek out knowledge of ancient things, northward is the way she would have gone. Still, the paths she knew would not help her in coming to Chamferton. She had not been that route before.

Bidding a polite farewell to the innkeeper she stepped onto the road and walked northward on it. The night's storm had given way to a morning of pale wet light and steamy green herbage dotted with flowers. Far to the west she could see Cagihiggy Creek in a plaze of webwillow, yellow as morning. It was calming to walk, stride on stride, aware of the day without worrying where night would find her. She yawned widely as she turned aside from the road onto the wooded slope of the hills.

She was now a little east of Pfarb Durim, ready to run in fustigar shape along these eastern hills until she came some distance north of Hell's Maw. Having walked into that labyrinth once, she had no desire to see it or smell it again. Once she was far enough north, she would climb down the cliff in order to reach the Lake of the Faces, a new feature upon the maps, created, so it was said, only within recent years. She had a mind to see it, to learn if what was said of it was true, though half her mind mocked the rest of her with believing such wild tales. Still, there would be no time wasted. The Lake of Faces lay in the valley below the entrance to the canyon where the Demesne of the High Wizard Chamferton would be found. She felt the map, tightly folded in her pocket. Once she abandoned her clothing, she would make a pocket in her hide for it.

Soon she was lost among the trees, invisible to any eyes except small wild ones peering from high branches or hidey holes among the roots. Keeping only the little leather bags which held her supply of coin, she put her clothing into a hollow tree, the boots dropping against the trunk with a satisfying clunk. Fur crept over her limbs, sensuously, slowly, so she could feel the tickling emergence of it; bones flexed and bent into new configurations. She dropped to all fours, set eyes and nose to see and hear the world in a way her own form could never do. A bunwit flashed away among the bushes, frightened out of its few wits by this sudden appearance of a fustigar. Mavin licked her nose with a wet tongue and loped away to the north. A bunwit like that one would make her supper, and she would not necessarily feel the need to cook it.

Dark came early, but she did not stop until she had reached the edge of the cliff and crawled down it in a spidery bundle of legs and claws. Once at the bottom she could smell water and hear many trickling falls, thin and musical in the dark. A shaving of moon lit the Lake of Faces and made silver streamers of the water dropping into it from the cliffs above. The spider shape yawned, Shifted; the fustigar yawned, Shifted. Mavin stood in her own shape upon the shore, ivory in the cool night. She scratched. Whatever shape one Shifted into, the skin stayed on the outside and all the dirt of the road stayed on it. The water welcomed her as she slid beneath its surface, relishing its chill caress.

The lake had been so inviting she had taken no time to look around her. Now, floating on her back with her hair streaming below her like black water weed in the moonlight, she began to see the Faces.

White poles emerged from shadow as she peered into the dark, an army of them in scattered batallions on the shore, in the shallows, marching out into the fringes of the forest. One such stood close beside her, and she clung to it, measuring it with hands which would not quite reach around it, finger to finger, thumb to thumb. She lay on the water and thrust herself away from the pole so she could look up into the face at its top, white as ivory, blind-eyed, close-lipped, its scalp resting upon the top of the pole, a thin strap extending from ear to ear behind the pole and nailed there with a silver spike.

It was a woman's face, a mature woman, not thin, not lovely but handsome. The face had no hair, only the smooth curve as of a shaved skull, pale as bleached bone.

Though it seemed no more alive than a statue and was no more real, it troubled her. She swam away a little, found another of the white posts and confronted a man's face, weak-jawed and petulant-looking, the blind eyes gleaming with reflected light. The moon had come higher, making the pale poles stand out against the dark of the forested cliffs like a regiment of ghosts.

From high above the cliffs, a scream shattered the silence; the harsh, predatory cry of some huge bird. Mavin looked up to see two winged blots circling down toward the lake. Shifting herself, she sank beneath the waters to peer at them with protruding, froglike eyes.

Harpies! She edged upward, let her ears rest above the water in the shadow of the pole, drawn by something familiar in the cry. Yes. Though she had not heard that voice for twenty years, she could not mistake it. One of the descending forms was Pantiquod – Pantiquod who had brought the plague to Pfarb Durim, who had almost killed Mertyn, who should have been far to the south at Bannerwell with her evil children – screaming a welcome to another child.

"Well met, daughter! I thought to find you during new moon at the Lake of Faces. And here you are, at old Chamferton's oracle. Does he send you still to question the Faces?"

The voice in reply was as harsh, as metallic, with an undertone of wild laughter in it. "Pantiquod, mother-bird, I had begun to think you too old to take shape. What brings you?" The two settled upon the shore, folding their wings to stalk about on high, stork legs, bare pendulous breasts gleaming in the moonlight. Mavin became aware of a smell, a poultry house stink, chemical and acrid. Shifting her eyes to gather more light, she saw that the shore among the poles was littered with Harpy droppings, white as the masks themselves.

"Not too old, daughter. Too lazy, perhaps. Since Blourbast is dead, I have luxuriated with no need to Game or bestir myself."

"And how are my half sister and brother," the younger Harpy cried, voice dripping venom. "The lovely Huldra, the lovelier Huld?"

"Well enough, daughter. Well enough. since Huldra bore a son, Mandor, she has had little to do with Huld. She hates him, and he her, and both me and I both. I do not let it trouble me. I stay with them for the power and the servants and the comfort. In the caves beneath Bannerwell there is much pleasure to be had."

"I can imagine. Years of such pleasure you've had already. More years than I can remember, yet never a word from you since Blourbast died. Why now, mama? Why now, loathsome chicken?" And she cawed with wild laughter, at some joke which Pantiquod shared, for the older Harpy shrilled in the same tone.

"Oh, does Chamferton call you that still? And me as well? I came not before, dear daughter, because I do not serve him still and would not be caught again in his toils. I come now because you do serve him still and I want to borrow *it* from you. For a moment or two."

"I do not serve him. He holds me, as he once held us both. And you want to borrow it? The wand? Foolishness, mother-bird. He would know it in a minute."

"Would it matter if he did? After eight long years, is he still so violent? Would he punish you? For granting a small request to your own mother?"

The younger Harpy lifted on her wings, threw her head back and screamed with laughter, jigged on her stork legs, wings out, dancing. "Would Chamferton punish me? Would Chamferton punish me? What a question, a question!"

Mavin paddled her way closer to the shore. They were talking more quietly now, the screaming greetings done, and she thrust her ears upward to catch each word.

"I will not lend it to you, Mother. Do not ask it. Try to take it and I'll claw your gizzard out and your eyes as well. But I'll use it for you, perhaps, if you have not any purpose in mind Chamferton would find hateful enough to punish me for."

"It is no purpose he would care a thrilpskin for. Does he care for Huld? Is the Face of Huld still here?"

"He cares nothing for Huld, and the Face is still here, where he had you put it, Mother. Long ago."

"He has probably forgotten it. But I have not forgotten, and I need to know from it a little thing. Ask it for me: Will it grow and flourish like webwillow in the spring? Or will it shrivel and die? Ask it for me, daughter. And I will then do what is best . . . for me."

The two stork-legged shapes moved away among the poles, Mavin after them flat as a shadow on the ground, invisible as she crept in their wake. They wound their way through the forest of poles, searching for a particular one. At last they found it, cawing to one another excitedly. "Oh, it is Huld's Face, as he is today. He was handsomer when young, daughter. For a time I thought him a very marvel of beauty, before Blourbast changed him and made him what he is."

"Ahh, cahhh, ah-haa, mate a Ghoul with a Harpy and blame the Ghoul's influence for what comes out. Well, Mother. Shall I ask?"

There were whispers. Then the younger Harpy stood back from

the pole with its Face and called strange words into the silence of the place, striking the pole three times with a long, slender wand she had drawn from a case on her back. Three times she repeated this invocation. On the ninth blow, the lips of the Face opened and Huld's voice spoke – Huld's voice as it would have come from another world, beyond space. It was the timeless ghost of his voice, and it made shivers where Mavin's backbones might have been.

"What would you know?"

"Will you live or die, Huld?" asked the Harpy. "Will you flourish or wilt into nothing?"

"For a season I will flourish. I will lose that which I now hold precious and discover I care not. I will heap atrocity upon atrocity to build a name and will lose even my name in a dust of bones." The lips of the Face snapped shut with the sound of stones striking together. The young Harpy spun on her tall legs, snickering.

"So, Mother? Is that enough?"

"It is enough," Pantiquod said in a dry, harsh voice. "I felt something of the kind. A pity. If one would choose, one would choose a son who would not be so ephemeral. Still. It is he who will dwindle and die, not I. There is time for me to protect myself. I will be leaving Bannerwell, daughter."

"And your other daughter, lovely Huldra?"

"As she will. She may choose to stay, or go."

"Where will you go?"

"If I do not wish to share Huld's eventual ruin, away from him. Into the Northlands, I think. I have heard there are fortunes to be made and damage to be done in the Northlands. And I will not go empty-handed."

"Ah-haw, cawh, I would think not. Will you wait with me now, Mother, while I do Chamferton's bidding? Will you keep me company?"

"We were never company, daughter," said Pantiquod, rising on her wings and making a cloud of dry, feathery droppings scud across the ground into Mavin's face. "But I fly now to Chamferton's aerie, and you may return there before I go. Maybe he will have news for me of doings in the north." She flew up, circling, crying once at the top of the spiral before wheeling north along the valley.

Now the younger Harpy moved among the Faces, chattering to herself like a barnyard fowl, full of clucks and keraws. Three times she stopped before Faces and demanded certain information of them. Three times the Faces replied before returning to their silent, expressionless masks. A man with a young-old Face was asked where he was and answered, "Under Bartelmy's Ban." It was a strange Face and a strange answer. Both stuck in Mavin's memory. An old woman's Face opened its pale lips and chanted, "Upon the road, the old road, a tower made of stone. In the tower hangs a bell which cannot ring alone. . . " There was a long pause, then the lips opened once more. "The daylight bell still hangs in the last tower." The Harpy chuckled at this before going on to the next Face, that of a middle-aged man with a missing eye who announced that the Great Game being played in the midlands near Lake Yost would soon be lost for all who played, with only death as a result and the Demesne of Lake Yost left vacant.

By the time Mavin had heard the words of invocation said three times for each of these, she could have quoted them herself. The moon was high above. The young Harpy seemed to have finished her assigned duties and now moved among the poles and Faces only for amusement, Mavin still following doggedly, her curiosity keeping her close behind.

She almost missed seeing Himaggery's Face, her eyes sliding across it as they had a hundred others, only to return, shocked and fascinated. It was the face of a man in his mid years, perhaps forty, with lines from nose to mouth and a web around his eyes. And yet – and yet see how those lips quirked in a way she had remembered always, and the lines around his eyes were those her fingertips remembered. He looked as she had dreamed he would, as she had known he would, and that second look told her it was he beyond all doubt.

She came up from the guano-smeared soil in one unthinking movement, grasping the Harpy with fingers of steel before she could react.

"I will take the wand, daughter of Pantiquod."

The Harpy did not reply, but began a wild, wheeling struggle, beating her wings against Mavin's face, thrusting with her strong talons. When she found she could not escape, she began screaming, raising echoes which fled along the lake-shore, rousing birds who nested there so that they, too, screamed in the night. Mavin felt the distant beating of wings, heard a cry from high above, knew that fliers there could plunge upon her in moments.

"Call them off," she instructed breathlessly. "At once. I have no desire to kill you, Harpy, unless I must."

There was only a defiant caw of rage as the Harpy redoubled her struggles. Mavin shook her, snapped her like a whip, raised her above to serve as a shield – and felt the talons and beak of whatever had plummeted from the sky bury themselves in the Harpy's body. Abruptly the struggles ceased.

Mavin dropped the body. Perched upon it was a stunned flitchhawk, its dazed, yellow eyes opaque. Mavin pulled it from the Harpy's throat and tossed it away. It planed down onto the soil to crouch there, panting.

Mavin turned her back on the bird. She drew the Harpy's wand from its case. The battle had driven the words of invocation from her memory, and it took a moment to recall them. Then she stood before Himaggery's Face and chanted them, striking with the wand three times, three times again, and a final three.

The stony lips opened. "What would you know?" asked the ghost of Himaggery's voice.

"Where are you?" she begged. "Where are you, Himaggery?"

"Under the Ban, the Ban, Bartelmy's Ban," said the ghostly voice, and the lips shut tight.

She had heard that meaningless answer before! She tried to open his lips again with the wand and the words, but it did no good. She wandered among the Faces, to see if there were others she knew. There were none. At length her weariness overtook her, and she returned to the water to wash away the harsh, biting smell of the place. After that was a long time of sleep on a moss bank, halfway up the cliff, where no Harpies had come to leave their droppings. And long after that, morning which was more than halfway to noon.

She went down to the lake for water. The Harpy lay where Mavin had thrown her the night before, dried blood upon her throat and chest. That chest moved, however, in slow breaths, and the wound had clotted over. Mavin mused at this for some time before turning to the water. When she had washed herself and found something juicy for her breakfast, she returned to the Harpy's unconscious form and took it upon her back. "I will return you to your master," she announced in a cheery tone, Shifting to spider legs which could carry them both up the precipitous cliffs around the lake. "You and your wand – the Wizard's wand. It may be he will be grateful."

"And if he is not?" asked some inner sceptical part of her. "And if Pantiquod is there?"

"Well then, not," she answered, still cheerily. "He can do no worse than try to enchant me, or whatever it is Wizards do. I can do no better than Shift into something horrible and eat him if he tries it. So and so. As for Pantiquod . . . likely she will have gone on by now. She did not intend to await her daughter's coming."

The spider shape gave way to her lean, fustigar form when she reached the cliff top. Before her the canyon stretched away in long diagonals where the toes of two mountains touched, northwest then northeast then northwest once more. The small river in its bottom was no more than a sizeable creek, bright shallow water sparkling over brown stones and drifts of gravel. Fish fled from the shallows where she stood and something jumped into the water upstream, bringing ripples to her feet.

She lapped at the water, feeling it cool upon her furry legs. The water joined her breakfast to add bulk, making the body on her back less burdensome. Squirming to get it more comfortably settled, she trotted up the canyon into the trees, which grew thicker the farther north she went.

At noon she put her burden down, caught two ground-running birds, Shifted into her own form and cooked them above a small fire as she watched the smoke, smelled it, smiled and hummed. The mood of contentment was rare and inexplicable. She knew she should feel far otherwise, but as the day wore on, the calm and content continued to grow.

"Enchantment!" her inner self warned. "This is enchantment, Mavin."

"So," she purred to herself. "Let be. What will come will come."

It was dusk when she rounded a last curve of the canyon to see the fortress before her, its battlements made of the same stone it stood upon, gray and ancient, as though formed in the cataclysm which had reared the mountains up. There was a flash of light from the tower, like a mirror reflecting sun from the craggy horizon. In that instant, the mood of contentment lifted, leaving behind a feeling of dazed weariness, as when one had drunk too much and caroused too late. She knew someone had seen her, had weighed her up and determined that the protection of enchantment was not necessary any longer. She snarled to herself, accepting it.

After waiting a few moments to see whether anything else would happen, she trotted forward. A road began just before her, winding, grown over in places, but a road nonetheless. She followed it, tongue out and panting. The way had been long and mostly uphill. Breakfast and lunch were long gone.

The fortress stood very high upon its sheer plinth of stone. From the canyon floor, stairs wound into darkness up behind the pillar. Mavin dropped her burden and lay down at the foot of these stairs, first nosing the Harpy to determine whether she still lived. She stretched, rolled, then began licking sore paws. She would stay as she was, thank you, until something definitive happened. She was not about to get caught in any shape at all on that dark, ominous staircase.

"Is that as far as you intend to bring her?" asked a hoarse, contentious voice from the stairs.

She looked up. He stood there, framed against the dark, in all respects a paradigm of Wizards. He had the cloak and robe, the tall hat, the beard, the crooked nose and the stern mouth. She was silent, expecting sparks to fly from his fingers. None did. He seemed content to stand there and wait.

Mavin fidgeted. Well. And why not? She Shifted, coming up from the fustigar shape into her own, decently clothed, with a Shifted cloak at her shoulders. Let the man know she was no savage.

"I had need to borrow her wand," said Mavin flatly. "She fought me."

"So you wounded her. Considerably, from the look of her."

"She called down a flitchhawk from the sky. It wounded her. I thought her dead until this morning. Then, when I saw she breathed, I decided to return her to you."

"What did you expect me to do with her in that state?" There was a movement behind the Wizard as someone emerged upon the stair, a tall, gray woman in a feathered headdress – no longer in Harpy's shape. Pantiquod.

Mavin shrugged elaborately, pretending not to see her. "If she has value, I presume you will have her Healed. If she has none, then it doesn't matter what you do. In any case, I have returned your property. All of it." She took the wand from her shoulder and laid it upon the Harpy's breast where it moved slowly up and down with her breathing.

Pantiquod screamed! She started down the stairs, pouring out threats in that same colorless voice Mavin had heard her use in Pfarb Durim, hands extended like claws, aimed for Mavin's throat. "Shifter bitch! It was you killed Blourbast! You who set our plans awry! You who have wounded my daughter, my Foulitter. Bitch, I'll have your eyes. . . ."

The Wizard gestured violently at the Harpy, crying some strange words in a loud voice, and the woman stopped as though she had run into a wall. "Back," the Wizard shouted. "Back to your perch in the mews, loathsome chicken. Back before I put an end to you." The woman turned and moved away, reluctantly, and not before casting Mavin one last, hissing threat. Mavin shivered, trying not to let it show.

Somewhere nearby a door banged. There were clattering footsteps, and several forms erupted from the dark stairway. Servitors. The Wizard pointed to the limp body.

"Take her to the mews. Maldin, see if the Healer is in her rooms. If not, then find her. Fermin, take that wand up to the tower and hang it on the back of the door where it belongs." He turned to Mavin and gestured toward the stairs. "Well, Shifter, you had best come in. Since you have taken the trouble to return my property, it seems only fitting to offer some thanks, and some apologies for a certain one of my servants."

Mavin stared upward. The castle loomed high above her, an endless stair length. She sighed.

He interpreted her weariness correctly. "Oh, we won't climb up there. No, no. We use that fortification only when we must. When Game is announced, you know, and it's the only appropriate place. It's far too lofty to be useful for ordinary living. Besides, it's impossible to heat." He turned to one of the servants who still lurked in the shadowy stair. "Jowret, tell the kitchen there'll be a guest for supper. Tell them to serve us in my sitting room. Now, just up one flight, young woman, and through the door where you see the light. To your left, please. Ah, now just open that door before you. And here we are. Fire, wine, even a bit of cheese if hunger nibbles at you this early."

He took off his tall hat and sat in a comfortable-appearing chair before the tiled stove, motioning her to a similar one across the table; and he stared at her from under his brows, trying not to let her see that he did so.

Uncomfortably aware of this scrutiny, Mavin cut a piece of cheese and sat down to eat it, examining him no less covertly. Without the tall hat he was less imposing. Though there were heavy brows over his brooding eyes, the eyes themselves were surrounded with puffy, unhealthy-looking flesh, as though he slept too little or drank too much. When she had swallowed, she said, "I overheard the two Harpies talking. I know Pantiquod from a former time, from the place they call Hell's Maw. She called the other her daughter."

"I doubt they spoke kindly of me," he said sneeringly, reaching for the cheese knife. "Both of them attempted to do me an injury some years ago. I put them under durance until the account is paid. Pantiquod was sly enough to offer me some recompense, so I freed her, in a manner of speaking. The daughter was the worse of the two. She owes me servitude for yet a few years."

"She questioned the Faces. I heard her doing it. Three of them for you. One for Pantiquod." Mavin hesitated for a moment, doubting whether it would be wise to say more. However, if she were to find any trace of Himaggery, some risk was necessary. "And then I took the wand away from her and questioned one myself."

"Someone you know?" His voice was like iron striking an anvil.

"Someone I'm looking for. He set out eight years ago to find you. His friends have not seen him since."

"Oh," he said, darting one close, searching look at her before shrugging with elaborate nonchalance. "That would be the Wizard Himaggery, I think. He stopped here, bringing two old dames with him from Betand. Foolish." He did not explain this cryptic utterance, and Mavin did not interrupt to ask him to clarify it. "He'd been collecting old talks, songs, rhymes. Wanted to solve some of the ancient mysteries. Well. What are Wizards for if not to do things like that? Hmmm? He wanted to go north. I told him it was risky, even foolish. He was young – barely thirty? Thirty-two? Hardly more than a youth." He shook his head. "Well, so you found his Face." He seemed to await some response to this, almost holding his breath. Mavin could sense his caution and wondered at it.

"You put it there?" She kept her voice casual. There was a strange tickle in her head, as though the man before her sought to Read her mind. Or perhaps some other person hidden nearby. She had never heard that Wizards had that Talent.

"Well, yes. I put it there. It does them little damage. Scarcely a pinprick."

"How did you do that? What for! " Still that probing tickle.

"How do I make the Faces?" He leaned back, evidently reassured that she carried the question of Himmagery's Face no further. "It would take several years to explain. You said your name was? Ah. Mavin. Well, Mavin, it would take a long time to explain. It took me several decades to learn to do it. Suffice it to say that the Lake is located at some kind of – oh, call it a nexus. A time nexus. If one takes a very thin slice of person and faces it forward, just at that nexus,
then the slice can see into its future. That is, the person's future. Some of them can see their own end, some only a little way into tomorrow. And if one commands a Face to tell – using the right gramarye, a wand properly prepared and so forth – then it tells what it sees. Believe me, I use only a very thin slice. The donors never miss it." Again he seemed to be waiting some response from her.

Why should he care whether I believe him or not, she thought. This question seemed too dangerous to ask. She substituted another. "Why did you want to know his future?"

He paused before answering, and Mavin seemed to hear a warning vibration in her mind, a hissing, a rattle, as when something deadly is disturbed. She leaned forward to cut another piece of cheese, acting her unconcern. This misdirection seemed to quiet him, for the strange mental feeling passed as he said, "Because he insisted in going off on this very risky endeavor. Into places no one knows well. I thought it might yield some new information about the future, you know. But none of it did any good. He went, and when I questioned his Face a season later, all it would say was that he was under the Ban, the Ban, Bartelmy's Ban.I have no idea what that means. And his quest into the old things is not what I am most interested in." Again that close scrutiny, that casual voice coupled with the tight, attentive body.

Some instinct bade Mavin be still about the other Face which had also spoken of Bartelmy's Ban. Was it logical that the Wizard would have two such enigmas in his Lake of Faces?

"That surprises me. I was told that the Wizard Chamferton was interested in old things, that he had much information about old things, that he had much information about old things." She pretended astonishment.

"So Himaggery said. Which is why he brought the old women from Betand. Lily-sweet and Rose-love." He paused, then said with elaborate unconcern, "Well, at one time I *was* interested. Very. Oh, yes, at one time I collected such things, delighted in old mysteries. Why, at one time I would probably have been able to tell you everything you wanted to know about the lost road and the tower and the bell. . . ."

Still that impression of testing, of prodding. What was it he wanted her to say? What was it he was worried about her knowing? Mavin chewed, swallowed, thanked the Gamelords that she knew nothing much, but felt herself growing apprehensive nonetheless. She went on, "Do you mention roads, towers, bells by accident? One of the Faces your Harpy questioned spoke of a tower, of bells." She quoted all she could remember of what she had overhead, all in an innocently naive voice, as though she were very little interested.

"Old stories." He dismissed them with a wave of his hand. "The old women Himaggery brought – they were full of old stories." He would have gone on, but the door opened and servants came in to lay the table with steaming food and a tall pitcher of chilled wine. Bunwit and birds, raw or roasted, were all very well, but Mavin had no objection to kitchen food. She pulled her chair close and talked little until the emptiness inside her was well filled.

"Well," she said finally, when the last dish had been emptied – long after Chamferton had stopped eating and taken to merely watching her, seemingly amazed at her appetite; long after the mind tickle had stopped completely, as whoever it was gave up the search – "I must learn what I can from you, Wizard. Himaggery is my friend. I am told by a friend of us both that he came in search of Chamferton because he desired to know about old things and it was thought that you had some such knowledge. Now, you say he went from you on some risky expedition you warned him against. The story of my entire life has been spent thus – in pursuit of kin or friends who have gone off in pursuit of some dream or other. I had not thought to spend this year so, but it seems I am called to do it."

"Why? For mere friendship?" Prodding again, trying to elicit information.

Mavin laughed, a quick bark of laughter more the sound of a

fustigar than a person. "Are friends so numerous you can say 'mere,' Wizard?" What would she tell him? Well, it would do no harm to tell him what Pantiquod already knew. "A long time ago, a Gamesman helped my younger brother during the plague at Pfarb Durim. You heard of that? Everyone south of King Frogmott of the Marshes heard of it!" And especially Pantiquod, who caused it, she thought.

"I heard of it," he agreed, too quickly.

She pretended not to notice. "Well, I am fond of my brother. So, even if there were no other reason, in balance to that kindness done by this Gamesman, I will do him a kindness in return. He is Himaggery's friend and wants him found."

The Wizard's tone was dry and ironic, but still with that underlying tone of prying hostility. "Then all this seeking of yours, which you find so wearying, is for the Seer Windlow."

"That is all we need consider," she said definitely, seeming not to notice his use of a name she had not mentioned. So, Himaggery had talked of his personal life to this Wizard. Of his life? His friends? Perhaps of her? "Anything beyond that would be personal and irrelevant."

"Very well then," he replied. "For the Seer Windlow, I will tell you everything I can."

As he talked, she grew more certain there was something here unspoken, something hidden, and she little liked the feel of it. However, she did not interrupt him or say anything to draw attention to herself, merely waiting to see what his voice would say which his words did not.

"Himaggery came here, eight years ago. Not in spring, but in the downturn of the year with leaves blowing at his heels and a chilly wind howling in the chimney while we talked. He had a map with him, an interesting one with some features on it I didn't know of though they were near me in these hills. He told me about Windlow, too, and the old books they had searched. Himaggery had been collecting folk tales for six or seven years at that point. He wanted to hear the ones I knew, and I told him he might have full liberty of the library I had collected. Old things are not what I am most interested in now. Now I am interested in the future! It has endless fascination! Himmagery admitted as much, but he didn't share my enthusiasm. Nonetheless, we talked, he told me what he had found in the books, and we dined together and even walked together in the valley for the day or two he spent here. I took a mask from him for the Lake of Faces, which amused him mightily.'' He fell silent, as though waiting for her to contradict him, but Mavin kept her face innocent and open.

''So! What sent him on? Where did he go from here?''

''Ah. Well, truthfully, he found very little helpful here. I was able to tell him about the road. There is a Road south of Pfarb Durim, with Monuments upon it. Do you know the place? Yes? Well, so did he. And when I told him that the Road goes on, north of Pfarb Durim, hidden under the soil of the ages, north into the Dorbor Range, then swinging west to emerge at the surface in places – when I told him that, he was all afire to see it.'' He nodded at her, waving his hands to demonstrate the enthusiasm with which Himaggery was supposed to have received this information. ''Like a boy. All full of hot juice.''

There was something false in this telling, but she would not challenge it. She sought to pique his interest, perhaps to arouse enthusiasm which would override his careful talk. ''The Road south of Pfarb Durim that has Monuments on it – I saw them dance, once. The shadowpeople made them do it.''

''So Himaggery said! You were there then? I would like to have seen that. . . .''

''My point, Wizard, is that we were not harmed. Some are said to have been driven mad by the Monuments, though I don't know the truth of that, but I have never heard that any were killed. Yet you told Himaggery it was risky? Dangerous?''

''So I believed.'' He poured half a glass of wine, suddenly less confiding, almost reticent, as though they had approached a subject he had not planned for.

''Come now. You must tell me more than that. You know something more than that. Or believe you do.''

''You are persistent, '' he said in a tone less friendly, lips tight. ''Uncomfortably persistent.''

Mavin held out her open hands, palms up, as though she juggled weights, put on her most ingenuous face. ''Am I to risk my own life, perhaps Himaggery's as well, rather than be discourteous? If it is something which touches you close to the bone, forgive me, Wizard. But I must ask!''

"Very well." He thought it over for a time, hiding his hesitation by moving to the window, opening it to lean out. There he seemed to find inspiration, for he returned with his mouth full of words once more. "There are many stories about the old road, Mavin. Tales, myths – who knows. Well, I had a . . . brother, considerably younger than I. He was adventurous, loved digging into old things like your friend Himaggery. I was away from the demesne when he decided to seek out the mysteries of the old road. I did not even know he had gone until much later, and my own search for him was futile."

"Ah," said Mavin, examining him closely, still keeping her voice light and unchallenging. "So, if the truth were told, Wizard, perhaps you did not warn Himaggery so much as you might? Perhaps, respecting him as you did, you thought he might find your brother for you?"

"Perhaps," he said with easy apology. "Perhaps that is it. I have searched my mind on that subject more times than I care to remember. But I do remember warning him, not once but many times. And I do remember cautioning him, not once but often. And so I put myself to rest, only to doubt again on the morning. I believe I did warn him sufficiently, Shape-shifter. But he chose to go."

She rose in her turn to investigate the open window. It looked out upon the valley, moonlit now, and peaceful. A cool wind moved the budding trees. Scents of spring rose around her, and she sighed as she closed the casement against the cool and turned back into the firelight. "Your Harpy questioned three of the Faces, Wizard. One was an old woman who spoke of a bell. What does it mean. 'The daylight bell hangs in the last tower'?"

He gestured to say how unimportant a question it was. "I told you Himaggery brought two old story-tellers with him from Betand. I took a Face from one of them – her name was Rose-love – shortly before she died. It was her Face you heard in the lake, saying words from a children's story. Old Rose-love told stories to the children of Betand during a very long life, stories of talking foxes and flying fish and of Weetzie and the daylight bell."

"Weetzie?" She laughed, an amused chirrup of sound.

He barked an echoing laugh, watching her closely the while. "Weetzie. And the daylight bell, not an ordinary bell, but something very ancient. Himaggery had heard of it, and of another one. He called it 'the bell of the dark,' the 'cloud bell,' the 'bell of the shadows.' Have you heard of that?" His voice was friendly, yet she felt something sinister in the question, and she mocked herself for feeling so, here in this quiet room with the fire dancing on the hearth. The man had said nothing, done nothing to threaten her. Why this feeling? She forced herself to shake her head, smilingly. No, she had not heard of it.

He went on, "Nor had I. Well, he had found out something about these mysterious bells from old Rose. I question her Face once or twice a year to see how long it will continue to reply. It says only the one thing. First a little verse, then 'The daylight bell hangs in the last tower.' "

"The Blue Star is on the horns of Zanbee."

"It is not," he said. "That time is just past and will not return for many seasons yet." His voice was harsh as he demanded, "Where did you hear that?"

She remained nonchalant. "It was something Himaggery said once. The night the Monuments danced on the Ancient Road south of Pfarb Durim. They danced when the Blue Star was on the horns of Zanbee – the crescent moon. Now we have, 'The bell is in the last tower.' They both sound mysterious, like Wizardly things."

He relaxed. "I suppose they are Wizardly things, in a sense. Certainly your friend Himaggery thought so. My . . . brother, too."

"What was his name?" asked Mavin, suddenly curious about this unnamed brother. "Was he a Wizard?"

"Ah . . . no. No, he was not a Wizard. He was . . . a Timereacher. Very much a Timereacher." He smiled, something meant to be a kindly smile, at which Mavin shuddered, speaking quickly to hide it.

"His name?"

"Arkhur. He was . . . ah . . . quite young."

"And so, Wizard." She rose, smiling at him, letting the smile turn into a yawn to show how little concerned she was with what she said or what he replied. "You can tell me only that there is a road northwest of this place. That there is a bell somewhere, called variously, which Himaggery talked of. That Himaggery's Face says only what I heard it say. That your brother Arkhur is gone since his youth. That all of this, you think, is connected with ancient things, old things, things beyond memory. You think. You believe."
"And that it is risky, Mavin. Dangerous . . . "

"Everywhere I have gone they have told me that. 'It is risky, Mavin. Dangerous.' I have sought Eesties and battled gray oozers and plotted with stickies and crept through Blourbast's halls in the guise of a snake. All of it was risky, Wizard. I wish you could tell me something more. It is little enough to go on."

"If you had not interrupted me, I would have gone on to say there are others seeking the road you seek." He seemed to wait for her comment or question, to be dissatisfied by her silence. "Also, the other old woman brought here by Himaggery still lives, still chatters, still tells her stories. It is too late to disturb her old bones tonight, but if you will wait until morning, she will tell you one of her stories, no doubt. Perhaps there is something in her story which will enlighten you."

You mean, she thought, that perhaps it will convince me of your friendship, Chamferton, and make me talk more freely. Well, little enough I know, old fox, but I will not tell you more than I need.

She nodded acceptance of the invitation to hear the storyteller, weary to her own bones. The night before had not been restful, and since she had drunk those last few sips of wine she had been weighted down with sleep. She bowed, an ordinary gesture of respect. He patted her on her shoulder, seeming not to feel her flesh flinch away from him, and then tugged the bell near his hand.

Chamferton's servants took her to a room with a bed far softer than her bed of moss had been. There was a tub full of hot water on a towel before the fire. She did not linger in it. The shutters were open at the high window, letting the night air flood the room to chill her wet skin, and she shut them, fumbling with the latch to be sure it would not blow open again. She remembered only fleetingly that Chamferton had spoken of someone else on the trail she followed, thinking that curiosity over this might keep her awake. It did not. She did not even dry herself completely before falling asleep between the sheets, as though drugged.

CHAPTER THREE

Very early in the morning, just before dawn, she woke thinking she had heard some sound – a scratching, prying sound. She sat up abruptly, calling out some question or threat. The shutters were open, a curtain waving between them like a beckoning hand, and she rose, only half awake, to look outside. Around the window were thick vine branches, one of which was pulled away from the wall, as though something heavy had tried to perch upon it. She saw it without seeing it, for in the yard at the base of the stairs a group of horsemen was preparing to depart. Even with her eyes Shifted, she could not make out their faces in the dim light, but there was something familiar about one of them – something in the stance. Chamferton she could identify by his tall hat, and he stood intimately close to the familiar figure, their two heads together in conspiratorial talk. Mavin widened her ears, heard only scattered phrases. " . . . While she is here . . . easy enough to get rid of . . . "

Then the horses walked away, not hurrying their pace until they had gone well down the valley, and Mavin knew it was for quiet's sake, so that she would not hear. "Shifter ears, Wizard," she yawned. "Never try to fool Shifter's ears."

After watching the men ride out of sight, she closed the shutters firmly once more, then returned to bed to sleep until the sun was well up.

In the morning she found Chamferton on a pleasant terrace behind the plinth on which the castle stood. There she ate melons grown under glass, the Wizard said, so they ripened even in the cold season. He was all smiling solicitude this morning, and Mavin might have accepted it from one who did not employ Harpies as servants. They were creatures of such malice, she could not believe good of one who kept them, though she asked him whether the injured Harpy lived, trying to sound as though she cared.

"Foulitter is recovering," he told her. "She bears you much malice. Or perhaps me, for not punishing you. I told her her former plots against me earned her whatever damage you had done to her, and to hush and do my bidding." He smiled at Mavin, showing his teeth, which were stained and crooked. It was not a nice smile, and she did not find it reassuring.

"I would not like to have her behind me when I go," said Mavin, cursing herself silently for having said so the moment the words left her mouth.

"I will see she does not leave the aerie for some time," he promised with that same smile. "She is fully under my control. I am less worried about her than about some others who seek the same road you do."

Mavin put down her spoon with a ringing sound which hung upon the air. "You mentioned that last night. I was so weary, I could not even think to ask who it would be."

"Did you ever meet King Prionde's eldest heir? Valdon Duymit, son of the King Prionde?" His voice was deceptively casual, as it had been the night before.

Valdon! Of course. That had been the familiar stance she had recognized. So. Valdon had been the Wizard's guest until the predawn hours – and he had left surreptitiously. She deducted another portion from Chamferton's reputation for truth. Do not say too much, Mavin, she instructed herself. But do not lie, for he may know part of the truth already. "I have," she admitted. "I was there when he and Himaggery came almost to Game duel between them. They did not like one another."

"So much I guessed," he said. "Nonetheless, he came here, so he said, in search of Himaggery."

"Did he say why?" She spooned up melon, trying not to seem interested in the answer to this question.

"Oh, he gave me some reason or other. He lied. However, I encourage my servants to gossip. Sometimes it is the only way to get at the truth. My servants told me he fancied himself wronged for some reason connected with the school set up by Prionde. Do you know anything about that?"

"I know of the school, yes." She spoke of it as anyone might who knew nothing beyond its location and that Prionde had sponsored it, thinking meantime that it was undoubtedly the Harpy whom he counted upon to gossip among the guests. In her own shape, she was probably not uncomely.

"So I had some knowledge of the school," she concluded, "though I am told it is not a large one. That is all I know."

"You are succinct. Would that more of my informants were so terse. Well, I gathered that Valdon has some unfinished anger which moves him. He desires Himaggery's embarrassment, perhaps even his destruction. I knew that. I could read it in his voice; I did not need a Face from him to learn it." An expression of annoyance crossed the Wizard's face, was wiped away in an instant as though he became aware of it and did not want the world to see it.

"How long ago was Valdon here?"

"Oh, a year or two. No. Little more than a year. I tell you so you may be warned." He turned toward the stairs while Mavin made note he had told her yet another lie.

"Ah. Look over there to the steps. See the old woman, the very old woman being carried up in the chair? She is two hundred years old, that woman. So she says, and so I do believe. Old as rocks, as the country people say. That is Lily-sweet, sister to Rose-love, whose Face you saw in my lake. I have had her carried up here in the sun, which she much enjoys, and promised her all the melon she can eat if she will tell you a story. She and her sister told stories in Betand for all their long lives, stories learned from their great grandmas, who also, if the stories about them be true, lived to be very old. If she were still young and strong, she could talk about Weetzie for several days, for Weetzie had more adventures than a thousand years would have given him time for. Somewhere in all that mass of story-telling is a little verse which says something about there being a road, and on the road a tower, and in the tower a bell, which cannot ring alone. That verse much intrigued your friend Himaggery. You may choose to ask for the story of Weetzie and the daylight bell. She will say she is too old to remember, too tired, that it is only a children's story, a country tale. You must persist." He was playing with her now, Mavin knew. All this was so much flummery, to keep her occupied.

"This is the story you mentioned last night."

"Yes. If you seek Himaggery, you may find something in it. He pretended to do so. If you are to get her to to tell you anything you must say her name in full, caressingly, and do not laugh."

Chamferton went back to his melon, waving her away.

She rose almost unwillingly, strongly tempted to challenge his lies and his foisting nonsense upon her in the guise of information, and yet unwilling to pass by anything in which Himaggery had been interested. That much, at least, might be true and she, Mavin, might find help in it that Chamferton did not intend. So she strolled across the high terrace to the chair where the old woman sat wrapped in knitted shawls against the slight chill of the morning. She was so old her face and arms were wrinkled like the shell of a nut, like the fine wavelets of a sea barely brushed by wind. Thin flesh hung from her arms and neck. Wisps of white hair fringed the edge of her cap. Her eyes were bird-bright though she pretended not to see Mavin's approach. "Well then," thought Mavin, "we will lure her as the birder does the shy fowl of the air".

"Lily-sweet," she begged, "the High Wizard Chamferton says that you know a tale known to none other in all the lands. The tale of Weetzie and the daylight bell."

The old woman stroked her throat, made a pitiful shrug and shook her head wistfully. "Ah, girl, but one's throat is too dry and old for telling tales."

Mavin rose without a word and went to Chamferton's table. "I need to borrow a teacup," she told him, returning with it to the old woman.

"Wet your gullet, Lily-sweet. This is the High Wizard's own tea, and while it is not good enough for softening the throat of a true story-teller, still, it is the best we have."

"You are a well spoken child, for all your outlandish appearance. In my day the women wore full trews and vests to show their bosoms. None of this tight man-breeching and loose shirts." Lily-sweet tugged at Mavin's shirt, and inside that tug, Mavin twitched. The shirt was herself.

"So my own grandmama has said, Lily-sweet. And much we regret that those days are past." She sighed. "If we dressed now as true women did in the days of your youth, chance is I would have a . . . companion of my own."

"You'd have a husband, child, and thankful for it. Ah, and well, and sorry the day. What was it you wanted to know of again?"

"The story of Weetzie and the daylight bell?"

"Ah. A children's story, was it? I'm not sure I remember that one."

"Oh, it would be a tragedy if you did not, Lily-sweet, for none but you can be found to tell it rightly. Oh, there are those in Betand who pretend to know the story, but the mockery they make of it is quite . . ."

"None know that story save me!" The voice was suddenly more definite, and the old hands quivered upon the arms of the chair. "Since sister Rose died, none but me."

"I know," Mavin soothed. "So says the Wizard Chamferton. He says the women in Betand are liars and scrape-easies, that you are the only one who has the truth of it."

"And so I do," said the old woman. "And so shall you be the judge of it." She took a deep breath.

"One time," she quavered, gesturing with a claw to indicate a time long past, "one time a time ago, was a young star named Weetzie, and he went out and about, up and down, wet and dry, come day come night till he got to the sea. And there was a d'bor wife, grodgeling about in the surf, slither on slither.

"And Weetzie spoke polite to her, saying 'Good morn to you, d'bor wife. And why do you slither here near the shore when the deep waves are your home?'

"And the d'bor wife, she struck at him once, twice, three times with her boaty flappers, flap, flap, flap on the sand, but Weetzie jumped this way and that way, and all that flapping was for nothing. So, seeing she could not get Weetzie that way, the d'bor wife began to sing in her lure voice, 'Oh, I grodgel here in the surf to find the daylight bell where the shadows hid it.'

"And Weetzie was greatly taken with this idea, so he came close to the d'bor wife and began to help her grodgel. And whup, the d'bor wife wrapped Weetzie up in her short reachers and laughed like a whoop-owl, 'Oh, little star, but I have you now, I have you now.'

"And Weetzie was sorry to have been so silly, for Weetzie's forepeople had often said that trusting a d'bor was like betting on the wind. So Weetzie thought quick, quick, and said, 'But why did you stop me, d'bor wife? Quick, grodgel down, grodgel down, for just as you caught me, I saw the very edge of the daylight bell.'

"And the d'bor wife was so excited, she dropped Weetzie in the instant and began to grodgel again, with the water flying. And Weetzie took his bone and twanged it, so the d'bor wife was all wound up in her tentacles and tied in a lump. Then he sat down and sang this song:

'Daylight bell in water can't be;
Tricksy lie brings tricksy tie.
Give a boon or else you die.'

"And the d'bor wife cried loudly, until all the seabirds shrieked to hear it, and begged the little star to be let go. So Weetzie said, 'Give me the boon, d'bor wife, and I'll untie you.'

"So they talked and talked while the sun got high, and this was the boon: that Weetzie could go in the water and breathe there as did the d'bor. So he twanged his bone to turn the d'bor wife loose and went on his way, up and down, over and under, back and forth in the wide world until he came to a forest full of tall trees.

"And there in the top of the tallest tree was a flitchhawk in a nest, grimbling and grambling at the clouds as they flew past. And Weetzie cried out, 'Ho there, flitchhawk, why are you grimbling and grambling at the clouds?' And the flitchhawk said, 'Because I'm looking for the daylight bell which is hung up here in the mist where the shadows hid it.'

" 'I'll help you, then,' cried Weetzie, and he climbed the tall tree 'til he came high up, and he stood in the nest and reached out for the clouds to grimble and gramble them in pieces. But the flitchhawk screamed and grabbed Weetzie in his huge claws and then laughed and cawed as though to raise the dark, 'Little star, I've got you now.'

" 'Why did you grab me, old flitchhawk,' cried Weetzie 'just as I was grambling the clouds? I caught a glimpse of the daylight bell just there where I was grambling when you took hold of me!' And when he heard that, the flitchhawk dropped Weetzie and went back to grimbling and grambling the clouds, looking for the daylight bell and crying, 'Where is it? Where did you see it?' But Weetzie took his bone and twanged it and sang this song:

'Daylight bell in water can't be
Daylight bell in treetop shan't be
Tricksy lie brings tricksy tie.
Give a boon or else you die.'

"And flitchhawk was tied wing and claws so he couldn't move, and he begged to be let loose, but Weetzie would not until the flitchhawk gave him a boon. And the boon was that Weetzie could fly in the wide sky as the flitchhawk had always done. So then Weetzie twanged his bone and turned the flitchhawk loose.

"Up and down he went, in and out, under and over, until time wore on, and Weetzie came to a broad plain where there was a gobble-mole druggling tunnels, coming up with a snoutful of dirt and heaving it into little hillocks. So, Weetzie said, 'What's all the tunneling for old gobble? More tunnel there than a mole needs in a million.'

"And the gobble-mole says, 'Druggling to find the daylight bell, little star. I know it's right down here somewhere in the deep earth where the shadows hid it.'

"So Weetzie says, 'Well, then, I'll help you druggle for it,' and he started in to druggle with the mole. But the mole pushed Weetzie in a hole and shut it up so Weetzie couldn't get out.

"And Weetzie cried, 'What did you do that for, old mole? I caught sight of the edge of the daylight bell, just then, before you covered it up with your druggling.'

"Old mole said, 'Where? Where did you see it?' and he uncovered the hole where Weetzie was so Weetzie could twange his bone and sing this song:

'Daylight bell in water can't be.
Daylight bell in treetop shan't be
Daylight bell in earthways wan't be
Tricksy lie brings tricksy tie.
Give a boon or else you die.

"And the gobble-mole was all tied up, foot and snout, so he couldn't move. So the gobble-mole decided upon a boon, and the boon was that Weetzie should be able to walk in earthways as the mole had always done. Then Weetzie twanged his bone and let the mole loose.

" 'Well now,' said Weetzie. 'All this talk of the daylight bell has made me curious, so I'll take my three boons and go looking for it.' And all the creatures within ear-listen laughed and laughed, for none had ever found the daylight bell where the shadows had hidden it, though the beasts had had boons of their own for ever since. But Weetzie danced on the tip of himself, up and down, in and out, over and under, as he went seeking."

The old woman sighed. Mavin put the teacup to her lips, and she supped the pale brew, sighing again. "That's the story of

Weetzie and the daylight bell, girl."

"Is there more to the story, Lily-sweet?"

"Oh, there's enough for three days' telling, girl, for it may be he found the bell at the end of it, but I'm weary of it now. Let be. He that calls himself Wizard there may tell it to you if you've a mind to hear it. I told it to him, and to that other Wizard – real, he was, sure as my teeth are gone – and to people in Betand, and to children many a time when they were no more than mole-high themselves." And she leaned back in the chair, shutting her eyes. So the old woman did not much care for Chamferton, either. "He that calls himself Wizard . . . "

Back at the table where Chamferton sat smiling at her as a fox might smile at a bird, she continued to play the innocent. "I wonder what all that was about?"

"I think it's about Eesties, Shifter-woman, though I'm not certain of that. Eesties, Eestnies, the Old-folk, the Rolling Stars. Whatever you choose to call them . . . "

"They say 'Eesty' among themselves," said Mavin, without thinking. Then her throat closed like a vice and she coughed, choking, gesturing frantically for air.

"You mean you've spoken to them, seen them? Gamelords, girl, tell me of it!" His face blazed with an acquisitive glow, and his hand clutched her arm. *Now*, she thought through her suffocating spasm, *now* I see the true Chamferton.

She shook her head, trying to breathe as her face turned blue. Then the spasm passed, and he nodded with comprehension, handing her a cup. "Don't try to talk then. I understand. What you've seen, what you've heard, they don't want talked about. Well. Pity." He took paper from a nearby table and wrote on it, "Have you ever tried to write it out?" He turned the paper for her to read.

She shook her head, drawing deep breaths as her throat opened reluctantly.

He put the pen and paper near her hand. She wrote a trial sentence. "I have talked with an Eesty at Ganver's Grave. . . ." Nothing happened. She turned the paper to face him, and he nodded eagerly.

"Well, Shifter-girl, there is a bit of additional information which I will trade for an account of your . . . experience." He nodded toward her hand, resting upon the paper as he turned the page toward her again. He had written, "If you will write me an account of your experience, I will tell something else about Himaggery – also, I will pay you well for the account."

Mavin shook her head in pretended indecision. "You know, Wizard, from time to time I have been asked to Game for this King or that Sorcerer. All have offered to pay me well, but none has yet told me what I am to do with the pay. What do Shifters need, after all? I cannot eat more than one meal at once, nor sleep in more than one bed at a time. I have little need to array myself in silks or gems. What payment would mean something to me?"

"Perhaps hospitality," he suggested. "A place to rest, or eat cooked food, or merely to stare at the hills."

"No. It is not tempting," she said, having already decided what she would give him which might both allay his suspicions of her and make him careless. "But I will do it because you have something to tell me about Himaggery, and for no other reason."

He nodded, then remarked in passing, almost as though it did not matter. "And – when you go to seek Himaggery, will you seek Arkhur as well? At least, do not close your eyes to him if you see him on the road? And if you see any sign of him, will you send word to me? Again, though it may take time to agree upon a coin, I will pay you well."

She smiled. Let him take that for assent if he would. She would do no more than write what she had seen of the Eesties and of the dancing Monuments and the shadowpeople upon the hills. She made it brief, leaving most of what had happened out, unwilling to put anything in his hands he might use for ill – as he would. She did mention that the magical talisman, Ganver's Bone, had been taken back by the Eesty who gave it, believing that it would go ill for the shadowpeople if Chamferton thought they still had it, though why she was so certain of that, she could not have said. When she had finished, it was a very brief account, though Chamferton nodded his head over it, almost licking his lips, when she had finished.

"This goes in my library, Mavin." Then, after a pause, as though to assure her of his good intent. "And should you not return in a fairly short time, I'll see that a copy of it goes to Windlow."

She nodded, in a sober mood. If she did not return in a fairly short time, she doubted Windlow could do much about it. Also, she thought Chamferton would not bother to do anything, no matter what he had promised, unless for some reason of his own. "I'm off north, now, Wizard, so tell me now what thing it is you know."

For a moment she thought he would deny the bargain, but he thought better of it. "It is only this one fact, Shifter. There are runners upon the road to the north. Strange runners. They come in silence, fleeing along the Ancient Road, without speaking. It was those runners Himaggery followed, and if you see them, they may lead you to the place he went."

So. She wondered what else he might have told her if he had wished to. How much he had left untold. How many other things he had lied about. Why say Valdon had not been there for a year when he had left only this morning? Why all that careful questioning, that covert watching? What had he hoped to learn?

Well, she would not find out by moping over it. Of the two of them, Mavin had probably learned the more. She went down and out of the place, the door shutting behind her with an echoing slam of finality. She started to turn toward the north, then whirled at a sound behind her.

It was Pantiquod, in Harpy shape, her head moving restlessly on its flexible serpent's neck, and her pale breasts heaving with anger. Yellow-eyed Pantiquod. Mavin set herself to fight, ready to Shift in the instant.

"Oh, no, fool Shifter," the Harpy hissed. "I will not attack you here under Chamferton's walls, where he may yet come out and stop me. Nor in the forest's shadow, where you and I might be well matched. No, Shifter-girl. I will come for you with my sisters. When I will. And there will be no more shadowpeople singing to help you, or tame Wizards to do your bidding, nor will Shiftiness aid you against the numbers I will bring."

There was hot, horrid juice in Mavin's throat, but she managed somehow to keep her voice calm. "Why, Pantiquod? What have I done to you? Your daughter is recovering, and it was she who attacked me, not I her."

The Harpy's head wove upon its storklike neck, the square yellowed teeth bared in a hating grimace. "It was you killed Blourbast, though Huld put the knife in his throat. It was you robbed us of Pfarb Durim. It was you and your forest scum friends who sang away the plague, Shifter-girl. Now it is you who has wounded my daughter, Foulitter. Did you think the Harpies would not avenge themselves?''

"You have not done much for twenty years, loathsome chicken," Mavin said. "But threats are easy and promises cheap. Do what you will." Her knees were not as strong as her voice as she turned her back upon the bird, opening a tiny eye in the back of her head to be sure she was not attacked from the rear. Pantiquod merely stood, however, staring after her, her yellow eyes burning as though a fire were lit behind them. Mavin shivered, not letting it show. When she was a wee child, she had been afraid of snakes. Her worst dreams had been of touching snakes. The Harpy moved her with a similar revulsion. She did not want to be touched by that creature. She could not think of fighting it because she would have to touch it. Still, so long as she could Shift, she could not utterly fear the Harpy – even if there were more than one. So long as she could Shift, it would not pay the sag-breasted bird to attack her.

When she had come out of sight of the tower, she entered the trees. There she crouched upon the ground, looking back the way she had come. Two sets of wings circled high above the tower, moving upward upon warm drafts of air. When they had achieved considerable height, they turned toward her and the wings beat slowly as the two figures closed the distance between them. Though she had not shown fear before Pantiquod, now Mavin watched the wings come nearer with a feeling of fatalistic fascination which paralyzed her, that nightmare horror of childhood, that ancient terror children feel when they awake in the dark, sure that something lurks nearby, so immobilized by that knowledge that they cannot move to escape. Only when the Harpies had come almost within hailing distance did she stir herself, melting back into the shadows and changing her hide into a mottled invisibility of green and brown. There had been something hypnotic in the Harpy's stare, something like . . .

"I would advise you, Mavin," her internal voice said calmly, "that you not look into a Harpy's eyes again. It would be sensible to kill them now, but if you find them too repulsive even for killing, then you should get moving. If you don't want to fight the creatures, avoidance would be easier if they didn't find you."

This broke the spell and she ran, under the boughs, quickly away to the north, deep in small canyons and under the edges of curling cliffs, until she had left the Harpies behind her, or lost them, or they had gone on ahead. In any case, the feeling of paralysis had passed – at least for the time. Her voice had been right. She should have killed them then. "I must be getting old, and weak, and weary," she cursed herself. "Perhaps I should settle on a farm, somewhere, and grow thrilps." This was not convincing, even under the circumstances, and she gave it up. Enough that she had not wanted to touch the beasts. Leave it at that.

She had come some little distance north when she saw the first travelers, paralleling her course to the west. They were higher on the sides of the hills, running with their heads faced forward – though there was something odd about those heads she could not precisely identify, even with sharpened vision, as the forest light dappled and shadowed. They were naked, men and women both, with long, shaggy hair unbound flapping at their backs. At first she saw only four or five of them, but as she went on others could be seen in small groups on the hillsides, emerging into sunlight before disappearing momentarily into shade once more.

There was a sheer wall ahead, one which stretched across her own path and that of those on the hill, a fault line where the land on which she walked had fallen below that to the north, leaving a scarp between, that scarp cut by tumbling streams which had left ladders of stone in their wake. The westernmost such path was also the nearest, and as she went on she saw the others gradually shift direction toward the rock stair, toward her own path, toward intersection. Prudence dictated she not intrude upon a multitude though the multitude seemed utterly unaware of her, so she dawdled a bit, trotting rather than striding, letting the others draw ahead.

When she came at last to the stream bed which led upward to the heights, they were assembled there, squatting on the ground in fives and sevens, small intent circles faced inward. She crept into the trees above them from which she could watch and listen without being observed. Their heads were bent. The chant started so softly she thought she imagined it, then louder, repeated, repeated.

"Upon the road, the old road,
A tower made of stone.
In the tower is a bell
Which cannot ring along.
One. Two. Three. Four. Five . . ." The voices went on, breathy, counting, seemingly endlessly. At last they faded into silence on

number one thousand thirteen, as though exhausted. After a time they began again.

"Shadow bell, it rang the night,
Daylight bell the dawn,
In the tower hung the bells,
Now the tower's gone.
One thousand thirteen, one thousand twelve, one thousand eleven . . ." and so on until they came to one again.

Some of the heads came up. She saw then what had been so odd. They were blindfolded, their heads covered as far as their nostrils with black masks, like flitchhawks upon the wrist, hooded. They were silent, faced inward, hearing nothing. Mavin rustled a branch. They did not respond. Then, all at once, without any signal which she could see, they stood up and began to run once more, up the stone ladder toward the heights.

Intrigued, she Shifted into something spidery and went up the wall in one concerted rush to confront them at the top of the scarp. They went past her as though she did not exist, not hearing her challenging cry. She fell in behind them, not needing to keep up, for their tracks were as plain as a stream bed before her. There were hundreds of them, sometimes running separately, sometimes together. She set her feet upon their trail and thought furiously about the matter.

Somehow, without sight, they knew where they were going. But sometimes they ran together, sometimes not. Therefore, her curious mind troubled at the thought, therefore? Sometimes the way was single, sometimes separate? Like strands of rope, raveled in places, twisted tight in others? But where were the signs of it? She put her nose up and sharpened her eyes. Whatever it was that guided them, it couldn't be smelled.

Now they were running all together, in one long clump, straggling a bit, yet with the edges of the group smooth, feet falling cleanly into the tracks of those before. Something along the edges, then. She paused beside the track, peering, scratching with her paws.

Tchah. Nothing she coud see. Nothing she could feel. She stopped, puzzled, scratching her hide where the dirt of the road itched it. Perhaps from above.

She Shifted, lifted, beat strong wings down to raise her into the soft air, circling high, above the trees, sharpening sight so that she could see a tick upon a bunwit's back. Circle higher, higher, peering down at the runners, separated again now. She could see their trail cleanly upon the earth, a troubling of the grass, a line of broken twigs. Leaves crushed. Dark then light.

And more!

Along their way a scattering of stones. No. Not scattered, tumbled. Heaved up. Some washed aside in spring rains, but still maintaining their relationship to one another. Lines of stones. A slightly different shade of gray than the natural stones of the hills. Lighter. Finer grained. Like the stones of the Ancient Road south of Pfarb Durim. She dropped like a plummet, down onto those stones, then Shifted once more.

Yes. Now she could see the difference. But how did the runners know? She laid her palm upon the stone, shut her eyes, concentrated. It was there, a kind of tingling, a small, itchy feeling as of lightning in the air. Experimentally, she Shifted a human foot and laid it upon the stone. Yes. She could feel it. So then. She did not need to follow the runners, she knew where they would go. They would follow this road, this road, broken or solid.

Satisfied, she trotted in the tracks of those who ran, wanting to see what they would do when night came.

Had Himaggery come this way in pursuit of the runners? Or had he followed the map, which would likely have brought him to the same place? And where was that place? A tower, she thought. There is always something magical about a tower, a stone tower. Magicians and Wizards live in towers. Kings are held captive in towers. Signals come from towers, and dragons assault towers. So it is fitting that on this old road there should be a tower. But now the tower's gone. So sang the runners. Then what were they looking for?

"Shadow bell, it rang the night, daylight bell the dawn, in the tower hung the bells, but now the tower's gone," she hummed to herself between fustigar teeth. Not really gone, she thought. Gone, perhaps, but not really gone. Just as Himaggery was gone, but not really gone. Somewhere. Somewhere. Somewhere.

It became a chant, a kind of prayer which accompanied each footfall. Somewhere. Somewhere.

CHAPTER FOUR

The way of the Ancient Road lay across hills and valleys, sometimes with the slope, sometimes against it, as though the Road had been there first and the valleys had come later to encroach upon it. Sometimes trotting, sometimes scrambling, Mavin followed the way, the tracks of the runners going on before her, the sun crossing above her to sink into the west so that long bars of shadow stood parallel to her path, making a visible road along which she and the runners moved in a silence broken only by far, plaintive birdsong. Beside the road bloomed brilliant patches of yellow startle flower – no seed-pods yet to startle the traveler with noonday explosions. Beneath them lay the leafy lacework of Healer's balm, a promise that great purple bells would swing above the moss toward the end of the season. Clouds had sailed in from the west all day, full of the threat of rain, but none had fallen. Instead the gray billows had gone on eastward to pile themselves into a featureless veil covering the Dorbor Range. The east was all storm and rumbling thunder while the west glowed softly in sunset. The shadow road was as clear before her as an actual road would have been.

It was a moment before she realized that she ran upon the surface of an actual roadway. In this place the tingling stones had never been covered, or perhaps they had come up out of time to lie upon the earth once more. Among the trees she could catch glimpses on either side of huge, square stones which might once have supported monuments like those which arched the road outside Pfarb Durim. The light glared straight into her eyes from the horizon, blinding her, and she almost strode across the naked runners before she saw them. They lay upon the roadway, prostrate in their hundreds. She stood for a moment, troubled at the sight of so many figures lying as though dead upon the road, barely breathing.

The light faded into dusky gray-purple. The runners heaved

themselves onto all fours and crawled into the surrounding forest, scavenging among the litter on the forest floor for the moist carpets of fungus which lay in every sunny glade. Seeing them moving about, Mavin felt less pity for them and set to follow their example, making a pouch in her hide to gather this crop as well. The mushrooms were both delicious and nourishing, known among gourmands as "earth's ears" both for their shape and raw texture, crisp and cartilaginous. Both the flavor and texture improved when they were cooked, which Mavin intended to do. The sight of the runners groveling offended her, and only after she had found a place to suit her remote from them did she build a fire at last, laying the wood against a cracked stony shelf beside a small pool. Her firestarter was the only tool she carried, the only tool she needed to carry – though she had heard it said in Danderbat Keep that one Flourlanger Obquisk had learned to Shift flint and steel in some long forgotten time. Mavin had never believed it a practical solution. Since one would have to Shift flint and steel into one's body to begin with, why not simply carry them and have done.

She sat warming herself, lengthening her fur to hold body heat from the evening cool, turning the thin sticks on which the fungus was strung, watching it crisp and brown. A strange sound pervaded the quiet, a soft whirring, as though some giant top hummed to itself nearby. She crouched, trying to decide whether it conveyed some threat, whether the fire should be put out or she herself put remote from it. She compromised by leaping to the top of the shelf and collapsing there into a pancake of flesh, invisible upon the stony height.

Something came into the clearing, a whirlwind, a spinning cloud, a silvery teardrop gyring upon its tip. It glinted in the light of the fire, twirling, slowing, the long silver fringes of its dress falling out of their spiral swirl into a column, the outstretched arms coming to rest, one hand clasped lightly in another. It wore a round silver hat from which another fringe settled, completely hiding the face – if there was a face.

Upon the stone, Mavin stirred in astonishment and awe. She had never seen a Dervish before, for they were rare and solitary people, devoted, it was said, to strange rites in the worship of ancient gods. Still, she could not fail to recognize what stood there, for the dress and habits of Dervishes figured often in children's tales and fireside stories. Wonderful, remote, and marvelous they were said to be, but she had never heard they were malign. She dropped from the side of the stone and came around it to the fire once more, reaching to turn the splints on which the mushrooms roasted. Let it speak if it would.

"I smelled your fire," it said. Mavin could not tell if it was man or woman, for the voice was scarcely more than a whisper. "The runners build no fire, so I knew someone followed them. I came to warn."

Mavin chose to disregard the warning. "Will you sit down?" Mavin gestured at a likely rock beside the flames. "I would be glad to share my supper."

"Thank you, no. I seldom sit. I seldom eat. Like those poor runners on the road, I go on and on, without thinking about it very much." There was a breathy sound beneath these words which, after a time, Mavin interpreted as laughter.

"My name is Mavin," she offered. "Mavin Manyshaped."

"A Shifter," the other breathed. "I could tell from your fur. A pretty beast, you, Mavin Manyshaped. An unusual one as well. Most beasts do not cook their earth's ears."

"They taste better cooked," said Mavin, testing one with her fingers to see if it was done. "Also, when they are cooked, they do not make that noise between one's teeth that makes one believe one is eating something still alive and resisting."

"Ah," laughed the windy voice, "a pretty, sensitive beast. Are you following the runners?"

"I am." She saw no need for dissimulation. "I am seeking someone – someone who followed these runners eight years ago. Someone who has not been seen since, but who the Rancelmen and Pursuivants say still lives. Have you seen him?"

The figure before her shrugged. "Perhaps, Mavin Manyshaped. I have seen many since first I watched the runners go past. That time, the first time, they sang nine hundred years and twenty. This time they sing one thousand and thirteen. In that time, I have seen many, Mavin Manyshaped."

Mavin set the splint to one side to cool a little. "These runners – they run each year?"

"Each year, beginning when the Blue Star approaches the horns of Zanbee, from the south city upon the Ancient Road, north, west, then south and east until they come to the south city once more. Many die upon the way, of course. Every year, many die."

"The road makes a circle?"

"A circuit. Yes."

"And where is the south city?"

"It is only ruins now. A place in the hills, at the headwaters of the River Banner, north of Mip and Pouws. Do you know that land?"

"I never heard of any ruined city there."

"No. They hide it well, these devotees. Still, when the Blue Star rises, they assemble in that place for the run. Those who die upon the circuit are assured of bliss, so they say. Even those who live to return to the lands of the south have earned great merit."

"But . . . " Mavin took a mouthful of mushroom and sucked in the juice which spurted on her lips. "What is it all for?"

There was that hint of breathy laughter once more. "What is it for? What is anything for, Mavin Manyshaped. There is something in their eschatology which speaks of rebuilding the tower. You will say, 'What tower?' and I will say, 'What tower, indeed?' " The Dervish paused, seeming to invite response or comment.

Mavin felt the question, chose not to indicate interest. "The tower that is gone, I suppose," she said flatly. "Except that it isn't gone. I think."

"What makes you think that?"

Now there was no mistaking the oddly expectant tone in that whispery voice. As though they had been talking in riddles. As though the Dervish were seeking some particular answer. Mavin decided to let the matter go no further. If Dervishes were not malign, still they were not understood. Least said, best handled. For now.

She nodded over her meal. "Oh, just that it seems likely there must be some tower around someplace or other. Sufficient to keep the legends spinning. Don't you think?"

Something wilted in the Dervish's stance. Still, it persisted. "Have you come this way before, Mavin Manyshaped? Upon this road? Or any other?"

Surprised by the question, Mavin answered it honestly. "I have not come this way before, Dervish." She finished chewing, swallowing. "Now. Dervish without a name, can you help me find the one I seek?"

"Perhaps," said the Dervish with a disappointed breath. "Perhaps." It began to spin, at first slowly, arms rising until they were straight out from the shoulders, fringes rising, whirling, the figure moving faster and faster. When the fringe rose from the face, Mavin caught a look at it, skeletally thin, huge-eyed, lips curved in an eternal, unchanging expression of calm, and yet – Mavin thought she saw something of disappointment in the face, too, though it blurred into motion too quickly for her to be sure. The Dervish hummed, spun, began to move away through the trees. Mavin let it go.

"If you will, perhaps," she whispered to herself, "then do, perhaps. Though why you should have expected me to say anything else, I do not know. So, if you will help me find him, do. If not . . . well, I will find him by myself." She lay back upon the mosses, replete, weary, not suddenly full of new thoughts. If the Ancient Road merely bent upon itself and returned to the south, then was Himaggery likely upon it or aside from it? Would he – could he have joined the runners? She would not have thought to look for him there.

Groaning, she rose to her feet and made a torch to light her way. Back upon the road the runners lay sprawled, unconscious, driven into exhausted sleep. She moved among them, making an orderly pattern in her mind to assure that she examined them all. Men, women, even some who were little more than children. Lean as old leather straps, bruised and scratched from the road, with soles on their feet like cured d'bor skin, hard as wood. She turned over lax bodies, pulled hoods aside to peer into faces, and replaced them. There were hundreds of them, and the task took hours. Dawn paled the eastern sky before she was finished. The clouds of the night before had gone; now there was only clear sky to the eastern horizon, flushed with sickly rose. Mavin threw down the torch with a growl of disgust and wandered back to her fire to curl close around the coals and sleep, not caring that the runners woke, chanted, and ran on into the west. She could find them if she wanted to. She was no longer sure she wanted to.

Late evening she wakened, stretched, scratched, built up her fire once more, gathered a new supply of earth's ears thinking furiously the while. Himaggery had followed the runners. He had come, as she had, to this place on the road. Likely he, as she, had encountered the Dervish. The Dervish who had "come to warn." The Dervish who had said that the runners would return to the south would likely have said as much to Himaggery. Who had not, at that time, joined the runners. At least he was not among them now. So he had turned aside, say.

"As good a supposition as any other," she encouraged herself. Himaggery had turned aside, then, after meeting the Dervish. Why?

"Because," she answered herself, "he, too, would have said something about the tower. Being Himaggery, he would not have done as I did, merely put the subject aside. No, he would have said something curious, something more Wizardly than mere chitchat. And if he did, then the Dervish would have replied with something sensible, also, and off Himaggery would have gone. So. Perhaps. At least it is worthy of examining further." She covered the fire with earth and Shifted into fustigar shape. The Dervish would not be difficult to track.

The trail was like a swept path, leaves and litter blown to either side by the Dervish's spinning, a little drift on either side marking the way. The path led away north of the road, down quiet moon-silvered glens and through shadowed copses, up long, dark inclines where the black firs sighed in the little wind, quietly moving as in the depths of a silent sea. Though the way rose and fell, she was neither climbing nor descending overall. Streams fell from higher tablelands into the valleys, ran there as quick streams away into the lowlands beyond. She wove deeper and deeper into the hills.

She could not recall ever having come that way before, and yet there was something familiar about a distant crest, the way in which a line of mountain cut another beside a great pinnacle. There was something recognizable in the way a bulky cliff edged up into the moonlight, catching the rays upon one smooth face so that it glowed like a mirror in the night. She stopped, tried to think where she had seen it before. It must have been some other similar place, though it teased at her, flicking at the edges of memory.

From this place the trail led upward, over a ridge. On either side were great trees, those called the midnight tree because of its black leaves and silver bark. The trees were rare, had always been rare, and were rarer now because of men's insatiable use of the black and silver wood, beautiful as a weaving of silk. Mavin shook her head, troubled. She had seen . . . seen such trees before. Not –

not from this angle, but the bulk of them seemed somehow familiar, painful, as though connected with something she did not want to remember. Still, the trail led between the trees and down.

Down. There was velvet moss beneath her feet. She could feel it, smell it. The moss was starred with tiny white blossoms which breathed sweetness into the night. Other blossoms hung in long, graceful panicles from the trees, and a spice vine twined up a stump beside the way. Here the Dervish had slowed, stopped spinning. He – she, it had walked here quietly, scarcely leaving a trail. Across the valley was a low stone wall, and behind that wall a small building. Mavin could not see it, but she knew it was there. Discomfited, she whined, the fustigar shape taking over for a moment to circle on the fragrant moss, yelping its discomfort. Across the valley a pombi roared, softly, almost gently, like a drum roll.

The fustigar fell silent, Shifted up into Mavin herself, wide-eyed and bat-eared upon the night, no less uncomfortable but more reasoning in her own shape. "Now, now," she soothed herself. "Come now. It may be enchantment, or some malign influence or some Game you know nothing of, Mavin. Hold tight. Go down slowly, slowly, into this valley." Which she did, step by step, pausing after each to listen and sniff the air.

A pool opened at her side, ran lilting into another. The path crossed still another on a bridge of stone which curved upward like a lover's kiss. Down through the blossoming trees she could see the valley floor, laced with streamlets and pools, like a silver filigree in the light. Beside one of the pools stood a glowing beast, graceful as waving grass, with one long horn upon its head.

Mavin ceased in that moment, without thought.

The place from which she came ceased, and the runners on the road. Windlow and Throsset ceased, and the cities of the world. Night and morning ceased, becoming no more than shadow and light. There was water, grass, the unending blend of foliage in the wind. There was whatever-she-was and the other, two who were as near to being one as had ever been. She was in another shape when she called from the hill, there from the crest where the great black trees bulked like a gateway against the stars, called in her beast's voice, a trumpet sound, silvery sweet, receiving the answer like an echo.

He ran to meet her, the sound of his hooves on the grass making a quick drum beat of joy. Then they were together, pressed tight side by side, soft muzzles stroking softer flanks, silk on silk, this joy at meeting again no less than the joy they had had to meet at first, that other time, so long ago. But that-which- they-were did not think of so-long-ago, nor of the time-past-when-they-were-not-together, nor of the moment-yet-to-come. Time was not. Before and after was not. The naming of names was not, nor the making of connections and classifications of things. Each thing was its own thing, each song in the night, each shadow, each pool, each leaf dancing upon its twig against the sky.

They simply were.

Sometimes, in the light of morning, when they had walked slowly across the soft meadows, he would call in that voice she knew, and she would flee, racing the very clouds away from him, ecstatic at the drum of his hooves following; never so fast to flee as he to pursue. Then they would dance, high on their hind hooves, whirling, manes and tails flourishing in a fine silken fringe to veil the light, their voices crying fine lusty sounds at the trees, coming into a kind of frenzy at one another, lunging and crying, to settle at last with heaving sides, hearts thudding like the distant thunder.

Sometimes they would lie in the deep grass, chewing the flowers, head to tail as they whisked the glass-winged flies away, talking a kind of stomach talk to one another, content not to move. Then they would rise lazy at midday to stroll to the pools where they would swim, touching the pebbly bottoms with their feet, rolling in the shallows as they tossed great wings of spray against the trees. And at dusk, when the whirling, humming thing came from the stone building at the edge of the rise, they would stand at the gate to let it stroke them and sing in tune with that humming, a song which the birds joined, and the pombi of the forest, and the whirling creature itself.

And sometimes they would run together, outdistancing the wind, fencing the air with their graceful horns, leaping up the piled hills of stone to stand at last like carven things on the highest pinnacles, calling to the clouds which passed.

Sometimes. Time on time.

Until one night the whirling thing came to the place they lay sleeping. It stopped whirling, and sat on the ground beside them and laid one hand upon her head. Her, her head. Her head only. And began to speak.

"This is the garden, Mavin. The garden. Come up, now, out of this place you are in, the wordless place. Come up like a fish from the depths and hear me. This is a garden you are in – the garden, most ancient, adorable, desired. All here is limpid and bright, all details perfect. There are pure animals here, and trees bright with blossom and fruit, streams which sing a soft incessant music and birds which cry bell sounds of joy. There are lawns here, Mavin, green as that light which burns in the heart of legendary stones, and there are other creatures here as well. They lie upon the knolls soft with moss, garlanded with flowers, eating fruits from which a sweet scent rises to the heights.

"Hear me, Mavin. In this land walks also the slaughterer, Death. He comes to an animal or an other and kills it quietly, leaving the body to be eaten by the other beasts and the bones to bleach in the twining grasses. There is no outcry when he comes, for no creature in the garden sees the slaughterer or knows his purpose or anticipates his intent. No one here knows the end of his action, for none in this garden know one moment from another, none know the next moment from the moment at hand. None fear. None are apprehensive for the coming hour, or the morrow, and none hunger or thirst, but all eat and drink and mate and bear in the perfect peace which this garden has always within its borders. Mavin, do you hear me?

"Listen to me, Mavin. There is only peace, tranquility, and simplicity here. And the end of it is Death, Mavin. Only that. Come up out of that dreamless place, Mavin, and think into yourself once more . . ."

And the peace was destroyed. Not all at once, for she rose and trumpeted her song and ran across the meadow to leave the words behind, but they pursued her, slowing her feet. And when she swam in the pool, she looked into the depths of it and thought of drowning, making a panicky move toward the bank. And when evening came again, she did not lie upon the grasses beside him but stood, head down, musing, unaware that she was changing, Shifting . . .

The Dervish stood before her, summoning her with a quiet hand. "Come."

A voice which she did not recognize as her own said, "I cannot leave . . . him . . ."

"For a time," said the Dervish. "Come." And they walked away up the hill toward the low stone building behind the wall.

Inside it was only white space, simple as a box, with a single bench and a cot and a peg upon the wall where clothing could be hung, and one small shelf. The Dervish brought clothing to Mavin, trousers, a shirt, a cloak, a belt and knife. "Put these on."

Mavin looked stupidly down at her nakedness, began to Shift fur to cover herself, was stopped by an imperative "No," from the Dervish. "Put them on." While Mavin was occupied with this, the Dervish took a cup from the shelf, filled it from a flask and gave it to Mavin. "Sit. Drink. Listen to me, Mavin Manyshaped."

"I must go . . . "

"Listen." The voice was hypnotic, quiet, almost a whisper. "Who is it who lies yonder on the grasses, Mavin Manyshaped?"

"I . . . I don't know. Not a person . . . "

"You know better, Mavin Manyshaped. Who is it who runs trumpeting with you through the glades? Who swims with you in the pools of the garden? Who is your companion?"

"Don't . . . I don't know."

"Come, woman. Do not try me too far. Did you lie to me? You were here before. Eight years ago. You found him here then because I had brought him here. He had enraged the shadow, and it came after him. There is no way to flee from the shadow, only a way to hide – or be hidden. So, I hid him here in shape other than his own, safe for a time, only for a time . . . .

"Then I had to go away. There were things I had to do, great goings on which required my attention. When I returned I found him here and took him away, out of the valley, to a place where it would be safe to change him into his own form. *He would not change.* He could not change. He could not get out of the shape I had given him. So, I brought him back here, thinking to find whatever – whoever it was which had enchanted him more deeply than ever I had intended. I looked here in the valley, but there was no one here. Signs, yes. Tracks so like his own they were made by his twin. But of that beast itself no trace. Whoever had been here was gone.

"And it was you! You who came to him eight years ago! It had to have been a Shifter. Who else? What else!" The Dervish rose, began to spin, to him, the very walls humming with it as though enraged. After a time it calmed, settled, whispered at her once more. "Mavin Manyshaped, what have you done?"

Mavin sat frozen, like curdled stone, only half aware of what was said, what was meant. Eight years ago Himaggery had disappeared. Eight years ago she, Mavin, had found an idyll in this place. With . . . with . . .

"Himaggery!" she sobbed, at once grieved and joyed, lost and found, the world spinning around her as though it were the Dervish. "Himaggery!"

"Ah." Now the Dervish was quiet. "So you didn't know. And perhaps you told me the truth when you said you had not been upon the road before? Hmmm. But you had come here, and found him here, and changed, not knowing who he was. Well, having loved you here, my girl, he would not leave the place, would not give up his shape. You did not know it was he. I wonder, somehow, if he knew it was you. Well. Knowing this, perhaps now I can save him."

"Save him for what?" Mavin cried, anguished. "Save him for what, Dervish? Were we not content as we were in your garden? Could you not have left us as we were?"

"Think on that, Shifter-woman. True, I have set some in this garden who will never leave it. But the slaughterer will come, woman. Age will come, and Death. The youthful you will go, and there will be no joy of the mind to make up for it. Think of it. What would Himaggery have you do, if he could ask?"

Mavin leaned her head in her hands. How long had this gone on? All she wanted to do was return to the garden, leave this simple house and return. If she could not do that? What then? Could she take Himaggery with her?

"Oh, Gamelords, Nameless One. Tell me your name, at least. Let me curse you by name!"

"I am Bartelmy of the Ban, Mavin. It is beneath my Ban that Himaggery was saved from the shadow, within my Ban he has lived these eight years."

"Can we get him out of it?"

"I believe so. I believe you can. Now."

"Well then, Dervish, let us do it. All my body longs only to go back to your garden. Oh, it is a wicked enchantment to make such a longing. See. I am sweating. My nose is running as though I had a fever. Yet inside my head is boiling with questions, with summons, with demands. I would be content to leave it, but it will not leave me. Let us get on with it."

"You are too quick, Shifter. Too quick to Shift, too quick to change, too quick to decide. You came here the second time, and even though I half expected you, you were too quick. Now you would pull Himaggery back into his self without knowing why he was hidden, why that hiding was necessary. No. I will not accept this. Before we try, you and I, to get Himaggery out of the garden I put him in, you must understand why he went there. He was on a search, Shifter. He found at least part of what he was looking for."

"I don't care," Mavin sobbed. "Himaggery is like that. He must understand everything. It doesn't matter to me, not half of what he cares about. If a thing needs to be done, let us do it."

The Dervish made a gesture which froze her as she sat, and the voice which came was terrible in its threat. "I said, too quick, Shifter. I, Bartelmy, will say what you will do. It is for your good, not your harm, and I will not brook your disobedience. You may go willingly or I will take you, but you will see what it was Himaggery saw."

The voice was like ice, and it went into Mavin's heart. There had been something in that voice – something similar to another voice she had heard long before. When? Was it in Ganver's Grave? The Eesty? She drew herself up, slowly, feeling the inner coils of her straighten to attention, readying themselves for flight or attack. Oh, but this was a strange person who confronted her. It was both weaponless and fangless, and yet Mavin shuddered at it, wondering that she could be so dominated in such short time.

It commanded. There was no energy in her to contest its commands, no strength to assert her own independence, her own autonomy. Almost without thought, she knew that this one had a will to match her own – perhaps to exceed her own. Too much had happened, too much was happening for her to consider what might be best to do – so let her do what this Dervish demanded. And if a thing must be done, then better seem to do it willingly than by force. She forced down her quick, instinctively shifty response to sit silent, waiting.

"Beyond the crest of the hill, Mavin, is a path leading to the south. Walk upon it. You will go three times a rise, three times a fall. On the fourth rise look away to your left. Something will not be there. Seek it out. Examine it. When you have done so, if you still can, return here.

"If you do not draw its attention, it will not follow you." The Dervish began to spin, move, away and out the door of the place, down the meadow and into the trees. Mavin looked among those trees for the silver beast, the lovely beast, the glorious one, her own. A pain too complex to bear broke her in two, and she gasped as she ran toward the crest of the hill. Gamelords. She would not live to finish this journey.

Once at the crest, it was some time before she could gather her attention to find the southern path. Once on it, her feet followed it of themselves, counting the rises, the falls. She burned inside, an agony, uncaring for the day, the path. The third rise, the third fall. Gasping like a beached fish she came to the last crest and fell to her knees, tears dropping into the dust to make small dirty circles there. At last she stood again and looked off to the left, wondering for the first time how one could see a thing which was not there.

Her glance moved left to right, to left, to right once more, swinging in an arc to that side, only slowly saying to her brain that there was one place in that arc where no message came from the eye. A vacancy. Nothing. She sat upon a log and stared at it. It vanished, filled in with lines of hill and blotches of foliage. She scanned along the hill once more, and it vanished once more. Her throat was suddenly dry, hurtfully dry. There was a streamlet in the valley below, and beyond that stream a hill, and beyond that the upward slope. She struggled down toward the water, catching herself as she slid, somehow not thinking to Shift or unable to do so. At the stream she drank and went on.

As she reached the last hill, she fell to her belly to crawl the last few feet, masking her face with a branch of leafy herb. Below the hill was . . . a road. A side road, a spur leading from the south to end in this place. Upon the road a tower. She thought it was quite tall, but the wavering outlines made it uncertain. If one could get closer . . . It seemed almost to beckon, that wavering. One should get closer.

No! It was as though the Dervish's voice spoke to her where she lay. Himaggery would have gone closer. Being Himaggery, he would have been unable to keep himself away from it. He went down there, saw – something. Something terrible, which did not want to be seen. Something which pursued him.

Then he ran. She could see him in her mind, fleeing down the steep slope, falling, scrambling up to run again, panting, his throat as dry as her own. Run. To the path at the top of the hill, down three times, up three times, growing wearier with each fleeing step, with some horror coming after him. Until he reached the great midnight trees at the entrance to the valley where the Dervish waited. . . .

Whatever had pursued him from this place could not be misled or outrun. So much she had gathered; so much she understood. No. He could hide from this pursuing horror only by giving up everything which made him Himaggery.

So, go no closer, Mavin, she told herself. Watch from here. Find out from here what is there.

Nothing was there.

Nothing boiled at the edges of vision, blurring and twisting like the waves of heat she had seen on long western beaches, making a giddy swirl of every line. For a time there was nothing more than this impression of boiling nothingness to hold her attention, making her feel so dizzy and sick that she gripped the ground beneath her, digging her nails deep into gravelly soil which seemed to tilt and sway. Then, when time passed and her eyes became accustomed to the unfocused roiling, she saw there was substance – if not substance, then color – to whatever shifted and boiled. It was not another hue. Greens were not bluer or yellower, browns not more red or ocher. It was, instead, as though all color was grayed, darkened, becoming mere hint and allusion to itself, a ghostly code for the shades and tints of the world. This allusive grayness piled upon the roadway, flickered around the outlines of the tower she believed she saw, coalescing into writhing mounds, fracturing into fluttering flakes.

Breaking away, one such flake flew upward toward her, coming to rest upon the littered slope. Behind it as it flew the trees lost their gold-green vitality to appear as a brooding lace of bones against the sky; at first an entire copse, then a narrower patch, then a thin belt of gray which striped the trees. As it came to rest, the shadow became wider once more, the copse behind it showing gray and grim. After a chilly time, her mind translated this into a reality, a thing seen if only in effect; something leaf-shaped, thin when seen edge on but broad in its other dimensions, something which could lift or fly and was, perhaps, like those other flakes crawling in nightmare drifts upon the roadway.

Shadows. Shadows which moved of themselves. She put her face into her hands and lay there silently, unable to look at them because of the vertiginous dizzyness they caused. She was helpless until the nausea passed, leaving a shaky weakness in its place. Then she could breathe again, and she opened her eyes to watch, not daring to move.

There were birds nesting in the trees behind her. She heard them scolding, saw their shadows dash across the ground as they sought bits of litter and grass. One of them darted near her face. It hopped toward a bunch of grasses on which the shadow flake lay, gathering dried strands as it went. There was plenty of grass outside the shadow. The bird half turned, as though to go the other way, but a breeze moved the grasses. Within the shadow, they beckoned. The bird turned and hopped into the shadowed space. The grasses dropped from its beak. It squatted, wings out, beak open, then turned its head with horrid deliberation to peck at one wing as though it attacked some itching parasite.

All was silent. Mavin lay without breathing, prone, almost not thinking. Before her on the slope in the patch of shadow a bird pecked at its wing, pecked, pecked.

After a time the shadow lifted lazily, hovering as it turned, becoming a blot, a line, a blot once more as it rejoined the clotted shadow at the tower. Behind it on the slope a bird stopped pecking. With a pitiable sound it stumbled away from its own wing which lay behind it, severed.

Mavin drew upon the power of the place without thinking. She Shifted one hand into a lengthy tentacle, reached out for the bird and snapped its neck quickly to stop the thin cry of uncomprehending pain. The piled shadows heaved monstrously, as though someone had spoken a word they listened for. They had noticed something – the draw of power, her movement, the bird's death. She could not watch any longer. Head down, she wriggled back the way she had come.

When she had returned to the road, she saw shadows there as well, one or two upon the verges, a few moving across the sky from tree to tree. At the top of each rise were a few, and in each hollow. As she approached the great midnight trees at the entrance to the valley, she saw others there, more, enough to shimmer the edges of the guardian trees in an uneasy dance. Between them stood the Dervish.

"You have seen." It was not a question. It was a statement of fact. Mavin knew what she had seen showed in her face; she could imagine the look of it. Ashamed. Terrorized.

"I have seen something," she croaked. "I do see. They lie in the trees around us."

"I know," the Dervish replied. "In usual times, they lie only upon the tower as they have done for centuries, hiding it from mortal eyes, hiding the bell within. I have seen them, as have others before me. But Himaggery was not content merely to see. He attempted to penetrate, to get into the tower."

"How is that possible?"

"To a Wizard, anything is possible," the Dervish said with more than a hint of scorn. "Or so they lead themselves to believe."

"If you think so little of Wizards, why did you save him from the shadows at all?" Mavin asked this with what little anger she could muster.

"I counted it my fault he went there. He asked about the tower and I answered, not realizing his arrogance. I did not warn. Therefore this disturbance was my responsibility, Shifter. At least for that time. Now it is one I will pass on to you, for it is you who thwarted my releasing him. You will take him away with you. His presence, and yours, disturb my work."

"If you'll put him into his own form," agreed Mavin, not caring at the moment what the Dervish's work might be. "Though he may immediately try to go back to the tower and finish whatever it was he started. . . ."

The Dervish hummed a knifelike sound which brought Mavin to her knees, gasping. "Not in his own form! And he will not go back to that tower! How far do you think these will let him go in his own form?" The Dervish gestured at the shadows, making a sickening swooping motion with both arms, then clutching them tight and swaying. "They would have him tight-wrapped in moments. No. It must be far and far from here, Mavin Manyshaped, that he is brought out of that shape. Come!"

There were no shadows in the valley, at ieast none that Mavin could see. There was a silvery beast waiting beside the flowery pools, and she fought the instinctive surge toward him, the flux of her own flesh inside its skin. There was a pombi there as well, huge and solemn beside the low wall, leaning against it, an expression of lugubrious patience upon its furry face.

"Come out, Arkhur," commanded the Dervish.

The pombi stood on its hind legs, stretched, faded to stand before Mavin as a sad–faced, old youngster dressed in tattered garments. Mavin gasped. It was the face she had seen at the Lake of Faces, the other which had spoken of Bartelmy's Ban. So here was Chamferton's brother, wearily obedient to this Dervish.

"Go back, Arkhur," said the Dervish.

The youth dropped to all fours and became a pombi once more.

"I didn't know anyone could do that," grated Mavin. "Except Shifters, and then only to themselves."

"No one can, except Shifters, and only to themselves. He only believes he is a pombi. You believe it because he believes it. He believes it because I believe it. Even the shadows believe – no, say rather the shadows do not find in him that pattern they seek. When Himaggery went to the tower, he found this one nearby,enchanted, perhaps, or drugged, or both. When Himaggery fled, he carried this one out with him, though he would have been wiser to go faster and less encumbered. I hid him as I hid Himaggery, though it is probable it was not as necessary. Now both must go. Those you meet upon the road will believe he is a pombi.

"So, too, with the other. He believes he is the fabulous beast he appears to be to others. You believe it also. All others will believe it. The shadows will not sense in him the pattern they seek. But you must go far from here, very far, Mavin Manyshaped. No trifling distance will do. You must be several days' journey from your last view of the shadows before you bring him out into himself once more. Do it as I did. Call his name; tell him to come out. *Make him hear you,* and he will come out."

"A place far from here." Mavin staggered, too weary to stand. "Far from here."

"A place well beyond the last shadow, a place where no shadow is," the Dervish agreed.

She took up a halter which was hanging upon the gate, and wondered in passing whether it was real or whether she only believed she saw it. Whichever it might have been, the fabulous beat believed he felt it, for he called a trumpet sound of muted grief as they went up the road past the guardian trees, the pombi shambling behind them.

CHAPTER FIVE

They could not go far enough. Mavin stumbled as she led the beast, dragged her feet step on step, looking up to see shadows in every tree they passed beneath, on every line of hill, in every nostril of earth. Still, she went on until she knew she could go no farther, then tethered the beast to a tree and coaxed him to lie down as a pillow for her head. The pombi lay beside them without being coaxed, and warmed by the furry solidity she rested. The smooth body beneath her cheek breathed and breathed. She forced herself not to respond to that gentle movement, though she passionately desired to lie right against that body and abandon herself to the closeness, the warmth. Something in the beast responded to her, and he turned to bring her body closer, touching the soft flesh of her neck with a muzzle as soft. She forced herself away, trying to find a position which would not so stir her feelings, found one of sheer weariness at last. Thus they slept, moving uneasily from time to time as night advanced, and it was in the dark of early morning that she woke to begin the trek once more.

The thought of food began to obsess her. She did not know what the beast could eat. She remembered eating grass when she had been his mate, but she had actually Shifted into a form which could eat grass. What did Himaggery eat in this strange shape he thought he bore? Did belief extend to such matters as teeth and guts? Could she feed such a beast on grasses which would not keep the man alive? The pombi did not wait upon her consideration. He shambled off into the forest and returned with a bunwit dangling from his jaws, munching on it with every appearance of satisfaction. Soon after, they passed a rainhat bush. Mavin peeled a ripe fruit and offered it from her hand. The beast took it with soft lips and a snuffle of pleasure. Had it not been for the shadows clustered around them, she would have felt pleased.

"I cannot call you . . . Himaggery," she whispered, giving no voice to the name itself. "Not even to myself. To do so starts something within me I cannot hold. And I may not think of you as I did when I was your mate within the valley, for to do so melts my flesh, beast. So. What shall I call you?" She considered this while they walked a league or so, the pombi licking bunwits blood from his bib of white hair, she feeding the other two of them on fruit and succulent fronds of young fern which thrust their tight coils up among the purple spikes of Healer's balm. Only the rainhat bush bore fruit so early, and she gave some thought to the monotony of the beast's diet if, indeed, it could not eat grass or graze upon the young leaves.

"I will call you Fon," she said at last. "For you were Fon when we met. Or I will call you Singlehorn."

The beast stopped, staring about himself as though in confusion, and she knew her words had reached some inner self which was deeply buried.

"Fon," she said in pity. "It's all right. It's all right, my Singlehorn."

It was not all right. The shadows had only multiplied as they went, as though attracted by some ripe stink of passion or pain. Something in the relationship among the three of them, perhaps, or between any two of them. Something, perhaps, which sought to surface in either Arkhur or . . . Fon. Something, perhaps, which sought expression in herself. She thought of the bird which had severed its own wing, wondering what had motivated the shadow to cause such a thing, or whether any creature, once it had invaded the shadow, would have acted so automatically. Yet Himaggery had sought to invade the tower and had somehow escaped.

The bird had simply gone into the shadow.

How had Himaggery gone?

The shadows had not sought the bird. Or had they?

The shadows were seeking something now. Seeking, following, but not attacking. She wondered at their passivity, knowing they could attack if they would. Their failure to do so was more frightening than the actuality, making heart labor and breath caw through a dry throat without purpose. Running would not help. Conversation would make her feel less lonely, but there was no one present who could answer her. Even her words were dangerous, for either of the beasts beside her might rise to an unintentional inflection, an unmeant phrase, rise into that pattern which the shadows sought.

So, in a forced silence, for the first time since leaving the valley, she began to consider where they were going. Somewhere without shadows. And where might such a place be found?

"We need a Wizard," she whispered to herself. "One walks at my back, and I cannot use him. Chamferton is far to the east of us. Besides, I cannot like him, dare not trust him. So. Perhaps instead of a Wizard, I need . . .a Seer. To find the shadowless place. And who would be more interested than Windlow, Fon-beast, eh? Far and far from here, down the whole length of the land to the mountainous places of Tarnoch. Still, I could rely upon him. And once there – once there we could rest."

Even though the shadows did not attack, they were present. Weariness followed upon that fact, a weightiness of spirit, a heaviness of heart and foot and hand so that mere bodies became burdens. Mavin wondered dully if she could Shift into something which would be less susceptible to this lassitude and was warned by some inner voice to stay as she was, not to change, not to draw upon any power from the earth or air, for it was such a draw upon the power of the place which had stirred the shadows in her presence once before.

"As we are, then," she sighed. "As we are, companions. One foot before another, and yet again, forever. Gamelords, but we have come a wearying way."

They had not come far and she knew it. They had gone up and down a half-dozen small hills, tending always south, toward the road of tingling stones where the blind runners had been. She did not know why she had set out with that destination in mind except that it was a real place, a measurable distance from other places she knew, not so far that it seemed unattainable even to a group as weary as this one.

One rise and then another. One hollow and then another. Trees blotted dark on a line of hill. Rocks twisted into devil faces; foliage in the likeness of monsters. Clouds which moved faster in the light wind than they three moved upon the earth. Each measure a measure of a league's effort to cross a quarter of it. Until at last they came to a final rise and saw the pale line of the road stretching across its feet.

The day had dawned without sun and moved to noon in half light.

They could go no further, but she led them on until the road itself was beneath their feet. Once there, they dropped into a well of sleep as sudden as a clap of thunder. No shadow moved on this road. No shadow moved near this road. Pale it stretched from east to west, the stones of it cracked into myriad hairline fissures in which fernlets grew, and buttons of fungus, their minute parasols shedding a tiny fog of spores upon the still air. Mavin lay upon them like a felled sapling, all asprawl, loose and lost upon the stones, the beasts beside her. In their sleep they seemed to flatten as though the stones absorbed them, drew them down, and when they woke at last they lay long, half conscious, drawing their flesh back up into themselves.

It was music which had wakened them, far off and half heard on a fitful wind, but music nonetheless. A thud of great drum; a snarl of small drum; blare and tootle, rattle and clash, louder as it continued, obviously nearing. There were no shadows nearby though Mavin saw flutters against a distant copse. She dragged herself up, tugging the beasts into the trees at the side of the road. They stood behind leafy branches, still half asleep, waiting for what would come.

What came was a blare of trumpets, a pompety-pom of drums, three great crashes of cymbals, thrangggg, thranggg, thranggg, then a whole trembling thunder of music over the rise to the east. They saw the plumes first, red and violet, purple and azure, tall and waving like blown grass. The plumes were upon black helmets, glossy as beetles, small and tight to the heads of the musicians who came with their cheeks puffed out and their eyes straight ahead, following one who marched before them raising and lowering his tall, feathered staff to set the time of the music. Mavin felt the Fon-beast's horn in the small of her back, up and down, up and down, marching in time to the music. Looking down, she saw pombi feet, Fon feet, and Mavin feet all in movement, pom, pom, pom, pom, as the bright music tootled and bammed around them.

The musicians were dressed in tight white garments with colorful fabric wrapped about them to make bright kilts from their waists to below their knees, reflecting the hues of the plumes as they swished and swung, left-right, left-right. Polished black boots thumped upon the stones; the musicians moved on. Behind came the children, ranks and files of them, some with small instruments of their own, and behind the children the wagons, horses as brightly plumed as the musicians were, the elderly drivers sitting tall as the animals kept step, legs lifted high in a prance.

She could see no shadows anywhere near, not upon the road nor within the forest, perhaps not within sound of the music. Mavin moved onto the roadway behind the last of the wagons. From the back of it, an apple-cheeked old woman nodded at them with a smile of surprise, tossing out a biscuit which the Fon caught between his teeth. Mavin got the next one and the pombi the third, throwing it high to catch it on the next step, marching as it chewed in the same high, poised trot the wagon horses displayed.

"Are you Circus?" cried the old woman from a toothless mouth. "Haven't seen Circus in a lifetime!"

Mavin had no idea what she meant, but she smiled and nodded, the Singlehorn pranced, and Arkhur-pombi rose to his hind legs in a grave two-step. So they went, on and on, keeping step to the drums even when the other instruments stopped tweedling and flourishing for a time. The sun dropped lower in their faces, and lower yet, until only a glow remained high among the clouds, pink as blossoms.

Then the whistle, shreeee, shreee; whompity-womp, bang, bang. Everything stopped.

A busy murmur, like a hive of bees. Shouts, cries, animals unhitched and led to the grassy verges of the road. Fires started almost upon the road itself, and cookpots hung above them. Steam and smoke, and a crowd of curious children gathering around the Fon-beast and Arkhur-pombi, not coming near, but not fearful either, full of murmurs and questions.

"Are they trained, Miss? Can you make them do tricks? Can you ride them? Would they let me ride them? Are you Circus?"

"What," she asked at last, "is Circus?"

"Animals," cried one. To which others cried objection, "No, it's jugglers." "Clowns." "Acrobats, Nana-bat says." "It's marvels, that's what."

An older child approached, obviously one to whom the welfare of these had been assigned, for he wore a worried expression which looked perpetual and shook his head at the children in a much practiced way. "Why are you annoying the travelers? One would think you'd never seen an animal trainer before. We saw one just last season, when we left the jungle cities."

"Not with animals like this, Hirv." "Those were only fustigars, Hirv." "Nobody ever told me you could train pombis, Hirv." "Hirv, what's the one with the horn. Ask her, will you Hirv."

"That beast is a Singlehorn," Mavin replied in an ingratiating tone. "The pombi was raised by humans since it was a cub." Which is true enough, she told herself. Arkhur must have been raised by someone. "I am not their trainer. I am merely taking them south to their owner." She had thought this out fairly carefully, not wanting to be asked to have the beasts do tricks. "If it would not disturb you, we would like to go along behind you for a time. Your music makes the leagues shorter." And she provided another ingratiating expression to put herself in their good graces. The children seemed inclined to accept her, but the one who was approaching next might be harder to convince.

He was the music master, he of the tall, plumed staff and the silver whistle. He thrust through the children, planted the staff on the pave and looked them over carefully before turning to the child-minder. "What does she want?"

"Only to follow along, Bandmaster. She says it makes the leagues shorter."

The Bandmaster allowed himself a chilly smile. "Of course it does. The Band swallows up the leagues as though it had wings. Music bears us up and carries us forward. In every land in every generation."

The children had evidently heard this before, for there was tittering among them; and one, braver than the rest, puffed himself up in infant mockery, pumping a leafy branch as though he led the marching.

"What is your name?" the Bandmaster demanded.

"Mavin," she said, making a gestured bow. "With two beasts to deliver to the southland."

"I assume they are not dangerous? We need not fear for our children?"

Mavin thought of the murdered bunwit and looked doubtfully at Arkhur-pombi, who returned the gaze innocently, tongue licking his breast hairs, still slightly stained with bunwit blood. "I will keep it near me, Bandmaster. Can you tell me where you have come from? I have traveled up and down this land for twenty years, and I have not run across your like before."

The Bandmaster smiled a superior smile, waving his hand to an elder who lingered to one side, arms clutched tight around a bundle of books. "Where have we been in twenty years, Byram? The Miss wishes to know."

The oldster sank to his haunches, placing the bundle on the ground to remove one tome and leaf through it, counting as he leafed back, stopping at last to cry in a reedy voice, "Twenty years ago we were on the shores of the Glistening Sea nearby to Levilan. From there we went north along the shore road to the sea cities of Omaph and Peeri and the northern bays of Smeen. And from there," leafing forward in his book, "to the Citadel of Jallywig in the land of the dancing fish, thence north once more along Boughbound Forest to the glades of Shivermore and Creep and thence south to the jungle roads of the Great Maze. Oh, we were on the roads of the Great Maze ten years, Miss, and glad to see the end of them at last in the jungle cities of Luxuri and Bloome. And from there south across the Dorbor Range onto the old road where we are now. We have played the repertoire forty times through in twenty years. . . ."

"How long have you been doing this?" she asked. "Traveling around this way?"

"How long have we been *marching*," corrected the Bandmaster. "Why, since the beginning, of course. Since disembarkation or shortly thereafter. At first, so it is written, there were few roads and long, Miss, but as we go they ramify. Ah, yes, they ramify. Used to be in time past, so it is written, we could make the circuit in five years or so. Now it takes us seventy. In time, I suppose, there will be children born who will never live to see their birthplace come up along the road again. Jackabib, there, with his leafy bough pretending to mock the Bandmaster, why, it may be he will never see the city of Bloome again."

Jackabib did not seem distressed by this thought. He only flushed a little and ran off into the trees where he peeked at them from among the leaves like a squirrel.

"Well then, I would not have seen you," agreed Mavin. "You have not been this way in my lifetime. I am mighty glad you came this way now, however, for it is a sight I will always remember." And a sound, she thought, aware of the ache in her legs. The sound had carried them step on step, and never a sign of weariness or hurt until the music stopped. "This pombi is pretty good as a hunter, as am I. May we contribute meat for the pot?"

This was agreed to with good cheer, so she led Arkhur beast into the trees and set him on the trail. She poised, then, ready to Shift herself into hunting fustigar shape, only to stop, listening, for it seemed she heard a deep, solemn humming in the trees. The sound faded. She took a deep breath, began the Shift, then heard it once more. The voice came on the little wind like a sigh. "Do not Shift, Mavin. Stay as you are. You risk much if you Shift, the shadows not least."

When it had spoken, she was not sure she had heard it. When she readied herself once more, however, she knew she had heard it, for her flesh twinged away from the idea of *Shift* as though it had been burned.

"Well then," she said to herself, not ready yet to be worried at this. "I will do as the children of Danderbat Keep were taught to do. I will set snares."

Arkhur-pombi returned to her from time to time with his prey, like a cat bringing marshmice to the door. Each taime Mavin patted him and took the proferred bunwit with expressions of joy, as though he had indeed been some young hunting beast she sought to train. She laughed at herself, yet went on doing it. Her snares, set across burrow runways, were also useful; and they returned to the wagons some hours later, Mavin's arms laden with furry forms, even after feeding two of them to Arkhur to assure the safety of the children.

She found the people of the band occupied with a myriad orderly duties, cooking, cleaning their musician dresses, polishing boots and helmets, copying strange symbols by firelight on squares of parchment which they told her conveyed the music they played. Mavin had not seen written music before, and she marveled at it, as strange and exotic a thing as she could remember ever having seen. Others of them gathered food from the forest by torchlight, rainhat berries, fern fronds, fungus to be sliced and dried before the fires. "When we play in the cities," she was told, "we are given coin, and we use that coin to fill the meal barrels and the meat safes. Between times, we must live upon the land."

The Fon-beast, tethered to a tree, was suffering himself to be petted and decked with flowers by a tribe of children. Mavin offered fruit and bread from her hand, only to be copied by all the young ones. So she could leave the Singlehorn without guilt in their tender hands and sit by other fires to hear what these people knew. She ended the evening telling stories of lands across the sea, of giant chasms and bridge-people who lived below the light, and stickies – one of whom, at least, probably remembered the days of disembarkation. "His name is Mercald-Myrtilon," she said. "And he has memories in him of that time a thousand years long past." There was much expression of interest and wonder at this, and the Bandmaster even began to talk of taking a ship to that farther shore to march there, until Mavin told him there were no roads at all.

After which she slept beside her beasts along with half a dozen children who had fallen asleep while petting or feeding one or both. When they woke, it was a brighter world than on any recent morning.

"Come, Arkhur-pombi," she teased the beast up and into motion. "There are no shadows near this road, and I must risk us both to learn something sensible." She took him off into the trees, not far, watching all the time for that telltale darkening of foliage or sky, seeing nothing but the honest shadows cast by the sun. There in a sweet clearing full of unrolling ferns she told him in the closest approximation of the Dervish's voice, "Arkhur, come out!"

It was some time before he did, rising on his hind legs, dropping again, circling uneasily, then at last seeming to set his mind on it. The figure which materialized out of the pombi's shape was no more impressive than before. It still had that young-old expression of apologetic intransigence, a face which said, "I know you all think this a stupid idea, and perhaps I do also, but I must get on with it." When he was fully before her, he seemed to have no idea what to do with his hands, but stood waving them aimlessly, as though brushing flies.

"You are Arkhur?" she asked in a gentle voice, not wanting to startle him. "Younger brother of the High Wizard Chamferton?"

She might as well have struck him with a whip. His eyes flashed; his back straightened; the hands came down before him in a gesture of firm negation.

"I am Arkhur," he said in a furious tenor. "I *am* the High Wizard Chamferton, younger brother of a foul Invigilator who despised his Talent and sought to usurp mine!"

"Ahh," she breathed. "So that was it. And how came you to this pass, Arkhur – or should I call you High Wizard, or sir? I called your brother by your name, I'm afraid, but it doesn't surprise me to learn the truth. He had a slyness about him."

"I trusted him," the pombi-man growled, so suddenly angry he was almost incoherent. Mavin had to struggle to understand him as he spat and gargled. "I trusted his pleas for understanding and rest. He told me he was an old man. Beyond scheming anymore, he said. Beyond treachery. Wanting only warm fires and warm food, cool wine and quiet surroundings. And so I took him in. And he stayed, learned, Read me when I least expected it, then drugged me deep and sent me to be Harpy-dropped where the shadows dance. Fool! Oh, much will I treasure vengeance against him, woman. But well will I repay the Gamesman who brought me away from the shadows and the tower." He seemed to savor this for the moment then demanded:

"Where is he?"

Mavin assumed he meant Himaggery. She shook her head. "He is near, but worse off than you, Wizard. Now, before you say anything more, tell me a thing. The Dervish who hid you told me to bring you out of the pombi shape '*where no shadow was.*' Well, there is no shadow here, but I doubt not they are somewhere perhaps within sight of us. Are you in danger in your shape? And if so, shall I return you to beastliness?"

At first the High Wizard Chamferton understood none of this and it took considerable time for Mavin to explain it. By the time he had climbed a tree to see for himself where shadows lay upon the line of hills, smells of breakfast were wafting from the fires along the road, and they were both hungry.

"My brother used a certain drug on me, Mavin. He knows little enough of his own Talent, and even less of mine, or he would have realized that in that drugged state, the shadows would pay me no more attention than they might pay a block of wood. Though I could see them and even consider them in a dreamy way, I had no more volition than a chopping block. No. They did not care about me and will not be attracted to me. I am certain of that."

"Certain enough to risk our lives?" she persisted.

He nodded, again solemn. "Certain."

"Well, that's something the Dervish didn't know." This made Mavin cheerful for some reason. It was good to think that there were some things a Dervish might not know. "Well then, how do

I explain the loss of the pombi?''

"Don't explain it. Put me back as I was, woman, and let us part from these good people amiably. Perhaps in time we will want their friendship. Then, when we have separated from them, you can bring me out again. Next time it will not be such a task, for I will set myself to remember who I am, even in pombi shape.''

Mavin, well aware of the lure of forgetfulness which came with any beast shape, did not totally believe this optimistic statement but was content to try it. "Go back, Arkhur,'' she said, needing to say it only once. They emerged from the trees to the welcoming bugle of the Singlehorn and in time for breakfast.

"Have you a map of the way you are going?'' she asked the old man, Byram, who seemed to be totally responsible for all matters of record. "Perhaps I might rejoin your party farther on?''

He sniffled, scuffled, laid the map out on a wagon's hinged side and pointed out to her the way they would go.

"Well, here's the way of it, girl. Last time we were by here, I was a youngun. 'Prentice to the manager before me, just as he was to the one before him clear back to disembarkation. He took the notes and went over 'em with me, and I took 'em down myself, just to have another copy – he used to say that a lot: 'one copy's a fool's copy,' meaning if you lost the one, where'd you be? Eh? Well, so I always had my own copy made from then on. Now, though, after fifty years, try and read it! So look here. It goes from where we are on west, and west, bumpety-bump, all through these whachacallems forests. . . .''

"Shadowmarches,'' offered Mavin. "This whole area west of the Dorbor Mountains and east of the sea, north of the Cagihiggy Creek cliffs, all the way to the jungles.''

"Sha-dow-mar-ches,'' he wrote laboriously, spelling it out. "Well now, that's good to know. So, westward, westward for a long straight way, then we come to the coast and turn away down south. No road north from there, just trails. At least fifty years ago was just trails. Maybe won't be any road south either, now, but we can usually find flat enough to march on.

"Anyhow, the road goes south and south until it comes to this long spit of land heading right out into the sea, down the west side of this great bay, almost an inland sea. Well, the road goes along south. East across the bay you can see a town, here, at the river mouth. What d'ya call that?"

"Ummm," said Mavin, puzzling out the map. "That's Hawsport."

"Right! See, those little letters right there. That's what they say. Hawsport. So you know it's been there a while, don't you? Well, we go on until we're well south of Hawsport, then the spit of land turns east a little, coming closer to the mainland, closer and closer until it gets to a bridge."

"I don't think there's a bridge there," said Mavin. "Not that I remember." She tried to summon bird memories of the coast as seen from above, as she had crossed it again and again in the long years' search for Handbright. No bridge. Certainly not one of the length the old man's map called for.

"Now then, isn't that what I said to the Bandmaster! I said, likely that bridge's gone, I said. There was a storm not long after we were here before that would have been a horror and a disaster to any bridge ever built. Even if it isn't gone, likely it's in a state of sorrowful disrepair. Oh, the bridges we've gone over that trembled to our step, girl, let me tell you, it's no joke when a band must break step to keep a bridge from collapsing. And the ones we've not dared tread on and have had to go around, ford the stream, march along the river to a better place. Bridges! They're the bane of my life."

"I truly don't think there's one there," she repeated. "What will you do if there isn't?"

"Well that's not my problem," he said, folding the map with small, precise gestures. "I've told Bandmaster, told him in front of half the horn section just this morning, and he paid me no mind. So we get there and no bridge? Well, that's his problem, not mine."

"You'll have to go back?" she asked.

"Likely. And wouldn't that make him look silly." The old man giggled into his hands in a childlike way, then harumphed himself into a more dignified expression. "If you don't find us on the shore, Mavin, you look for us across the great bay. Likely we'll be there, waiting for boats!"

Mavin had to be satisfied with this. She felt she could take twenty days or more and still meet them somewhere on the road, across the bay or this side of it, safe from shadows. Or so she told herself to comfort the cold sorrow with which she left them. Perhaps she would only bring Arkhur into his own shape and let him go east alone. Perhaps, she told herself, watching him shamble along behind the wagons, that solemn expression upon his face, as though he considered all the troubles of the world.

After the noon meal she left the Band, turning aside on a well traveled track as though such a destination had been intended from the beginning.When the Band had tootled itself away into the west, no more than a small cloud of dust upon the horizon, she stood upon the ancient pave and said, "Arkhur, come out." This time he was less hesitant, and he did remember himself – which somewhat increased her respect for Wizards, or at least for this one – so that their way east could begin immediately. Only Singlehorn stood behind them, crying into the west as though he could not bear the music to be gone. Mavin had to tug him smartly by the halter before he moved, and even then it was with his head down, his horn making worm trails of gloom in the dust.

"There is the one who saved you, Arkhur. We are not far enough from the shadows to restore him to his own shape, but his name," she whispered, "is Himaggery, and you may choose to remember it. You will want to return to your own demesne. There is probably little I could do to help you there, and since it is not our affair, we will go on south."

"It is not your affair," he agreed in a troubled voice, "if you are sure my brother has not your Face at the Lake of Faces, yours nor Himaggery's. I need not search the place to be sure he has mine!"

"He does have Himaggery's," she confessed. "Though he said it did not hurt those from whom he took them. No more than a pin prick, he said."

"No more than a pin prick at the time, no more than a year's life lost each time he questions the Face thereafter. He need only send evil Pantiquod or her daughter Foulitter, to question a Face some forty or fifty days running, and the life of even a youngish person would be gone. I am sure he questions my Face from time to time, to no purpose so long as I was in the Dervish's valley. What would it have said?"

The question had been rhetorical, but Mavin answered it. "It said the same as Himaggery's did; that you were under Bartelmy's Ban."

He thought deeply, hands covering his eyes as he concentrated upon this information. "Well, I think it likely that such an answer did not shorten my life nor Himaggery's. But my brother Dourso will not cease questioning. He may be there now, or tomorrow, asking of my Face. And when he hears I am no longer under – what was it you said? – Bartelmy's Ban, will he not strip me of what life I have left as soon as he may? And he will not neglect to take yours, Mavin, and Himaggery's as well. Do not ask me why, for I do not know, but it is no coincidence that all three of us came from Chamferton's aerie to the Shadow Tower." He gloomed over this, seeking a solution. "No. We must go quickly to the Lake of Faces, you as well as I, for either one of us alone might be unable to complete the task. Run as we may, are we not six days, eight days from the Lake of Faces? More perhaps?"

"You, perhaps," she said. "Not I." Even if she could not Shift, dare not Shift, for some reason only the Dervish understood, she could lengthen her legs and her stride. That was not truly Shifting. It was only a minor modification. "It is likely he has my Face as well. I slept deeply when I was there, too deeply, now I think of it. Perhaps he took my Face. . . "

"I think it probable, " Arkhur said. "More than probable. In my day I had a dozen Faces there, no more, all of them of evil men and women whose lives are a burden to the world. Even so, I questioned them seldom and only in great need. Not so my brother! I doubt not he has filled the Lake with them, and the forest as well." Seeing Mavin's expression, he nodded, confirmed in his belief. "Well then, we must move as quickly as we can. You must go there swiftly, Mavin. Take our masks down from the posts on which they hang and press them deep into the Lake. They will dissolve. Once gone, they are no danger."

"Can you run faster as a pombi?" she asked, wondering whether he would know.

"No faster than when I am not." he said, "except that I may run safer."

"Will you bring Singlehorn as quickly as you can? I can go faster without either of you. It will perhaps save a day or two – a year or two. . ."

The High Wizard Chamferton looked at her with serious eyes, and Mavin knew she could trust him with her own life or any other she could put in his keeping, to the limit of his ability. She nodded at him. "I will make a trail for you to follow. Watch for signs along the road." Then she spoke as the Dervish had done once more. "Go back, Arkhur."

She ran away to the east without looking behind her, lengthening her legs as she went. There were still no shadows near nor on the road. It stretched away east, straight and clear, edged by long, ordinary sun shadows from the west, seeming almost newly built in that light. She fled away, stride on stride leaving them behind, hearing the shuffle of pombi feet and the quick tap of Singlehorn hooves fade into the silence of the afternoon.

CHAPTER SIX

She had not gone far before discovering that it was one thing to run long distances when one could Shift into a runner – whether fustigar shape or some other long-legged thing – and quite another thing when one must run on one's own two legs, even when they were lengthened and strengthened a bit for the job. The road was hard and jarring. She stepped off it to run on the grassy verge, seeing the shadows lying under the trees, wondering if they were of that same evil breed she had seen around the tower, knowing they were only a flutter away from her if they chose to move. The fact that they did not made them no less horrible.

She fell into a rhythm of movement, a counting of strides, one hundred then a hundred more. It seemed to her that she felt weariness more quickly than she had done on other similar occasions. Was it age? Was it only having to run in her own shape? Was it the fact that she ran eastward toward the Harpies once more, toward that paralyzing fascination she had felt once and dreaded to feel again? Was it the presence of the shadows? Was it that other thing – whatever it was – which prevented her Shifting? And what was that other thing? A mystery. Inside herself or outside?

Eighty-five, eighty-six, eighty-seven . . .

It isn't the Dervish who speaks to me, telling me not to Shift, she told herself. Even though I hear that strange Dervishy humming all around, it isn't the Dervish. If the Dervish had known a reason I should not Shift, the Dervish would have said so, just as it said too many other things.

Besides, when she had pulled power there on the hillside above the shadowed tower the chill had attracted their attention, or it had seemed to do so. So it might be her own dream-mind telling her to be careful, telling her things her awake-mind was too busy to notice. Too busy to notice. As for example, how relieved she was to have left the Fon-beast behind. . . .

"That's not true!" she tried to tell herself. "That's nonsense."

The denial was not convincing. It was true; she was relieved to have left him behind. There was too much feeling connected with his presence, a kind of loving agony which pulled first one way then another, making her conscious of her body all the time. It was easier not to worry about that, easier to be one's own self for a time.

"Selfish," she admonished herself. "Selfish, just as Huld and Huldra were thinking only of themselves."

"Nonsense." Some internal monitor objected to this. "You have lived for thirty-five years on your own, mostly alone, not having to worry about another person every day, every hour. Thirty-five years sets habits in place, Mavin. It is only that this new responsibilty disturbs your sense of the usual, that's all."

But it was not all. If that had been all she could have left the Fon-beast at any time for any reason, and so long as he was cared for, she should have felt no guilt. If that had been all, it would not have mattered who cared for him. But as it was, she knew she would not leave the Fon-beast unless it were necessary to save his life. He was now her responsibility. Set into her care. Given to her. Foisted upon her. She could no more turn her back on that than she could have turned her back on Handbright's children. "But I did not agree to that," she said to herself in a pleading voice. "I did not agree to that at all."

Seventy-one, seventy-two, seventy-three . . .

"You agreed to meet him. Of such strange foistings are meetings made."

She did not know where these voices came from, familiar voices, sometimes older, sometimes younger than her own. They had always spoken to her at odd moments, calling her to account for her actions – usually when it was far too late to do anything about them. "Ghosts," she suggested to herself. "My mother's ghost? Ghost of all the Danderbat women, dead and gone." It was an unprofitable consideration which distracted her attention from covering the leagues east. She tried to think of something else, to concentrate upon counting her strides.

One hundred, and a hundred more, and a hundred more . . .

Responsibilty. Who had taught her the word? Handbright, of course. "Mavin, it is your responsiblity to take the plates down to the kitchen. Mavin, you are responsible for Mertyn. Don't let him out of your sight. Mavin, you must acquire a sense of responsibility. . ."

What was responsibility after all but a kind of foisting? Laying a burden on someone without considering whether that person could bear it or wanted to bear it. Dividing up the necessaries among the available hands to do it, though always exempting certain persons from any responsibility at all. Oh, that was true. Some were never told they must be responsible. Boy-children in Danderbat Keep, for example.

So it was some went through life doing as they chose without any responsibility or only with those responsibilities they chose for themselves. Others had it laid upon them at every turn. So Handbright had tried to lay responsibility upon Mavin, who had evaded it, run from it, denied it. She had not felt guilty about that in the past. Why then did she feel guilt because she relished being on her own again, away from the thin leather strap which tied her to the Fon-beast, linking her to him by a halter of protection and guidance, a determination to bring him to himself safely – one hoped – at last. And it was not really the Dervish who had laid it on her; she had it laid on herself – laid it on with that promise twenty years ago.

"Every promise is like that," she whispered to herself as she stopped counting strides for a moment. "Every promise has arms and legs and tentacles reaching off into other things and other places and other times, strange bumps and protrusions you don't see when you make the promise. Then you find you've taken up some great, lumpty thing you never knew existed until you see it for the first time in the light of morning." It was easier not to think of it.

Thirty-five, thirty-six, thirty-seven . . .

A great lumpty thing one never saw before. Not only ecstasy and joy and an occasional feeling of overpowering peace, but also guiding and protecting and watching and hoping, grieving and planning and seeing all one's plans go awry. "I did not agree to be tied to any great, demanding responsibility," she said, surprised at how clearly this came. "I don't want to be tied to it."

"Come now," said a commentator. "You don't know what it is yet. You think it's likely to be lumpty, but it might not be that bad. You haven't seen it. How would you know?"

"I know," said Mavin, scowling to herself. "Never mind how I know, I know."

"She knows," said the wind. "Silly girl," commented the trees. Her inner voices agreed with these comments and were silent.

She tried to estimate how far she might be from the Lake of Faces. Two days perhaps, or three. The Lake was a good way south of Chamferton's aerie, of course, and the road lay north. It was probable a great deal of distance could be saved if she could cut cross country southeast to intercept the canyons north of Pfarb Durim. Shadows lay beneath the trees to the southeast. Everywhere except on the road. Benign or malign. Both looked superficially the same until they moved, quivered, flew aloft in sucking flakes of gray. Better not tempt them. Run on.

Ninety-nine, one hundred, start over.

"You loved him as Fon-beast," her internal commentator suggested, as though continuing a long argument. "When you ran wild in the forest. Why do you disavow him now, at the end of a halter?"

"Because," she hissed, "I am tied to the other end of it! If he is tied, we are both tied. Now, voices, be still. Be done. I will think on it no more, care about it no more, worry it no more. I have leagues to run again tomorrow. I run to save my life and Himaggery's life and Arkhur's life, and there is no guilt in that, so be done and let me alone."

This exorcism, for whatever reason, seemed efficacious. She ran without further interruption to her concentration until darkness stopped her feet. She thought she would have no trouble sleeping then, though the stone was of a hardness which no blanket was adequate to soften. She would still sleep, no matter what, she thought, but that supposition was false. She lay half dozing, starting awake at every sound, realizing at last that she heard a Harpy scream in each random forest noise. When she realized that, she remembered also that she was traveling back toward the Lake of Faces, back toward the Harpy's own purlieus. It would be impossible to avoid them there. Impossibe to avoid those eyes, those mouths, those long, snaky necks. She fell at last into shuddering dream, in which she was pursued down an endless road, Harpy screams coming from behind her, and she afraid to turn and see how many and how near they were.

She woke to music, thinking for a time in half dream that the Band had come to chase the Harpies away, or had not gone on, or had come back for her.

"Now we sing the song of Mavin," a small voice sang. Actually, it sounded more like "Deedle, pootle, parumble lalala Mavin," but she knew well enough what it meant. In half dream she knew that voice as from a time long past when she had wandered the shadowmarches with the shadowpeople, hearing their song. Half awake, she identified it.

"Proom?" she called, sitting upright all in one motion. "Is that you?" only to have the breath driven out of her as something landed on her lap. Proom. Plus several other shadowpeople, their delighted faces beaming up into her own from between huge, winglike ears while others of their troop pranced and strutted around her.

"Proom, you haven't grown older at all." She was astonished at this, somehow expecting that he would have turned gray, or wrinkled, or fragile. Instead he was as wiry, sleek and hungry as she remembered him, already burrowing into her small pack to see what food she had to share. "There's nothing there, Proom. I'll have to go hunting. Or you will."

He understood this at once, rounding up half his troop with a few high-pitched *lalalas* and vanishing into the forest. She started to cry out a warning, then stopped. There were no shadows within sight. What had seemed ambiguous the day before was clear enough today. Where the shadowpeople had gone there were no shadows except the benign interplay of sun and shade.

A pinching made her gasp, and she looked down to find two of the shadowperson females with their huge ears pressed tight to her stomach. "I know I rumble," she commented, a little offended. "I'm hungry."

The two leapt to their feet, smiling, caroling, dancing into and out of her reach in a kind of minuet. "Obbla la dandle, tralala, lele, la," over and over, a kind of chant, echoed from the forest, "lele, la." They were back in a moment, one with ear pressed against her belly while the others paraded about miming vast bellies, sketching the dimensions of stomachs in the air. "Lele, la," making a great arc with their hands. "Lele, la."

She did not understand. Even when their miming became more explicit she did not understand. Only when Proom emerged from the trees to caress one of the females, gesturing a big belly and then pointing to the baby she carried, did Mavin understand. "No," she said, laughing. "You're mistaken."

"Lele, la," they insisted, vehemently. "Lala, obbla la dandle."

"Oh, by all the hundred devils," she thought. "Now what idea have they swallowed whole. I am not lele la, couldn't be. I haven't . . ."

"In the lovely valley," sang one of her internal voices, using the tune of a drinking song Mavin remembered from Danderbat Keep. "In the lovely valley, see the beasties run. . . ."

"That's not possible. Himaggery was a Singlehorn. I was a Singlehorn. I mean, he thought he was. I really was. Besides, I was only there a day or two. Or ten. Or . . . I don't know how long I was there. How could I know?"

"Lele, la," sang the shadowpeople, seeing her tears with great satisfaction. In their experience human people cried a lot over everything. It took the place of singing, which, poor things, most of them seemed unable to do. There was one group of humans who sang quite well – all males, back in a cliffy hollow west of Cagihiggy Creek. And there was a house of singers in the city of Leamer. Other than the people in those places, most humans just cried.

One of the females crawled into Mavin's lap and licked the tears off her cheek. "Lele, la," she affirmed. "Deedle, pootle, parumble, lalala Mavin."

She, Mavin, even while being sung of at great length and with considerable enthusiasm; she, Mavin, awaiting breakfast; she, Mavin, still disbelieving, stood up to look about her at the world. Some clue was there she had missed. She had been so focused on the shadows, she had not seen the purple lace of Healer's balm under the trees, the seedpods nodding where yellow bells of startle flower had bloomed twenty or thirty days before. So. It was not a matter of a day or two. The startle flower had carpeted the forest north of Chamferton's tower. Now it was gone to greenseed, the pods swelling already.

"It's not possible." She said this firmly, knowing it was a lie, trying to convince herself.

"Lele, la," sang the female shadowpeople, welcoming the males back from their foraging in the woods. They came out singing lustily themselves, bearing great fans of fungus, skin bags full of rainhat fruit, and the limp forms of a dozen furry or feathered creatures.

"Celebration," she said to herself in a dull voice of acceptance. "We're having a celebration."

Fires were lit. Mavin was encouraged by pulls and tugs to help prepare food; there was much noise and jollification until she laughed at last. This was evidently the signal they had waited for.

The shadowpeople cheered, danced, sang a new song, and came to hug Mavin as though she had been one of their children.

"Well, why not," she wept to herself, half laughing. "Why not. Except that I should not Shift for a time, it is no great burden. And perhaps a child will be company."

"Of course," soothed an internal voice. "Except that you should not Shift for a time." Which was what it had been saying all the while. So she had known it herself. With a Shifter's intimate knowledge of her own structure, how could she not have known it? Known it and refused to admit it.

And that was it, of course. Her protection, her Talent, her experience – all useless for a time. Singlehorn and Arkhur behind her, depending upon her to do a thing which would be easy for a Shifter but perhaps impossible for someone without that ability. Harpies before her, threatening her, quite capable of killing her. If not easy, it would have been at least possible to defeat them so long as she could Shift. And now . . . now!

If Shifting were simply impossible, the matter would be simpler. If she couldn't do it, then she couldn't – there would be no decisions to make, no guilty concerns about choices that should have been made the other way. She would live or die according to what was possible. But the ability to Shift was still there. If she abstained it was only that an internal voice had told her to abstain – in order to protect what lay within. Old taboos, childhood prohibitions, little brother Mertyn's voice coming back to her out of time, "Girls aren't supposed to, Mavin. They say it messes up their insides. . . ."

Was that true? Who knew for sure? And how did they know? So now, Mavin, believe in the old proscriptions and you will not Shift until this child is born. So now, Mavin, do not Shift and it may be you cannot accomplish what you have set out to do, in which case Himaggery could suffer, even die because of it. Protect the one, lose the other.

"I did not want this lumpty thing all full of hard choices," she cried, tears running down her face. "I did not want it,"

"Lele, la," sang the shadowpeople, happy for her.

When the food was cooked, they ate it. The shadowpeople preferred cooked food, though they would eat anything at all, she suspected, including old shoes if nothing else were available. They licked juice from their chins and munched on mushroom squares toasted above the fires, nibbling rainhat berries in between with dollops of stewed fern.When they had done, with every bone chewed twice, they sat across the ashes, stomachs bulging, and looked expectantly at her. This was Mavin Manyshaped of whom a song had been made, and they would not leave her unless they determined that nothing interesting was likely to happen. There were babies present who had never seen her before, this Mavin who had been to Ganver's Grave, who had saved the people from the pits of Blourbast. So they sat, watching her with glowing eyes, waiting for her to do something of interest.

At last, in a bleak frame of mind which simply set all doubts aside for the time, she stood up, brushed herself off, and waited while they packed up their few bits and pieces; a pot, a knife, a coil of thin rope, the babies clutching tight to their neck fur. Then she went to the side of the road and built a cairn there with a branch run through its top to point a direction. All the shadowpeople understood this. She was leaving a sign for someone who followed. They chattered happily at this opening gambit, then went after her as she ran off the road toward the southeast, shadows or no shadows. She thought it likely the particular shadows she most feared did not come near the shadowpeople. Perhaps the shadowpeople were immune. Perhaps, like the people of the marching Band, they created an aura which shut such shadows out. For whatever reason, she believed herself safe while with them and chose to use that time in covering the shortest route possible.

The hearty breakfast made her legs less weary, the day less gray than before. The members of the troop gathered foods as they ran close about her, the little ones darting ahead to leap out at them from behind trees or dangle at them from vines broken loose from the arching tres. Mavin stopped from time to time to leave sign along their way, though a blind man could have tracked them by the plucked flowers and the dangling vines. A warm wind came out of the south, carrying scents of grass so strong she might have been running beside mowers in a haymeadow. "Diddle, dandle, lally," the people sang, skipping from side to side. One who had not heard their songs translated might think them simple, perhaps childish. Mavin knew better. Childlike, yes. But never simple. Their tonal language concealed multiple meanings in a few sounds; their capacity for song carried histories in each small creature's head.

"Diddle, dandle, lally," they sang, and Mavin made up a translation, wishing the translator-beast, Agirul, were present to confirm it. "I sing joy and running in the bright day, glory in the sun, happiness among my people." She would have wagered a large sum that it was something like that. "I sing babies playing hide and seek in the vines."

This was a good song to run by, and it kept her mind away from her destination. Away from Harpies. The shadowpeople were an excellent distraction and she blessed them as she ran, thanking their own gods for them. It was hard to be really afraid among them, for they faced fear with a belligerent, contagious courage.

When they rested at noon, she acted a play for them, showing herself sleeping first, then acting the part of one who came and stole her face, taking it away, placing it upon a high pole. When she had acted it twice, one of the people began to chatter, dancing up and down, gesturing at the trees, climbing one to a point above her head, hanging there as he mimed a face hanging there, touching the eyes, then his eyes, nose, then his nose, the mouth, then his own, showing them what hung upon the tree. At this they all fell into discussion some pointing eastward of the way they ran, others to the south, waving their arms in violent disagreement. When it was obvious they could not agree, Proom spoke sharply, almost unmusically, and a young one climbed the nearest tall tree to sing from the top of it toward the south and east. After a time, they heard a response, a high, faint warble like distant birdsong. Time passed. The people did not seem distressed or hurried. More time passed. Then, when the sun stood well after noon and Mavin was beginning to fidget, the high, faint birdsong came again, and the shadowman above them warbled his response before plunging down among the branches. He gestured the direction and all of them pounded into movement again, this time guided by infrequent calls which seemed to emanate from distant lines of hill.

Somewhere, Mavin told herself, there are shadowpeople who know the Lake of Faces – perhaps even now they are near there. So the call goes out and is relayed across the forests until someone responds, and then that response is relayed back again. Song-guided, we go toward a place we cannot see. So they went until evening fell and the shade of the trees drew about them. Once more the fire, the foraging, the songs, the laughter. Once more lele-la, and choruses of joy. "I am unworthy of the great honour you do me," said Mavin, bowing until they fell over one another in their amusement. "I am deeply touched."

In the night she dreamed once more, starting upright in the darkness with a muffled scream. In dream the Harpies had laid their talons upon her, she had felt their teeth. The dark around her bubbled with small cries of concern, small soothing songs. Poor lele-la, they sang. She is not used to it yet. After a time, the songs became a lullaby and she slept.

When morning came, they could hear the guiding calls more clearly, this time with something of warning in them. Proom pulled at Mavin's leg, asking to be taken up on her shoulders as he had ridden in the past. At first she thought he was weary of the long run, then she realized he wished to gain height in order to see better what lay before them. Two of the shadowmen ran far ahead this day, darting back from time to time. As noon grew near, they came back from their scouting with a rush of whispered words, and all the troop then went forward at a creep, silent through the brush, seeing light before them at the forest's edge. It was not only the edge of the trees, but also the edge of the land where it fell away in steep cliffs down which streams trickled in a constant thin melody.

She had not seen it from this angle before, but when she looked down, screening her face behind a small bush, Mavin knew where she was. The Lake of Faces lay immediately below them. Had she been able to Shift, she could have swarmed down the cliff and finished her business within the hour. Had she been able to Shift – had the place been untenanted.

It was not only occupied but guarded. At the edge of the trees below were high, square tents of crimson stuff, main poles poking through their scalloped roofs like raised spears. From these poles limp pennants flapped, the device upon them raising old memories in Mavin. She had seen that Game symbol before. It had been blazoned on the cloak and breastplate worn by Valdon Duymit long ago in Pfarb Durim. So. The Demesne of the High King in the person of his thalan-son, Valdon.

Aside from these tents and the armsmen lounging outside them, there were other occupants of the place. She shuddered, sank her teeth into her arm and bit down to keep from crying out. They were there, like giant storks, their white breasts flapping as they walked among the faces, their heads thrown back in crowing laughter so that she seemed to look down their throats, their endless, voracious throats. And he whom she had called the High Wizard Chamferton, strolling there without a sorrow in the world. Mavin stopped biting herself with a deep gulping sigh. She had hoped it would be easy; she had hoped it would be *possible*. Now what?

She rolled away from the rim of the cliff into the mossy cover of the trees, the shadowpeople following her, silent as their name.

CHAPTER SEVEN

When she had recovered a little, the first thing which came into her head was that she wished to hear what Valdon and the false Chamferton – what had his brother called him? Dourso? – what those two would talk of. The fact they were here together said much: much but not enough. There was Game afoot, Game awing, Game doing something and going somewhere. Shifty Mavin was angered enough by that to ignore all the lumpty responsibilities and hard choices in an instantaneous retreat to a former self. "I need to get where I can hear them," she growled to the shadowpeople, adding to herself – purely as an afterthought – "Without being seen by the Harpies. And without Shifting."

Proom seemed to understand this well enough, even without an Agirul translator present or a lengthy mime session. Perhaps spying out the ground was a routine first step prior to any interesting thing – a bit of sneaking and slying to learn what was going on. At any rate, he fell into discussion with his fellows, much whispered trilling and lalala, hands waving and eyebrows wriggling, ears spread then cocked then drooped, as expressive as faces. Several of them ran off in various directions, returning to carry on further conversation before inviting her in the nicest way to accompany them. She was not reluctant to go, though doubtful they had found any suitable way down those precipitous cliffs, and was thus surprised to find almost a stair of tumbled stone leading down behind one of the falls. The bottom of it was screened behind a huge wet boulder, and this way led to a scrambly warren among the stones and scattered trees at the foot of the cliffs which emerged at last within two strides of Valdon's tent, the whole way well hidden.

Proom had his neck hair up and his ears high, both expressing self-satisfaction, so she bowed to him, then he to her, then both together, trying not to make a sound, at which all the others rolled on the ground with their hands clamped over their mouths.There was nothing funny in the situation but she relished their amusement. They lay beneath the stone together, waiting for dark. Mavin could hear the Harpies screeching away at the far edge of the lake. They were a good distance away and she could relax enough to plan.

Tomorrow the pombi should reach them, the pombi and Singlehorn. She hoped it would be sooner rather than later, the help of the Wizard being much desired. If she had been able to Shift, she told herself, she would have crept into Valdon's tent at once, strangled him, then swumbled up his men at arms. Then . . . then she would have laid some kind of nasty trap for the Harpies. Yes. Something clever, so that she would not have to touch them. After which the Faces could have been taken care of with simple dispatch. As it was . . . well, as it was she would have to think about it.

Just as dark was beginning to fall, there was a clucking Harpy chatter from the shore of the lake, and the false Chamferton came strolling along the water to be greeted by one of Valdon's men. He disappeared into the nearest tent. The Harpies who had followed him scratched among the poles, pausing now and then to caw insults at the silent Faces. Foulitter carried the wand in its case upon her back. Soon they went back the way they had come, disappearing among the white poles in the dusk. Mavin unclenched her teeth and wriggled from behind the stones, barely aware of the shadowpeople who followed, each mimicking her movements as though they reflected her in a mirror. When she reached the back of the tent she lay still, head resting upon her arms as she strained to hear whatever was said inside.

The false Chamferton was speaking. "Two days ago . . . knew something had happened . . . should have at the time . . ."

"You should have done many things at the time!"

Valdon's voice was raised, easy to hear, stirring memories in her of a long ago time. He sounded no less arrogant now than he had done twenty years before.

"Had you the wits the gods gave bunwits, you would have done many things differently. Eight years ago you engaged upon this elaborate scheme concerning your brother, the Wizard Chamferton. Why did you not merely kill him? Dead is dead, and it is unlikely a Necromancer would seek him out among the departed. But no. You must do this painstaking stupidity, this business of drugging him and having him dropped by Harpies. Why?''

''Because it could have been to our advantage, Prince Valdon. I set him where he could observe the shadow and the tower, the tower and the bell. I kept his Face here to answer my questions. So we might have learned much of mystery and wonder. . . .''

''Dourso, you're a dolt! Mystery is for old men teaching in schools because they have no blood left to do otherwise. Wonder is for girls and pawns. But power and Game – that is for men. Save me from puling Invigilators who seek to outplay their betters. . . .''

''You are in my demesne, Prince.'' The voice was a snarled threat. ''Shouldn't you mind your tongue.''

''I am in my own demesne wherever I go, Dourso. You ate my bread and took my coin for decades among the least of my servants. Oh, it's true you had some small skill in treachery. Nothing has changed. You have had possession of a tower for a few years. You have learned a few tricks for a time. Do not overestimate the importance of these trifling things.''

''I have them at your instigation,'' Dourso hissed again. ''Let us say at your command. It was you bid me come here and rid the land of the High Wizard Chamferton, taking his place in order that Valdon, King Prionde's son, might have an ally to the north.''

''Well, and if I did? I said rid the land, not encumber it further with enchantments and bother. Let be. What is the situation now?''

''It is no different than it was an hour ago, or a day ago. When I drugged my brother – half brother, and on the father side, which makes it no kind of treachery – I had my Harpies drop him in the valley where the Shadow Tower is. None can come near that place without being shadow-eaten, so it seemed safe enough. . . .''

''Seemed,'' snorted Valdon in a barely audible voice.

''Seemed safe enough,'' repeated Dourso. ''I took his Face before he was drugged, but I never questioned it. There was no need to question the Face. I knew where he was. The Harpies swore to it under pain of my displeasure. That same year came the Wizard Himaggery in search of Chamferton, as you had said he would.''

''In pursuit of an old tale I had taken some pains to see he learned of. His eccentricities were well recognized among more normal Gamesmen. It was not difficult.''

"Well, so he came, bringing with him two old dames from Betand. I fed him the stories we had agreed upon, all of which are true enough, and he went off in pursuit of the runners and the tower. I took his Face before he left, also – though he did not know it – and the Face of one of the old dames as well. She was so far gone that the taking killed her, so it is as well he did not know of that either."

"So Himaggery came and went, and after a time . . ."

"After a time, not long after he left, his Face began to answer that it was under Bartelmy's Ban. Then I thought to question the Face of my brother, and so spoke the Face of Chamferton also. Thus I knew one fate had taken them both. So, I said to myself, Himaggery and Chamferton have both been shadow-eaten, and my friend and ally, Valdon, will be mightily pleased. As you were, my Prince. As you were. It is not long since you feasted in my tower and told me so."

"As I might have remained," sneered Valdon, "if he had not returned from the shadow gullet after eight years like one vomited up out of the belly of death."

There was a pause. Mavin could almost see Dourso's shrug. "It was that Mavin, I suppose. You told me years ago she would probably follow Himaggery."

"As I thought she would eventually. Long and long ago she promised to meet him. My brother Boldery told me of it, full of romantic sighs and yearnings – the young fool. And with her gone there would have been only two left upon my vengeance list – her younger brother, Mertyn, and the old fool, Windlow, at the school in Tarnoch."

"Why such enmity? If her brother is much younger than her, he must have been a child at the time. Was it not at the time of the plague in Pfarb Durim? Twenty years ago?"

"Child or not, Mertyn is on the list. Senile fool or not, Windlow is there as well. Woman or not, Mavin shares their fate. What care I what they may have been. They offended me. They did me an injury. If it had not been for Himaggery, and Windlow, and Mavin and her brother, Pfarb Durim would have fallen into the hands of my friend, and thence at least partly into mine. So my friend tells me. And if I had the wealth of Pfarb Durim in my hands, I would not be grodgeling now about the northern lands in search of allies."

There was a long strained silence. After a time, the false Chamferton spoke again. "Well, so, Mavin came as you know, interrupting your own visit to me. And I did the same with her, feigning friendship and helpfulness, giving her bits and pieces of the story, telling her at the last about the runners. And I took her Face as I had the others and sent her off."

"But she did not die, and the others returned from the dead." Prince Valdon spat the words, working himself up into a fury.

"Which is impossible." Dourso was vehement. "No one returns from the tower. It holds fifty generations of questing heroes sleeping the shadow sleep at its gates."

"What is it, this tower?"

Again, Mavin could extrapolate the shrug from the expressive silence. "Something old, from the time before men came to these parts. Something to do with the Eesties. You say you do not care for such things. Well then, it doesn't matter what it is. It is easy enough to stay away from."

"And to get away from, seemingly. At least your brother and Himaggery and Mavin seem to have done so."

"We don't know that. We know only that when Chamferton's Face was questioned yesterday, it did not speak of the Ban as it has spoken in the past. It said other garbled things, speaking of pombis and music. And when Mavin's Face was asked, it, too, spoke of beasts and music. Only Himaggery's face said what it has said for years, that it is under Bartelmy's Ban."

"So it may be they have only exchanged one death for another?" Valdon asked, rather more eagerly than Mavin thought mannerly. "Then they may yet be dead, or as good as."

"I consider it likely. My Harpies consider it probable. They have been full of celebratory laughter all afternoon. I think you have little to concern you, Prince Valdon. Still, we will let tomorrow come and question the Faces once again."

"You will wait until tomorrow comes and question them, yes," Valdon grated in a harsh, imperious voice. "And the day after that, and the day after that, until you have used up whatever lives they might have left in the answering, Dourso. There are more ways to plant a hedge of thrilps than by poking the dirt with your nose, and your maybe this, maybe not approach has not proved satisfactory."

"As my Prince commands," said the other, conveying more ironic acquiescence than obedience. "I had intended to do so in any case."

Well, thought Mavin, squirming back from the tent into the gloom of the rocks. Isn't he a carrier of long grudges. Twenty years of vengeful thought over a few boyish disagreements. "And a lost city," reminded an internal voice. "At least part of one."

She looked over the area. Dark had come with a sliver of moon, enough light to find a Face, perhaps. She thought she could remember where Himaggery's had been, on the far shore of the lake, about halfway between the water and the trees, roughly in line with a great boulder. Where might her own Face be? Somewhere in that forest, hard to see in the dim.

A soft touch on her shoulder turned her. Proom, reaching out to touch her face, then gesturing away to the poles. Touching her face once more, gesturing away, that questioning gesture. She nodded in great chin-wagging agreement and reached up behind her ears as though she untied something there. She moved her hands forward as though she stripped a mask away, then pointed at the mimed mask and said, "Mavin's." She indicated the poles, then gestured to Proom and his fellows as she raised her eyebrows. Could they find her Face? Could they get her Face? There was colloquy among them while she thought further.

Proom had seen Himaggery once, on the side of a hill above Hell's Maw. She reached out to him, went through the dumb show once more, this time naming the mask, "Himaggery's." He cocked his head, thinking. She did it again. "Himaggery's."

Aha. His face lighted up, and he turned to his troop with a lilting quaver of words. "Maggeries, gerries, ees, ees." Proom was becoming Himaggery, miming him, walking with a graceful stride, chin tilted a little in diffidence, face drawn down in a serious expression. For someone only knee high, he looked remarkably like her memory of the tall Wizard. Mavin tittered, smothering the sound, but it had been enough to set them off. In the instant Proom had a parade of Himaggeries, winding their way among the stones. Mavin lay back against a narrow mossy strip between the rocks, weary beyond belief. So. Perhaps they could find her Face, hers and Himaggery's. She would have to look for Chamferton's Face herself. There was no way to describe him to Proom.

The moon sank toward the west. Night birds called from the cliff tops and were echoed from the river bottom. One of the Harpies screamed in the forest, a quavering screech that brought Mavin upright in terror, making her head ache. She pressed her head between her hands, but the pain only worsened, two sharp, horrible stabbings around her ears, as though two knives were inserted there. Just when she thought she could bear it no longer, that she must scream, the pain weakened, became merely sore, throbbing rather than agonizing. Trembling, she dipped a handkershief in the trickling fall and bathed her face and eyes. Tears spilled onto her cheeks. She was reluctant to move her head. Pressing the cold, wet cloth around her ears helped a little. She brought it away red with blood.

She was still staring stupidly at the stains when Proom wriggled back through the rocks, holding a thing at arm's distance from him, his lips drawn back in an expression of distaste and fear. He let it fall at her knees, and she recoiled as her own face looked blindly up at her, ragged holes chewed at ear level. Proom had gnawed the strap away which held it to the post. His lips were red, and he bathed them in the stream with much spitting and wiping. When Mavin showed him the wounds at her ears, he recoiled in mixed dismay and horror.

The mask was paper light, like the shed skin of a serpent, fluttering in the light evening air with a kind of quasi life. She held it under the falls, feeling it squirm weakly beneath her hands, suddenly slick as frogskin and as cold. It became a slimy jelly in her hands, then began to dwindle in the cold water, becoming totally transparent before it dissolved and washed away. As it did so, the pain in her head almost disappeared though a quick touch verified that the wounds remained.

Another of the shadowpeople squirmed through the stones bearing a mask. Yes. Himaggery's. Ragged about the upper face as her own had been.

"Gamelords," she cursed to herself. "Did it hurt him as it hurt me?" Knowing even as she said it that it would, that it already had. "He will not understand," she whispered. "Oh, Chamferton, pray you have tight hold upon him!"

Once more she held a mask in the flowing water, feeling the foul sliminess of it soften into jelly before it vanished. The shadowpeople observed this closely as they talked it over among themselves, and

Mavin knew that they were resolving to steal others of the Faces now that they knew what to do with them. Not now, though. Now was time for sleep. She had not the energy to do more tonight.

They climbed the stones beind the falls and found a softer bed among the trees. There was no fire tonight, but she lay pillowed and warmed among a score of small bodies, sleeping more soundly than she had upon the Ancient Road.

She was wakened by a startled vacancy around her, a keening cry of panic which dwindled at once into shushed quiet. There was hot breath on her face. The pombi face which stared down into her own had a broken strap in its mouth and an expression of sad determination in its eyes. She struggled out of dream, trying to remember the words of exhortation.

"Come out, Arkhur," she said at last, still struggling to get her eyes fully open. The pombi shape shifted, lifted to its hind feet, solidified into the figure of Chamferton, the strap still in his mouth.

He spat it out. "I lost him. Last night, not far from here. He screamed as though he were wounded, and then dashed away into the trees. The strap broke. I thought of going after him, but it was too dark to trail him and I knew you might need me here."

The first thought she had was that she should feel relieved. She had wanted to be away from the Fon-beast – wanted not to be responsible for him. Now he had gone, and the matter was settled. Except, of course, that it was not. Her eyes filled with tears which spilled to run in messy rivulets down her face, puffy from sleep.

"He ran because he was wounded when one of the shadowpeople chewed his mask from the pole. I didn't know that's what would happen, but it did to me as well." She lifted her hair from the sides of her face to show him. "The masks are spiked to the poles, and the little people couldn't pull out the spikes, so they chewed the masks off. We'll have to find him, Chamferton, but it must wait a little. There is Game here against you and Himaggery and me. You were right that we need you here."

She led him to the cliff's edge. They lay there, peering down at the encampment, and Proom's people, puzzled but reassured by the pombi's disappearance, came to lie beside them, waiting for whatever came next. "I don't know how many times they've questioned your Face in the past, Wizard, but they intend to question it every day from now on. More often if they can."

"They can't," he said flatly. "And I doubt if any of the questioning done while I was in the valley will deprive me of life. I feel stronger than when I last saw this place, the strength of anger, perhaps, but nonetheless useful. Now what is to be done?" He began to list. "First – to get my own Face down from that obscene array. Second – to eliminate one Dourso, and his allies if necessary. Third – to find Singlehorn. Can you think of anything else?"

"Harpies," said Maviin. "I have some cause to think they are dangerous. Pantiquod brought plague to Pfarb Durim, many years ago. Her daughter Foulitter tried to kimm me when I was here last. And Pantiquod has threatened me."

"Harpies," he said, as though adding this item to his list. "The first thing I need is my wand. We have no strength to oppose Valdon and his men until I have the wand. Dourso has probably hidden it somewhere in the fortress."

"He has given it into the keeping of Foulitter," she said. "Look beyond the largest pile of stones, against the trees. See where she struts about there. Look on her back when she turns. See! That is the wand. He gave it to her so that she might question certain of the Faces. I caught them at it when I came here first."

"The fool! To set such a thing in a Harpy's hands. They would as soon turn on him as obey him!"

"He has some hold on one of them," Mavin said. "Pantiquod flies free but her daughter's in some kind of durance. He told me he would hold her for some time yet."

"Still a fool. He learned a few words, a few gestures, and fancied himself a Wizard. What he learned was only thaumaturgy, gramarye. Children's things. Well, even children's toys may be dangerous in the hands of a fool, so we must go careful and sly. I need that wand."

Mavin forced herself to move. She wanted nothing to do with the Harpies, but something had to be done. She made a long arm to touch Proom and tug him toward her, pointed at the Harpy, moving back from the cliff edge to mime the storklike walk, the bobbing neck, the head thrown back in cackling laughter. The shadowpeople took this up with great enthusiasm, becoming a flock of birdlike creatures almost instantaneously. She pointed out the wand, then pretended to have one such on her own back, removing and replacing it. Finally, she led them off through the trees. Chamferton had time to grow bored with the view below him before she returned.

"Come on," she said. "We need simple muscle, and all of it we can get. The shadowpeople will lead her into a kind of trap, but they are not big enough to hold her."

The plan had the virtue of simplicity. If the Harpy were typical of her kind, she would pursue any small creature with the temerity to attack her, which Proom or one of his people would do. They would flee away, and the Harpy would follow.

"They'll try to get her when she's alone, not with Pantiquod. It seems the shadowpeople aren't particularly afraid of them one at a time, but they don't want to tangle with two or more. At least that's what I think all their lalala-ing was about. Proom is down there behind the biggest pile of stones. The others are scattered in a long line leading to that rockfall. The tricky part will be at that point. The shadowman will drop down into the rocks. Then another one will show himself halfway up the slope, then another one at the top. If they time it right, it should seem to be one small person the whole time. She can't walk up that slope, but if she's angry enough, she should fly to the top, at which point they'll lead her between these two trees. Then it's up to us, Wizard. Proom left us a knife, and some rope. . . ." She said nothing about her nausea, her revulsion.

"Rope if we can," hissed Chamferton. "I've a use for her alive. But knife if she starts to scream."

Mavin nodded her agreement. From their hiding place they could see between leafy branches to the valley floor. Mavin sharpened her eyes, not really Shifting, merely modifying herself a little, to catch a glimpse of Proom – she thought it was Proom – perched near the edge of the stones. The Harpy was prodding at some bit of nastiness on the ground nearby. Pantiquod had wandered toward the tents. There was a scurrying darkness, a darting motion, and the Harpy leaped into the air like some dancing krylobos, screeching, head whipping about. Proom had bitten her on the leg. Mavin could see the blood. A palpable bite, a properly painful bite but not one which would cripple the creature.

No! Not cripple indeed. She strode toward the stones, head darting forward like the strike of a serpent, jaws clacking shut with a metallic finality. On the cliff top, they gasped; but she had missed. A small furry form broke from cover and fled toward the cliff. The Harpy crowed a challenge and sped after it.

The shadowman fled, darted, dropped into hiding. From another hidey hole not far away, another form popped up and fled farther toward the cliffs. The Harpy strode, hopped, struck with her teeth at the stones, hurting herself in the process so that her anger increased.

"Watch now," hissed Mavin. "They're coming to the cliff."

The quarry disappeared into a cleft between two large stones wet with spray. The Harpy thrust her head into the cleft, withdrew it just in time to see her prey appear briefly halfway up the slope, fleeing upward. It turned to jeer at her, increasing the Harpy's frenzy. She danced, clacked her jaws, spread her wings to rise in a cloud of spray and dust. The quarry on the slope disappeared, only to reappear at the top of the cliff.

"Get your head down," Mavin directed.

They could hear Foulitter's approach, the whip of wings and the jaws chattering in rage. A furry shadow fled between the trees, and the Harpy came after. As she passed between the trunks, Mavin and Chamferton seized her, Mavin holding tight to the wings as she tried to avoid those venomous teeth – without success! The serpent neck struck at her, and the teeth closed on her hand. Fire ran through her, as though she had been touched by acid or true flame, and she cursed as she slammed the striking head away. Chamferton thrust a wad of cloth between the teeth and threw a loop of rope about her feet which he then wound tight around the wings. When he had done, they stepped back breathlessly. The Harpy glared at them with mad yellow eyes, threatening them with every breath.

"She will kill us if she can," said Mavin, gasping, cradling her hand; it felt as though it was burned to the bone.

"She would," agreed Chamferton. "If she could." He took the wand from its case, drawing it from among the coils of rope. "If you watch me now, you must promise never to . . ."

"Oh, Harpy-shit, Wizard! Oath me no oaths. I've seen more in your demesne recently than you have. I am no chatterbird and you owe me your life. So do what you do and don't be ponderous about it."

"Did she bite you?"

"Yes, damn it, she did." Mavin stared at him stupidly. "How did you know?"

"Because you suddenly sounded Harpy bit. We'll take care of it before you leave – must take care of it, or you'll die. Harpy bite is deadly, Mavin. But you're right. I have no business demanding secrecy oaths from one who has saved my life. So go or stay as you like."

She was curious enough to stay, not that she learned anything. She could not concentrate because of the pain in her hand, now moving up her arm. All she saw was waving of the wand, and walking about in strange patterns, and speaking to the world's corners and up and down, and sprinkling dust and sprinkling water, at the end of which time he removed the rag from the Harpy's mouth and turned her loose. "You are my servant," he told her in a voice of distaste. "My unworthy servant. Now you will serve me by giving me the name of one of those you have questioned down below – the name of any one."

The Harpy answered in a toneless voice without pause, "I have questioned Rose-love of Betand."

"Very well," said Chamferton. "When you next hear the words 'Rose-love of Betand,' your servitude is over and you have my leave to die. Do you understand?"

The Harpy nodded, its pale, pendulous breasts heaving. "When I hear the words 'Rose-love of Betand,' I have your leave to die."

"And you will die then," said Chamferton. "Quickly and without pain."

"And I will die then," agreed the Harpy. "Quickly and without pain."

Chamferton turned away from the empty-faced creature. "The first thing I must do is obtain my own Face." Turning to the Harpy, "Go to my Face, Foulitter. Pull the silver spike which holds it to the pole, gently, with your teeth. Bring the Face to me here."

Without a sound the Harpy walked away to the cliff's edge and dropped from there on quiet wings to the regiment of pale poles on which the Faces hung. To Mavin, accustomed to the constant cluck and keraw of the Harpies, this quiet evoked more foreboding than sound might have done.

"Is she completely at your command?" Somehow she still doubted this.

"Completely. Though nothing would have put her completely at my command unless she had attempted to injure me first – or had succeeded. There is a rule of Wizardry called the Exception of Innocence. We are not allowed to bind the will of one who has never done us ill or attempted it. It is somewhat inconvenient at times.''

''I can imagine it would be,'' she rasped, glad she had done the High Wizard Chamferton only good. ''And what of those who have actually helped you, aided you?''

''No true Wizard would be so unmannerly as to enchant one such,'' he replied with a smile. It was an ominous smile, for all his appearance of grave, childlike stubbornness. Still, she took it as sufficient encouragement to ask a further question.

''You said something earlier about Dourso having learned only thaumaturgy, gramarye – children's things. Does that mean such things are not the Talent of Wizards?''

''Such things are not. Such things are mere tricks, like the Faces. They are dependent upon a particular place, perhaps a particular time. Did Dourso tell you about the lake? About the nexus here? Blame my stupidity that I bragged to him about it, crowing at my discovery. The crux of the thaumaturgy lies with the lake, with the forces around it. I chose my demesne because of the forces which are here, not the other way around. Away from this place I am no more or less Wizardly than any of my colleagues. Only this place – and that arrogant aerie built halfway to the clouds – gives me the name 'High Wizard'.''

''How did you ever learn to . . . to do things. Make the faces. Or bind Harpies. Or whatever?'' It was hard to think through the pain in her arm, but she doubted that Chamferton would often be so patient with questions.

''I have speculated about that,'' he mused. ''It is my theory that the forces of the place desire expression. That they, themselves, are my tutors, suggesting to my dream-mind what I should try or do.'' He gave her another of those quick, ominous looks. ''You have said you are no chatterbird, Mavin, and I rely upon that. I do not want half the world of the True Game camped upon my steps, attempting to learn what I have learned, or – worse – finding out and using it to make more pain and tragedy in this world.''

She returned him an enigmatic smile. She had already given him her word; it was not necessary to give it again. Besides, the sound of wings returning drew their eyes to the cliff edge where Foulitter now perched, her teeth broken and bloody around the silver spike and limp Face she carried. Arkhur took it without a word, carrying it to the stream where he pressed it deep into the chill water to let it dissolve, shuddering slightly as he did so.

"I think the shadowpeople intend to remove more of them," Mavin remarked, more to break the silence than for any other reason.

"It won't be necessary,' he growled with sudden determination, shuddering again at the feel of the slimy tissue under his fingers. "There will not be any left after today. I have decided that because a thing can be done is not always reason enough to do it." He rose from the stream, face pale, a small muscle at the corner of his eye twitching again and again. "Do you have any idea whose Faces he has taken down there? Dare I hope they are mostly villains? Gamesmen Ghouls, perhaps? What of that one the Harpy named? Rose-love of Betand?"

Mavin shook her head, almost sorry to tell him the truth. "I think it unlikely they are Ghouls and villains, Wizard. Rose-love is one of the old women Himaggery brought from Betand, a story- teller. I overhead Dourso say he had taken her Face and killed her doing it. Her sister still lives at the aerie – or did when I was there half a season ago. She, too, is full of old tales. Neither of them were Gameswomen. They were merely . . . people."

"So Dourso has taken Faces from peaceful folk, pawns, perhaps even goodly Gamesmen, Healers and the like?"

"I would not doubt it," she agreed.

"And some of them have lost life, perhaps much life. Some, like old Rose-love, may have lost all life. Whatever is done must seek to set that right. Certainly whatever is done must not put them at further risk. Ah well. I have my wand. I can do what must be done. However, there is a counter spell, and it may be that Dourso has learned it. His understanding is not great, but his sense of power and treachery are unfailing. If he has learned it, then the Faces would be caught between my power and his, possibly injured or destroyed, and their owners would suffer even more."

"But you have the wand!"

"The counter spell would not require a wand though perhaps he does not know it. Would you risk that?"

Mavin thought of the Faces as she had seen them first in moonlight, unconscious, taken from who knew what persons abroad in the world. "No," she admitted. "I wouldn't risk hurting them any more. Not if there were some other way."

"We will think of some other way. Perhaps we can lure Dourso away from here, back to the aerie, leaving me here alone for a short time . . . . Yes. Back to the aerie with Valdon. Hmmm. Let me think on that."

He strode away toward the cliff top, ignoring the Harpy half crouched there, her nipples almost brushing the ground. The Harpy's face was not unlike those on the poles, blind and unaware, yet full of some enormous potential which was almost palpable. In this case, the potential was for evil, thought Mavin, turning her back on the creature, trying not to vomit at the sight of her. Her arm throbbed and she was full of pain and hunger and annoyance. Waiting on another to take action was foreign to her nature, and she fought down her irritation. She should be away from here, searching for Himaggery.

"Searching for Himaggery," she snarled. "I have done nothing else since first arriving at Pfarb Durim."

A tug at her leg made her look down into Proom's face, wrinkled with concern. Was she sick, unhappy, miserable? Poor Mavin. What would Mavin do now?

"I'm hungry," she announced, rubbing her stomach and miming eating motions. "Let's have breakfast."

He was immediately ready for a feast, slipping away full of song to summon the others. It was not long before they had a fire going, hidden behind piled stones, with chunks of mushroom broiling. Someone had brought in a dozen large, speckled eggs. Surprisingly they were fresh, probably purloined from some farmyard. When the High Wizard finished his solitary walk and sought them out, they were fully engaged in breakfast with little enough left for him.

"I have a plan," he said.

Mavin nodded, her mouth full. She would listen, the nod said, but she didn't feel it necessary to stop chewing.

"You will go to the aerie," he said, ticking this point off on one palm with a bony finger. "Seek the Healer. Tell the ones there you have been Harpy bit, need Healing, and have a message for the High Wizard Chamferton – his demesne is threatened from the north. That should get their attention. Someone there will know where the supposed High Wizard is. Insist that a message be sent immediately. Can you ride horseback?"

The question seemed a meaningless interpolation, and it took her a moment to respond. "After a fashion. Why?"

"There is a farm a little east of here where you can borrow an animal in my name. Ride hard as you can to get to the aerie by early afternoon. They will send a messenger back here – to my loving brother, Dourso – that messenger arriving by evening. If the message is properly portentous, Dourso will leave here at once for the aerie, arriving there about midnight. It may be Valdon will go as well, but in any case Dourso will go. That will be enough for my purposes."

"What am I to do there? Merely wait? Or depart again?"

"Well, you are to find the Healer, as I said. You must not let that Harpy bite go untended. The mouths of the creatures are poisonous as serpents'. It is not precisely venom which they hold, but some other foulness which comes from the filth they eat when they are in Harpy shape.

"So, you find the Healer, in private, and tell her I sent you. Say 'Arkhur' so she will know which Wizard you speak of. After she has healed you, secret yourself somewhere within sight of the aerie. It may be you will want to see the end of this matter."

"How will I know when that is?"

"You'll know," he said in a flat, emotionless voice. "You will know." He pulled her to her feet and pointed the direction to the farm he had mentioned. She wiped one hand upon her trousers, cradling the other in her shirt, and awkwardly tied back her hair. Proom had his head cocked in question, and she nodded to him. Yes. She wanted the shadowpeople to come with her. No further word or action was needed. They were packed and ready to go within moments.

She found the farm without trouble. The farm wife heard her out, then went to the paddock and whistled to a sleek brown horse which came to her hand, nuzzling her and her pockets.

"Prettyfoot," cooed the wife. "Will she carry the nice lady and her pet? Hmmm? High Wizard wants us to help the nice lady. Will Prettyfoot do that? Oh, wuzzums, she will, won't she?"

Mavin stared in astonishment at this, but Proom – the only one of the shadowpeople to have accompanied her into the yard – stood nose to nose with Prettyfoot and seemed to sort the matter out. The farm wife went so far as to try to pet him. Proom growled deep in his throat, and her gesture became a quick pat of Prettyfoot instead.

"She'll go best for you at an easy jog," she said, suddenly all business. "Not fast, but steady. When you're arrived where you're going, turn her loose and she'll find her way back to me. I trust you not to abuse her, woman, you and your pet. The High Wizard has not often asked a favor before, though we owe him much at this farmstead."

Mavin promised, helped with the saddle and bridle, and got herself and Proom astride, Proom bounding up and down behind her, making her dizzy by tugging at her sides. Then they were away, and Mavin merely sat still while Prettyfoot jogged off toward the north, tirelessly, and happily for all Mavin could tell. They stopped briefly only once, to drink from a streamlet they crossed, and it was still early afternoon when she saw an aerie towering above a low hill. If she were to talk of threats from the north, she would have to arrive from the north, so she circled widely to the east before dismounting, tying the reins loosely to the saddle and patting Prettyfoot on her glossy flanks. The little horse shook her head and cantered back the way she had come, seemingly still untired. Mavin memorized the animal's shape. It was one she thought she might have use for in the future.

She left Proom in the trees with a stern injunction to stay where he was. Previous experience had taught her to verify this, and she walked part of the distance to the tower backwards, making sure he was not following her. She had no doubt the rest of his family would be with him by the time she returned. If she were able to return. She was staggering rather badly, and her arm felt like a stone weight.

The fortress was as she had seen it last, brooding upon its high plinth, the sun flashing from the narrow windows, the stairway making a pit of darkness into the stone. She approached it as she had before, hammering upon the heavy door with her good hand, hearing the blammm, blammm, blammm echo up the stony corridors within. It was some time before there were other sounds, pattering, creaking, and then the squeak of a peephole opening like an eyelid in the massive wood.

"I come with an important warning for the High Wizard Chamferton," she intoned in her most officious voice, somewhat handicapped by the fact that the world was whirling around her. "Tell him Mavin is here."

"Babble babble, Wizard not at home, babble, grumph, go away."

"When he learns you have disregarded my warning, he will want to know the name of the person who told me to go away. I have no doubt he will repay you properly." She saw two faces at the peek hole but knew there was only one person there. She held up one finger and saw two. "Healer," she begged silently. "Please be at home."

Scuttle from inside, a whiny voice trailing away into distant silence, then the approach of heavier feet. "What do you want?"

"I bring a warning for the High Wizard. First, however, I must make use of his Healer."

The door creaked reluctantly open. "High Wizard isn't here."

"The High Wizard is somewhere," Mavin snarled. "I have no doubt you know where to find him. Best you do so very quickly. Before giving the message, however, I need to see the Healer. Now!"

Orders were shouted in a surly voice. A search took place. There was running to and fro and disorderly complaints. "Is she in the orchard? Beggle says look in the melon patch. Get Wazzle to come up here."

Mavin sat herself wearily. The world kept fading and returning. At last they found her. Mavin retreated with her into the privacy of a side room, pulling the door firmly shut behind her.

"Harpy bit?" the Healer questioned. "Nasty. Here, give me your hand."

"Arkhur sent me," whispered Mavin, dizzy, distracted, sure there were ears pressed to the door.

"Ahhh," murmured the Healer, gratified and moist about the eyes. "Is he well?"

"Now he is. Now that his Face is taken down from its pole."

"That is good news. Be still, please. I am finding the infection." She nodded at the door, indicating listeners. Mavin sat back and relaxed. There were a few peaceful moments during which the pain lessened, becoming merely a slight twinge, a memory of pain. The throbbing which had pounded in her ears was gone. She sighed, deeply, as though she had run for long leagues.

Then they had done holding hands. The Healer passed her fingers across the wound, already half healed, then across those shallow scrapes around Mavin's ears. These, too, she Healed, making them tingle briefly as though some tiny, marvelous creature moved about raking up the injured parts and disposing of them.

"Now, what's afoot?" the Healer asked, brushing the tips of her fingers together as though to brush away the ills she had exorcised. "What can I do?"

"A message must be sent to . . . the High Wizard Chamferton telling him his demesne is attacked from the north." This was loudly said.

"Ah. Do we know who attacks?"

"The attacker is unspecified," murmured Mavin. Better let Dourso respond to some unknown threat than discount a threat he might know to be false. Loudly: "Unspecified but imminent. He should return here as soon as possible."

"A messenger sent to him now will reach him by dusk. If he left there at once, the . . . High Wizard might return here by midnight."

"Whatever," Mavin yawned. "Now, if you have no further need of me, I will take my leave. Send the message quickly, please. Much may depend upon it."

The Healer gave her one keen glance, then moved away, opened her door to give firm orders to some, quick instructions to others. As Mavin left the place she saw two riders hastening away south in a cloud of dust. She rubbed her face. The area around her ears itched a little, and she smoothed her hair across it self-consciously. Shifters did not make much use of Healers. It had not been as bad an experience as she had thought.

Proom was where she had left him, Proom and his family and his friends. A much wider circle of friends than heretofore. They seemed to enjoy the afternoon, though most of it was spent watching Mavin sleep and explaining to the newcomers that this was, in fact, the Mavin of which many things were sung. Undoubtedly something of interest would occur very soon, and the newcomers were urged to pay close attention. Mavin heard none of it. She had decided to sleep the afternoon away in order to be up and watching at midnight

Night fell, and there was a foray for provisions followed by small fires and feasting. Smoke rose among the trees, dwindled to nothing and died. Mavin rose and led the shadowpeople forth to find a good view of the aerie. Even as they settled upon their perch, Dourso came clattering up to the fortress with Valdon and Valdon's men making a considerable procession upon the road, two baggage wagons bringing up the rear. A large, grated gate opened at ground level to admit the wagons, the horses and most of the men. Valdon and Dourso climbed to the door Mavin had used, and not long afterward she saw lights in the highest room of the tower.

"May neither of them have time to get their breath back," Mavin intoned, almost enjoying herself. She had found a grassy hollow halfway up the outcropping on which the aerie stood. She could see the road, the aerie, the doorway – even the roof of the melon patch gleaming a glassy silver in the moonlight. "Now Dourso will be looking north to see what comes." She sipped at the wine the Healer had given her, offering some to Proom. He took a tiny taste and handed it back, nose wrinkled in disgust. "Well, beastie," she commented, "to each his own taste. I've never really liked those stewed ferns everyone cooks each spring, though most people consider them delicious. Now. What's that upon the road?"

It was an ashen shadow, a bit of curdled fog, a drift of clotted whey. It moved not with any steady deliberation but in a slow, vacillating surge, like the repeated advance of surf which approaches and withdraws only to approach once more. Though Mavin sharpened her eyes, she could see no detail. It came closer with each passing moment, the shadowpeople staring at it with equal intensity.

"Lala perdum, dum, dum," Proom whisper-sang. "Ala, la perdum."

"I don't know what perdum is." Mavin stroked him. "But I'm sure we're going to find out."

"Perdum." Proom shivered as he climbed into Mavin's lap. She had seen him thus disturbed only once before, many years ago in the labyrinth under Hell's Maw, and she closed her arms protectively around him. "It's all right, Proom. Whatever it is, it isn't coming for us."

The cloud came nearer, still in its clotted, constant surge and retreat. She peered in the dim light, suddenly knowing what it was. "Faces," she cried. "All the Faces. There must be thousands of them. And they have their eyes open!"

Through the milky cloud she could make out Arkhur's form on horseback, with the striding Harpy behind him as he set the pace for the floating Faces in their multitude. Proom whispered from her lap, a hushed, horrified voice. She could see why. The mouths of the Faces were open as well, hungering.

From the high tower the northern windows flashed with light, now, again, again. Whoever watched from there did not see the threat approaching on the southern road. Mavin had time to wonder how the Faces would assault the fortress, or whether they would simply besiege the place. She did not wonder long. The cloud began to break into disparate bits, a hundred Faces there, a dozen here, here a line trailing off up the stony plinth like a dim necklace of fog, there a small cloud gathering at the foot of the great door. There was no frustration of their purpose. The door presented no barrier to their paper thinness. They slipped beneath it easily, as elsewhere they slipped through windows and under casements, between bars and through minute cracks in stone. Within moments all were gone.

Silence.

Silence upon the height, the light still flashing to the north.

Silence within the aerie, the stables, the armories.

And then tumult! Screams, shouts, alarm bells, the shrill *whee*ing of a whistle, the crashing sound of many doors flung open as people tried to flee.

Did flee. Down the steps of the fortress, out of the great gates. Beating with arms and hands as though at a hive of attacking bees while the Faces clustered thickly upon those arms, those hands, around mouths, clamped upon throats. A man ran near the hollow where Mavin sat, screaming a choked command as a Face tried to force its way into his throat. It was Valdon, all his arrogant dignity gone, all his Princely power shed, running like an animal while the Faces sucked at him with pursed, bloody lips, to be struck aside, only to return smiling with manic pleasure as they fastened upon him once more.

Mavin turned away, unsure whether she was fascinated or sick. On the flat below ran a half-dozen others, Dourso among them, so thickly layered with Faces it was only their clothes which identified them. Some of Valdon's men. Some of Dourso's. Yet even as these ran and choked and died beneath the Faces, others walked untouched. The Healer, quiet in her white robes, came down the steps to stretch her hand toward Arkhur, to cling first to his hand and then to his body as though she had not thought ever to see him again. So, thought Mavin. So that is what that is all about. Something in her ached, moved by that close embrace.

Valdon had fallen. One by one the Faces peeled away, eyes closed once more, mouths shut. Misty on the air they hung, fading, becoming a jelly, a transparency, a mere disturbance of sight and then nothing. Unable to stop herself, she went to the place the body lay, prodded it with her foot. It swayed like a bundle of dried leaves, juiceless, lifeless.

"There are two ways to dispose of the Faces," said Chamferton's voice from behind her. "To dissolve them in running water, or to let them regain whatever life was taken from them. Come in and we will see what has been done." He turned toward the fortress and Mavin followed, the shadowpeople staying close by her feet. The Harpy stalked behind them without a sound, but still Mavin shuddered to come near her. They passed up the great stairs, through the door, down a long, echoing corridor to stop before a narrow door behind an iron grate. On this door, Chamferton knocked slowly.

"Who's there," quavered an old voice. "Who is it there?"

"Who is it there?" Chamferton responded.

"I?" asked the weak old voice, wonderingly. "I? Why I am Roselove of Betand. . . ."

Behind them the Harpy slumped dead to the floor.

"What's in there?" asked Mavin, not really wanting to know.

"The tombs of my demesne," said Chamferton. "Healer? Will you have her taken out of there and up to her sister's room? Chances are she will not live out a year, but such time as it is, it is hers. Recovered from Dourso's blood and bone.

"None of the Faces has lost life. The Faces themselves are gone. Valdon and Dourso are dead. Foulitter is dead. Only Pantiquod was left behind at the lake, and she fled before I could bind her. I believe she has gone to the south, Mavin. It is unlikely she will return to the north."

Mavin heard him without hearing him. She wanted to believe what he said.

They found the room Mavin remembered from her prior visit, and there were summoned the people remaining in the place, many of them suffering from wounds or minor enchantments. Some were Healed, some disenchanted, wine was brought, and while the shadowpeople roamed about the room, poking into everything – surprisingly free of the place, inasmuch as Mavin had never seen them enter human habitation before – Chamferton turned the talk to Singlehorn.

"It will be a search of many days, I fear," he said in a tired voice, obviously not relishing further travel. She saw the way his eyes searched the shelves, the corners, knowing that he found it defiled and would not be content until he could replace it as it had been. "A search of many days."

"No," Mavin said. "It shouldn't take that long. I could find him almost at once if I could only tell the shadowpeople what he looks like. I can convey only so much in mime. Trying to describe the beast is beyond me."

The Healer had followed all this with interest, though never moving from Chamferton's side. For his part, he seemed to be conscious of her presence as he might be conscious of his own feet or ears, giving her no more of his attention than he paid those useful parts. She laid her hand on his arm.

"Old Inker is still here, Arkhur. Couldn't he do a picture for the little people?"

So in the end it was very simple. Mavin described while an old, sleepy man drew a picture, this way and that until he had it right; then he put it in her hand and staggered back to his bed.

"I will come with you," offered Chamferton without enthusiasm, examining a pile of books.

"No," she said, knowing he would be little help. If he came with her, his mind would be here. "The shadowpeople will find him. I have only to follow. But I would like to know one thing, High Wizard, before I go."

"If I know whatever it is."

"What is the tower? The one where you were dropped? What are the shadows? Why did Himaggery want to find it, and how did he get in without being eaten?"

He stared at her for such a time that she felt he had stopped seeing her, but she stood under that gaze neither patiently or impatiently, merely waiting. Proom and his people were lying quietly about, silent for once, perhaps composing a song to memorialize the destruction of the Lake of Faces.

When he replied it was not in the ponderous, Wizardly voice she had begun to associate with him. It was rather doubtful, tentative.

"Do not talk of it, Mavin. When Himaggery is brought back to himself, discourage him from having interest in it. Though I have read much, studied much, I understand very little. I will say only this . . .

"Before men came to this world – or to this part of the world, I know not which – there were others here. There was a balance here. You may say it was a balance between shadow and light, though I do not think what I speak of can be described in such simple terms. One might as well say power and weakness, love and hate. Of whatever kind, it was a balance.

"There was a symbol of that balance. More than a symbol; a key, a talisman, an eidolon. A tower. In the tower a bell which cannot ring alone. Ring the bell of light, and the shadow bell will sound. Ring the shadow bell and the daylight bell will resonate. So was the balance kept. Until we came. Then . . . then something happened. Something withdrew from this world or came into it. The tower disappeared or was hidden. The bell was muffled. . . .

"An imbalance occurred. Does the real tower still exist? Is the bell only muffled? Or destroyed? Does something now ring the shadow bell, something beyond our understanding?

"Mavin, do not speak of this. In time the balance must be restored or the world will fail. But I think the time is not now, not yet. Any who attempt it now are doomed to death, to be shadow-eaten. So – when you have brought Himaggery to his own once more, do not let him seek the tower."

Mavin heard him out, not understanding precisely what he attempted to say – and knowing that he understood it no better than she – yet assured by her own sight and hearing that he spoke simple truth as it could be perceived by such as they. She, too, had seen the shadows. She, too, had heard the sound of their presence. It was not the time.

"I will remember what you say, Arkhur," she promised him. Then she took leave of the Healer, accepting many useful gifts, and went out into the dawn.

CHAPTER 8

At Chamferton's invitation – though it was actually the Healer who thought of it – Mavin took several horses from the stable beneath the rock. None was the equal of Prettyfoot, but any at all would be easier than walking. She rode one and led three, the three ridden – or better, she thought, say "inhabited" – by Proom and his people. They did not so much ride as swarm over, up and down legs, around and across backs. The horses, at first much astonished and inclined to resentment, were petted into submission. Or perhaps talked into submission. Mavin had a sneaky belief surpported by considerable evidence that Proom spoke horse as well as fustigar, owl, flitchhawk, and a hundred other languages.

She showed Proom the picture of Singlehorn only after they had found the place from which the Fon-beast had bolted, a place in the woods still some distance northwest of the Lake of Faces (former Lake of Faces, Mavin said to herself, trying to think of a good name for it now). He looked at it with obvious amusement, then passed it around to the accompaniment of much discursive lalala, snatching it back when one infant attempted to eat it.

The search was immediately in motion, with a dozen shadowpeople up as many trees, all twittering into the spring noonday. They descended after a time to swarm over their steeds once more, pointing away to the west and urging Mavin to come along. Calls kept coming throughout the afternoon, always from the west, as they proceeded into the evening until the forest aisles glowed before them in long processionals of sun and shade, the sky pink and amber, flecked with scaly pennants of purple cloud. None of them had slept for a full day and night. Though the guiding song had not yet fallen silent there was general agreement – not least among the horses – that it was suppertime.

They built a small fire and ate well, for the Healer had sent packed saddlebags with them, bags full of roast meat and cheese, fresh baked bread and fruit from Chamferton's glasshouses.Then they curled to sleep – except that they did not sleep. The shadowpeople were restless, getting up again and again to move around the mossy place they had camped upon, full of aimless dialogue and fractious small quarrels. Finally, just as Mavin had begun to drift away, one of them cried a sharp, low tone of warning which brought all of them up to throw dirt upon the coals of the fires.

"Sssss," came Proom's hiss, and a moment later tiny fingers pressed upon her lips.

It took time to accustom her eyes to the dark, though she widened them as much as she could to peer upward in the direction all the little faces were turned, ears spread wide, cocked to catch the least sound.

Then she heard it. The high, shrill screech of a lone Harpy. A hunting cry.

"Pantiquod," she whispered, questioning their fright.

"Sssss," from Proom. A shadowperson was pouring the last of Mavin's wine on the fire while others peed upon it intently, dousing every spark and drowning the smoke.

"Why this fear?" she asked herself silently. "They played tag with Foulitter upon the hill near the lake. They led her into a trap without a moment's hesitation, yet now they are as fearful as I have ever seen them."

The horses began an uneasy whickering, and a dozen of the little people gathered around them, talking to them, urging some course of action upon them and reinforcing it with much repetition. Mavin did not understand their intention until the horses trotted away into the darkness, returning as they had come.

"No!" she objected. "I need . . ."

"*Ssss*," demanded Proom, his hands tightening on her face.

Then she saw them. A line of black wings crossing the moon, beat on beat, as though they breathed in unison, moving from the northeast. From that purposeful line fell a single hunting call, as though only a lone Harpy hunted there upon the light wind. Beat on beat the wings carried them overhead, and as they passed directly overhead Mavin heard a low, ominous gabble as from a yard of monstrous geese.

They waited in silence, not moving, scarcely breathing. After a long time, Mavin tried again. "Pantiquod?"

Proom showed his teeth in a snarl. "Perdum, lala, thossle labala perdum."

"Perdum," she agreed. "Danger." The little ones took this word and tried it out, "ger, ger, ger," decided they did not like it. "Perdum," they said, being sure all of them were in accord. Mavin thought not for the first time that she must learn Proom's language. Perhaps – perhaps there would be a time of peace while she waited for her child to be born. Perhaps then. She considered this possibility with surprising pleasure. It was ridiculous not to be able to talk together.

Be that as it may, she could appreciate the danger. One Harpy could be teased, baffled, led on a chase. Perhaps two or three could be tricked or avoided. But more than that? All with poisonous teeth and clutching talons? No doubt Pantiquod had learned of Foulitter's death and was out for vengeance. "Fowl, bird-brained vengeance," she punned to herself, trying to make it less terrible. Proom had sent the horses away because they were large enough to be seen from the skies. So long as those marauders ranged the air, travel would have to be silent, sly, hidden beneath the boughs. She hoped that Singlehorn was not far from them and had not chosen to wander down into the plains or river valleys where there would be no cover.

At last, having worried about all this for sufficient time, she slept.

Proom shook her awake at first light, and they made a quick, cold breakfast as they walked. The twittered directions came less frequently today, and more briefly. Obviously other shadowpeople went in fear of the Harpies as well. Rather than travel today in a compact group, they went well scattered among the trees, avoiding the occasional clearings and open valleys. When it was necessary to cross such places, they searched the air first, peering from the edges of the trees, then dashed across, a few at a time. Mavin judged that the Harpies were too heavy to perch at the tops of trees – and the thought made her remember the broken vine outside her window at Chamferton's castle – but they could find suitable rest on any rock outcropping or cliff. Proom, well aware of this, kept them far from such places, and they did not see the hunters during the daylight hours.

Nor did they see Singlehorn. That night as they ate another cold meal without the comfort of fire, Mavin remembered that forlorn, bugling call the Fon-beast had sent after the Band as it marched away west. If Singlehorn were following the Band, then he might be moving ahead of them at their own speed. If that were the case, they might not catch up with him until he came to the sea, a discouraging thought. Though the shadows had little interest in him in his present shape, she wondered if the Harpies did.

At midnight she woke to the sound of that lone, hunting cry. There was an overcast, and she could not tell if there were more than one. Around her, the shadowpeople moved restlessly in their sleep.

So they went on. On the third night nothing disturbed them. Proom began to be more his usual self, full of prancing and jokes. The fourth and fifth night passed with no alarms. Mavin had convinced herself that the Harpy flight coming so close to her own path was mere coincidence. As Chamferton had said, Pantiquod had likely gone south to Bannerwell by now. Or somewhere else where her habits and appetites could be better satisfied.

They began to travel on the road which they had paralleled for many leagues. Now they came out upon it, staying close to the edge, still with some nervous scanning of the skies. They could move faster on this smooth surface, and by the time the sixth night fell, Mavin smelled the distant sea.

And on the following morning, a friendly family of shadowpeople drove Singlehorn into their camp, head hanging, coat dusty and dry, tongue swollen in a bleeding mouth. The broken strap of the halter still hung from his head, making small, dragging serpents' trails in the dust. Mavin lifted Fon-beast's head and looked into dull, lifeless eyes. She growled in her throat, hating herself for having wanted him gone. There were swollen sores around his ears, and remembering her own pain and the gentleness of the Healer, Mavin cursed her impatience with him. And with herself, she amended. It was not the Fon-beast himself, but her feelings about him that disturbed her. "I will forget all that," she resolved in a fury of contrition. "I will forget all that and concentrate on taking care of him until we get to Windlow's."

They gave him water. She squeezed rainhat fruits into his mouth. Obviously he had not eaten well in the days he had been gone, or rather he had tried to graze on common grasses. Though he thought himself a grazing beast, the grasses had not been fooled. They had cut his mouth and tongue until both were swollen and infected.

Mavin made a rich broth of some of the meat they had carried and dropped this into his mouth from a spoon while infant shadowpeople rubbed his dusty hide with bundles of aromatic leaves.

She had not noticed that Proom had left until he returned with a group of the older shadowpeople carrying bags full of herbs and growths, most of which she had never seen before. These were compounded by the tribe in accordance with some recipe well known to them all. It resulted in a thick, green goo which Proom directed be plastered around Singlehorn's mouth and upon the open sores. Some of it trickled into the Fon-beast's mouth as well, and Mavin was restrained from wiping it away. Finally, when everything had been done for him that anyone could think of, she covered him with her cloak and lay down beside him. After a time the smell of the herbs and the warmth of the day made them all drowsy – they had been much awake during the past nights – and they slept once more.

When they awoke in the late afternoon, the Singlehorn was on his feet, pawing at the ground with one golden hoof, nodding and nodding as though in time to music. Dried shreds of the green goo clung around his mouth and ears. Beneath this papery crust the flesh was pink and healthy-looking, the swelling reduced; and while his eyes were still tired, he did not look so hopeless. There was a pool a little distance away, and while the shadowpeople yawned and stirred, readying for travel, Mavin led him there. She let him out to the length of the new rope she had tied to his halter but did not release him. "No more running away," she said firmly. "Whatever I may feel about this whole business, Fon-beast, however impatient it makes me, we are bound together until we reach safety." And to herself, she said, "And when we reach Windlow's – then we'll see if there is a true tie between us."

Singlehorn, rolling in the shallow water, tossing his head and drinking deep draughts of cool liquid, did not seem to care. She let him roll, unaware of the sun falling in the west, enjoying the peace of the moment. When she returned to the road, the shadowpeople were gone.

"Hello?" she cried. "Proom?"

Only silence. Perhaps a far-off twitter.

"Goodbye?" she called.

No answer.

Well. They had observed and assisted while Mavin had done several interesting things. They had introduced their children to this person. They had, perhaps, made a new song or two – the Lake of Faces was surely good for at least a brief memorial – but now the shadowpeople had business of their own. Mavin had found the creature she sought, and now they might be about their own affairs. She sought the edges of the road for any sign, any trail, but saw nothing.

Nothing . . .

Except a grayness lying quiet beneath a tree. And another superimposed in fluttering flakes upon a copse, wavering the light which passed through it so it seemed to shift and boil.

Her soul fell silent. Shadows from the tower come to haunt her once more. Not upon the road, which still prevented their presence, but nearby. Perhaps the shadowpeople had been shadow-bane, but without them the bane prevailed no longer.

There was nothing for it except to get on to the south. They must come to Tarnoch at last, or so far from the tower that the shadows would give up. Though what they would give up, or how they were here, she could hardly imagine. Was it she who drew them, or Singlehorn? Were they set to follow any who left the Dervish's valley? And if so, until when? Until what happened? Perhaps this was only conjecture. Perhaps they had not followed at all but were everywhere, always, ubiquitous as midges.

To which an internal voice said, Nonsense. You have not seen them in your former travels because they were not in this part of the world before. Now they are, because they have followed you here from the Dervish's valley. But follow you where they will, they did not harm you when you were with the shadowpeople, and they do not harm you if you stay upon the road.

As she walked away, leading Singlehorn, it was to the steady double beat of those words; the road, the road, the road. *"On the road, the old road, a tower made of stone. In the tower hangs a bell which cannot ring alone. One, two, three, four, five . . ."* When she reached one thousand she began again. *"Shadow bell rang in the dark, daylight bell the dawn. In the tower hung the bells, now the tower's gone."*

Why a stone tower? Was it important? She hummed the words, thinking them in her head, then saw all at once how thickly the shadows lay, how closely to the road, how they piled and boiled as she sang.

Gamelords! Was that verse of the weird runners a summoning chant? It could be!

Sing something else. Anything. A jumprope chant. *"Dodir of the Seven Hands, a mighty man was he; greatest Tragamor to live beside the Glistening Sea. Dodir raised a mountain up, broke a mountain down. See the house where Dodir lives, right here in our town. One house, two house, three house, four house . . ."*

The shadows were not interested in this. They dwindled, becoming mere gray opacities, without motion beneath the softly blowing trees.

"Dodir of the Seven Hands, a mighty man to know, every tree in shadowmarch, he laid out in a row. One tree, two tree, three tree, four tree . . ."

It was true. The shadows were fewer. "Well, Mavin," she said, "Chamferton told you not to think of it, so best you not think of it. Sing yourself something old and bawdy from Danderbat Keep or old and singsongy from childhood, and keep moving upon the southern way." She soothed herself with this, and had almost reached a comfortable frame of mind when she heard the scream, high and behind her. She spun, searching the air, seeing clearly the dark blot of Harpy wings circling upon a cloud.

Pantiquod had found her at last.

Oh, damn, and devils, and pombi-piss. And damn you, Chamferton, that you let her get away.

And damn you, Himaggery. Damn you, Fon-beast. I should raise you out of that shape and let you fight for yourself. Why must I do everything for you?

The Harpy circled lazily and turned away north. Mavin knew she would return. That had done it! There was no way she could face even one Harpy without Shifting. Being Harpy bit taught that. Even a scratch could be deadly. There being no help for it, she went on walking, singing over in her head every child's song she remembered, every chanty learned in the sea villages, even the songs of the root-walkers she had learned in the deep chasm of the western lands across the sea, and these led her to thoughts of Beedie which led in turn to nostalgic longings to be wandering free again. She had not truly wandered free for five years, not since bringing

Handbright's babies back to her kin, and the longing to break away from the rigid edges of the road became almost hysteria by nightfall.

Off the road, beneath the trees, her mind sang, *shadows piled up to your knees. Safe from shadows on the road, and you'll feel the Harpy's goad.* She had not seen Pantiquod again, but she knew the Harpy would return in the dark, or on the day which followed, and she would not return alone.

"Now, Mavin," she harangued herself angrily, "this hysteria does not become you. Were you nothing but Shifter all these years? Were you a Talent only, with no mind or soul to call upon except in a twist of shape? Your Shiftiness is still there, may still be used if we need it. It is not lost to us, but by all the hundred devils, at least try to figure out if we're Shifty enough without it. So, stop this silliness, this girlish fretting and whining and use your eyes, woman. Think. Do."

The self-castigation was only partly effective. She tried to imagine it having been administered by someone else – Windlow, perhaps. That lent more authority, and she forced herself to plan. There were narrow alternatives. If she stayed upon the road to be protected from shadows, she would be exposed to the air. *However!* "We came a long way from the Dervish's valley to this road, and though the shadows swarmed all about us, we were not hurt. Use your head, woman!"

She set herself to watch the shadows instead of ignoring them. How did they lie? How did they move? She watched them for many long leagues, and it seemed to her they moved only in random ways, piling here and there, singly here and there, floating like fragments of gray glass between copses and hills. She tried to foretell where floating flakes would fall. Beneath that tree or upon that clump? Upon the other shadow, or beside it? Where that flock of birds sought seeds among the hedgerows, or beyond them? After a time, she thought she was beginning to be able to predict where the shadow would fall. There was a strange, hazy pattern, if not to their movement, at least to their disposition upon the earth.

If there were any sizeable living thing – any bird or small beast, the shadow would not descend upon that place but in a place near adjacent. The large the animal or bird, the more thickly the shadows would pile around it, but never upon it and never completely surrounding it. There was always a way out, a trail of light leading through the dark.

She remembered the bird upon the hill. The shadow had not fallen upon it. The shadow had lain there, waiting – waiting for the bird to intrude upon the shadow. And then. . . .

Himaggery had intruded upon the shadow. So said the Dervish.

So had the drugged Chamferton, presumably, though in such a condition that the shadows had not recognized him as a living thing. She saw that the shadows did not seem to bother very small forms of life – beetles and worms went their way beneath the shadow undisturbed.

But larger creatures near which the shadows fell almost always chose the unshadowed way as they hopped about, even when that way was very hard to see – as when the sun was hidden behind clouds, or when the haze of dusk made all things gray and shadowlike.

So. So. One could walk, if one were careful, among the shadows. One could walk, if one were alert, safely away from the road. She stopped to get food from her pack, to feed Singlehorn, all the time keeping her eyes fixed upon patches of gray in a little meadow to the west of the road. There were gobble-mole ditches druggled through the meadow, dirt thrown up on either side in little dikes, a shower of earth flying up from time to time to mark the location of the mole as it druggled for beetles and worms and blind snakes. The tunnel wound its way among the shadows as though the mole had a map in his snout which told him where they lay.

Could the shadows be sensed in some other way than sight? Perhaps even in the dark? Did they exist in the dark? If one were unaware of the shadows, would one find a safe way among them, without even knowing it? Useless consideration, of course. She did know about them, all too well. But did Harpies – ah, yes, she thought – did Harpies know about the shadows?

Dusk came at last, but well before that she chose the place they would spend the night; a half cave beneath a stone which bulged up from moss and shrub into a curled snout. Shadows lay about it, true, but not in it, and a tiny pool of rainwater had collected at the foot of the stone. They would be comfortable enough, well fed enough, with water to drink and to wash away the dust of the road. They would be unseen from above also, and could lie quiet against the stone, invisible beneath the mixed browns and grays of Mavin's cloak.

Deep in the night she awoke to the first Harpy's cry. Now the variety of cries was unmistakable; the Harpies had returned in force. Why they flew at night she could not tell, unless they relied upon some other sense than sight to find their quarry. Perhaps they, like the huge ogre-owl of the southern ice, cried out to frighten and then struck at the sound of things which fled. Perhaps they did it only to terrify.

"It won't work on me, Pantiquod," she said between gritted teeth. "Go eat a Ghoul or two and die of indigestion." Ignoring the fact that her nails had bitten bloody holes into her palms, she forced herself to sleep. When next she opened her eyes it was day.

Dull day, overcast day, day in which nothing moved and no shadow could be seen against the general murk. She stood at the mouth of the cave, refusing to feel hopeless about the matter but tired beyond belief, wondering what path they might take back to the road. "No panic," she grated. "No hysterics. Quiet. Sensible. You can camp here for days if need be. . . ."

She drew the Singlehorn close beside her, feeding him from her hand. "Fon-beast, sit here by me and keep me warm. We must take our time this morning. I have trapped us by being clever. We must spy out a path."

Which they did, little by little, over the course of an hour, spying where moles moved in the grass, where birds hopped about, where a bunwit mother ran a set of quick diagonals, her two furry kits close behind. They stepped onto the road at last, Mavin with a feeling of relief, the Singlehorn placidly walking behind her. Twice during the afternoon Mavin thought she heard Harpies screaming, but the sound came from above the overcast, remote and terrible, making the Singlehorn flinch and shy against the halter as though he connected that cry with pain.

Toward evening the sky began to clear; and by dusk it held only a few scattered traces of cloud, tatters of wet mist upon the deeper blue. They came to the top of a rise which overlooked a league or more of road, endless undulations of feathery forest, and to the west the encroaching blue of the sea. Mavin began to put landmarks together in her mental map of the area. Schlaizy Noithn lay to the east. Below them the coast began its great eastward curve, and several days to the south they would come to Hawsport, lying at the mouth of the River Haws, full of little boats and the easy bounty of the ocean. Her heart began to lift as she thought of protective roofs and solid inns, sure that the shadows could not gather thickly where there were so many men.

Her elation lasted only for a few golden moments, long enough to make one smothered cry of joy and draw the Fon-beast close to surprise him with a kiss. Then the cry came from the sky behind her, triumphant and terrifying. The Harpies once more.

Harpies. Many more than one. They would not give her time to reach Hawsport and safety. They had played with her long enough, followed her long enough, and now that she was almost within sight of safety they were readying for the kill.

The kill.

Which she might defeat, even now, by Shifting into something huge and inexorable. They were still circling, still flying to get above her. There were a few moments yet. There was time, still, to gain enough bulk for that. Tie the Fon-beast somewhere hidden. Retrieve him later. Build oneself into a wall of flesh which could gather in one Harpy, or a dozen, or a hundred if need be.

An easy, accustomed thing to do.

And then there might be no Himaggery's child and her own.

She considered this for some time. It was by far the easiest solution. Behind her, Singlehorn tapped the stones with his hooves, a jittery dance from one side of the road to the other. Mavin went on thinking, adding to a plan half formed the night before.

"Himaggery," she said at last. "This is as much your doing as mine, and you must share the risk. Come out, Himaggery." She remembered the Dervish's words: *Make him hear you*, and her voice was high-pitched in fear that she would not be able to, in haste and danger.

But the Singlehorn reared to his hind legs, faded, took the form of the man she remembered, the face she had seen a thousand times in reveries, had imagined night and morning over twenty years. His face was full of confusion and doubt. Beyond him on the hillside the air was suddenly alive with shadows, boiling in a frenzy, collecting more thickly with every moment – as she had hoped.

"Go back, Himaggery," she commanded in a stentorian voice allowing only obedience. "Go back!" The man dropped to all fours to become the Fon-beast once more. It stood with its head dragging, discomfitted at this abrupt transformation. The shadows, seeming confused, piled in drifts at the side of the road. The Dervish had been right. The shadows had been seeking Himaggery, and now they were fully alerted to his presence. Her hazardous play depended totally upon what these alert and ravenous shadows would do now with any creature which intruded upon them.

The Harpy cries came once more, nearer. Whirling around, she saw them descending from the north, close enough that she could recognize Pantiquod in the fore. The next step, she reminded herself. Quickly. Do not look at them, do not become fascinated by them. Do not think of them at all, only of what you must do next.

She spun to search the area near the road. There had to be an appropriate battleground near the road, a patch now occupied by some living thing which the shadows had left clear. It had to be close! And it must have a clear trail of light back to the road. She searched frantically, hearing the sound of wings in the height, the cawing laughter of the Harpies as they circled, savoring their intended slaughter.

There it was! A gameboard of light and shadow to the left of the road. A bunwit's burrow in the light, the shadow piled deeply about it, alternate bits of shadow and light leading to it, jump, jump, jump. She pulled the Fon-beast close behind her – he unresisting but unhelpful, subdued, his usual grace gone, almost stumbling after her – hauling him by main strength to keep him away from the shadowed squares, only remembering when she straddled the burrow that she could have tethered him at the road. Well and well. No, the Harpies might have attacked him there. Here at least they stood together upon this tiny patch of sunlight surrounded by piled shadows on every side.

She pushed him to the ground and stood astride him, bellowing a fishwife's scream at the falling fury of wings. He lay dumbly, nose to the ground. "Ho, Pantiquod! Filthy chicken! Ugly bird! Die now as your foul daughter did, and her kin, and her allies. Come feel my claws. . . ."

She had Shifted herself some claws and fangs, needing them badly and considering it no major thing. It was only fingers and teeth, nothing close to the center of her. If so little a thing could destroy the baby within – well, then so be it. Without this much, there would be no chance at all. She danced over the recumbent

Singlehorn, screaming abuse at the skies, trying to make the women-creatures furious, frantic, mad with anger, so they would fall to encircle her, come to the ground to use their teeth and talons. They must not drop directly upon her if she could prevent it. She made a long arm to snatch up a heavy branch from the ground, whirling it above her head.

She had succeeded in infuriating them. Their screams were shattering. They slavered and shat, the nastiness falling around her in a stinking rain. Their breasts hung down in great, dangling udders, swaying as they flew. Beneath Mavin's knees the Fon-beast trembled at the sound of them, even dazed as he was, drawing his legs tight against his body, as though to get out of her way. Mavin whirled the branch above her and taunted them. "Filthy bird. Stinking fowl. Drag-breasted beast!"

Directly above her, Pantiquod folded her wings and dropped like a flitchhawk. Remembering that other flitchhawk which had dropped upon her at the Lake of Faces, Mavin whirled the branch in a whistling blur of motion.

The whirling branch stopped Pantiquod in her stoop, wings scooped back to break her fall. Around her the other Harpies touched ground, started to strike with talons and teeth only to stop, half crouched, mouths open, panting, panting. Almost all of them had landed in the shadow. Those few which had not beat their wings and leaped on storklike legs to come at Mavin, stepping across their sisters as they did so. Then they too squatted to pant, tongues hanging from wide-opened mouths before they turned their heads to bite at themselves. Then all but the one were so occupied.

She, Pantiquod, was still in the air, still fluttering and screeching threats at Mavin, eyes so closely fixed upon her prey she had no sight to spare for her sisters.

"Filthy chicken," Mavin grated again from a dry throat. "Cowardly hen. When I have finished with you, I will seek out your other children and put an end to them . . . " This broke the bonds of caution which had held the Harpy high, and she plummeted downward again like a falling stone.

"Strike well, girl," Mavin instructed herself, holding the branch as she had done as a child playing at wand-ball. The stink of the birds was in her nostrils. Her skin trembled with every moment. She gritted her teeth and ignored it. "Strike well . . . "

As it was, she waited almost too long, striking hard when the foul mouth was only an armspan from her face, swinging the branch with all her strength, unwinding herself like a great, coiled spring.

The branch caught the Harpy full upon her chest. Mavin heard the bones break, saw the body fall away, half into the shadow. Only half. On the clear ground the head and feet. In the shadow the body and wings. Slowly, inexorably, while the mouth went on screeching and the talons grasped at nothing, the wings drew back into the shadow, back until they were covered.

Mavin looked at her feet. She herself stood within the width of one finger from the shadow. Gulping deeply she drew herself away, drew the Fon-beast away, carefully, and slow step by slow step found a safe path back to the road.

Once there she looked behind her, only once. The shadows were lifting lazily, as though well fed. Behind them on the grass the Harpies flopped, as headless chickens flop for a time, not knowing yet they are dead. Pantiquod was eating herself, and Mavin turned from that sight. Something within her wanted to call out, "Remember the plague in Pfarb Durim, Pantiquod? This is your payment for bringing that plague, Harpy!" She kept silent. She was sure that no creature within the shadow could hear any outside voice. She prayed she would never hear the voice that Pantiquod must be hearing; the voice of the shadow itself.

For a long time she lay on the road, at first heaving and retching, then letting her stomach settle itself. The Fon-beast was utterly quiet, not moving at all except for a tiny tremor of the skin over his withers. At last she drank some water from her flask, gave the Singlehorn a mouthful from her palm, then went away down the long slope, pausing to rest once more at the bottom of it as she smelled the salt wind from the sea.

After a time she raised her head, habit turning her eyes to inventory the shadows. She sought them first where they had been easiest to see, along the edges of the road. None. Reluctantly, she looked behind them, seeing whether the shadows followed them only now from that battlefield at the top of the hill. None beneath the trees, or on the stones of the hill. None moving through the air in that lazy glide she had learned to recognize.

None. None at all.

Well, Mavin thought, it is possible. Possible they sought a certain creature; possible they found that certain creature, thus triggering some kind of feeding frenzy. Then they had fed. Would the shadows know that the creature which triggered their frenzy was not the one they ate?

Possibly not. Only possibly. Mavin wondered if they had really gone for good. She considered bringing Himaggery back again. She thought of it, meantime stroking the Fon-beast who had at last recovered his equanimity enough to tug at the halter, eager to be gone.

"No, my love," she said at last, patting him. "I can handle you better as you are. Let us come to Windlow's place and ask his help before we risk anything more. Truth to tell, Singlehorn, I am mightily weary of this journey. In all my travels across the world, I have not been this weary before. I do not know whether it is the child, or my own doubts, or you, Fon-beast, and I do not want to blame you for my weariness."

Which I might do, Himaggery. Which I would do. She had said this last silently to herself, wary of using his name. She believed the shadows were gone, but she could be wrong. Himaggery had come out of the Fon-beast shape more easily than she had expected. She would not risk it again. It would be foolish to assume . . . anything.

"I will remember what you told me, Chamferton," she vowed. "There is much I will tell Windlow when I see him at last, and there is much I will not tell Himaggery at all. Let him find some other quest to keep him busy."

They came into Hawsport on a fine, windy day, the wind straight across the wide bay from the west, carrying elusive hints of music; taran-tara and whompety-whomp. Singlehorn danced, tugging toward the shore to stand there facing the waters, adding his own voice to the melodic fragments which came over the waves.

Mavin bought meat and fruit in the market place, where children pursued the Fon-beast with offers of sweets and bits of fruit. "Is there a bridge south of here?" she asked the stallholder. "One which connects the shore with that long peninsula coming down from the north?"

"Never was that I know of," said the stallholder offhandedly, leering at her while his fingers strayed toward her thighs, making pinching motions.

Mavin drew her knife to cut a segment from a ripe thrilp and did not replace it in her belt. The stallholder became abruptly busy sorting other fruit in the pile. "No bridge there," he said, putting an end to the matter.

"Oh, yes," creaked someone from the back of the stall. "Oh, yes there was. It was built in my granddaddy's time. My granddaddy worked on it himself. They took boatloads of rock out into that shallow water and made themselves piers, they did, and put the bridge on that. Fine it was to hear him tell of it, and I heard the story many times when I was no bigger than a bunwit. It had a gate in the middle, to let the boats out, and the people used to go across it to all the western lands . . . "

"What happened to it?" Mavin asked, ignoring the stallholder's irritation at his kinswoman's interruptions.

"Storm. A great storm. Oh, that happened when I was a child. Sixty years ago? More than that even. Such a great storm nobody had seen the like before. Half of Hawsport washed away. They say whole forests came down in the east. Dreadful thing. My granddaddy said a moon fell down . . . "

"A moon fell down!" sneered the stallholder. "Why don't you stop with the fairy tales, Grandma. I didn't even know there was a bridge. Was you planning to go over there? My brother has a boat he rents out. Take you and the beast there in a day or so." He leered again, less hopefully.

"No," Mavin told him with a measuring look. "Can't you hear the music? The Band will need to get over here."

"The Band?" queried the old voice again. "Did you say Band? Oh, my granddaddy told me about the Band. They came through when my daddy was a boy. Before the storm, when I was just a babby, while the bridge was still there. My oh my, but I do wish I could see the Band."

"Since there is no bridge," Mavin said, "I should imagine that if the fishermen of Hawsport were to sail over to the far side, they might find a full load of paying travelers to bring back. It's only a suggestion, mind, but if the fishermen are not busy with their nets or hooks at the moment, and if they have nothing better to do . . . "

She was speaking to vacancy. The stallholder had hurried away toward the quay, shouting to a group of small boys to "Go find Bettener, and Surry Bodget and the Quire brothers . . . "

"'Tisn't his brother's boat at all," quavered the old voice. "He only says that to save on taxes. Pity you told him about it. He'll only cheat those Band people, whoever they are, and I would so liked to have seen the Band."

"That's all right, Grandma," Mavin soothed her. "The Band people have been traveling this world for a thousand years. They probably know tricks your grandson hasn't thought of yet. There's an old man named Byram with them. He probably remembers the moon falling down. I'll bring him to meet you, and you two can talk about old times."

She wandered down to the shore, cutting bits of fruit for herself and for the Fon-beast, counting the little fishing boats which were setting out to sea. Not enough. They would have to make two trips or more. The far peninsula lay upon the horizon, a single dark line, as though inked in at the edge of the ocean. The boats were tacking, to and fro, to and fro. Well, say four or five days at the outside. Time enough to rest and eat kitcheny food. She fingered the coins in her pocket. Time enough to buy some clothing for herself. If she couldn't Shift fur or feathers when she wished, then she would need more than the Dervish's cast-offs to dress herself in. Time enough to let the Fon-beast finish healing. She stroked him, feeling his soft muzzle thrust up to nuzzle at her ear. Tempting. Very tempting.

"Not until we get to Windlow's," she said, Sighing, she went to find an inn.

CHAPTER NINE

Mavin and the Singlehorn came to Windlow's school early of a summer evening. Though the way had been wearying, there had been no fear or horror lately, and the companionship of the Band people had replaced fear and loneliness in both their minds. Singlehorn did not shy at the sound of hunting birds any longer. Mavin did not often wake in the night starting bolt upright from dreams of gray shadows and screaming Harpies. Night was simply night once more, and day was simply day. They had come down the whole length of the shoreline from Hawsport, past the Black Basilisk Demesne, and on south to the lands of Gloam where the road turned east once more. Thence they had come up long, sloping meadows to the uplands of Brox and Brom, and there Mavin had left the Band to turn northward along the headwaters of the Long Valley River.

They left the river at last to climb eastward into the hills, and at some point in this journey, the Fon-beast began to lead them as though he knew where they were going. At least so Mavin supposed, letting him have his way. When they came over the last shallow rise looking down into Windlow's valley, she recognized it at once. Though she had never seen it, Throsset had spoken of it, and Windlow himself had described it long ago in Pfarb Durim. There was the lone white tower, and there the lower buildings which housed the students and the servants. Even from the hill she could see the sparkle of light reflecting from a fountain in the courtyard and a shower of colorful blossoms spilling over the wall.

Singlehorn gave an odd strangled but joyous call, and Mavin saw a small bent figure in the distant courtyard straighten itself and peer in their direction. Windlow was, after all, a Seer, she reminded herself. Perhaps he had expected them. If that were so, the tedious explanations she had dreaded might not be necessary. She had done things during the past season which she found it hard to justify to herself. She did not want to explain them to others.

Fon-beast led the way down the hill, tugging at the rope. She pulled him up for a moment to take off the halter, letting him gallop away toward the approaching figure. Of course he was tired of being tied. So was she. It might have been only stubbornness on her part which had insisted upon it all those last long leagues, but she had not wanted to risk his running away again. Day after day when Singlehorn had looked at her plaintively, wanting to run with the children, she had refused him. "Not again, Fon-beast. I am weary of searching for you, so you must abide the rope for a time." *However*, she had told herself, *however*, that isn't the real reason. The real reason is you would go back to that same form with him, Mavin, if you could. "You must learn to abide it," she had said aloud, ignoring the internal voices.

In time he had learned to abide it. Now that time was done. She watched his grace of movement, the flowing mane, the silken hide, knowing she had appeared the same when they had been together. They had had perfection together. Was there anything else in life which would make the loss of that bearable?

Well and no matter, she told herself. That person coming toward you is Windlow, and he is hastening his old bones at such a rate he may kill himself. Come, Mavin. Forget the past. Haste and put on a good face.

So she greeted him, and was greeted by him, and told him what person lay beneath the appearance of Singlehorn and something of what had passed, saying no more than she had to say, and yet all in a tumble of confusing words. He passed his hand across his face in dismay. "But in my vision, long ago, I saw you together at Pfarb Durim!" He had aged since she saw him last, though his eyes were as keen as she remembered them.

"I'm sorry, Windlow. It must have been a false vision. We did not meet in Pfarb Durim. We met in a place far to the north, of a strangeness you will not believe when I tell it to you over supper."

"And this is truly Himaggery?"

"It truly is."

"Is he bound in this shape forever? Is it an enchantment we may . . . "

"No and yes, Windlow. I will bring him out of that shape as soon as you have heard what I must tell you." And she stubbornly clung to that, though Windlow said he thought she might release Himaggery at once, and so did Boldery, who was there on a visit, and so did Throsset of Dowes who was likewise.

"I will tell *you*," she said to Windlow, granting no compromise. "And then I will release Himaggery and all of you may say whatever you like to him and may tell him everything he should know. When he has had a chance to think about it all – why, then he and I will talk . . . "

"I don't understand," said Boldery in confusion. "Why won't she bring him back to himself now?"

"Let her alone," Throsset directed, unexpectedly. "I imagine she has had a wearying time. It will not matter in the long run."

So there was one more meal with Himaggery lying on the hearth in his Singlehorn guise during which Mavin told them all that she knew or guessed or had been told about Himaggery's quest and subsequent captivity, carefully not telling them where the Dervish's valley was, or what had happened to her there, or where she had seen the tower.

"Chamferton says Himaggery must leave it alone," she concluded. "I believe him. The shadows did seek Himaggery, and it was a great part luck and only by the narrowest edge that they did not eat us both. The shadows fed upon Pantiquod and her sisters and did not seem to know the difference, but I would not face such a peril again – not willingly." The telling of it still had the power to bring it back, and her body shook again with revulsion and terror. Throsset put a hand upon hers, looking oddly at her, as though she had seen more than Mavin had said. Mavin put down her empty wineglass and rose to her feet, swaying a little at the cumulative effect of wine, weariness, and having attained the long awaited goal. Her voice was not quite steady as she said, "Now, I have told you everything, Windlow. I will do as I promised."

She laid her cheek briefly against Singlehorn's soft nose. "Come out, Himaggery," she said, turning away without waiting to see whether the words had any effect. She left the room, shutting the door, while behind her a man struggled mightily with much confusion of spirit and in answer to a beloved voice, to bring himself out of the Singlehorn form and to remain upright on tottery human legs. For Mavin, there was a soft bed waiting in a tower room, and she did not intend to get out of it for several days.

The knock came on her door late, so late that she had forgotten what time it was or where she was, or that she was. Aroused out of dream, she heard the whisper, ''Mavin, are you asleep?'' and answered truthfully. ''Yes. Yes I am.'' Whoever it was went away. When she woke in the morning, very late, she thought it might have been Windlow. Or perhaps Himaggery.

She had bought clothing in Hawsport, during the days spent there waiting for the Band to be ferried over from the peninsula. Skirts – she remembered skirts from Pfarb Durim a time before – and an embroidered tunic, cut low, and a stiff belt of gilded leather to make her waist look small, though indeed it was already tighter than when she had bought it. When she was fully awake – it might have been the following day or several days, she didn't know – and after a long luxurious washing of body and hair, she dressed herself in this unaccustomed finery and went into Windlow's garden.

Someone observed her seated there and went to tell someone else. After a time she heard halting steps upon the stone and turned to find him there, neatly trimmed of hair and beard, walking toward her with the heasitant stride he was to have for some years, as any four-footed creature might if hoisted high upon two legs and told to stay there.

She was moved to see him so familiar, as she had pictured him a thousand times. ''Himaggery. For a time, you know, I had not thought to set eyes upon you in human shape again.'' She was unprepared for his tears, and forgave him that he was not her silken-maned lover any longer.

They sat in the garden for some time, hours, talking and not talking. He had heard of the journey and was content to ask few questions about it.

She was less content. ''Do you remember anything at all about being the Singlehorn?'' she asked. ''Do you remember anything at all about the Dervish's valley?''

He turned very pale. ''No. And yet . . . sometimes I dream about it. But I can't remember, after I've wakened, what the dream was about.''

She kept her voice carefully noncommittal. "Do you desire to return there?"

"I don't think so," he faltered. "But . . . it would be good to run, I think. As I ran. As we ran. We were there together, weren't we?"

She waited, hoping he would go on to speak of that time, even a few words. He said nothing more. After a time he began to talk about other things, about plans for his future, things he might do. He asked about the Lake of Faces, and she described it as she had seen it in moonlight, with the Harpy questioning the Faces. She told him of Rose-love's answer, and of the man who spoke of the Great Game taking place around Lake Yost. This piqued his interest, for he remembered the place, and they spoke for a time comfortably about things which did not touch them too closely.

When the bell rang to tell them supper was served in the tower, he took her hand and would not let her go. "May I come to your room tonight?" Not looking at her, dignified and yet prepared for her refusal, hardly daring to ask her and yet not daring to go without asking. She was more moved by that pathetic dignity than she would have been by any importunate pleas.

"Of course. I hoped you would." That, at least, had been the truth. Later, deep in the ecstatic night, she knew it was still the truth, and more than the truth.

Several days later she sat with Throsset in that same tower room, lying upon a pile of pillows, a basket of fruit at her side. Throsset had been nervously stalking about for some minutes, picking things up and putting them down. Now she cleared her throat and said, "You're pregnant, aren't you? I've been watching you for days. All that nonsense on the road with those Harpies! Any Shifter worth a trip through the p'natti could have handled a dozen Harpies without being touched. But you didn't Shift. You haven't Shifted once since you've been here. Not even to fit yourself to a chair or lie comfortably before the fire. How far along are you?"

"I don't know," Mavin replied, almost in a whisper. "I was Shifted when it happened, not myself. In the Dervish's valley. It could have been a season I was there with him, or a few days. I don't know." She did not mention the time she had visited that valley eight years before. She wondered if Himaggery would ever remember how it had been, they two together in the valley.

Somehow it seemed terribly important that he remember it – without being reminded of it.

"Shifted when it happened! Well and well, Mavin. That leaves me wondering much. Time was we would have assumed it an ill thing and believed that no good issue could come of it. I'm not certain of that any more. Still it's interesting. And you don't know how long ago? Well, we can figure it out. I left you near Pfarb Durim early in the season of storms. You traveled from there how many days before you found him?"

Mavin counted. "One to the Lake of Faces. One to Chamferton's tower – or to him who said he was Chamferton. I don't know after that, three or four days, I think, following the runners. Perhaps two days to find the Dervish, then time got lost."

"So, the earliest it could have happened would have been still during the season of storms. Only a few days after you left me. Then how long to come south?"

"Forever, Throsset. Days at Chamferton's tower, straightening out that mess. Days searching for Singlehorn. Days running from shadows. Days trying to hide from Pantiquod, until the shadows ate her. Days and more days following the Band as it came south along the shore. Days following the river courses. Then across country, through the mountains. To here. And the time here, these last few days."

"So. Perhaps about one hundred days ago. Perhaps a bit more. Not really showing yet, but I can tell that you feel it. Any Shifter-woman can feel it almost from the beginning, of course. A kind of foreign presence telling one not to Shift."

"You have had . . ."

"Two. A son, a daughter. Long ago. Neither were Shifter, so after they came of age I left them with their father's kin. Better that way. Still, sometimes . . ."

"Did you use a forgetter?"

Of course not. They were grown, and fond enough of me. They forget soon enough on their own, and if they're ever ashamed of having a Shifter mother, then bad luck to them." She laughed harshly enough to show that the thought of this hurt her. "What are you going to do?"

"Do?"

"Do. Are you going to stay with Himaggery? He wants you to go with him to build a great demesne at that place he talks of, near

Lake Yost. The place with unlimited power. He says anything is possible to one with a demesne at such a place."

"And if I go with him, what?" Mavin asked in a bleak voice. Then, rising to stride about, her voice becoming a chanting croon in the firelight. "When I think of him, Throsset, I am afire to be with him. My skin aches for him. It is only soothed when I am pressed tight against him, as tight as we can manage. My nipples keep pushing against my clothes, wanting out, wanting him to touch them. Then, when we are together, we make love and lie side by side, our arms twisted together, and there is such wonderful peace, like floating – quiet and dusky, with no desires for a time. And then he talks of his plans. His plans, his desires, his philosophy. Of things he has read. I listen. Sometimes I think he is very naive, for I have found things in the world to be different from his beliefs, but he does not hear me if I say so.

"So I merely listen. I fall asleep. Or, if not, my head starts to hurt. Soon I ache to be away, in some quiet place with the wind calling, or in some wild storm where I could fly, run, move. And so I go into the woods and am peaceful away from him for a time, until I am brought back like a fish upon a line. . . .

"If I go with him, what?" she asked. "I keep asking myself that. He has never asked me what I would like to do."

"That's not true," objected Throsset, "I heard him ask you as we dined last evening. . . ."

"You heard him ask me, and if you listened, you heard him answer his own question and go on talking. He asked me what I would like to do, and then he told me how useful a Shifter would be to him. He has heard the story of our journey south, but he has not questioned why I could not Shift. He has not questioned why I have not Shifted in the time we have been here."

"That's true," Throsset sighed. "Men sometimes do not see these things."

"So." Mavin nodded. "Since they do not see these things, if I were to go with him, then what?"

"You're planning to go to Lake Yost, aren't you," Windlow asked Himaggery. "You haven't stopped talking about it since you first heard about the place. Not even when you're with Mavin, at least not while the two of you are with anyone else. Why all this sudden interest in the place?''

''At first I was afire to go back norther,'' Himaggery said, laying the pen to one side and shuffling his papers together. Couldn't wait to try that tower again. I figured out how I got caught the first time, and I had all sorts of ideas that might have worked to outwit the shadows – or distract them. I don't think they have 'wits' in the sense we mean. But the longer I thought about it, the more I decided you were right, Windlow. The time isn't right for it. So, the next best thing is to set up the kind of demesne you and I have talked of from time to time. And an excellent place to do it is at Lake Yost. There's more power there than any collection of Gamesmen can use in a thousand years, enough to make the place the strongest fortress in the lands of the True Game.''

''Mavin told you the place has been emptied?''

''She learned of it at the Lake of Faces. Actually, I already knew of Lake Yost. A marvelous location but it was held by a troop of idiots, True Game fanatics, wanting only to challenge and play, come what might of it. They called Great Game a season ago, a Game so large we haven't seen its like in a decade. With the unlimited power of the place, they succeeded in killing all the players, every Gamesman. The place is emptied and dead, ready for my taking.''

''And will Mavin go with you?''

''Of course! We can't lose one another now, not after all this time.''

Windlow went to the tower window, stood there watching the clouds move slowly over the long meadows to the west. There were shadows beneath them on the grasses, and he wondered if *the* shadows hid in these harmless places unseen, when they did not wish to be seen. ''Have you thought she might have something else she would like to do?''

''Ah, but what could be more important than this, old teacher? Eh? A place where your ideas can be taught? A place where we can bring together Gamesmen who believe in those words of yours, where we can work together! Wouldn't anyone want to be part of that?''

''Not everyone, my boy. No. There are many who would not want to be part of that, and that doesn't make them villians, either.''

''Mavin will want to come with me,'' he said with satisfaction. ''Windlow, we are so in love. I imagined it, all those years, but I could not imagine even a fraction of it. She wouldn't lose that anymore than I would."

"You've asked her, I presume."

"Of course I have! What do you take me for, old teacher? Some kind of barbarian? Kings and other Beguilers may hold unwilling followers – or followers who would be unwilling if they were in their own minds – but Wizards do not. At least this Wizard does not."

"I just wondered if it had occurred to you – a thought I've had from time to time, a passing thing, you know – that love behaves much as Beguilement does. Mertyn, for example. Do you remember him at all?"

"Mavin's brother. Surely I remember him. A nice child. Boldery's friend. Of course, he was only eleven or twelve when I left the School, so I don't remember him well. . . ."

"Mertyn had the Talent of Beguilement, you know. Had it early, as a fifteen-season child, I think. And it was Mertyn who kept Mavin's sister from leaving the place they lived, not a very pleasant place for women to hear Mertyn tell of it. He blamed himself, you know, crying over it in the night sometimes. And I asked him if his sister loved him, even without the Beguilement, and he told me yes, she did. So – mostly to relieve the child's mind, you understand – I said it could have been love did it just as well. And he was not responsible for that. We may be responsible for those we love, but hardly ever for those who love us. Takes a saint to do that." He turned from this slow, ruminative speech to find Himaggery's eyes fixed on some point in space. "Himaggery?"

"Um? Oh, sorry. I was thinking about Lake Yost. There's a perfect site for a community, as I recall, near the place the hot springs come up. I was trying to remember whether there was a little bay there. It seems to me there was, but it's not clear. You were saying?" He turned his smiling face toward the old man, eyes alight but already shifting again toward that distant focus.

"Nothing," Windlow sighed. "Nothing, Himaggery. Perhaps we'll talk about it some other time."

'I wanted you to have this account of the Eesties," said Mavin, handing the sheets of parchment to the old man. "Foolishly, I betrayed myself into giving one such account to the false Chamferton. He was very excited over it. I think he would have tried to hold me in some dungeon or other if I hadn't cooperated with him so willingly."

She sat upon the windowsill of the tower room, waiting while he read them over, hearing his soft exclamations of delighted interest, far different from Chamferton's crow of victory when he received his copy. The washerwomen were working at the long trough beside the well, and a fat, half-naked baby staggered among them, dabbling in the spilled water. She considered this mite, half in wonder, half in apprehension.

"And you can't speak of this at all?" Windlow asked at last.

"Not at all," she said. "And yet nothing prevents my writing it down."

"Let's see," he murmured. "You went to Ganver's Grave and . . . ahau, ghaaa . . ." He choked, coughed, grasped at his throat as though something were caught there, panted, glared around himself in panic. Mavin darted to him, held him up and quiet as the attack passed. He sat down, put his head upon his folded arms. "Frightening," he whispered. "Utterly frightening. The geas is laid not only upon you, then, but upon anyone?"

" To speak of it, yes. But not to write of it. That fact makes me wonder strangely."

"For a start, it makes me wonder if the . . . they do not choose to be spoken of by the ignorant. They don't mind being read of by literate people, however. Remarkable."

"I thought so, too," she agreed. "Except that the pawns have a thousand fables about the rolling stars and the Old Ones and the Eesties. Nothing stops their throats. Nothing stopped old Rose-love when she told me the story of Weetzie and the daylight bell."

"Because fables are fables." He nodded, ticking the points off to himself. "And facts are facts. You could probably tell the story of your own meeting with them, Mavin, if you fabulized it."

"Girl-shifter and the Crimson Egg," she laughed. "The story of Fustigar-woman and the shadowpeople."

"Quite wonderful. Are you going back there? Seeking the Eesties again?"

"Of course," she cried in unconscious delight of which Windlow was altogether conscious. "Who could not? Oh, Windlow, you would like that place. As full of marvels as a shell is full of egg. And there are other things, things having nothing to do with the Eesties. There's a place below the ridge by Schlaizy Noithn like nothing you have ever seen. I call it the Blot. Traders come there

– Traders some say. I think them false gifters, myself – and I want to explore it one day. And I left a girl-child friend across the sea. Her I would see again, before I am old, her and her children."

"And what about your child?" he asked, head cocked to one side, gentle as the wind as he said it.

"How did you know?"

He shrugged. "Oh, I'm a Seer, Mavin. Of one thing and another. In this case, however, it was a case of using my mind and my heart, nothing more. Himaggery doesn't know, does he?"

"Anyone might know," she replied in a sober voice. "Anyone who used mind or heart. Throsset knew."

"You won't allow that he's simply afire to get on with his life, so much of it having been spent in a kind of sleep?"

"Why, of course!" she answered in exasperation. "Why, of course I'll allow it. Do I constrain him to do other than he will? He lost eight years in that valley. Should I demand he turn from his life to look at me? Or listen to me? Windlow. That's not the question to ask, and you know it."

He nodded, rather sadly, getting up with a groan and a thud of his stick upon the floor. "Surely, Mavin. Surely. Well. Since it seems you'll not be Shifting for a time – do I have it right? That is the custom? More than custom, perhaps? – call upon me for whatever you need. Midwives perhaps, when the time comes? I have little power but many good friends."

"I do not know yet what I will need, old sir. Midwives, I guess, though whether here or elsewhere, I cannot say."

"You'll risk that, will you?"

"Risk Midwives? I would not do other. It is a very good thing the Midwives do, to look into the future of each child to see whether it will gain a soul or not. The great houses may scoff at Midwives if they will, caring not that their soulless children make wreck and ruin upon the earth. Of such houses are Ghouls born, Gamesmen like Blourbast and Huld the Demon." She did not mention Huld's son, Mandor. Years later, deep in the caves beneath Bannerwell, she was to curse herself for that omission. If Windlow had known of Mandor . . . if Mertyn had known of Mandor . . . "Of course I will risk Midwives, and count the risk well taken to know I have born no soulless wight who may grow to scourge the earth and the company of men."

He smiled then, taking her hand in his own and leaning to kiss her on the cheek, a sweet, old man's kiss with much kindness in it. "Mavin, perhaps I erred when I had that vision of you and Himaggery in Pfarb Durim. It seems to me that in that vision your hair was gray. Perhaps it was meant to be later, that's all." He sighed. "Whatever you need, Mavin. Tell me." Then they left the place and went to their lunch, spread on a table in the courtyard among the herb pots and the garden flowers. For a quiet time in that garden, Mavin told herself she would stay where she was, for the peace of it was pleasant and as kindly as old Windlow's kiss.

"You might remember that he's eight years younger than he seems," commented Throsset. "All that time in the valley. He didn't live then, really. In fact, he may have gone backwards . . . "

"To become what?" Mavin asked, examining her face in the mirror. She had never before been very interested in her own face, but now it fascinated her. One of Windlow's servant girls had asked if she could arrange Mavin's hair, and the piled, sculptured wealth of it made her look unlike herself. "Become a child, you mean?"

Throsset swung her feet, banging her heels cheerfully against the wall below the windowsill where she sat, half over the courtyard, defying gravity and dignity at once as she tempted the laundress's boy-child with a perfect target for his peashooter. "Children are very self-centered, Mavin. They are so busy learning about themselves, you know, that they have no time for anything else. You were like that, I'm sure. I know I was. Himaggery, on the other hand, went straight from his family demesne into Windlow's school, and straight from that into continuous study – books, collections. Not Gaming. Not paying attention to other people, you know."

" 'Among,' but not 'of,' " commented Mavin, touching the corner of her eyes with a finger dipped in dust-of-blue. She turned. "Do you like that? It's interesting."

"I like the brown better," Throsset advised. "Better with your skin. What are you up to with these pawn tricks, anyhow?"

Mavin turned back to the mirror, wiping away the blue stain to replace it with dust-of-brown. She had bought the tiny cosmetic jars from a traveling Trader and was being self-consciously experimental with them. "I'm finding out whether I can get him to look at me."

"He looks at you all the time. He's in love with you."

"I mean see me. He doesn't care whether I'm Mavin the woman, a fustigar hunting bunwits, or a Singlehorn. He's in love with his idea of me." She applied a bit more of the brown shadow, then picked up the tiny brush to blind herself painting her lashes.

"Your eyelashes are all right!" Throsset thumped down from the window, brushing at her seat, not seeing the pea which shot through the opening behind her. "When are you going to tell him?"

"I'm not." She was definite about this. "And you're not to tell him either."

"Oh, Mavin, by all the hundred devils but you're difficult. Why not?"

"Because, dear Fairy Godmother" – The proper designation for one with both Shifting and Sorcery was "Fairy Godmother." Mavin had looked it up in the Index and had been perversely waiting for an occasion to use it. Now she took wicked pleasure in Throsset's discomfiture – "*dear* Fairy Godmother, what you saw and what Windlow saw you saw by observation. Himaggery is not innocent. He knows where babies come from. He does know we were together in the Valley. It is a kind of test, my dear, which may be unfair, but it is nonetheless a test I am determined to use."

"And if he passes it?"

"If *he* passes it, with no advice from either you or Windlow – whom I have been at some pains to silence – then I will go with him to Lake Yost, and see what it is he plans to do there with his thousand good Gamesmen. And I will not Mavin at him, will not flee from him, will not distress him."

"And if he fails . . . "

"Then, Throsset of Dowes, I will know that it really does not matter to him much. He is in love with the idea of me, and that idea will content him. He will be reasonably satisfied with memory and hope and a brave resolution to find me once again – which he will put off from season to season, since there will always be other things to do." She looked up at Throsset with a quirk of the eyebrows. "Listen to me, Throsset, for I have made a discovery. It may be that Himaggery will *prefer* the idea of me to the reality – *prefer* to remember me with much romantic, sentimental recollection, at his convenience, as when a sweetly painted sky seems to call for such feelings of gentle melancholy. In the evenings, perhaps, when the sun is dropping among long shadows and the air breathes sadness. On moonlit nights, with the trees all silvered . . .

"A remembered love, Throsset of Dowes, does not interfere with one's work! A lovely, lost romance is a convenience for any busy man!"

"You're cynical. And footloose. You simply don't want to sit still long enough to rear this child."

"I'll sit still, Throsset! Where I will and when I will, and for as long as is necessary. And if Himaggery sees the meaning behind this paint on my face or realizes I am carrying his child, well then I will become dutiful, Throsset. So dutiful, even Danderbat Keep would have been pleased." She made a face, then rummaged in her jewel box for some sparkling something to put in her hair. "I have discovered something else, Throsset of Dowes. And that is that men give women jewels when they have absolutely no idea what might please them and are not willing to take time to think about it."

They sat beside the fountain beneath the stars. Out in the meadow other stars bobbled and danced, lantern bugs dizzying among the grasses.

"I used to imagine this," said Himaggery. She lay half in his lap, against his chest, watching the lights, half asleep after a long, warm and lazy day.

"What did you imagine? Sitting under the sky watching bugs dance?"

"No, silly. I imagined you. And me. Together. Here or somewhere like here. I knew how it would be."

"This isn't how it would be," she said, the words flowing out before she could stop them. "This is an interlude, a sweet season. It's no more real than . . . than we were before, in the valley."

"How can you say that?" He laughed, somewhat uneasily. "You're real. I'm real. In our own shapes, our own minds."

She shook her head. Now that she had started, she had to go on. "No, love. I'm in *a* shape, a courtyard shape, a lover's shape, a pretty girl shape, a romantic evening shape. I have other shapes for other times. With those other shapes, it would be a different thing . . . "

"Not at all. No matter what shape it might be, it would always be you inside it!" His vehemence hid apprehension. She could smell it.

She soothed him. "Himaggery, let me tell you a story.

"Far on the western edge of the land, there's a town I visited once. Pleasant people there. One charming girl-child I fell in love with. About nine years old, I suppose, full of joy and bounce and love. She was killed by a man of the town, a Wolf. Everyone knew it. They couldn't prove it. They had locked him up for such things before, but had always let him go. It was expensive to keep him locked up and guarded, and fed and warm. It took bread from their own mouths to keep him locked away . . . "

"What has this to do with . . . " he began. She shushed him.

"So, though everyone knew he had done it, no one did anything except walk fearfully and lock up their children. I was not satisfied with that. I took the shape of one of his intended victims, Himaggery, and I ended the matter."

There was a long pause. She heard him swallow, sigh. "As I would have done, too, Mavin, had I the Talent. I do not dispute your judgment."

"You don't. Well, the people of the town suspected I might have had something to do with it, and one of them came to remonstrate with me that such a course of action was improper. So I asked why they had not kept him locked up, or killed him the first time they had proof, and they told me it would have been cruel to do so. And I asked then if it were not cruel to their children to let the Wolf run loose among them. They did not answer me.

"So then, Himaggery, I took their children away from them. All. Far to the places of the True Game. For at least in the lands of the True Game people are not such hypocrites. I thought better those children chance a hazardous life knowing who their enemies were than to live in that town where their own people conspired with their butchers."

There was another long silence. "You were very upset at the child's death," he said at last.

"Yes. Very."

"So you were not yourself. If you had had time to think, to reflect, you would not have acted so."

Then she was silent. At last she said with a sigh, "No, Himaggery, I was myself. Completely myself. And if I'd had longer to think on it, I would have done worse."

He tried to tell her she was merely tired, but she changed the subject to something light and laugh-filled. Later they made love under the stars. It was the last conversation they had together.

Midmorning of the following day, Throsset of Dowes rode with Mavin northward along the meadow edge. They had brought some food and wine with them, intending to take a meal upon the grassy summit which overlooked the canyon lands before Throsset left for the south. Throsset had decided to go visiting her children soon, away in the Sealands. It was a sudden decision.

"I decided they would scarcely remember me unless I went soon. I haven't gone before because I feared they would reject me, a Shifter. But if I don't go, then I have rejected them. So better let the fault lie upon their heads if it must lie anywhere. I will go south tomorrow. I have not run in fustigar shape for a season and a half, not since I met you outside Pfarb Durim. I am getting fat and lazy."

Mavin hugged her. "You will be here tonight then? Good. You will be able to tell them that I have gone."

"Ah," said Throsset, a little sadly. "Well. So you have made up your mind."

"When we have had our lunch, you will ride back and I will ride on. Tell Windlow I will repay him for the horse sometime."

"Windlow would have given you the horse. Where are you going? Why are you going?"

"I am going because I do not want this child to be born here, or at Lake Yost, to serve as a halter strap between me and Himaggery. I am going because Himaggery does not see me as I am, and I cannot be what he thinks I am. I am going because there is much distraction here, of a wondrous kind, and I want two years, or three, to give to the child without distractions.

"As to where. Well. North. Somewhere. I have friends there. I will find Midwives there. And when the time is right, I may see Himaggery again. Windlow now thinks his vision was of a later time. We may yet come together in Pfarb Durim."

"What am I to tell them?"

"That I became restless. That I have gone on a journey. Don't say much more than that. Himaggery will be quite happy with that. Each day he will think of going off to find me. Each day he will put it off for a while. Each night he will dream romantic dreams of me, and each morning he will resolve again – quite contentedly.

"Don't tell him I'm expecting a child. If he knew, he would first have to decide how to feel about it, and then what actions such a feeling should create. Better leave him as he is. After all, the Midwives may not let the child live. So don't take his smile from him, Throsset. Strangely though I seem to show it, I do love him."

They drank the wine. When they had done, Throsset threw the jug against a stone, shattering it into pieces. She wrote her name upon a shard and gave it to Mavin, accepting a similar one in return. So were meetings and partings memorialized among their people, without tears.

After Mavin rode down into the canyon lands, Throsset sat for a long time staring after her. She was not sad, not gay, not grieving or rejoicing. She went boneless and did the quick wriggle which passed for comment in Danderbat Keep; Mavin could not Shift for a time, but she was still Mavin Manyshaped, and Throsset did not doubt she would return.

"Good chance to you," she whispered toward the north. "And to your child, Mavin." Nothing answered but the wind. Putting the shard into her pocket as one of the few things she would always carry, she went to tell them that Mavin Manyshaped had gone.

'Do you think I'd be on this coach if I'd known that I'd have to face you every day for a fortnight?'

Dane's dark head was abruptly lowered so that it was level with her own. Dark eyes channelled cold scorn. 'When did *you* develop a conscience? At the same time that you learned to control that temper?' he mocked.

Joanne flinched from the contempt in his tone, annoyed with herself for the swift, sharp riposte that betrayed her chagrin. What was it about this man that challenged her fierce spirit as well as her senses in the same old way? 'You really hate me, don't you?' she countered.

His lip curled and a pulse beat an angry tattoo in his lean cheek. 'I've certainly no reason to love you,' he ground in a savage undertone.

Lynne Collins has written twenty-six Medical Romances based on personal experience of hospital life, backed by research and information from her many friends in the medical profession. She likes writing about hospital settings, with their wealth of human interest. Married with one son and now living on the Essex coast, Lynne enjoys travel, meeting people, talking, walking, and gardening. She has also written several Medical Romances under the pen-name of Lindsay Hicks.

Previous Titles

BEAT OF THE HEART
STAR SURGEON
SURGEON AT BAY

REPENTANT ANGEL

BY

LYNNE COLLINS

MILLS & BOON LIMITED
ETON HOUSE 18–24 PARADISE ROAD
RICHMOND SURREY TW9 1SR

All the characters in this book have no existence outside the imagination of the Author, and have no relation whatsoever to anyone bearing the same name or names. They are not even distantly inspired by any individual known or unknown to the Author, and all the incidents are pure invention.

First published in Great Britain 1990
by Mills & Boon Limited

This edition 1990

ISBN 0 263 76844 9

Set in 10 on 11½ pt Linotron Plantin
03-9006-53589
Typeset in Great Britain by Centracet, Cambridge
Made and printed in Great Britain

CHAPTER ONE

THE sharp squeal of brakes still had the power to freeze her blood and turn her legs to jelly, after all these years. Joanne spun to glare at the powerful car that shot through the gateway and came to a halt in a vacant parking bay only yards from the coach that waited, engine on the thrum, for the last arrival.

A ragged cheer went up from those already in their seats. Anneliese, busily supervising the stowing of luggage and wheelchairs in the belly of the coach, looked relieved. 'He's a Dane!' she exclaimed, and hurried to meet him.

As if that excused his lateness, Joanne thought drily, busily folding yet another wheelchair. The revelation of the man's nationality didn't excite her at all, for she was used to the polyglot mix of people associated with the Red Cross. Anneliese was German and it was her organising abilities that had got this holiday in Austria for a disabled group off the ground when everyone else had been declaring that it was impractical. Her gift for treating obstacles as if they simply didn't exist and her boundless enthusiasm for the project had marshalled a motley crew of helpers, Joanne among them. She had volunteered to be one of the nurses so essential to the venture, taking time off from the hospital where she and Anneliese were both ward sisters.

She glanced at the couple standing beside the expensive Mercedes. The newcomer was tall and lean and surprisingly dark for a Scandinavian. Anneliese had said little about him except that he had agreed to be the last-minute replacement for the doctor who had broken his leg in an inter-hospital rugger match at the weekend.

His back was to Joanne, and as he raised the car boot to take out a case and a leather holdall, she saw the ripple of muscles beneath his lightweight jacket. Those splendid shoulders would serve him well in the next two weeks, Joanne decided. There was a lot of lifting and carrying in store for the helpers on this unusual holiday and, doctor or no, he would be expected to do his share.

She turned to take a case from Lionel, one of the first to help in any situation. 'Thanks. That's the last, isn't it? I think you should take your seat now, Lionel. We should be leaving in a few minutes.' She smiled warmly at the gentle giant. Over six feet tall and powerfully built, blessed with very blue eyes and an enchanting smile, he was a general favourite.

'Lionheart' was Joanne's private name for the profoundly deaf man whose difficult speech could be understood by those who had the patience to listen. She had met him at the local PHAB Club, where she had been lured along by Anneliese one evening to entertain the members with her guitar and some folk songs. It had become a regular event and she had come to know several of the youngsters, who were craning their necks on the coach and beginning the 'here we go' chant of football fans in excited voices.

Anneliese and her friend walked towards the coach, and Joanne wondered if he was also disabled as she saw that he was slightly lame. Her glance travelled upwards to a lean, good-looking face, and she stepped back in sheer horror, stumbling over the suitcase she had just taken from Lionel and set ready for the coach driver.

Cal steadied her with a hand on her arm. 'All right, lass?' He was a Yorkshireman, good-hearted and reliable and, more important, at ease with the disabled. Employed by the company who supplied coaches for PHAB outings and had provided the holiday coach free of charge when approached by the persuasive Anneliese, he had volunteered to go along as driver-cum-helper.

Joanne mustered a smile. 'I'm fine. Just half-asleep still and falling over my own feet,' she quipped, her gaze on the late arrival.

He wasn't a Dane. He was *Dane*! Dr Dane Gregory, last seen in the Intensive Care Unit at Brook's, threatened with possible amputation of a leg and seriously ill with head injuries as a result of a car crash that she had caused.

She saw the flicker of shock in deep-set dark eyes, the fade of his smile and the sudden tensing of his sensual mouth as he recognised her, although it was nearly seven years since she had been a slightly plump first-year with a mass of unruly curls and a temper to match their blaze. Now, she was enviably slim, her hair was a smooth cap of gleaming auburn silk and her temper had been tightly chained since the dreadful night when the man she had loved had looked at her with loathing and had told her to get out of his life.

Unaware of the trauma in the totally unexpected encounter between two of her closest friends, Anneliese clung happily to Dane's arm, beaming. 'Here's Dane!' she declared once more and with obvious delight. 'His car wouldn't begin!' Her English tended to slip at moments of anger or excitement. 'This is Jo, who works with me at Monty's and is coming along as one of our nurses. I think I have spoken about her. . .?'

Joanne held her breath. Would he admit that they had once known each other? Or would he snub her, cold-eyed and unsmiling, setting the pattern for the next two weeks?

'I think I expected a male nurse—Joe with an E.' Dane brushed past to put case and holdall with the rest of the luggage, nodding to Cal, necessary haste excusing him from smiling or shaking hands with a girl he had never wanted or expected to see again.

Clever micro-surgery had saved an almost severed leg, but he had been left with a slight limp and a degree of pain that was a constant reminder that women could be dangerous, particularly redheads. A head injury had kept him drifting in and out of coma for days, too. When he had finally come round, expecting an anxious Joanne to be at his bedside, he had learned that she had left Brook's.

Young, impulsive and irresponsible, she had seemed an unlikely candidate for a nursing career, so he was surprised to find that she had finished her training at another hospital and had duly qualified.

'No, no! I confused you with so many names, perhaps! *Owen* is our male nurse. See—on the coach, with Richard.' Anneliese indicated the young Welshman, who waved back at her from his seat beside his main charge, the eighteen-year-old multiplegic who had fallen from a tree when he was seven and was now totally dependent on others for all his needs.

Cal closed and locked the luggage compartment. 'That's the last, is it, Annie? Because we ought to be moving.' As he swung himself into the driving seat, a great cheer went up, almost drowning Anneliese's urgent demand to know if everyone had their passports. As it was the third time of asking and they were all confident that nothing had been forgotten, no one took any notice.

As she said goodbye to Red Cross friends who had been so supportive with funds, advice, accommodation arrangements and helpers, a little anxiety tugged at

Joanne. If only Gary hadn't played rugger that weekend and had ended up in traction! If only Anneliese's anxious scouting for a substitute hadn't turned up Dane Gregory, of all people! With so much on her conscience, could she enjoy the carefully planned adventure in Austria?

Beaming faces greeted her as she boarded the coach. Moving down the aisle, she was constantly checked by clasping hands, eager questions, a demand for a kiss or a hug from the mix of lively, affectionate and uncomplaining young people. As she slid into her seat next to Becky, a girl in her mid-twenties born without normal legs as a result of thalidomide given to her mother to combat pregnancy problems, Joanne told herself sternly to stop making a mountain out of a molehill.

So Dane Gregory was coming along too. That was no reason to let his presence spoil things. This holiday had been lovingly planned down to the last detail with people like Becky and Richard and Lionel in mind, and it was only a working holiday for helpers like herself. Personal feelings would simply have to take a back seat for the time being.

'I thought today would never come!' Becky's pretty face was flushed with excitement as she shifted her bulky body on the cushions that made her as comfortable as possible for the long journey. 'Are you looking forward to Austria, Jo? Did you bring your guitar?'

'And my lederhosen,' Joanne joked, with a sparkle of the smile that endowed her with a captivating beauty. 'I'm planning to add some Tyrolean folk songs to my repertoire, so it should be a very noisy musical evening next month, with all of you stamping and clapping.

Leaning across the gangway, Lenny was promptly prevented by Patrick, a Red Cross helper, from falling out of his seat as the coach started off. He was one of the 'walking wounded', as Cal cheerfully called those who didn't need assistance to get on or off the coach. He had a good pair of legs and one good arm. The other arm, paralysed since birth, was supported by a permanent sling. 'Let's practise, Becky. . .you stamp and I'll clap,' he suggested irrepressibly, the broad grin making light of their respective disabilities in the way that Joanne had come to expect from the happy-go-lucky crowd from the PHAB Club.

As the coach eased through the gates, family and friends waved and called last-minute injunctions amid a flurry of renewed excitement. But shortly, as the coach sped towards Dover, the excitement began to subside. The early start to the day was taking its toll and, here and there, eyes closed and limbs lolled as people dozed. Joanne listened idly to snatches of conversation between wakeful members of the party, her gaze on the back of a dark head that reared above the seat in front.

Dane's crop of waving jet-black hair reminded her vividly of days when she had loved to twine her fingers in the tight, tempting curls. A faint waft of expensive aftershave told her that his tastes hadn't changed since she had bought him Givenchy for his birthday, just days before that fateful night had put paid to their love-affair.

He sat with a partially sighted girl who was incredibly lovely but so shy that she seldom spoke. This was her first holiday without her family and she was obviously nervous. It had taken much persuasion to get Nadine and her parents to agree to the holiday, and Joanne wondered how the shy girl would get on with the dour, unsmiling doctor who had walked past a one-time love without a word.

She couldn't blame him, in the circumstances. He must have been as shocked and as shaken as herself when they had come face to face without warning. But it wouldn't be a very comfortable trip if he continued to ignore her so pointedly.

The young disabled were observant and outspoken, and they had often embarrassed her before she'd grown used to their eager interest in her affairs. Their lives were often so limited that they had to enjoy a vicarious excitement through able-bodied friends, and if Becky learned that Joanne and Dane had once been lovers then she wouldn't rest until she had thought up a way to thrust them back into each other's arms—and neither of them could want that!

Once, Joanne had been headlong in love with the handsome doctor, swept off her feet by his looks and charm, and thrilled to realise that he cared for her too. But now he was a part of her past that she preferred to forget, and they must both be very different people after seven years.

He was apparently still single, like herself. She had steered clear of romance since the disaster of her affair with Dane. But she had thought him long since married, for women had run after him in droves and he was very attractive, tall and dark and beautiful, with a smile that could charm any woman into giving him what he wanted.

Joanne could have drawn that remarkable face from memory without stealing a single glance at the reality. Darkly expressive, lean and sensitive and intelligent, its classic planes might have been immortalised by Michelangelo in earlier times. The deep-set dark eyes with their penetrating perception could smoulder with anger or passion, smile with humour or loving tenderness, shine with enthusiasm as he talked of his work, his patients, his aims and his plans for a future that Joanne had once hoped to share with him.

The warm, sensual mouth could sweep a woman into

paradise with its sweet seeking, its power and its promise, but there was an obstinate set to the lean jaw and a touch of arrogance in the way he held his handsome head. Both proud and stubborn and quick to anger, they had clashed fiercely and often during their brief relationship, and it had probably been meant that they should never marry, she told herself sensibly, ignoring a tug at her heart.

Anneliese left her seat to make the first of many sorties to check that everyone was comfortable. She wore a bright orange tracksuit so that she was easily spotted in a crowd by anyone who became separated from the main party en route or when they were on one of the many planned excursions.

'To match my eyes,' she had declared laughingly when someone had commented on her gaudy attire. And they *were* amber, unusually large and sparkling in a lively, lovely face.

She paused to speak to Dane. 'Is there enough room for your long legs? Are you comfortable? Later, we can sit together for a while, perhaps. I want all those who can to change seats occasionally so that we all know each other well by the time we reach Pleydorf. That will be best, I think. Are you all right in there, Nadine? Not too crushed by this giant? Tell Dane or Jo behind you if you have any problems.'

As she leaned across Dane, a fall of her corn-coloured hair toppled across her bright face. Dane brushed it back and curved his hand briefly about her cheek in an unmistakable caress. Anneliese smiled at him with a warmth that left Joanne wondering about their relationship. The warm-hearted German girl fell in and out of love with an ease that astonished the more circumspect Joanne, but perhaps it was the real thing this time. For both of them.

'So many plans and problems, but we're really on our way at last.' Anneliese sighed happily, moving on to come level with Joanne. 'We are going to have a wonderful holiday, all of us—and the weather forecast is good,' she added, loud enough for all to hear. 'The sun will shine for us. By personal arrangement.'

'And you vill enjoy yourselves!' Lenny capped loudly, cheerfully, teasing her slight accent.

'You certainly vill!' Anneliese retorted with a laugh, rumpling his hair. 'Or I shall want to know vy not!' She turned back to beam at Joanne's companion. 'Oh, Becky—I see that you are looking after Jo! Good! She needs you to keep an eye on her or she'll have too much schnapps or too many cream cakes, or she'll run off with a muscular young Austrian in too-tight lederhosen!'

'You're a spoilsport,' Joanne reproached as Becky giggled. 'I was looking forward to running amok.'

'Along with Richard and Lenny and a few others, no doubt,' Anneliese returned, mock-severe. 'I don't know why I brought such tearaways on holiday.'

'We're not tearaways!' It was said in unison, loud, cheerful rebuttal of the teasing words.

'Oh, yes, you are!'

'Oh, no, we're not!'

Anneliese conceded defeat with a smile and a shrug and continued to the back of the coach. Sensing waves of disapproval from the man in front, Joanne impulsively leaned forward. 'I suppose you think it's all very juvenile.'

Dane half-turned, a spark of irritation in his dark eyes at the tart challenge. 'I'm beginning to wonder what I've let myself in for, certainly,' he agreed, goaded by her presence and too many bitter memories, and a feeling that he would regret his last-minute consent to join the group.

'Annie can be very persuasive.' Joanne's tone implied her suspicion of the persuasion that her friend had probably applied to get him to come on this most unlikely holiday for a man of his standing and temperament.

'I dare say it will be good for my soul,' Dane drawled with deliberately infuriating smugness.

'It might even teach you a little humility!' she snapped unfairly, and sank back, flushed and trembling. The first words they had exchanged in nearly seven years and they were back to quarrelling. Nothing had changed, she thought wryly.

Becky glanced at her curiously. Joanne smiled in rueful apology. 'Don't take any notice of us, Becky,' she said brightly, making light of the brief spat. 'Dane and I are old friends.' That was true enough. It didn't have to imply that they were still friends. The spark of animosity made it clear that friendship was out of the question these days. She felt too guilty about the past—and it was only too obvious how Dane felt about her.

'He's smashing,' Becky whispered admiringly. 'Very good-looking. Annie has some great-looking friends. Where does she find them?' She sounded envious. She had lots of admirers of her own, but most were disabled, like herself. Able-bodied men were drawn by her pretty face and bright personality, but were reluctant to become too involved with a girl who spent her days in a wheelchair. She studied Dane with thoughtful interest while he tried to encourage Nadine into conversation, and then she leaned forward. 'Nadine won't talk to men. She doesn't talk to anyone very much. But she likes Jo. Why don't you change places with Jo? You'd like that, wouldn't you, Nadine?'

A shy smile peeped as the girl nodded assent. Dane promptly got up. A little reluctantly, Joanne stood up at the same moment that Cal braked sharply to avoid a car that swung in front of the coach from the fast lane. She was thrown against the man, who instinctively put out a hand to steady her. His touch was too much, sending remembered excitement shivering along her spine, alarming and annoying in its intensity.

Fiercely she shrugged off his hand and plumped into the seat next to Nadine.

By the time they reached Dover, the girl had uttered no more than two sentences, but Joanne felt confident that she would emerge from her shell during the two weeks with a crowd of lively, uninhibited youngsters.

Behind them, Becky chatted in her usual bright fashion, and Joanne caught the occasional drift of Dane's deep voice, the low chuckle of amusement. The conversation flew back and forth across the gangway as Lenny and Patrick joined in, and it was obvious that Dane was fast making friends. He had always got on well with people, one of the first essentials for a doctor. He was warm and caring and genuinely interested in the whole person and not just the problem that they brought to him for solving.

Before the accident, he had been a junior registrar at Brook's, clever and ambitious. Mutual friends had kept Joanne informed of his gradual recovery and eventual return to work. Relieved, reassured that he had got over the car crash and was getting on with his life, Joanne had felt that she could crush the last of the lingering memories and concentrate on her own future in nursing. She had gradually lost touch with the people who had known both her and Dane in the days of that doomed affair, and it was some years since she'd heard anything about him. She had often wondered if he would ever turn up as a new member of staff at the Montgomery

General Hospital where she had eventually realised her ambition to become a ward sister.

They might have found themselves working together. Now they would simply be thrown together for a short time, and it ought to be possible to get on with each other. For the sake of the group. Joanne was prepared to meet him more than halfway, but she couldn't convince herself that he would take even one small step towards co-operating. He had a lot to forgive, she reminded herself ruefully. The stcel in the dark eyes and thc grim set to his mouth told her plainly that he hadn't forgiven at all.

On arrival at Dover, the coach was sped through Passport Control by considerate port officials who had been warned to expect them by the Red Cross. Cal drove the coach up the ramp and into the vast bowels of the car ferry to park in the allocated space close to a lift for the disabled. Some of the 'walking wounded' were glad to stretch their legs and head for the upper decks and the duty free shop, but only a few of the chairbound opted to leave the coach during the short journey across the Channel. Helpers ferried some to the toilets while Joanne and Anneliese went to the self-service cafeteria on an upper deck to get hot drinks for those who wanted them. Some munched sandwiches or crisps or chocolate bars, having been unable to fancy breakfast at an earlier hour.

Joanne doled out medication to those who were due for it according to the carefully detailed list in her notebook. Some needed pills or regular injections, and the small, secure case she had brought contained all the drugs and equipment she would need on the journey. She had agreed to be responsible for that side of things, as Anneliese had enough to do with organising meals and drinks en route and supervising the progress of the party across the Continent.

Temporarily occupying an empty seat at the rear of the coach, Joanne checked her list against the remaining pills and capsules and medicine levels with the conscientiousness of the trained nurse before she closed and locked the case with the key she carried on a thin chain about her neck. She looked up as a shadow fell across her and a hand thrust a steaming cup of coffee under her nose.

'Oh, thanks. . .' Dane's offering was welcome, for she, like Anneliese and Owen, had been so busy tending others that she'd had little time for her own needs. Grateful, wondering if it was an olive branch, she tried a smile, but it was met with an uncompromising coldness in the dark eyes.

'I'm only the delivery boy,' he said brusquely. 'The tall guy—Leonard, is it. . .?'

'Lionel.'

'Whatever. He brought half a dozen coffees from the cafeteria and asked Anneliese to hand them round to the carers.'

'That's like him,' Joanne said warmly. 'He's very thoughtful.' Glancing through the window, she saw Anneliese gratefully gulping coffee while she talked to Cal. Shouts and bangs and furious activity announced that they were approaching Calais, and it would soon be necessary to count heads and settle people in their seats before they disembarked for the next stage of the long drive to the purpose-built holiday complex in the Tyrol that was owned and run by the International Red Cross.

'Want this out of the way?' Taking the medical case from her lap, Dane stowed it on the shelf with automatic, meaningless courtesy.

Briefly, his powerful body swung towards her and

Joanne saw the ripple of muscles in his deep chest and flat belly, and his warm, male scent mingled with deodorant to flood her nostrils and stir her senses in the old, remembered way.

Tensing, she drew back. From the man and the memories. But the squeal of brakes and the shatter of glass and the groans of an injured man in a welter of blood were loud in her ears. . .

CHAPTER TWO

LOOKING down at Joanne's sleek auburn head, the taut figure, the slim hands curving defensively about the polystyrene cup, Dane wondered what twist of fate had thrown them together again.

It had taken a long time to put her out of his heart and mind. He might have forgiven her for losing her temper, with such dire consequences, because he had loved her very much. But no man could be expected to overlook the callous disregard for his injuries and his feelings that she had shown. She hadn't cared enough to visit, to enquire about him or to support him through the long, traumatic weeks of recovery, and it still rankled. Dane had no recollection of having seen or spoken to her since she ran his car off the road. All he knew was that she had left Brook's in a hurry, unable to face the consequences and, totally without caring or conscience, had walked out of his life.

'I've brought a supply of the usual drugs—Panadol, insulin, beta-blockers, that kind of thing,' he said, briskly professional even as he wondered at the silver badge of the registered nurse that she wore on the collar of her neat navy dress. How had a madcap, hot-tempered first-year ever made it to ward sister, no less? 'So if you should run out of anything. . .'

'I'm pretty well stocked. It takes a lot of advance planning for a trip of this kind.' Joanne knew that she sounded cool, stilted. It wasn't easy to talk naturally to a man she had nearly killed.

'I came along at such short notice that there was little

time to plan anything. Or to learn who was on the passenger list,' he added pointedly.

'Annie didn't tell me about *you* either,' Joanne flared defensively. 'I had no idea that you knew each other.' Sapphire eyes sparked fire. 'Do you think I'd be on this coach if I'd known that I'd have to face you every day for a fortnight?'

Dane's dark head was abruptly lowered so that it was level with her own. Dark eyes channelled cold scorn. 'When did *you* develop a conscience? At the same time that you learned to control that temper?' he mocked.

She flinched from the contempt in his tone, annoyed with herself for the swift, sharp riposte that betrayed her chagrin. What was it about this man that challenged her fierce spirit as well as her senses in the same old way? 'You really hate me, don't you?' she countered.

His lip curled and a pulse beat an angry tattoo in his lean cheek. 'I've certainly no reason to love you,' he ground in a savage undertone.

As if she needed the reminder of a nightmare that she had relived too many times, waking in a cold sweat from the shake of jealous rage, the torrent of accusing words, the flood of tears that had temporarily blinded her and the frozen moment of terror as she had lost control of the car and it had careered across the lonely road to up-end in a ditch.

'I'm sorry. . .' What else could she say to a bitter, hostile man?

As Dane turned abruptly to limp down the gangway to his seat, his back expressive of loathing, Joanne shrank into a corner, feeling totally unable to cope with questions or demands for a few moments. Her heartbeat was heavy with dismay as a barrage of memories battered at the unwilling door of her mind

* * *

The evening had begun so well. Her new dress had been the blue of her eyes and she had worn her proudly flaming hair in a knot of curls, threaded with ribbon of the same sapphire shade. Dane had whistled softly with awed admiration as she'd run down the steps of the nurses' home and into his eager arms, and her heart had soared in the confident belief that tonight, at last, he would ask her to marry him.

Joanne had had no reason to doubt that it would prove to be a very special birthday celebration, a little late because they had both been working on the actual date. Dane had been tender, loving, attentive, obviously proud and pleased to show her off to his friends at the club that had been a favourite venue for off-duty Brook's staff.

'This will be a night to remember for as long as we live, sweetheart,' he had declared extravagantly as they'd danced. He had been high on alcohol and ambition, for he had been promised a senior registrar's post, another cause for celebration for a dedicated, ambitious doctor.

He had held her like a lover who had enjoyed the intimate knowledge of her body and expected to enjoy it again before the night was over. Joanne had thrilled to his touch, the look in his dark eyes, the hunger in the lean body pressed against her own. Loving him as she did, it had proved impossible not to give him everything he had wanted. Loving him, she would go on giving until the end of time, she had vowed passionately.

She had wanted to marry him with all her heart. It hadn't mattered that they had quarrelled almost as often as they had made love. They had both been quick to anger, equally quick to cool and regret, and making up had been sweet and tender, adding a new dimension to their lovemaking. Once they were married, there would be none of the tensions that led to quarrels, she had told herself optimistically. Then, she'd lived in the nurses' home with all its restrictions. Dane had shared a flat with two other doctors. Both had worked long, unsocial hours and off-duty times had seldom coincided, and their affair had seemed to consist of snatched moments and rueful apologies and inevitable anxiety.

Joanne had been jealous, suspicious of any girl who had looked twice at Dane, terrified that he would tire of her and charge off in hot pursuit of one of the many good-looking nurses who had smiled so encouragingly at him.

Dane had been jealous too. The demands of his job had left him little time for the girl who had swept him into loving and thoughts of marriage for the first time. He hadn't expected her to sit in and forgo the fun that her friends enjoyed just because he had been on duty. But that fun had inevitably been shared by colleagues who fancied the pretty, personable redhead, and she had been young, impetuous, newly awakened.

His smiling, easy-going tolerance had seemed like indifference at times, and Joanne had been afraid of losing him. Halfway through the evening that had begun so well, that fear had erupted when Rona, the former girlfriend whose ghost she had still been trying to exorcise, had turned up unexpectedly

Rona had been everything that she had envied: tall, beautiful, worldly-wise. It had seemed inconceivable to Joanne that Dane could have willingly broken off the relationship. They had still been friends, she'd known—and to her jealous mind it had been an indication that he would have leapt at a chance to go back to her. Feeling overshadowed and resentful as the more dominant personality of the other woman had commandeered Dane's attention, she had got up to dance with Melvin without the usual, questing glance for approval. She had been swept off to the dance floor before she'd realised the smoulder in Dane's dark eyes. Seeing him extend his hand to Rona, she had thought that she understood his failure to object, as she had been whisked away to dance by another man.

In that moment, the spell of the evening had been shattered along with the promise of happiness. Studying them as they had danced, she had sickened as Rona had clung and laughed into Dane's smiling eyes and wound her arms about him in blatant, provocative reminder of past intimacy.

And with the sickness of hurt and jealousy had come a growing anger. . .

'Is Jo here? Has anyone seen Jo?'

Anneliese's voice carried down the length of the coach, startling Joanne back to the present. Blinking, she straightened the cup of cooling coffee that threatened her skirt with its tilting contents. 'I'm here, Annie,' she said quickly, showing herself above the seat back that had hidden her from view. Teasing tracked her every inch of the way as she swept down the gangway to her proper seat.

'Catching up on your sleep back there, Jo?'

'You got a man tucked away in that corner, Jo?'

'Keeping out of the way of the work, weren't you, Jo?'

Anneliese looked her over with a hint of concern in her amber eyes. 'Not feeling seasick, are you, Jo?'

'No, I'm fine.' She had almost forgotten that they were on board a cross-Channel ferry. It had been a very smooth crossing.

'You're looking peaky, lass. The smell of the diesel down here upsets some people,' Cal said kindly. 'But we've docked and we'll soon be on dry land. You'll feel better then.'

She put a friendly arm about his neck. 'I'll sit up here by you and get some fresh air, I think.'

'Aye, you're welcome. You can take over the wheel, if you like,' he suggested with a grin.

Joanne shuddered, the tremor rippling through her slender frame, and the blanch of remembered horror struck her cheeks. As if she could ever drive any vehicle again after that awful night when she had insisted on taking the wheel of Dane's powerful car because he had been drinking and might be over the limit!

Cal sensed her shivering unease. 'Someone walking over your grave, lass?' he sympathised.

The words washed over her. Against her will, she swivelled her head to look at Dane, who must have seen and heard and understood her reaction to Cal's light words. She looked at his handsome face and saw it covered in blood that welled and poured over her fingers in the moonlight as she touched him, screaming his name in blind panic and screaming again when he made no reply. . .

Shocked and dazed from the initial impact, breasts bruised by contact with the steering-wheel, Joanne had heard Dane groaning at her side. Then an ominous silence had convinced her that he was dead. Sobbing, almost hysterical, she had torn at his clothes and run a hand over his chest to find a heartbeat, and had flooded with relief that he was still alive, after all.

Somehow, panic-stricken but unhurt except for a few cuts and bruises, she had scrambled through the shattered windscreen in time to flag down the crowded car of medical students that had followed them from the club. Too far behind to witness the accident, they had arrived promptly enough to extricate Dane and give him immediate first-aid. While someone had looked after the shocked and shaking Joanne, someone else had driven to the nearest telephone box to summon an ambulance.

Dane had come round briefly as the paramedics had shot morphine into a vein and set up a life-saving drip, and Joanne had shivered in a bright red blanket on the nearby seat of the ambulance that had wailed through silent streets to the Accident and Emergency Department at Brook's, where a team had been alerted to expect the critically injured registrar.

Seeing the flicker of eyelids and the twist of pain that had crossed his face, Joanne had thrust past the paramedics to kneel on the floor at his side. 'I'm sorry. . . I'm so sorry!' she'd wailed along with the siren.

Dark eyes had opened abruptly to glower at her with intent and unmistakable loathing. 'Damn you, Jo!' he'd said thickly, savage with pain and fury. 'Just get out of my life and stay out! I never want to see you again, you stupid bitch!'

As the drug had taken effect, slurring the last words, Joanne had been lifted from her knees by a kindly ambulanceman, who had encouraged her to sob out her heartbreak against his chest. 'Take no notice, miss. He doesn't mean it. People say all sorts of daft things in shock and pain. He doesn't know what he's saying,' he'd comforted.

But Dane *had* known and meant every word, she'd felt, knowing that even if he recovered she had lost his love and his respect. She could never hope to redeem herself, and the best thing she could do was to get out of his life, just as he'd urged—as soon as she was sure that he still had a life to lead. . .

* * *

Joanne looked at Dane's impassive face as he sat beside Nadine, and his eyes seemed to be twin daggers of dislike, piercing her heart. The pain was so sharp, so intense, that she suddenly knew that she hadn't forgotten, hadn't got over him, hadn't ceased to love him. She had merely closed her mind to memories and her heart to feeling. Now, with the jabbing intrusion of past into present, she wondered how she would get through the fourteen days before they were back in England and she could escape from the silent rebuke in those dark eyes.

There was little time to dwell on the problem of Dane during the day, with its succession of stops and starts, the business of unloading wheelchairs and party for a meal, some fresh air and a look at the local scenery before folding and stacking chairs and getting everyone back into their seats, and the many minor problems that part-responsibility for a disabled group seemed to present, as the coach ate up the miles.

Spirits were high, in spite of the long hours of travelling. To pass some of the time, Joanne took down her guitar and played evergreens, and everyone sang until they were hoarse. Almost everyone, anyway. Nadine smiled and clapped her hands to the music. Lionel couldn't hear it, but beamed with delight as he sensed the enjoyment of his friends. Dane closed his eyes and might or might not have slept as cheerful voices were raised in song, but was obviously in no mood to applaud her playing. Having taught herself the guitar since leaving Brook's, Joanne had half expected him to show surprise if nothing more. She wasn't a brilliant musician, but she had a true, sweet voice and she played and sang with heart.

At last they reached the hotel on the Rhine where they were staying overnight. Their arrival was chaotic, with the transfer of wheelchairs and luggage to the respective rooms, unpacking of bags and the inevitable discovery of forgotten items, marshalling the group for dinner and then assisting with baths or showers and settling the severely disabled for the night. Thankfully, Joanne made the final round of various rooms with pills or injections or other necessary requirements, making sure everyone was comfortable and without worries, and then escaped to her room, looking forward to stealing between the sheets.

Standing under the shower, she revelled in the slick of hot water over shoulders and back and thighs, chasing away the aching weariness of mind and body. Pivoting her head on her slender neck beneath the cascade, eyes closed, she felt tension draining away with the water and began to feel that she could cope with Dane on top of everything else in spite of the seemingly impenetrable barrier of his chilly contempt.

Things would be easier when they got to Pleydorf. She wouldn't be able to avoid him entirely, but at least they wouldn't be quite so involved with each other as they were on the journey, helping with wheelchairs, assisting people on and off the coach, advising and supervising and being constantly on call. Fortunately, the general busyness and the holiday atmosphere camouflaged the fact that two of the carers never spoke to one another if they could avoid it, she thought drily.

Feeling a little guilty that she had been so long under the shower, she turned off the taps. Or rather, tried to turn them off. The cold tap presented no problem, but the hot tap seemed to be fixed in one position and the more she tried the more impossible it seemed to turn. Becoming impatient, she tugged and pulled with each hand in turn while hot water continued to stream from the shower head, filling the small bathroom with steam and threatening to scald her.

Perhaps because she was tired and in unfamiliar surroundings, Joanne began to panic. If she couldn't turn off the tap, there would probably be no hot water left for anyone in the hotel by morning! Snatching up a towel, she wrapped it about her and ran out of the bathroom. She hesitated to reach for the telephone. It was nearly one o'clock and she didn't want to rouse the night porter with something so trivial and so absurd as her inability to turn off a tap! Besides, she knew very little German and it might be difficult if not impossible to explain her predicament.

Gingerly, she opened her room door and peeped out, hoping that Patrick or Owen or Cal or some other capable member of the group would be about, although it seemed unlikely. Everyone had been in their rooms when she had last patrolled the long, silent corridor.

A familiar figure turned from a doorway, key in hand, arcing a dark eyebrow at her near-nudity. 'Oh, Dane!' So great was her relief that she would have welcomed the devil himself at that moment. Dane would know what to do, she thought thankfully, visibly relaxing and almost losing the thick towel about her breasts.

He frowned as she hoisted her unconventional attire. 'What's the problem?' He might want nothing more to do with her, but it wasn't in his nature to ignore a maiden so obviously in distress.

'It's the shower. I can't turn it off.'

'What do you mean? Why not?'

'It won't budge! I know it sounds silly——'

'It sounds like a job for a plumber,' he said dismissively, turning away.

'I know. But at this hour—and I don't want to wake the entire hotel! I feel such a fool, anyway! Can't *you* do something? I hate to ask. . .' Joanne trailed off, feeling uncomfortable as she saw the glimmer of amused scorn in the dark eyes. He had always despised helpless women who went to pieces at the first sign of a crisis, and here was she, a nurse trained to cope in any emergency, running around in near-panic because she couldn't cope with a bathroom tap!

Dane's glance lingered on the clinging cap of damp-darkened hair, the pretty face flushed with anxiety and embarrassment and the thick towel that scarcely covered the gentle swell of breasts and shapely thighs. He was unwillingly reminded of the delights of her body, once so intimately known, recalled so tantalisingly often in his dreams.

What man could forget the sweet, generous warmth of her giving, the breathless kisses, the untried caresses, the blossoming of shy virgin into eager, loving woman who met his needs so joyously? There had been other women, for seven years was a long time in any man's life, but there had never been anyone like Joanne.

Theirs had been a rare ecstasy, a mingling of hearts and minds as well as bodies, a sharing of tenderness as well as passion. Without love, the only key, there was no way into that particular heaven, and he had never loved anyone but the girl who had let him down so badly that love had been swamped by the hot lava of anger.

Steeling his body not to stir along with the memories, Dane brushed past her, into the bedroom. 'Let's have a look. . .'

Wisps of discarded lingerie lay across the bed. Her perfume was everywhere, heady and feminine, disturbingly evocative.

Joanne padded after him into the mists of steam, too anxious about the gushing shower to think about her *déshabillé* or its possible effect on a man whose sensuality had once overwhelmed a token resistance.

Wrapping a towel about his hand, Dane plunged an

arm into the cubicle and groped for the offending tap. It was stiff but not immovable. With a deft twist of the wrist, he turned it in the opposite direction to the one that Joanne had struggled so vainly to achieve, and the flow of water eased from a torrent to a trickle and then stopped.

Joanne stared in surprise. 'But that's the wrong way——' She broke off, feeling even more foolish, for it so obviously *wasn't*.

'Alternative plumbing. Cold tap turns one way, hot tap turns the other. I've met it before on the Continent. It isn't very common, but it can be confusing.'

'So the more I tried to turn off the wretched thing the more I turned it on!' She followed him from the bathroom and shut the door on the steam. 'I'm sure I tried it both ways,' she said in lame defence.

'I expect you did. It was very stiff,' he conceded.

Bright red, Joanne was ready to sink through the floor. Dane spoke as if he thought she had contrived the situation, and she wondered if he suspected her of calling him into her room on a pretext. Crisis over, she was suddenly conscious of her scant covering. Blushing even more fierily, she clutched at the towel that threatened to expose even more of her body. 'I'm very grateful,' she said brightly. 'I didn't know what to do. I can't speak German and no one seems to be around. Thank you for coming to the rescue.'

The finality in her tone urged him to leave. She was sure he must hear the uneven thud of her heart. Deep down, she was clamouring for his remembered touch and the nearness of him, the body that had never known any other man newly aroused in sudden, bitter-sweet yearning.

'You're lucky it was someone you knew in the corridor at this hour,' Dane told her reprovingly. 'A stranger might have read an invitation into your dilemma. Particularly as it was so easily solved. You seem to be as wildly impulsive and irresponsible as ever, Joanne. Who else would rush out of a hotel room in the middle of the night wearing nothing but a towel to waylay the first man who came along!'

'It wasn't quite like that,' Joanne protested. 'I only put my head round the door!' It seemed an unkind quirk of fate that it had been Dane who had come to her aid. Cal—or Patrick or Owen—would have done so without making her feel foolish or that she was throwing herself at a man who didn't want her, she thought, aggrieved.

'Another man might have taken advantage of the situation,' Dane said tensely, prolonging the conversation unnecessarily, painfully aware of her femininity and of the need he had quietened in other arms but never entirely suppressed, and which he now discovered to be as quick and insistent as in the past. Joanne was in his mind and in his blood, and he wanted her in his arms once more, even if there was no longer any place for her in his heart.

She had distanced herself from him, instinctively, but he had only to put out a hand to touch her, to stroke the silk of her bare shoulder, to draw her close. A moment more and he could taste the remembered sweetness of her mouth and know the thrust of taut breasts against his chest and shudder with desire as her slender frame moulded itself to his lean body in newly kindled longing.

Joanne looked up at the man she still loved and needed, looming tall and masculine and rather too near, studying her with an inscrutable gleam in his dark eyes. She wanted to hurl herself into his arms and feel them tighten about her, welcoming her home. She wanted his mouth to fasten on her own and transport her to a remembered heaven. She wanted the sweeping, skilful exploration of tender hands and the slow build of ecstasy until it culminated with the powerful explosion of mutual passion.

More than anything, she wanted the love she had lost.

CHAPTER THREE

THANKS to too many memories and the feeling that she had made a fool of herself, Joanne didn't sleep very well. She still felt uncomfortable at the thought that Dane might have mistaken her motives in inviting him into her room, wearing nothing but a towel. The worst part was knowing that she would have welcomed his lovemaking—and suspecting that he knew it too!

She was careful not to meet his eyes across the long breakfast table with its gleaming linen, the array of hams and cheeses and fresh-baked rolls, the jugs of delicious coffee. Sitting next to Lenny, Dane unobtrusively helped with the buttering and filling of rolls, the pouring of coffee and the discreet retrieval of dropped items as if he was totally at home with the needs of the disabled.

Knowing their proud sensitivity, Joanne had been just a little anxious, remembering him as impatient and arrogant at times, but her fears had obviously been groundless. Like herself, he had long experience of the sick and disabled, she reminded herself.

Patrick was dividing his time between Lenny, Becky and his own breakfast. Becky could look after her own needs, but she was obviously enjoying the attention of a good-looking young man, and Patrick seemed drawn to her as he exchanged smiling banter with the girl who never allowed her disability to dampen her spirits.

A holiday romance in the offing, perhaps, Joanne thought with a qualm. They were fine in their way, but they could lead to heartache, and Becky was more vulnerable than most. It might be as well to keep a close eye on the situation.

Her own breakfast finished, she slid into the empty seat on the other side of Richard, who was having muesli spooned into him by his dedicated carer. 'I'll take over now, Owen,' she said. She knew that his breakfast was neglected while he fed Richard.

Caring for a multiplegic was a full-time job, and there had been one or two dissenting voices when it had first been suggested that Richard should be invited to go on the Austrian holiday. Owen had insisted that he went and promised to be wholly responsible for him. Sharing a room meant that he was on call day and night, but he made light of the work. Now, he smiled gratefully at Joanne as he relinquished the spoon and the bowl of cereal.

'That's more like it,' Richard approved as Joanne shifted her chair closer. 'But where were you when I had my bath this morning? That's when I really needed a pretty nurse around.' Grey eyes danced with mischief.

Joanne's heart went out to him, although she knew he detected and disliked any trace of pity. Like so many disabled, he was highly intelligent, but often suffered the indignity of being treated as retarded by the general public because he was confined to a wheelchair and mostly helpless. He could be very scathing about the public ignorance of disabilities at times, having all the outspokenness of youth combined with a great many frustrations. He had black moods and moments of anger—but that wasn't confined to the disabled, of course.

At eighteen, Richard was going through the difficult process from boy to man with all the extra problems of his disabilities, and he had fallen for Nadine's delicate loveliness and sweet smile. The partially sighted girl backed away from his helpless body and unthinkingly brash tongue, embarrassed and confused and desperately shy at the best of times. Joanne hoped this holiday would allow them to get to know each other better so that Richard wasn't continually hurt by Nadine's unaware rejection, and she learned how to cope with feelings she unwittingly aroused.

'Who is that guy who keeps trying to chat up Nadine?' Richard demanded aggressively as Joanne buttered a roll for him, jealous eyes on the couple, who sat together, Dane's dark head dipped towards Nadine. 'He was hanging round her all day yesterday.' A very natural resentment of his own inability to follow the girl wherever she went tinged the words.

'He's a doctor,' Joanne said, as if that made it all right. 'Gary was supposed to come with us, but he broke his leg, playing rugger. Annie asked Dane to take his place.'

Richard scowled. 'Daft name!'

Privately, Joanne had always thrilled to its masculine ring, feeling that the name suited the man, strong and full of character. 'Unusual, anyway,' she compromised.

'Is Nadine talking to him?' Richard was unable to turn his head to look at the couple as they strolled across the dining-room.

'I shouldn't think so. Nadine doesn't talk to many people, does she?' Joanne glanced at the lovely girl in her stylish cream blouse and skirt and elegant, high-heeled shoes as Dane escorted her from the room with a hand hovering at her elbow. It might be the discreet guidance so necessary to her impaired vision. It might also be the desire to touch of a man who found himself irresistibly attracted by the girl's fragile, feminine beauty.

Nadine loved fashion and wore some lovely clothes

and a great deal of inexpensive jewellery. She loved hats, too. A chic French beret topped her gleaming black hair that morning, ready for the second stage of their journey to Pleydorf. She had the looks, the figure and the flair of a model, but her poor sight and chronic shyness prevented her from pursuing the much-cherished ambition. Even at that early hour, she was beautifully made-up and immaculate from head to toe.

Knowing her visual problems and the time it probably took Nadine to appear at her very best, Joanne felt quite guilty about her own flick of a brush through her auburn hair and hasty dab of lipstick. She had packed her uniform, feeling she would be more suitably dressed in such hot weather in a floral cotton skirt and matching sleeveless top, the vivid colours in sharp contrast to the sober navy blue of the previous day. Bright lipstick matched the row of beads she wore around her neck, cheap and cheerful adornment but a birthday present from Lenny that she had put on to please him. The way his grin had lit up his face as she had walked into the dining-room had assured her that he was delighted.

Joanne had been given many such inexpensive gifts from the members of the PHAB Club, evidence of their affection and assurance that she would enjoy the Austrian holiday in their company. And so she *would*, in spite of Dane, she told herself staunchly—and nearly jumped out of her skin at the unexpected sound of his deep voice in her ear.

'Cal wants to know if your case is ready for loading.' Dane's hand almost brushed her shoulder and, as he bent his dark head, his cheek almost brushed the smooth silk of her hair.

A shiver of awareness rippled down her spine. 'Oh. . .not quite. I've some last-minute packing to do,' she said hastily, cursing the betraying warmth in her face and hoping he would attribute it to anything but his nearness.

'You were asked to bring it down with you,' he reminded her impatiently. 'Anneliese wants to get away as soon as possible—apparently she has something planned for this morning. If you could let Cal have your case. . .?'

'Richard hasn't finished his breakfast.' He had the healthy appetite of a young man and was taking a long time over the meal. Joanne had no intention of rushing him for anyone, and certainly not a peremptorily arrogant man who couldn't wish her a friendly good morning or find her a smile!

'I think I'll have another roll, Jo.' Richard supported her stand, not because he was still hungry but because he had taken a jealous dislike to Dane Gregory. 'And some more coffee,' he added for good measure.

'OK, I'll see to it. Go and finish your packing, Joanne.' Dane recognised rebellion when he saw it and knew how to quell it.

Resenting the note of authority, Joanne found herself responding to it like a well-trained nurse. But, as she hurried from the room, she discovered that she had no qualms about leaving Richard to Dane's tender mercies. Whatever his faults, he was caring and considerate and he seemed to have a gift for anticipating needs.

A slightly breathless Anneliese hailed her while struggling to manoeuvre a wheelchair from a lift. 'Have you seen Dane, Jo?'

Joanne hurried to help. 'He's giving Richard the last of his breakfast. I was doing it, but he sent me to get my case.'

'He is very commanding,' Anneliese approved happily, having felt much more relaxed about the projected holiday ever since she had persuaded Dane to accompany them. 'I thought he would be useful, apart from being a medical man, and I am right. What do you think of him, Jo?'

'Commanding,' Joanne agreed drily. 'Have you known him long?' She knew most of her fellow sister's friends, but there had never been any mention of Dane.

'For many years, since I was a child and he stayed with my family as a student on an exchange visit to improve his German. He speaks very good German, which is why I thought of asking him to takc Gary's place.'

It was so matter-of-fact that Joanne's heart lifted. Perhaps they *were* just good friends and there was no more to their relationship than that, she thought hopefully, although it was obvious that even an uncommitted Dane was unlikely to feel anything for *her* after so long.

Except for brief forays into the dining-room on one mission or another, Anneliese had scarcely been seen that morning, being responsible not only for the group as a whole but also for Clair, who needed nearly as much attention as Richard.

Joanne smiled warmly at the thin girl while holding open the foyer door so that Anneliese could wheel Clair out to the waiting coach. Clair tried very hard to be cheerful, but pain was etched into her thin features and every move was an obvious effort to the girl who had been a dancer until multiple sclerosis had eroded her strength and her spirit.

Not for the first time, Joanne counted her blessings as she went away to pack. She felt a little guilty about having had a room to herself, for the other carers had shared with someone who might need attention in the night. Even Dane had shared with Howie, an arthritic who was still reasonably mobile but needed help with dressing and getting in and out of his chair.

Joanne had originally meant to share with Becky, but the girl had begged to have Marcia with her as they were special friends. She suspected that the two girls had gossiped and giggled late into the night, seeing shadows beneath their eyes, but that was all part of the holiday, of course. She made a mental note to check that they didn't also indulge in late-night snacks, for Marcia was a diabetic who tended to take chances with her diet.

Coming out of her room, burdened with suitcase and shoulder bag and the locked medical case, she almost collided with Dane. 'Where's Richard? Who's looking after him?' she instantly demanded with the instinctive concern of a ward sister who could seldom trust junior nurses not to abandon a patient at the worst possible moment.

'He's in good hands. Owen and Cal are getting him on to the coach while I collect luggage.' He reached for her case. 'I'll take that.' He was brusque, resenting the wave of wanting that had swept him at the sight and scent of Joanne in the flamboyantly pretty outfit.

'I can manage. . .' But, seeing the flicker of impatience that crossed his handsome face, she relinquished the case without further protest. 'Thanks very much.'

Dane looked down at her with a lift of a dark brow that mocked the unexpected surrender. She was learning to subdue her stubborn pride, he thought drily—and then felt compelled to concede that she must have learned a whole lot more than that to become a ward sister at a busy hospital.

'I thought you'd opted out of nursing,' he said abruptly, following the trend of his thoughts.

Joanne was heartened by the voluntary mention of the

past. 'It was something I'd always wanted to do.' Until she had met Dane and thought of little else but marriage and children and happy ever after, she thought with a pang. 'I'm a very good nurse,' she added, as if something in his tone had implied doubt.

He nodded. 'So I gather.'

She looked at him quickly. Then he had discussed her with Anneliese—but when? She wondered if he had told her friend about the brief, unhappy affair that had almost ended with a tragedy. 'Does Annie know. . .?'

He shook his head, impatient. 'She knows about the car crash, of course. She knows a girl was involved. I didn't mention your name in that connection, because I know she would be horrified to realise that she'd unwittingly thrust us into each other's company for a fortnight.'

As they talked, they walked towards the stone stairway, leaving the hotel lifts free for the disabled and their helpers. There was a bustle of last-minute activity as everyone vacated their rooms. Joanne's burnished head was just level with Dane's shoulder, her silky hair dancing with each step. Small breasts peeped above the low neck of her colourful blouse, and he wondered if she was aware of their provocation and the smothered stir of his senses.

He had lain awake for some time, feeling that he should have swept aside everything but the moment and taken her, for she was no longer a half-grown girl, unaware of her own sexuality, unused to men and their needs. No doubt she had known just what she did when she had stood before him in that scanty towel, allowing it to slide from her beautiful body, her breath quickening in unmistakable betrayal.

The love they had shared was dead, but desire still sparked between them, and perhaps he was a fool not to have seized the offered opportunity to ease a renewed hunger in her arms. But it would certainly have led to complications.

'Richard was singing your praises as soon as you left the room,' he commented with a slight smile as they descended the stairs. 'Apparently you're a cross between his favourite sex symbol and an angel.'

Joanne glanced back. 'I expect you told him that I'm a fallen angel as far as you're concerned,' she retorted, feeling that the only salvation for their present relationship was to be as light-hearted as possible about the past.

Dane's mouth twisted with ironic amusement. It was an apt description, for he had set her on a pedestal all those years ago, loving her, admiring her bright spirit and her zest for life, and she had fallen at the first challenge to the love that she had claimed to feel for him.

'My angel,' he had breathed in moments of glorious content, head on her breast, arm flung across her body as they had lain together in the golden aftermath of loving. Precious moments that flooded into his mind at the most inconvenient of times. He had never felt so tenderly for any other woman, for Joanne had been special, heaven-sent, meant only for him—or so he had believed.

'I don't deserve you,' he had once declared, humbled by the power of love. And perhaps it had been true. Or maybe the listening gods had resented his worship of a mere mortal and had seen to it that his idol had been promptly shattered.

Dane felt it would be flying in the face of destiny to try to pick up the pieces. She had hurt him enough and he could never trust her again, he reminded himself sternly.

Joanne came to a sudden halt. 'I didn't think—your

leg! We should have waited for the lift!' she exclaimed in contrition.

'Don't fuss me, Joanne. There isn't much wrong with my leg these days. Go *on*!' he urged in sudden irritation as she looked up at him with luminous eyes expressive of sympathy. Damn her! How dared she pity his lameness? Where had she been when he'd needed her, called her name, held out his hand and touched air?

Rounding a turn of the staircase, making himself useful where needed as always, Lionel almost ran into them. He stopped short, his face brightening at the sight of Joanne. 'I've been looking for you, Jo!'

She almost fell on his neck in gratitude for defusing the explosive tension of the moment. Dane had glowered at her as if he hated her—and her heart was sure that he *did*. So it was heart-warming to see the warm look in Lionel's eyes and hear the affection in his slow, toneless speech.

'Afraid I'd be left behind?' She smiled at him. 'There's no danger of that happening while you can be relied on to make sure the coach doesn't leave without me!'

'Excuse me, you two—Cal's waiting for these cases.' Dane found it surprisingly hard to sound pleasant as he brushed past the couple who blocked the stairway, smiling into each other's eyes.

He had never expected to feel again the sharp sting of jealousy, for surely that only came with loving. But its stab seemed strangely muddled with impatience and an intense irritation as he glanced back to see Lionel take Joanne's medical case and guide her gently down the remaining steps. Dane had already observed that she reserved a special warmth for the man. There was something about him that most women found attractive, he suspected, and it seemed that his deafness and difficult speech was no bar to something more than ordinary friendship between Lionel and Joanne.

Damn it, he *was* jealous! He had been Joanne's first and should have been her last and only lover, he felt on a rage of resentment, tormented by a vision of her perfumed and sensitive body in his arms, her generous nature expressing itself in sweet kisses and soft caresses and her willingness to learn all the mysterious craft of loving at his eager hands.

It was almost a physical effort to thrust the thought of her from his mind as he hurried to help Cal to load luggage and lift the severely disabled on to the coach and into their seats.

Having counted heads, Anneliese held up a hand to silence the excited ripple of conversation. 'I have a surprise trip for you this morning,' she announced happily. 'Part of the journey will be along the Rhine as far as Boppard. It is all arranged.'

Concerned with cramming as much as possible into the holiday, she had been busy since waking to another day of golden sunshine. A quiet talk with Cal, a telephone call to the company whose boats cruised up and down the Rhine and another to Frau Meyer in Pleydorf to warn that they would arrive later than expected, and she was able to delight everyone with an addition to the itinerary.

Cal drove the coach to the nearby landing-stage and willing hands trundled wheelchairs down the gangway, lifted them on board and arranged them on the shady lower deck at the rear of the vessel, staff rushing to remove tables and chairs to accommodate them. Other passengers viewed the proceedings with interest and some came to help, language no barrier in their care and concern for the disabled.

'I thought Annie was coming with us!' Joanne said in

surprise as her friend waved them off, her lively face wreathed in a smile of satisfaction.

Dane shifted Clair's chair to a slightly better position to give her the best possible view of the panoramic scenery. 'She decided to travel on to Boppard with Cal. I said we could manage without her.'

'We can, of course,' she agreed brightly. '*Lenny*!' Don't hang over the side like that or we'll lose you! Are you desperate for the loo, Becky? If you could just wait until we get everyone settled. . .'

For some minutes, it seemed like chaos as people milled about and Dane vanished from view, leaving her to manage alone. But eventually Joanne felt that things were under control and she could begin to enjoy the trip.

Leaving the chairbound to the reliable care of Owen and Patrick, she mounted the steps to the upper deck where some of the 'walking wounded' had found seats to enjoy the rolling vista of hills and vineyards and nestling villages and the occasional *schloss* set on a jagged peak. The riverside trains and the fast-moving traffic on the road that ran the length of the Rhine, and the flotilla of small boats and river steamers and the occasional beach crowded with holidaymakers all vied for her attention, and Joanne leaned against a rail, her hair ruffled by a welcome breeze, the kiss of the sun on her face, drinking in the beauty of her surroundings.

'Magical, isn't it?' Dane came to stand at her side, the hard knot of anger in his breast softening as he saw the enchantment etched on her lovely face. Briefly, it seemed an eternity and a world away from the traumas of the past.

Joanne nodded. 'I'm so glad Annie thought of this! I'm sure everyone's enjoying it—and the weather makes it perfect.' She sighed. 'I don't know how she could bear to miss it!'

'A trip on the Rhine would be no novelty for Anneliese, apparently.' He handed her a can of ice-cold Cola and she took it in grateful surprise. 'And she seems to get much more pleasure from knowing that the rest of us are having a good time.'

Joanne turned to look at him, a wry smile in her sapphire eyes. 'And *are* you? In spite of me?' An unexpected relenting of his distant manner gave her the courage to ask.

'What can't be cured must be endured,' he said lightly. 'A favourite saying of an elderly aunt. It seems applicable in the present situation, don't you think?'

'Things aren't going to be easy for either of us for a couple of weeks,' she pointed out carefully.

Dane shrugged. 'We're old enough to cope, I imagine. We can't be the first ex-lovers to meet again in awkward circumstances.' Cola fizzed and gushed as he tore off the sealant by its ring.

'If it was only *that*——' She broke off, biting her lip. Then, suffused with guilt and concern, she put an impulsive hand on his arm. 'Does your leg still give you a lot of pain?' She wished she dared to take his handsome face in her hands and kiss the deep scar that furrowed his brow, so dangerously near the temple. He was still so dear and she was so desperately sorry for what she had done.

Dane shook off her hand, rejecting more than her touch, swept with a sudden longing as she looked up at him, her loveliness catching at his heart and battering at the indifference that was his only defence against loving her again. He might want her with an intensity that shocked and alarmed him, but he would despise himself if he gave in to the weakness of that wanting or let her know that it had survived her desertion of him.

'It's rather late in the day for you to be worrying about me,' he said drily, hardening his heart.

'Do you think I haven't worried and wondered about you? Many, many times,' Joanne returned indignantly.

His lip curled in patent disbelief. 'I was dead, for all you knew. Or cared, I suspect.'

'That's unfair! I knew you were getting on all right. Melvin——' She broke off as his face darkened.

'Supplied you with regular bulletins, did he? Obliging of him to ease your conscience and save you the trouble of coming to see how I was faring,' drawled Dane, ice in his deep voice, former jealousy flickering anew at the reference to a colleague who had admired Joanne and had apparently continued to see her after she had left Brook's, without mentioning the fact.

'You said you didn't want to see me, so I stayed away.' It was defiant.

Dark eyes narrowed. 'Rubbish! I never said anything of the kind. Why would I? You just didn't want to stay involved with someone who might be crippled for life—even if it was your fault,' he told her bluntly.

'If that's what you've believed about me all these years then no wonder you despise me! I was only eighteen,' she reminded him tautly. 'It was all too much for me. I just couldn't handle it. I was afraid, too—of being prosecuted, of going to prison, perhaps. . .'

'You had nothing to worry about,' Dane said curtly. 'The police investigation proved that the car had a mechanical fault. But, by running away, you allowed them and everyone else to assume that *I* drove us into that ditch!'

CHAPTER FOUR

JOANNE couldn't fight Dane's anger or his bitterness when there seemed to be so little to say in her own defence. Obviously he had no recollection of having sent her away and he didn't believe her reminder. He thought she had fled from the consequences of that terrible accident. In fact, she had run from the look in his eyes and the feeling that his love had been irrevocably lost.

Now, looking into his lean, darkly furious face and seeing nothing but a continuing contempt in the glowing depths of his dark eyes, Joanne had no reason to hope that the past would ever be forgiven and forgotten.

'You make it sound as if I deliberately crashed your car!' she protested.

'Perhaps you did. You were beside yourself with temper at the time,' Dane reminded her brutally.

'*Oh!*' Her eyes widened in dismay as the words hit her with all the force of a blow.

He relented slightly. 'OK, so it wasn't your fault that there was something wrong with the steering. But if you hadn't lost your temper over a trifle you'd have known that something was wrong with the car in time to stop it from going off the road. As it was, I paid the price for your stupid show of jealousy.'

He was so harsh, so unforgiving. But the fault hadn't been wholly hers! 'I was provoked,' she said stiffly, remembering. . .

Having given in to her insistence that she should drive, Dane had sat in the passenger seat and criticised her driving. 'Slow down, Joanne. These roads can be tricky at this time of night. Cars loom up out of nowhere.'

'I know what I'm doing.' Deliberately, she had trodden on the accelerator to prove she was capable of handling the powerful car.

'You'll have us off the road!' he had warned.

'No, I won't. I'm a very good driver.'

'You'll argue with St Peter at the gates of heaven if you do kill us both, hothead!'

She had been silent, brooding on the impatient note in his deep voice. Was he tiring of her? Was he hankering for the old days with Rona? No doubt *she* always kept her cool and *never* argued with him!

'What's wrong with you, anyway? PMT?' Dane's tone had softened as he'd glanced at her taut profile and sparkling eyes, illumined by the full moon that had danced in the night sky as the car had traversed the narrow country road.

'You know perfectly well what's wrong!' Pique had flounced in her lilting voice, in the indignant turn of her head.

He'd smiled indulgently. She had been very young, still unsure. 'I committed the crime of dancing with another woman.'

'Not just another woman—*Rona*! You said it was over!'

'So it is.'

'You were all over her on the dance floor!' Actually, it had been the other way round, she'd admitted fairly, but he hadn't seemed to mind.

'You were enjoying yourself with Melvin.' It hadn't been a serious spurt of jealousy. For he had trusted Joanne, and he'd known she had only been paying him back for an imagined slight. She should have trusted him, too, knowing it hadn't been in his nature to brush off a girl he had once cared about and who had still cared for him.

'I hated every moment!'

Dane's answering smile had infuriated her with its implication of incredulity. How dared he mock her agony of heart and mind when he ought to be doing his utmost to reassure her? He'd begun to whistle, very softly, the tune of a ballad currently in the charts. Their song. A beaty ballad that sang of hearts beating as one, of lovers knowing each other at first glance, of lasting love. At any other time, Joanne would have recognised a peace-offering, a reminder to soften her heart and quiet her temper, an invitation to make up a foolish quarrel in his welcoming arms.

Maybe his timing had been wrong. For it had merely seemed a deliberate reminder of an image that would be etched on her memory forever—Dane and Rona dancing to that same tune with their arms wrapped about each other, smiling into each other's eyes, surrounded by a cloak of former intimacy that all her loving and giving had apparently failed to shed.

She had boiled over, unaware that she had trod down on the accelerator as she had done so. 'I think you're still in love with her!' she had accused hotly.

Dane had shrugged. 'I'm not going to argue with you, Joanne.' He had been hurt by her lack of trust, the unnecessary resentment of Rona, the widening rift and had been beginning to doubt that she had loved him as much as she had thought and said she did.

'You *can't*! Because it's true! I've just been second-best all these weeks, obviously. Well, you'd better go back to her!' Even as the hot words left her lips, spurred by anger and pride and dismay, she lost control of the speeding car at a bend in the road and was swamped by a sickening horror. . .

* * *

'The provocation was all in your mind,' Dane said brusquely, unaware that Joanne had relived the worst moments of her life in the few seconds between her words and his curt reply. 'But I've no intention of rehashing what happened over and over again. We went our different ways after that night, and I doubt if either of us wanted to meet again in this way. However, there's no harm done as long as we both accept that the past is dead and buried.'

'Some good might even come of it,' Joanne said brightly, ever the optimist. 'I can't have been one of your favourite people all these years. Maybe this is my chance to make amends, Dane.'

'Don't even try.' He backed from the glow in those beautiful eyes, the temptation of her lifted face and slender figure, the stir of tender recollections that undermined his resolve to keep her at a safe distance. 'Just leave things the way they are.'

Turning, he walked across the sunny deck to join Lenny and Nadine, his limp more marked than usual, as always when his emotions were under stress.

Joanne sipped her Cola and smiled at Lionel as he joined her, hoping she successfully hid her chagrin. But perhaps it had been too much to hope that Dane would accept the offer of an olive branch so soon.

Having rejoined the waiting coach at Boppard, they travelled on towards Austria, stopping for a picnic lunch at a spot that provided a magnificent view of the Alps. Every stop, however brief, involved much time and effort. Patrick, Owen and Dane were invaluable when it came to helping Cal with the unloading of chairs and passengers and then, before they could continue the journey, doing it all in reverse, folding and stacking the cumbersome wheelchairs and lifting their owners into the coach.

Anneliese knew that this holiday could not have been achieved without their cheerful willingness, and it seemed to her that Joanne in particular failed to realise how grateful they should all be to Dane, who had given up a prearranged holiday with friends to join them at very short notice. The warm friendliness that she extended to everyone didn't seem to embrace Dane, for some reason, and Anneliese could tell that he was chilled by her fellow sister's offhand attitude. But no doubt they would be friends by the end of the holiday, she told herself comfortably.

Cal was worth his weight in gold, she thought warmly as the coach driver came up behind her and draped his own jacket about her shoulders, seeing her shiver in the unexpected chill of the high vantage point. She turned to him with a smile. 'Thank you. You are very kind.'

He *was* kind, very thoughtful. Although only really responsible for the storage of luggage and the safe conveyance of coach and party, he was friend, helper and cheerful support when she flagged under the weight of responsibility. Anneliese found it easy to lean on the rock-like Yorkshireman with his earthy sense of humour, warm good nature and commonsense solution to a number of problems that had arisen. She didn't know how they would manage without him, in fact.

'I think we should make a move, Annie. Some of the group feel the cold more than we do, lass,' he reminded her.

She linked a hand in his arm. 'Yes, of course. People become cold when they cannot move about to keep warm, as we do,' she agreed. 'You are right—we must get them together now. Jo, would you round up the walking wounded, please.'

Watching them stroll away, Joanne realised how well they got on. They had become friends when Cal had driven members of the PHAB Club on outings, but now they were being thrown together for very long hours. Sitting in the courier's seat, talking to him as the coach ate up the miles of motorway, Anneliese was drawing closer to the rugged Yorkshireman.

He was possibly the only person who could sway the strong-minded girl from a decision that might not benefit the party as a whole, although she had an in-built resistance to any change of plan by anyone but herself, Joanne knew. It was Cal who had originally shortened the pretty name to Annie, and now most of the group did the same. Cal wasn't afraid to argue with her, and she seemed to enjoy it. He could jolly her out of a momentary irritation, and he often teased her on particularly Teutonic traits in her character, and Anneliese laughed and liked it and leaned on him more and more.

Having seen the warm affection in Dane's eyes and manner for her friend, Joanne wondered how he felt about that growing closeness. Apparently they had known each other for years. He must be fond of her to fall in so readily with a request to take Gary's place on this trip. He might even love Anneliese, she thought, resolving to be cheerful about the unpalatable fact that there could no longer be any place for *her* in his life. What can't be cured must be endured, she reminded herself, quoting his own words.

Rounding up those who had wandered some distance from the coach, she paused to look at a tableau that gave her more food for thought. Patrick crouched beside Becky, her hand resting on his shoulder as he pointed out the views. She seemed more intent on his good-looking profile than the jagged outline of the Alps, Joanne thought drily, wondering if there were problems looming that neither she nor Anneliese had anticipated when this trip to Austria had been mooted.

Walking past the engrossed couple, she touched Lenny's shoulder. He was engrossed too, having discovered two fine bays cantering about a field that bordered the road. They had come at his call and he was happily feeding them apples bought from a service station shop, his face aglow.

'Time to go, Lenny.' Joanne hated to spoil his rapt pleasure in the moment.

He stroked the white blaze on the bigger bay's nose. 'I'm going to have a horse of my own one day, Jo.'

The wistful words touched her heart, for he came from a very poor background and it was most unlikely that he would ever be in a position to keep a horse. But there was no reason why he shouldn't learn to ride, she decided, chiding herself for not discovering his love of horses before. The subject had never arisen at the PHAB Club, surprisingly. 'There's a local scheme for riding for the disabled. I'll make enquiries for you as soon as we get home,' she promised.

'I'd like that,' Lenny said simply.

'In the meantime, there may be horses in Pleydorf. Mucking out before breakfast should make it a perfect holiday for you,' she teased as she led the reluctant lad towards the coach.

He grinned. 'You don't mean it, but that's just what I *would* like. *Are* there horses where we're going?'

Joanne hoped she hadn't raised his hopes only to have them dashed on arrival. 'I'm not sure,' she admitted. 'But it's a village, so there must be farms, and where there are farms there are sure to be horses. We'll work something out.'

'You're a nice girl, Jo,' he said, rather bashfully. 'Everyone likes you.'

Embarrassed, she laughed and blushed and then hugged him. 'It would be nice to think so, but we all have our critics,' she returned lightly, and met the uncompromising eyes of the man who was probably her sternest critic.

Having just lifted the slight Clair from her chair, Dane waited for Cal to take her and carry her along the gangway of the coach to her seat. He was very tender with the ex-dancer and, in spite of the lassitude that was symptomatic of her illness, Clair responded like any other woman to his masculinity. She wound thin arms about his neck and smiled up at him as he joked about her weight, pretending to sag beneath his burden.

As she watched, Joanne's heart welled with love. Dear, caring, kindly Dane, so much a man, so strong and so splendid! A new realisation of her loss ripped through her along with a surge of unwarranted envy.

Jealousy was the evil that had attacked their joy in each other in the past, she reminded herself fiercely. She might love him still, but that didn't give her the right to resent the way he cossetted Clair and cuddled Becky, coaxed Nadine and teased Marcia and smiled with special warmth at Anneliese.

Everyone was travel-weary by the time they arrived to a warm, friendly welcome from the Austrian staff of the holiday complex in the small Tyrolean village.

Lenny was anxious to explore. 'It's smashing, Jo!' he enthused, returning from a first foray to take her arm and drag her off to look at well-designed buildings and well-kept gardens in a lovely setting, the evening sun slanting across the valley to dapple everything with gold. 'And there *are* horses! Come and look!'

'Later,' she promised, detaching herself, for she was needed to help to settle everyone in their rooms. Most of the carers were sleeping in the main building, for it was felt that they deserved a restful night away from their charges after being constantly on call during the day. But Owen had chosen to share Richard's room in the annexe, with its ramps and rails and specially equipped bathrooms and telephone links to the main building. In an emergency, a member of staff or a carer could be quickly on the scene.

The first few days were hectic, for there was so much to see and do. Pleydorf was enchanting, with its quaintly spired and richly decorated church, its scatter of shops and farms, and a number of pretty timber chalets with carved and painted balconies and masses of bright geraniums at each window. A river ran through the village, spanned by a bridge. Set in a valley, it was easy walking and pushing, and Joanne took the chairbound along winding river paths and country roads to admire the chalets and farmhouses that sprinkled the meadows beneath gently sloping mountains.

Each day began with glorious sunshine and soaring bird-song and the tinkling of cow-bells as the cattle were led through the village to grazing land. The splendid surroundings, the sweetness of new experience, was enhanced for Joanne by the daily sight and sound of Dane, coaxing Nadine to talk, cheering Becky as she competed in a wheelchair slalom with Clair and Richard and Howie, teasing Lenny, talking football with Ian and Paul, supporting a giggling Marcia as she floundered in the pool or tickling a dozing Suzy as she lay on the sun-drenched lawn. He seemed tireless, busy from early morning to late evening to make the holiday as enjoyable and as memorable as possible for everyone.

Rounding a corner with Howie, Joanne fell in with Dane as he pushed Clair to the dining-hall for lunch. As they walked side by side along the tree-lined path, she was very conscious of him, tall and tanned and attractive in white shorts and lemon, open-necked summer shirt, straight from the tennis courts where he had indulged Suzy in a knock-about game that had had the chair-bound spectators in fits of laughter. He had greeted her with a smile and a light word, and she felt that things were improving between them. Perhaps friendship, at least, wasn't out of the question after all, and that thought was balm to a heart that loved him so much.

He was warm-hearted, caring and concerned for others in so many admirable ways, she thought on a wistful welling of emotion. She found that loving at twenty-five went deeper, demanded more, than loving at eighteen, when she had been so enchanted by his looks and charm and cleverness and perhaps, most of all, by his ability to create heaven on earth for her with his subtle, sensual lovemaking.

Dane studied the slender, self-contained girl, so pretty in her rainbow-striped frock, bare arms and legs glowing from golden sun. She seemed tense, a little tired, and he wondered if she was doing too much. She was here, there and everywhere all day, taking on far more than her share of work and responsibility, and, as a doctor, he recognised that the need to be busy was a sign of inner anxiety. Now, having parked Howie next to Clair in the dining-hall, she was about to dash away to collect Becky.

He detained her with a light hand on her shoulder. 'Slow down. Let Marcia look after Becky—she's quite capable of pushing her such a short distance,' he said firmly. 'Try to delegate some of the chores. You don't have to run the entire show on your own, Joanne.'

She smiled in wry admission that there was some justice in the well-meaning rebuke. 'I don't think of them as chores, Dane. I enjoy being useful.' But she allowed him to sit her down on the stone balustrade of the terrace to await the arrival of Becky and Marcia, her body still tingling from his touch, her heart lifting that he had noticed her efforts.

He perched beside her, long legs outstretched, relaxed and confident. 'Take some time off for yourself occasionally. You're on holiday too.'

'This is my idea of the perfect holiday,' she assured him blithely. 'I'm loving every minute.' The glow in her face confirmed the claim.

'As a sister, you must know how to delegate. Anneliese tells me that you're in charge of a ward at the Montgomery.'

Joanne was heartened by the unexpected show of interest, the hint of admiration. 'Ellis Ward—men's surgical, twenty-four beds and a constant turnover of patients. It's a demanding life, but I like it—and I'm very lucky to have the back-up of a splendid team of nurses.'

'An efficient team implies an excellent ward sister.'

'I'm good at my job,' Joanne agreed without false modesty. 'I've worked hard for my sister's cap.'

'Work isn't everything. Anneliese says you live on your own. No husband, no live-in lover, no friends? I'm surprised.' The light words hid concern, for he felt that she was too lovely, too vulnerable, to spend her life without a man.

During this Austrian adventure, Dane was getting to know Joanne very much better than in the days when they had been madly in love but circumstances had allowed them little time to be together. He sometimes felt that he had loved a dream rather than a real person. Now he was fighting the tug of his heart and the feeling that Joanne had matured into the kind of woman that any man would welcome in his life.

'I've plenty of friends,' she said stoutly. 'I'm just not

interested in anything permanent.' There was no need to tell him that she had never met a man who could take his place in her heart and her life. 'No time, for one thing—and I'm too independent, anyway. No man would put up with me for long!' On the laughing words, she darted across the lawn to Lionel, who was struggling to understand an increasingly frustrated Richard, who wanted to go back to the annexe for something before he was trundled to the dining-hall.

For the first time, Dane had softened, allowed a warmth to touch his heart, felt that something might yet be salvaged from the debris of the past. The brief relenting was dashed as she sped to be with Lionel.

It would be absurd to regard him as a rival, but it was obvious that Joanne had a special fondness for the deaf man. Dane told himself that Lionel's physical limitations were no insurance against a challenge, and there was no reason why he should feel sorry for someone who obviously lived life to the full in spite of his disabilities.

Joanne's senses quickened when he was near, he knew, and there was nothing to stop him from taking her if he so desired. Except pride. She hadn't cared enough to stay by him when he had needed her. She no longer cared for him at all, and if she went into his arms it would only be because of a newly kindled desire or a feeling that she ought to make amends. Dane didn't want her on those terms!

His lameness was slightly more marked than usual as he strode to relieve the struggling Marcia of responsibility for Becky's wheelchair.

The afternoon was spent by the pool, some of the group in the sparkling water and others relaxing to read or write postcards or chat to each other on the surrounding lawns.

In a brief black bikini, Joanne lay on her stomach, chin cradled in her hands, watching the fun, watching Dane. He was very popular, much in demand. Marcia followed him round with a devotion usually reserved for her favourite pop star, hanging on his every word, and he was endlessly patient with her. Day by day, he was coaxing Nadine further out of her shy shell. He spent time with Clair, who came to life, forgetting pain and sadness, encouraged to talk about her days as a ballet star. Joanne had warned others to avoid the subject, thinking it would upset the girl, but now she realised that Clair had believed her early success forgotten and as wasted as the rest of her life. Dane's different, caring approach brightened the days for the stricken dancer, who hadn't particularly wanted to come on this Austrian holiday.

Becky had eyes only for Patrick, or she might have fallen victim to Dane's unconscious charm too. As for Anneliese. . .well, it seemed to Joanne that her friend cared a great deal for Dane, but her days were so filled with ensuring the enjoyment and comfort of everyone else that she had no time for personal pleasures. Perhaps the nights came into their own, Joanne thought with a pang, remembering occasions when she had caught the inflections of her friend's voice through the wall.

Dane's room was next to her own, linked by a wooden veranda with a magnificent array of flower-filled window-boxes. Sliding glass doors opened out to the veranda, and sometimes Joanne could hear Dane's deep voice, carrying clearly on the still air, if he had left his door open. Occasionally she heard Anneliese's unmistakably accented voice in reply and rushed to shut her own door to escape the hurtful implication of intimacy.

Sometimes he stood out on the veranda for a few minutes before going to bed, and Joanne, unable to sleep and hearing the distinctive shoosh of the glass door as he slid it back, stole from her bed to gaze at his tall figure, his powerful frame, the set of his handsome head against the sky, and wish that she could go to him and know herself forgiven as his arms closed about her.

Sweet, impossible dream. . .

Lionel scooped her with his effortless strength and swept her to the edge of the pool. Dangled over the water, Joanne kicked and struggled in mock terror, her lovely face alive with merriment, her blue eyes dancing as she clung to the man who couldn't hear her laughing protests but shared her enjoyment.

He held her firmly, close to his thudding heart, and suddenly she sensed a change in him and knew that the teasing intent had been replaced by the tension of male desire. A shudder of shock ran through her slight frame as she realised that he also had his dreams.

CHAPTER FIVE

'PUT me down, Lionel,' Joanne said unsteadily.

He held her all the closer, his gaze on the distant range of mountains rather than on her troubled face as he struggled with the surge of his emotions.

Joanne tugged at his shoulder. 'Put me down!' She was sure that everyone was staring, and the blush seemed to start at her hairline and ripple all the way down to her bare toes. Conscious of her skimpy bikini and its possible provocation, she was annoyed that she had overlooked the fact that Lionel was very much a man. The sudden realisation of his sexuality cast a forbidding shadow.

'Throw her in, Lion!' Lenny's gleeful shout came from the direction of the water-splash. Unencumbered by his useless arm, having a strong pair of legs, he could be equal to the others in the water, and was thoroughly enjoying himself as he shot round the curves of the fun-chute that ended in shallow water for safety reasons. Newly installed, it was popular with those who could mount the steps to the tower supporting the framework of the slide.

Lionel lowered Joanne to the ground, very gently, literally deaf to the plea in her voice but sensing her discomfiture. 'I wasn't going to do it,' he assured her warmly. 'Surely you trust me, Jo?'

She did trust him. But, like most men, so far and no further, she thought drily as he went back to his deckchair and she sat on the poolside, dangling her feet in the water. Calming down, she felt that her irritation might have been slightly over the top. No one seemed to have taken any notice of the incident, intent on their own water games.

It was a very hot day, the sun glinting from a cloudless sky, its rays reflecting in the pool to dazzle the swimmers. A hoist enabled even the severely disabled to join in the fun, and Becky, supported by a wide rubber ring, happily bobbed up and down in the water, holding tightly to Patrick's willing hands.

Marcia had attached herself to Dane, who had good-naturedly agreed to teach her to swim. The deep scar that ran from thigh to ankle of his lame leg stood out starkly against the bronze of his skin, a reminder of a time that Joanne would prefer to forget. He was magnificently male, scooping water from his jet hair as he surfaced from a dive, water streaming over powerful back and shoulders, laughing at Marcia as she hurled water at him with both hands like a boisterous child.

She *was* childlike in some ways, but her youthful body in the clinging satin swimsuit was all woman, and Joanne didn't doubt that the sensual Dane was aware of her nubile charms. She was sure that, as a doctor, he was well used to the lures and wiles of women, who found him attractive not only for his good looks and splendid physique and enchanting smile but also because of his profession. Medical men seemed to have a special fascination for women in much the same way that male patients chased the nurses on her ward!

Richard was also in the pool, supported and watched over by Owen, who guided him across the pool to Joanne.

The boy butted her foot with his head, grinning. 'I want to go on the chute, Jo!' He flopped a hand towards Lenny as the lad shot down the plastic slide once more with a yell of '*Geronimo!*' and a huge, delighted splash. 'Like Lenny.'

'Oh, I don't think so, Richard.' She exchanged doubtful glances with Owen. 'Lenny can look after himself better than you can,' she qualified gently, doing her best to soften the refusal.

'I'll never have another chance,' Richard urged. 'I *want* to try it, Jo. It can't hurt me, can it? It's only a slide, and someone can catch me at the bottom.'

'How can we get you on it, though?' Joanne glanced at the tower platform and the steps with a rueful smile.

'Owen and Cal could get me up there,' he declared confidently. 'I know they could.'

'I'd rather not try,' Owen said bluntly. 'If there was an accident——'

'There won't be! Just put me on it and see! How can you say no, Owen? It's all right for you—you can do anything you want! I have to be helped with every little thing.' A deep-seated frustration began to bubble to the surface. 'This is something I can do by myself once I'm on the chute.'

'I don't know what your parents would say if we allowed you to take such chances,' Joanne pointed out reasonably.

'My mum wouldn't stop me! She says I *should* try things—even the impossible. She says it's the only way to live. *She* doesn't treat me like a useless kid!' It was bitter.

Joanne looked round for moral support. Anneliese sat in the shade of a tree, avoiding the sun on her fair skin, discussing another outing for the group with Cal. Head bent over the large illustrated map of the Tyrol spread out on her lap, she seemed oblivious to the tussle of wills. Dane had left the pool and was walking towards the building, a towel about his shoulders, obviously on his way to dress. And Patrick had eyes and ears only for Becky.

'Cal! Can you spare a minute?'

The Yorkshireman looked up at Richard's eager shout. 'What is it, lad?' He approached the edge of the pool.

'He wants to go on the chute. We keep telling him that it can't be done,' Owen explained.

'Of course it can. Let the lad have a go,' Cal said indulgently. 'I'll put him on at the top and you can be ready to catch him as he hits the water. Nothing to it—and you'll enjoy it, won't you, Richard?'

'Oh, Cal!' Joanne protested. 'How will you get him up those steps?'

'Easy, lass—one of us on each side of him. Me and Lionel, say. He's a strong chap. Never say die, eh, Richard?'

Her protests brushed aside, Joanne watched doubtfully as the determined coach driver and the ever-helpful Lionel hoisted Richard's helpless body up the steps between them, his thin, useless legs dangling. His wide grin told the world of his delight at being enabled to do something that the able-bodied took in their stride.

It took some time to achieve their object, and Cal had to choose just the right moment to release his firm hold on Richard. The boy's young face was wreathed in joyous satisfaction as he hurled down the curving slide, floppy limbs all over the place, and landed with a huge splash in the shallow water, totally out of control. He submerged and surfaced, gasping and spluttering but still grinning as Owen grabbed him by the hair and then clutched at his floundering body.

Thankful that no harm had come to him, but fearing the shock to his sensitive nervous system of so much excitement, Joanne did her best to applaud an achievement that obviously meant a lot to him, then hurried him away to be dried and dressed and allowed to rest. Warmly wrapped in a flurry of thick towels, Richard was taken off to the annexe by his devoted carer, and she turned to face the wrath of the approaching doctor.

Rage thundering in his breast, Dane limped around the pool to reach her, horrified by the scene he had returned in time to witness but not to prevent, almost too angry to react to the allure of her femininity in the provocative bikini.

'What the devil has been going on?' he demanded, appalled, angry enough to shake the girl who turned a seemingly defiant face to him. 'What were you thinking of to allow that to happen? Don't you know the dangers of putting multiplegics at risk in that fashion? What kind of a nurse are you?'

'It wasn't my idea,' she flared defensively, resenting the unfairness of the attack. 'I did try to talk them out of it, but no one would listen!'

Dane wasn't listening to her either. 'I'm well aware that you're irresponsible and impetuous, but that was sheer bloody insanity!' he accused. 'We're supposed to be looking after these people, not exposing them to danger, for God's sake! How would you have explained things to his parents if that boy had drowned?'

'There was no danger of that. There were too many of us looking out for him,' Joanne said coolly, refusing to shrink before the blaze in his dark eyes, the lash of his tongue. He didn't understand. He hadn't seen the look on Richard's face and known that the venture was worth every ounce of the risk to give him the experience of a lifetime. 'He loved it,' she swept on, face illumined by the recollection. 'If you'd only been here——'

'I'd have stamped on such a stupid idea. Which is

exactly what *you* should have done,' he told her in uncompromising tones, stifling a stir of appreciation of that lovely, brightened face and sparkling eyes.

Unable to follow the torrent of words, Lionel saw from the doctor's angry face and Joanne's defensive attitude that she was being scolded. He hastened to intervene. 'Don't blame Jo. She did her best to talk us out of it——'

Dane rounded on him with uncharacteristic roughness. 'Keep out of this, Lionel. This is between myself and Joanne.' He turned back to her. 'I'm the senior medical officer in this party and should be consulted before anything so dangerous to life and limb is attempted. In future, you refer to me in all things. Is that understood?'

'Perfectly,' Joanne said grittily, hot with humiliation at the public set-down, blazing with the temper she had thought completely under control until Dane contrived to stir the embers with his arrogance and unfeeling attitude.

Anneliese rushed to pour oil on troubled waters. 'What is this upset?' she asked, laughing, putting a soothing arm about each of them. 'Richard wanted to be like everyone else—and why not? It made him feel good, and surely that is all that matters? Cal wouldn't have helped if there was danger!'

Dane bridled. 'I wasn't aware that he's a medical man or that he has specialised knowledge of the needs of multiplegics,' he said drily. 'I imagine I may be a slightly better judge of what is best for Richard!' He had nothing against the Yorkshireman. In fact, he liked him, but he did object to having his professional standing undermined by a coach driver, however genial and good-natured!

Anneliese wrinkled her nose at him, pricking the

bubble of an uncharacteristic pomposity. 'You would have disappointed him. Perhaps you are wiser than we are. But it seemed harmless fun. There isn't much fun in Richard's life, and now he has something to remember, a happy memory of a good day with his friends. You are too serious sometimes, Dane—and you have upset poor Jo,' she declared.

'It doesn't matter.' Joanne was annoyed that her friend had drawn attention to the tears that stung her eyes. She moved away from Anneliese's encircling arm. 'I'm feeling cold. I'd better go and dress. . .'

Dane caught up with her as she sped around the side of the pool. 'I may have over-reacted,' he said stiffly.

'If that's an apology, then don't bother,' Joanne returned coldly, convinced that he had been prompted.

He scanned her stormy face, the over-bright eyes. 'I *thought* they were tears of temper,' he mocked. 'Nothing changes, does it?'

Joanne boiled over. 'Get lost!' She thrust at him with both hands as if she wanted to thrust him out of her life forever. Taken by surprise, he stepped back, unwarily.

Led by the incorrigible Lenny, a loud, delighted cheer went up as Dane plunged into the pool, fully clothed. As he surfaced, he struck out for the side where Joanne stood, unsure, wanting to flee but rooted to the spot by remorse. Once again she had yielded to ungovernable rage, and although this time he had suffered nothing worse than a ducking, it was obvious he would regard her with even deeper distrust in future.

Hauling himself from the water, Dane lay flat on his face on the paved surround, fighting for the breath that had been shocked out of him, torn between annoyance and amusement.

Joanne bent over him, anxious. 'I'm sorry,' she said contritely. 'I really didn't mean to do that.'

He sat up, sleeking wet hair from his handsome face, dark eyes alight with laughter. 'Heaven help me if you ever plan to do me an injury,' he said drily.

Hot colour stormed into her face. 'That isn't funny!' She was pained by the reminder that she had once done him an injury she could never expurgate, for all her regret. Or her lingering love.

'Just be grateful that I can still laugh at the crazy things you do, hothead!' Drawled in his deep, vibrantly amused voice, the familiar term was an endearment, uttered in a moment of weakness. With a hint of the awkwardness of his slightly lame leg, he got to his feet in squelching shoes, once immaculate trousers and carefully laundered shirt clinging wetly to his powerful body. He greeted another cheer from Lenny with a grin and a wave.

Anneliese hurried up, relieved to see that they were almost smiling at each other. '*Ach, gut*! Now you are friends again,' she announced, beaming.

It wasn't so, but perhaps there was reason to think that they might be in time, Joanne felt with a lift of her heart. She had dented Dane's dignity, but he had taken it surprisingly well, and the unexpected smile in his dark eyes and the indulgent humour in his deep voice gave her new hope for the future. But the most she dared to hope for was a return to a liking that had dawned before love. . .

Lying back against an incline, Joanne breathed in the delicious scent of meadowland and pure mountain air and luxuriated in the warmth of the sun on bare arms and legs, shorts and sun-top a vivid splash of yellow contrasting with the verdant green of the grass beneath her body.

'Great holiday, isn't it, Jo?' Lenny echoed her

thoughts with unmistakable content as he sat at her side, cross-legged, eating the hard-boiled egg she had peeled.

Joanne agreed. Nursing was rewarding, but these days with the young disabled was much, much more. They were such fun, laughing at themselves, meeting every challenge head-on, overcoming obstacles with admirable grit—and Anneliese was admirably intent on giving them all a wonderful holiday.

Fractionally shifting position, she could just see her friend in another of her colourful tracksuits, fair head very close to Dane's dark one as he stretched at her side, snatching a rare moment of rest. She suppressed a twist of envy, a stab of pain. There was nothing but heartache in store for her if she continued to hanker for a man who didn't want her, she told herself firmly. Dane had no time for a fallen angel.

'Everything all right, Becky?' she asked brightly.

But Becky didn't hear, dreaming in her wheelchair, sandwiches lying forgotten in her lap as her adoring eyes followed Patrick as he toured the group with plastic beakers and a five-litre carton of milk. They had brought a picnic lunch on a tour of the Tyrol and Cal had parked the coach in an open meadow at the side of the mountain road. A wide area of flat ground suited the 'wheelchair brigade', as he called them, and above them reared the beautiful Wilderkaiser, craggy peaks tipped with snow.

Nearby, a chair-lift creaked and swung a succession of sightseers up the mountainside for a breathtaking view of the superb Austrian scenery. The beauty and the peace of their surroundings was a far cry from the Montgomery General with its hustle and bustle and relentless demands. Joanne wondered briefly how they were getting on without her on Ellis Ward—if Mr Murray had got over his artery bypass and if Mr Emerson had been discharged as expected and how Staff

Nurses Hammond and Wynn and Baxter were coping with the new influx of patients in her absence. Then she forgot everything to drowse in the warm sunshine and listen to the murmur of voices and the lilt of laughter, Dane's deeply vibrant tones and very distinctive chuckle surmounting all others to her ultra-sensitive ear. Suddenly, startled heart on the leap, her eyes flew open at the brush of a man's mouth on her lips.

Lionel grinned down at her, blue eyes dancing.

Laughing, she sat up. 'Wretch! I was having such a lovely nap!'

'Lenny told me to wake the sleeping beauty with a kiss.'

'Lenny *would*!' She aimed a mock punch at the boy, who was highly delighted with the success of his strategy. 'He wouldn't dare to do it himself, though!' She held out a hand to Lionel. 'Help me up.'

She was thistledown compared to his great strength. For a moment, disorientated, Joanne leaned against him as her head swam, laughing up at the good-looking giant who was framed against a backcloth of glorious mountain peaks.

He had overcome the problem of his deafness with a long study of lip-reading, and he apparently had a gift for interpreting facial expressions and mannerisms. Joanne often marvelled at how well he coped with most situations, but it must still be an isolated world for him at times, she felt, wondering if he was a lonely man. His handicap must make it difficult for him to establish an intimate relationship with any woman, for so much of loving was conveyed by the sensitive nuances of speech that would escape Lionel.

Dane felt compelled to interrupt an obviously tender moment. It annoyed him that Joanne was so blatant in her liking for the man, insensitive to the feelings of others in the group who didn't have Lionel's physical advantages or the opportunities for courting a pretty girl. It would be a rare man who didn't respond in some way to her attractions and the unconscious charm of her lovely smile, he felt—and Lionel was aggressively masculine in a way that would appeal to many women, but there was no need for them to flaunt their interest in each other!

'Cal suggests that we take some of the group on the chair-lift, Joanne. What do you think?'

Unaware of Dane's approach, unable to hear the brusque words, Lionel continued to clasp Joanne to his broad chest, looking down at her with a smile and a glow in his blue eyes that betrayed his feeling for her. Drawing from that protective arm and the tender gaze, Joanne turned to look at Dane, surprised that he consulted her. 'Oh, I'm all in favour. Nothing is too dangerous for the disabled to attempt, in my view, surely?' she quipped drily, still smarting slightly from an accusation of irresponsible behaviour that had been so undeserved. 'I'd send them to scale Everest in a milk float, given the opportunity!'

Unexpectedly, Dane laughed. 'I believe you would too! You and Anneliese are a pair! She marches right over obstacles and you simply don't see them,' he said in mock despair.

'Does Annie think it's a good idea? So do I,' she said promptly, and turned to Lionel, who was looking puzzled, having missed the essential ingredient of the conversation. 'We're talking about the chair-lift.' She indicated the swinging chairs suspended from strong cables supported by steel pylons stretching up the side of the mountain. 'Annie thinks some of you might like to try it.'

He instantly agreed. 'It's a double-seater, so someone

like Clair can ride with me or a carer,' he pointed out, as practical as ever.

'Don't you dare to leave me behind,' Becky warned from her wheelchair. 'I'll ride with Patrick.'

'Try anything once, won't you?' Dane teased gently.

'Twice, if I like it,' she retorted with a sparkle of mischief lighting up her pretty face.

Dane was smiling, dark eyes dancing, handsome face lit with laughter as he glanced at Joanne, and for a split second she was embraced by the warmth ignited by Becky's deliberately provocative reply. It was a rare moment of shared amusement and admiration for the girl's spirit. Heart on the tilt, she instantly fell even deeper into love with the man who seemed to be her inescapable destiny.

Dane looked into luminous blue eyes that had once swept him along on a frenzy of loving and the belief that he couldn't be happy without her. He had since proved that he *could*, but it hadn't been easy—and there were many degrees of happiness, he thought wryly. He was finding it hard to maintain dislike and disapproval and a pretence of indifference when she was so pretty, so appealing, the girl he had once loved turned into a fine and caring woman. Deliberately, in sheer self-defence, he reminded himself of the dangers in falling for her lovely face and warm femininity all over again.

'We seem to have some takers,' he said abruptly. 'Perhaps you could count heads, Joanne.'

'I can go, can't I?' Lenny demanded anxiously, afraid he would be barred because of his disability.

Dane laid an arm about the thin shoulders. 'Of course. Who else would I trust to lead the Pleydorf Commandos on their intrepid assault on the Wilderkaiser?'

As he led the boy towards the boarding-stage, Joanne looked after him and realised anew how good he was with the young disabled, sensing their anxieties and frustrations and knowing just how to counter them with the right word or gesture. How could she help loving such a man?

Eager hands flew into the air when she put the suggestion to the rest of the group, and Anneliese arrived to announce that the chair-lift operator had offered them a very generous discount. She was delighted, for funds were limited and had to be stretched as far as possible on each excursion.

Some opted not to go, either unwilling to trust the seemingly flimsy structure or nervous of heights. Joanne volunteered to stay with them, but she was overruled.

'I have seen the view many, many times,' Anneliese said firmly. 'It is not to be missed, and you are needed to ride with one of the disabled.'

As it was arranged as a round trip, no one would get off at the top, where another operator oversaw the smooth running of the chair-lift. One after the other, with Lenny and Paul in the lead, the double-seated chairs rose, lurching slightly on their metal rods at the beginning of the ascent. A gleeful Becky set off with Patrick, her excited cries ringing out on the air as they were carried up and away from the slowly dwindling group on the ground.

Between them, Dane and Cal settled Richard securely in a chair and Owen rode with him, providing the assurance of his presence and a strong arm about him, determined that even a multiplegic shouldn't miss yet another experience of a lifetime. Clair trusted herself to Cal's common sense and kindly manner, and soon only Nadine and Marcia were left to take their places in the constant procession.

Dane planned to ride with the rather excitable Marcia, and Joanne had promised to look after the nervous

Nadine in spite of her own qualms. At the last moment, both girls backed out.

'I don't like heights!' Marcia wailed, and ran to Anneliese's protective embrace.

Dane turned to Nadine, hand outstretched. 'You'll ride with me, won't you?' he encouraged with his warm smile.

The shy girl evaded his hand. 'No, thank you,' she whispered, anxious not to offend him, but adamant.

'All right, Nadine,' he soothed. 'Nobody does anything they don't want to do on this holiday.'

Anneliese gave Joanne a little push towards Dane. 'You two must ride together,' she urged, her provident soul recoiling in horror from the thought of money wasted on unused tickets. 'You will enjoy it.'

'Oh, I don't think so,' Joanne demurred, afraid she would shame herself if she *didn't* enjoy the chair-lift. Riding with Nadine, she would have been compelled to overcome her own nervousness or at least make light of it. Alone with Dane, suspended in the sky, she might cower and cling to him in sheer panic, although the waving hands and cheerful shouts of those already on the way up implied that there was nothing to fear. Joanne suspected that much of it was bravado!

'Beautiful view,' the operator said firmly, taking her arm. 'And it is quite safe.' Caught off balance, an empty chair nudging the back of her knees, Joanne sat, instinctively clutching at Dane as she did so.

He was drawn down with her, willy-nilly, and, before she realised what was happening, the operator dropped the safety bar across them and the chair began its slow, lurching ascent.

CHAPTER SIX

THEY looked at each other in startled, wary, half-smiling surprise. 'I'm not too happy about heights, either,' Joanne admitted wryly, clutching at the rail to avoid clutching at Dane's arm.

But the mountainside was still only feet below them and trees lined the first part of the ascent, reassuringly close, and it was really rather fun to look down on grazing cows and cyclists and wooden mountain huts and the dwindling coach and left-behind people as they were carried unrelentingly into the sky.

'There's nothing to worry about, Joanne. You're perfectly safe,' Dane assured her, tempted to put a reassuring arm about her but knowing it would tax his self-control to the very limit. She was so pretty, so provocative, in the colourful shorts that showed off her lovely legs and the skimpy, sleeveless top that clung to pert, peaked breasts and exposed much of her sun-kissed skin.

Having had no chance to settle herself comfortably and apparently not daring to shift her position as the chair swung unnervingly on its metal rod, she sat much too close to him. Dane was conscious of her weight against his shoulder and her thigh pressed hard against his leg, the perfume of her in his nostrils. The old magic persisted, it seemed, stirring his blood.

'Oh, I know! These things have a thousand and one safety regulations, don't they? But I'm jelly just the same!' Joanne shivered with a mix of excitement and nerves and cold as the ground veered away beneath them and the unexpected chill of the mountains struck at her exposed flesh. At the same time, she was euphoric, sitting so close to Dane, conscious of his disturbing masculinity and breathing in the male scent of him with a kind of hunger.

'You never did like heights. You screamed at the top of your voice when we were stuck for ten minutes on that Ferris wheel at the local fair,' Dane reminded her lightly.

'You were so embarrassed!' Joanne turned to him, glowing, forgetting, and then swallowed a rush of emotion as she remembered that those lovely, light-hearted, loving days were gone. How young she must have been to be so sure that they would last for ever!

Dane resisted the impulse to capture the slender hand that gripped the protective rail so fiercely that her knuckles were white. 'I threatened to throw you over the side,' he recalled, remembering the girl with her flame-coloured, flyaway hair and laughing eyes and the exciting challenge of her lovely body as she'd clung to him in real or pretended terror while the Ferris wheel had swung them to and fro, high in the night sky. Wasn't that the moment when he had known that he had loved her?

'You kissed me instead.' Her voice was unsteady.

'So I did.' Days long gone filled his head and his heart with memories. His body clamoured too, filling with the hunger that tormented him at nights when he lay in his room, next to Joanne's, craving her kiss and her touch and her joyous response to his need. 'Let me know if you feel like screaming,' he drawled, taking refuge in teasing.

The twinkle in his dark eyes and the smile that lurked about his lips tempted Joanne to take him at his word. She ached for the warm kisses, the sensual caresses, that had swept her into a world of indescribable delight in the days when they had been lovers. Instead, she pointed out the breathtaking array of peaks and valleys, the silver ribbon of winding river, in a determined attempt to hide her feelings.

'You're cold,' Dane said suddenly.

'No, I'm fine.' But her voice wobbled on the lie. She was terrified as well as cold. It was taking every ounce of her courage not to think about the awesome drop beneath them, and the rush of the wind that touched bare arms and legs with icy fingers seemed to threaten their precarious perch with every gust. 'I didn't expect it to be so windy,' she said through chattering teeth. 'It's so lovely down there. . .' It was a mistake to look down, she discovered too late, hastily closing her eyes. The ground was such a long way below them.

Dane unbuttoned his shirt and took it off to drape it about her shoulders. 'It's only cotton, but it should keep you slightly warmer.'

'But now *you'll* be cold.' It was a feeble protest as she clutched gratefully at the shirt, warm from his body. The wind tore hungrily at the thin stuff, almost whipping it away, and the shirt frolicked about her as Dane struggled to secure it at her throat by the top button, each movement causing the chair to swing and filling Joanne with fresh terror.

The shirt continued to flap, sleeves waving excitedly, as if it enjoyed the experience much more than she did, Joanne thought with wild, almost desperate humour. She relaxed only a fraction as Dane put an arm around her to keep the shirt in place. His arm was warm and comforting, like his nearness, and she longed to bury her face in his powerful chest as they began the slow and even more alarming descent. She wondered if anyone else was as nerve-racked as herself. She was too far away to see faces clearly, and the shouts that were drowned by the wind might have been cries of delight or shrieks of terror for all she could tell!

'They'll have to prise my fingers off this bar when we finally get back to earth,' she declared ruefully. 'They're absolutely frozen!'

'You aren't enjoying this at all, are you? Whatever will Annie say?' teased Dane, intensely aware of her and grimly fighting the realisation that the years had done nothing to diminish the wanting. His heart still yearned for her and his body still desired her sweet and generous welcome.

'She'll say I'm a coward—and so I am!' Joanne tried to laugh.

He touched his cheek to the silk cap of bright hair that was blown about her lovely face. 'We all have our weaknesses,' he comforted, knowing that she would always be his greatest and dearest weakness. However, a hard-earned lesson in loving kept him from attempting to repair the shattered image of a fallen angel. He had trusted her with his heart and his happiness, and he would never do so again, he vowed, strengthening a resolve that was close to crumbling.

Dane's warm breath was sweet on her face as he brought down his dark head, and for a breathless moment Joanne thought he meant to kiss her, making all right between them. As she turned her face to him in trembling invitation, he jerked away before their lips could touch. Her cheeks burned from more than the stinging wind as they finally docked at the boarding-stage to cries of welcome from the waiting group.

Handing back his shirt with a stiff smile, Joanne walked towards the coach, leaving Dane to assure Anneliese that they had both enjoyed the experience—and perhaps to explain why his arm had been around

Joanne and their heads so close together as they neared the ground.

Lenny almost fell over his own feet, rushing to meet her. 'Did you like it, Jo? Wasn't it smashing? We were over a mile high, Annie says. Did your ears pop? Mine did!'

'I didn't notice,' Joanne admitted. She had been far more concerned with a stomach full of wildly fluttering butterflies and a throbbing heart than popping ears, she thought drily. It seemed that everyone but herself felt that it had been a memorable experience. Joanne hoped she would never have to ascend a mountain by chair-lift again for as long as she lived—unless she could be sure that Dane would be there to comfort her with a strong arm and a kiss!

Getting off the coach on their return to Pleydorf, Nadine missed a step that she couldn't see very well with her limited vision. Cal's hand shot out too late to save her as she crashed down on the gravelled forecourt.

'Don't move her!' Dane shouted, abandoning Howie, who leaned heavily on two sticks as he waited for his wheelchair to be assembled. In two strides, Dane was beside Nadine, crouched on his haunches, while those still on board the coach craned and jostled each other to find out what had happened, blocking Joanne's effort to return for her medical case.

Nadine huddled, grey-faced with pain and shock, terrified of being touched by any hands other than Dane's. She trusted him, but she whimpered like a child as he ran experienced hands over her, checking for damage, reassuring her in his deep, gentle voice. The fall from such a slight distance might have only bruised and shaken someone less vulnerable, but Nadine's brittle bones were only one of the reasons why her anxious parents had been reluctant to let her join the

Austrian holiday. Anneliese had promised with her hand on her heart that no harm should come to their delicate daughter. Now, coming back from wheeling Becky to the annexe, she found an anxious group surrounding the coach.

'What has happened? What is it?' She pushed her way to the centre with some difficulty. '*Ach, liebe Gott*! Is she broken?' As was usual in moments of stress, her excellent English had temporarily deserted her.

'Impossible to tell without an X-ray. Frau Meyer is telephoning the Haupmann Clinic to warn them that we shall need to make use of their facilities.' Although he was a qualified doctor, Dane had no standing in Austria, but the clinic in nearby St Johann was available in cases of accident or sudden illness and he had already made himself known to the doctor in charge. 'All right, Nadine. Don't worry, sweetie—I'm going to give you something for the pain and then you'll be more comfortable.' He nodded to Joanne, who took a syringe and a capsule from her case and began to prepare the injection. He stroked the tousled hair from Nadine's beautiful face, knowing that she hated even a single strand of it to be out of place.

'Where's my hat?' she whispered, a hand fluttering to her uncovered head, more concerned about one of her beloved hats than a possibly broken bone, a commonplace event to a girl who had spent much of her life in plaster.

'Hat. . .?' Dane looked blank. He had something more important on his mind, for, noticing that she winced slightly with each breath, he suspected a fractured rib and possibly worse.

Lionel bent to retrieve the pale straw boater with its trailing navy-blue ribbons that had been Nadine's pride and joy when they had set off that morning. 'I'm afraid

I trod on it,' he said ruefully, showing the crushed and torn crown and the dirtied ribbons. In his rush to help, he hadn't seen the delicate piece of finery beneath his large foot.

Nadine burst into tears.

Joanne hastily bundled the once-cherished straw out of sight and handed the prepared hypodermic to Dane. As he gave the pain-killing injection to Nadine, Joanne closed and locked the medical case, slipped the key on its chain over her neck and scrambled to her feet.

'Now, come along, everybody,' she said in the briskly authoritative tones that were so effective in marshalling dawdling juniors on her ward. 'This won't do. Cal wants to put the coach away, and some of you should be resting.' She sent Lenny and Paul and Ian off to the games room, handed Howie into Lionel's reliable care and gave the hovering Marcia an encouraging pat and a push in the direction of the annexe. 'Go and keep Becky company, there's a good girl. She's due for her rub, and I'll be along with your insulin shortly. Nadine will be well looked after—and all the sooner if everyone gets out of the way,' she added firmly as Frau Meyer hurried up with a stretcher trolley and the news that an ambulance was on its way and Herr Doktor Schwodler alerted to receive a patient.

Later that night, having done the final round of pills and medicines and injections and given Becky her bath, Joanne crossed the lawn with Lionel, met on her way to her room, just as a taxi drew up to disgorge Dane, finally back from the clinic, where Nadine had been admitted with two fractured ribs and a Colles' fracture of the wrist.

Murmuring a quick goodnight to Lionel, she hurried to speak to him. 'Is Anneliese staying at the clinic?'

'It seemed sensible.' Riffling through a wad of Austrian schillings to pay the taxi driver, Dane scarcely glanced at her, but he was well aware of the tall man in the shadows, watching them. He had no real dislike of Lionel, but he was becoming slightly incensed by the hovering that Joanne seemed to encourage. He had also spent a very dull evening, listening to Anneliese and the tall, blond Austrian doctor who had been at Heidelberg University with one of her brothers talking to each other over dinner. Their delighted flow of German had exhausted him, and he had left them to a happy exchange of personalities as soon as he could.

Joanne fell into step beside him as he turned to enter the building, stealing a glance at his shadowed face and wondering why he seemed so cross. 'Poor Nadine! What a thing to happen,' she said warmly.

He rounded on her abruptly. 'How *did* it happen?'

Joanne was taken aback. 'Why, she fell——'

'I know she *fell*! But how did she come to fall? Why wasn't someone looking after her? Where were you? Where was Patrick—or Owen? Or even Lionel, usually getting under everyone's feet in the rush to help even when he isn't needed?' he added on an irrational surge of jealousy.

The hot blood stormed into her face. 'Are you saying that *I'm* responsible?'

'*Irresponsible* seems more appropriate in your case.' It was an unjust, unfair and totally unreasonable desire to punish her for strolling about the grounds in the moonlight with another man, instantly regretted as he saw her flinch from the words.

With an effort, Joanne kept her temper. 'I don't see how you come to that conclusion, Dane,' she said evenly. 'I wasn't anywhere near Nadine.'

'Then you should have been. A half-blind girl with

little sense of balance and poor co-ordination was left to get off the coach without assistance, and those who should have given an eye to her were apparently too concerned with other things. Or people,' he added cuttingly and with unmistakable implication. 'Lionel was around to give *you* a hand, no doubt.'

She didn't recognise the taunt as a jealous one, but she flew instinctively to the defence of her gentle giant. 'Lionel is not an official helper,' she reminded him grittily. 'Too many people expect him to be available to lift and carry and push wheelchairs and look after the walking wounded. There are times when I don't know what we'd do without his help, but I won't have him taken for granted, and it's most unkind to imply that he ought to have been watching out for Nadine!'

Dane's mouth hardened at the support that confirmed her affection for the man. 'You misunderstand me,' he said coldly, punching the button for the lift. 'I mean that it's *you* who ought to have been watching out for Nadine.' He walked into the lift. 'Fortunately, things aren't as bad as they might have been,' he relented as he looked down at her from his superior height. She was lovely, with that delicate flush in her face, the militant sparkle of luminous blue eyes and the tremulous sweetness of her mouth catching at his heart.

But the swift spark of indignation reminded him of the ungovernable temper that still simmered beneath the surface of an acquired control. Until she mastered it completely then the happiness or peace of mind or even the physical safety of any man in her life couldn't be guaranteed, he told himself, backing away from the brink of loving her all over again.

'I had visions of her being flown home by air ambulance,' Joanne admitted, cooling but still cross with him for being so hard on her and so scathing about Lionel. Didn't he make allowances for anybody any more?

'Things aren't that serious. Both ribs should heal satisfactorily within a few weeks, although she'll have some discomfort at first.' Dane spoke with the briskly dismissive manner of the medical man that overlooked her status as a ward sister. 'The fractured wrist shouldn't present any problems, and it has been well and truly plastered by a most efficient nurse.'

'How long will she be in the clinic?' Joanne followed him into the lift and the door slid shut, enclosing them in a cocoon of intimacy.

'Schwodler wants to keep her for a few days.'

'It seems a shame that it had to happen to someone as shy as Nadine.' She clung to the subject of Nadine because it was safe, impersonal and had no link with the past, so much in her mind at that moment.

Dane shrugged. 'She seems more relaxed than I've ever seen her. She's well used to hospitals, isn't she?' He ushered her into the corridor and they strolled towards their adjoining rooms. 'Most of the nurses seem to speak very good English, but Anneliese will stay with her, in any case. More for her own sake, I fancy,' he added with a slight smile. 'It seems that she and the Herr Doktor have a number of things in common.'

Joanne gazed at the door that had shut him from her sight with such finality. He had spoken lightly, but she wondered if his attack on her and Lionel had been prompted not so much by concern for Nadine but by a dislike of the rapport between Anneliese and an Austrian doctor.

The planned expedition to the historic Summer Palace on the outskirts of Salzburg went ahead without Anneliese, at her urging. She had been many times, and the group must not miss its splendours or the famous Water Gardens with their cleverly devised surprises and playing fountains and ancient statuary, she insisted. Everything was arranged.

It was another very hot day, and the cool, walled gardens with their amusing traps for the unwary, and the enchanting models set in niches and grottoes, provided a welcome shade after they had strolled around the flower-filled palace grounds with its lake and tree-lined walks. Manipulating wheelchairs and ushering the walking wounded along narrow, damp pathways and up and down worn stone steps, and admiring each new ingenuity, took up so much of Joanne's attention that she didn't notice that Becky was unusually subdued or that Lionel pushed her wheelchair for much of the time instead of the normally attentive Patrick.

She did notice that Marcia scarcely left Dane's side as he manoeuvred Clair's chair around the gardens, and she marvelled at his unfailing patience with the girl. At the same time, she wondered if he was storing up trouble all unknowingly. A brush-off might seem unkind, in the circumstances, but kindness could be construed as encouragement by the immature Marcia.

'We miss Annie, don't we, Jo?' Lenny trailed in her wake as they approached the exit from the Water Gardens.

'It isn't the same without her,' she agreed. It had been an enjoyable outing, but things were always more fun when Anneliese was with them. Perhaps Joanne was too anxious, too inclined to raise objections or recognise potential obstacles, while for Anneliese problems just didn't exist or, if they did, were dealt with so efficiently that the group was unaware that they had ever arisen.

'Or Nadine,' Richard contributed over his shoulder.

'I know she doesn't say much, but it's nice to have her around. When is she coming out of hospital, Jo?'

'Tomorrow, I believe.' She hurried to help with Richard's chair, which had to be negotiated up the few but curving steps to the exit. Slipping on the wet stones, she felt the wrench of an ankle and 'Ouch'ed in pain.

Having parked Howie's chair safely at the top, Cal came bounding down to her assistance. Wincing, she tried her weight on the injured ankle as he supported her. 'Bad, is it, lass?' he asked, concerned.

Joanne clung to his arm, smiling in spite of the pain in her ankle, which throbbed unpleasantly. 'Oh, I don't think so,' she said brightly. 'It will be fine in a few moments, I expect. I'll just sit on this wall until the pain eases off, if you'll give Owen a hand with Richard. . .' Feeling slightly sick and very stupid, she hoped that she hadn't disabled herself for the remainder of the holiday.

'I said I'd be back to help with Richard. You should have waited,' Cal scolded in his kindly way. 'A lass like you shouldn't be tugging and heaving at these heavy chairs. You try to do too much, Jo.'

'What's wrong?' Dane caught up with them.

He had coped efficiently with Clair's chair as well as the clinging Marcia, but, watching him as he had guided them along the last of the narrow, dimly lit pathways, Joanne had seen the drag of his lame leg and knew he was tired.

'Jo's hurt her foot—she slipped on these steps. She says it doesn't pain her, but you can see that it does,' Cal told him bluntly.

'Let's have a look.' Crouching beside her, Dane ran his hand over the rapidly swelling ankle. 'Why on earth did you wear such stupid shoes for this outing?' he demanded with the impatience of concern, tapping the high wedge heel of the rainbow-striped sandals that matched her dress. The blaze of the colourful outfit had stood out sharply in the gloom of tall trees and grey stone and cool green water of the gardens, drawing his eye again and again, giving yet another twist to the screw of longing. 'You should have worn flat heels, knowing that so much walking would be involved.'

'Well, I didn't,' Joanne muttered, resenting the unhelpful criticism and hurt by the impersonal indifference of his touch and his tone. She stifled another 'Ouch' as his strong fingers probed a tender spot.

'That hurts, does it?' He probed again, more gently.

'I think I'm broken.' With a wry smile, she echoed Anneliese's clumsy English and was rewarded by the flit of a smile across his lean, handsome face.

'I doubt it.' Unfastening the narrow strap, Dane eased the sandal carefully from her foot, watched by the fascinated few crowding the path behind him.

Bare, mud-splashed, shamefully grubby from the heat and dust of the day, her small foot lay in his palm, and his touch sent a shiver of excitement from the tip of those dusty toes to the top of her smooth, shining head.

Hot with embarrassment, Joanne felt just as foolish as he probably thought she was to have missed her footing so carelessly on the wet steps. 'I feel like Cinderella,' she joked, putting her hand on his broad shoulder and drawing comfort from the feel and the warmth of his flesh through the thin summer shirt.

'I'm right out of glass slippers at the moment.' With a professionalism that masked the strong stir of tenderness, Dane checked the delicate bones and then manipulated her small toes, one by one, watching her expressive face for reaction. 'Nothing more than a wrench,' he diagnosed confidently. 'Painful, but not serious. The best thing you can do is to walk on it as much as possible.'

'Walk on it!' Joanne was horrified. 'But it hurts!'

'Am I the doctor or are you?' Dane challenged lightly but with an implacable note to his deep voice. 'Believe me, the more you use that foot the less it will hurt and the sooner it will heal.'

'It doesn't seem very likely——' She broke off, capitulating as she saw the light of battle in his dark eyes, remembering that Dane's hackles had always risen if his medical judgement was questioned. 'Oh, very well. I'll try your theory,' she said grudgingly.

Still crouching, he eased her foot into the sandal and fastened the strap, his touch so impersonal that there was no justification for the wanton weakness of desire that rippled through her. She stood as Dane straightened, and the brush of his strong shoulder almost knocked her off balance.

'Sorry. . .' He put an arm about her waist to steady her and she leaned on him, gingerly testing her weight. 'OK?'

To her surprise, her ankle seemed slightly less painful for his ministrations and the brief rest. Like many good doctors, he had the healing touch. 'It's much better, Dane. Thanks very much.'

Lionel pushed through the huddle of people about them, eager to help. 'Let me carry you back to the coach, Jo.'

She smiled and shook her head. 'Dr Dane says I mustn't be a baby and that I'm to use my foot as much as possible,' she told him lightly.

Almost before the words had left her lips, she was scooped into a pair of determined arms and had to curve an arm about a powerful neck to keep her balance as she was swept up the few stone steps to the top, where Cal waited with Clair and the others.

CHAPTER SEVEN

HELD close to a heart that seemed to thud more heavily than the brief ascent merited, Joanne observed the pulse that throbbed in a lean jaw and the grim set to a sensual mouth that hinted at a struggle for self-control, and her own heart shuddered with the wild hope that he might not be as indifferent as he seemed to be, after all.

'You certainly know how to sweep a girl off her feet,' she murmured wickedly, a dancing invitation in her sapphire eyes.

'I couldn't trust you not to slip again in those ridiculous shoes,' Dane returned curtly, setting her down, wondering why he had felt compelled to forestall the well-meaning Lionel, and if she knew what it had cost him to appear unmoved as he'd held her against his heart. 'But you should be all right on level ground. However, let me know if it becomes too uncomfortable and I'll strap it up for you.' His tone was brisk, professional.

'Thank you, Doctor,' Joanne said meekly, firmly put in her place by the rebuke of his tone, still shaken by the brief but disturbing contact with a body that had once been the harbinger of ecstasy for an unawakened girl.

Turning away, she took charge of Clair's chair for support and hobbled along the path towards the open-air cafeteria that was their next port of call. Pride forced her to make light of the discomfort of her wrenched ankle, and she found it easier with each step, just as Dane had predicted.

Enjoying a superb ice beneath the colourful umbrellas of the terrace tables, she saw Patrick and Marcia disappearing in the direction of the lake and glanced round automatically for Becky. The girl's chair was parked at a nearby table and she was toying with a huge banana split in a splendid silver dish. Lenny and Paul were looking after her and she seemed happy enough, but at the back of Joanne's mind was a little, niggling anxiety. Something was wrong, she felt.

'Sit with me, Jo,' Becky invited unexpectedly as Joanne eased along the gangway of the coach on her way to a seat at the back for the return to Pleydorf. 'I want to show you my postcards.'

Expecting to vacate the seat as soon as Patrick finished helping to stack wheelchairs, she dutifully admired the postcards and agreed that the Summer Palace had been well worth the visit. She was surprised when Patrick found himself another seat without a word of protest, for the couple had been virtually inseparable since the start of the holiday. But Becky, chatting away in her usual voluble fashion, appeared not to mind the defection.

At least he hadn't chosen to sit with Marcia, Joanne thought thankfully, vaguely troubled by a possible complication should both girls have taken a fancy to the same man. Then, seeing Marcia plump herself down beside Dane, she reminded herself drily that the highly strung girl seemed to have eyes for no one but the much older doctor.

Later that afternoon, the cool, sun-spangled water looked very inviting as Joanne passed the pool on her way to the annexe. She had a number of things to do, for her duties as a carer were doubled by Anneliese's absence, and she envied the few who had headed for the pool as soon as they had got back to Pleydorf.

Eager for another lesson, Marcia had coaxed Dane to accompany them, and now she earnestly attempted the breast-stroke with his hand beneath her chin—and one foot firmly on the blue-tiled floor, Joanne suspected, although Dane was making encouraging noises as if he pretended to believe that Marcia was actually trusting herself to the water.

'Coming in, Jo?' Lenny was poised at the top of the water-splash, a wide grin splitting his boyish face.

'Not at the moment. Too busy,' she called back. There was no sign of Becky, although Patrick was behind Lenny on the chute. Knowing him to usually be well informed of the girl's whereabouts, she waved to him. 'Is Becky in her room, Patrick?'

He hit the water with such force that the surge and the splash drowned her words. Joanne gave him the benefit of the doubt, anyway, as he struck out across the pool as if he hadn't heard. Marcia had looked round, however, wrenching her chin from Dane's supporting hand. She promptly sank and surfaced, choking.

'Sorry,' Joanne said contritely.

'She was doing so well, too,' Dane reproached, holding the spluttering girl upright with one hand. 'Now don't give up, Marcia. You managed three strokes entirely on your own. Have another try,' he urged.

'Becky wasn't feeling well,' Marcia managed as soon as she recovered her breath. 'She said she had a headache.'

'Oh, dear. Too much sun, I expect. I'll go and see how she is now. . .' Joanne glanced back, envying the girl who was enjoying so much of Dane's time and attention on this holiday.

Once he had been just as patient and tender and kind with her, and she had adored him in much the same way that Marcia did now, knowing little about loving and where it could lead or the heartache it could bring. If only she could turn back the clock. . .

Collecting some paracetamol, she made her way to the room that Becky shared with Marcia. The patio door stood open and Becky had placed her chair so that she had a clear view across the lawns to the pool, the shouts and laughter carrying clearly on the still summer air, the bright colours of shorts and swimsuits identifying the swimmers. Her pretty, plump face was wet with tears and her shoulders heaved with sobs as she stared at the scene.

Instantly, Joanne was on her knees beside her. 'Whatever is it, lovey? Is your head very bad?' Her trained mind immediately began to tick off all the various illnesses of which a severe headache might be the first symptom, while she prayed that the holiday wasn't threatened by another disaster, another urgent call to the Haupmann Clinic.

Enveloped in warm and kindly concern, Becky broke down completely. 'Oh, Jo, I'm s-so m-miserable!' she wailed, fresh tears welling.

'I can see that you are. But why? Tell me what's wrong and I'll do my best to put it right. Is it Marcia?' She wondered if the two friends had quarrelled over a trifle that had taken on mountainous proportions.

Becky shook her head, looking forlorn. 'No. It's P-Patrick. He s-says he doesn't want to get involved. He says there's a g-girl at home who wants him to m-marry her. But I know it isn't that, Jo. It's b-because I haven't any l-legs,' she sobbed, tears streaming.

Joanne put both arms about the unhappy girl. 'I'm sure that isn't true,' she soothed. 'It doesn't sound at all like Patrick. Perhaps he just needs a little more time. . .'

'He's b-been avoiding me all day!' Becky's head sank on to Joanne's comforting shoulder on the heartbroken words. She had tried to hide her hurt and disappointment during the day, but it had become too much for her as she'd sat and watched and listened to her friends as they enjoyed the pool. She tried not to feel sorry for herself as a rule, for the situation couldn't be altered, but she was only human and she had really felt that at last she had met someone who didn't feel that her freak of a body was a turn-off.

That was the niggle that had troubled her throughout the outing to the Summer Palace, Joanne realised. Usually glued to Becky's side, Patrick had been missing each time she'd glanced at the girl, other members of the group taking it in turns to push her from place to place. Deep down, she felt it wouldn't be surprising if Patrick *was* backing away. It took a rare man to accept without question all the problems that could attach to loving a severely disabled girl. But she had really believed that it would be a match, for the couple had seemed so close, so devoted, so happy to be together since the very first day of the holiday. Perhaps it had been much too soon for either of them to see the future clearly or realise the pitfalls. But how long did it take to fall in love? Or to be sure that it would last forever?

Hadn't she known at first sight that Dane would be the one and only love of her life?

'It's been one of those days, Becky,' she said warmly, doing her best to comfort and reassure. 'Nobody realises how much Annie does until she isn't with us, and we've all had to rally round and fill the gap. Patrick has had to look after other people when he would much rather have been with you, I expect. I'm sure you've got it all wrong.'

Perhaps it wasn't wise to build up her hopes, but Joanne knew how desperate a girl could feel when she saw her happiness slipping away and couldn't do anything to prevent it happening.

She left Becky slightly cheered, charged with the unenviable task of talking to Patrick and finding out how he felt about the situation. There were times when Joanne felt slightly out of her depth, although she had known the members of the PHAB Club for some months. The disabled youngsters talked freely of their feelings, rather too freely at times, she thought drily, and seemed to have come to terms in most cases with the limitations that disability set on their lives. Anneliese had taken them on holiday before and knew what to expect and how to cope if feelings got out of hand, but Joanne wondered if her friend had ever been faced with so many emotional problems.

Richard and Nadine. Patrick and Becky. Marcia and Dane. Even Lionel and herself, she admitted ruefully, knowing she must hurt him in the end. She suspected that he was beginning to care for her, but although she was very fond of her dear Lionheart she could never love him—and that had nothing whatsoever to do with his deafness or his difficult speech.

Her inability to respond to any other man in the last seven years and the instant revival of dormant emotions when Dane had walked back into her life told her plainly that he was the only man she could ever, would ever want.

The slight heaviness about her heart persisted when she stood out on the veranda later that night, wrapped in a thin silk dressing-gown, looking across the roofs of the complex and the surrounding village to the distant and very beautiful Wilderkaiser. The moon hid behind a bank of cloud and the jagged mountain peaks were just a darker shade of night against the horizon. Here and there, throughout the silent valley, a light shone out brightly, telling her that she was not the only one who couldn't sleep on this hot, still night.

Heart and mind and body were caught up in a tangle of longing and loneliness. Only yards away but with so much more than distance separating them lay the man she loved and ached to hold and touch and kiss. She wished she had the courage—or the shamelessness—to walk into his room and slide into bed beside him and wake him with a kiss that spoke of her hunger to be crushed in his arms, swept along on the roller-coaster of his forceful lovemaking and up, up, up to the glorious peaks of ecstatic fulfilment, and then to lie against his heart, held close in the golden glow of after-loving, exchanging the sweet tenderness of endearments that sprang so instinctively to the lips of lovers.

The evening had been so still and airless that most of the group had gathered on the terrace. They had been tired from the day's excursion, and conversation had flagged. Hearing some of the Austrian staff mention an impending storm, Joanne had gone for her guitar to distract the youngsters from the increasing portent of the atmosphere, and they had gone off to bed in happy mood after an hour of their favourites.

On an impulse, she reached for her guitar now and sat down to strum at it, forgetting everything but long-gone days as her fingers found the strings of the ballad that had once meant so much to her and Dane. Sometimes there was a comfort in evoking the past in spite of its shattered dreams, and she recalled the days when Dane had loved her and held her close as she softly played the song that had cemented their romance.

Dane strode out to the veranda, running a hand through the rumpled waves and curls of his black hair, and shot a dour glance at the girl and her guitar. A throbbing ache in his lame leg and a persistent desire for her sweet love had kept him awake more than the threatening storm. It was impossible for lovers such as they had been to wholly ignore the tug of long-ago intimacy, and he suspected that she was as stirred as himself by the hint of sexuality in every encounter. He had only to reach out and she would be in his arms. . .

'Must you play that damn tune?' he growled.

Joanne's clever fingers were stilled. Her heart almost stopped too, as she glanced the length of the veranda to the tall, shadowy figure in the white towelling robe. Lost in the music and her memories, she was abruptly jolted back to the present. Suddenly, throbbingly aware of him, of love and longing and desperate wanting, she gazed at the just-visible planes of his handsome face, the powerful thrust of shoulders, the muscular and potently masculine body beneath the knee-length robe.

'Did I wake you? I'm sorry.' It seemed incredible that the soft sound of her playing could have reached his sleeping ears.

'I was already awake. Too tense to sleep.' He sent her a sidelong glance. 'Aren't you?'

Joanne supposed he meant the threatening storm. Certainly, his words were accompanied by a low rumble of thunder in the distance. 'A little,' she admitted, smiling.

Dane moved towards her, hands clenched and jammed into the pockets of his robe to still their trembling need to touch and take. He fought the stir of his body as he studied the slender, pretty girl, her glorious hair haloed by the light from the room behind her, a thin wrap clinging to the curves of beautiful breasts and parting to reveal the long, provocative line of a thigh as she moved to lay down her guitar.

'I don't mind the music,' he said abruptly as the silk fell away to expose the sweet swell of a naked breast.

Longing surged even more strongly. 'You play very well.' The need to control his fierce and demanding desire harshened his tone.

'Oh, I don't know. It's only a hobby. . .' Joanne began to feel slightly breathless, her heart skipping a beat as he came nearer, looming above her, a tension she couldn't help but sense in his tall frame.

'Never mind. Your playing gives people a lot of pleasure—I saw that tonight.' He crouched beside her low chair. 'Just don't play that particular song when I'm around, Joanne.'

Her name lingered on his lips like velvet, but she heard the steel behind the quiet words and nodded, understanding. 'I'm surprised you recognise it.'

'Some things can never be completely pushed from mind.' Like the memory of her in his arms, loving and giving, Dane thought achingly. Like the magic of her kiss and her sweet, shy caress, moving him in a way he had never known before or since.

Like her foolish jealousy and mistrust and wild flight from a man who had no recollection of telling her to go, Joanne thought wryly. Like the pain and anxiety and anguish she had left him to suffer alone when concern and contrition and her continued love for him might have made amends.

'I should have stayed. . . I thought you hated me,' she stumbled. 'I didn't know what to do. I thought you might die—and if you didn't that you wouldn't want me near you.'

'I loved you, Joanne,' he said roughly.

'I loved you.' It was a whisper in the past tense when her heart longed to cry out loud that she loved him still and always would.

'First love—young love. It didn't stand up to the first test. Perhaps I asked too much of you,' he conceded, his heart smiting him as he remembered just how young and untried and vulnerable she had been at eighteen.

It was the first sign of forgiving, more than she had dared to hope. She wondered if she dared to put her arms about him.

'How's that foot?' Dane asked abruptly, seeking to break the spell of her femininity that threatened to enchant him all over again.

He enclosed her ankle in his strong, warm hand, and Joanne's heart beat so high and so hard in her throat that she was sure he must hear it. 'It seems to be fine,' she said brightly. Did he know what he did to her with his touch, his nearness? Oh, of course he did! Hadn't he always known and delighted in her weakness and swept her laughingly, lovingly, into bed on the strength of his potent sensuality? Wasn't the offer of an olive branch only the prelude to the lovemaking that he so obviously desired?

Dane moved his hand along her calf in slow, familiar caress and her body shrieked a warning, although heart and mind were past caring about anything but the need to be in his arms once more. Hypnotised by the glow in his eyes, the warmth in his face, the nearness of him, she leaned towards him in unconscious invitation for his kiss, his embrace, his urgent response to the flood of her own desire.

Women sent out signals that any experienced man could read, Dane knew. *Touch me not*—or *touch me now*. . .and Joanne's signal was coming over loud and clear. He slid his caressing hand towards her soft, seductive thigh and felt the tremble of her body. He stilled the clamour in his loins with sheer strength of will. She needed time, he felt. Seven years couldn't be wiped out all in a moment, even with a kiss.

His dark head came close in unmistakable intent and

Joanne waited, her breath quickening, for the kiss that would wipe out all the pain and bitterness of the past. The sky exploded with a zig-zagging streak of brilliant blue lightning that danced off the mountain peaks, and a loud crash of thunder announced the eruption of the storm.

Joanne's thoughts flew to the highly strung Marcia, who became hysterical with the advent of any storm—and this one threatened to be a particularly violent one. Another flash of lightning lit up the sky, and she pushed Dane away and leaped to her feet. 'Marcia must be terrified. I ought to go to her. . .'

Dane trapped her in strong arms. 'Let someone else do the worrying for a change,' he said with the brusqueness of his body's urgency. 'It's going to be a spectacular night. Share it with me.' The moment and the mood were right and there might never be another opportunity. Joanne would shrink back behind the defensive shell of guilt, and he would remember all the very good reasons why he ought not to give anything of himself to her ever again.

He looked for a long, searching moment into eyes that were limpid with desire. Touched by the trembling that betrayed the fire he had kindled, he kissed her, at first with a tender hunger and then with all his pent-up passion.

His body was hard and urgent against her as they clung together in that long, long kiss. His hands gripped her so fiercely that she would have to camouflage the bruises, but Joanne didn't care. His mouth stifled any protest that she might have wanted to make—but protest was the last thing in her mind. Sighing, she melted, giving him kiss for kiss, her slight body straining for the ultimate closeness.

Dane laid her gently on her bed as a fresh blaze of

lightning struck the sky and skipped up and down the mountainside, lighting up the village and the holiday complex. The boom of thunder echoed back from the distant Wilderkaiser as he stretched at her side, sliding the silk wrap from her body. He kissed her breasts with reverent lips, paying homage to their peaked beauty.

Joanne's fingers twined in his jet hair, teasing, delighting in the crispness of his curls as she breathed in the warm male scent of him that mingled with the lingering aftershave and the laundry-freshness of his robe. She thrust back the folds of his robe and touched her lips to his bare shoulder and ran her hands over the muscular chest and back, a little shyly, familiarising herself again with his body, eager for its potent ability to give her pleasure. Touching him, she felt the quickening of his flesh beneath her shy fingers and revelled in the age-old power of a woman to make a weakling of even the strongest man with mutual desire.

Dane lifted his head to look at her, with a smile in the depths of his smouldering eyes. She knew what he asked, and she smiled back at him in swift, spontaneous answer and felt his arms tighten about her abruptly, gladly. Long, clever fingers stroked the silk of her bare breast, trailed lower to the round of her hips and the flat of her belly and found the warmth of her womanhood. As he kissed her, Joanne sighed against his lips, betraying the craving that his expert touch evoked. With a sudden, aching groan, he swept her beneath his compelling body and took her, exultant, triumphant male claiming his woman, and the storm raged above their heads while they joyously renewed past delight in each other, oblivious to the blitzkrieg, bodies illumined by each flash of lightning, the pound of their pulses drowning the barrage of angry thunder.

He was a sensual and thoughtful lover, with an

unerring instinct for knowing and satisfying a woman's every need, and Joanne's love for him enhanced their union beyond even her wildest dreams.

Wisely, even at the height of ecstasy when a storm of emotion accompanied the joyous surge of breathless fulfilment, she stifled the words that wanted to tumble from her heart, instinctively knowing that they would lessen the moment and the strength of her feelings. For how could she put into words what she felt about Dane and her gladness at this reconciliation?

And, even more wisely, she kept from prompting him into murmuring things he might not mean as he lay, sated, across her breast, proud body gleaming with sweat and satisfaction, dark hair falling over his brow and heavy lids guarding the eyes that she might try to scan for some sign of an emotion he couldn't feel.

If Dane ever loved her again, that would be a blessing beyond anything in life and much, much more than she deserved, Joanne felt. But she didn't expect a miracle. He hadn't reached out and taken her because of any past or present love for her, she realised, refusing to build dreams on such an insecure foundation. She had simply given a sensual man what he briefly happened to want again, and it would be a mistake to attach importance to the totally unexpected stir of his senses and his need for satisfaction in her arms.

Take what the gods offered and be content, she told herself firmly—and wasn't she more than thankful to have lain once more in Dane's arms, to have enjoyed his passionate and powerful lovemaking and to know with utter and instinctive certainty that no other woman had ever delighted him as she did?

Maybe it wasn't loving as she knew it. But it might be a basis for some kind of friendship between them in the future.

CHAPTER EIGHT

SLIDING into sleep, heart and mind at peace for the first time since they had left England, Joanne roused abruptly to the buzz of the bedside telephone. In the middle of the night, it could only be an emergency of some kind, she knew.

Grateful that she had been allowed to enjoy the magic of Dane's lovemaking to the full before she was summoned, she eased herself from beneath his body, heavier still in slumber, and reached for the receiver. 'Sister speak—sorry! I mean—it's Jo,' she amended hastily, needing those few moments to orientate herself and identify the caller. 'What is it, Owen?'

A crash of thunder almost drowned the voice in her ear, and with it came the sharp staccato of rain on the windows. The skies had opened and it was very welcome, for the atmosphere had been dry, electric and dangerous, rather alarming to anyone unused to mountain storms.

Attending to a wakeful Richard, Owen had heard someone banging on the dividing wall between their room and the one shared by Becky and Marcia, he explained. Richard wasn't feeling well and he couldn't leave him to find out what was wrong. Could Joanne investigate?

'I can and will. Right away,' she assured him briskly, wondering why neither girl had picked up the telephone to call for assistance. Panicking too much to think clearly, no doubt, she decided.

She was reluctant to shatter the magical spell of a

precious intimacy, but training told and she knew that she had no choice. Recalled to her responsibilities, she felt rather guilty about Marcia and one or two others who had probably been just as disturbed by the violence of the night, needing her reassuring presence and comforting words, while she selfishly but oh, so marvellously revelled in the strength and satisfaction of Dane's embrace.

She shook him, very gently. 'Dane! I'm sorry to wake you, but there seems to be some problem with either Becky or Marcia and I'm needed in the annexe. I think you ought to go back to your own room now.'

He was instantly awake, a hangover from his days as a junior doctor at Brook's when he had been on constant call and had had to snatch the odd hour or two of sleep whenever he could. 'Can't someone else deal with it?' he grumbled, sliding an arm about her and attempting to draw her back to his side, his sensual body remembering and thrilling and throbbing with a renewal of desire.

Lovely, lovely Joanne, his love, his angel, back in his arms and his heart where she belonged, he thought on a drowsy tide of content—and then the warning bells rang.

Picking up the pieces wouldn't work. She was still the same hot-headed girl who had let him down. He had managed to survive without her in his life for seven years, and a busy, dedicated doctor didn't need the hassle of loving someone with the twin faults of jealousy and a quick temper, he told himself sternly. He weakened briefly as she relaxed against him, kissed him with those sweet lips before she reluctantly edged from his arms.

He wanted her. He needed her. Having found her again so unexpectedly, could he let her walk away from him a second time as she no doubt would when they got back to England, going back to her job and her friends on the other side of the city? *Yes*, he decided, hardening his heart against the tug of longing. Their lives lay in different directions and, like himself, she had made a new beginning after the accident. She seemed perfectly content with things as they were, and he was far from convinced that she was capable of love as he knew it.

'I have to go,' Joanne said ruefully, unaware of the tussle between wanting and will that had decided her chance of happiness in the future. 'Apparently, Owen can't leave Richard, and Becky wouldn't want Patrick anywhere near her at the moment.'

Hands behind his head, Dane lay back and admired the lovely lines of her body as she pulled on bra and briefs. 'Shall I go? Marcia would welcome me with open arms,' he drawled with a twinkle in his dark eyes.

'You'd never get out alive!' Laughing, Joanne reached for her tracksuit.

Dane stretched, sighed, smiled with a lazy charm as she pulled the tracksuit top over her head and shook out the silken cap of her hair. 'Poor Marcia. She really thinks I'm God's gift to any woman, doesn't she? Someone should tell her that I'm the love 'em and leave 'em type.'

Alerted by the warning that she read into the light words, as he had no doubt intended, Joanne looked up, fingers stilled in the act of tying the lace of a trackshoe. 'You never used to be!' He had been so steadfast, so loyal—and the loyalty to a past girlfriend had been beyond her understanding and tolerance and temper, she thought wryly.

Dane shrugged and sat up, reaching for the robe that lay in a crumpled heap on the floor. 'People change, Joanne. Either through age or experience or circumstances. There was only one time in my life when I wanted something permanent. It didn't work out.' It was a careful, deliberate reminder, without bitterness or anger but ruthless in its implications. 'Now, my attitude is that women are great to have around, but not all the time. When one of them starts to get serious that's the time to move on, in my book.'

'Oh, I agree!' Pride prompted the light, slightly brittle retort. 'Heavy involvement is out for me too. My job is far more important to me than any man these days.'

Oh, she was a fool, an absolute idiot! Joanne castigated herself as she hurried along the corridor to the lift. She had thought a kiss would make them friends again, so the trembling ecstasy that they had just shared should have turned them into real and lasting lovers once more. It hadn't.

Dane had made it very plain that he had taken her on a storm of wanting that he might have felt for any woman who was available and willing. Love hadn't played any part in that bitter-sweet tumult of love-making. She hadn't really expected anything else in the circumstances, and she had schooled herself not to dream of a future shared with him—but wasn't it unnecessarily cruel of Dane to spell it out for her so bluntly even before the bed they had shared was cold?

The storm that had seemed to be dying out had obviously paused only to gather itself for a fresh onslaught of fury. Collecting a member of the night staff on her way through the annexe, Joanne arrived in a breathless rush to find Becky on the floor, having fallen out of bed and hit her head so that she was dazed as well as helpless, and Marcia cowering beneath the sheet, screaming in terror at each renewed flash of lightning or roll of thunder, totally useless in an emergency.

Joanne didn't blame the shattered girl. She was much too busy blaming herself for lying in Dane's arms when she ought to have been with her disabled charges. To her, the electric atmosphere of a summer storm, the passion and rage of nature expressed in those vivid streaks of blue and orange and gold and purple across the night sky, and the crash and clash of celestial cymbals amid the mountain peaks, had seemed a very exciting accompaniment to the power and glory of a shared passion between two mortals who had found each other again after a long time. But the violence of the storm had obviously been very frightening to others, and she felt guilty that she had ignored their fears.

Fortunately, Becky didn't seem to be badly hurt. 'I was trying to get to the telephone,' she explained as Joanne and the care attendant lifted her back into bed and settled her against the mound of pillows that she needed for her comfort. 'I thought someone ought to be doing something for Marcia.'

Joanne winced at the implied reproach as yet another bright shock of lightning hurtled across the room, to be followed by another terrified shriek. Marcia's bed shook with her fearful trembling, and the Austrian nurse hurried to comfort her, cuddling and patting and soothing with a flow of hushing German, just as if she were a child. And, in fact, Marcia had reverted to infancy in her terror, crouching in the foetal position, hands locked tightly about her head. She would need a sedative as soon as she had attended to Becky, Joanne decided.

'Do you feel sick? Dizzy? Does the light hurt your eyes?' As she treated the nasty bump on Becky's head, she went through the routine questions to check for any sign of concussion, and was relieved by the reassuring replies.

It took some time to coax Marcia to swallow the proffered pill, but eventually she succeeded. She sat with the frightened girl, holding her hand, talking quietly of the things they had done in the last few days and the excursions still to come, doing her best to distract her until she finally fell asleep. Having checked the others, Joanne was thankful that there were no other problems. Owen had coped with one of Richard's fortunately rare fits, triggered by the storm, and reported that he was sleeping soundly.

The storm raged until the early hours, and Joanne dozed in a chair, feeling that she had done her best to redeem an earlier neglect. Before breakfast, she found time to return to her room for a shower, sluicing away the last traces of Dane's male scent from her body, bracing herself for the inevitable awkwardness of first meeting.

Whatever he said or did, she must be as casual about that brief idyll as he obviously meant to be. There was no need for him to know that she had welcomed and warmed to his lovemaking because she still loved him.

The tense atmosphere in the night, prelude to that summer storm, had created a sexual tension between former lovers that nothing short of an earthquake could have prevented from seeking and attaining its release, she told herself sensibly. Driven by a powerful and primitive need, they had gone into each other's arms and delighted each other as man and woman had done since the beginning of time.

There was no need for regret or reproach or any sense of obligation on either side, through love or guilt or the broken bonds of the past. Joanne determined to be very cool, very matter-of-fact, thoroughly modern about the whole thing.

By chance, they emerged from their adjoining rooms at exactly the same moment. Dane paused to lock his door, buoyant and handsome in cream linen slacks and cream short-sleeved summer shirt, more attractive than ever to Joanne's love-bemused eyes and quickened pulses.

He glanced at the slender girl in the peppermint-green cotton skirt and sleeveless blouse, perfect foil for her gleaming hair and lightly sun-tanned skin, and resisted the urge to reach out and enfold her and try to recapture some of the previous night's magic. They had both been caught up in a kind of enchantment, but Joanne couldn't have wanted to be reminded so forcibly of the past, any more than himself. After all, she had never really loved him or she could never have left him to rot after the accident which had turned doctor into patient!

He wasn't sure of her reactions, Joanne decided as he fiddled interminably with the key in the lock. His body had betrayed a resolve to keep her at arm's length, but his heart hadn't been in that tempestuous lovemaking, and now he was afraid they might not be able to return to the comfortable indifference of the past week.

'Hi!' she said brightly, blazing a trail for him to follow. 'It's a lovely morning after the storm.'

'So it is.' Lightly tossing the room key from one hand to the other, Dane strolled towards her, his dark eyes veiling the memory of her in his arms and the insistent feeling that it was where she belonged, in spite of the past and the doubts of the present. 'Everything all right?'

'Everything's fine.' And so it *was*, while she could see and hear him every day and hope that a surprisingly forgiving friendliness would turn to love. But she knew she would miss him terribly when they were back in England, leading their separate lives once more, unlikely to meet again.

'What was it all about last night?'

'Sorry. . .?' Blue eyes widened in shock as he boldly marched in where not even a fallen angel dared to tread.

'The cry for help,' he enlarged, ushering her before him into the waiting lift. 'What was the problem? No one sent for me, so I assume it wasn't serious.'

'Oh!' She should have known that their lovemaking would be a closed book to Dane, and perhaps that was the only way to regard it. A one-off, a clutch at the past that had turned out to mean nothing in the present. 'Becky fell out of bed and banged her head, not badly enough to need professional attention, fortunately. Marcia had hysterics and I gave her a mild sedative. Richard had a fit, but Owen coped with that. Quite an uneventful night, really.' She smiled up at him. 'The storm went on for hours. I suppose you slept through the second half?'

It was surprising that she could speak so lightly, smile so brightly, gloss over those moments of shared passion as if they had never happened. But if he could pretend, then so could she!

Returned to the fold with her arm in plaster, Nadine was proud of the little amount of German she had picked up from the kindly nurses at the Haupmann Clinic, and seemed unexpectedly anxious to air it. Encouraged as she was by the men who clustered about her, her small, sweet voice was heard more than it had been at any time during the holiday.

Richard's chair was parked at her side on the sunlit terrace, and his unwavering gaze rested on Nadine's beautiful face beneath the pert Tyrolean hat, complete with green feathers and bright silver badge, that Cal had bought for her on his way to the clinic that morning, replacement for the irreparable straw.

Joanne noticed that Nadine was finding it easier to accept Richard's admiration, however badly expressed because of his youth and his inability to do much more than speak of it. She was gradually becoming part of the group instead of one on her own, and Joanne gave Dane much of the credit for that because he had taken pains to coax the girl out of her shy world ever since they had left England.

She sat at another of the white-painted tables, writing postcards with the sun warm on her bare shoulders while she kept an eye and an ear on the group. She heard the irrepressible Lenny boast that he knew German and would teach Nadine, but it soon became clear that the words he had in mind were rude ones, and Dane's deep voice was raised in amused reproof from his perch on the balustraded stone wall.

Leaning on the back of Howie's chair, Patrick was one of the lively group, while Becky sat at the other end of the terrace, as far as possible from the good-looking carer, nursing her heartache. Joanne felt sorry for the girl, who pretended to be absorbed in Marcia's chatter while unable to resist the occasional wistful glance in Patrick's direction.

It was a very delicate situation. Joanne had tried to talk to Patrick, sounding out his feelings about Becky in the hope of giving her a little comfort, but he had shied from her tactful approach and she suspected that he was as unhappy about things as Becky herself. Without well-meaning interference from others, they might be able to sort out the problem for themselves, she thought hopefully.

Cal and Anneliese rounded the corner of the main building, hands breaking apart but still linked by the obvious warmth of their affection for each other. During the few days of her absence from Pleydorf, Cal had found a variety of reasons to borrow Frau Meyer's car and drive in to St Johann, making no secret of the fact that he had called at the clinic to see Anneliese, and reporting Nadine's satisfactory progress on his return.

Joanne saw Dane glance at the couple as they approached and wondered how he felt about their growing closeness, and if chagrin about Anneliese's obvious preference for the coach driver had played some part in driving him into the arms of a former love.

Drawing out a chair as Cal crossed to speak to Dane, Anneliese sat down to face Joanne with a militant look in her amber eyes. 'You had an exciting night,' she said, coming directly to the point. Joanne's heart jumped until she realised that her friend referred to the storm and its various effects on the group, rather than the loving hour that Dane had spent with her in her room. 'How is Becky now?'

'No harm done, luckily.' But, even from that distance, the faint smudge of bruising on Becky's forehead was visible, just a hair's breadth from the temple, and she knew it could have been much more serious.

Smiling at Anneliese, she thought how typical it was that she had ferreted out all the events that had taken place in her absence within minutes of her return.

Well, almost all. . .

'What happened?' Primarily responsible for the safety and welfare of the group she had brought on holiday, Anneliese needed to know the details of every accident, however minor.

'Marcia had an attack of nerves, and Becky was anxious about her. Trying to reach the phone to call someone, she tumbled out of bed,' Joanne explained, her tone making light of something that could have been a disaster for the severely disabled girl. 'In normal circumstances, it wouldn't have been much of a fall, but she hit her head on the locker and stunned herself. Marcia wasn't much help, but she did bang on the wall for Owen, who realised something was wrong and rang me. Richard was having a fit, so he couldn't leave him.'

'But why were Becky and Marcia on their own? Where were you, Jo? You must have known that they would be very frightened.'

She winced at the bewildered reproach in her friend's voice. 'I was in bed.'

'You slept through such a storm!' Anneliese was sceptical. 'You are a nurse, Jo. You know how people react to such weather and that the disabled often feel vulnerable and nervous. It was your business to be with them at such a time!'

Joanne was thankful that Anneliese didn't know how much more cause she had for irritation. She seemed to regard Dane as no more than a friend, after all, but although she might not resent it she would strongly disapprove of a sexual liaison between two of her carers on this holiday for the disabled. Thank heavens that her usually too perceptive friend hadn't made the obvious connection between her tardy arrival in the annexe and the fact that Dane hadn't shown up at all during the storm!

'I'm sorry, Annie,' she said contritely. 'I went to the girls as soon as Owen called me.'

'Do you know that Lenny spent most of the night in the stables?' Anneliese was even more reproachful as she pursued another tack. 'He thought the horses might need him! He could have been trampled to death!'

'I didn't know anything about that until it was mentioned at breakfast,' Joanne admitted ruefully, feeling just as guilty as Anneliese intended, although it was Patrick who should have known the boy was missing from his bed and gone in search of him. No doubt his mind had been more on Becky than the boy who was his particular responsibility while they were in Austria. 'It was dangerous, but absolutely typical, don't you think? He loves those horses and spends every possible moment with them.' Her smile was conciliatory. 'Perhaps they did need him, Annie. Lenny has a wonderful way with them, and they were probably much calmer once he got in with them.'

'He could have been killed. I don't think you realise our responsibility for these young people—and Cal says that you hurt your ankle in Salzburg,' Anneliese added for good measure.

'Oh, that was just a wrench. I can walk on it perfectly well now,' Joanne assured her hastily.

It wasn't strictly true, for her foot still twinged with each step and a dark bruise was just beginning to show. But the ache in her ankle was nothing to the ache in a heart that still hungered for the content she might have known with Dane if she hadn't lost her temper and then foolishly fled from the consequences.

It must have seemed to him, injured and angry, that she hadn't cared about him at all, and heaven knew how Melvin, with an axe of his own to grind, had represented their continued friendship after she'd left Brook's. But he had merely been useful, keeping her informed of Dane's recovery and slow convalescence in those first months, and she had never thought of him or any other man as a replacement for Dane.

If only there were some way to convince him that her love for him had been real and lasting and still survived. But he had made it painfully clear that he didn't want to know. . .

Anneliese sighed. 'Cal says I must not do another holiday like this one. It is too much worry.'

Joanne glanced at the curly headed coach driver who was so kind, so helpful in a number of ways, so concerned and caring towards her friend. 'It's been a wonderful holiday for everyone, in spite of one or two mishaps,' she soothed.

'You have enjoyed it?' Anneliese looked doubtful.

'Very much. It won't be easy to settle down to ward routine after these two weeks, though. It's been a lot of fun and I've loved it. A holiday to remember,' she said firmly.

If only because of Dane. . .

'Something is wrong with Becky,' her friend announced. 'All the light has gone from her face.'

It was apt, for Becky's pretty face usually shone as if a bright candle burned at the back of it, her eyes always on the merry dance and unquenchable spirit in her smile. Looking at the slump of her shoulders and the bow of her head, and the hands that lay so helplessly in her lap instead of flying hither and thither as she talked, it was just as if someone had blown out that candle.

'She's tired, I expect. The storm. . .and the fall—she didn't get much sleep last night.'

'No, no! She is not happy. Is it Patrick? Have they quarrelled? I have been so afraid for her.'

Reminded that little escaped Anneliese's observant eye, Joanne warned herself to be even more careful whenever she spoke to Dane or looked in his direction. 'I don't think they've quarrelled, exactly,' she said carefully, unwilling to break a confidence, although it appeared that Anneliese knew exactly how things stood.

'Patrick is a nice man, but weak,' she declared, not at all bothered that her ringing tones carried to the carer's ears. 'He has a girl at home, you know. He had no right to make love to Becky and encourage her to care for him.' In her book, black was black and white was white, and she did not approve of compromise.

'I rather think he couldn't help himself, Annie.'

Joanne knew all about the inexorability of loving. 'Somehow I think it will come right for them in the end. I think Patrick is torn, trying to do the right thing by one girl and anxious not to lose the other, doing his best not to hurt either of them,' she said sagely. 'I'm sure he's really very fond of Becky.'

Having seen them together for much of the holiday, Joanne felt that they were two halves of a whole, born for each other, whatever the world might feel about the problems inherent in a close relationship between an able-bodied man and a severely disabled woman.

'I will ask Cal to talk to him. He will know what to say, and Patrick will listen and be helped to choose,' Anneliese said confidently. 'All will be well.'

'I hope you're right.'

Amber eyes twinkled as the German girl pushed back her chair. 'When am I ever wrong, Jo?'

Joanne laughed. 'Not even destiny would dare to argue with you,' she agreed, smiling.

'I feel what is right for people and try to make it happen for them, that is all,' Anneliese demurred modestly.

But did she know what was right for *herself*, any more than anyone else? Joanne wondered as her friend joined the group about Nadine, and Cal turned to smile and engage her glance for a meaningful moment.

A woman followed where her heart led, but loving wasn't always the path to happiness.

CHAPTER NINE

As he lowered his tall frame into the vacated chair, Lionel's blue eyes held a warm smile. 'All alone, Jo?'

'I've been writing the last of my postcards.' As she shuffled them together, Joanne smiled back, feeling that she would have to be totally insensitive not to know that he cared for her, and finding his unquestioning affection something of a balm for her disappointment over Dane.

His liking and admiration had been evident from the first meeting, but she had done her best to discourage feelings she couldn't reciprocate. However, they had become friends in recent months and she had gone out with him occasionally, for dinner, for a drive to the coast, for a walk beside the river. Now, she realised that his attitude had changed. She was no longer someone to admire from a distance but someone he could touch, hold, even kiss if she gave him the opportunity.

Perhaps she needed someone like Lionel in her life, too. He was kind and generous and undemanding, a very understanding man. Somehow she felt that he knew she had only one heart to give and no longer owned it. Sometimes she was sure that he knew her heart belonged to Dane. He was possibly the only man she would ever meet who would be happy to marry her on those terms.

Joanne backed from the startling thought, for he deserved better than a wife who could never love him. In any case, it would never occur to the modest, self-effacing man to suggest marriage to her, she knew.

So the suggestion would have to come from her. . .

'I'm going to walk into the village and post these

before lunch,' she said, knowing she ought to offer to take Becky and that Marcia would be sure to tag along and there were others who would enjoy a walk, but feeling that she needed some time away from the group. Thoughts and feelings were in a little turmoil that morning.

'Do you want company?' Lionel asked, happy to go with her if she wished and just as happy to accept a refusal. Whatever Joanne wanted would always be right in his eyes, he felt with the tenderness of a love that he would never attempt to offer.

'That would be nice.' He was undemanding company, and she could talk or not as she chose, Joanne knew.

'Perhaps we should meet at the gate. . .?' If they were seen to leave together, there would be a barrage of eager questions and demands to accompany them, and she had earned a brief respite. She had taken very little time for herself on this holiday, he knew.

Lionel sensed that she had something on her mind, although she seemed her usual bright self, and he hoped she would confide in him during the walk to the village. They were good friends and he had a strong shoulder for her to lean or cry on, if necessary, but if she preferred to keep her problems to herself then he wouldn't probe.

Joanne touched his hand in a gesture of gratitude before she picked up the small stack of postcards and her bag and strolled away. Perhaps it was Lionel's deafness, cutting him off from the distractions of the world that could numb sensitivity in others, but he seemed to have an instinctive ear for what people *didn't* say. He was the most understanding man she had ever known—and perhaps the idea that had popped in and out of her head wasn't so insane, after all.

Did she really want to spend the rest of her life as a ward sister at Monty's? Never knowing the love of a husband and the comfort of a shared home and the blessings that children could bring? At times, the future stretched before her like an empty road leading to a lonely old age, but, with someone like Lionel at her side, she need never be lonely or afraid.

If she did marry him then she would do all in her power to make him happy. For seven years she had smothered the thought of Dane and the longing for him. Surely she could spend the rest of her life refusing to think about him and learning to love someone else?

As she crossed the strip of lawn beyond the terrace, postcards in hand and obviously on her way to post them in the village, Dane was tempted to follow and endeavour to make his peace with the girl who lay so heavily on his heart and his conscience. Earlier that morning, a mix of feelings had kept him silent, but he deeply regretted the words that had sent her rushing from the room in the middle of the night.

He had allowed her to think that he had merely used her, when it had been a compulsion of the heart that had swept aside every other consideration and led him to take her into his arms.

Joanne's smiling attitude implied that she had no regrets, but he remembered a vulnerable, sensitive girl, who had been so anxious that he shouldn't think less of her because she had finally yielded to his ardent, experienced persuasions.

Dane didn't believe that even seven years could have turned that shy, sweet virgin into the kind of woman who indulged in casual sex with past or present lovers. She must have felt *something* for him last night. It couldn't have been merely guilt that had made her welcome him into her arms.

Seeing Lionel strike out across the grass in her wake with a nonchalance that betrayed intent to the doctor's narrowed gaze, Dane wondered if he was heading for an arranged rendezvous with Joanne or simply dogging her footsteps, as usual. He decided that he needed to know.

More worldly-wise than Lionel, he went by a roundabout route, to arrive within view of the gates in time to see them greet each other, Joanne tucking her hand into the other man's arm in warm welcome and looking up at him with a smile and a loving word.

Swept by a storm of jealous rage, Dane could hardly stop himself from rushing at Lionel and knocking him to the ground, as he followed the couple to the village and back again.

Last night, Joanne had lain in his arms and given him more joy, more sweet content, than he had known in seven years. Last night, he had known himself dangerously near to loving and drawn back from the brink. Now he knew without a shadow of doubt that the passion of wanting she had inspired in him was akin to the torment of love and longing that had never really left him when she had, all those years before.

He loved her still. He loved her more than ever now that she had matured into the beautiful, temperate woman he had believed she would become in time when he had given his heart to the eighteen-year-old Joanne. She was his love, his fate, his woman for all time.

But her readiness to play one man off against the other—and a disabled man at that!—was proof that she still couldn't be trusted, he felt. Loving her, needing her more than ever, Dane was angry and bitterly disappointed as he realised that he couldn't risk putting his happiness, his life, his future into those unreliable hands a second time.

It would have been better if he and Joanne had never met again. For, even patched up with love, a fallen angel would still be flawed. . .

Turning from sending Lionel to the stables in search of Lenny, who would miss a meal rather than miss a moment with his beloved horses, Joanne was waylaid by Dane, on his way to the annexe, like herself.

'Enjoy your walk?'

'It's very hot.' She didn't wonder why he looked at her so coldly. She knew. The brusque tone and the steely glint in those dark eyes warned her to forget what had happened in the night. They had both lost their heads and briefly forgotten that their lives were no longer linked by love, and now he was reminding her that a sexual encounter made no difference to the way he felt about her these days. Someone to bed but never to wed, she thought in wry acceptance, knowing she had forfeited all right to his love.

Her hair snaked in tiny damp tendrils on her brow and about her pretty face, betraying the curl that she had cut and brushed almost out of existence, as if the severe cap of burnished auburn silk matched the careful image of the well-trained nurse that she had become in the intervening years. 'It's cold and damp in England, and we'll soon be on our way back,' Dane reminded her smoothly.

'Yes.' Face and neck and gentle swell of breasts above the scoop neckline of her thin blouse glowed with perspiration from the brisk walk back from the village. Bare feet in bright red sandals were dusty from the country roads, and low heels forced her to tilt back her head to look up into his handsome, remote face. 'It's been fun, but I can't say that I'll be sorry to go home,' she admitted frankly. 'This holiday has been rather more than I bargained for, what with one thing and another. . .'

'And me.'

'And you,' she agreed with a wry half-smile.

'I could have done without the complication of you on this trip too.'

Joanne winced at the deliberate harshness of the words, the hard look in his eyes. Her quick temper flared at such injustice, for *she* hadn't been responsible for what had happened between them during a summer storm. *She* had been doing everything she could to keep her distance and not remind him of the past!

'Oh? What about last night?' she demanded hotly, although she had sworn to herself that wild horses wouldn't drag the slightest mention of that lovemaking from her if he was so determined to dismiss it as unimportant.

Dane shrugged. 'It was always the same, wasn't it? We could never meet without wanting to fall into bed, but it was only sex, after all. A kind of chemistry.' Could it have been anything more on her part when she had fled at the first hint of a greater demand on her emotions—and when she had melted into his arms at the first approach, seven years later? He couldn't condemn her for a weakness that had attacked his own stern resolve. But he wanted more than that from Joanne, and it seemed that she was still incapable of giving it.

Joanne was infuriated by that bald dismissal of the love they had once shared. He dragged all her precious memories of past togetherness into the dust with that careless contempt for the loving and giving, the sharing and caring and the heartfelt desire for his happiness above all else.

His claim that it had been no more than sexual attraction that had brought them and kept them together for those few weeks devalued the love that had kept his image in her heart and mind long after she should have forgotten him. Damn him! What did he know of love, its highs and lows, its reliefs and anxieties, its pleasures and its pains? Like most men, he thought it all boiled down to sex, she thought angrily. Let him think what he would! A rankling bitterness prevented him from thinking any good of her these days, anyway!

'I expect you're right. I was very young and silly in those days, and I just couldn't resist the fatal attraction that you had for all the girls. But we were obviously never meant to be together for ever. Not then or now, so perhaps we should stay out of each other's lives in future.' She spoke as if it wouldn't tear her to pieces never to have him kiss her or touch her or hold her again. Pride could be a real comfort in the face of a final death-knell for their on-off-on-again relationship. '*Lenny*! Don't you dare to go in to lunch in that state!' She spun away from Dane on the words to intercept the youngster, who had come from the stables with face and hair and clothes streaked with mud. 'What on earth have you been doing?'

She hustled Lenny into his room in the annexe to wash and change and, out of the corner of an eye, saw Dane pass the door a few minutes later with Clair. He bent his dark head to speak to the girl in the wheelchair, his handsome features softened by the tenderness he felt for the less fortunate, and perhaps something of Joanne's wistful longing showed in her face.

For as she whipped the shirt over Lenny's head, he said quietly, 'You like Dane, don't you, Jo? Really like him, I mean. Marcia says you fancy Lionel, but I reckon you like Dane better.'

'Everyone likes Dane,' she said firmly, whisking a clean shirt from a drawer and shaking it out while Lenny dragged a soaped flannel across his bespattered face. 'Annie and I have known him for a very long time. He's a very good doctor.' It was as impersonal as she could make it, and she felt it safer to bracket herself and her friend as old acquaintances of the man who could still wreak havoc with his charm.

'Will he come to club nights when we get back, do you think?'

'Probably not. He lives a long way from us and I expect he's very busy. Has he said that he might?' Joanne steeled herself not to look for such a visit on an evening when she might be at the PHAB Club, for nothing was likely to change between her and Dane and she wanted to settle down again to a life that didn't include him at all.

'So Marcia says. But she could have been making it up. She talks a lot of rubbish about Dane,' Lenny said scathingly.

'Does she?' Joanne smiled, but she was vaguely disturbed by the information as she gently eased his crippled arm into the sleeve of his shirt.

'Nobody believes her, though.'

'How are the horses now? Calmed down?' she asked, to distract him from the subject of Marcia's passionate interest in Dane.

Shortly, she left him to make his own way to the dining-hall and hurried along the corridor to see if Becky was still in her room and needed help. She found her alone, listlessly drawing a brush through soft, fair curls and looking a very different girl from the bright-eyed, sunny-natured Becky of previous days.

'Where's Marcia? Didn't she wait for you today?' she asked brightly, but suspicion stirred at the girl's absence.

'No. She wanted to go with Dane. She saw him pushing Clair and ran after them.'

Joanne frowned. 'That was a little naughty of her, leaving you to fend for yourself.'

Becky shrugged. 'I told her not to wait. I don't think I want any lunch, Jo.'

'This heat tends to spoil one's appetite, I must admit,' Joanne agreed lightly, as if she wasn't well aware that the weather had nothing to do with Becky's lack of interest in food or anything else. 'But most of us can manage a salad and some fruit. Do your best, Becky.'

As she wheeled Becky's chair along the tree-lined path to the dining-hall, Joanne was a little troubled by the confirmation of Marcia's growing attachment to Dane. Girls of that age could make something out of nothing, assisted by wishful thinking, and his kindness could so easily be misconstrued.

Doctors were always at risk from accusations of sexual overtures by emotionally disturbed women, but it would be too bad if an unsuspecting Dane was being slandered by an over-imaginative girl simply because he wasn't firm enough with her clinging demands for attention.

Joanne felt that she ought to warn him to be more circumspect in his dealings with the immature, romantically minded Marcia. Even if, with her track record, she was accused of a dangerous jealousy.

'I know how to handle Marcia,' he said impatiently. 'She's just a child.'

'She's eighteen.' The same age that she had been when she'd first met and fallen in love with Dane. 'A child in some ways, but she has all a woman's feelings, and I'm afraid that you're stirring them up,' she told him bluntly, having waylaid him as he walked to the pool where everyone else had gathered on that blazing afternoon.

'My fatal attraction,' he suggested drily, echoing her earlier words. 'I don't think it works on every woman, Joanne.'

She felt the warmth creep into her face. 'It's all very well being modest, Dane. But I'm concerned about Marcia—and the effect on your reputation if she says some misleading things about the fuss you make of her,' she said crisply.

'Do I make a fuss of her? I thought I was just doing my job as a helper,' he protested.

'Overdoing it,' Joanne stressed warmly. 'You let her take advantage of you.'

'I'm too good-natured,' he agreed. 'It's always been my downfall. Look what happened when I let *you* run away with my heart.' It was light reminder and firm assurance that he had no intention of allowing it to happen again.

She smiled, just as he expected. But she heard and understood the warning. He had given her his heart in good faith but had taken it back when she'd let him down, and she had no hope of winning it again. At least she knew where she stood. At least she knew better than to waste the rest of her life in wanting when there was someone like Lionel only too ready to love and look after her, she thought on a swift surge of defiant pride.

Hurrying on, she waved to the tall man in the pool and dived directly into the cool blue water, to surface close beside him. Lionel held out his hand and she grasped it firmly, allowing him to draw her up and out of the water and against his broad chest. Smiling, she put both arms about his neck, and for a moment they clung together and she could feel the heavy thud of his heart against her breast. She ignored the prick of her conscience. Just now, she needed Lionel. His affection, his unspoken need of her were balm to a wounded pride and a welcome camouflage for the painful hunger for another man.

'Are you two lovers?'

With one foot glued to the tiled bottom, still unable to swim for all Dane's patient teaching, Marcia dog-paddled towards them, her curious, eager voice resounding across the pool and the surrounding lawns to reach the ears of Cal and Anneliese—and Dane, where he had flopped down beside the couple. For once, Joanne was thankful that Lionel was deaf. She was embarrassed enough for them both.

She pulled away, hot-faced. 'Don't be so silly, Marcia,' she snapped, although she knew the girl hadn't meant any harm with the unthinking words.

'They're just good friends. Aren't you, Jo?' Lenny defended promptly, making matters worse, a broad grin wreathing his cheeky face.

'And we all know what that means, don't we?' Paul jeered mischievously.

Feeling the bore of Dane's dark eyes on her, Joanne struck out for the side of the pool, and Lionel swam after her, anxious to make amends, for he sensed her annoyance and was sure that he had offended her with that instinctive embrace.

He reached her as she tried to haul herself from the water and fell back as her foot slipped on the wet rail. He caught her, smiling. She didn't smile back. 'What's wrong, Jo?' he asked, believing she had sensed the strength of his love and desire. 'Are you annoyed with me?'

'No, of course not. It isn't you!' Joanne knew she had over-reacted and had possibly wounded the last man in the world she wished to hurt. 'I'm just a bit sensitive to teasing, that's all.'

'Teasing?' Belatedly, he realised the laughing faces and read some of the encouraging words on the lips of the interested youngsters. 'I guess I missed something,' he said drily.

'Oh, you know what they're like.' Joanne mustered a smile. 'They see romance round every corner. They know we went to the village on our own before lunch and now—in the pool. . . Oh, they're just being silly!'

'Do you mind so much?' he asked quietly. 'I expect you know that I wish it were true.' With a thrust of powerful arms and shoulders, he levered himself out of the water and lowered a hand to Joanne. He swung her up and on to the paved surround with effortless ease, and she padded wetly at his side towards the array of colourful towels stretched out on the grass, only a few yards from where Dane sat with the others.

She didn't look in his direction. Lowering herself to the ground, she stretched at Lionel's side, arms folded across her breasts in unconscious protection, eyes closed.

Lionel supported himself on an elbow, studying her lovely face, waiting for her to speak and wondering if he had blown it completely with those unguarded words. He loved her, but he had never meant to let her know it and never dared to hope that she found him attractive. Women did, briefly, but soon lost interest when they had to struggle with his deafness, the difficult speech. Joanne was different. With her, he forgot that he couldn't hear and that every word was an effort. But liking and understanding and empathy wasn't love, and he never expected it could be. If the girl at his side stayed his friend then that was all he asked.

Joanne's heart thudded at the thought of the man at her side and the enormity of what she was about to do. Perhaps it wasn't the time or the place to commit herself, but there might never be a better moment. She had been cross with Marcia and Lenny and Paul, but perhaps they had done her a favour, for Lionel had been driven into an admission that he might otherwise never have made.

His words opened a door to a different future from the one she had once hoped to share with Dane—and had dared to dream about again on this holiday, until he had made it clear that a brief and meaningless idyll was all she could expect from him now. Perhaps it would be better for her to marry Lionel than to spend the rest of her life hankering for a lost love.

Lionel would surround her with a tender, all-embracing love that forgave and forgot anything she said or did to cause him pain, for he was that kind of man, gentle and generous and good-hearted. Unlike the unforgiving Dr Dane Gregory, who had never loved her enough in the first place and certainly didn't love her any more, Joanne thought proudly.

Without opening her eyes, she said softly, 'Marcia wanted to know if we were lovers. I said no. But perhaps we ought to be. For I suppose we do love each other and just haven't got around to saying it.'

His hand moved involuntarily towards her face as if he would like to lift the words from her lips and secrete them forever in his heart. In fact, he wasn't at all sure that he had read them aright, and he had never cursed the fact of his deafness so soundly as in that moment.

'Are you saying that you love me, Jo?' he asked, almost afraid to put the question in case he was making a terrible and very embarrassing mistake, but desperately needing to know.

Joanne rolled over to face him and put her arms about his powerful, still-damp body, smiling into the diffident blue eyes of a man who had always undervalued his sterling qualities where she was concerned. She gave him a kiss for answer and hoped the warmth of her lips would be more convincing than the words she found impossible to speak, for all her new-found resolve.

There were many kinds of loving, she told herself, stifling the qualm of conscience, and she did love him—in a way. It might not be the way he hoped and deserved, but she vowed to make it enough in the future. For what more could she ask than for someone like this 'parfait gentil knight', her dear Lionheart, to love and look after her for the rest of her life?

The scream that pierced the air, shattering the golden serenity of the scene, brought her swiftly to her feet, startled and afraid.

CHAPTER TEN

BECKY'S wheelchair hurtled down the slight incline where it had been parked in the shade of the trees. Joanne's first thought was that the brake had slipped off, and then she saw that Becky's hands were on the wheels, rotating them at furious, determined speed as she propelled her chair towards the water with grim intent all over her pretty face.

It was Marcia who had screamed at her friend, alerting everyone to the impending disaster. Joanne froze, as did everyone else in that split second before Becky and chair shot off the surround to crash into the pool on a surge and a cascading flurry, to sink instantly out of sight.

Marcia continued to scream. Dane and Cal dived from a running dash across the grass, both fully clothed, while Patrick abandoned Howie, with a curt command to Paul and Ian to look out for him, and struck out desperately for the deep end.

Lionel couldn't hear Marcia's screams or the anxious shouts and cries of others or Anneliese's urgent instructions, but he sped to join those who were already struggling to extricate Becky.

There seemed to be absolute chaos for some minutes, while a frightened group huddled together anxiously in the shallow end and Joanne joined them to try to quieten the shocked, hysterical Marcia. Anneliese knelt on the surround, urging on the men who struggled to release Becky's strapped body from her chair on the tiled bottom of the pool. A frantic Patrick came up briefly for air, then plunged again to struggle with the several knots that Becky had tied in her strap before making her suicide bid.

It had been a cry for help and attention rather than a serious attempt to kill herself, Joanne was sure, or Becky wouldn't have chosen a time when people were in and around the pool and on hand to rescue her. But that didn't make things any better.

Poor Becky, so desperately unhappy that she could do such a thing! Joanne felt consumed with guilt, for she had been too concerned with her own mixed-up feelings to remember Becky and her heartache or to realise the awful intent in her mind.

On the perfectly valid grounds that he was needed to watch over Howie and Lenny and the rest, Patrick had been virtually ignoring the girl who had sat in her wheelchair, watching the fun and the frolics. Her friends enjoyed themselves, forgetful of her and apparently indifferent to her low spirits, and suddenly it must have seemed all too much to bear for a girl who had always been denied a normal life and was unhappily convinced that her disability had cost her the one chance of happiness with a man she had loved at first sight.

It seemed an eternity of waiting and hoping and silent urging on of the rescuers beneath the blue water before Becky was finally brought to the surface, lying limp and grey-faced in Dane's strong arms. The powerful muscles of back and shoulders strained as he lifted the heavy, impaired body to the surround.

Anneliese promptly began artificial respiration, while the men struggled to regain their breath and their bearings, lying face down with heaving chests. Dizzy from lack of air and despairing anxiety, Patrick clung wearily to the rail, having neither the energy nor the will to clamber out of the water, afraid to face the shock announcement that all their efforts had been in vain.

Owen came running across from the main building with an armful of blankets and the news that Frau Meyer had been alerted and asked to summon an ambulance.

'She's dead. . .oh, she's dead! I know she's dead!' Marcia wailed over and over again as Joanne held her, soothing and patting and reassuring even though a familiar dread clutched at her own heart as Dane thrust Anneliese aside to take over the seemingly futile attempt to resuscitate Becky.

'*Is* she dead, Jo?' Lenny asked anxiously, wading closer. 'It took them an awfully long time to get her up, didn't it?'

'What about her chair? She'll need her chair,' Howie exclaimed, with thoughts of his own invaluable 'wheels'—and then everyone looked at everyone else in horror as it struck them all anew that Becky might never need her chair again.

'Oh, they'll get that up between them,' Joanne said briskly, refusing to allow such morbidity. 'Now, come along—it's time we were all out of the water. Lenny, you're turning blue with cold! Hot drinks all round as soon as everyone's dried and dressed, I think! Paul, will you stay with Howie until Patrick can come to help you?'

Sensibly, she rounded up the youngsters and chivvied them from the pool, knowing there was nothing she could do for Becky at the moment and it was better to make herself useful in another direction.

It was a struggle to persuade Marcia to get out and wrap her shivering body in a towel, but she managed it just as the sound of an ambulance siren carried through the complex, the vehicle on its way through the village.

Pushing Clair's chair with a still-wailing and weeping Marcia clinging to her arm and a subdued Lenny in tow, Joanne glanced back to see that Cal and Lionel and

Patrick had begun the business of retrieving Becky's wheelchair from the pool. Frau Meyer and a nurse were hurrying towards Dane as he carried Becky, her bulky body wrapped in the blankets that Owen had thoughtfully rushed to provide. Anneliese ran at Dane's side, calling urgent explanations in her native language as they crossed the lawn to the complex gates to await the arrival of the ambulance.

It wasn't possible for Joanne to see Becky's face, turned towards Dane's broad chest and shielded by a fold of blanket, but there was an urgency in his stride and a hint of relief in Anneliese's tone that conveyed that there was still hope for the apparently lifeless girl.

The ambulance siren trailed off mournfully as the vehicle came to a halt. Joanne saw Dane break into a run, heading for the attendants, who jumped down from the back, and her nursing experience told her that Becky was in urgent need of oxygen or a fresh resuscitation attempt.

She was longing to abandon her charges and hurry over to see for herself what was happening, but she couldn't leave people who were shocked and horrified and as full of dread as herself. There were plenty of others to attend to Becky and her first concern must be for the distraught Marcia, and then she must set about dispelling the belief that Becky had meant to kill herself.

An accident, it must be stressed with all the authority she had acquired during her years of nursing—and see to it that that was believed. It would be dreadful if the young disabled were to return to homes and families with an account of a suicide attempt by one of their number among their memories of an Austrian holiday!

She must do what she could to comfort and reassure Patrick, too. Denied the right to accompany Becky in the ambulance, not knowing what was happening but realising that his neglect and seeming indifference must have played a big part in influencing her actions, he was probably suffering terribly from a mixture of guilt and anxiety.

Returning some minutes later for Suzy and Nadine, Joanne saw the back of the departing ambulance through a gap in the trees that shielded the holiday complex from the road, and sent up another silent prayer that Becky would come back to them, safe and well.

Another patient for the Haupmann Clinic and Dr Christian Schwodler, she thought ruefully—and yet another blow to everyone's high hopes for the holiday. . .

Anneliese telephoned with the news that Becky was alive but still unconscious, but they knew nothing more until Dane came back later that evening. Joanne flew to meet him, heart pounding, followed by an equally anxious Lionel, who had given her moral support throughout the waiting hours.

Cal's beaming smile sent a shock-wave of relief rippling through her from head to toe. 'It's good news, Jo,' he called reassuringly from the driving seat of Frau Meyer's small car, borrowed to collect Dane from St Johann. 'The lass will be all right.'

Dane unfurled his tall frame from the passenger seat. 'It's going to be touch and go for a few days yet,' he temporised. 'But the general opinion seems to be that she'll do.' He used the traditional term for patients who were expected to make a full recovery from illness or injury.

'Thank goodness,' Joanne breathed.

Lionel put a warm hand on Dane's shoulder. 'Well done,' he applauded. 'You saved Becky's life.'

Dane shrugged off the warm commendation along

with the man's big hand. 'It was a joint effort. Everyone did what they could.' Tired and drained from the events of the day, he was in no mood to tolerate even the well-meaning geniality of the man that Joanne had been kissing at the very moment that one of her charges was heading for near death.

Somehow, even in the most anxious moments as he had worked to save Becky, he hadn't been able to shake the image of that tender moment from his mind.

'Frau Meyer says that a meal will be ready for you whenever you want it.' Joanne saw strain in his dark eyes, the drag of his lame leg as he turned towards the building. He must be exhausted, she felt, longing to put her arms about him and draw him down to rest on her breast.

'Tell her thanks, but I've eaten.' Dane glanced back to see that Lionel had put an arm about Joanne's shoulders as she lingered to talk to Cal before he garaged the car. It was a very proprietorial gesture, he felt. The man must be very sure of her affection and his place in Joanne's life to make such a public statement, he decided on a surge of jealous fury.

Half an hour later, fresh from the shower, he opened his door to Joanne's knock, hastily drawing his robe about his lean, muscular frame, rubbing at wet hair with a towel.

'I've brought you some coffee. . .' Without waiting for an invitation, she walked past him into the room and set the tray on a table.

He noticed that she had set two cups on the tray. 'Why don't you join me?' he suggested drily.

A smile warmed her wide blue eyes. 'I think I will.'

They took their coffee out to the veranda, where the setting sun touched the valley with gold fingers and created a halo for her beautiful head as she leaned against the rail, smiling at him. Dane fought the desire to kiss her. She was lovely and feminine and appealing in the navy and white striped cotton trousers and navy cotton shirt, the casual clothes enhancing the formal prettiness of face and hair and figure.

The anger that burned just beneath an outwardly cool surface stifled the impulse. For Dane felt that if she had been less concerned with snaring the poor besotted devil whose deafness probably made him grateful for a beautiful girl's interest and affection, she might have been more aware of Becky's disturbed frame of mind and acted to avert a near tragic incident. As it was, it seemed that she still couldn't be trusted not to put self before everything else, and he had come close to losing his head—and almost his heart again—because of a girl who just wasn't worth the cataclysmic upheaval of his emotions at every encounter.

Joanne hadn't changed. Her feelings, her own selfish interests and desires, were still all-important to her. Dane was deeply disappointed by that seemingly irreparable flaw in her character.

'You haven't said much about Becky,' she prompted gently. 'Is she very ill?'

'She's a very sick girl. Her heart stopped twice and it took some time to resuscitate her the second time, in the ambulance on the way to St Johann. I really thought we'd lost her,' he admitted with a wry shake of his dark head. 'And there was a considerable amount of water in her lungs when we finally got her out of the pool.'

'So there's a serious risk of chest infection?'

'Yes. She'll need to be carefully watched for a few days.' He turned to look at her intently. 'Why the devil did she do it?'

'She's very much in love with Patrick.' It was a careful reply. 'She's terribly upset because he's cooled off. You must have noticed! I think it was an impulse, instantly regretted.'

'Well, perhaps she'll come round with a better sense of perspective. I sympathise with her feelings, but one brush with death certainly taught *me* that life's too sweet to throw away. Even for love,' Dane added with an ironic twist to his sensual mouth. 'Travelling home with the rest of us at the end of the week is obviously out of the question. I've been in touch with the Red Cross people in Salzburg and they've been very helpful. They'll provide an air ambulance to fly Becky and Anneliese home and alert the Montgomery General to admit her on arrival in England.'

'Oh, that's splendid,' Joanne enthused. 'You must be very relieved to have that settled.'

He nodded. 'It means a lot of extra work for all of us, travelling back without Anneliese, but it can't be helped.'

'Oh, we'll manage, Dane. Lionel will help in lots of ways,' she assured him confidently.

Dane's mouth hardened at the mention of the man who seldom seemed to be far from her mind. 'I'm sure he will.'

Unaware of the contained anger behind the smooth words, Joanne leaned on the veranda rail and looked across the pretty village to the splendid mountains. 'The thought of going home makes me realise how much I'll miss this lovely place, in spite of all the problems,' she said wistfully, knowing she could never forget the tranquil beauty of Pleydorf or the mixed blessing of Dane's unexpected presence on the holiday. 'It's so lovely, isn't it? I'd like to come back one day.'

'On a honeymoon, perhaps.'

She threw him a startled glance, her heart on the leap, but there was nothing more than mockery in the dark eyes that regarded her so steadily. 'I'm not planning to get married, Dane,' she said lightly.

'Friend Lionel appears to have other plans,' he said, with a smile that concealed the thunder in his heart at the mere thought of her as another man's wife.

Abruptly reminded of thoughts and feelings that had been banished by Becky's plunge into the pool, Joanne felt her heart sink slightly at the implication that he wouldn't care if she *did* propose to marry Lionel, wouldn't say one word or make one move to prevent her from becoming lost to him forever.

A light laugh camouflaged her dismay. 'I'm a career woman—I told you,' she reminded him brightly. 'I'm not thinking of marrying anyone at the moment.'

Except *you*, dearest of all men—dearer than ever since the long, filled days in his constant company had deepened her love for him. But that was and always would be an impossible dream for a fallen angel.

'I've a feeling that he'll wear you down. These patient, faithful types always seem to get the girl in the end,' Dane drawled with convincing indifference. 'Don't tell me you haven't considered him as a possible husband, Joanne, because I won't believe you.'

Her face flamed. But her voice was admirably cool as she returned, 'Women consider all their options, don't they? And Lionel doesn't make any secret of his feelings. I expect you're not the only one to think that we're on the verge of an engagement.'

She began to stack the empty coffee-cups on the tray, her hands shaking along with her dismayed heart. How little he cared! How foolish of her to have tumbled into love with him all over again, the last man in the world to care for her, to trust her, to want her in his life!

'He wouldn't be very happy about it if he knew that you'd been to bed with me this week, would he?'

Joanne turned swiftly to look into the taut, handsome face and gently mocking eyes. 'There's no reason for him to know, surely?' she challenged.

'Oh, I've no intention of telling him,' he assured her with a slight smile. 'He's bigger than I am!' Dark eyes met suddenly militant blue ones without any trace of the blaze of love and longing he felt in their inscrutable depths. 'Besides, I've no wish to spoil things for either of you, Joanne. He's a great guy and I'm sure he'll make a great husband.'

'Giving us your blessing, Dane?' It was tart.

He smiled down at her. 'Why not? I've no hard feelings any more, and I'd like you to be happy.'

Then take me in your arms and tell me that you love me, can't live without me, for that's all I'll ever need for my happiness! Stifling the anguished cry of her heart, Joanne scooped up the tray and turned towards the open door of her own room, further along the veranda. 'I'm happy as I am,' she said firmly. 'And it's time for the medicine round.'

She escaped before anger broke its bounds. That hot, swiftly sparked temper was in every line of her taut, trembling body, in the mulish set of her pretty face and in the leaping flame of her blue eyes. How dared he? How could he? The man she loved more than anything in the world to hand her over so generously to another man without the blink of an eyelid, the slightest hesitation, the smallest hint that the gesture cost him more than he cared to admit.

In that moment, Joanne never wanted to see or speak to Dane Gregory again. But she would die rather than let him know how much he had hurt her with that cool, indifferently careless magnanimity. 'No hard feelings any more', he had said in that generous fashion. So she was forgiven. But the ardently desired gift of his forgiveness had turned to ashes in her mouth by the very nature of its giving!

Temper died down, but the hurt remained. However, she was kept much too busy to brood over Dane's unthinking and uncaring attitude. She worked hard to make the remainder of the holiday as pleasant and as relaxed as possible for the shattered group, organising paper games and table tennis tournaments and wheelchair slaloms, shopping expeditions and short drives through the Tyrol, and no one minded that the weather had turned cool and cloudy, keeping them away from the pool with its painful reminders.

With Frau Meyer's help, she arranged an outing to a local Folk Festival, but the music and dancing and cheerful, noisy atmosphere did little to lighten the shadow of everyone's anxiety about Becky. Those minutes under water, trapped in her chair, had taken their toll on her delicate lungs and she had developed an acute respiratory infection that gave some cause for concern. By the end of the week, she was a little better, and the fear that she would have to remain in the Haupmann Clinic after the party had left Pleydorf was lifted.

On the day that Dane went to Salzburg to finalise arrangements with the International Red Cross for Becky's transport back to England by air ambulance, Joanne drove into St Johann with Cal to see Becky and also to relieve Anneliese for a few hours, feeling that her friend must be heartily sick of the place where she had spent the better part of the holiday.

Cal swept Anneliese off to lunch, determined to make the most of their short time together. Watching them go, Joanne envied the steadily growing bond between her fellow sister and the kindly Yorkshireman, obviously unaffected by the blatant admiration and interest of the

Austrian doctor which had alleviated Anneliese's extended stay at the clinic.

Suddenly, Dane seemed not merely aloof but anxious to thrust her into Lionel's arms at every opportunity, and the message was unmistakable, Joanne thought wryly. Regretting a momentary weakness, he had no intention of yielding to it again and he was keeping her and temptation at a safe distance.

Becky was still in a private room in the Intensive Care Unit. Used to sick people and their anxieties, Joanne was still alarmed by the girl's feverishly high colour, the difficult breathing that necessitated the constant presence of an oxygen cylinder beside the bed, and the listless indifference to her survival. She knew that such apathy was due as much to heartache as her seriously ill condition, and wondered what had happened to the supreme spirit that had always enabled Becky to meet obstacles with a cheerful determination to overcome them.

Love had an awful lot to answer for at times. . .

'You're going to be fine,' she said warmly, drawing up a chair and clasping the nervously fretting fingers. 'You're looking much better already.'

Plump shoulders lifted in a near shrug. 'It doesn't matter, does it? I really don't care, Jo.' Becky's eyes filled with tears that belied the hopeless words. 'I suppose Patrick doesn't want to see me.'

'I'm sure he does. But you aren't allowed visitors yet,' Joanne soothed.

'Aren't you a visitor?'

'Oh, I don't count.' Joanne smiled. 'I'm only a nurse.'

'Then Patrick *does* want to see me? He has asked to come?'

The instant flicker of hope tugged at Joanne's heart, for she knew the tendency to clutch at straws, however feeble. 'He's very fond of you, Becky.' She didn't dare to say more than that for fear of raising false hopes. Patrick seemed stricken, but that might be simply remorse, she thought shrewdly. 'Look at these gorgeous flowers and this beautiful bed-jacket I've brought for you—both from Patrick. That speaks for itself, surely,' she encouraged.

'He's just sorry for me.' Becky fingered the fragile petals and stroked the softness of the exquisitely embroidered little coat without interest.

'He never wanted to hurt you,' Joanne assured her gently. 'He just wanted to slow things down for a while, I think.'

She wished she could believe that Dane had a similar motive for setting up a seemingly impenetrable barrier, with his austere smiles and cool manner and the aseptic attitude that doctors knew so well how to adopt towards a nurse but that was so hurtful after that unforgettable idyll of shared intimacy.

'So he could kiss me goodbye when we got home, go away and forget all about me.' Becky's bitter words instantly dragged Joanne's mind away from her own problems. 'Oh, I know, Jo. It's happened before. It never mattered so much before, though. I never felt like this about anyone but Patrick.' Slow tears coursed down her cheeks and she turned her face to the wall on a choked-back sob.

Joanne understood, perhaps better than most. For Dane wouldn't even kiss her goodbye, she knew. At the end of this eventful holiday, he would simply walk away and out of her life and forget her all over again.

Sometimes, it seemed very hard that she would have to pay for the rest of her life for that fearful flight from a man she had loved but had hurt so badly when she had been only eighteen.

* * *

She was back in Pleydorf in time to take some of the group to the village shops for souvenirs and last-minute items for the journey, now looming very near. Most people were ready to pack and go home, she felt, except perhaps for Lenny, who had been able to indulge his passion for horses to the full and would certainly miss his stint in the stables and the riding that had become the highlight of his holiday.

Later, parking Clair in the lounge, with Nadine and Marcia to look after her, she went to change the navy blue uniform dress for a cool, loose-fitting tunic of bright yellow silk that would see her comfortably through the evening.

It was a warm day in spite of the persisting clouds that wreathed the peaks of the Wilderkaiser, and she flopped into a chair on the veranda for a few minutes, feeling that all her nerves were strangely at full stretch, just as if she was waiting for something more to happen—or to go wrong, she thought with a wry smile.

No one could say that the holiday hadn't been full of incident!

CHAPTER ELEVEN

STEPPING through the sliding doors Dane frowned at the girl who lazed on the veranda when there were many more worthwhile ways in which to spend her time. He had just seen Clair by herself in the lounge, looking forlorn. He had caught a glimpse of Marcia wandering about the grounds, looking lost and lonely. With Anneliese tied up at the Haupmann Clinic and himself having to spend almost the entire day in Salzburg, dealing with all the necessary red tape of an emergency flight back to England, Joanne ought to be doing more to help!

'Nothing better to do?' he challenged, the dry words shafting towards the slender girl in the bright dress who looked so young and pretty and deceptively vulnerable as she relaxed in a chair. 'You might remember that people like Clair are dependent on us for her enjoyment of this holiday, Joanne. She's stuck in that restricting chair, by herself in the lounge, while everyone else has gone off to do their own thing. Including you!'

Joanne sat bolt upright, indignation sparking along with a natural annoyance with Marcia and Nadine, who had promised to stay with Clair for the time being. 'Are you accusing me of neglecting Clair?'

'I think you could give a little more thought to those who need your attention and give rather less of it to those who don't—like Lionel.'

She glowered. 'I haven't seen Lionel all day! I've been to the clinic to see Becky and I've just got back from taking Clair and some of the others to the village shops. This is my first chance to put my feet up, and I'm damned if I'll let you make me feel guilty!' She lay back in her chair, a defiant set to her pretty face. 'Go to hell, Dane!'

'Oh, I've been *there*. And back,' he said smoothly. 'Thanks to you.'

Joanne was dismayed by the jibe. All her loving and giving and regretting, all her efforts to make things right between them, hadn't made a scrap of difference to the way he felt about her. He was still full of hate and bitter memories. 'You won't let me forget, will you?' she said hotly.

The quick spurt of a temper that he had good reason to remember and resent triggered another gust of irritation. 'Do you think *I* can forget?' He slapped the long, lean thigh of a permanently lame leg and limped towards her on a sudden surge of fury. 'I've a perpetual reminder of what you did to me,' he declared on a savage blast of pent-up pain and anger.

Joanne leaped to her feet, alarmed by the blaze in those dark eyes. He was always so cool, so controlled, so much in command of himself. This was a Dane she didn't know, furious, uncontrolled and potentially dangerous, she felt, backing from the angry man.

'I never meant. . . I didn't want. . .oh, Dane, it would never have happened if I hadn't loved you,' she blurted.

As if all the love in the world could excuse the damage she had done to his beautiful body and his pride, she thought achingly, knowing that forgiving and forgetting had proved to be beyond him, after all.

'*Love*!' Dane struck out blindly. 'When did you ever know the meaning of the word? Heartless, unfeeling and totally self-centred just about sums you up!'

She winced from the words, more brutal than a blow. 'I suppose you feel I deserve that,' she said quietly, making no attempt to defend herself. If all the bitterness poured out of him in angry words then perhaps, when he was empty of hate, there might be room for a different attitude. Not love—she could never hope for that from Dane, she knew. But a new understanding of the girl she had been, afraid and unsure and ill-equipped to cope with circumstances so unexpectedly thrown at her.

'My God, I do! And can you blame me?' he grated harshly, his handsome face suffused with remembered pain and present fury. 'I know just what you are and what you can do to a man, and I'm sorry for the poor devil who thinks the sun rises and sets with your smile. So did I, once—and, heaven help me, you nearly fooled me into thinking you were worth caring about again. You're not! You're still the selfish, scheming, cold-hearted little bitch that you were seven years ago!'

Long-ago hurt and dismay swamped present-day considerations, swept aside everything but the desire for revenge. Damn it, he thought, she had made it impossible for him ever to love anyone else, and he wanted to punish her for that in a way she would never forget. Just as he had never, ever been able to forget the love and the need for this beautiful, bewitching girl who had come back into his life only to taunt him with the might-have-been.

Gripping her shoulders with fingers that bit deep into the soft flesh, he crushed her to him with a hunger that belied the contemptuous tone and the anger in his heart. He held her and kissed her, bruising the startled, quivering mouth, savage with the desire to take her and make her his own just once more.

Joanne tried to prise herself from the angry, determined embrace. 'Dane. . .*please*!'

He was in no mood to listen. It was doubtful if he

even heard the breathless plea as he forced her back against the rigid frame of a window-box, his mouth hard and brutally demanding, his hands keeping her firmly captive while his raging body urged a response to the powerful, primitive need that she and his anger had fired. Her lips remained resolutely cold and the stiff rejection of her slender body fuelled his anger and abruptly reinforced the urge to avenge injured pride and heart and body.

Rage and passion mounting in him so tumultuously that he no longer knew which was uppermost, Dane spun her round and propelled her through the open door into her room.

She struggled to escape the vice-like clench of his hands on her arms, telling herself that this was *Dane*, the man she loved, and not a threatening stranger who meant her harm. 'Oh, come on!' she exclaimed with a shaky laugh, desperately trying to defuse the situation. 'You wouldn't be such an idiot. . .oh!' The last, shocked exclamation was bounced out of her as he picked her up bodily and dumped her on the bed.

Beginning to be seriously alarmed, Joanne looked in wide-eyed astonishment at the man who looked back at her with grim, uncompromising intent in steely dark eyes. As she scrambled to get up, he pushed her down again with both hands on her shoulders and bent to kiss her, taking her lips without any trace of tenderness.

Joanne seized handfuls of black, crisply waving hair and tugged, as he pinioned her to the bed with his weight. She resisted him with all her lesser strength, and, as his mouth lingered on her own, fought the stir of love and longing which undermined her anger that he should besmirch precious memories of previous love-making with this furious attempt to force her into giving what she had never yet wanted to deny him.

His impatient hands tore at buttons, thrust at her skirt. 'Don't do this, Dane,' she implored, for his sake rather than her own, knowing that he would despise himself—and *her*—more than ever, if he persisted. 'Do you want me to hate you?' She hoped the desperate words would give him pause.

Dane leaned up on an elbow to look into her stormy, beautiful face, a wry smile to his sensual mouth. 'I'll notice the difference, will I?'

He saw the flicker of hurt widen her blue eyes and the tremor of her soft, expressive mouth. But it was too late to take back the words and too late to stem the torrent of a desire that disregarded everything but his need for a girl who had left him once in spite of her claim to love him, and couldn't be trusted not to do so again.

Roughly, he kissed her. Roughly, he bared the lovely breasts, cupping his hands about their tender curves and commandeering the peaked tips with impertinent lips and tongue, his body still urgent but less angry as the reluctant love he had tried so hard to banish stole through his veins along with the heat of passion.

Reluctant shafts of dark, delicious desire shivered along her spine and she melted to his kiss, his touch. Even in anger, he was a skilled and sensual lover, coaxing rather than insisting, bent on giving as well as taking pleasure, and it was impossible not to respond, to yield, to delight in his ardent embrace.

As his powerful body reared above her, potent with promise, Joanne welcomed his slow, sure descent with a sigh of loving surrender, for perhaps the tempestuous lovemaking would give him ease of mind and spirit as well as body, purging the pain of the past and renewing the joy in each other that they had once known.

Then she lost thought and time and place and all else in the shuddering delight that consumed her as her senses began the joyous ascent to the ultimate peaks of ecstasy in his demanding arms.

Joanne wasn't sure when the blind, unthinking rage of passion turned into a sensitive and tender loving, but she was glad of it when Dane finally lay on her breast, spent and breathless and shuddering, slowly coming down from the glorious pinnacle that they had climbed and conquered together, sweat trickling down his handsome face to pool on his powerful neck and shoulders. But that moment of altered intent had turned a near-rape into something lovely and forever memorable, after all.

Apparently Dane didn't share that rose-coloured view.

'Now we both have something to forgive,' he told her harshly, reaching for the clothes that lay in crumpled heaps on the floor, anxious to escape before he should read reproach and contempt in the blue eyes that regarded him so steadily. 'I wonder if you'll be any better at forgiving than I am.'

He left her on the curt, clipped words, suddenly a stranger once more in the dark glower of his mood. Joanne took her shaken, still trembling and tingling body into the shower and lifted her flushed, bright-eyed face to the cascade, her heart filled with a new hope in spite of that abrupt departure and the brusque parting words.

Dane had behaved very badly, taking her on a wild and foolish storm of passion that had overruled even a half-hearted protest, but he had only levelled the score, she felt. Now perhaps things really could come right at last.

Maybe it was possible for her to dream of being enfolded once more in the love she had forfeited, of being restored to a once-cherished place in his heart and life, of being sure of the destiny that had been her heart's desire since her first meeting with the dashing Dr Dane Gregory.

Loving him, she could wait for as long as it took. . .

Cramming the last of Becky's clothes into a suitcase which had surely shrunk in size since it had left her home in England, Joanne turned from the task of packing for that day's flight home at the sound of her name.

'Jo! I have looked everywhere for you! It is arranged that you will fly back with Becky,' Anneliese declared with the authoritative manner that had made her a sure bet for the eventual role of ward sister from her very first day as a junior nurse at the Montgomery General.

'*I* am?' Joanne stared in astonishment.

'Dane says that Becky will prefer to have you with her on the plane, and he is right, of course. She is so fond of you—and really I shall be much needed on the coach journey.'

And it will be a wonderful experience for me to go home by air ambulance, Joanne thought drily, mentally forestalling her well-meaning friend. 'Then I'd better go and pack for myself,' she said levelly, knowing that it would be pointless to protest. Between them, Dane and Anneliese had settled her immediate future, but with very different motives.

Anneliese simply wanted to make up for lost time with Cal. But Dane wanted to be rid of her reminding presence. There was the steel of suppressed anger in every line of his tall, taut body, in every glance from dark, guarded eyes, and in every word he addressed to her, although they had been few enough since he had limped from her room with his clothes under his arm, she thought wryly.

She had ached to reach out to him, to assure him that nothing he said or did could turn her against him, but she knew that he found it doubly hard to forgive himself after the years of failing to forgive her for a past injury and that his anger was directed solely against himself. Nevertheless, he didn't want to see or speak to her until he had mastered that anger and brought himself to seek forgiveness, Joanne realised with the understanding of her love for him, and she had avoided any attempt at a showdown, although it was impossible to leave things as they were.

Now, faced with leaving Pleydorf at less than an hour's notice, she felt a surge of panic. For supposing she never saw Dane again!

'I know you will not mind taking my place, Jo,' Anneliese swept on confidently. 'It is really my responsibility to accompany Becky, but I wish very much to travel back with the group.' Unexpectedly, a blush stole into the fair face.

Joanne smiled at her warmly. 'Cal will be pleased. You haven't had much time to be together, after all.'

'We did not come on this holiday to be together,' Anneliese declared firmly. 'It is a bonus that we like each other and get on so well, but my first consideration is always for the group.'

'No one could doubt it.' Joanne hastened to smooth slightly ruffled feathers. 'Actually, I thought at first that Dane was the attraction,' she added tentatively as she closed and locked Becky's case after a slight struggle with the bulging contents.

'*Dane?*' Amber eyes glowed with amusement. 'No, no! We are friends, that is all. He has always been kind and interested since I went to England to be a nurse, but it is not romantic, Jo. Besides, he doesn't believe in love, you know,' Anneliese added with a twinkle. 'That is why he will never marry, he says. I tell him that a doctor should have a wife and that one day he will eat his words, but he only laughs.'

Joanne was aware that Dane had very good reason to distrust love, relieved that he had never talked of loving Anneliese or pressed her to marry him as she had feared, and heartened to realise that while his heart was no longer open to her it was closed to other women too.

'There was a girl. . .years ago——' The German girl broke off suddenly to stare into guarded blue eyes. 'It is *you*, Jo!' she exclaimed as a missing piece of jigsaw fell neatly into place. She didn't like mysteries, and the one that had puzzled her since the start of the holiday now seemed to be solved. If she had not spent so much time away from the group, she would have solved it sooner, she thought confidently. '*You* are the girl he will never talk about! I know I am right! There has been a tension between you since the day we left. He has seemed to dislike you, which is strange when you are so popular and you—oh, Jo! You are still in love with him,' she said softly, in sudden and sympathetic realisation.

'Don't tell me I'm wasting my time. I know.' Her friend's feelings for Cal must be making her even more receptive to the signals that people unconsciously gave out, Joanne thought ruefully. Denying her love for Dane was unthinkable, but she wondered how he could be so blind and deaf to her feelings when they were apparently so obvious to everyone else. 'So I don't at all mind about going back with Becky,' she went on with a wry smile. 'I shall get away from Dane all the sooner and I won't feel so envious of you and Cal.'

She smiled to assure Anneliese that she wasn't desolate about Dane. She had got on with her life without him for the past seven years and could do so again, she told herself stoutly.

But she didn't like to think how much harder it would be for her now.

'And your friendship with Lionel will have time to cool down,' Anneliese suggested sagely.

'I'm sorry about that.' Joanne's tone was rueful. Was there anything that had happened on this holiday that her perceptive friend hadn't noticed? she wondered. 'I like him so much, but I really didn't mean to encourage him to care for me, Annie.' Becky's accident—as everyone had resolutely referred to what had happened to avoid all kinds of repercussions, both here and at home—had been opportune in one respect. For she couldn't be expected to think about the future or make plans for spending it with Lionel or anyone else when she was so anxious about Becky. She had realised a change in his attitude, a new confidence and a hint of possessive pride, but he hadn't referred to the moment when she had come so recklessly close to committing herself. It was something to sort out when they were all back in England, she knew. She had thought that time and experience had cured her of impulse, but it seemed that she had been sadly mistaken!

'I'm sure he understands very well the situation, Jo. Lionel is a very good man,' Anneliese soothed.

'Then you think he knows how I feel about Dane? I've tried to hide it from him. I didn't want him to be hurt,' Joanne said anxiously.

'I expect he thinks that you lost your head a little in such lovely surroundings. People do, don't they? On holiday? Perhaps Cal and I are just another holiday romance.' Anneliese's smile and the shine in her amber eyes belied any belief in the light words. 'I don't want to know about you and Dane—that is your business. But you must have been very dismayed to see him, Jo. Why didn't you say something to me when you knew he was coming with us? I would have found a reason to put him off.'

'It was too late. I didn't know he was Gary's replacement until he arrived to board the coach.' Joanne glanced doubtfully at her friend as they left the annexe to hand over Becky's case to Cal. 'I had no idea that you were friends, Annie,' she reminded the German girl. She hesitated. 'Did he never mention *me*?'

'As the girl that he hoped to marry? No, not by name. There was a car crash and a bad injury and he was ill for a long time. After, he didn't speak of the girl again, and I thought he had fallen out of love or she had found someone else. These things happen. But that was when he began to say that he would never marry and I felt he had been badly hurt, deep inside him.'

'Yes. I did that to him,' Joanne said baldly. 'And he can't forgive me for it. . .'

Leaving Anneliese, she hurried on to pack her things as quickly as possible, for Cal was waiting with the car to take her into St Johann to link up with Becky at the clinic.

She stole a few seconds to stand on the veranda for the last time, remembering all the good and bad things about this holiday in the pretty Austrian village. The sun slanted across the mountain to strike the gold cross of the church, and she took it as a symbol that the silent prayer of her heart would eventually be answered.

About to get into the car, she looked across to the terrace where most of the group had assembled for the afternoon. Nadine sported another new hat; a paper one, this time, fashioned by Dane's clever hands out of a newspaper. Lenny and Ian were hurling paper darts in an attempt to topple it, and Nadine was actually laughing out loud as she tried to snatch the shafts of newspaper before they reached the target. It was another victory over the girl's shyness that she had begun to accept and respond to such light-hearted teasing, Joanne felt.

Bereft of Becky, Marcia had attached herself to Suzy, who would probably be glad of her company to pass the long hours on the coach as they travelled home. Both in their chairs, Clair and Howie sat talking, having become firm friends in the last two weeks. Lionel was on the edge of the group, a loner in some ways because of his deafness, but never lonely, for he was a self-sufficient and strong-minded man who had rarely felt that he was held back by his disability. Joanne wondered at the impulse that had almost hurtled her into something she would certainly have regretted, much as she liked him. Fortunately, Lionel wasn't the kind to remind her that she had turned to him for comfort and support because her heart ached for another man. He would just go on being a very good friend.

The others were her friends too, and she was sorry to miss the trip back to England in their company. She had said her farewells, giving and receiving hugs and kisses all round, and now she sent them all a last wave and turned away, knowing that Dane had deliberately avoided her send-off.

Cal released the handbrake. 'All right, lass? Got everything?'

'I think so. . .' Everything but her heart, and that remained with the man who showed no sign of ever wanting it again.

The car moved slowly towards the gates and the road to St Johann, where an ambulance waited to take her and Becky to Innsbruck Airport. She was leaving Pleydorf, perhaps never to return, but she took with her a cluster of memories. Craning her neck, she looked up at the flower-bedecked veranda that she had shared with

Dane—one last look in the hope of glimpsing him. A slight movement caught her eye and she stiffened.

Dane *was* there, watching, stepping swiftly out of sight as if he sensed her wistful gaze and didn't mean to admit that he looked after the car that had swept her from his life once more. Was he relieved? she wondered—or as heartsore as herself?

'Oh. . .*stop*! Do stop, Cal! I *have* forgotten something. . .!' Her feet hit the gravel even before the car came to a complete halt and she ran back to the main building to take the stairs two at a time to the second floor. His room door stood open and she burst in without the ceremony of knocking. 'You didn't say goodbye!' she exclaimed, breathless and indignant.

Dane turned to look at her, unsurprised by her impulsive dash from the departing car to confront him with a challenge in her sparkling blue eyes. Impulse and Joanne still seemed to be synonymous, he thought with a flicker of tender amusement, studying the avenging angel in her crisp navy blue dress with its distinctive white piping at collar and cuffs, small waist spanned by the wide, silver-buckled belt, bright blaze of hair vying with the blaze of angry accusation in her lovely face.

'I didn't think you believed in goodbyes. You didn't bother with them the last time we went our separate ways, as I remember,' he returned drily.

'But that's just it! You *don't* remember! You were in ICU and in no state to know if I was there or not,' she said hotly, desperate to straighten out a misunderstanding that he had nurtured for much too long. 'You didn't feel my kiss or taste my tears! I wish you *could* remember that you told me to go, said you never wanted to see me again! You might think less badly of me!'

'I was probably half dead and delirious at the time, but it suited you to take me at my word.'

'Oh, Dane! Try to put yourself in my position for once, please! I was in a dreadful state, frantic with fear and guilt, terrified that you'd die, and that it was all my fault, and convinced that you'd never forgive me if you didn't—and I was right! You haven't!'

'The crash would have happened if I'd been at the wheel,' he conceded. 'The car had a faulty steering pinion, as I said. But to run away—from *me*, from everything. . .' His mouth hardened. 'I never thought you were a coward, Joanne. That's what I find so hard to forgive.'

'Love can make cowards of us all,' she said wryly. 'I loved you too much to face your anger—and your hate. I can't help it if you don't believe me, Dane. I've tried to make you understand. I've tried to make amends. You just don't want to forgive, to be friends.' She held out her hand. 'So I guess it really *is* goodbye this time.'

It took courage to smile, to meet those hard eyes without flinching, to accept that she would never kiss him or touch him or hold him again and that their paths were unlikely to cross again. Destiny had given them a second chance—but a third would never come along, she felt.

At eighteen, she had taken refuge in cowardly flight, but now, older and wiser, she was walking away from the man she loved for a very different reason. Not because he needed her and she couldn't cope with the demands he might make on her, but because he didn't need her at all.

CHAPTER TWELVE

LOOKING back on those two weeks in Austria as the air ambulance carried her and Becky safely through the skies, Joanne felt that they had all the elements of a dream. Moments of magic, interspersed with alarm and confusion and nightmare, sudden storms and oases of tranquillity, tears and laughter—and through it all the thread that was Dane, love from the past that had touched the present with a mix of happiness and heartache.

And, like a dream, it had ended abruptly, the magic and the mystery evaporating in the cold light of the reality that was Becky's harsh breathing and high temperature and restless mood. Surrounded by the array of essential medical equipment and accompanied by a highly skilled team of paramedics during the short flight across the Continent, Joanne felt that her presence was superfluous as the sick girl was rushed to a hospital in England to be treated near home and family. But Becky was glad of the comfort of a familiar face, and Joanne knew that the coach journey with the rest of the group would have been harder going home than it had been on the way to Austria, for in the meantime she and Dane had been lovers again, a bitter-sweet interlude to make the holiday even more memorable.

Becky was admitted to Russell Ward after the short journey to the Montgomery General by ambulance from the airport, and Joanne stayed to talk to the doctors who examined her, took details of her medical history and the accident and her treatment in the Haupmann Clinic.

Becky had been exhausted by the flight and the emotional toll of parting with Patrick, allowed to see her for just long enough to cheer her with the promise of visiting her as soon as he was back in England with the rest of the group, and it was obvious that the severely disabled girl would be in hospital for some time, recovering from the chest infection she had contracted as well as the strain on her nervous system.

When Becky's anxious parents arrived at the hospital, Joanne had to recount the details all over again, carefully omitting Becky's frame of mind at the time. She assured them that their daughter had been in excellent hands after the accident and that her reaction to the flight was only a minor setback, and she did her best to convince them that Becky had enjoyed the holiday along with everyone else until that unfortunate afternoon.

The sister in charge of Russell Ward was a friend who had been interested in the venture long before it became a reality, and she invited Joanne into her sitting-room for some tea, wanting to hear all about Austria as well as the accident. It was long after the air ambulance had landed at the airport when Joanne finally let herself into her flat and dumped her suitcase in the hall. As she had returned earlier than expected, there was no bread or milk or other essential food items that a neighbour had promised to provide, and that meant a trip to the corner supermarket that fortunately opened until late.

After the excitement and the company of the last two weeks, things had fallen very flat, and she wandered aimlessly about the flat, thinking of the friends she had left behind in Pleydorf, trying not to conjure up wistful images of Dane—talking to Clair and Suzy and Cal, teasing Marcia, coaxing shy, sweet Nadine into conversation, listening patiently and with real interest to Lionel's difficult speech, reining Lenny's wilder urges.

She had telephoned from the hospital to tell Anneliese of their safe arrival and Becky's admission and present condition, ringing off after the brief exchange, unsatisfied because there had been no mention of Dane.

Since she had spent so many days with him, it was inevitable that she should miss him. They had almost become friends once more, and she couldn't help wondering if she had said this or done that whether things might have turned out differently. As it was, she would have to get used to blanking him from her mind and heart all over again, Joanne told herself firmly—and the best thing she could do was to return to work as soon as possible. It would be better to fill her days with the familiar routines of her job and a caring interest in the patients on Ellis Ward than to spend them in wishful thinking and vain longing.

'Hello, Sister! How was Austria?'

'Is that an all-over tan, Sister?'

'Nice to see you back, Sister!'

Joanne made her first round of the ward on her early return to work to an accompaniment of friendly greetings from those patients admitted before her holiday and still not well enough for discharge. She paused to talk, to hear news of home and families, to pass on information from the doctors. She plumped up pillows, picked up a newspaper that had slipped to the floor, adjusted a drip for one patient and a dressing for another, supported an elderly man while he struggled into a dressing-gown to take the first reluctant steps after a major operation.

As she moved from patient to patient, her trained eye took in every detail of the long, bright room with its two rows of beds and cheerful chintz curtains, the polished lockers that were cluttered with personal items as well as vases of flowers and water-jugs and get-well cards, the long windows through which the sun streamed its golden rays on another glorious morning. Nurses carried out the quiet, ordered routines of dressings, medicine round, tube-feeds, blanket-baths and regular observations of post-operative patients.

Soon it seemed to Joanne that she had never been away, as the hours whisked by while she worked on the ward with her nurses or talked to doctors who came to examine their patients and discuss test results, treatment, progress or lack of it with her. Porters took patients to Theatre and brought others back from the recovery room after surgery. The telephone rang incessantly. The hustle and bustle of the busy surgical ward left her very little time to think of anything else, in fact.

It was good to be back on the ward that had become her responsibility and her pride. Nursing was a very important part of her life—and that was just as well, when it promised to be the only thing in her life, Joanne thought sensibly as she settled for sleep at the end of the day.

Nothing could change the past, not even love, so she must simply get on with the present and face the future with the cheerful attitude that people expected of a Monty's nurse, she decided as she switched off the bedside lamp.

But good resolutions didn't prevent her from mentally following the progress of the holidaymakers from country to country to cross-Channel ferry over the next few days, and she was waiting to welcome them when the familiar blue coach turned into the grounds of the local Red Cross Headquarters with Cal at the wheel.

Heart thumping, Joanne scanned faces for a glimpse of Dane. Her last words to him in Pleydorf had been a goodbye to hoping and dreaming rather than a belief that they would never meet again, for he had an ongoing friendship with Anneliese and it was possible that he would keep up the new association with some members of the PHAB Club.

He would be very busy at first, helping with luggage and wheelchairs and getting people off the coach, and then he would probably be caught up in introductions to relatives and friends who were milling about the coach. But they might have a moment or two to speak before he got into his car and drove off to a world where she no longer belonged, and Joanne was desperate to bridge an abyss of misunderstanding—and surely the right words would spill from her heart when they were so sorely needed?

Lenny nearly fell off the coach in his haste to get to her and throw his one good arm about her, his youthful face brimming with affection. 'I knew you'd be here to meet us, Jo! We missed you!'

She hugged him. 'I expect you miss the horses more than me,' she teased. Surrounded by her friends, exchanging a warm smile with Lionel as he assembled Howie's wheelchair, admiring the bright tartan cap that had been Nadine's last and most unlikely purchase before they left Calais, she struggled to look over heads for a sight of Dane's tall figure. 'Where's Dane?' she was finally forced to ask, trying to keep everything but casual interest from her tone. 'You didn't lose *him* too, I hope!' she said with a smile, having just heard about Paul's adventure in Cologne. The music-mad youngster had wandered away from the group when they'd stopped for lunch and a visit to the cathedral, and it had been a panicky half-hour before Lenny had found him at the record counter in the nearby Woolworths.

'He got off at Monty's with Patrick,' Cal paused to explain as he carried Clair from the coach to her brother's car. 'They both wanted to see Becky, so I made a detour to pass the hospital.'

Pushing Howie across the forecourt to his parked invalid car, Anneliese overheard. 'Dane has been in daily contact with Dr Hunt by telephone, but he wished to see for himself that Becky is making progress,' she added with a hint of warm understanding in her smile. Basking in the rosy glow of her own probable future with Cal, she could still sympathise with the dismay in her friend's blue eyes. 'He will be sorry to have missed you, Jo. But we are to leave his luggage with Mrs Wren for him to collect when he comes for his car.'

'Oh, I see.' Joanne rallied. 'Becky's much better now, and seeing Patrick will be the best possible tonic for her.' Years of training had taught her to conceal her emotions behind a bright smile and a brisk manner, but she felt all the irony of the situation. For she had rushed off duty to be on time to meet the group on their return—and Dane was at the hospital at that very moment!

She wondered if he had been as sure as everyone else that she would be at the Red Cross Headquarters to meet the coach—and taken steps to ensure that he wasn't on it. . .

It took some time to match each person with the right luggage, to say farewells and exchange telephone numbers and promises to meet in the near future, to wave everyone off by car or taxi or PHAB mini-bus. But eventually only Joanne and Lionel were left in a near-empty forecourt as the coach set off for its company garage with Cal and Anneliese on board.

It was like Lionel to be of help to the very last, Joanne thought warmly, turning to him with a grateful smile. 'Well, that's it—until the next time. The end of the holiday.'

'It was a happy holiday for most people, Jo. And the start of many new friendships.'

'Everyone got on so well, didn't they? Annie and I were relieved about that, because there were a lot of different personalities on the coach,' she admitted.

'Clashes were few and far between, thanks to the way you and Annie worked to keep everyone happy and interested.' He reached for her hand. 'I'm very glad that I went, for one. It was a wonderful holiday, Jo.' He paused, so much that he would never say in those smiling blue eyes. 'I hope we shall always be friends,' he said quietly.

'I'm sure we will.' Joanne was relieved that she had no need to explain, to apologise, to extricate herself from a difficult situation. He understood and accepted, and didn't mean to tie her down to something said and done on impulse in the Austrian sunshine.

'Are you going home now?' he asked. 'Would you like a lift?'

Joanne hesitated. If she refused, it would mean two bus changes to reach her flat. If she accepted, she would miss her last chance of seeing Dane, who must surely arrive for his car and his luggage before the headquarters closed for the night. She glanced across at the dusty Mercedes, parked between two Red Cross ambulances. 'Thanks very much, Lionel. But I want to have a word with Mrs Wren and I may be some time. Don't bother to wait for me. Come and have a meal on Wednesday at the flat, if you're free,' she invited on yet another impulse.

His face brightened. 'I'd like that very much,' he agreed.

'About seven-thirty, then.'

She walked with him to his car and then bent to brush

his cheek with friendly lips just before he drove away and just as a taxi turned into the forecourt.

Dane got out and glanced across at her, then waved a friendly hand to Lionel in the departing car before he limped towards Joanne. 'What are you doing here?' he demanded. 'I expected you to be at the hospital.'

There was nothing lover-like about the greeting, but Joanne's heart gave a huge bound of relief. He had looked for her at Monty's! He had wanted to see her again! 'I left early to be here when the coach arrived. But you weren't on it,' she said simply.

He didn't need the betrayal of the words to tell him that she was glad to see him. It shone in her eyes and her smile, a forgiving and a welcome that he didn't deserve. But the spectre of Lionel still haunted him, and he had just seen her kiss the guy before he left! Dane couldn't get to the bottom of that relationship, but it wasn't going to stand in his way when he had just spent two days mentally urging the coach along every mile of autobahn with all the desperation of a man in love—even if he wasn't yet ready to admit it!

'I need some English money to pay the taxi driver. I changed some schillings on the ferry, but I've run out. I didn't realise that it was such a distance from the Montgomery General to this place, I'm afraid. Can you let me have ten pounds, Joanne?'

It was the easy, unembarrassed request that a friend might make of another in similar circumstances, and she instantly rummaged for her purse in her shoulder bag. 'Of course.'

Watching him as he returned to the waiting vehicle, she saw the rueful expression on his handsome face as he glanced at his car. Recalling the immaculate, highly polished condition of the sleek Mercedes when he'd arrived to board the coach and had given her such a shock, Joanne guessed that Dane was grieved by the grime it had acquired during the two weeks that it had stood in the well-used forecourt.

She walked to meet him. 'Cal put your luggage in the office, by the way. No one knew what time you were likely to get here this evening, so it was thought best to store it in a safe place,' she explained. 'I'll let Mrs Wren know you've come to collect it.'

'Becky only had eyes for Patrick, just as you'd expect,' Dane told her as they strolled towards the main entrance of the Red Cross Centre. 'As soon as I'd said hello and satisfied myself that she was really on the mend, I left them to it. There didn't seem to be any point in hanging about at the hospital.' Once he had learned that Sister Ellis had gone off duty, he thought but did not add. The hope of seeing Joanne, if only for a few minutes, had been his prime reason for accompanying Patrick, although he had also genuinely wanted to check on Becky and have a word with the doctor in charge of her case.

Joanne introduced him to the commandant who was still working in the office, and they retrieved his case and holdall. 'I expect you're anxious to get home,' Joanne said tentatively, watching him stow both in the boot of his car.

Wherever that is, she added silently, taken aback to realise how little she knew about him nowadays. It seemed that reality had taken a back seat during the holiday, when she had lived only for each day and the delight of spending some of it in his company. There were so many things she wanted to know about the man she loved, so much she might have asked when he was in friendly, communicative mood, but they had never entered her head at the time. Perhaps she had been afraid of spoiling those rare, sweet moments when he had looked and smiled and spoken with a friendly warmth that had seemed to have forgotten a past injury.

She had been walking on eggshells every time circumstances had allowed them to be alone together for a few minutes, she admitted ruefully—and she was still far from confident about approaching a man who had become a stranger in seven years.

Dane shrugged the powerful shoulders that had made light of the demands made on his strength in the last fortnight. 'Not particularly. Why?' Home was a penthouse apartment in a riverside development on the other side of the city, comfortably furnished with all the trappings of an expensive and well-ordered lifestyle, with little evidence of the women who had occasionally shared it with him until the relationship had turned sour because there had only ever been one woman who had really mattered to him, even if he had never expected to find her again.

Having found her, he had been like a boy in love, saying and doing all the wrong things, falling into jealous rages, making too many demands and allowing his pride to obscure the fact that she was and always had been his destiny.

Having found her, could he bear to lose her again?

'Oh, no reason! Except. . .there's a wine bar just over the road—I mean, you must want something to eat, Dane. Or a drink, perhaps?' Joanne was floundering, and he wasn't helping, looking down at her with that dark, inscrutable gaze!

'I left my credit cards at home, and I doubt if they'll accept Austrian schillings, so——'

She didn't let him finish. 'It doesn't matter, of course!' Her smile was bright, hiding the hurt of a rebuff. 'It was just an idea. . .' One that obviously didn't appeal to him, she thought ruefully, turning to leave him.

Dane checked her with an arm draped lightly about her neck that drew her close in quite masterful fashion. 'So it looks as if I shall be in your debt for more than a taxi fare,' he continued firmly. 'You'll have to give me your address so I can send you a cheque.'

Joanne looked up at him. 'You could deliver it in person,' she suggested with the ghost of a smile in her blue eyes, meeting him more than halfway as she recognised an olive branch.

The small, dimly lit wine bar with its dark red décor and indifferent comfort was a sombre setting for a reconciliation, but Dane saw only the blaze of her beautiful hair and the glow of her lovely smile, not too sure at first but lighting her face more frequently as she began to relax over the meal and the wine and his careful handling of her sensitivity.

He felt his heart contract with love and longing, the same heart that had believed it could banish her completely and been proved so wrong. Having allowed her to leave Pleydorf on an unhappy note, too proud and still too bitter to admit his lasting love and need, he had castigated himself for it all the way back to England. Now, he desperately wanted to make amends, but if she chose to reject him after all that had happened then it would be no more than he deserved, he knew.

They talked, carefully feeling their way towards a new and better understanding, discussing the holiday and smiling together over a few of the more amusing moments, recalling with mutual tenderness some of the more appealing facets in Lenny and Marcia and Paul, regretting some of the distressing incidents that had bedevilled the Austrian venture and uniting in their admiration of Anneliese's efforts and enthusiasm and caring qualities.

Unthinkingly, Joanne referred to the night of the storm that had swept over the mountains to spend its electric fury on the village in the valley, and then found that she couldn't meet Dane's smiling eyes as she remembered a tempest of lovemaking.

He sensed her thoughts and guessed at her confusion, and reached a hand to her chin, gentle fingers turning her averted face towards him. 'That's a good memory,' he said softly. 'Don't push that one away, Joanne. All I ask is that you try to forget another time when I made love to you, because that shouldn't have happened the way it did. I won't ask you to forgive, because I don't see how you can,' he added wryly.

She kissed the fingers that traced the curve of her mouth with such loving tenderness. 'Forgiving isn't so difficult when you care for someone, Dane.' The way I care for you, with all my heart, and I can't make it any plainer and still hang on to a little of my woman's pride! she thought.

Dane's sensual mouth twisted, remembering. 'No one could have loved you more than I did, but it didn't make it any easier for me to forgive you.'

She stifled a pang at his use of the past tense. If they were to go on seeing each other then there would be many such moments of hurt, and she would have to live with them, for nothing could change the pattern of the past.

'I wasn't around to be forgiven,' she reminded him levelly. 'And, because you had no memory of sending me away and believed that I didn't care, you went on being bitter and angry all those years. I don't blame you, Dane. I just think we ought to make a pact to stop talking about forgiving and forgetting and what happened. We could simply go on from here and now. . .that's if you want to, of course,' she added hastily.

Dane leaned to kiss her, the merest brush of his warm lips. 'I want to,' he said, smiling into eyes that held a promise he had never expected to see again in those expressive blue depths.

He collected his car just in time to prevent it from being locked inside the grounds of the Red Cross Headquarters for the night.

'You'll have to direct me,' he told Joanne as he nosed the car through the gateway into the stream of traffic. 'I don't know this part of the city at all.'

It was a strange feeling to be sitting at his side in a car again after so long and with so many memories, and she was sure that he was remembering too.

Her hands locked tightly in her lap, she was tense with the effort not to remember, but her mind's eye followed a long-ago scenario. Narrow, winding road and weird shapes and shadows of trees and hedges thrown up sharply in the twin beams of powerful headlamps and the feel of the accelerator pedal through the thin sole of her evening sandal. The echo of angry voices and a shout of warning, the sickening thud and crunch of metal and the frightening shatter of glass and a sudden silence. The shock of pain in bruised breasts and a failure to breathe, the numb disbelief of mind and heart and body—and then blood and tears and indescribable panic.

The nightmare had returned. Dane, injured and possibly dying, slumped at her side in a crashed car, was the ghost that she still couldn't exorcise. . .

Hearing the soft catch of her breath, aware of her thoughts because he shared many of those horrifying memories, Dane instantly swung the car into the side of the road and brought it to a halt.

'Stop it,' he commanded. 'Blank it out, Joanne. You said yourself that we can't stay in the shadow of the past for the rest of our lives!'

Suddenly sure that only the reassurance and security of his love for her could ease and erase the guilt and the anxiety, he pulled her into his arms and made it impossible for her to think of anything but the warm sensuality of his lips and the tender touch of his hands.

Joanne clung to him with a full heart, deeply thankful for the final forgiveness that she found in his kiss, scarcely able to believe that fate had been kinder than she deserved in bringing Dane back to her, whole and well and wanting her still.

She lay in his arms in her bed throughout the night, and they found each other again in the sweet talk and exchange of kisses and the tumult of loving that healed the wounds and wiped out the bitterness of the past.

He was gone when she woke and stretched her still glowing, deeply satisfied body in remembered delight. 'Clinic at ten,' he had scrawled across the plastic-coated reminder board in her tiny kitchen. 'Will be in touch.'

Joanne smiled, content with the promise of the words even though he had yet to tell her that he loved her. Deep down, she knew that they were meant to be together, and she meant to take good care not to let her temper or jealousy or anything else get in the way of a future that had to be better than the past.

CHAPTER THIRTEEN

HALFWAY along the ward, Joanne helped her senior staff nurse with the medicine round, carefully checking patients against drugs and dosages, doling out pills and medicines and noting those that were running low and would need to be re-stocked from Pharmacy.

Her trim figure was set off by the dark blue dress with its white piping, and the frilled organza cap of a Monty's ward sister sat securely on her shining auburn head, and an inner contentment was reflected in the warmth of her smile and the confidence of her manner as she talked to staff and patients.

Dane was courting her with telephone calls and flowers, but she had yet to see him, for he was extremely busy after the two weeks away from Brook's, catching up on his patients and a huge pile of correspondence, keeping engagements he had made before he'd left for Austria. Joanne knew that she couldn't expect to be instantly absorbed into his life as if she had never left it, for he had friends that she had never met and interests that she didn't share. There was possibly a girlfriend very much in the offing too, she told herself sensibly. She didn't want to rush things any more than Dane did, of course. It was enough for the moment that they had met again and were friends once more.

She had stressed the importance of her job on more than one occasion. I'm not interested in marriage, she had told him. I'm a career girl. . .and it wouldn't be surprising if Dane had taken her at her word, accepting and approving that independent stance. Joanne longed with all her heart to be his wife, but it was just another unlikely dream. For if he'd shown no inclination to marry in seven years then it was improbable that a chance encounter with a former love could change his mind—and hadn't he warned her that he wasn't interested in a permanent relationship? She didn't have the conceit or the confidence to assume that he had been lying in his teeth, like herself!

'Excuse me, Sister.' A junior nurse approached the drugs trolley, the single blue stripe of a first-year adorning her starched cap. 'There's someone to see you, Sister. I said you were busy, but he said he'd wait. . .'

Joanne glanced towards the grey-suited man who stood at the end of the ward, tall and lean and tanned and with all the marked authority of his profession in his attitude, and her heart skipped a beat. But training told.

'Thank you, Nurse,' she said crisply. 'Stay here and help Nurse Wilson with the medicine round. Staff, can you take over from me? Nurse Bennet will give you a hand. It seems that I've a visitor. . .' She didn't hurry towards Dane, although she felt as if she had wings attached to her heels. 'Good morning, Dr Gregory. Would you come into the office?' He might have been any one of the many medical men who had business on Ellis Ward, and her cool smile was for the benefit of interested juniors who were hovering to admire the darkly handsome doctor.

'I'm impressed,' he murmured as he followed her into the room with its glass wall overlooking the ward. 'Every inch the potential SNO!'

'I'm not sure that's a compliment!' She smiled from behind her desk, needing to distance herself in case she followed the impulse of her heart and fell into his arms in full view of everyone on the ward. Much as she loved him, she couldn't risk her job or the respect of the juniors by flouting hospital rules so blatantly. 'I wish I'd known you were coming. I'm on duty till six,' she told him regretfully.

'I wasn't sure of my plans. As I said on the phone, things are really hectic at the moment. But your Professor Lang has just published a very interesting article on renal disease in *The Lancet*, and it occurred to me that he might be able to help one of my patients. He suggested that we meet to talk about it, and it was too good an opportunity to miss.' He touched the slim hand that lay on a pile of folders on her desk. 'It's been a long week, Joanne.'

'The flowers were beautiful,' she said, although she had already thanked him for the surprise bouquet that had arrived earlier in the week.

'I believe in showing appreciation.' There was a twinkle in the dark eyes that became a smile as she blushed. The telephone broke the warm intimacy of the moment. 'You're busy,' he said hastily as she reached to silence its shrill note. 'And I'm due to see Lang in five minutes. Dinner tonight?'

'I'd love it. . . Sister Ellis speaking. Would you hold on, please?' She covered the mouthpiece with her hand. 'Where shall we meet. . . Oh!' She had suddenly realised that it was Wednesday and she was expecting Lionel that evening. 'Dane, I can't! I'm sorry, but——'

'You already have a date. OK—fair enough. We'll make it another time.' He was disappointed, but he knew it would be unreasonable to expect to slot back into her life at a moment's notice. Naturally, Joanne had friends and interests that he didn't know about. Just as naturally, she felt free to make plans to meet those friends and pursue those interests without referring to him.

Dane accepted that it was early days in a new-found relationship and that he had no claim on Joanne just because he loved her more than ever. He wasn't even sure that the way he felt about her was welcome or reciprocated, in spite of her loving and generous reception on his return from Austria. For all the maturity and sophistication acquired in the years between first-year nurse and efficient hospital sister, she was still the impulsive, warm-hearted and eager-to-please girl of long ago, he felt.

Glancing at his watch, he moved to the door. 'I must go or I'll be late for my appointment with Lang. We'll talk later,' he said, more brusquely than he intended.

'Dane! Just a minute—let me explain!' The querulous voice in her ear vied with the obvious coolness in Dane's deep tones, recalling her to a sense of duty. 'I'm sorry to keep you waiting—just one more moment, please,' she said briskly into the telephone, and lowered the receiver. Dane had paused at her plea, a dark eyebrow slanting towards the crisply curling black hair that concealed the reminding scar. 'I've asked Lionel for a meal and I can't put him off.'

She was tempted to do just that, but knew it wouldn't be fair to disappoint Lionel when she hopefully had the rest of her life to agree to everything that Dane asked of her.

'You can, but you'd rather not,' Dane amended drily. *Lionel*! Drat the man, continuously cropping up at the most inconvenient of moments, forcing him to wonder if Joanne was fonder of him than she admitted. Certainly it seemed to his jealous heart that she cared too much to relegate Lionel to second place in her life!

'I can't keep every evening free on the offchance that you'll turn up with an invitation,' Joanne protested reasonably, feeling that he could have warned her with a telephone call in time for her to alter her arrangements, angry at his obvious resentment of Lionel when he ought to be well aware that he had no rivals. How could Dane suppose that she cared for anyone but him after all she had said and done to show how much she loved him? she thought indignantly.

'There's no reason why you should, of course,' he agreed smoothly, quick with pride, sensitive to the slightest hint of rebuff. 'I know you're very popular. I'll just have to take my chance along with all the others, obviously.'

He was gone on the curt words and, unable to run after him and mend matters, Joanne turned her attention to the anxious relative on the other end of the telephone line. But all the time that she was offering reassurance and answering familiar questions, she was wondering if and when she would see Dane again.

He was waiting outside the ward when she went off duty that evening, startling her by falling into step at her side and taking her arm in a possessive grasp when her mind was on an essential trip to the supermarket for the things she needed for her meal with Lionel.

'I'm sorry, sweetheart,' he said abruptly. 'I'm a jealous idiot, but I can't stand the thought of you with someone else!'

'Oh, Dane!' Joanne's heart lifted. 'It isn't like that! Lionel's a *friend*.'

'He's crazy about you.'

'He's fond of me,' she corrected. 'We get on well and we've things in common, that's all.' She looked up into his handsome face. 'I expect I've more reason to be jealous than you have,' she said with a wry smile.

'Meaning Anneliese? Then she's told you that I'm taking her to dinner as you've turned me down?' he said airily.

'No. I haven't seen her.' With an effort, she steadied her voice. 'That seems a good idea. She says that she doesn't see enough of you these days.'

Dane had noticed the tremor, the careful coolness that concealed the shock of hurt. He bent to kiss her and two juniors from her ward, going off duty at the same time, stared and giggled and whispered to each other as Sister Ellis blushed to the roots of her hair. 'Cal's coming too, of course. It seems that I can't have one without the other—and the woman I really want prefers the company of another man,' he teased.

It was a few days before Joanne heard from him again, days of doubt and disappointment and wondering if she ought to have heeded his warning that he was unreliable and uninterested in serious involvement in spite of the reassurance of his words and his kiss and more flowers. Then he telephoned to apologise for not telephoning, explaining that he had been called out of town by a family emergency, and asking her to go to the coast with him that weekend.

'I wish I could,' she sighed. 'But it isn't possible, Dane. I'm going home for the weekend.' Home was in North Wales, a long train journey and an expensive fare away, but her parents were expecting her, a promise made before she went to Austria. It would be nice to take him with her, she thought wistfully, but she was reluctant to force him into any kind of a commitment, and she knew what her parents would make of the situation if she turned up with a former fiancé.

'Then I can't make it until Wednesday.'

'I'm expected at the PHAB Club that night!' Joanne almost wailed. 'It's the musical evening and I can't——'

'Let them down,' he finished wryly. 'I know.' He

sighed. 'This is an impossible situation, Joanne. Either you'll have to transfer back to Brook's or I'll have to take a job at the Montgomery General! Or we'll never get together, it seems to me!'

'I'm not sure if it's what you really want, anyway,' Joanne said tentatively, taking her courage in both hands, desperately needing to hear three words that he hadn't once uttered since they had met up again.

'If you knew how I curse the fact that I'm a doctor with too many demands on any one man's time, then you wouldn't doubt it,' he exploded uncompromisingly. 'Damn it, I can't stop thinking about you, wanting you! My work's shot to hell, I can't concentrate on anything and I resent everything and everyone that keeps me from seeing you!' He drew a deep breath. 'All right, I'd forgotten the PHAB night. They're expecting me too. For God's sake, don't make arrangements to go home with Lionel or any other of your lame dogs!'

She didn't have time to promise before he rang off. It seemed an eternity until Wednesday, with a weekend in Wales to get through as patiently as possible. All the members of the club would be delighted to see him again, but no one would be happier than herself to see him walk into the room.

She saw Anneliese on the following Monday morning, returning to the ward from her coffee break, and paused to speak to the friend she had scarcely seen since Austria, for they were both busy people on duty and the German girl seemed to be spending every free moment with Cal. He had become an enthusiastic helper at the PHAB Club, with a number of new ideas for excursions and entertainment and fund-raising, and there wasn't the slightest doubt in Joanne's mind that the holiday had set the pattern for *their* future, at least.

'This week we have our musical evening,' Anneliese

reminded her anxiously. 'You will be there? Everyone is looking forward to some music to remind them of Austria.'

Joanne had scarcely touched her guitar since leaving Pleydorf, for the first bars of any tune seemed too redolent of Dane and those two weeks in his company, painful reminder of how much she missed him. 'I'll be there,' she promised.

'Good. We have a little surprise for you, Jo.'

'What kind of surprise?' It was wary, for the German girl's expectations of delight didn't always coincide with her own.

'If I tell you then it is not a surprise. But you will like it,' Anneliese said confidently as the lift doors closed on her. Joanne hurried back to Ellis, to be greeted by an emergency of a haemhorraging post-operative patient that instantly drove the words from her mind.

Those members of the club who had been on the Austrian holiday with her crowded eagerly around Joanne when she arrived on Wednesday evening. She had seen one or two of them since, but most were outside her usual orbit and she relied on Anneliese for news of them.

She was delighted to learn that Lenny had enjoyed his first visit to the riding club that she had arranged for him to join, as promised. Nadine was there, without even one of her many hats, much to everyone's mock astonishment, and she took the kindly teasing with a smile that proved her increased confidence.

Becky and Patrick arrived together, their radiant faces announcing that they were engaged even before Becky told the news and showed off her ring and declared that they were all invited to the wedding.

Marcia had a huge folder of photographs to pass round, for she had carried her camera everywhere while they were away. She was particularly proud of an excellent shot of Richard, taken as he hurtled around a curve in the watersplash, capturing the look of glee that would certainly reassure his anxious family that he had loved every moment of the experience.

She handed Joanne a snap that she had taken of her and Dane on the chair-lift. 'You can have that one, Jo.'

Joanne scanned it eagerly, studying Dane's dear, handsome face and windblown hair and bare, bronzed chest, his arm cradling her so comfortingly as she huddled against him, the sleeves of his shirt whipped by the stiff breeze and the frozen smile on her face showing none of the terror and tumult that she had felt at the time.

'This is really excellent, Marcia,' she admired. 'They all are! Have you ever thought of a career as a photographer?'

'I'd love it, but I don't know how to go about it.'

'We'll find out,' Joanne said immediately, for she felt that any talent, however small, should be brought out and warmly encouraged with a view to providing a lifelong interest if not a career for a disabled youngster.

'When you are ready, Jo?' Anneliese was busily organising chairs into a circle and rounding up people to sit on them.

Stifling her disappointment that there was no sign of Dane, after all, Joanne reached for her guitar and took it to the chair that Anneliese had placed for her, facing her waiting audience. She picked out the first notes of the first song just as Cal arrived, and she shot him a smiling glance before she saw Dane following him into the room, and felt her heart shudder to a halt. Smiling, he blew her a kiss with an unmistakable warmth in his dark eyes, and a breathless mixture of relief and delight set her small, sweet voice faltering as she started to sing.

Tall, tanned, smiling as he talked to Cal and Anneliese at the back of the room, their heads close together in some kind of conspiracy, he was so dear to her yearning eyes that it was a physical pain in her breast to have him so near and yet not be able to run headlong into his welcoming arms.

An hour had never seemed so long, and for much of that time Joanne was conscious of the dark, piercing gaze that rested so intently on her as she sat with her guitar slung across her shoulder, wearing the pretty dirndl skirt and low-necked embroidered blouse that she had bought in St Johann with this evening in mind. She played and sang all the favourites, and the rafters rang with the stamping and clapping and shouting when she rounded off her amateur concert with one of the folk songs that had been so popular with the group on that memorable holiday.

Anneliese stepped into the circle to hush the cheers of enthusiastic applause. 'That was splendid, Jo. Now, we have something for you.' She produced a package from behind her back, beaming. 'All your friends wish you to have this small memento of our happy time in Austria and to thank you for everything you did to make it so enjoyable.'

Joanne slowly unwrapped the unexpected gift, to expose a long, velvet-covered jewel case. Opening it to the eager urging of her friends, she found a silver bracelet with a number of small enamel emblems of various places in the Tyrol that they had visited.

It was a most unusual souvenir, something to treasure, something to remind her of the courage and spirit and cheer of disabled friends, who would probably travel very different paths from herself in the years to come but would always have a very special place in her affections.

'It's beautiful!' she declared through a slight haze of tears as she admired the brightly coloured discs and the delicate links of the bracelet.

'It was Dane's idea,' Marcia announced with a sly emphasis on his name.

Joanne's gaze flew to the lean, handsome face of the man who had carved a place for himself in her heart long ago, her love now and forever. He met her eyes and his sensual mouth curved into the beginning of a special smile, and something sparked in the dark eyes that told her she was loved in return.

'It was a lovely idea,' she said with an unsteady smile. 'But I really didn't do anything more than anyone else. . .'

'Our names are on the backs,' Lenny told her eagerly, too impatient to wait for her to find out for herself. 'That was *my* idea.'

'Oh, how marvellous!' Joanne began to turn over each silver-backed emblem in turn to read each name. *Becky. Lenny. Richard. Clair. Lionel. Marcia. . .*

'Dane arranged for the engraving,' Anneliese said, delighted that the bracelet was such a success.

Joanne wasn't listening. For she had found the Pleydorf emblem with Dane's name on its back and beneath it were the words that would be engraved on her mind and heart for ever.

My love, my life, for always.

What more could any man say? Joanne began to tremble at the realisation of a dream that had never left her in all those long, lonely years. Dane was back in her life, to stay.

Again she met his eyes. This time there was a question that demanded an answer in his compelling gaze, and she knew that he was in an agony of impatience to know if she had yet come across his name among all the others.

She wanted to leap to her feet and rush to his arms, but she was surrounded by a clamouring group who wanted to admire the bracelet and see for themselves that each name had been correctly and clearly engraved. Laughing, her heart soaring with the certainty of future happiness with the man she had loved for so long, Joanne yielded to their eager demands and found each name in turn among the emblems.

At last she was free to go to the man who waited for her with evident tension in his tall frame. She was a little tempted to pretend that she hadn't yet found his name and his meaningful message on the bracelet, but she knew that someone as proud as Dane had only been able to admit his love and his need by such means.

Later, the words might come easily to his lips when she lay in his arms once more, against his heart, but the initial surrender must have been hard for a man who had been so determined not to forgive nor to fail in the attempt to prove that he could be happy without her.

With all her heart, Joanne was thankful for a love so sure and so strong that it had transcended everything but a mutual need.

'Dane. . .' She spoke his name on a breathless rush of love and longing that no man could mistake.

'I've missed you so much, angel.' He took her slim hands to his lips, one after the other, paying homage, promising her tender, loving care for the rest of her life if she allowed him back into her heart.

The look in his eyes sped a shock of happiness through her, from tip to toe. 'Take me home,' she said simply, and both knew that further words were unnecessary when eyes and hands and soaring senses conveyed the love that had survived all the hazards.

It took a little time to get away, for so many wanted to wish them goodnight. Joanne was grateful that the usually outspoken Marcia forbore to comment on her departure with Dane, but she saw the unmistakable gleam of romance in the teenager's eyes. Lionel shook hands with Dane in a way that wished him well and sent her a smile that announced his total abdication of all claim to her affections.

Cal and Anneliese accompanied them to the outer door when they finally left. 'We are having a party soon for all our friends. You must come,' Anneliese urged. 'You will enjoy it.'

Dane avoided the unholy twinkle in Joanne's lovely eyes at the familiar words, and carefully controlled the twitch of his own lips. 'Let me know the date in good time,' he warned Anneliese as he kissed her. 'Don't forget I'm a busy doctor.'

'It will be a special occasion,' she hinted with a swift, smiling glance for Cal.

'No prizes for guessing what our Annie has up her sleeve,' Dane murmured drily as he ushered Joanne out into a wet evening with an arm about her slender waist. 'Someone could make a fortune if they bottled that mountain air and sold it as a love potion!'

Joanne looked up at him, smiling. 'Was it only the mountain air that made you want me again?'

'When did I stop wanting you?' he demanded with an ache in his dark velvet voice. 'I can't remember a time when you weren't in my heart and my blood. I never stopped loving you, Joanne—*never!*'

He drew her into his powerful body to protect her from the worst of the weather, and she clung to him as they picked their way through a minefield of puddles to his parked Mercedes. Briefly, he bent his head to kiss her soft cheek, his breath warm and sweet against her face, and his nearness and dearness sent shivers rippling down her spine. Joanne clutched at the bag that swung from her shoulder, containing her lovely bracelet and its even lovelier message of love and promise.

Producing his keys, Dane opened the car doors and laid her guitar case on the back seat. Then he turned to her and, heedless of the rain that shimmered in the light of a street lamp, swept her into his arms, needing the sweet reassurance of her kiss, taking her warm and willing lips with a tenderness that spoke of real and lasting love.

Strong frame trembling, shaken by the force of his feelings for this sweet, spirited, stubborn tempest in a woman's beautiful body, Dane neither saw nor heard the approach of a speeding motor-cyclist. Gathering her closer, he held Joanne to his heart, raindrops glistening on the deep waves of jet hair that she put up a hand to stroke.

It was Joanne, golden content breathing magic into the moment as Dane murmured the promise of happiness into her receptive ear, who looked over his broad shoulder to see in sudden, appalled dismay that the motor cycle had skidded on the rain-soaked road and was careering towards them, out of control.

With split-second reaction and a strength she hadn't known that she possessed, she thrust Dane to safety, her slight body propelling him headlong towards the shops at their back. The motor cycle crashed into the Mercedes and toppled, throwing its rider to the pavement.

For some moments, there was confusion as youngsters leaving the club rushed to the scene and passing motorists stopped to offer assistance. Meanwhile, doctor and trained nurse had reacted instinctively, speeding to aid the injured boy, his needs overcoming their own sense of shock.

Incredibly, he wasn't badly hurt, protected by his

crash-helmet and thick leathers. Blood streamed from a cut on his face and Dane diagnosed a dislocated shoulder, but he was conscious. Soon, police and an ambulance arrived, names and addresses and details were given and the boy taken off to hospital, and the crowd melted away, leaving Dane and Joanne with his battered but still roadworthy car.

They reached for each other in relief. 'I think you may have saved my life,' Dane said quietly, marvelling that such a slip of a girl had swept him out of danger.

'I owed you that one,' Joanne reminded him with a shaky smile. 'Perhaps now the slate really is wiped clean at last.' She clung to him, weak with longing and relief. 'Oh, Dane, I love you so much. I couldn't bear it if anything happened to you!'

He cradled her lovely face in both hands and smiled into her shining eyes. 'Then you'd better marry me and keep me out of danger. I promise that you *will* enjoy being Mrs Dane Gregory,' he said with a twinkle lurking in his dark eyes.

Joanne sighed happily. 'I never really wanted to be anything else. . .'

Dane kissed her. She was his love, his life, his beloved angel. It no longer mattered that she had once fallen from the pedestal where his youthful, too demanding love had set her, all those years ago.

For her place was not on a pedestal but in his heart.

Eden
PENNY RICHARDS

DREAM SONG TITLES COMPETITION

HOW TO ENTER

Listed below are 5 incomplete song titles. To enter simply choose the missing word from the selection of words listed and write it on the dotted line provided to complete each song title.

A. ....DREAMS — LOVER
B. DAY DREAM.......................... — ELECTRIC
C. DREAM.......................... — CHRISTMAS
D. ....UPON A DREAM — BELIEVER
E. I'M DREAMING OF A WHITE........... — ONCE

When you have completed each of the song titles, fill in the box below, placing the songs in an order ranging from the one you think is the most romantic, through to the one you think is the least romantic.

Use the letter corresponding to the song titles when filling in the five boxes. For example: If you think C. is the most romantic song, place the letter C. in the 1st box.

	1st	2nd	3rd	4th	5th
LETTER OF CHOSEN SONG					

MRS/MISS/MR..

ADDRESS..

....

POSTCODE......................COUNTRY......................

CLOSING DATE: 31st DECEMBER, 1990

PLEASE SEND YOUR COMPLETED ENTRY TO EITHER:

Dream Book Offer, Eton House, 18-24 Paradise Road, Richmond, Surrey, ENGLAND TW9 1SR.

OR (Readers in Southern Africa)

Dream Book Offer, IBS Pty Ltd., Private Bag X3010, Randburg 2125, SOUTH AFRICA.

- -

Please retain this section.

RULES AND CONDITIONS

FOR THE COMPETITION AND DREAM BOOK OFFER

1. These offers are open to all Mills & Boon readers with the exception of those living in countries where such a promotion is illegal, employees of the Harlequin Group of Companies, their agents, anyone directly connected with this offer and their families. **2.** All applications must be received by the closing date, 31st December, 1990. **3.** Responsibility cannot be accepted for entries lost, damaged or delayed in transit. Illegible applications will not be accepted. Proof of postage is not proof of receipt. **4.** The prize winner of the competition will be notified by post 28 days after the closing date. **5.** Only one application per household is permitted for the Competition and Dream Book. **6.** The prize for the competition will be awarded to the entrant who, in the opinion of the judges, has given the correct answers to the competition and in the event of a tie a further test of skill and judgement will be used to determine the winner. **7.** You may be mailed with other offers as a result of these applications.